THE WARNING

The phone rang.

"There is nowhere you can run that I can't follow," a voice told me. "There is nowhere you can hide that I can't find you."

The voice startled me. The malice it conveyed was unmistakable and I had to remind myself that it was merely a voice on the phone. *It can't hurt you.* Besides, I had heard it before.

I turned on the light to read the number on my caller I.D. attachment, but the field was empty.

"Did you hear me?" the voice asked.

"There's nowhere I can run that you can't follow, there's nowhere I can hide that you can't find me. Anything else?"

The voice hesitated as if it was unsure of itself. "John Barrett must not be allowed to run for the Senate," it replied in a rush.

"Okay. Thanks for sharing."

A moment later, the connection was severed, leaving me staring at the silent receiver.

This is what happens when you agree to do favors for old friends.

Other *Leisure* books by David Housewright:

TIN CITY
A HARD TICKET HOME

PRETTY GIRL GONE

DAVID HOUSEWRIGHT

LEISURE BOOKS NEW YORK CITY

For Renée,
as always.

A LEISURE BOOK®

April 2007

Published by

Dorchester Publishing Co., Inc.
200 Madison Avenue
New York, NY 10016

ISBN-10: 0-8439-5847-2
ISBN-13: 978-0-8439-5847-8

Printed in the United States of America.

Visit us on the Web at www.dorchesterpub.com.

ACKNOWLEDGMENTS

I would like to thank all those whose invaluable aid and insight helped make this book possible: Cara Engler, Chris Engler, Coon Rapids City Attorney Tammi Fredrickson, Dr. D. P. Lyle, Rhonda Martinson, Tom McGlynn, David Peterson of the Minnesota Bureau of Criminal Apprehension, Alison Picard, John Rock, Ben Sevier, Michael Sullivan, and Renée Valois.

PRETTY GIRL GONE

PRAISE FOR DAVID HOUSEWRIGHT!

TIN CITY

"Twists and double-crosses, exciting car chases and gun battles, leavened by plenty of laughs."

—*The Boston Globe*

"Channeling Raymond Chandler with tongue-in-cheek humor, Housewright delivers plenty of action, a pinch of romance, and more than a few surprises."

—*Publishers Weekly*

"An amiable throwback to Marlowe/Archer. Housewright has a keeper in McKenzie."

—*Kirkus Reviews*

"This series may be seriously habit-forming."

—*Booklist*

"A nicely crafted combination of procedural and character-driven crime story."

—*St. Paul Pioneer Press*

A HARD TICKET HOME

"A true son of Spenser."

—*Publishers Weekly*

"Captivating…a series worth watching."

—*Booklist*

"An exciting, action-packed thriller."

—The Best Reviews

"David Housewright has written a stunning novel."

—William Kent Krueger, author of *Blood Hollow*

"I didn't so much read *A Hard Ticket Home* as inhale it. The action is superb, and the tour of the Twin Cities is a delight."

—Nevada Barr, author of *Hunting Season*

"David Housewright's McKenzie is a smart-alecky, wise-cracking, two-fisted, soft-hearted, and very human addition to the PI field. Get to know him—you'll be glad you did."

—S.J. Rozan, author of *Absent Friends*

Chapter One

The Degas was real.

I had seen the painting of the ballerina at the Minneapolis Institute of Art about a year earlier. The Institute sold it at auction soon after, despite much criticism, claiming it required the income to cover overhead and pursue new acquisitions. Only the auction was less public than MIA members had been led to expect, and gossip swirled that the man who eventually purchased the painting had simply seen it, wanted it, and used his considerable connections to get it.

I was admiring the painting in the lobby on the top floor of that man's bank, thinking it actually looked pretty good hanging there. My escort stood close by. He was wearing a gray trench coat with the belt cinched at the waist, looking like an extra in a bad Humphrey Bogart movie—actually, there are no bad Humphrey Bogart movies, but you get my drift. He gestured for me to move along with the pocket of the trench coat. There was a gun in the pocket, a stainless steel Charter Arms .38

wheel gun, but I ignored him. If he didn't shoot me when we were alone, I doubted he would do it now, in a lobby filled with purposeful business people. I spoke loud enough for most of them to hear.

"Hey, pal. Do you have a gun in your pocket or are you just happy to see me?"

My escort's face went from pale to crimson so quickly you would've thought I bitch-slapped him, which I had every intention of doing at the first decent opportunity.

I heard the gallop of footsteps behind me, followed by a woman's voice.

"You're late."

"Come," my escort said, taking my arm. I shook it free and pointed at the Degas.

"Have either of you ever stopped to look at this painting? You've probably passed it a thousand times, but have you ever taken a moment to really look at it? The lines, the blending of color, the woeful expression on the ballerina's face? Critics didn't like the ballerinas that Degas painted. They said he was vulgar and cruel. But he was neither. It's just that while everyone else at the time was painting dancers in all their resplendent glory, Degas wanted to capture them offstage, catch them when they were worn down by tedious tryouts and exhausting rehearsals. He wanted to show us the pain they endured, the suffering that went into their art. Perhaps he thought it would help us to appreciate them more."

"Don't tell me," the woman said. "You're the expert on nineteenth-century art we were told to expect."

"Merely a gifted amateur."

"You be sure to give Mr. Muehlenhaus your opinion of French Impressionists. I'm curious to hear his reaction."

"Let me guess. Muehlenhaus is one of those guys who knows nothing about art but knows what he likes."

The woman stared at me with smart brown eyes and an expression that suggested I was mad.

"*Mister* Muehlenhaus knows when he has been kept waiting for thirty minutes. This way."

She moved toward a pair of glass doors; I could see offices and workers beyond them. I followed. It was only polite. After all, the man had gone to such extremes just to meet me. The woman opened the doors for us and my escort gave me an unnecessary shove through them.

"You're pushing your luck," I told him, but I don't think he believed me.

Immediately, I could detect a soft, pleasant hum—the noise of many people performing complicated tasks with the efficiency of a Maytag. Voices rose and fell as I passed small offices and cubicles and there was an occasional peal of laughter. I wondered what would happen if I suddenly shouted, "Help! I'm being kidnapped!" Would anyone come to my rescue? Would someone tell my escort, "Unhand that man"? I was tempted to give it a try, but the woman turned abruptly, leading us down a narrow corridor.

There was a large double door at the end of the corridor made from wood I didn't recognize. The woman rapped twice and opened one side. My escort nudged me forward into a large, richly appointed conference room. It looked as if the decorator had been admonished to fill the room with an air of grandeur, which he accomplished with a floor-to-ceiling bookcase filled with leather-bound books and drawings by Picasso that could have been originals for all I knew. The far wall was entirely glass and provided a panoramic view of downtown Minneapolis with the Mississippi River beyond. In front of the window was a gleaming wood table long enough for a dozen English lords to have sat around while discussing the colonial tea tax two hundred and fifty years ago. A handful of men sat at the table, four at the end farthest from the door, a clear pitcher of water and several long-stemmed glasses arranged on a sterling silver tray in front of them. A much older fifth man was seated alone at the near end of the table, his ancient hands folded on top of a black leather file folder. Like the room, the inhabitants also were richly appointed, each in a suit that cost more than season tickets to the Vikings. Truth be told, I would have been impressed with both the room and the men if not for a persistent odor that for some reason reminded me of the inside of a shoe store.

My escort said, "Here he is," and shoved me again.

"Thank you, Norman," the older man said.

Enough is enough, I decided.

I pivoted swiftly on my left foot and drove my right fist just as hard as I could into Norman's solar plexus. The shock and pain doubled him over. I stepped behind him, yanked down the top of his trench coat, pinning his arms against his body, reached into his pocket and pulled out the .38. I shoved him toward the table. He lost his balance, fell against the table, hitting his face on the gleaming top, and slid to the floor.

I pointed the .38 more or less at the table. The four men at the far end were on their feet now and looking helpless. The fifth man never stirred from his chair. He looked at me with an expression of quiet curiosity.

Norman managed to free himself from his trench coat and struggled to his feet. He didn't want to take me on, but he would have if he were told to. The old man shook his head, and my escort made his way to a chair against the far wall and sat down. He fingered his nose, apparently relieved that it wasn't broken.

I held up the gun for everyone to see. The four men at the end of the table were obviously frightened. I liked that. I broke open the wheel gun and dumped the five cartridges on the carpet one at a time, making a production of it, then flicked the gun shut and tossed it on the table. I arranged myself in a nonthreatening posture in a chair opposite the old man, right elbow resting on the arm, my chin cupped in my palm, adopting an expression that I hoped said, "Bored."

"*Mister* Muehlenhaus, I presume."

Muehlenhaus was elderly-looking but fit—or at least as fit as someone on the far side of eighty years could be. His face was the color of old paper and framed by wisps of silver hair. He had the strong eyes of a man who knew what he wanted and usually got it, yet when he smiled—which he was doing now—he became the kindly uncle who always had toys and candy hidden in his pockets for the kids.

He said, "Was that necessary?"

"Given the nature of our relationship, I thought it was prudent to make a statement early."

The other four were sitting again, but they didn't seem comfortable. Three of them were in their sixties and looked like the only exercise they ever engaged in was walking to their limousines. The fourth was younger—I guessed late forties.

One of the older men was wearing a politician's uniform—dark blue suit, white shirt, and solid red tie. He said, "What statement?"

The old man answered for me.

"He's not afraid of us."

"He should be," the politician said.

I grabbed the .38 and skipped it hard across the table. It bounced twice before smashing into the pitcher and two of the glasses. Water and glass shards spilled over the tray, table, and the four men. They jumped to their feet and brushed at the debris like it was acid.

"I'm sorry," I told Muehlenhaus. "Was that crystal?"

"Your behavior is inappropriate, Mr. McKenzie."

"Someone might say that your behavior is even more—what's the word—indecorous? I'm not suggesting for a moment that you gentlemen are above kidnapping and assault, but to do it so openly? To bring it into your office? In front of witnesses? Someone with experience in these matters might think you were putting him to some sort of test. Or playing a practical joke, although none of you look like you have much of a sense of humor. So, which is it? Why did you bring me here?"

Muehlenhaus carefully opened the leather folder in front of him. He looked down on the white sheets of typed paper therein as he slipped a silver fountain pen from his pocket and prepared it to write. I couldn't recall the last time I had seen one. When I was a kid at St. Mark's Elementary School the nuns made us use fountain pens thinking it would help us learn to write with a graceful hand, except I kept breaking off the nibs.

Muehlenhaus said, "You were a member of the St. Paul Police Department, respected, decorated, poised for promotion, until you killed a perpetrator—"

"Suspect," I corrected him. "They only say perpetrator on television."

"Suspect, thank you. You killed an armed suspect in a convenience store robbery. There was some trouble concerning the use of unnecessary force—you killed him with a shotgun. You have, in fact, killed several men. . . ."

"None of this is answering my question, Muehlenhaus. Why am I here?"

A lightning hit of anger flared in his eyes, but passed quickly. I don't know if he disliked being interrupted or if he expected to hear a "mister" in front of his name, probably both. He continued reciting the details of my life.

"You quit the police force in order to collect a reward for recovering money stolen by a rather industrious embezzler named Thomas Teachwell. I knew Thomas. I remain astonished by his audacity. The finder's fee amounted to several million dollars, which you have since doubled due to some rather insightful investments. Very impressive."

I tilted my head at the compliment, even though it was misplaced. For practical purposes, I was financially illiterate. All my so-called insightful investments had been made by a twenty-seven-year-old former homecoming queen living in a houseboat on the St. Croix who played the market the way some people played Texas Hold 'Em.

"You are known for doing favors for friends," Muehlenhaus continued. "We are aware of your dealings with the so-called Entrepreneur's Club, for example, and with the Federal Bureau of Investigation last spring."

"Do you have a point, Mr. Muehlenhaus?" I don't know why I used the "mister." Maybe it was because, bravado aside, he *was* starting to frighten me.

Muehlenhaus carefully screwed his fountain pen back together and returned it to his pocket. He hadn't written a word. He closed the leather folder and folded his hands on top of it. It was a clever ploy, making me wait, playing off my insecurities. I was beginning to think he was clever in other ways, too.

"You are currently performing a favor for the first lady," he said.

It wasn't a question, so I didn't answer.

"You met with her this afternoon."

I had no reason to deny it.

"You are *friends*." Muehlenhaus made the word sound like an accusation.

I stood slowly, trying to maintain the same bored expression. Norman did the same. Despite the bloodstained handkerchief he held to his nose, he looked like he was perfectly willing to go another round. I gestured toward the Picassos on the wall.

"Gentlemen, do I need to break more stuff?"

"Mr. McKenzie, please." The youngest of the four men at the end of the table moved toward me. "Please." He gestured toward my chair. I took a seat.

"First, allow me to apologize for the clumsy manner in which we brought you here today," he said, but there was neither remorse nor regret in his voice. "We were all quite anxious to speak with you and to judge for ourselves your capabilities."

"Capabilities?"

"Indeed," Muehlenhaus said.

"I'm Troy Donovan. Allow me to introduce my colleagues."

While Donovan recited the names, I attached numbers gleaned from the *St. Paul Pioneer Press* business section—something I never read until I became filthy, stinking rich. Through his banks and investment groups, Muehlenhaus held paper on a large chunk of the metropolitan area. If the Twin Cities were a corporation, he'd be the senior partner. Prescott Coole ruled an empire of over two hundred convenience stores and gas stations throughout Minnesota and Wisconsin. Glen Gunhus made a quarter from every railroad car that rolled into and out of the state of Minnesota. Carroll Mahoney, probably considered middle class by his colleagues, was founder and first president of the 22,000-member Federation of Minnesota State County and Municipal Employees and therefore a valuable friend regardless of income. I had never heard of Donovan, yet somehow I didn't believe he had gained access to this exclusive circle by selling magazine subscriptions door-to-door. Collectively, they and their friends were known as the Brotherhood by us peons, and they moved and shook the Twin Cities into whatever shape that suited them.

Each of the men nodded when he was introduced to me, but none smiled and none of them made an attempt to shake my hand. Except for Troy Donovan. He rounded the conference table, took my hand, and gave it a firm squeeze. He smiled. True, it was a smile devoid of humor or goodwill and the tone of his voice was politely demanding, like he was speaking to a trespasser, but at least he made an effort.

"I'll be blunt, if I may." Donovan glanced at Muehlenhaus. The old man nodded and Donovan said, "We have been informed that the first lady has been made quite upset over something the past few days and we wish to learn what it is."

I felt the icy grip of panic on my shoulder. The answer Donovan sought was folded twice and resting inside my jacket pocket.

Lindsey Bauer Barrett was the most attractive first lady in the history of Minnesota, maybe in the history of all fifty states. The week after her husband was elected governor they were both featured in *People* magazine. The following week it was *Glamour*. By my estimate, her face must have appeared at least a dozen times in national publications during the two years since the inauguration and Lord knows how many times in the local media. Which made the heavy knit hat and sunglasses all the sillier. Who was she kidding?

I found her sitting alone at the Groveland Tap in an old-fashioned wooden booth, the kind with high backs that you can't see over. It wasn't hard.

"Honestly, Zee. You need to work on your disguise."

"McKenzie," she whispered. She grabbed my wrist and pulled me into the booth while glancing around to see if anyone had noticed her.

The Groveland Tap was a neighborhood joint in St. Paul where you could get a cold beer, a bowl of chili, watch the ball game on one of a half dozen TVs, and shoot some stick in the back room. In the evenings it was crowded with college kids from St. Catherine, St. Thomas, and Macalester. During the day it belonged to the families and business folk that lived and worked in the Macalester-Groveland area. The lunch hour crowd filled most of the tables and booths, but no one paid attention to Lindsey except a heavyset man with relentless eyes who sat alone near the door.

I sat across from her. She removed the sunglasses and smiled, her eyes sparkling like ice water. Lindsey had always possessed a kind of Renaissance quality that came very close to real beauty. Not the kind of fragile beauty flaunted so carelessly by teenage rock princesses, beauty that erodes inexorably with time. Rather it was a lasting beauty, the kind that inspires the imagination, like the canvas of a Pre-Raphaelite master that a discerning collector might study for hours, days, perhaps even a lifetime; examining, evaluating, analyzing each line, each curve, each brush stroke until he falls helplessly, hopelessly, permanently in love. I had thought so even when I was a kid, even before I knew what fine art looked like.

"It's good to see you," I said.

"Long time," she told me.

A waitress appeared, set two menus before us, and asked for drink orders. Lindsey requested iced tea after first being assured that the Groveland Tap brewed its own. I had the same.

The waitress grinned brightly. "It'll be just a moment, Mrs. Barrett." Lindsey nodded her approval. The waitress departed and Lindsey sighed deeply, pulled off the knit hat, and dropped it on the bench next to her.

"Ah, the joys of celebrity," I told her.

"I wanted our meeting to be secret."

"Why?"

The waitress reappeared. I wondered when I had last seen such brisk service.

"Here you go, hon," she said, setting the beverages before us. "Would you like to order now?"

"Later, perhaps," Lindsey said.

"I'm Terry, Mrs. Barrett. You just give me a wave when you're ready."

"Thank you, Terry."

The waitress left without once looking at me.

Lindsey frowned.

"Shake it off, Zee," I said, like she was a teammate who had just gone down swinging. "You grew up not far from here. People would recognize you even if you weren't the first lady."

"Zee. Now that's a name I haven't heard in a good, long time."

"How's Linda?" I asked, just to be polite.

"Working on her fourth marriage."

"Too bad."

"She should have stayed with you."

"We were children when we knew each other. If we had stayed together, it would have only ended up being the *first* marriage for both of us."

"You never did marry, did you?"

"No."

"What's holding you back?"

"I'm still waiting for you to realize that I'm the man you've been searching for your entire life and that you made a terrible, terrible mistake marrying Barrett. That's why you called, right?"

"McKenzie, you are a terrible flirt."

"When you say that, do you mean I flirt a lot or that I don't do it well?"

"Both."

"Why did you call?"

She didn't reply. Instead, she gazed at our drinks for a few moments, and then at the walls of the booth and finally at me. She was dressed in silk and cashmere; a long, charcoal-colored wool coat hung on the hook next to the booth. She looked like she had never wanted for anything, but that was merely a carefully cultivated illusion. I knew her when she worked the camera counter at Walgreen's to put herself through school.

"What is it, Zee?"

"Probably nothing. It's just—It just makes me so angry."

"What does?"

"I heard that you do favors for people."

"Sometimes. For friends."

"Am I a friend?"

"You know you are."

"Perhaps you can do a favor for me—for old time's sake."

"Sure."

"Be careful. You haven't heard what it is yet."

"Doesn't matter. *If* I can help you, I will—for old time's sake."

Her voice was serious, yet her mouth formed a smile that was almost giddy, as if she had gone some time without hearing good news. Lindsey reached into her bag and brought out an 8½ by 11 sheet of white paper folded twice and slid it across the table to me. I unfolded it. It was a hard copy of an e-mail. It read:

> *John Allen Barrett murdered his high school sweetheart, Elizabeth Rogers, in Victoria, Minnesota, and the police covered it up so he could become a basketball hero. If he runs for the U.S. Senate, I will expose him to the world.*

"Whoa," I said.

"It's a lie." She spoke the word like she had just discovered its meaning. "A big lie."

"I should hope so."

I examined the e-mail more closely. It was unsigned. The gobbledygook in the "from" field was unpronounceable. It had been addressed to Lindsey Bauer and sent at 6:57 P.M. Friday, three days earlier. The subject line was empty.

"Lindsey Bauer," I said.

"It was sent to my dot-com account," Lindsey said. "I have a dot-gov address through the state, but this was sent to my private e-mail address."

"How many people have your private address?"

"I don't know. Not many."

I folded the paper and slid it across the table to her. "What do you want me to do?"

She slid it back. "This is political, I know it is. Someone is trying to mess with Jack through me, and I want to know who."

"You want to know who sent the e-mail?"

"Exactly."

"That's it?"

"Can you do it?"

"Sure, but . . ." I gestured toward the heavyset man near the door. "Why not use your own people?"

"Because then it becomes public record. My e-mails through the state, all of Jack's e-mails—that's public record. You can get copies through the Freedom of Information Act. But what's sent to me personally, that's private."

"Unless you make it public."

"It could be that's what all this is about. It would make a nice headline, wouldn't it: First Lady Asks Bureau of Criminal Apprehension, 'Is the Governor a Murderer?' "

She smiled slightly, and in that moment I knew she was hiding something. I didn't know why I knew, yet I did. Probably it was because I had seen her smile often when she was younger and I recognized that it wasn't the same. All of my internal alarm systems fired at once. The noise was so loud in my head I was amazed that everyone in the restaurant wasn't diving for the door.

"What the e-mail says, is it true?"

Her eyes were sharp, but not angry, as she considered the question.

"Of course it's not true."

"Because that would have been my first question."

"It's an outrageous lie."

"Not who sent it, but if it's true."

"I'm sure that's exactly what the writer wants you to ask."

"Have you spoken to the governor about it?"

"Certainly not."

"Does he even know about the e-mail?"

"He has enough to worry about without this nonsense."

The alarm bells just kept getting louder and louder. I felt sweat on my forehead and trickling down my back. I considered removing my bomber jacket, decided to leave it on.

"Was the e-mail sent to anyone else? To the governor?"

"I don't know. If Jack received one, he didn't tell me."

"Why send it to you?"

"To drive a wedge between us."

"Between you and the governor."

"Yes."

"If that was the case, why accuse the governor of murder? Why not just say he's sleeping with one of his assistants?"

"If I knew who sent the e-mail, maybe then I'd know the answer to that, too."

She had me there.

"Is Jack running for the Senate?"

"People have been asking him about it, only he hasn't decided, yet. That's confidential, by the way."

"Apparently not." I slid the paper off the table and

into my inside jacket pocket. "It doesn't make a lot of sense, though. The threat goes into effect if Jack runs for senator, not governor."

"I've been thinking about it almost constantly since I received the e-mail. I have no answers. You will help me, though, won't you, McKenzie?"

"You know I will. But, Zee, I gotta ask, why me?"

"I told you."

"You told me why you didn't go to the state, not why you came to me."

"You're smart. You're tough."

"C'mon, Zee."

"If I've learned one thing as a politician's wife, I've learned this—plausible deniability. I go to a private investigator, someone that can be compelled to talk, and the media learns about it, what can I say, what can I do? I go to you, an old friend from the neighborhood, who's to know, and if they did . . . ?" She shrugged.

"I could rat you out?"

"No. Not you."

"How do you know?"

"Because you never told anyone why you broke up with my sister the evening of the senior prom, not in all these years." She smiled at me. "It's true, isn't it? You've never told anyone. Not even your good friend Bobby Dunston."

"Not even Bobby."

"And you never told anyone about us."

"No."

"Most men would have. Certainly most men who were seventeen years old would have. They'd have bragged about it every chance they could. Not you."

"Not me."

"You're an honorable man, McKenzie. You were an honorable man even when you were a kid."

I supposed she was paying me a compliment, so I said, "Thank you."

"Do you ever think of that evening?"

"Yes."

"What do you think?"

The question made me squirm against the back of the wooden booth. "Let's just say I cherish it and let it go at that."

"Do you really?"

I nodded.

"I always feel guilty."

"Why?"

"I used you."

"In what way?"

"The night of the prom when I learned that my sister was sleeping with my boyfriend, that they had been together that entire spring—you know, I would have married Michael that spring if he had asked me."

"That's what made it so—is 'sordid' the right word?"

Lindsey nodded and stared at her tea. When she looked back at me her eyes were moist.

"I didn't behave much better," she said. "The evening I invited you over to the house, it wasn't to return all those gifts that my sister had taken from you—your records, your sweatshirt. It was because she had taken something from me and I wanted to prove I could just as easily take something that belonged to her."

"I didn't belong to her, Zee. That evening I was all yours, body and soul. And I have to tell you—even though it happened only that once—it's like the song says, 'I feel a glow just thinking of you.' "

"You will help me then."

"Of course I will."

In the back of my mind I was thinking, *You're a schnook.* Lindsey was using the memory of that one night we spent together to hook me into doing her bidding, and I was going to let her.

"So, are you going to the gala tonight? Jack's big charity do? I know you have an invitation. I saw your name on the guest list."

"I'm not a gala kind of guy."

"You should come. I'll introduce you to the governor. You'll like him. I know you will."

"I'll think about it."

"Oh, no, I'm running late," Lindsey said suddenly. "I have to go." She was standing now, pulling on her coat. The heavyset man at the door was standing as well. Lindsey gestured at the drinks. "I always forget to bring money. Can you get these?"

"Sure."

Lindsey leaned into the booth and kissed my cheek.

"It was so good to see you again, McKenzie."

She put on her hat and sunglasses and moved toward the door. The heavyset man held it open and icy air swirled into the restaurant. I called to her.

"How do I reach you?"

"Don't worry about it. I'll find you."

"Zee. The e-mail? How can you be sure it's not true?"

Lindsey turned. I couldn't see her eyes for the sunglasses. She said, "You're a dear," and hustled out of the door.

I don't care for cell phones and the lack of privacy they represent and for a long time I resisted them, a conscientious objector in the telecommunications revolution. But over time I gave in, just as I surrendered years earlier to CDs after vowing vinyl today, vinyl tomorrow, vinyl forever. Guess I'm just a wimp when it comes to peer pressure.

I opened the tiny phone book I carry, found the correct page, and thumbed ten numbers on the keypad of the cell.

"McKenzie," Kim Truong shouted after two rings. I guessed she had read my name on her caller ID. "How are you, you stud muffin?"

"Same old, Kimmy. Same old. How are you? Staying out of trouble?"

"What can I say? Thank God for the morning-after pill. Tell me you called because you dumped the girlfriend."

"Oh baby, oh baby," I answered and Kim chuckled. I had never known a woman to speak the way she did, but then I've never known a woman quite like her, either—young, petite, pretty, a transplanted Vietnamese computer genius with a barroom personality that would make a sailor blush.

"Whaddaya need?" she asked.

"I have a job for you."

"Hmm, I like the sound of that."

"Can you track down the owner of an e-mail address?"

"Easy."

"With just the address?"

"Easy. What is it?"

I recited the long, seemingly meaningless series of letters and numbers in the "from" field on Lindsey's e-mail.

Kim was using her surfer's voice, carrying on a conversation with me while simultaneously surfing the web, reading e-mails or trading instant messages, so I wasn't surprised when she said, "Wait, wait, wait . . ." Seconds later Kim said, "Tell me again."

I did.

"When did you get the e-mail?"

"Three days ago."

"Shoulda called then, Mac. We coulda tapped into the ISP's short-term memory cache before new records replaced the old records, know what I mean?"

I pretended that I did.

"Don't worry. If your friend's using a route account with a concrete street address like Eudora or Outlook, it'll be like looking up a phone number. If he's using a Web-based account like Yahoo or Hotmail that exists only in cyberland, or even an anonymizer, one of those sites created to mask information about the original sender—and right now I'm thinking that's what this looks like—it'll be tougher, but a babe like me, I can handle it."

"How long will it take?"

"About ten minutes."

"Really?"

"Ten minutes once I start. Can't do it now. Some delinquent launched a particularly nasty little virus and my accounts are screaming for me to purge their systems before the entire Western economy collapses around them, so I'm gonna have to get back to you."

I had often wondered if Kim had ever launched a few viruses of her own in order to drum up business—it would have made for a nifty extortion racket—but I never asked.

"As soon as you can get to it, I'd appreciate it," I told her.

"So, McKenzie. This e-mail. You got a stalker?"

"No."

"Would you like one?"

"I'll let you know if there's an opening."

"Here's the thing," Kim said. "I can hack an ISP and trace the route back to the original sender, or at least to his computer. No muss, no fuss. Only we're talking the violation of several federal privacy statutes. . . ."

"I figured."

"For that kind of exposure, I'm gonna have to charge you."

"You're on. Just don't go crazy out there, Kim. Protect yourself, okay?"

"Nothing to it."

"Send me a bill."

"What bill? I tell you how much it costs and you pay me in cash. It's not called the underground economy for nothing. 'Course, I might take the price out in trade, if you know what I mean."

"You've got my number."

"I wish."

"Hey, Kimmy?"

"Yeah."

"Pleasure talking to you."

"See ya."

The sky was cloudless and pale; the sun fierce and white and glistening on the snow piled along the streets and sidewalks. Except the prettiness of the afternoon was just bait to lure unsuspecting prey out of doors. The sweat on my forehead froze so quickly in the frigid air when I left the Groveland Tap that the fingertips of my brown leather gloves came away encrusted with frost when I brushed my brow. I began to shiver as the rest of the perspiration on my body chilled, and it took an effort to keep my teeth from chattering.

At five degrees below zero—not to mention the minus

twenty-three-degree windchill—Minnesotans understand that Nature gives the body a choice. Either lie down and die or run to some place warm. Me, I was running. I broke into a slow trot when I left the Tap, moving along St. Clair Avenue to my Audi parked half a block up. Not for the first time I marveled at those eccentric men and women who dash out of saunas, roll around in the snow or leap into a nearby frozen pond, then hurry back to the sauna before frostbite settles in.

I had just about reached my car when a man on the other side of the street called, "Excuse me." He was dressed for business in a gray trench coat over black dress slacks and wingtips. He was carrying an unfolded map in both hands and looked hopelessly lost. It was one of the oldest ploys in the book, but I didn't see it until he crossed the street and shoved the .38 into my gut. I blamed the weather. After all, how many muggers prowl the streets at five below looking for vics?

"My employer wishes to speak to you," he said politely, his warm breath rising like mist.

"He could have called," I said. "I'm in the book."

A combination of cold fear and hot anger thrilled through me as he pressed the muzzle under my ribs. It was a dangerous combination for all involved—frightened, angry men don't always do what's in their best interests. I carefully reviewed his words in my head. "*My employer wishes to speak with you.*" I took that to mean that he didn't want me killed, whoever *he* was—at least not for the time being. I decided to keep it uncomplicated, give my escort no reason to make any fatal mistakes. So, a moment later when a black Park Avenue pulled up, I said, "Is this our ride?"

My escort yanked open the back door.

"Inside," he said calmly.

"After you," I told him.

He gave me a gentle poke with the gun.

"Well, since you asked nicely."

A few minutes later, we were on I-94, crossing the Mississippi River into Minneapolis—"Sin City" some of us St. Paulites call it, and not always in jest. A few minutes more and we were deep inside downtown Minneapolis, pulling into the parking ramp of one of the newer glass-and-steel towers. It was when we were on the public elevator with three other people going up that I realized the kidnapping was all for show and that I had little to fear.

"You're new at this kidnapping thing, aren't you," I told my escort.

A panicked look spread across his face as our elevator mates glanced at him while pretending not to.

"I gotta tell you, though, the trouble with shooting through your pocket? You can't really be sure where the gun is pointing."

My escort's face became a shade of red that you don't often see in nature. Yet he didn't speak. Nor did he take his hand out of his pocket. Instead, he stood motionless, watching the floor numbers change on the electronic display. Once the doors slid shut after our final companion departed the elevator, he turned toward me with an expression of snarling anger.

"Uh-uh," I grunted and pointed toward the upper corner of the car. My escort followed my finger to a small security camera.

"You could end up on *America's Funniest Home Videos*."

He faced the door again and said nothing.

"Seriously," I asked him. "What did you do before you got into this line of work?"

Now Norman, my escort, was sitting in a chair against the wall, nursing his pride. The three men at the far end of the table were all leaning forward, waiting to hear what I had to say. Muehlenhaus was sitting back in his chair, his arms folded across his chest like he already knew. Donovan was pacing, his hands behind his back like he was an eighteenth-century naval commander bestriding the deck. There was a streak of vanity in the man, I decided. It was long and wide.

"If the first lady is upset, I am unaware of it," I announced calmly.

Mahoney—he was the one wearing the politician uniform—grunted loudly and looked at me as if he didn't believe me, as if he hadn't believed anything anyone had told him in years.

Donovan apparently agreed with him. He said, "I think you're lying."

I said, "I don't care."

The pain in his expression was so severe, you'd think I shot him.

"Whom do you think you're talking to?" he demanded.

"I'll tell you when I get to know you better."

The tension in the room was suddenly a thin wire stretched too tight. Just the slightest pressure and it would snap.

"Gentlemen, gentlemen," Muehlenhaus repeated in an attempt to calm us.

"Gentlemen, gentlemen," I said. "Under what scenario

can you imagine that I would betray the confidence of my friends to you?"

"We know how to reward *our* friends," Gunhus said.

"I bet. But we're not friends. We're not even acquaintances, and if someone doesn't start volunteering information in a hurry, I'm going to leave."

Coole, Gunhus, and Mahoney looked at each other to see who would speak first. Donovan beat them all to it.

"Can we rely on your discretion?" he asked.

"Not even a little bit."

They didn't like my answer. I watched the five men discuss it with glances and gestures. Not a word was spoken—it was as if they communicated with ESP. I rotated in my chair and faced Muehlenhaus.

"What is it you want of me?"

He in turn made a nearly imperceptible gesture with his bloodless hand.

Donovan read it and said, "Mr. McKenzie, we have an assignment to discuss with you. One that requires fine sensibilities and good judgment, one that requires the utmost in secrecy."

"You have already proven to us that you can keep a secret," Muehlenhaus informed me.

I leaned back in my chair and crossed my arms and ankles. *And people say I watch too many movies.* I half expected the theme from *Mission: Impossible* to begin wafting through the room from hidden speakers.

"Do you know the governor?" Donovan asked.

"We've never met."

"Do you like him?"

"We've never met," I repeated.

"We have a great deal invested in Governor Barrett."

"A great deal," Mahoney confirmed.

"Just so," said Muehlenhaus.

"We made him governor," Donovan added. "We would like to make him a U.S. senator."

"Why stop there?" I asked.

"Why indeed?"

Jesus.

"We—as I'm sure you'll appreciate—are prepared to protect that investment."

"When we say 'we,' we're referring to the party," said Muehlenhaus.

"After decades of being in the minority, the party has made great strides in Minnesota," said Coole. "Much of that is due to Governor Barrett. He's comparatively young. Attractive. Charismatic. He's well known in the state and becoming well known throughout the nation—a high school sports hero, a self-made man rising above small-town poverty to become successful in business, respected for his philanthropic activities. He has been a splendid standard-bearer. So much so, that many people are considering him for higher office, perhaps the highest office."

"He's also willing to spend as much as twenty million dollars of his own money on his campaign," added Mahoney.

"There's that, too," said Coole.

"So, what's the problem?" I asked.

"You tell us," Donovan said.

Muehlenhaus leaned forward.

"The first lady asked you to do a *favor* for her—please, don't deny it. The favors you perform for your friends don't always bear up well to public scrutiny. We would like to understand what this particular favor entails, but we will no longer press you on the matter. We wish only to impress you with this one fact: If there is a problem with the first lady, we can make it go away. We are determined to make it go away. In that regard, are we not allies?"

"Mr. McKenzie," said Donovan. "We are not asking you to help us. We are asking that you allow us to help you."

"We'll reward you well for your cooperation," added Mahoney.

A feeling of excitement grew in my stomach and a kind of hollow feeling, too, that I couldn't give a name. I couldn't do anything about the feeling and wasn't sure I wanted to. Like most people, I have been on the outside looking in while men and women I didn't know manipulated events and made decisions that affected my life, sometimes gravely. Now I was being asked to participate, albeit in a somewhat roundabout manner. It made me feel the way I had when I was a freshman in high school and the "cool" kids invited me to lunch at their table. It made me feel important.

Then Donovan had to ruin it all by saying, "At the same time, we will not allow you or anyone else to devalue our investment in the governor."

Suddenly, I was a guy who found himself lost in an elaborate maze without a ball of string or a trail of bread crumbs to lead him to safety. The voice in the back of my head that I had learned to trust long ago was now screaming at me. *These men can't be trusted.* 'Course, I knew that before I even walked into the room.

"Gentlemen, I don't know what you're talking about." I stood and rolled my chair under the table. "The first lady is my friend, that's true. But if she has a problem, as you say, I am unaware of what it could be. 'Course, if I did know, I wouldn't discuss it with you or anyone else.

That's a promise I make to all of my friends and I never break my promises. Just to prove it, I'll make you a promise. You fuck with me or my friends, I'll fuck with you. I won't pretend that you and your resources don't scare me. They do. But you know what? I can be pretty scary, too." I pointed at the file in front of Muehlenhaus. "Ask around."

Coole, Gunhus, and Mahoney looked at each other to see if they were even remotely frightened by my remarks. Apparently not. Muehlenhaus seemed delighted. He clasped his hands together and laughed. Donovan laughed with him, just not as vigorously.

I was astonished by their reaction and probably looked it.

The old man said, "You'll do, McKenzie. You'll do fine."

The thought I had at the Groveland Tap pushed itself from the back of my brain right up front. *You are a schnook.*

Chapter Two

Normally, I would eschew the Minneapolis skyway system. Only normally it wasn't five degrees below zero and normally the wind that seemed to gain velocity as it was funneled between the downtown skyscrapers wasn't powerful enough to lift you off your feet.

The skyway system was a network of streets in the sky, connected to each downtown office building with an enclosed pedestrian bridge or skyway that spans the street below. The original purpose was to allow pedestrians to travel from one building to another without suffering the cold and wind of Minnesota's winters or the heat and humidity of its summers—neither of which was nearly as brutal as their reputations suggest, although have you been outside lately? Yet, over time, the skyway virtually took over downtown Minneapolis as people abandoned the city streets for its artificially controlled environment. Most businesses followed the pedestrians. In fact, very few businesses other than restaurants and shopping centers still had entrances on the street. It had reached the point where one intrepid magazine writer of my acquaintance wrote how he was able to "live" on the skyway for an entire month—working, lodging, eating, shopping, dating, and generally entertaining himself—without once allowing the warmth of the sun or the cool of moonlight to touch his face. Personally, I don't think the man's been the same since.

Muehlenhaus had offered me transportation back to St. Paul, but I didn't want him to believe for a moment that we were partners. Nor did I trust Norman. The look on his face—call me paranoid, but I had a feeling he was the type who held a grudge. So, I decided to hoof it to a hotel where a cab could be found that would take me back to my Audi.

It was getting close to the rush hour and most of the people in the crowded skyway moved relentlessly as they completed last-minute errands or rushed to parking ramps in hopes of beating the traffic. When I slowed to punch the numbers for directory assistance into the pad of my cell phone, and then later the first lady's office, the human current jammed up behind me like debris caught against a rock in a fast-flowing river.

I wanted to warn Lindsey that her cover had been blown. The Brotherhood knew exactly where we had met and when, which meant there was a leak on her end. Only he or she didn't know what we spoke about, which meant the source wasn't necessarily someone close to Lindsey. My chief suspect was her bodyguard or driver or whatever the big guy was. But I couldn't get through to her. I was passed from a receptionist to an assistant to an aide until I finally connected with a senior aide who took my name and number. I had the impression that she took a lot of names and numbers without passing them on.

I didn't think it was possible to just show up at the

front door of the Governor's Mansion on Summit Avenue in St. Paul, but there was another option. I used the memory function on my cell to dial Nina Truhler's number. She answered on the fourth ring.

"Rickie's, how may I help you?"

"Nina, you answer your own phones now?"

"I've even been known to sweep out the place. How are you, Mac?"

I could hear music in the background. Hoagy Carmichael. "Stardust." Nina owned and managed a jazz club on Cathedral Hill in St. Paul that she had named after her daughter.

"Very well, thank you, especially now that I'm speaking to you."

"Oh, you sweet-talker. What's going on? Anything interesting?"

"Yes. Interesting. That's a good word for it."

"You're off on another one of your adventures, aren't you? I can tell by your voice. It always sounds excited when you're into something."

"Am I that obvious?"

"To me you are. What is it? Can I help?"

"I can't tell you what it is. Truth is, I'm not exactly sure myself, yet. But yes, you can help."

"How?"

"Can you get away tonight?"

"I could be talked into it."

"Remember that $3,600 dress you gave yourself on your birthday."

"Yes."

"Would you like a chance to wear it?"

Turned out she did.

After arranging the logistics for our date, I said good-bye, deactivated my cell phone, and slipped it into my jacket pocket. Almost immediately afterward, a man grabbed me. Strong fingers closed around my right hand and yanked violently, twisting and pulling it up between my shoulder blades. The pain in my shoulder forced me to cry out, a moment of weakness I immediately regretted. At the same time another hand pressed hard against my spine, steering me out of the skyway traffic, driving so hard and fast I didn't even think of ordering my legs to resist.

He flung me up against the thick glass wall of an office that sold life insurance and leaned his full weight against me, pinning me there. My forehead was mashed against the glass and the point of my elbow was wedged between my body and his, making the pain in my shoulder even more excruciating.

I couldn't see his face, but I felt his lips close to my ear.

"Do the right thing," he hissed.

"What? What do you mean?"

"Do the right thing," he repeated.

"What is the right thing?"

He stepped back and shoved hard again, using his weight and leverage to bounce me against the glass wall. He released me.

I wasn't thinking now, merely reacting. I spun around into a fighting stance, my legs wide apart, the outside edge of my heels more or less lined up with my elbows, my feet at forty-five-degree angles, my body sideways, my hands curled into forefists and held high in front of me. It's called a "horse" stance and exposes few vulnerable targets to an opponent. Only there was none.

I craned my neck searching for a target. A few pedestrians had stopped and were staring at me. I tried to look around and past them, spotted a man with brown hair and a dark blue jacket—it could have been a Minnesota Twins baseball jacket—swiftly bobbing and weaving away from me through the skyway traffic, and then he was gone.

I brought my left hand up to massage the ache in my shoulder. Pedestrians continued to stare at me.

"What the hell," one of them said.

My sentiments exactly.

I kept the thermostat set at sixty-eight degrees. Even so, it cost a small fortune to heat my English Colonial and not for the first time I wondered if it wasn't time to move on. It was big, something like 2,650 square feet of living space, including bathrooms and a finished basement. Yet just four rooms were furnished and I lived in only three of them. Shelby Dunston had once called it "the biggest, most expensive efficiency apartment" she had ever seen. I bought the house because, at the time, I wanted my father to live with me, and so he did, until he died six months later. Afterward, the kitchen, my bedroom, and what my father used to call "the family room"—where I kept my PC, TV, VHS and DVD players, CD stereo, and about a thousand books, some of them even stacked on the shelves—were all the space I needed.

A few minutes after I arrived home, I settled in front of my computer with a coffee mug emblazoned with the logo of the St. Paul Police Department that Bobby Dunston had given me. It had not occurred to me to take souvenirs when I left the job, and Bobby had been supplying me with sweatshirts and other paraphernalia ever since. Sometimes I wished I could go back and get my own.

I fired up the PC and began dragging databases. Kim

Truong had taught me how. An ex-girlfriend named Kirsten had hired Kim to develop a specialized research program for Kirsten's business. She introduced us, mostly, I think, because she had wanted to prove that she was broad-minded when it came to hiring minorities. Kim didn't like her. After a while I didn't, either.

Later, I hired Kim to teach me how to conduct computer investigations of people my travels brought me into contact with. She proved to be a persistent and uncompromising instructor. Under her tutelage I soon mastered the full spectrum of credit reporting, public records searches, database access, medical information retrieval, and how to explore the countless other nooks and crannies where personal information lies hidden. No amount of information—privileged or otherwise—was safe from my prying eyes. Kimmy's massive tip sheet made it easier—I had had it laminated—along with other helpful hints on what to look for and how. Yet even without them, I soon became pretty adept at exposing an individual's history with only a few strategic keystrokes and cursor movements. I am continually amazed by the depth and breadth of data available out there.

Take John Allen Barrett. I didn't have his social security number. Yet that didn't prevent me from learning that he was born on November 30, at 1:13 A.M. C.S.T., in the State of Minnesota, in the County of Nicholas, in the City of Victoria, in Nicholas County Hospital to father Thomas Robert Barrett, age twenty-eight (at time of birth) and mother Kay Marie Barrett, age twenty-six (at time of birth), whose mailing address was 1170 County Road 13, Victoria, Minnesota. Or that C. T. Brown, M.D., certified that he had attended the birth of the child who was born alive at the place and date stated above. Or that, except for treatment of a sprained knee when he was a shooting guard coming off the bench for the University of Minnesota Golden Gopher basketball team, it was the only time that Barrett had ever been hospitalized for any reason.

Nearly a quarter of the U.S. population has a criminal record of some kind, but not Barrett. According to the Bureau of Criminal Apprehension's database—which I accessed for only a $5 charge to my credit card—he had never been arrested for a felony or gross misdemeanor of any kind. Nor could I locate any juvenile police incident reports with his name on them. 'Course, if there had been, I was pretty sure his political opponents would have exploited them long ago.

The Department of Motor Vehicles database listed two speeding tickets and one accident on Barrett's driving record: he had rear-ended a Ford Taurus during a sleet storm. No one was injured, no citation was issued, and his insurance promptly paid for the damage. He currently owned three vehicles: a Lexus sedan, an SUV, and a 1965 Ford Mustang for which he had purchased "collectible" plates. It was a modest fleet considering his vast wealth. 'Course, the state was chauffeuring him around these days at public expense.

A visit to the Web site of the secretary of state gave me more information about his businesses and partners than I knew what to do with. Barrett wasn't on the board of any corporation except his own—Barrett Motels, one of the top five motel chains in the nation. He had been among the initial twelve investors who brought the Minnesota Wild National Hockey League team to St. Paul, and he had briefly pursued partial ownership of the St. Paul Saints minor league baseball team, only nothing came of it.

The Ramsey County Property Tax Web site indicated that Barrett owned a 6,249-square-foot house built in 1967 on Pleasant Lake Road in the city of North Oaks with an estimated market value of $1,069,400. It was the only residence Barrett owned in Minnesota that I could discover and, of course, he divided his time between there and the Governor's Mansion. His polling place in North Oaks was the East Rec Center, where he had voted in every election in the past decade.

Barrett continued to contribute to numerous and varied charities and nonprofit organizations, including the American Cancer Association, the Children's Heart Fund, Big Brothers, Minnesota Public Radio, the Loft Literary Center, the St. Paul Chamber Orchestra, and the Minnesota Institute of Art. I wondered what he thought of Muehlenhaus's purchase of the Degas.

Most of the other information I gleaned came in the form of newspaper and magazine articles, starting with the most recent events in his life and working backward. I skipped everything that dealt with politics or the governor's office, staying strictly with his personal information before he ran for office:

John Allen Barrett rejects Marriott's latest offer. Barrett Motels remain the top independent in the upper Midwest, according to the *Wall Street Journal*.

John Allen Barrett's fiftieth birthday party on November 30 attracts over 350, including many celebrities.

John Allen Barrett hailed as a financial guru for predicting the sudden decline in tech stocks traded on NASDAQ.

John Allen Barrett visibly embarrassed during the dedication of Barrett Hall, the addition to the University of Minnesota's Business School that he helped finance with a $25 million contribution.

John Allen Barrett congratulated in the business section of the *St. Paul Pioneer Press* upon the grand opening of his fiftieth motel.

John Allen Barrett and his bride, the former Lindsey Bauer, mugging for the cameras following their nuptials . . .

I lingered here for a few moments, examining an electronic photograph of Barrett and a startlingly lovely woman in a white gown that someone estimated cost over $50,000. Yet Zee wore it as if she was either unaware or unconcerned by that fact. Barrett, a half-dozen years older than Zee, was wearing a tuxedo cut in the English style with matching gloves and hat. Still, the way they smiled and clung to each other, I could believe they would have been just as happy if they had been married in burlap sacks.

And on and on it went.

John Allen Barrett forms partnership to build motels for travelers on a budget.

John Allen Barrett to provide color commentary during TV broadcast of the Minnesota State High School Boys Basketball Tournament.

John Allen Barrett returns to the University of

Minnesota after a brief professional basketball career in Europe to gain his master's degree in business administration.

John Allen Barrett agrees to play for Milan in the European basketball league.

John Allen Barrett in tears after the University of Minnesota Gophers basketball team is eliminated in the first round of the NCAA Basketball Tournament.

John Allen Barrett triumphant after leading the "Victoria Seven" to a 52–50 victory over heavily favored Duluth Central to win the Minnesota State High School Boys Basketball Championship before a raucous sellout crowd at St. Paul Auditorium.

The Victoria Seven were as well known in Minnesota as the 1980 "Miracle" Olympic hockey team was to the rest of the nation. Seven kids from tiny Victoria High School overcame incredible odds to win the tournament. This was before the state high school league divided the schools into four different classes, back when there was only one state champion, when it was still possible to have upsets and underdogs and Cinderella stories, when it was still possible to build a legend.

There was surprisingly little information about the team on the Internet, probably because the game had been played so long ago—over thirty years. Most of the stories that mentioned the Seven were connected to the governor's election campaign, although there was one stand-alone piece written on the eve of the team's thirtieth anniversary. In it, the writer praised the team for the heroic manner in which it faced adversity throughout the season, *including the brutal murder of Victoria High School cheerleader Elizabeth Rogers one week prior to the state tournament.*

So, there was an Elizabeth Rogers, and she had been murdered. I attempted to learn more. Had anyone ever been arrested or convicted of the crime? I accessed the Web sites of both the *St. Paul Pioneer Press* and the *Minneapolis Star Tribune* and browsed their archives. Both papers had stories, but they were short and to the point: A seventeen-year-old high school cheerleader was found murdered in the tiny town of Victoria, according to authorities, with little additional information. Each article linked the woman to the Victoria Seven, but not to John Allen Barrett personally. There were no follow-up stories that I could find.

I switched gears and began searching for intel on the Brotherhood. There was surprisingly little information about Muehlenhaus. Apparently the man shunned publicity, although I unearthed a nice joke about him: "Muehlenhaus is so cheap when he walks onto a green he picks up all the dimes." Mahoney, Gunhus, and Coole, on the other hand, seemed to enjoy publicity, although they didn't do much that anyone would be interested in. Troy Donovan was a bit harder to read. He had been everywhere for a while and then apparently decided to keep a lower profile, not unlike Muehlenhaus. I learned that he was single, that he had inherited a $7 million stationery business from his father and grew it into a $60 million concern, and that a few years ago he began exploring the possibility of building a Kinko's-like copy and print shop franchise throughout the Upper Midwest. I wasn't interested enough to read how it turned out.

I was staring at the computer screen, wondering what to do next, when my phone rang.

"Oh baby, oh baby, oh baby," Kim Truong's voice chanted.

"Hey, Kimmy. Long time, no see."

"At least five and a half hours."

"Seems longer."

Kim thought that was pretty funny. After she finished chuckling, she said, "I have what you're looking for."

"We're talking about the information I was needing, right?"

"Well, that, too. Write this down: one six zero point nine seven point two eight six point one eight seven."

"What's that?"

"The number of the computer that sent your e-mail."

"That doesn't exactly help me, Kimmy."

"How 'bout this, then. The computer is located at— Are you writing this down?"

"I am. I am writing it down."

"The computer is located at 347 Second Avenue, Victoria, Minnesota."

"Do you have a name?"

"No, just a location."

"Victoria, Minnesota."

"Yeah."

"Makes sense."

"In what way?"

"It's the scene of the crime."

Chapter Three

The Sixteenth Annual Charity Ball to raise money for the Governor's Endowment for a Drug-Free Minnesota was held at International Market Square, an enormous brick-and-mortar warehouse on the outskirts of downtown Minneapolis. Listed on the National Register of Historic Places, it had been remodeled to house 135 upscale home furnishing showrooms, designer studios, architectural firms, remodeling resources, and advertising agencies as well as a spectacular atrium located at the heart of the Square beneath a huge glass and steel girder roof.

After depositing our winter coats and Nina's boots at a makeshift coat check just inside the entrance of the building, we made our way from the lobby down a corridor toward the atrium. There were several retail businesses located along the corridor, all shuttered for the evening, and Nina could see our reflections in the windows as we passed.

She stopped. I was two steps past her when I felt Nina's hand slip from mine and turned about.

"What is it?" I asked.

My first thought was that she had halted to admire her gown. It was what she was doing when I arrived at her home earlier, posing this way and that in front of a full-length mirror like a model at a photo shoot. Red velvet stretched lovingly over her thighs, hips, waist, and chest, and a shawl, attached to the bodice, rose up from under her arms to hug her neck. There was plenty of exposed flesh both front and back. The hem of the gown grazed the bottom of her ankles and the side slit was high enough to expose much of Nina's leg, yet not so high as to cause her embarrassment.

I searched my vocabulary for a word and found it. "Sinuous," I said aloud. The dress was full of devious curves. She liked the word and repeated it twice as she examined herself over her shoulder.

I enjoyed watching Nina, enjoyed her short black hair, high cheekbones, narrow nose, and generous mouth; enjoyed the curves she refused to diet away; enjoyed the way she moved so smoothly and effortlessly. But mostly I was charmed by her eyes, the most arresting eyes I had ever seen in a woman. From a distance they gleamed like polished silver. Up close they were the most amazing pale blue.

Watching her own movements in the shop window, Nina reached out for me. I took her hand, marveling not for the first time at how comfortable it felt in mine.

"What is it?" I asked.

"We make a nice-looking couple."

"You make anyone look good," I told her, although I had to admit the tuxedo I wore helped some.

She didn't reply.

"Nina?"

"Hmm? Nothing. It's just . . ." She curled her arm around mine. "Nothing."

Which meant *something*. I knew she would get around to it when she was ready.

Nina tightened her grip on my arm and we moved to the edge of the atrium. The band was in full swing, playing a cover of one of Elvis's early recordings for Sun Records. Yet while Elvis was content with guitar, bass, and drums, this orchestra added trumpets, saxophones, trombones, clarinets, violins, and piano to the mix—so many instruments that musicians were in danger of being crowded off the makeshift stage set up in front of the glass elevator. Directly across from it on the other side of the atrium, red-vested waiters and waitresses stood guard behind long buffet tables garnished with trays of hors-d'œuvres, pastries, and salads and shallow pans with silver lids and tiny fires glowing beneath them. A sunken pebblestone floor sprawled between the orchestra and the food. A temporary wooden dance floor in front of the orchestra took up half of it. Dozens of small round tables covered with white linen and adorned with fresh flower centerpieces filled the other half. More tables and chairs were scattered on the perimeter of the sunken floor, and long bars were strategically located in every corner. Most of the tables were occupied and the bars were crowded. Looking up, I could see the moon and a few of the brighter stars through the glass ceiling. It was jarring to think that on the other side of the glass was a world where it was cold almost beyond measure.

We glided to the steps and waited for several couples to descend before us. I studied the throng. All the women wore expensive gowns or cocktail dresses and the men were dressed in tuxedos or elegant suits. They had paid a thousand dollars each to be there. Their affluence was great, but while others might feel small and out of place among them, I did not. In the past few years I had come to understand money and I wasn't intimidated by it.

Finally, Nina and I descended the short flight of stairs and twisted and turned our way across the dance floor and through the maze of tables beyond. Eyes and occasionally entire heads turned toward us as we passed. Nina pretended not to notice. Eventually, we found an empty space between tables. At least a dozen partygoers glanced our way. Some smiled to indicate they liked what they saw.

"Hey," I said. "People are watching us."

"Of course they are. We're all dressed up," Nina told me.

"So are they."

"Yes, but we're pretty."

"That's true."

"Besides, at the risk of sounding even more conceited than I am . . ."

"You're not conceited."

"When I dress up like this, I expect to be watched."

"Seriously?"

"Why else would I dress like this? Are you telling me you don't ogle pretty girls as they walk by? Don't lie, McKenzie. I've seen you do it. I've even seen you do it when you were out with me."

"I didn't think women noticed."

"Of course we notice. You guys are so obvious. Besides, a woman—we can feel it. It's almost instinctual. We don't have to look around for it. We just know."

"Doesn't it piss you off, guys always checking you out?"

"No. I find it flattering, as long as they don't cross the line."

"What line?"

"If you want to give me a smile, an unobtrusive nod, the clandestine glance when you think your date isn't looking, that's cool. Only don't speak to me unless we're introduced. Don't give me, 'Hey, babe.' Don't give me, 'It must be jelly cuz jam don't shake like that.' That's just plain rude. And don't stare. It makes me nervous when guys stare. Especially the guys who give you that million-mile stare, who don't reveal anything in their expression or body language, who just stand there—they scare me most of all."

"I hadn't thought of that."

"No reason why you should."

Nina glanced about the atrium.

"Do you know these people?" she asked.

"Some to nod at. You?"

"I don't know anybody. Wait. Yes, I do."

"Who?"

"The band."

Nina shaded her eyes with her hand.

"That's Bobby DeNucci playing piano," she said. "Nick Weiland. Abby Hunter on violin. Joey Anthonsen and his brother Mark. You've heard these guys."

"I have."

"Most of them have played my place at one time or another. Played jazz. Tonight, though, they seem to be playing a primitive kind of music that's popular with young people today. I think they call it rock 'n' roll."

"Philistines."

"Barbarians."

"Maybe they'll let you sit in."

"Puhleez."

"Why not?"

"It's one thing to let me play with them when they're

in my club—it's my customers we're driving away. Not here." Nina shook her head. "Let's dance."

I draped my arm over her shoulder and gazed demurely into her eyes.

"How 'bout I buy you a drink, sweetheart."

"You never dance with me anymore."

"I'll dance with you. I just thought a drink first. . . ."

"Fine. But we are going to dance."

"Of course," I told her while wondering how I could get out of it. I don't like to dance. The way I dance is sort of like potatoes falling out of a sack.

I selected the bar that seemed least crowded and went toward it. The orchestra swung into a cover of the B-52's "Love Shack" with Abby Hunter and Mark Anthonsen supplying vocals. Unfortunately, an opera of loud chatter and laughter rose up around me in opposition to the music, and midway through the song I gave it up.

As Murphy's Law would have it, the line I picked moved slowest. I engaged in some people watching while I waited my turn. It wasn't nearly as interesting as it was at, say, the Minnesota State Fair. Too many women wore black, and while some of their hairstyles demonstrated boldness and imagination, most did not. Women enthusiastically greeted other women whose names they couldn't recall while men nodded stoically and offered perfunctory handshakes during introductions that were quickly forgotten. Small groups formed, swelled with importance, dissolved, and reformed at the next table. Alliances were forged and broken, plans were made and abandoned, and suggestions on how to squeeze even more fun out of the evening were proposed, debated, and rejected. Meanwhile, a handful of wanderers drifted from group to group in search of a familiar face.

Something caught my eye and I turned toward it.

A small hurricane of people swirled and grew larger as it tracked slowly along the atrium opposite where I was standing. At the eye of the hurricane was a man I recognized immediately. John Allen Barrett. Governor of the State of Minnesota. He was part of the crowd, yet seemed to stand apart from it at the same time, as though some trick of light brightened the area immediately around him while casting everyone else in shadow. It was a wondrous trick, and I tried to determine how he managed it. He certainly had the size to have once played college basketball, and instead of the pale cast of most Minnesotans in winter, his skin had the glow of good health. I could see the blue in his eyes all the way across the room, and his smile, which never seemed to leave him, threw off sparks like a welding torch you're not supposed to view with the naked eye. Yet it was more than physical appearance that attracted. It was attitude. Barrett had the look of victory about him.

Standing next to him, Lindsey seemed both young and not so young. Her face was as flawless and smooth as when it was new, yet I detected in her eyes an intelligence and thoughtfulness that came only with time and hard lessons learned. She wore a simple black silk sheath with a high, square neck, low back, and long skirt and no ornament save the star that sparkled on her left hand, yet she seemed to shimmer like moonlight on dark water. For a moment I was alone with her in the living room of her parents' home, the house empty except for us, Miles Davis on the stereo, Lindsey smiling her lovely smile and saying, "Can I get you anything?"

I didn't become a man because of Lindsey, I reminded myself. But she did make it a lot easier.

Barrett exchanged greetings easily with the people who gathered around him, shaking hands with his right while his left circled his wife's waist and held her in a protective embrace. Occasionally, she would slip free and drift away from him as the hurricane surged forward. When that happened, Barrett would reach back for her, refusing to acknowledge anyone until she was once more safely at his side.

That's what love looks like, my inner voice told me.

Miraculously, the Barretts found an empty table and the crowd began to disperse. The hurricane was soon downgraded to a squall and Lindsey was able to sit, which brought an expression of relief to her face.

Only relief soon gave way to something else that I couldn't name. Lindsey's face was still as lovely, yet suddenly it seemed hard. I watched her eyes. They were locked on an object far away. I tried to locate it, failed, and then realized that Lindsey wasn't looking at something, but purposely looking away from something. I had no idea what it could be. I searched the faces of the people around Lindsey until I found one I recognized.

Troy Donovan.

He stood above and behind Lindsey with one hand on the railing of the second-floor balcony while the other gripped the stem of a wineglass. He was watching her, yet his face revealed nothing—neither pleasure nor pain, neither joy nor reproach. It was the million-mile stare that Nina had explained to me, the one that unnerved her so.

I finally bought our drinks and returned to Nina.

"Sorry it took so long," I told her. "Apparently, the Sixteenth Annual Charity Ball for a Drug-Free Minnesota doesn't consider alcohol a drug, because there sure are a lot of people lapping it up." I offered one of the drinks to Nina. "Not that we're hypocrites or anything."

"Of course not." Nina took the drink. "What is this?"

"Vodka martini, shaken not stirred."

"You didn't actually order that."

"Sure, I did. I'm wearing a tuxedo. What else would I drink?"

"What did the bartender say when you ordered it?"

"Oh, he thought it was hilarious."

"I bet. I hope you tipped him."

"Does James Bond leave tips?"

"Now that you mention it, in all his movies I don't think I've ever seen him pay for anything."

"Well, then."

Nina sipped the drink and shuddered.

"Wow," she said.

"It might be a tad strong."

"You're not trying to get me drunk and take advantage of me, are you, McKenzie?"

"*Moi?*"

"That's what I thought."

I took a sip of my martini and gazed back toward Lindsey Barrett. Barrett had disappeared, leaving his wife in the company of a woman who had joined the table and was waving her arms with great animation. She was wearing what resembled a ballerina's costume, a fitted slip dress on top and layers and layers of black tulle on the bottom. The dress and waving arms reminded me of a spider. Whatever tale she wove must have been quite enthralling, because Lindsey never looked away from her.

I did lift my eyes, however, scanning the second-floor balcony. Troy Donovan had gone. But he hadn't gone far.

"What are you doing here?" he wanted to know. Donovan was standing directly behind Nina, speaking to me over her shoulder as if she wasn't there.

"Good evening," I replied.

"What are you doing here?"

"Supporting a worthy cause. How 'bout you?"

"You're being flip."

"It's one of my hobbies. Why are you here?"

Donovan chuckled.

"Supporting a worthy cause," he said.

"And so . . ."

"I apologize," Donovan said. "To you and your date." He moved next to Nina and held out his hand. "Good evening, I'm Troy Donovan."

"Nina Truhler," she replied, taking his hand.

"Ms. Truhler, if I seemed rude earlier it is because the matter we discussed this afternoon with Mr. McKenzie is quite important to me, to us, and when I found him here I panicked a little."

"Who is *we* and what matter did you discuss?" Nina asked.

"You don't . . . He didn't . . . Of course not." Donovan pivoted toward me. I was beginning to think he wasn't very bright—one of those guys who couldn't make scrambled eggs without an instruction manual.

I said, "I haven't discussed our business with Ms. Truhler, but, please, feel free."

He nodded. His smile reminded me of the blade of a knife gleaming in sunlight and I realized it had been a test. The sonuvabitch had been testing me. Again.

Donovan bowed his head toward Nina and said, "A pleasure to have met you. Have a good evening."

"You're not doing a favor for him?" Nina asked when he was out of earshot.

"Not even at gunpoint."

"Who, then?"

I turned my attention back toward Lindsey. She was sitting at the same table, still listening to the same woman.

"Mac?"

"I can't say," I answered absently.

Nina followed my gaze to Lindsey.

"Can I guess?"

"Forgive me, Nina, but there's something I need to do." I handed my drink to her. "I'll be right back."

"Don't forget. You promised to dance with me."

"I know."

I walked in a straight line to where Lindsey sat. The woman in the spider outfit said, "That's not even the half of it—"

"Excuse me," I said and offered Lindsey my hand. "Mrs. Barrett. Would you care to dance?"

"Mr. McKenzie," she said. "I would be delighted. Please excuse me, Evelyn."

Evelyn didn't seem even remotely happy to have been interrupted, but said, "Of course," just the same.

I led Lindsey to the dance floor. Nina watched us. She was frowning.

"Thank you, thank you," Lindsey chanted just above a whisper. "Thank you for getting me away from that dreadful woman."

"My pleasure," I said.

I took her lightly in my arms. It was the first time I had held her in nearly twenty years, yet the thrill of electricity that flowed through me was the same as it had been that evening in her living room. I tried to ignore it. She was a married woman after all.

Lindsey was wearing perfume or cologne—I never understood the difference—which made her smell vaguely like a pine tree. People smiled at her and nodded their heads. If they noticed me at all it was to wonder, "Who's that guy?"

The orchestra segued into a full arrangement of Edwin McCain's rock ballad, "I'll Be." I led Lindsey into a waltz step as best I could. She followed without effort.

"You dance very well," she said.

"Stop it."

"I'm surprised to see you here. I thought you weren't a 'gala kind of guy.' "

"It was the only way I could think of to speak to you. Your aides wouldn't put me through."

Lindsey's body stiffened beneath my hands.

"Do you know who sent the e-mail?" she asked.

"Not yet. I did learn where it was sent from."

"Where?"

"An address in Victoria."

"Victoria, Minnesota? Jack's hometown?"

"Yes. I'll run down there tomorrow and check it out. There is something else you should know."

"We can't talk here on the dance floor," she insisted.

"I'm open to suggestions."

"There's a restroom at the end of the far corridor. Meet me there five minutes after the dance is over."

We continued to twirl on the floor in time to the music, floating between other couples that mostly danced in tiny, graceless circles. I looked over Lindsey's shoulder for Nina. I couldn't find her. Instead my eyes rested on Troy Donovan. He was glaring at me. Lindsey and I spun a few times and I lost sight of him. When I saw him again, his eyes appeared serene and were directed elsewhere. I watched cautiously. A moment later, Donovan looked at us again. The expression that flamed across his face—if only for an instant—was curiously familiar, one that I had seen on a man's face before, and it didn't take long for me to recognize it. Jealous anger.

Why?

The answer became painfully clear when Lindsey said softly, "I miss my old friends," and rested her head against my shoulder. Donovan witnessed the move, grimaced, and turned away.

You're kidding, my private voice said. *You are absolutely kidding.*

The song ended. I stopped dancing and released Lindsey from my embrace. We applauded politely along with the other dancers.

Lindsey whispered, "Five minutes."

She left the dance floor while I stood there watching, a post in the ground.

I searched for Nina, but couldn't find her. After a few minutes, I headed for the restrooms farthest from the atrium. Along the way I snatched a long-stemmed glass filled with white wine off a silver tray carried by a waiter. I didn't know if the glass was meant for someone else and I didn't care.

The noise from the ball that followed me down the corridor became blessedly hushed by the time I reached the restroom.

Lindsey's driver—the man I had seen at the Groveland Tap—stood watch at the door. He could've been one of the guards at Buckingham Palace for all the acknowledgment he gave me when I paused next to him. I sipped from the wineglass. Chardonnay. I didn't like chardonnay. Too dry. I drank it anyway and stepped inside.

I had never been in a woman's restroom before. It seemed larger than most men's restrooms and there was a long sofa with black cushions hard against the wall opposite the sinks and mirrors. Lindsey had slumped down into it.

"You'll wrinkle your dress," I told her.

"Oh, God," she said and stood up, smoothing the silk with her hands. "It's been a long day."

"It's not over yet," I reminded her.

Lindsey went to the mirror, examined her face carefully, and slipped her hand into her clutch bag for lipstick even though she didn't need it. She dabbed her upper lip while her eyes, as clear and sharp as a sunny day in July, examined my reflection with polite curiosity.

"What do you want to talk about, McKenzie?" she asked.

I told her about the Brotherhood, the fact they had me kidnapped five minutes after she left the Groveland Tap, that lacking any other suspects, I blamed her driver for ratting her out. She didn't seem a bit surprised.

"Tell me the truth, Zee. What exactly is going on?"

Lindsey pretended to tend to her makeup and I pretended to watch. After a few moments, she slipped her lipstick back into her clutch bag.

"You know everything I know," she said.

"Do I?"

"I don't know what you're asking."

I told her about my assailant on the skyway.

"Are you all right?" she asked.

"Five minutes, Zee. Five minutes after I left the Brotherhood he came at me, which means he was waiting. Just like the guy outside the Groveland Tap had been waiting. Now, why do I have a feeling that everything that's happened today was staged for my benefit? Like I'm a minor piece being maneuvered around a chessboard."

Lindsey paused for a moment before saying, "If you're being maneuvered, then so am I."

"I don't know what to do about it."

From the expression on her face, Lindsey didn't have a clue, either.

"This is bigger than it seems," I told her.

"You will help me, though, won't you, Mac? You'll help me despite everything?"

"Everything?"

"The Brotherhood and all that."

It was back—the feeling I had had at the Groveland Tap that Lindsey wasn't telling me the truth, at least not the whole truth—but I said yes just the same, for old time's sake.

"Good."

"Zee," I asked innocently.

"Yes?"

"Tell me about Troy Donovan."

"What do you mean?"

"How well do you know him?"

"Not well at all," she answered easily. "We're acquainted through events like this, but I don't think I've spoken more than a dozen words to him. Why?"

"The way he looked at you when you first arrived. . . ."

"You'd be amazed at the way some men look at me."

"The way he looked at us when we danced together."

"I don't know what to say."

"Okay."

"Is it?"

"Sure."

"What happens next?"

"Good question."

I gave Lindsey a head start before leaving the restroom and making my way back to the atrium. I searched unsuccessfully for Nina, wondering if she had become so fed up with me for ignoring her that she left the ball. Couldn't say I blamed her.

The orchestra was taking a break and there was no one on the dance floor. It was getting late for a weeknight. Wives were looking at husbands the way they do when they want to go home, and husbands, at least for the time being, were pretending not to notice. Yet the exodus would soon begin. The couples with younger children would depart first, followed shortly by those with older children, followed by the single and the childless. Most of the partygoers would be gone by the time the orchestra finished its final set.

I thought the set might be about to begin when Bobby DeNucci walked to the microphone at center stage.

"Ladies and gentlemen," DeNucci announced. "We have a treat for you while the orchestra takes a few moments to catch its breath. Please welcome Nina Truhler."

Oh my God.

Sparse applause followed Nina across the stage. She briefly hugged DeNucci and sat at the piano and immediately began to play. I moved to the edge of the sunken floor while a few partygoers ventured onto the dance floor itself. They were met there by a piece of classical music, one of the variations on Bach's *Goldberg Variations;* I didn't know which one. The would-be dancers glanced at each other as if to say, who is this woman? *Wait for it, wait for it,* I urged them silently.

After a full minute of playing the slow, melodic music, Nina's left hand began to beat out a hard rhythm. The dancers looked up at her in anticipation. People who weren't listening suddenly were. DeNucci and a few of the other musicians gathered next to the stage. I was sure I heard Abby Hunter exclaim, "Bring it, girl." Nina brought it. After establishing the baseline with her left hand, her right abandoned Bach's sweet sound for something much grittier—Jay McShann's bluesy "My Chile." When she squeezed as much out of the song as she wanted, Nina segued without pause into "Cow Cow Blues" by Meade Lux Lewis. Soon a few of the musicians joined her on stage—she had percussion, a bass keeping time for her, and Abby Hunter's violin lending unexpected shadings to the melody she riffed. The floor began to fill, yet the people didn't dance so much as they swayed and hopped to the sound Nina was laying down. At the edge of the sunken floor, I clapped my hands in delight.

Nina dropped out and let Abby take four choruses. When she came back she was playing Otis Spann's hard-driving "Spann's Stomp." I wasn't all that surprised that the other musicians were able to follow her so well. Unlike most rockers, jazz musicians know how to listen to each other. Still, how was she going to get out of this? I wondered. Nina must have had a plan because she said something to Abby, who relayed her message to the bass and drummer. After three more choruses, Abby dropped out with a flourish, followed by the drummer. That left

Nina and the bass talking to each other, one taking the lead, then the other, and when Nina nodded, the bass dropped out and she retreated to the *Goldberg*, ending it with her right hand playing Bach and her left hand pounding out a blues rhythm.

A moment of silence was followed by loud applause. Nina waved at the audience, curtsied elaborately, and waved some more. She crossed the stage, stopping only to shake hands and to hug Abby. DeNucci returned to the stage, took up the microphone, and pointed at her.

"Miss Nina Truhler," he said, and the audience applauded louder.

"We'll be right back," DeNucci added.

Nina shook some more hands while I watched from my spot at the edge of the floor. There was a lump in my stomach that floated up through my chest and lodged in my throat, making speech impossible. It wasn't a hard lump, but soft and squishy, and it seemed to vibrate, causing my body to hum like a tuning fork. I recognized it for what it was. Pride. I was proud of Nina Truhler.

I continued to watch her. She gave me a half wave and a smile and I grinned in return. After a few moments, she detached herself from her admirers and attempted to make her way along the perimeter of the sunken floor to where I stood. However, before she could reach me, she was stopped by still another fan.

John Allen Barrett offered his hand and Nina shook it casually. Barrett said something and Nina laughed. Nina said something in reply and Barrett laughed. A moment of panic seized me, I don't know why. The e-mail accused him of being a murderer but it couldn't possibly be true, so why should I worry that he was chatting with my girl?

Nina waved me over and I joined them, hoping none of the trepidation I felt had touched my face.

"Mac," said Nina, as she slid a hand behind my neck. "Allow me to introduce Governor Barrett. Governor, this is Rushmore McKenzie."

"I've heard that name," Barrett said. "You're an old friend of Lindsey's."

"I am."

"There's a story she told me about your name." He turned toward Nina as if for confirmation. "He was conceived at a motel in the shadow of the Rushmore Monument when his parents took a vacation through the Badlands."

She said, "But it could have been worse."

"It could have been Deadwood," they both said in unison.

"I definitely need new material," I told them.

"It's a pleasure to finally meet you, Rushmore."

"Thank you."

"Just call him McKenzie," Nina said. "He doesn't like Rushmore."

"Who can blame him?"

Everyone seemed to be having a wonderful time at my expense.

"It *is* good to meet you," Barrett said. "Lindsey said you were one of her most trusted friends from the neighborhood." He took my hand and gazed directly into my eyes, and in that instant I felt as though John Allen Barrett had attended this ridiculous, self-indulgent ball for the sole purpose of meeting me. I couldn't explain it. Or why I felt a pang of jealousy when he released my hand and directed his attention to Nina.

"What you played reminded me of the blues you'd hear in Chicago," Barrett said, as if he was continuing a conversation already in progress.

"Some of it was," Nina said. "Otis Spann and Meade Lux Lewis were from Chicago. Lewis used to play boogie-woogie piano at rent parties when he was a kid and Spann probably did, too. The first bluesman I played, though—Jay McShann—he came out of Kansas City in the thirties. Charlie Parker used to be one of his sidemen."

"I didn't know that." Barrett spoke in a way that made me believe that freely admitting ignorance didn't faze him a bit. It was a small thing, yet filled with courage, and suddenly Barrett seemed less wealthy, less intimidating, less like the improbable icon I had been researching all afternoon.

"I presume you play professionally," Barrett told Nina.

"Goodness no," said Nina.

"Yes," said I.

"I used to play a bit when I was a kid," Nina added. "Not so much anymore."

"What do you do now?" asked Barrett.

"I have my own club."

"Really? Where?"

"Rickie's on Cathedral Hill in St. Paul."

"I've been there," Barrett insisted. "It has two levels, a kind of lounge on the first floor and a restaurant on the second."

"That's right," said Nina. "You should come again. We'll take good care of you."

"I have an idea. I have a radio program for an hour on WCCO Friday mornings. I'm going to give you a call—not this week, but the next. We'll talk about your club on the air."

"That would be wonderful."

Barrett smiled at Nina like a doting father praising his child. I watched him smile. His unexpected interest in Nina reminded me of something—a sentence, a phrase, a fragment of words that I had heard or read when I was younger. Except it stayed tantalizingly out of reach and I gave up the struggle for it, and then there it was, a line of Wordsworth from a long-ago English Lit class:

That best portion of a good man's life,
His little, nameless, unremembered acts
Of kindness and of love.

"Jack," said Lindsey.

She had appeared behind Nina and crossed in front of her to reach Barrett. She wore the regal and slightly forced smile of a homecoming queen and if she felt any anxiety over seeing her husband conversing with Nina and me, there was no sign of it that I could detect.

Barrett's eyelids pricked up like an animal's ears when he heard his wife's voice, and he reached for her the way a child might reach for a butterfly. He took her hand, nodded toward me, and announced, "Look who I found."

"McKenzie," Lindsey said and kissed my cheek. "But I saw him first. We danced together earlier."

"Yes, I noticed," Barrett said. "Danced awfully close, I thought." To me, he added, "You'll be getting a call from the Minnesota Department of Revenue in the morning."

"Hey," I said. "Look at the time. We should be going."

"Don't even think about it," Nina told me. "We're going to dance."

"Forgive me," said Barrett. "Lindsey, this is Nina Truhler."

"Nina, I enjoyed your performance very much," Lindsey told her as they shook hands.

"Thank you," said Nina.

"What a lovely gown."

"You're very kind."

"I'm also very tired," said Lindsey. "Excuse me, but we're heading home."

"We are?" said Barrett.

"Jack," Lindsey said. "You made me promise to drag you home before midnight no matter how much fun you were having."

"Why would I do that?"

"Because you're flying to Washington in the morning."

"Don't worry about it. Let's dance."

Lindsey turned to Nina and me.

"You kids," she said. "I bet you could dance until they rolled up the floor, go out for a nightcap, maybe a moonlit walk . . ."

"Hummida, hummida," I said.

"And still get up at the crack of dawn and be fresh as a daisy." She turned back to her husband. "Remember when you could do that?"

"Are you calling me old?"

Lindsey crossed her arms over her chest.

Barrett sighed. "Message received," he said. "Good night, Nina. McKenzie. And hey," he added, looking first at Nina and then glancing at me, "do the right thing."

I felt my body stiffen at the phrase and then go soft as I watched John and Lindsey Barrett disappear down the corridor beyond the bandstand. *It can't be*, my trusted voice announced. *There is just no way*. Followed by, *What the hell is going on?*

"Mac, are you okay?"

I took Nina's arm and pulled her close. She rested her head against my shoulder.

"Mac?"

"I'm okay. A little dizzy. I had some bad chardonnay before."

"Are you sure?"

"Yes."

The orchestra returned to the stage and Nina asked, "Would you care to dance?"

"Yes," I told her.

And we did, until they rolled up the floor.

At 1:15 A.M. it was actually warmer in the parking lot of the International Market Square than it had been when we arrived, such was the weather in Minnesota. My arm was around Nina's waist and her arm was curled around mine, and we walked slowly and silently as lovers do toward my Audi. We had arrived late, so the car was parked in the farthest, darkest corner of the lot. The lot had been plowed down to the asphalt and the heels of Nina's boots made nice clicking sounds as we walked.

I was escorting Nina to the passenger door, car keys in hand, when a voice called out.

"McKenzie."

We stopped in front of the car. I edged Nina behind me, shielding her with my body.

"Who is it?"

"Is that your girl? Nice." The voice came from out of the darkness between the two SUVs parked directly in front of me. It was masculine. Disguised. Unsettling.

"What do you want?"

"To give you a warning. To give you *both* a warning."

"What's that?"

"There is nowhere you can run that I can't follow. There is nowhere you can hide that I can't find you."

"You're telling me this—why?" I moved my thumb over the key chain.

"Barrett cannot be allowed to run for the U.S. Senate."

"Why not?"

"Because I said so."

I pressed the red panic button on my key chain. Immediately, a loud, piercing alarm reverberated across the parking lot. The Audi's headlights flashed on and off, illuminating the space between the two cars. The man standing there brought his arm up to guard his face. It wasn't necessary. His face was encased in sheer nylon and I couldn't make out his features. He screamed an obscenity and started running in the opposite direction. He was wearing a brown leather coat instead of the blue jacket worn by my assailant on the skyway. I watched him hit the street, turn right, and disappear down the block.

I wonder who he works for?

I turned around and embraced Nina. I searched her face for a suggestion of fear or anger, but there was none.

She said, "Governor Barrett is running for the Senate?" over the noise of the car alarm.

"Shhh. It's supposed to be a secret."

Nina had nothing to say during the drive home, which I took as a bad sign. It meant she wanted to have a *serious* conversation and was just waiting for the right moment to begin. I pulled into her driveway and put the Audi into park, letting the engine idle.

"Would you like to stay the night?" Nina asked.

"Isn't Erica home?"

"Yes."

"Then, no."

"I have to think Rickie knows we're sleeping together."

"Maybe so, but that's a lot different than seeing me in her mother's bed when she's getting ready for school. It's tough enough raising a teenage daughter, teaching her the things she needs to know, without explaining that. Besides, it's like what my dad used to say. 'The best lesson is a good example.' "

Nina leaned across the seat and kissed me.

"I knew you were going to say that," she said.

"That's because I've said it before."

"I like constancy in my men."

"I have to tell you, that dress you're wearing makes me consider the virtues of inconstancy, if you get my meaning."

"I take that as a compliment."

"Please do."

"How long have we been together, Mac? Fourteen, fifteen months?"

"Closer to sixteen."

"In all that time, we've never discussed the M word."

"Do you want to discuss it now?"

"Do you?"

"You're the one who brought it up."

"We make a terrific couple."

"You said that earlier."

"But I don't want to get married."

"You don't want to marry me?"

"I didn't say that. I said—I've been married. It wasn't fun. Even now I think about it and my hands begin to tremble. Look."

Nina held her hand flat in front of me and it was trembling.

"I'm not your ex-husband," I reminded her. "It wouldn't be the same."

"I know but—Listen, you don't want to get married, either."

"I don't?"

"No. I don't *need* to be married. I've been married and I learned the hard way that I can be happy without a ring on my finger. You're the same way."

"I am?"

"Most men, they *need* to be married. They need someone to take care of them. When they're kids, they have their mothers. When they get older, they find wives. That's why when a man and woman get divorced, the man usually remarries within a year or something like that. It's because they can't be alone. They can't take care of themselves. My ex-husband—Well, enough about that. But you, McKenzie. Your mother died when you were very young, so you and your dad, you guys took care of yourselves and did a pretty nice job of it, too, if you ask me. You're the best cook I know who doesn't do it for a living. You don't *need* to be married."

"There's needing and then there's needing."

"I know. Only we haven't reached that point yet."

"Speak for yourself."

"C'mon, McKenzie. Think about it."

"I think you don't want to marry me and now you're trying to convince me that I not only don't want to marry you, I don't want to get married at all."

"Do you want to marry me?"

"I've thought about it."

"That doesn't answer my question."

"You're starting to annoy me, Nina."

"Why can't you just say it? You don't want to get married."

"I don't want to get married tonight."

"Neither do I. So, we're both on the same page. What's the problem?"

"I might change my mind tomorrow."

"If you do, let me know. We'll work something out."

"What happens in the meantime?"

"Nothing happens in the meantime. We just keep on going the way we have been."

This is a good thing, my inner voice told me. *You don't want to get married. The beautiful, intelligent, successful woman you've been sleeping with doesn't want to get married, either. Yet she still wants to sleep with you. Most guys would kill for a relationship like this.*

So why was I angry?

Despite her protests, I insisted on walking Nina to her door. I stood back while she unlocked it and slipped inside.

"Come in for a moment while I disarm the security system," she said.

A few moments later she returned. She had removed her overcoat and her red velvet dress shimmered in the light behind her.

"Thank you for coming," I told her.

"Thank you for inviting me."

I hesitated for a moment.

"When you played piano, tonight—that was for me, wasn't it? You were performing for me."

"I just wanted to remind you that I was there."

"I'm sorry I left you alone for so long."

"It's all right."

"I should have been more attentive."

"Yes, you should have."

Nina stepped forward and kissed me. The kiss was warm and moist and lasted a long time.

"I should go," I told her.

She held open the door and I stepped through it and made my way to the Audi. I had just about reached it when I turned. She was watching from the door. There was considerable distance between us now and she had to shout.

"I said I didn't want to get married and I meant it, but . . ."

"But what?" I shouted back.

"You'll never find anyone better for you than I am, Rushmore McKenzie. Never."

I lay in my bed a long time yearning for sleep that did not come. My brain was convulsed by too many thoughts and images that made me toss and turn and twist and continually flip my pillow to the cool side. The incident in the skyway. *Do the right thing.* Wasn't that a Spike Lee film? The parking lot. *There is nowhere you can run that I can't follow. There is nowhere you can hide that I can't find you.* If that wasn't a line from a movie, it should be. Jack and Lindsey Barrett, Donovan, Muehlenhaus, and the others. Nina. *Maybe I didn't want to get married, but what the hell!* Who could sleep through noise like that?

Eventually, I gave it up and padded in bare feet down the stairs and into my kitchen. In the freezer compartment of my refrigerator I retrieved a half-filled bottle of Stolichnaya. I poured two fingers of the icy vodka into a short, squat glass and took a sip. It was so cold it made my teeth ache, only, Lordy, it went down nice. I returned the bottle and glanced about. The kitchen appliances on my counter gleamed in the moonlight that filtered through my windows—blender, espresso machine, bread maker, ice cream churn, microwave, pasta maker, George Foreman grill. My sno-cone, mini-donut, and popcorn machines were stored in boxes on my kitchen table—I reminded myself to take them to the Dunstons.

I took another sip of vodka and drifted to the breakfast nook. I sat at the end of the table, surrounded by eight windows arranged in a semicircle, each window with a view of my backyard. The pond had been frozen over since early December; the ducks that lived there had been gone since late September.

Nina.

The first year there had been seven ducks, Tracy and Hepburn and their five ducklings that I named Shelby, Bobby, Victoria, and Katie, after the Dunstons, and Maureen, after my mother. Victoria and Katie returned with their mates the next year and had nine ducklings between them that I named after an assortment of friends. Yet I had never named one after Nina.

Why not?

The phone rang before I could answer the question.

"There is nowhere you can run that I can't follow," a voice told me. "There is nowhere you can hide that I can't find you."

The voice startled me. The malice it conveyed was unmistakable and I had to remind myself that it was merely a voice on the phone. *It can't hurt you.* Besides, I had heard it before.

I turned on the light to read the number in my caller I.D. attachment, but the field was empty.

"Did you hear me?" the voice asked.

"There's nowhere I can run that you can't follow, there's nowhere I can hide that you can't find me. Anything else?"

The voice hesitated as if it was unsure of itself. "John Barrett must not be allowed to run for the Senate," it replied in a rush.

"Okay. Thanks for sharing."

A moment later, the connection was severed, leaving me staring at the silent receiver.

This is what happens when you agree to do favors for old friends.

Chapter Four

The difference between five below zero and five above is mostly in the mind. The odds that your car won't start are just as slim at either temperature; the likelihood that your water pipes might burst is just as high; the danger of frostbite, of numbing death from exposure, is just as real. Yet there was something joyous in the fact that the Twin Cities had finally crept into positive digits. I could see it in the robust gait of pedestrians who no longer felt as anxious over the climate as they had the day before and I could hear it in the voices of the customers at the Dunn Brothers coffeehouse where I had stopped for a mocha. It made me glad to be about with a job to do and *a heart for any fate*, as the poet once wrote. I didn't even mind that the early morning rush hour traffic had forced me to rein in the 225 horses beneath the hood of my Audi as I made my way to Merriam Park. For once the prevailing traffic laws seemed perfectly reasonable to me.

I had moved to the suburbs. It was an accident. I thought I was buying a home in the St. Anthony Park neighborhood of St. Paul, but after making an offer I discovered I was on the wrong side of the street, that I had actually moved to Falcon Heights, though I won't admit it to anyone but my closest friends. Bobby Dunston, you couldn't get out of the city, not with a crowbar. He purchased his parents' home after they retired and was now raising his children in the house where he was raised directly across the street from Merriam Park, where he and I played baseball and hockey and discovered girls.

I parked on Wilder in front of his house. It took me a few moments to wrestle the popcorn machine out of the passenger seat. If I hadn't fumbled my car keys in the process and had to pick them out of the snow, I might not have looked up and seen the white Ford Escort parked about a block behind me, its exhaust fumes plainly visible in the cold air.

I carried the machine up the sidewalk, across Bobby's porch, and knocked on the door. While I waited, I directed my eyes across the street as if there was something in the park that interested me. It wasn't an abrupt gesture, but casual—for the benefit of my tail. I watched him out of the corner of my eye, or rather I watched the car. I couldn't see who was in it.

Shelby opened the door with a smile that could guide ships at night. Which in turn made me smile. I tried to picture her at sunrise, telling myself that in the morning's first light she would look as attractive as a wrinkled grocery bag, but failed. I had known her since college, known her, in fact, for three minutes and fifty seconds longer than her husband—the exact length of Madonna's "Open Your Heart," the song they were playing when we met—and she always looked good to me.

"What's that?" she asked, pointing at the box.

"A 2554 Macho Pop popcorn popper."

"Of course it is. Do you need help carrying it in?"

"I've got it. Can you get the door?"

I muscled the machine into her house and set it on her living room carpet.

"What's that?" Bobby asked.

He had come from the kitchen, a newspaper in his hand.

"Popcorn machine," Shelby told him.

"How did the Wild do last night?" I asked him.

"Lost 2–1."

"Nuts."

When I went back outside, he followed me. Bobby and I had started together at the very beginning and watched the world evolve in fits and starts, in disappointments and small victories. He was me and I was him and we felt exactly the same about most things most of the time, and since we lived in the same place at the same time forever, we were able to communicate volumes to each other with a single word or sentence fragment or a raised eyebrow.

He lifted my Belshaw Donut Robot Mark I, capable of making one hundred dozen mini-donuts per hour, thank you very much, while I grappled with my Paragon 1911 Brand Sno-Cone Machine. I do like my treats.

"Where's the Jeep Cherokee?" he asked.

"In the garage."

"I thought the Audi was going to be the summer car."

"It's just so damn fast."

Last spring a Chevy Blazer I was chasing outraced me on the freeway. The Audi satisfied my vow that it would never happen again.

"Why are you home?" I asked.

"Accumulated time off. I put in sixty-seven hours last week."

"Nice hours if you can get them."

"If people would stop killing each other, I might actually have time for the family."

"Where are the girls?"

"They had better be in school."

"Why wouldn't they be?"

"Gee, I don't know. Maybe because their surrogate uncle likes to tell them stories about how he and their father used to skip class to run around the city and they think it's cool."

"Sorry 'bout that."

"I can tell."

A few moments later, the machines were arranged side-by-side in the Dunstons' living room.

"I thought you were bringing these over Friday," said Shelby.

"I have to leave town and I'm not sure when I'll be back. I wanted to make sure the girls had them for their fund-raiser." I turned to Bobby. "That's why you don't have to worry about them skipping school. Because they're Girl Scouts and we—"

"We were never Scouts."

"Not even a little bit."

"Where are you going?" Shelby asked.

"Victoria, Minnesota."

"Why?"

"I'm doing a favor for Zee Bauer."

"No kidding," said Bobby.

"Who's Zee Bauer?" Shelby asked.

"Lindsey Bauer," said Bobby. "She's married to the governor now."

"Lindsey Barrett, the first lady? You know the first lady?"

"She used to live not far from here, near Summit Avenue, on what, Howell?" Bobby said. "McKenzie dated her younger sister, Linda, when we were seniors in high school."

"You called her Zee?"

"Lind-*zee*," said Bobby. "Not to be confused with Lind-*duh*."

"Linda wasn't the smartest girl in the class," I said.

"She was a slut," Bobby said.

"Hey, hey, hey, c'mon. . . ."

"Tell me I'm wrong."

I didn't. I couldn't.

"What are you doing for the first lady?" Shelby asked.

"I can't tell you."

"Figures."

"Does it have anything to do with the Ford Escort parked down the street?" Bobby asked.

"You noticed."

"I'm an experienced law enforcement professional."

"I heard that rumor. Didn't they just promote you to lieutenant of something?"

"A richly deserved reward for my many years of outstanding service working homicide."

"Want to do me a favor?"

"You don't know who's in the Escort, do you?"

"Not a clue."

Bobby sighed, said, "I'll make a call."

"When you find out, call me on my cell. I want to lead him out of the neighborhood in case there's trouble."

"Trouble?" Shelby said the word like she had just heard it for the first time. "Why does there always need to be trouble?"

I didn't know how to answer that.

"I understand why Bobby takes risks," Shelby said. "It's his job. But why do you?"

"We all take risks every day, Shel. We all walk down dark alleys without knowing what lurks in the shadows. . . ."

"Metaphorically speaking," said Bobby.

"We risk death riding in hurtling automobiles and by golf balls that are sliced out of bounds and from burritos that aren't cooked properly. There are diseases waiting for us out there that we've never even heard of and probably couldn't pronounce if we had—"

"Here we go," Shelby said like she had heard it all before, which, of course, she had.

"The thing is, ain't no one getting out of here alive, so we might as well have some fun while we can. Besides . . ."

"Live well, be useful," Bobby said.

"I bet I could learn to like you if I worked at it," I told him.

He said, "You're my hero. When I grow up I want to be just like you."

"You're both a couple of cowboys," Shelby insisted.

Who were we to argue?

I explained that instructions for using the machines were in the boxes as well as a hefty supply of ingredients. I told them if I wasn't back in time, they should call my cell with questions about setup and operation. Then I headed for the door.

I walked briskly to my Audi. I pressed a button on my key chain and the lights flashed and doors unlocked. Once inside the two-seat sports car, I started the engine and waited. The Ford waited, too. I pulled away from the curb. The Ford did the same. I led it to Marshall Avenue and hung a left. It followed.

He's not being careful at all.

I flashed on my assailant in the Minneapolis skyway, heard the voice of my late-night caller. I wasn't frightened. Nor was I particularly angry. Mostly I was curious.

I headed east until I hit Lexington and hung a right. The Ford closed on my rear bumper, then fell back again. At University I hung another right and drove west. The Ford stayed with me. I caught the traffic light at Hamline. The Ford was two cars behind me. My cell rang and I answered it.

"McKenzie?" Bobby said.

"Yeah."

"The license plate is registered to Schroeder Private Investigations. It's a one-man shop owned by Schroeder, Gregory R."

"PI, huh."

"Schroeder is five-eight, 160 pounds, brown hair, hazel eyes, age fifty-five."

"Practically a senior citizen."

"Do you need more? I can get you more?"

"No, that'll do. Thanks, Bobby."

"I'll have the girls call you later, thank you for the sno-cone machine and whatnot."

"That's not necessary."

"Of course it is."

Bobby's daughters—Victoria and Katie—were my heirs. If Schroeder, Gregory R., should put a bullet in my head, they'd get to keep my treat machines, and my cars and house, and all my money.

I deactivated the cell phone and dropped it on the bucket seat next to me. I glanced in the mirror. My assailant in the skyway had brown hair, I recalled.

Now what? I wondered.

It's like your dear old dad used to say, my inner voice replied. *If you don't ask questions, you'll never get answers.*

Ask what?

Let's start with, why is he following you?

Sounds like a plan.

I annoyed the drivers directly behind me by driving below the speed limit. As I had intended, I caught the long stoplight at University and Snelling, probably the busiest intersection in St. Paul. I put the Audi in neutral, set the brake, opened the door, and stepped out into the street. I left my Beretta in the glove compartment. I had put it there earlier that morning because it had been my experience that after threats usually comes violence. Only this didn't seem to be that kind of play.

The hard wind peppered my face with tiny, sharp snow crystals—it was as if the weather was warning me that this was not a smart idea. Instinctively, I closed my eyes and angled my head away from the wind.

I made my way along the line of cars to the Ford Escort. The driver of the first car I passed rolled down his window and shouted, "Hey, man, what the hell are you doing?" I ignored him.

Even though he must have seen me coming, the man in the Escort seemed surprised when I halted next to his door. I examined him through the windshield—brown hair, hazel eyes, not tall. I rapped on the driver's-side window. Schroeder rolled it down.

"Hey, Greg," I said. Schroeder's eyes grew wide.

"There's a fifties-style cafe just a few blocks up University at Fairview called Andy's Garage. Near Porky's. Know it?"

He nodded.

"Meet me there and I'll buy you a cup of coffee."

He nodded again.

I returned to the Audi before the light changed. My hands trembled just a tad, but I didn't know if it was because of the cold or because once again I was playing fast and loose with whatever luck I had left.

I arrived first at Andy's Garage and found a parking space in the restaurant's tiny lot. Schroeder appeared moments later and was forced to park up the street. I was already sitting on a stool at the counter when he entered. A pretty young thing with pink-and-purple hair was pouring coffee when he sat next to me.

"Coffee," Schroeder said like he was begging for an antidote to West Nile disease.

The waitress poured a generous mug.

"Bless you, child," Schroeder said.

"Are you two together?" she asked, a perky smile on her face. She seemed genuinely pleased when Schroeder answered, "More or less."

"Let me know if there's anything else I can get for you."

I paid for both coffees, but the waitress let the money rest on the counter when she left.

"So, why are you following me, Greg?" I asked.

"For practice."

"You need it."

"Think so?"

"I made you in what, ten minutes?"

"Try a day and ten minutes."

I didn't believe him.

"I picked you up at the Groveland Tap yesterday," he added.

Yes, I did.

"The guy in the Park Avenue—he was very mediocre," Schroeder said. "I was surprised when he got the drop on you."

"So was I."

I raised the coffee mug to my lips with both hands for no other reason than to keep them from shaking and studied Schroeder over the rim. His eyes were more green than hazel and they seemed tired. His hair was in want of a trim, he needed a shave, and judging by the way he poured it into his coffee mug, he had way too much sugar in his diet.

I asked, "Who are you working for?"

"Can't tell ya."

"C'mon, Greg. You don't have privilege. Private investigators have no more rights than the average citizen. Fewer, in fact, if you want to keep your license."

"That's true. If a judge orders it, I'll talk my head off. You wouldn't happen to have a subpoena in your pocket, would you? No? I didn't think so."

"I could get one."

"Sure you could."

"Your Honor, this man attacked me on the Minneapolis skyway and then stalked me."

"That wasn't me."

"You fit the description."

"It wasn't me."

"Say, 'If you run I'll catch you, if you hide I'll find you.' "

"Is that what he said?"

"Another guy."

"The one in the parking lot of the International Market Square?"

Jesus.

"And over the phone," I said. "His voice was disguised. It could've been you."

"It wasn't."

I believed him.

Schroeder decided his coffee wasn't sweet enough and added more sugar.

"How did you learn my name?" he asked.

"I'm psychic."

"Then you should know who I'm working for."

He had me there.

"I know who *you're* working for," he told me.

"Are you psychic, too?"

"No. I'm clever, just like you."

"We should start a club."

"I'll be president because I'm older and wiser."

"Greg, why would someone want Barrett to be governor, but not U.S. senator?"

"I'll bite. Why would someone want Barrett to be governor, but not U.S. senator?"

"Because someone wants the job but doesn't think he could win in a stand-up fight."

"That's one explanation."

"You have others?"

Schroeder nodded his head.

"Such as?"

"You tell me."

"You're starting to bore me, Greg."

"Just lulling you into a sense of complacency."

"Ah."

"Want some advice?"

"No."

"Tell the big boys Barrett's a helluva guy and get out while the gettin's good."

"What did you say?"

Schroeder smiled the way a parent might at a child who's made a mistake on his homework.

"The guy who attacked you—he wants you to flush Barrett, doesn't he?"

"One does, I'm not sure about the other."

"Now you know that there are people just as determined that you don't."

"Oh what tangled webs we weave when first we practice to deceive."

"That sounds like the title of a book," Schroeder said.

"I don't suppose you have a scorecard that identifies the players and their positions."

"Hell. I'm still trying to get your number."

"Swell."

"I'll tell you this, though. You're way over your head."

"It wouldn't be the first time."

I slid off the stool and put on my bomber jacket. Schroeder watched me while I searched my archives for something clever to say, a good parting line. Schroeder waited patiently.

"Ah, hell," I said and left the cafe.

I drove my car out of the parking lot before Schroeder could even reach his and went west on University. Schroeder's Ford entered the traffic lane and sped up behind me. I watched him in my mirror.

"I wasn't paying attention yesterday," I told his reflection. "You won't surprise me again."

To prove it I slipped Big Bad Voodoo Daddy into my CD player. "How about a little traveling music," I said and cranked the volume.

I had paid nearly $45,000 for the fully loaded Audi 225 TT Coupe because of the CD player. And the seven speakers strategically located within the car. And the Napa leather interior. And the light silver color. Mostly, however, I bought it because the 1.8-liter 225-horsepower four-cylinder turbocharged engine could propel the Audi from zero to sixty in 6.3 seconds—at least that's what the manual said. I had done much better on several occasions.

I turned left at the intersection of University and Highway 280, and took my own sweet time reaching the long, sweeping entrance ramp to I-94. Schroeder's Ford followed, just beating the light. As if on cue, Big Bad Voodoo Daddy began laying down the opening riffs to the hard swinging "Boogie Bumper." I downshifted and accelerated. By the time I reached the top of the ramp, I was doing seventy.

Back in what he referred to as his "sordid youth," my father raced stock cars. He and his pal, Mr. Mosley, had put together a team that competed on dirt, clay, and asphalt ovals throughout Minnesota and western Wisconsin. Arlington Raceway, Cedar Lake Speedway, Elko Speedway, Raceway Park in Shakopee, the Minnesota State Fair Speedway, and even Brainerd International Raceway—my father had raced them all. It was at Brainerd that he bested actor and racing aficionado Paul Newman by the length of his front bumper in a qualifying run. He had a photo to commemorate the event, Newman's arm draped around his shoulder, the Oscar winner laughing at an off-color joke that my father never told me. It had been one of his most prized possessions and now I owned it.

Then Dad got married. His bride was ten years younger than he and openly frowned on his dangerous hobby, and when I was born, she made him swear off racing altogether. "You have a family to think of," she told him. After my mother died when I was in the sixth grade, I thought he might take it up again, but he didn't: A promise was a promise. Yet, while he no longer drove competitively, my dad remained a loyal fan of auto racing. He took me to Cedar Lake and Brainerd and, one glorious Memorial Day, to the Indianapolis 500. When I was fourteen, he taught me how to drive a stick on the dirt roads up north. I was the best driver in my class at the police academy before I even met my skills instructor, and afterward, I was better still.

Now I was shifting through all six speeds as I raced around and past the midmorning traffic on I-94, crossing from St. Paul into Minneapolis, downshifting, accelerating through the turns. The sound of a few bleating horns followed the Audi, but Dad had taught me the difference between driving fast and driving reckless. By the time I was heading south on I-35W, Schroeder and his Ford were nowhere to be seen. I didn't care. I continued to weave in and out of traffic at speeds occasionally topping ninety miles an hour, even as I rehearsed my alibi: "Thank goodness you stopped me, Officer. I need help. A man I've never seen before has been chasing me for miles. He's driving a white Ford Escort, license number yada yada yada . . ."

I negotiated the congested Highway 62 interchange while Big Bad Voodoo Daddy went to town on "Go Daddy-O." I kept driving south on 35W, crossed under I-494 and headed into Bloomington. I didn't slow down until I was on the bridge spanning the Minnesota River and the band started playing "So Long-Farewell-Goodbye."

I was actually chuckling out loud. The things my father taught me.

Chapter Five

The radio was playing "Light My Fire" by the Doors. John Allen Barrett had probably listened to the same song—probably the same station—when he lived in Victoria an eternity ago. I shuddered at the thought of it.

I had lost all of my radio stations long before I reached the outskirts of the city and had already spun the two CDs I had thought to bring with me. Usually I listen to jazz or what the marketing mavens call adult contemporary and modern progressive, but none of that music seemed to penetrate deep into the southwestern corner of Minnesota. Instead, my scanner picked up two Christian stations, a "big" country music station and a "real" country music station—damned if I could tell the difference—an "active rock" station that sounded like it had been programmed by teenage girls living in Des Moines, and a talk station on which a man with a jeer in his voice ridiculed Democrats, liberals, feminists, environmentalists, the news media, the ACLU, Hollywood movies that didn't have lots of explosions, all minorities that didn't speak English, and bad drivers before cycling back to the "classic rock" station. I stayed with the oldies even though the station was now playing "Knock Three Times" by Tony Orlando and Dawn.

Two highway signs told me everything I needed to know about Victoria, Minnesota. The first bragged that it was the Home of the Victoria Seven, Minnesota State High School Boys Basketball Champions. The second announced that it was the first stop in "The Ride Across Minnesota," the five-day, 326-mile bike ride for charity that began in Pipestone and snaked its way across the width of the state from South Dakota to the Wisconsin border. The second sign was located at the bottom of a hill just inside the city limits. I didn't see the sign or the Crown Victoria police cruiser parked next to it until I had crested the hill, and by then it was too late. The cruiser's light bar was flashing at me before I had time to even touch my brakes.

"Good morning, Officer."

I smiled politely after pulling over and rolling down my window, my hands on top of the steering wheel where the officer could see them.

"May I help you?"

The officer rested her forearm on the roof of the car and bent down to look through the window. She removed her sunglasses dramatically and announced, "Sir, you were exceeding the posted speed limit." Wisps of frozen breath rose from her mouth and were immediately snatched away by the wind.

I liked her right away. She was five feet, eight inches tall, about 130 pounds, and she stepped out of her cruiser onto the icy shoulder of the highway like she was modeling police wear. The hard wind ruffled the strands of light red hair that escaped her fur-trimmed hat. Her name tag read D. Mallinger.

"I was?" I asked innocently.

"Seventy-six in a thirty-five-mile zone. That's awfully fast. Especially on an icy road."

"Thirty-five!"

"The speed limit changed at the top of the hill."

I had driven into an old-fashioned, small-town speed trap and there was no arguing about it. I said, "I'm so sorry, Officer. I didn't realize." I was grateful that the cold wind blew in my face. It made my eyes water and helped give me an expression of pleading innocence—at least that's what I was going for.

"Nice-looking car," Mallinger said.

"The salesman said the design was influenced by Bauhaus, whoever he is."

"Bauhaus is not a *he*. It's an influential German school of design that held that art should be practical as well as aesthetically pleasing."

"Wow. That's really smart. I bet you could go on *Jeopardy!* or something."

The officer smirked and gave her head a half shake.

"Some women might get away with the dumb blonde routine, but you're not a woman and you're not blond. Are you?"

"It was worth a try."

"Uh-huh."

"Would it help if I told you I was racing to the hospital to visit my poor, sick mother?"

"I'll need to see your driver's license, sir."

"How 'bout if I told you I was eleven and a half years on the job in St. Paul?"

"Driver's license."

I reached toward the opening of my bomber jacket with my right hand. Mallinger stepped backward, her hand moving to her holster. I stopped and said, "My wallet is in my inside jacket pocket."

I unzipped the jacket with my left hand and held it open for her to see. With my right I carefully removed the wallet. I found my license. Mallinger took the plastic card in her gloved hand.

"Wait here," she said and retreated to her cruiser.

I watched Mallinger's reflection in my mirror while I waited, watched her work her onboard computer. She was not only pretty, she was smart. Most of the women and all of the guys I knew probably thought Bauhaus was a bull. A few moments later, she returned.

"Mr. McKenzie . . ."

Here it comes.

"You have two speeding tickets over the past four months, but nothing previous. Why is that?"

Because the two tickets notwithstanding, most cops will give a retired police officer a break, I thought, but didn't say.

"It's a new car," I told her.

"Let me guess. It's fast."

"It has a top speed of 130. More if I fiddle with the electronics."

"You're a little young to be having a midlife crisis, aren't you?" I didn't answer and she said, "If I give you a citation the state'll probably revoke your driving privileges. I wouldn't want that to happen seeing how you were once on the job, so I'm going to let you off with a warning. 'Course, you've had warnings before, haven't you."

"One or two."

"Uh-huh. Where are you heading?"

"Victoria."

"That's my town," Mallinger confirmed. "I catch you speeding here again, I'll hammer you like a nail in soft wood."

Nice metaphor, I told myself.

"I'll be on my best behavior," I promised.

"Either grow up or get rid of the car."

Neither one us had anything to say after that and Mallinger returned to her cruiser. I waited until she was safely in her car before pulling off the shoulder and accelerating—slowly—to thirty-five.

"D. Mallinger," I said aloud as I watched her image recede in my mirror. "I wonder what the D stands for."

I don't know what I expected from Victoria. A quaint hamlet draped in sheets of pristine snow like something pictured on a postcard, I suppose. Instead, I found a tired, diminutive Twin Cities. A slaughterhouse and a lawn mower company were pumping enough money into the town to support a small hospital, a library, two elementary schools, a high school, city hall, fire station, and a law enforcement center, but none of them were new. There was a Wal-Mart, of course. A few fast-food joints, bars, convenience stores, and a tiny barn that sold Computers-Crafts-Miniature Golf lined Victoria's main drag. Christmas decorations still hung from stoplights and street lamps, but there was no joy in them. The evergreen boughs, gold garlands, and red ribbons appeared as gray and exhaust-stained as the drifts plowed along the boulevards.

Yet there was another side to the city as well—snow-covered baseball and soccer fields, several parks, three lakes with beaches closed for the winter, and the Des Moines River. A few blocks off Main Street I discovered a charming network of tree-lined streets, large and venerable houses with sprawling porches and tire swings in the front yard, rolling hills marked with the tracks of sleds, toboggans, and skis, as well as something I hadn't prepared for. How big the sky seemed. It stretched from the white water tower way up north to the grain elevators way down south with only the dome of the courthouse and a few church steeples for competition.

Now this is what a small town should look like.

Much of what I knew about Victoria I had learned from a city map I bought at the gas station where I stopped to fill my Audi. I had considered lunch; it was fast approaching noon. But first things first. Using the map, I navigated the streets until I found 347 Second Avenue and rolled into the parking lot. It was a small business. The large, illuminated sign above the door and windows read: FIT TO PRINT. The smaller sign in the corner of the window listed services: Black/White & Color Copies • Print From Disk/Color Laser Prints • Manuals, Reports & Newsletters • Flyers, Brochures & Transparencies • Binding, Laminating & Custom Tabs • Instant Posters, Banners & Exhibits • Business Cards & Letterhead • Invitations & Specialty Papers • High Speed Internet Access • PC & Mac Rental Stations.

I knew I was screwed before I even left my car.

The kid behind the counter looked like he was about sixteen. He smiled as if he meant it when he said, "Good afternoon, sir, how may I help you?" He was Hispanic, with dark hair, dark eyes, and a name tag that identified him as Rufugio Tapia. His accent was faint—you had to listen hard to hear it, but it was there. To the right of him there were eight copiers of various size and function; a woman was working one of them, copying what looked like newspaper clippings. To the left was an equal number of PCs and Macs separated from each other by soft privacy walls. Behind the counter I could see several large printers and a couple of machines I couldn't identify.

"You provide Internet access," I said.

"Yes, sir."

"Do you keep track of who uses your machines and when?"

"Sir?"

"Is it possible to learn who used your computers at any given time?"

The smile disappeared and his face closed down.

"No," he said.

"So, if I were to log onto one of your machines . . ."

"Sir, may I ask your name?"

"McKenzie. Now if I were . . ."

"Why are you asking these questions?"

Tapia wasn't angry, but he was getting to it.

"Perhaps you should let me speak to your supervisor," I said.

"I am the supervisor."

"The owner then."

"I am the owner."

"You're kidding?"

He crossed his arms over his chest, a classic defensive posture.

"It is not possible for a Mexican-American to own a business?" he said.

"How old are you?"

"Twenty-three."

"When I was twenty-three I owned a Dave Winfield autographed baseball glove, some hockey equipment, and a 1974 Chevy Impala. I was thinking of your age when I said, 'You're kidding.'"

"Oh. Yes. I understand."

"Listen," I said. "Here's my problem. An e-mail was sent from one of your machines Friday. I'm trying to figure out who sent it?"

"Why?"

"It wasn't a very nice e-mail."

Tapia inhaled through his teeth and exhaled slowly.

"All of our machines are self-service," he said. "Each comes with a self-service card reader. You access them by using a credit card or by buying one of our cards."

"How does that work?"

Tapia led me to a kiosk next to the PCs. The front of it had simple instructions printed in large type—plus illustrations—explaining how to slide ones, fives, tens, and twenties into one slot, press the appropriate buttons on a touch screen, and receive a coded self-service card from another slot good for photocopies and Internet access. You insert the card—or any of a half-dozen major credit cards—into the card reader, click a few icons with the mouse, and you have access, $6.39 for fifteen minutes, $25.56 for an hour.

"I never know who is on-line and I never know where they go while they're on-line," Tapia said. "I prefer it that way."

"There's no log, no . . . ?"

"Nothing like that, Mr. McKenzie."

"You have no way of knowing who uses your computers?"

"None. I suppose you could contact the credit card company."

"Which one?"

Tapia shrugged.

"Do you remember anything that was unusual Friday?" I asked. "A customer who acted odd? I'm talking early evening. Around seven."

"If it was a regular day, maybe I could tell you. But Friday we celebrated our first anniversary. I had an open house all day long. Prizes. Discounts on printing and copies . . ."

"Internet access?"

"That, too."

"Swell."

"People were coming and going all day. At five, I shut down my presses. I had cake and drinks for all of my employees, my business clients, my regulars. At one time there might have been as many as a hundred people in here. Any one of them could have used a PC or Mac and I would not have known it. Sorry."

"Don't worry about it. And, hey, congratulations on your year."

The smile Tapia had shown me when I had first arrived had returned.

"*Gracias*," he said.

The Rainbow Cafe had a worn linoleum floor, Formica tables, and metal chairs. The half-dozen booths arranged against the walls were upholstered in hot pink synthetic leather that was worn at the edges. A dozen stainless metal stools with seats covered in the same material were fixed to the floor along a lunch counter that stretched nearly the entire length of the building. There was a window cut in the wall between the dining area and the kitchen. Two waitresses wearing pink-and-white uniforms pinned their orders to a metal wheel fixed to the top of the window frame, shouted out a number, and spun the wheel toward the cook. When the order was ready, the cook slapped the plates on the windowsill, rang a squat metal bell, and repeated the number. In the corner, a jukebox was spinning Conway Twitty's "It's Only Make Believe." I felt I had stepped into 1958.

I found an empty slot at the counter and read the place mat while I waited to be served. The mat presented horoscopes based on the signs of the zodiac. It said the stars were aligned against me. "A difficult year both professionally and romantically can be expected." As if things weren't bad enough.

The waitress saw me frown as I studied the chart.

"The Mexican across the street is supposed to be delivering the new place mats later this week," she said while setting water and a menu in front of me.

It was only then that I noticed the horoscope was for last year. I was relieved by the news although when I thought about it, things professional and romantic couldn't have been much better last year. So much for astrology.

When the waitress asked, "What'll ya have?" I answered, "What's good?" She said, "Try the cheeseburger. We make it with blue cheese." So I did. It turned out to be one of the best burgers I had ever had—plump, juicy, the cheese melted just so, the onions grilled to perfection. To be honest, I wasn't all that surprised. The small, out-of-the-way joints have always been my favorite restaurants; their food is so much tastier than the chains.

While I ate, I plotted strategy. It didn't amount to much. I knew that the e-mail had originated in Victoria. That meant the governor's enemy was in Victoria. And, of course, Elizabeth Rogers had been killed in Victoria. The riddle was here. I decided that if I hung around long enough, asked enough questions, I might learn the answer to it—to all of it. Something else, probably more likely: If I couldn't find out who sent the e-mail, maybe if I made a big enough pest of myself, the e-mailer would find me.

It was awfully thin, I knew. But it wasn't like I had anything better to do. It's not like I actually worked for a living.

I turned my attention to the discussion going on in the corner. Over a dozen people, mostly old, mostly men, occupied a couple of booths and two tables. A man approaching fifty and wearing a jacket that read A-1 Auto on the back was talking loud enough for everyone to hear.

"Ten years ago you'd only see the Mexicans, the Hispanics, in the summer. Working on farms. Now"—he shook his head sadly—"fifteen percent, that's what they say. Immigrants—the Hispanics and the Somalis—ten years ago they were one percent of the population and now it's fifteen percent. That's why we're doing the Nicholas County Coalition for Immigration Reduction. That's why we're askin' you to join. We can't just let 'em invade our country like this, take our jobs.

"I was talking to a guy over to the meat plant. He said that immigrants comin' in, they're now thirty-five percent of the work force. If that ain't bad enough, they're drivin' down wages. In 1980, a guy could make $17 an hour as a meat packer—that's in today's dollars, adjusted for inflation. Now, it's only $12 an hour.

"This can't go on. If we don't do something about

these people—We gotta get *real* Americans back to work. They need jobs, too."

His audience nodded its collective head.

"As native-born Minnesotans," the mechanic continued, "we need to protect what we have. These people, bringin' in their culture, bringin' in their crime—we didn't have a drug problem in this city. We didn't have people dealing meth and cocaine and whatnot to our children. Where do you think that came from?"

I thought of Tapia, the kid across the street at Fit to Print, who worked hard enough to own his own business at age twenty-three. Yeah, I could see how he was a threat to the community, and I laughed. It wasn't a loud laugh nor did it last very long, but there were two kids about Tapia's age and dressed in the coveralls of an auto mechanic. They noticed it and instantly took offense. They nudged the mechanic. The mechanic spun around and gave me a hard look. I went back to my burger.

"Hey, you," said the mechanic. "You think something is funny?"

"Don't mind me. I'm just passing through."

"You got a problem?"

"Not at all. Go right ahead with your meeting."

"We're fightin' for the future of our community. Is that all right with you?"

"Honestly, pal. I couldn't care less. It's not my town, it's not my problem."

"No, but you're gonna sit there smirkin', thinkin' we're a bunch of dumb hicks who don't know any better. We deal in facts here and we don't like it when people, when outsiders treat us like the KKK or somethin', sayin' we're racist."

He took several steps toward me. At the police academy, I was taught that most people when they get worked up will display a series of behavior warning signals that indicate Assault Is Possible—head back, shoulders back, face is red, lips pushed forward baring teeth, breathing coming fast and shallow. The mechanic was burning through them like a highway flare.

"The things you're saying, it's been said by Americans before." I was trying to sound conciliatory, trying to defuse the situation. "That's why I was smiling. Not because I think you're a racist."

"Then you are sayin' we're racists."

There was no arguing with him because there was no substance to his complaints, only bitterness and defeat. How do you challenge that, and why would you? I gave it a shot, anyway. Silly me.

"No," I said. I could see his name stenciled in red above his left breast. I used it. "I'm not calling you a racist, Brian. It's just that what you're saying about the Hispanics, the Somalis, it's what people said about the Irish in 1860 and the Scandinavians in 1890. It's what they said about the Jews and the Germans and the Asians when they came here. Yet things somehow always managed to work out."

"You think we're racists *and* idiots, then."

"I think you're bored. I think that not much happens in a small town; there isn't much to talk about, so you spend all your time talking about this—the Great Immigrant Invasion."

Okay, that wasn't very conciliatory, but the mechanic was starting to piss me off with his racist talk. All I wanted was something to eat, not get dragged into his small town squabbles.

He stepped forward. His face went from red to white, his lips tightened over his teeth, his hands were closed and he began rocking back and forth as his eyes darted from my jaw to my stomach to my groin—target glances we call them. I slipped off the stool wishing I had an OC agent, wishing I could Mace the sonuvabitch before he took another step.

The men around him became still. Their eyes looked angry and their faces were rough and tired and disappointed. They seemed poised to take out their frustrations on someone—anyone—and were just waiting for a signal to strike. I was becoming very nervous.

The door to the cafe opened. Officer Mallinger stepped through it. She seemed to understand the situation immediately.

"Brian," she shouted. "McKenzie." Using our names, something I was also taught to do at the academy. "Look at me. I said, look at me."

We looked.

"If you can't do what you're about to do in front of me, you better not do it." The sentence seemed convoluted, but her meaning was clear.

The mechanic said, "He's an asshole."

"No law against that, Brian," Mallinger said. "If there was, I'd have to arrest half the people in town."

Just like that, the tension in the cafe gave way to words, smirks, glares, and grumbles. I decided Mallinger was very good at her job.

"Are you taking his side?" The mechanic spoke defiantly, but his posture had changed. His hands were in front of his body, palms out, and his head was slightly bowed—signals of submission. "You protecting this shithead?"

"I'm protecting the peace," Mallinger said. "It's what they pay me for."

"Yeah, well, just remember *Interim Chief*—the job ain't permanent yet."

"I know," Mallinger said. "I'm hoping I'll have your support and the support of all the rest of you, too"—she gestured at the mechanic's audience—"when the city council votes next month."

Mallinger turned away from the crowd and looked at me.

"Come here," she said.

She sat me down in a booth and leaned in close.

"Chief, huh?" I said.

"Take that stupid grin off your face."

I stopped smiling.

"Everyone's watching. Don't look at them. Look at me. Everyone's watching. They're expecting me to tear you a new one because even though Brian's an immense jerk, he lives in this town and you don't. Nod your head."

I nodded.

"Things are volatile enough around here. I got some asshole selling meth to high school kids. I got punks hassling citizens over the color of their skin. Yesterday I got a call to break up a knife fight at the meat plant. Two guys going at each other with these huge boning knives. Turned out they were fighting over a woman, but one was Hispanic and the other was white, so now it's a racial issue. I don't need this on top of it. I don't need riots in the Rainbow Cafe. Nod your head."

I nodded.

"Do you have business in Victoria?"

"Yes."

"Then why don't you get up, pay your tab, and get to it. Nod your head."

I nodded.

"Go."

I left the booth and I moved to the cash register. I gave the waitress a twenty and she gave me my change, along with some advice. "Why don't you go someplace warm, and I don't mean California." Apparently, she didn't like me. I couldn't imagine why, unless she was pals with the mechanic, or she didn't like outsiders causing trouble in her place, or she thought I should leave a bigger tip.

I asked her, "Do you have a newspaper in this town?"

"*Victoria Herald.*" She reached for a copy stacked next to the cash register.

"No. I meant, where is it?"

"Three blocks down and two blocks over," she said, using her hands to indicate which directions were down and over.

"Thank you."

"Go slip on the ice."

A few minutes later, I pulled into a small parking lot next to a flat, pale, one-story building. Inside, I found a chest-high counter made of blond wood. Behind the counter was a man who was my height and who even looked a little like me except that he was ten years younger. I, of course, was better looking.

"Excuse me," I said. "I would like to look at some past issues of the *Herald.*"

"How past?"

"Back when the Victoria Seven won the tournament."

"Let me guess. You're researching a book about the Seven, or maybe a screenplay like *Hoosiers*, the Gene Hackman movie."

"Do you get a lot of that?"

"Not a lot, but enough that no one is surprised by it. I'm Kevin Salisbury."

"McKenzie."

"This way."

Salisbury led me across the small, cluttered newsroom to a door labeled EMPLOYEES ONLY. Inside the windowless room, I found a series of wide, black-metal shelves shoved against a wall, each shelf stacked with past issues of the *Herald*. Three vending machines and two plastic trash containers labeled for recycling were arranged side by side against another wall. Baseball bats, balls, bases, and catcher's equipment were dumped in one corner and a life-size cardboard cutout of Bart Simpson saying, "Don't have a cow" was in another. In the center of the room there was a cafeteria-style table strewn with discarded newspapers and magazines and surrounded by metal folding chairs.

Salisbury quickly located what he was looking for—two thick files of yellowed newspapers held together by what resembled a giant three-ring binder. "February-March" and the year was written on the cover of the first in faded marker and "April-May" was written on the other.

"You'll probably want to start with these," Salisbury said. He set the files on the cafeteria table. "I've been telling the boss we should have put all these on microfiche years ago, but he doesn't listen to me."

"Thank you," I said. I slipped off my bomber's jacket, draped it over the back of a chair, and sat down.

I opened the first thick book and tried to find March 15, the day Elizabeth Rogers was killed. Only the *Herald* didn't publish on Saturday—only Sunday and Tuesday through Friday. I scanned the front page of the Sunday,

March 16, edition. The cover story was all about how the Victoria Seven had upset Minneapolis North High School for the right to advance to the state basketball tournament the following week. There was no mention of the murder of Elizabeth until Tuesday, March 18. The headline read: *Murder of Cheerleader Casts Shadow on State Basketball Tournament.* The subhead claimed *Victoria Seven Will Fight On Despite Loss.* Both stories were wrapped around a shot of the basketball players, which included an impossibly young John Allen Barrett.

A shot of Elizabeth, obviously her school photo, was tucked inside. The pose was typical, shoulders rotated slightly to the left, head turned to the right, chin up, eyes staring above and past the camera. Yet Elizabeth's youthful beauty seemed to transcend the mediocrity of the photographer and the ancient newsprint. She had straight, light-colored hair falling to her shoulders, a self-confident, almost smug smile, and large eyes. The cutline beneath the photograph said her funeral had been scheduled for early Wednesday morning so the basketball team could attend before boarding the bus to St. Paul.

I jumped ahead to the March 20 edition. There was extensive coverage of the funeral, yet again it was all about the boys, with plenty of photographs of them standing at the graveside looking uncomfortable and bored. It annoyed me that none of them appeared to be grieving. Included was a midrange shot of Barrett and a man the cutline identified as Coach Mark Testen. I was pleased to see what I thought were tears on Testen's face, but closer examination revealed that it was merely two narrow bandages running from his left eye to the middle of his cheek.

I returned to the Tuesday edition and began taking notes. Over twenty minutes passed before Salisbury spoke, startling me. I had forgotten that he was there.

"The case was never solved," he said.

"Excuse me?"

"They never found her killer. That's what you're interested in, isn't it? Not the Seven, the murder."

"Why do you say that?"

Salisbury pointed at my notepad.

"Like all good journalists, I can read upside down."

I glanced at the notepad. I had scribbled notes about Elizabeth, where her body was found, when, by whom, where she lived, and more. There was nothing about the basketball team.

"It's part of the story, isn't it? The story of the Victoria Seven?"

"I suppose it is," Salisbury agreed. "I wrote a piece about it myself a few years ago during the Seven's anniversary reunion."

"I'd like to read it."

"There's nothing there that you can't read here," he said, indicating the binder. "Except my contention that the chief of police screwed up, and didn't I catch hell for that."

"Chief?" I glanced at my notes.

"Leo Bohlig. He had been chief since the beginning of time. He retired last year and Danny Mallinger took over."

"Danny Mallinger?"

"Danielle. Know her?"

So that's what the D stands for.

"We met on the road," I said.

"Anyway, Bohlig was still chief when I wrote the story. He wouldn't answer any of my questions, wouldn't even let me read the files. Since the case was still active"—Salisbury quoted the air with both hands—"he said the public had no right to see the files. Personally, I don't know about that." Salisbury shrugged. "He screwed up and I wrote that he screwed up and that almost got me fired."

"What happened?"

"It's a small town newspaper and I wrote a story that gave the small town a black eye and the owner didn't like it. Simple as that. This paper—my boss doesn't want negative stories about Victoria in it. Last week a couple of kids got busted doing crystal meth. Should have been on the front page. We had three paragraphs on page five."

"Tell me about Bohlig's investigation."

"Elizabeth's body was found in a ditch along County Road 13. Next to Milepost Three, they found her, not far from the Des Moines River. It was within the Victoria city limits so Chief Bohlig claimed jurisdiction. Normally, a crime like that would automatically go to the Nicholas County Sheriff's Department regardless of where it was committed. Bohlig wouldn't give it up. He was pretty adamant about it. Why the county didn't just shove him out of the way, I can't say. I figured Bohlig must have pulled some pretty stout strings, collected a lot of favors. Anyway, he ran the investigation and came up with nothing. No one was arrested. No leads were developed. No one was even questioned hard as far as I could tell. Eventually, he announced that the murder was committed by transients who were just passing through."

"You disagree?"

"Hell, I don't know. I'm only saying that the investigation should have been handled by people who knew what they were doing, not some hick-town cop in a six-man department whose idea of a major crime was someone stealing fishing equipment out of a boathouse. There's been only one murder committed in Victoria in its entire history. One. It remains unsolved. Bohlig blew it. That's what I wrote. I was fresh out of JO school and just loaded with idealism, and I wrote that the city of Victoria's police chief was less than he should be and they damn near fired me for it. 'That's not the way we practice journalism,' they told me. I came down here hoping I could use the *Herald* as a stepping-stone in a long and storied journalism career. Now, I'm not so sure."

"Tell me what you can about the case."

Salisbury sat in the chair across the table from me. "Why do you want to know?"

"Like I said, it's part of the story of the Victoria Seven."

"I don't think so. You're on to something else."

I considered his hypothesis, couldn't concoct a lie that would refute it in such short notice, so I told him the truth. "I'm trying to find out what happened to Elizabeth Rogers."

"Why?"

"I can't tell you."

"Then why should I help?"

"There might be a story in it. Something big enough you might get a call from the Cities."

"I'm listening."

"I'll make you a deal."

"Oh, I love deals."

"If I can solve the crime, or at least come up with a better explanation of what happened to Elizabeth than the one Chief Bohlig supplied, I'll make sure you get the exclusive."

"Is that why you're here? To solve the crime?"

"No, I'm not. But I might have to solve it to get what I came to Victoria for."

"What is that?"

"See, now we're back to square one again."

"You can't tell me," Salisbury said.

"No, but you weren't that far wrong earlier when you said book or screenplay." I hoped the lie would give him something to think about.

Salisbury reached a hand across the table.

"Done."

I shook his hand, then retrieved my pen and notebook.

"What do you have?" I asked him.

"Saturday, March 15—This is all in the newspaper, by the way; you can look it up yourself. Anyway, the day after the Victoria Seven upset Minneapolis North for a berth in the state basketball tournament there was a party at the house of the mayor. Everyone was there, including the coach and all seven of his players. Jack Barrett, captain of the basketball team, was dancing with Elizabeth Rogers, captain of the cheerleading squad, his longtime girlfriend. In the middle of the dance, they start arguing—now that's something I developed on my own, it never was printed in the paper. Barrett and Rogers had an argument, and Barrett left the party early, leaving Elizabeth."

"Did Barrett leave alone?"

"Yes."

"Where did he go?"

"I don't know."

"Where did he live?"

"Outside town about four, five miles. His old man had a farm off of County Road 13."

"Did he have a car?"

"No."

"Then how did he get home?"

"Walked."

"Four, five miles? At night? In the winter?"

"This isn't the Cities, McKenzie. There's no bus service. People walk a lot, sometimes because they have to. Especially kids if that's the only way they can get around. Distance doesn't mean as much."

"What was the argument about?"

"Argument?"

"Barrett and Elizabeth."

"Oh, yeah, the argument. No one seems to know."

"What did Barrett say?"

"Nothing as far as I know. If Bohlig interviewed him, he's kept the conversation to himself. Anyway, Jack leaves, Elizabeth stays. This is around eight thirty, nine. The party goes on. Around eleven o'clock, which is late in Victoria even if you did just win a historic basketball game, Elizabeth leaves. Alone. Witnesses are pretty adamant about that."

"Where was she going?"

"The assumption is that she was going home, but like most assumptions . . ."

"Did Elizabeth live near the mayor's house?"

"A few blocks away. She never made it. Her parents were worried, but they didn't contact the police until after two."

"Did anyone leave the party just before or after Elizabeth?"

"No one remembers after all these years, and like I said, I can't get access to the police reports. All I know is what was reported in the newspaper at the time. They found Elizabeth's body at Milepost Three early the next morning. There was no sign of a struggle. Apparently, she had been dumped there. That's what Bohlig said—one of the few things he said for the record."

"How was she killed?"

"Manual strangulation."

"Hmm."

"What does 'hmm' mean?"

"Strangling someone with your bare hands is considered an intimate way to commit murder. Profilers will tell you that it usually indicates the killer had a personal relationship with the victim—usually, but not always."

Salisbury stared at me for a moment.

"Who are you?"

"What was the condition of the body?" I asked.

"What do you mean?"

"Was she dressed, was she . . . ?"

"Fully clothed. Boots, coat, purse nearby."

"Not raped. Was she robbed?"

"She only had a few dollars in her wallet, but it was still there. A locket was missing. Apparently she wore it around her neck on a silver chain, wore it everywhere, but that could have come off when she was strangled."

"Not robbed or raped."

"So where's the motive?" Salisbury asked as if the question had just occurred to him.

"What did the ME's report say?"

"Don't know. I never saw it. No one did. Bohlig said that releasing it would compromise the investigation. That's what he said during the investigation. Later, he wouldn't even tell me that much. I tried to get a copy from the county—the Nicholas County ME did the autopsy—but I was stonewalled."

"Was there any other evidence gathered at the scene?"

Salisbury shook his head.

"There's always something," I insisted, before reminding myself that the crime was committed over thirty years ago. That was practically the Dark Ages compared to today's forensic achievements.

"Who covered the original story?" I turned my attention to the ancient newspapers, found the byline William Gargaro. "Can we talk to him?"

"Conversation might be a little one-sided."

"What do you mean?"

"I mean I wanted to talk to him, too, only Billy's been dead for like twenty years. Most likely, though, everything he knew he put in the paper. That's what my editor said."

"Okay." I packed up my notes.

"What are you going to do?" Salisbury asked.

"Make a nuisance of myself. Oh, one thing. I want to add a codicil to our agreement."

"Which is?"

"You don't know me and you don't know what I'm doing."

"That's true enough."

Chapter Six

Victoria Area High School overlooked the Des Moines River. It was a comparatively new building—the date 1988 was carved into a cornerstone—with a football stadium on one side and a baseball stadium on the other. There was an empty field between the school and the river, and by the way the snow was trampled, I guessed that it was a popular place with the kids.

I parked my Audi in the lot behind the school. I had a difficult time finding a space because of all the cars there. I guessed that most of them belonged to the students—so much for Salisbury's theory of kids in Victoria hoofing it when they needed to get around.

The doors to the school were unlocked. I walked in and began wandering the halls, looking for the main office. No one stopped me; no one challenged my right to be there. I had to wonder if the school board had made a considered decision to operate its school like a school instead of the armed camp found in so many other schools in so many other towns, or if they were just being careless over security. Then I met the three women in the office and realized it was carelessness.

I asked for the names and whereabouts of any teachers who might have taught at Victoria when the Seven won the tournament, and they were happy to tell me—without checking my ID or, for that matter, even asking my name.

"Oh, you want to see Suzi Shimek," one woman told me.

"Where is Suzi?" the second asked.

"She has a free period, Room 238," answered the third after consulting a schedule pinned to the office wall.

I was given directions, yet no escort, and none of the women asked why I wanted to see Suzi.

Small towns seem never to believe they have a problem until the problem hits them square between the eyes, my inner voice concluded.

I eventually found Suzi Shimek hunched over a desk grading papers. Auburn hair fell along the side of her face and she pulled it back with her free hand and tucked it behind her ear. A pair of glasses sat on her head like a tiara. She was a well-made woman and my first thought was that when she was younger she must have had a difficult time keeping the minds of the teenage boys in her class on their work. Even now I could believe half of them would be in serious lust over her.

I introduced myself gently and Suzi assured me that she welcomed my interruption. She said she would love to chat about "those heady days when the Victoria Seven ruled the earth. Besides," she added, "after grading the same essay question on sixty-two tests, any break in the routine is a blessing."

Suzi offered coffee in a way that made it impossible for

me to refuse and led me to a teacher's lounge near the second-floor stairway. I had never been in a teacher's lounge before and was disappointed to discover that it was little more than a small lunchroom. There was a large round table, chairs, vending machines, coffeemaker, refrigerator, a CD/AM/FM stereo cassette recorder on top of the refrigerator, microwave, a bulletin board loaded with flyers, calendars, and memos, and two battered, but comfortable, sofas placed at a forty-five-degree angle to each other. Next to the sofas was a bookcase containing yearbooks as well as textbooks and other volumes. After pouring coffee, Suzi took one of the yearbooks from the shelf and began paging through it. Her spectacles were still perched on top of her head and I wondered if she wore them to see or strictly for show.

Suzi sat next to me on the sofa. Her eyes were soft blue and candid. I didn't think she'd be good at keeping secrets.

"They told me when I was going for my teaching certificate that I would always remember my first class, and they were right," Suzi told me. "I remember my students quite vividly. The Seven, of course, the ones I actually taught at least. Beth Rogers. I had a kid named Paulie who could juggle five balls simultaneously, and a girl named Rachel who threw up during midterms and eventually dropped out because she was pregnant—ah!"

Suzi turned the yearbook so I could see the page she found. There was a black-and-white photo of a young woman with dark hair that fell to her waist leaning against a classroom door with her arms folded across her chest. She was wearing bell-bottom jeans and a loose-fitting peasant blouse adorned with flowers.

"Now be honest, don't I look like I'm sixteen?"

"This was you?" I blurted.

"It's hard to keep order in the classroom when you look younger than your students."

Suzi turned the book so she could look at herself some more.

"How did you manage it?" I asked.

"Oh, I didn't," Suzi replied. "I was an awful teacher my first couple of years. Just terrible. I didn't realize that at the time, though. I thought I was better than Mr. Chips. I thought I was hipper than Sidney Poitier in *To Sir, With Love.*"

I decided I liked Suzi. Anyone who described herself in relation to movies nearly always got my vote.

"Here's another one." It was a photograph of her and a second woman just as young. "That's me and Monte, Grace Monteleone, but everyone called her Monte. We were both first-year teachers and we kind of gravitated toward each other out of self-defense. We became quite good friends. Now be honest, weren't we just the cutest things?"

I had to agree. She and Monte had looked like they were manufactured in the same factory—long hair, long legs, short skirts, and thin waists—although, while Suzi's face was open and exuberant, Monte's was guarded and had a sad kind of smile that reminded me of the painting of the ballerina hanging in Mr. Muehlenhaus's lobby.

"What became of her?" I asked.

"Monte didn't care too much for Victoria. She did at first. She seemed to love the town, seemed to welcome living here after growing up on the north side of Minneapolis. That changed around the beginning of February at just about the time people were getting excited about the Seven and started making heroes out of the kids. Jack Barrett had been one of her pet projects. He was ungodly smart. He would have been an honor student in any school in the country and Monte was determined that he go to college. Except, suddenly, it was all basketball, basketball, basketball and forget about school. Coach Testen lectured her for giving the boys homework and when she brought it to the principal, he sided with Coach. I think that took a lot out of her.

"Besides, look around. It's Victoria, Minnesota, for God's sake. Back in those days it wasn't even half as big as it is now. The school was this broken-down barn on the other side of town. Enrollment—we had ninety-two students, total. That's why the basketball team was so small. Seven kids played basketball and eleven played hockey. There was talk of closing the school and sending the kids to Windom. That ended after the Seven won the championship. Nobody wanted to be the one to say let's shut it down after that. Plus, we started getting industry. The lawn equipment people moved here. That generated 350 jobs. The meatpacking plant came two years later. That was another 475 jobs. The town was saved, the school was saved. We now have an enrollment of nearly six hundred. The Seven had a lot to do with that. They brought a lot of positive attention to Victoria at a time when the town badly needed it."

Suzi smiled broadly.

"Still, we were both twenty-two, Monte and I, single and pretty and living away from home for the first time, and we couldn't get a date with anyone who used vowels when they spoke besides eh! There was a sexual revolution going on out there and we were missing out. It didn't bother me so much. I was excited to be a part of it all, the Seven, the resurgence of the town. Monte—at the end of the school year, she moved to Mankato."

"Did you keep in touch?"

"Not at first," Suzi said. "I heard she got married, had a child—heard that her husband was killed in Vietnam. We didn't talk again until a few years later and I saw her name. Monte was conducting a seminar at a teacher's conference. She had kept her maiden name, which was a radical thing for a married woman to do in those days, but she was always a bit of a feminist. I saw her name and looked her up and we've been fairly close ever since."

"What about the other teachers that were here back then?"

"Gone. Some died. Some moved away. There weren't that many of us. As far as I know I'm the only one from back then who's still teaching."

"Maybe you can answer some questions for me."

"About the Seven?" Suzi asked.

"Yes, but mostly about Elizabeth Rogers."

Suzi thumbed through the yearbook, found a page and turned the book for me to see. The photograph covered nearly the entire page. It was the same shot that appeared in the newspaper, only in color. There was a black border around the photograph and beneath it Elizabeth's name was printed along with an epitaph.

God gives us all love.
But someone to love he only lends us.

"Beth," Suzi said. "She was what they used to call 'a dish.'"

I hadn't thought much about her when I first saw Elizabeth's faded black-and-white photograph in the newspaper. Just a pretty girl now gone. It was only her death that had held interest for me. Yet seeing the photograph in color, that changed. Elizabeth's face was smooth and gold tinted, her hair was a lustrous shade of gold that only nature could create, and her eyes—had they really been that brown, or was it merely a publisher's trick, a mixing of ink?

Elizabeth had been seventeen at the time of her murder. It must have seemed to her that all the good things in life were hers for the taking. She had only to reach out her hand.

Did she date much? I wondered, suddenly. Date boys besides Jack? My mother didn't have many dates when she was in high school. She told me most boys were afraid of her, afraid she would reject them. Or they had simply assumed she already had a boyfriend: someone who looked like her, of course she did. My mother had to wait for a man who was nearly a decade older than she, a man who had been with the First Marines at Chosin Reservoir in Korea, who wasn't afraid of anything, including a beautiful woman. Did Elizabeth have that problem, too? What about the other girls? Did they resent her because she had such pretty eyes, like they did my mom? Did she ever have the chance to be anything but a girl with pretty eyes?

Suzi turned the book around and stared at the photo for a few moments.

"Poor Beth. I sometimes wonder what she was thinking when—when it happened. Did she know she was going to die? Did she think she would be saved at the last moment? She must have been afraid. Alone and afraid. Did she beg for her life? Did she pray? Did she . . . ?"

Suzi closed the book and set it on the sofa next to her.

"Life should be a pleasure for those people lucky enough to be born pretty. That's what the poets tell us, and I believe it," Suzi said. "Only it isn't always so, is it? What did Shakespeare write? '*Alas, what danger will it be to us, Maids as we are, to travel forth so far! Beauty provoketh thieves sooner than gold.*' "

"I hadn't thought that much about it," I confessed.

"I have. Far too much. For months after Beth's death, I took every compliment as a threat, every invitation as— It was years before I felt comfortable enough to walk the streets alone, even here in crime-free Victoria. Truth is, I don't think I have really gotten over it. It was just too close to me.

"The sad thing, one of the truly sad things, is that we never really had the chance to mourn her. Excitement over the Seven took care of that."

"Were you at the party?" I asked.

"The night she was killed?"

"Elizabeth was dating Jack Barrett," I reminded the teacher.

"Beth. Everyone called her Beth. Yes, she was dating Jack. Of course she was. The prettiest girl dates the prettiest boy. That's the way it works."

"At the party, she and Jack had a fight. Do you know what it was about?"

"Who knows? Kids fight, don't they? I was gone by the time Beth left, anyway. We discovered that a lot of the kids had been drinking. The principal didn't believe it was wise for us to have any part of that. We were supposed to educate against that sort of thing. But he didn't want to ruin the party, so he asked us to leave a few at a time. Monte was the first to go. She was happy for the excuse. Monte was not a sports person. She left about, I don't know, eight-thirty. I left around ten."

"Were you close to the students?"

"Monte and I both were, probably because we were so close in age."

"If Beth was upset, distraught over Jack, and wanted to talk, who would she turn to?"

"Lynn Peyer. She was Beth's best friend."

"Was Peyer at the party?"

"Yes."

"When did she leave?'

"I don't know."

"Anyone else? Anyone she might have been going to see the night she was killed?"

"Me, I guess."

"Except she didn't come to you."

"No."

"How about Monte?"

"Very unlikely."

"Why's that?"

"Monte didn't approve of Beth. You need to understand. Monte, like I said before, she was a bit of a feminist. At least she was a feminist by Victoria, Minnesota, standards. She believed women could be, should be, whatever they wanted. Only back in those days, living in a small town like this, a woman who graduated from high school either got married or left for college. Beth, to put it charitably, was not going to college."

"Put it uncharitably."

"Beth could talk for an hour and not say a thing. She did all her thinking with her body. A lot of girls in small towns did. Maybe big towns, too. They spent their senior years looking for the man they were going to marry, and then spent the rest of their lives wondering what went wrong. That's just the way it was back then. Beth, like so many of the girls in Victoria, wanted only to get a ring on her finger as soon as possible."

"She expected to marry Jack," I said.

"Exactly. Anyway, if Beth had gone to Monte, Monte probably would given her a few college brochures and a lecture on self-esteem."

"Would Beth have gone to anyone else?"

"No one comes to mind."

"Chief Bohlig claims that she was killed by transients," I said. "That she was grabbed up off the street and killed."

"That's what he said."

"Do you believe him?"

"I want to believe him. I truly do. Otherwise Beth was killed by someone living in this town, someone who probably is still living in this town."

"You want to believe him, but you don't."

"No, I don't."

There didn't seem to be much more to say after that. After a few moments of silence, I asked to borrow the yearbook. Suzi said, "Sure."

"You know who you should talk to?" she added. "At least about the Seven? Coach Testen."

"Is he still in Victoria?"

"Are you kidding? Mark owns this town. He has a place near Jail Park."

"Jail Park?"

"Central Park," Suzi said. "Before they moved it, the county jail used to be located across the street and people called it Jail Park. Still do."

"Will Coach Testen talk to me?"

"Try to stop him."

* * *

Jail Park wasn't what I had envisioned. Instead of a few trees, well-trimmed lawn, playground equipment, maybe a baseball diamond, I found what resembled a wilderness preserve. I knew it was bordered on all four sides by narrow city streets, but the streets were far apart and I was unable to estimate its depth. It could have been as vast as Sherwood Forest for all I knew. There was a wide boulevard between the street and the trees, but no sidewalk. What looked like a path began about a hundred yards from where I had parked in front of Coach Testen's house and bent into the park, disappearing among dozens of trees and high, thick brush. There were areas like this in the Cities, too, I reminded myself. Pockets of wilderness, hidden, isolated, yet only five minutes from the nearest pizza joint.

Coach Testen lived in one of those newer homes designed to appear much older, larger, and grander than it actually was. It had a brick front, eccentric angles, high windows, pronounced gables, vaulted ceilings, and exposed staircases. It would have gone for $350,000 in my neighborhood, probably twice that in John Allen Barrett's. Even so, its dominant feature was an attached two-car garage and the wide asphalt driveway leading to it, the black of the asphalt in sharp contrast with the snow piled on either side. I walked up the driveway to a narrow concrete path that led to the front door and used a knocker that resembled brass but seemed lighter. Coach Testen opened the door as if he were expecting me and I wondered if Suzi Shimek had called him.

Testen was closer to seventy than he was to fifty, yet he looked as well preserved as Suzi. There must be something in the water, I decided. His eyes were bright and he still had plenty of light-colored hair that seemed to suit the sunny smile and aw-shucks demeanor he presented the moment he found me standing at his front door. I suspected the smile and easy manner were part of a carefully constructed facade, but it's already been established that I'm cynical.

Testen seemed overdressed for just hanging around the house—black loafers with tassels polished to a high gloss, neatly pressed black slacks, a brown, blue, and white cashmere sweater worn over a white cotton dress shirt, tennis bracelet on one wrist and gold watch on the other. Yet what surprised me more was his size. Testen was short—no more than five-five. I had expected a basketball coach to be taller.

Like Suzi, Testen welcomed my company.

"It's always a pleasure to chat about the Seven," he said.

"I, for one, enjoy meeting a local legend," I replied, laying it on a little thicker than probably was necessary.

"Please," Testen said, although he was obviously comfortable with the label. "Most of the people living in Victoria today probably don't even know who I am."

"I'm sure that's not true."

"Come with me."

I followed Testen down a corridor toward the back of the house.

"People in Victoria are pretty excited about the basketball team this year," he said. "We have a young man—a Somali named Nooh Mohamud Abdille—he's the real deal. There's talk that the NBA could make him a lottery pick right out of high school. Plenty of scouts have been following his development closely even though he's still a junior. I've encouraged him to play at least one year of D-1; spend a year in college before trying to make the transition to pro ball. But I'm not his coach. I haven't been on the bench for a couple of years. Instead, I'm the old coach now, emphasis on *old*. The kids don't listen to me."

Testen paused outside a closed door.

"Still, Mr. Abdille and his teammates will have to go a long way to achieve what we did."

With a flourish, Testen opened the door and waved me into the room. Two large windows all looked out on the backyard. The rest of the walls were covered with a banner that screamed GO WILDCATS!, several pennants, two basketball jerseys—one white with red numbers, the other red with white numbers—a Victoria High School letter jacket, framed pages from the Victoria, Minneapolis, St. Paul, Mankato, Rochester, and Duluth newspapers proclaiming the Seven's championship, and dozens of photographs, most in black and white, some in color, of Testen and his team in action. There were also shelves crowded with other memorabilia—two autographed basketballs, a half dozen trophies in assorted shapes and sizes, medals, and even more framed photographs. In the center of it all was a huge trophy mounted on a round platform.

I felt as if I were visiting a shrine.

"I collected most of what you see, but a lot of it was sent to me," Testen said. "People send me things. A few years ago during the thirtieth anniversary celebration, we put it all on display for the public. People seemed to get a kick out of it."

"All this for a basketball game?" I asked.

"It wasn't just a basketball game."

Testen moved slowly to the huge trophy and set his hand on top of it.

"This is a replica," he said. "The real trophy is locked away in the school." Yet the way he caressed the golden basketball made me think it was real enough.

"You have to understand something about the times we lived in to fully appreciate what the championship meant." Testen spoke as if he was reciting a speech he had given many times, yet never tired of. "We had just lost the war in Vietnam. Because of the growing Watergate scandal, Congress was preparing to impeach the president of the United States. OPEC triggered the first energy crisis in America—people who had never wanted for anything were suddenly waiting in long lines to pay soaring prices for gasoline if it was available at all, and our government's response was to encourage us to lower our thermostats and wear sweaters. The post–World War II boom was finally ending, inflation was rampant, and the nation began spiraling down into what seemed like an endless recession. The first Earth Day brought millions into the streets to demonstrate over the environment, there were riots in Boston over desegregation and busing, and feminists and anti-feminists protested just about everywhere over *Roe. v. Wade*.

"After all that, after the pain and confusion and frustration and anger and rebellion, what did we get? We got Jerry Ford. A good man. An honorable man. A lousy president. Believe me, people needed heroes, and at just that moment we found a few in the form of a ragtag team of smalltown American kids, ultimate underdogs who made it to the top. . . ."

I drifted through the room as Testen gave his speech, examining the memorabilia, studying the framed newspaper pages, each dominated by large photographs of jubilant teenagers hugging and dancing and raising their fingers in the air. *We're number one!*

"It wasn't noticed that much by the rest of the nation," Testen said. "Yet in Minnesota, I think the Victoria Seven was as huge as the Olympic hockey team that beat the Soviets and won the gold medal in 1980."

"I remember," I said.

"The funny thing is, we weren't that good. Jack Barrett was the only one on the team who was given a Division I scholarship. Dave Peterson played Division III at Gustavus Adolphus, but he was a walk-on. Gene Hugoson played JuCo for two years. The rest never played again. It shows in our record, too. We finished the season one game above .500. We never won a game by more than six points. We lost once by thirty-six."

"How did you manage to win the state championship?"

"People have asked me that question for over thirty years and I always tell them the same things—superior coaching." Testen chuckled in a practiced manner. "The truth is, I don't know. I only know that we won our last six regular season games, cruised into the sections, and kept right on going. It didn't matter who we played. It didn't matter how much size we gave up. It didn't matter if we trailed at the half or by how many points. We couldn't lose."

I halted in front of a photograph of the Victoria cheerleaders taken in the school gym. Elizabeth Rogers was in the forefront.

"I think it was psychological," Testen said. "Somewhere along the line the kids got it into their heads that they couldn't be beaten and so they didn't allow it to happen. Anyone who plays or knows sports will tell you that that's a goofy theory. What's the line? The race isn't always to the swift or the battle to the strong, but that's the way to bet? Still, after all these years, it's the only explanation I have. That and divine intervention. One sports writer compared us to the Amazing Mets of '69 that won the World Series."

"Still, it's getting to be a long time ago," I said. "Over thirty years."

"That's a long time only when you're looking forward. You look back and you wonder how the years passed so quickly."

"What about Elizabeth Rogers?" I asked abruptly to see how he would react. Testen continued without pause.

"Nothing is ever perfect, is it? The boys were very upset by Beth's death as you can imagine. . . ." I flashed on the photographs I had seen in the *Herald* and decided they had done an awfully good job of hiding it. "It was such a small school back then; everyone lived in everyone's pocket. But what were we going to do? Forfeit? People died the day the *Eagle* landed on the moon, yet that didn't stop Neil Armstrong from taking his giant leap for mankind. Do you think it should have?"

"No."

"No, no, of course not. Life goes on, just like it did after 9/11. Anyway, it's like you said, it was a long time ago."

So why does Elizabeth's murder trouble you so, my inner voice asked.

Because her killer is still out there.

What do you care?

It could be Jack Barrett.

What do you care?

I care.

Why?

I just do.

"You were at the party the night Elizabeth was killed," I said.

"I was the guest of honor. Me and the Seven."

"When did you leave?"

"It was late. Monte—Grace Monteleone—she was this hippy chick should have been running a flower store somewhere instead of teaching—she complained to the principal that the kids were drinking beer. Not my kids, I wouldn't have allowed that, but some of the other kids. She wanted the principal to put a stop to it. He refused. It was a celebration, after all. Instead, he suggested the teachers leave a few at a time, you know, pretend it didn't happen: out of sight, out of mind. Monte—she was the first one out the door, probably went home to burn incense or something. I stayed late because, well . . ."

"You were the guest of honor."

"Yes."

"Did you see Elizabeth at the party?"

"I'm sure I did, but honestly, I don't remember what I had for dinner last Monday much less who I saw at a party over three decades ago. Why do you ask?"

"I'm trying to learn who killed Elizabeth."

"After all these years?" Testen began to massage his temples and I knew he was regretting that he had opened his door to me. "I don't think I can help you with that. Why don't you talk to Chief Bohlig? Ask him about it. He'll tell you."

"Tell me what?"

"Tell you what happened. I have no idea. At the time, I was trying to win three consecutive basketball games."

"Did Elizabeth's murder help or hurt you in the tournament?"

"Help or hurt? That's actually a good question. Most people would be appalled to ask it, but— You look like you used to play some ball."

"Hockey and baseball," I told him.

Testen frowned, like I had failed an easy test.

"Not basketball?"

"Just pickup," I told him.

"Well, you play sports you learn about motivation. Sometimes the worst thing that can happen is the best. Josie Bloom, not our best player by any means, he's the one that carried us in the final. Seventeen points, eleven rebounds, four steals, including a big one at the end. He said before the opening tip he was dedicating the game to Elizabeth. Jack—I think Beth's death hit him the hardest—he *was* our best player, and he said the same thing. Yet in the championship game he didn't play well at all. 'Course, being double- and triple-teamed all night didn't help. So, to answer your question, I don't know. I just don't know.

"I'll tell you one thing, though," Testen said. "Linking what those kids achieved, linking their great triumph to something as sordid and tragic as Beth's murder annoys me. It's unfair to them."

Now was a good time to change the subject, I decided.

"Tell me about the players," I said. "Where are they now?"

Testen seemed relieved. He found a team photograph.

"Like I said earlier, they weren't that special." He was giving his practiced speech again. "It was only what they did that made them special. In many ways they were just typical kids who went on to lead typical lives."

He pointed to the boy in the middle of the photograph holding a basketball.

"Jack Barrett went on to become governor—you know

that. Before politics he was a millionaire entrepreneur, owning companies, making deals."

His finger moved to another boy at the far end of the photo with long hair that must have been pulled into a ponytail in order for him to play.

"Gene Hugoson went to prison for robbing a convenience store, assaulting the cashier, and stealing her car. He's now working on his family's farm."

Testen moved his finger along the line of basketball players, referring to each of them in turn.

"Dave Peterson, or I should say, Doctor David Peterson, is an optometrist working out of Mankato. Nick Axelrod owns and operates Nick's, a family restaurant here in Victoria. Brian Reif works as an auto mechanic. . . ."

Ah, my friend Brian, my inner voice said.

Testen sighed again and I wondered if he always sighed at this part of the presentation.

"We lost Tony Porter just a while ago," he said. "He was there for the thirtieth reunion of the team, but we all knew then that he was very sick."

Testen sighed some more, and pointed at the last of the Seven.

"Josiah Bloom. Well, I guess he's sick, too. He's an alcoholic, although the last I heard he was clean and sober."

Testen set the photograph carefully where he found it.

"Very much a microcosm of America."

"Just one big happy family," I said.

Testen laughed in reply.

"Lord, no. I said they were a microcosm of America. Sometimes they couldn't stand to be around each other."

"Why's that?"

"People can always find a reason to irritate other people, can't they?"

"What about Governor Barrett? How did he get along with the rest of the Seven?"

"Jack—he was the exception. Everyone loved Jack."

Everyone loved Jack. Well, not everyone, I reminded myself when I returned to my Audi and headed south. I was fumbling with my map, debating whom to annoy next when I encountered County Road 13. I hung a left and followed it to Milepost Three. I don't know why, certainly there was nothing to see after all these years. Curiosity, I guess.

When I reached the milepost, I stopped the Audi along the shoulder, put it in neutral, and set the brake. I sat and listened to the radio. After a few bars of country anguish, I switched it off. There were no structures that I could see and no traffic. It was as good a spot to dump a body as any.

I slipped out of the car. Only the wind whistling through the power and telephone wires that lined the blacktop and the gentle hum of the car engine disrupted the silence. Gray, snow-covered farmland stretched into the distance, merging with the gray sky—the horizon could have been a mile away, or it could have been a thousand. There was no color, except . . .

I moved to the edge of the ditch. I gazed at a spot of red just below the milepost.

What is that?

I stepped into the ditch and immediately descended into knee-deep snow. I could feel it lodge between my boots and jeans as I plowed my way to the red.

It was a flower. A red rose partially drifted over by blowing snow. When I pulled at it, a second bud appeared, and a third. I kept digging until I had recovered a bouquet of fifteen long-stemmed roses, frozen but still bright with color. Whoever had thrown them there had done it recently—I say "thrown" because there were no footprints in the ditch save my own.

I carried the roses back to my car. Once on the blacktop, I stamped my boots, shaking the snow free. I brought the flowers to my nose, but, of course, there was no scent.

"What in the hell are fifteen roses doing here?" I asked the deserted road. "Is it a tribute to Elizabeth?"

Maybe, my inner voice replied. *Either that or a message.*

Chapter Seven

T. S. Eliot called April "the cruelest month." T. S. Eliot never spent a January in Minnesota. If he had, he would have known that to us April is the light at the end of the tunnel. It is the promise of warmth; it is the bright and shiny future (not to mention the beginning of the baseball season). It is also a long way off. Which is why I took great pleasure from stepping into Fleur de Lis on Main, the only florist shop in Victoria. It smelled warm and damp and made me think of spring.

The woman behind the counter had enormous eyes that seemed to be in mourning. She spoke softly and for a moment I wondered if she was conducting a wake in the back room.

"May I help you?"

"Do you sell long-stemmed red roses?"

"We certainly do."

"How many in a bouquet?"

"Usually a dozen, but we can make up a bouquet of any size."

"Have you recently sold a bouquet of fifteen roses? Long-stemmed roses?"

"Fifteen?"

"Yes."

"I don't think so— No, I'm sure I haven't. Why do you ask?"

"I recently came across a bouquet of fifteen red roses, and I wondered if they came from here."

"No. No, I'm sure they haven't. I would have remembered an order of fifteen. It's an odd number."

"In what way is it odd?"

"There is a traditional meaning attached to the number of roses you give someone. For example, a single rose means 'Love at first sight,' or 'I still love you.'"

"Still love you? I thought it meant simply, 'I love you.'"

"No, that's three roses. Nine roses means 'We'll be together forever.' A dozen means 'Please be mine?' Two dozen means 'I'm forever yours.' Fifty roses professes 'Unconditional love.' Nine dozen means 'Will you marry me?' and nine hundred ninety-nine roses means 'I will love you till the end of time.'"

"What does fifteen mean?

"'Please forgive me.'"

A short time later I was again parked on the shoulder of County Road 13 opposite Milepost Three. I left the Audi, went to the edge of the road, and tossed the bouquet of fifteen red roses back where I found it.

"Who is it, Elizabeth?" I asked. "Who's apologizing to you? Or are the roses meant for me?"

If the flowers hadn't been purchased in Victoria, then they must have come from outside. As I had.

"I'm being played, sweetie," I said aloud. "I can feel it. I don't suppose you could tell me who's plucking the strings?"

Elizabeth didn't answer.

I stood alongside the ditch, not moving, not really thinking much, either. Someone driving by could have mistaken me for a cow in a pasture. After a few minutes I dropped a single white chrysanthemum next to the roses. The woman at the flower shop told me it meant "truth."

"It would be nice, Elizabeth," I said, "if we could find some."

The huge, overstuffed chair had been upholstered in blue mohair and the large sofa against the wall was covered in the same material. Both had ornately carved woodwork on the arms and along the backs. The large rug was a faded Persian. A coffee table made of ancient wood stood on the rug in front of the sofa and a matching end table had been placed at the elbow of the chair. There was a lace doily in the center of the end table and a crystal lamp in the center of that. Mounted on the wall in front of the sofa was a series of photographs. Mrs. Rogers identified the subjects—Elizabeth, her daughter, murdered by assailant or assailants unknown, Michael, her son, killed in a car accident, Thomas, her husband, dead of a heart attack.

"It has been very difficult," Mrs. Rogers said.

Her eyes had known anguish, yet suffering had not made them hard. Instead, they somehow had remained soft, even kindly and I wondered how Mrs. Rogers had managed it.

"After Beth was killed, my anger was powerful," she explained. "I hated. Since the Lord didn't show me whom to hate, I hated the world, I hated Him. I hid that anger, that hate, buried it deep inside because there were so many others who were hurting as I was, so many others who needed help. My husband, I needed to help him deal with our loss. My son—my son was so young at the time, only ten years old when his beloved sister was taken from him, and like the rest of us, he did not know why. So many others. Relatives. Friends. Neighbors who did not know Beth except as a cheerleader at the high school. They were all suffering, all desperate for comfort. I needed to be strong for them. When they no longer needed my strength, I tried to regain my anger, my hate; I went searching for it in the lowest part of my heart and discovered that it was gone."

"I can't imagine getting over something like that," I said.

"You do not get over it, you do not forget. It is not a photograph you paste in an album and put on the shelf to examine only on occasion. It is with you always, like the air you breathe. You must learn to accept it and move on in order to live life according to God's will."

"God's will?"

Mrs. Rogers smiled slightly and I realized that I wasn't the first person to question God's will in her presence.

"God does not murder young women, Mr. McKenzie. He does not tell children to drink and drive. He does not cause inactive, overweight men to die of heart attacks. We"—she tapped her breast—"are the cause of the world's ills. Not God. I do not hold him responsible."

I do! I didn't speak the words, yet Mrs. Rogers seemed to hear them just the same.

"Did you lose someone close, Mr. McKenzie? Someone you loved."

"My mother. My father."

"How did they die?"

"She died slowly of cancer when I was very young. He died quickly of a brain tumor a few years ago. They say the tumor could have been growing for years."

"For years," Mrs. Rogers repeated. "I wonder how many extra years he was given."

Not damn near enough, my inner voice answered.

"I didn't come here to talk about that," I said.

"What did you come here to talk about?"

"Elizabeth. I'd like to find out what happened to her."

"Chief Bohlig said—"

"I don't believe him."

"Why not?"

"Pretty young women are not kidnapped off the street and just killed, Mrs. Rogers. They are sometimes robbed and killed. They are more often abused and killed. Sometimes other things happen. But they are not *just* killed. Not by transients. Not by strangers. I think she was killed by someone she knew."

Mrs. Rogers shook her head.

"I have thought long about that, about the possibility that Beth was murdered by someone she trusted."

"What have you decided?"

"I do not believe that anyone who knew Beth could have hurt her."

"So, you think someone killed her at random for no particular reason?"

"Mr. McKenzie, do you believe in evil?"

I've heard the question before. It had often been bandied about in the squad room and in the corridors of the Ramsey County Court House. For most people, evil is abstract, a theoretical means of describing human behavior that is otherwise incomprehensible to them. To others it is very real, in the way drugs and guns and anthrax letters and airplanes crashing into skyscrapers are real. Only I had been a cop a long time and I knew better.

"No, ma'am," I said. "I do not believe in evil. I believe in motive."

Mrs. Rogers thought about that for a moment.

"Whom do you suspect?" she asked.

"Your daughter was seeing Jack Barrett."

"No," Mrs. Rogers said abruptly. "I do not believe that. I know Jack's heart. He could never have done such a thing."

I was surprised by how glad I was to hear Mrs. Rogers's defense of Barrett, yet just the same I said, "Witnesses said Elizabeth and Jack had an argument the night Elizabeth was killed."

Mrs. Rogers shook her head, refused to consider the possibility. I let it slide.

"Were there any other boys who were interested in your daughter?" I asked. "Boys who were jealous, perhaps?"

"I believe that most of the boys were interested in Beth and that many of them were jealous because she would date only Jack."

"Did any of them bother her?"

"No."

"Did any call, send letters, follow her?"

Again Mrs. Rogers shook her head.

"What about girls? Did Elizabeth have any enemies?"

"All high school girls have enemies. It is the politics of their age."

"Anyone in particular?"

"No."

"Afterward, did anyone act strangely? At the funeral

perhaps." I noticed something move behind the woman's eyes. "What?"

"The day after the Seven won the championship, just after the town threw them a parade, Josie Bloom came to see me."

"What did he do?"

"He hugged me. I opened the front door and found him there. He said, 'Mrs. Rogers, I am so sorry,' and he hugged me and he cried for a very long time. The entire town was celebrating the basketball team. It did not wish to be reminded of Beth. So, for Josie to do that—I was very touched."

Josiah Bloom the alcoholic, who dedicated his game to Beth.

"Mrs. Rogers, I found a bouquet of red roses at the site where your daughter's body was found."

"You did?"

"Yes."

"When?"

"About a half hour ago."

"How odd. Who could have left them?"

"That's what I was going to ask you."

"I have no idea."

"Has anyone left flowers at the site . . . ?"

"Since Beth was killed?"

"Yes."

"Like a shrine?"

"Yes."

"No. This is the first I've heard of anyone— Who would do such a thing? Why now, why after all these years?"

"I don't know."

Mrs. Rogers stared at me for a few beats as if she were seeing me for the first time.

"Why are you doing this?" she asked suddenly. "Why do you need to learn who killed my daughter?"

"Until this morning, I didn't. Yet somehow it's become very important to me."

"Perhaps you were sent by God to finally put the matter to rest."

"I doubt it." The very suggestion made me nervous.

"Why do you doubt it?"

"If God needed help, I'm sure he could find someone more competent than I. Besides, I haven't prayed, really prayed in many years."

"Since your mother died."

I nodded.

"The Lord works in mysterious ways, wondrous to behold."

"We'll see."

"I should tell you before you pursue this any further, Mr. McKenzie, that while I wish you well, I have already forgiven the person who killed my daughter."

I thought that was the most amazing statement I had ever heard.

I paused before turning into the parking lot of Fit to Print to allow a young woman wearing a ponytail and a Victoria High School letterman's jacket to cross the street in front of me. There were six patches sewn to her left sleeve representing basketball, speech, debate, band, scholarship, and track and field. When I was a kid she would have been labeled an overachiever. These days kids are expected to be Renaissance men, they're supposed to compete in sports, learn a language, play an instrument, write poetry, study physics and algebra. That's a lot of pressure. More than I grew up with. Still, I suppose it beats wasting their time in front of the television or playing video games.

"Pretty," I thought as she passed my car, even with the anxious expression etched across her face. I didn't look to see what made her anxious. Instead I waited for an oncoming vehicle to pass before wheeling into the lot. I silenced the Audi and opened the door.

The word was so loud and expressive that I was sure it was meant for me.

"Bitch."

I spun toward it.

Two young men, both dressed in jackets with A-1 Auto printed on the back, were blocking the woman's path. She tried to move past, but they kept sliding in front of her, forming a wall, nudging her backward along the sidewalk.

I recognized them immediately. They were the white guys whispering encouragement to Brian Reif in the Rainbow Cafe. The names stenciled over their breasts told me they were Mitch and Steve.

"You like those bean burritos, don't you," Mitch said. "You like those chili-shitters."

Steve lifted the woman's ponytail. She slapped at his dirty hand like it was a mosquito. He pulled it out of range and laughed.

"Does he wear Hispandex to bed?" Steve said, laughing at his own weak joke. "Does he go to the Latrino?"

They're hassling her because she's seeing a Hispanic, my inner voice said. *Well . . .*

I called to them in my best high school Spanish as I approached. "*¡Oyen, chicos! Por favor. ¡Dejen de molestar la chica!*" Hey, guys. Please. Stop bothering the girl.

They looked at me like I had come from Mars.

"What the fuck do you want?" Mitch asked.

I asked him if that was a nice way to talk. "*¿Eso es una manera agradable de hablar?*" My tone was deliberately mocking.

"Who are you?" Mitch asked.

"Ain't that the guy from before?" his friend answered.

"Are you okay?" I asked the girl.

She told me she was fine. As for the other two, I told them to go away.

"*Váyanse*."

"I knew you weren't no American," Mitch said.

That's when I backhanded him across the mouth. The force of the blow spun him on his heels and propelled him across the narrow boulevard against the side of a parked car. Steve spit "Bastard" at me, curled his fingers into a fist, and cocked his right arm. He took way too much time doing it. I grabbed Mitch by his collar and yanked him back, putting him directly between Steve's fist and me. Steve connected with the side of Mitch's face with a lot more force than I had. Mitch would have fallen if I hadn't been holding tight to his collar.

"Oh God, I'm sorry, I'm sorry . . . ," Steve repeated.

"Shit," said Mitch, cradling his face with both hands.

I shoved him hard. Steve had to grab him to keep him from falling.

"*¡Váyanse!*," I said to them. "*¡Ahora!*"

They took three steps backward before Mitch tore himself from Steve's grasp.

"This ain't over," he said. "You got a fight coming. It's coming soon."

I told them to stop it, they were frightening me. "*Dejen de hacer est. Me están dando miedo*." I smiled while I watched them scurry across the street toward the Rainbow Cafe. Only the young lady didn't share my joy. The name stitched to her letterman's jacket read JACE.

"What did that prove?" she wanted to know.

"That a young woman can walk the streets of Victoria unmolested?"

Her expression reminded me of Mount Saint Helens right before it exploded.

"Okay, it didn't prove a damn thing." I raised my hand to eye level, squinting through the space between my thumb and index finger. "But didn't seeing those bigots get theirs make you feel that much better?"

"Violence isn't going to change their minds," Jace said. "It isn't going to make the problem go away. It only makes it worse."

She had me there.

Jace looked both ways when she entered Fit to Print and smiled coyly at Rufugio Tapia. I followed her inside, but she wasn't paying any attention to me.

"Hi," she said as she moved toward him. It was a small word, yet she filled it with promise.

"Hello," Tapia replied.

They stared into each other's face, their eyes waltzing together in four-four time. She reached the counter and leaned halfway across it. Only he didn't bend to meet her.

"Aren't you going to kiss me, R.T.?" she asked.

Tapia gestured in my direction with his head.

"Don't mind me," I said. "Kiss the girl."

Tapia found something on the counter to interest him. The young woman looked down and away. They weren't going to kiss and the only explanation that I could think of was that she was white and he was Hispanic and there was a witness.

"Mind if I use this?" I asked, gesturing at the nearest Mac

"Help yourself."

I had stopped at Fit to Print to gain access to the Internet, using my credit card just the way my mysterious e-mailer must have. While I surfed, Tapia and the young woman bowed their heads toward each other and spoke softly. I tried to give them as much privacy as possible.

I had found all the names I wanted in the yearbook Suzi had lent me and was now looking for addresses. Dr. Dave Peterson was easy. He had his own Web site. I called his number in Mankato on my cell and arranged for an appointment the following morning. Grace Monteleone was now principal of West Mankato High School. I found her number easily enough, too, but I had to climb over three tiers of bureaucracy before I could arrange a meeting about an hour after I was set to speak with Dr. Peterson. Gene Hugoson, Brian Reif, and Nick Axelrod were all in Victoria. I recorded their addresses in my notebook and decided to visit them in person without calling first. It took a while to find Josiah Bloom. He was also in Victoria, but apparently he moved around quite a bit. I nearly gave up on Lynn Peyer before I found records of her numerous marriages and divorces. Unlike Monte, Lynn had changed her name three times and now went under the name Lynn Matousek. She also lived in Victoria.

I logged off the Mac. Tapia was standing next to me as I put on my jacket. The young woman was standing at the counter. She might have been waiting for a bus for all the attention she paid me. Tapia extended his hand and I shook it.

"I want to thank you for helping my girl."

I grinned.

He said, "What?"

" 'My girl.' I like the sound of it. I bet she does, too."

Tapia suddenly found something on the floor that needed looking at. Jace began to blush. Her cheeks were the color of a winter sunset.

"Have you two ever read *Romeo and Juliet*?" I asked.

"You mean the story about the two lovers who die because their families hate each other so much they can't be together?" Jace said. "That *Romeo and Juliet*?"

"Bad example," I told her.

"You think?"

"There has been trouble in town recently between Latinos and Somalis and the white residents," Tapia said.

"What kind of trouble?"

"Usual thing. Whites complain that immigrants are taking all the jobs, which is nonsense. The jobs they are taking—it's in the slaughterhouse. People coming up here are taking the dangerous, low-paying jobs—the hard work, low-prestige work—that the white, U.S. born residents just won't do. I don't blame them. My father, he worked hard, so very hard, worked two jobs when I was young so I could go to school, so I wouldn't need the slaughterhouse.

"I don't know," he added. "I didn't see much discrimination in college, but down here . . . Sometimes it is bad and sometimes it is not so bad. Right now it's bad because kids—children of immigrants—they were arrested for using drugs, using methamphetamine. Now people are saying that along with ruining the economy we're bringing in drugs. Yet people are also excited because Victoria might win another state basketball title after all these years because of the kid who plays center—a young man from Somalia. I just don't know."

"Did you ever think of leaving? The both of you going somewhere else?"

"Do you know a place where there is no discrimination?" Jace asked.

"The Cities," I said.

Tapia and the young woman looked at each other like they had simultaneously discovered I was a raving lunatic.

"I'm not saying you won't find any bigotry up there," I said. "You will. Of course you will. You'll find it everywhere you go. Only you'll find less of it. In a big city, a white woman dating a Hispanic, a Hispanic married to an African American, an African American dating an Asian, an Asian spending time with a Jew, a Jew with a Muslim, a Muslim shacking up with a conservative Republican—we see it all the time, and most people don't even notice, much less care."

"This is my home," Tapia said.

"Mine, too," said Jace.

Good for them.

I changed the subject. Pointing at the front of her letterman's jacket, I said, "Interesting name."

"It's short for J.C.," she said. "People called me J.C. when I was a kid but now everyone just calls me Jace. Sometimes they say Jacey with a long *e*. But I like Jace."

When she was a kid? my inner voice asked.

"J.C. and R.T.," I said. "Sounds like a match."

"We're just friends," said Tapia.

Who was he kidding? I wondered. *Not the punks out on the sidewalk.*

The young woman's eyes widened at the lie, but she said nothing.

"Listen, kids, there's something you should know. The earth spins on its axis at about a thousand miles an hour. You can't slow it down and you sure as hell can't stop it."

"What is that supposed to mean?" Tapia asked.

"It means, kiss the girl while you have the chance."

A few moments later I was standing outside. I zipped my jacket to my throat and looked up at the dirty gray sky. The weather geek on the radio had predicted snow and I figured that sooner or later he'd be right.

I walked to my Audi without once looking over my shoulder through the large windows of Fit to Print. It would have cheered me to see the kids making out on the counter, but I didn't think there was much chance of that happening.

What a shitty town.

Whatever was in the water that Suzi Shimek and Coach Testen were drinking, Lynn Matousek was having none of it. Her hair was thin and black with plenty of gray at the roots; she had a heavy, square body and a shiny face. She was only pushing fifty years old, yet could easily pass for sixty.

I introduced myself at the door and said, "May I ask you a few questions?"

"Are you a cop?" she asked.

"No."

"Are you a private investigator?"

"Something like that." It's illegal to pass yourself off as a law enforcement officer, but hell, anyone can be a PI.

"Which one of the assholes hired you?"

I was confused and probably looked it.

"My ex-husbands," she said. "Which one hired you?"

"How many are there?"

"Three. I got three ex-husbands."

"None of them hired me."

"I'm supposed to believe that?"

"Lady—"

"What're you doin' here? Lookin' for more shit t' use against me in court?"

"I want to ask some questions."

"You said that. 'Bout what?"

"Elizabeth Rogers."

That slowed her down. "Beth? Why? After all these years why would you ask about Beth?"

"I'm trying to find out what happened to her."

"Why? Why now? Is this for one of those TV documentaries or something? Is this for—Are you working for the governor? Is this for that shithead Barrett? If it is, you can just get your ass outta here."

I saw the opening and took it.

"It's time the people of Minnesota learned just what kind of man they elected to office," I told her. "I don't know what party you're affiliated with—"

"I ain't affiliated with no party."

"But I work for people who want to bring honor and integrity back to the governor's office."

"What people?"

"Real Minnesotans who want to take back their state."

Lynn's eyes grew wide. "Are you going to stick it to Barrett, that bastard?"

"This isn't about Governor Barrett. This is about the truth."

"C'mon in."

I followed Lynn into her home, dodging debris as I went. Apparently she kept house the way some college kids kept house.

"Want a drink?" she called over her shoulder.

"If it's not too much trouble."

"If it's not too much trouble," she mumbled. "Have a seat."

I found one behind a coffee table stacked with newspapers and the remains of Chinese takeout—beef lo mein, I guessed. A moment later, Lynn returned carrying a bottle of Phillips and two glasses. She set them on the table in front of me, poured a generous amount of vodka into one glass and took it across the room, leaving me to serve myself.

"You wanna know who killed Elizabeth Rogers?" she asked.

"Yes."

"It's 'bout time somebody did something about Beth. That bastard ain't never paid. You wanna know who killed Beth? I'll tell you. Jack fucking Barrett killed Beth. Jack Barrett killed Beth and everyone in town knows it. Only no one in the fucking town cares. They didn't care at the time cuz he was a fucking sports hero and they don't care now cuz he's the governor and they didn't care in between cuz . . . who the fuck knows? Cuz they let him get away with murder which makes 'em what? Accomplices? Ah, it don't matter. No one cares."

"I care," I said.

"Are you gonna get him? Are you gonna get him cuz of what he did to Beth?"

I smiled my most conspiratorial smile and said, "Tell me what you know."

Lynn brushed the debris from a chair next to mine, sat

down, and leaned forward, holding her vodka between her hands.

"People say there's no proof that Jack killed Beth. But there is proof. What you call irrefutable proof."

"Tell me."

"The locket. The locket Beth always wore. What was missing when they found her body."

"What locket?"

"The one he gave her. Beth wore a little silver locket in the shape of a heart. You open it up and there's this tiny picture of Jack on one side and a tiny picture of Beth on the other side. Jack gave it to Beth when they were juniors and Beth never, ever took it off. Even when she took a shower she wore it. She was wearing it at the party. I saw it. Only it was gone when they found her."

"There could be a lot of reasons for that."

Lynn shook her head vigorously.

"Jack took it," she said. "He killed her and took the locket. The fucking governor of the State of Minnesota. He did it."

"Why? What motive did he have?"

"Because, because . . . Just because. Look, the night of the party Beth had a fight with Jack Barrett."

"Do you know what it was about?"

"Jack was cheating on her."

"He was?"

"Yeppers."

"With who?"

"Beth didn't know. That's what the fight was about."

"If she didn't know who he was cheating with, how could she be sure?"

"You think we're stupid? I always knew when my husbands were cheating on me. They always knew when I was cheating on them. You don't need to be no rocket scientist."

"Did you ever learn who it was?"

"Nah. No one said nothing afterward. I wouldn't have said nothing, either."

"Someone at the party?"

"Fuck if I know."

"When Elizabeth left the party, she left alone," I said.

"She left alone," Lynn repeated and drained her glass of vodka. "Whew," she exhaled. "That was good." Good enough that she poured herself another hefty drink. She drank some more vodka and said, "Look. Jack did it. Everyone knows that. The whole fuckin' town knows that. So what are you gonna do 'bout it?"

Good question.

"When Beth left the party, where was she going? Do you know?"

Lynn shook her head.

"She didn't confide in you?"

"We were— We came together and we should have left together, but . . ."

"But what?"

Lynn drained her glass a second time.

"I haven't told but a half dozen people this, but if it'll help you get the governor. . . ."

"What haven't you told?"

"The reason Beth left the party alone. We were going to leave together. I should have been with her. I wasn't. Know why? You wanna know why? I'll tell you why? Because I was on my fucking knees in the upstairs bathroom giving the mayor a blow job when Beth decided to go home, that's why. Seventeen years old and this man married with two kids in my school and he, and he tells me—

Fuck. I believed every word he said. Fuck. That's why Beth left the party alone. Men can be such bastards."

I watched as Lynn poured herself another straight vodka.

"That's why I drink," she said. "That's the secret to my success. One of the secrets, anyway."

She drank some more.

"Worst thing that ever happened in this town was that fucking basketball tournament."

Nothing Lynn Peyer Whatever Whatever Matousek had told me proved that Jack Barrett had murdered Elizabeth. I could see why she believed it, why she wanted to believe it. Others in Victoria probably believed it, too. Yet the question remained: Who sent the e-mail? I didn't think it was Lynn. She didn't strike me as the e-mail type. If she had decided to threaten Governor Barrett, she would have done so far less subtly and at a much greater volume. Besides, how could she have possibly learned Lindsey Bauer's private e-mail address? I crossed her name off my list of likely suspects, but lightly, and in pencil.

I was idling at the intersection waiting on the light, debating which way to turn next. The traffic had an anxious feel to it, like all the drivers were afraid they were missing appointments. A black Mercedes pulled next to me, the engine revved impatiently. It was a new SLK 320 convertible with the top up, costing about the same as my car. I had taken a look at one a few months back before buying the Audi.

I recognized the driver immediately. Coach Testen. We glanced at each other and I nodded my head in greeting. He looked away. *Was the snub intentional or did he simply not notice me?*

The light changed and he was off in a hurry. I watched the Mercedes disappear around a corner.

A few minutes later I was on a county road heading out of town toward the South Dakota border. Both Lynn Matousek and Mrs. Rogers had asked why I cared about what had happened to Elizabeth. I wasn't sure myself. She wasn't the reason I had come to Victoria, although I was beginning to think she was the reason I was *sent* here. At the same time, it felt as if her eyes were watching me from on high as I drove Victoria's back roads. Perhaps she had been searching for someone to speak for her after all these years and finally found a man who might manage it. It was an incredibly arrogant thing for me to think, I know. Yet the idea pleased me just the same. It made me feel important.

At the same time, I recalled what Mrs. Rogers had said earlier. "Perhaps you were sent by God."

"Yeah, right. Me and God." I crossed my fingers. "We're like this."

I still had the map of the greater Victoria area that I had purchased at the convenience store and was now following it to the Hugoson farm. It was only 4:30 P.M., but dusk was already gathering. By five the sun would set. I had hoped to arrive at my destination before then. As it turned out, I drove past the farm and was nearly two miles down the road before I realized my mistake and doubled back.

I couldn't estimate the size of the Hugoson farm. It seemed huge, its snow-covered fields stretching toward the setting sun. The farm's driveway, however, was about two hundred yards long and plowed to the dirt. It started at the county blacktop and rose up a slight incline to a white two-story house with blue shutters that were badly in need of paint. There were two large pole barns flanking the house, both made of sheet metal. The driveway ended in a kind of courtyard framed by the three structures. I parked in the center, turned off the engine, and slid out of the Audi. The huge door to the nearest pole barn was open and I moved toward it. A hard crust had formed on the snow. It made each step sound like I had dropped my car keys.

Just inside the door, I could see the back end of a dark blue pickup. I called out and a man dressed for a tedious day's work in the hard cold stepped around the truck and into the courtyard.

I recognized him instantly. I had been trained by experience to recognize him by the way he restricted his movements, not turning his head or gesturing with his hands, relying on peripheral vision instead of normal eye movement. I recognized the way he controlled the muscles that gave his face expression and spoke in a restrained conversational range, neither low nor loud, excited nor dull. He was an ex-con, someone who had done the kind of time measured by many wall calendars.

"Mr. Hugoson?" I asked.

"Whatever you're sellin' I ain't interested in buyin' and by the looks of that car of yours, I doubt I could afford it, anyway."

"My name's McKenzie. I'd like to talk to you about—"

"I know what you want to talk about and I ain't havin' none of it. Get off my property."

"Mr. Hugoson—"

"You don't hear real good, do you, boy?"

He stepped nearer. Somehow he seemed to expand, becoming larger, straighter, harder, with eyes that held all the warmth of an ice pick. He stared at me without blinking so I would know that he was a dangerous man and certainly not squeamish about assaulting a trespasser. It was unnecessary. I already knew he was a dangerous man. I took a step backward as my right hand moved slowly to the spot on my hip where I would have holstered my gun if I hadn't been so careless as to leave it in my glove compartment.

"News travels fast in a small town," I said.

"Bad news does."

I turned to my right, but he was quicker, moving so that the setting sun was at his back and shining directly into my eyes.

"Why are you afraid to talk to me?"

Hugoson strung together a half dozen altogether filthy obscenities that suggested he wasn't afraid of anything, much less a big city punk of dubious sexual orientation.

"Does your mother know you talk like that?" I asked. It was a horribly lame retort, I know; it was the best I could come up with at the moment.

In response, Hugoson turned his back on me and stepped inside the barn. A moment later an unseen motor hummed and the huge door shuddered, shook, and rolled shut. I cursed out loud. I wasn't used to having doors slammed in my face, especially such big ones.

Brian Reif had a worn, weary expression that reminded me of a retired civil servant, someone who had been beaten down by ignorance and indifference and ingratitude. I found him inside A-1 Auto across the street from Nick's Family Restaurant and recognized immediately that he wouldn't talk to me. At least not civilly.

He was alone, wearing the same dungarees he had on at the Rainbow Cafe, and was working on a nearly new

SUV. He came into the office when I arrived, looked at me for about two seconds, turned around, and walked back into the garage. Without an audience, he had no use for a confrontation.

I followed him.

"How did the meeting go after I left?" I asked him. "Sign up any new members?"

He answered by taking an air wrench to the lug nuts of the SUV. The car didn't need tires, but then he wasn't changing them, just loosening and tightening the nuts with the air wrench, making noise.

"Mr. Reif . . ."

The noise was so loud I heard it in the soles of my feet.

"Mr. Reif . . ."

I decided I might as well be talking to a microwave oven. I was angry enough to consider whacking Reif on the side of his knee with the heel of my boot, except there was nothing to gain by it. Still, I might have done it anyway if I hadn't been distracted by the opening bars of "Don't Fence Me In" played on my cell in between blasts of the air wrench. I recognized the phone number on my display. I returned to the office and answered it.

"Hi, Nina," I said.

"McKenzie. Tell me you're not still angry."

"I'm not angry. I never was."

"Yes, you were."

"Was not."

"Was too."

"Nuh-uh."

"Then why don't you come over. I'll buy you dinner."

"I'd love to . . ."

"Prudence Johnson is singing tonight, one of your favorites."

"I can't."

"You are still angry."

"I'm not."

"Then why . . . ?"

"I'm not in the Cities."

"Where are you?"

"A couple hundred miles southwest, in Victoria, Minnesota," I explained.

"You rich jet-setters. The world's your playground."

"I really appreciate the invitation, though."

"What are you doing in Victoria and what is that godawful noise?"

Reif was still working the air wrench while he watched me, obviously wishing I'd go away.

"Nina, I can't talk right now."

"Okay, well . . ."

"I'll call you later tonight."

"Promise?"

"I promise."

"I love you," she said.

I deactivated the cell without replying. I closed the phone and slipped it into my jacket pocket. I gave an enthusiastic wave that Reif pretended not to see and stepped out of the office into the auto shop's parking lot. It was only about 5:30 but night was already a dark reality. Across the street the bright red neon sign of Nick's Family Restaurant beckoned to me.

Chapter Eight

I opened the door to Nick's, stepped inside, and let the door close itself. It was a big, heavy wooden door that could easily withstand a battering ram. It seemed to fit perfectly with the rest of the restaurant's decor—scarlet carpet, white stucco walls, false timber beams across the ceiling, and small, high windows built to discourage patrons from throwing one another through them. The bar was shaped like a horseshoe and surrounded by stools with black cushions. There were square tables with four chairs each arranged in the center of the room and a dozen highback booths along the walls. The lights were dim except for the neon signs behind the bar and mounted on the walls that advertised various brands of beer and tequila, and the air reeked of cigarette smoke and perfume sold for seven bucks a bottle. In the corner, a young woman stood in front of the jukebox, biting her nails as she studied the selections. Her companion at the nearest table watched her intently, as if he were afraid that the next button she pushed would end all life as he knew it.

Family restaurant? Not my family, I told myself.

Still, most of the booths were filled—most with families—and so were half the tables. Three waitresses moved between them, serving food and beverages. Two men worked the bar, one old, one not so old. I drifted toward the bar. Before I was halfway there the older bartender called to me.

"McKenzie. What'll ya have?"

That stopped me. There were joints where they actually knew my name. Just not this one.

While I thought about it, the bartender waved me over. He was bald, round, soft, and as milky white as mashed potatoes. Yet his eyes were bright and he smiled like a man who took it as a personal triumph whenever he could make someone laugh.

"I'm guessing you would be Nick Axelrod," I told him.

"At your service," he said loudly. It seemed everything he said was loud. He extended his hand and I shook it. His grip was firm but he didn't try to impress me with it.

"Since this is your maiden voyage aboard the Good Ship Nick, the first drink is on the house."

"In that case, make it a single malt Scotch."

Axelrod laughed boisterously.

"Good one," he said. "Glenlivet?"

"Perfect." I removed my jacket and draped it over the back of the stool.

"Water, ice?" Axelrod asked.

"On the side."

For some reason Axelrod thought that was funny, too.

"I'm guessing Coach Testen told you I'd be by," I said.

"Oh, yeah. Tried to be cool, but you could tell he was

all hot and bothered. Said a little prick in an expensive leather jacket was besmirchin' the good name of the Victoria Seven and I should throw your ass out."

"Why would he say that?"

"I don't know. You don't look so little to me."

"I meant about throwing me out."

"Coach is probably tryin' to protect his image. Thinks he's John Wooden, for cryin' out loud."

"He thinks he's in the same league as the Wizard of Westwood, a man that's won ten NCAA basketball championships?"

"What can I tell ya? Hey, you know what you need? Roast beef served open-faced on sourdough bread with garlic roasted mashed potatoes and gravy. Yum. Your mother couldn't make it better."

"That's no endorsement. My mother could barely make dinner reservations."

Axelrod thought that was hysterical.

"The woman could mess up Pop-Tarts," I added.

If he had been able to reach across the bar, Axelrod probably would have slapped me on the back. Instead, he rapped the bartop with his knuckles and proclaimed, "You're okay, kid."

I felt as if I had just passed some important initiation, which was what I was going for: Why else would I insult my mother's culinary skills?

"Seriously," Axelrod said, "You're not leaving here until you eat something."

"Do you have a salad bar?"

"No, we don't have a salad bar. This is Nick's."

"Someone has to make a stand against healthy food."

"Damn straight. Hey, Jacey."

A waitress seemed to appear out of thin air.

"This is my daughter, Jace," Axelrod said.

Of course I recognized her. The girl from Fit to Print.

"Hi," she said. Her smile was bright, but brittle. You could smash it with a word. Her eyes had the look of a small animal suddenly confronted by something much, much larger.

"Good evening, Jace," I told her. "My name is McKenzie."

"Mr. McKenzie."

"Jace. That's an interesting name."

"My real name is Judith Catherine, but since I was a kid everyone called me J.C. Somehow that was abbreviated to Jace."

"I like it very much. It's pretty."

Jace's smile became relaxed and warm, her eyes less frightened.

She was a good height for her age, about five foot seven. Her features were small and well turned, not yet beautiful, but beauty was there, like the buds on a rose bush. She smiled as though she had a lot to smile about.

"Don't tell anyone," Axelrod said, his voice taking on a conspiratorial timbre. "Jacey's too young to be working in a place that serves alcohol. Shh . . ."

"Daddy, what's alcohol?" Jace asked.

"We'll talk about that when you're twenty-six. Just remember, what do you do if the police arrive?"

"Buy 'em a drink and take them in the back room?"

"That's my little girl."

Jace rolled her eyes. "As if . . ." She turned to me, her pencil poised over the order pad. "What would you like for dinner?"

"It's called supper," Axelrod said. "He'll have the special."

"It's supper when you eat at home," Jace insisted. "When you eat out it's called dinner."

This time it was Axelrod's turn to roll his eyes.

Jace promised to return in a few minutes with my order. Axelrod watched her depart.

"I'm going to miss her," he said. "She's at that age now where she's actually pleasant company, where she has interesting things to say."

"Is she going somewhere?"

"College. In the fall. You think I want my daughter hanging around Victoria all her life? Don't get me wrong, Victoria is a great place to grow up and a great place to grow old. In between, for someone who wants to make something of herself—Jace'll be graduating high school soon. It's time to move on."

"You seem to have done all right," I volunteered.

"Yeah, well, all I ever wanted was right here. I guess you could say I was seduced by small dreams. Jace, though, Jace has big plans, big ambitions."

"What ambitions?"

Axelrod laughed loudly.

"They seem to change from week to week, but they're big. Very big." He laughed some more.

The restaurant continued to fill up until only a few empty seats along the bar remained. Glancing at the other patrons, I discovered that they were all white. I don't know why I found that so disconcerting, but I did. Maybe Jace had a very good reason to hide her relationship with the Hispanic kid at Fit to Print.

While Axelrod busied himself assisting the other bartender, Jace served the hot roast beef.

"Thank you," she said when she set the plate in front of me on the bar.

"For what?"

"For what. For not blowing my cover."

"I take it your father doesn't know about Tapia."

"Nobody knows. Not really."

"Is your dad a bigot? Will he not understand?"

Jace looked at me like I had just slapped her.

"My father is not a bigot."

"I'm sorry. I thought . . ."

"My father wants me to go to college, that's all."

"And you want to stay here?"

"Yes."

"Because of Tapia?"

She nodded.

McKenzie, my inner voice told me, *you're an idiot*.

Jace busied herself with other customers, while I ate. I had to admit, the roast beef was delicious, and while the mashed potatoes weren't quite as good as mine, I ate every forkful—no Atkins Diet for me! Jace eyed the empty plate before she cleared it, glanced at my waistline, then back at the plate again.

"Huh," she said. "You must work out."

"Not recently, unfortunately." I retrieved my wallet. "Should I pay you now?"

"Boss says it's on the house."

I opened my wallet, took out a fifty, and dropped it on the tray Jace was holding.

"I don't imagine that includes tips," I said.

"That's way too much."

"I remember what it was like to be a poor, starving college kid."

"Thank you," Jace said.

"You're welcome."

She moved away, stopped abruptly, and spun toward me.

"You're on his side."

"If I should have a daughter, I'd want her to go to college, too."

"Puhleez," Jace said.

Still, despite her outrage, she didn't return the fifty.

In between drink orders, Axelrod came to visit. He told a lot of jokes—most could be heard by the rest of his patrons—while I behaved like I had taken Good Cheer 101 in college. Eventually, I asked the questions I had come to ask.

"Beth was pretty," Axelrod said in reply to one of them. "Only she wasn't very bright and she took herself way too seriously. At least that's what I always thought. 'Course I think everyone takes themselves way too seriously."

"How about Coach Testen?"

"Him most of all. He pretends that winning the championship ranks as one of the greatest sports achievements of all time. I can understand. I mean, it's the only thing he's ever done. Only you know what? It wasn't nearly as exciting or earth-shattering as Coach and some others make it out to be. Don't get me wrong. I don't mind that he's nurtured it, made a legend outta it. Around here some people treat me like I'm a celebrity cuz of it. It helped me make a go out of this place." He gestured at the restaurant. "So, believe me, I don't mind.

"What you gotta remember, small towns are different from big towns. The past is more important to us. We tend to live there longer. That's why Coach gets nervous when he thinks someone might tarnish the legend he's created. Have you seen his museum? Good God."

"Yes, I've seen it."

"So you know what I mean."

"Tell me about the night Elizabeth Rogers died," I said.

"You're not gonna let that go, huh? Okay."

Axelrod added very little that I didn't already know except this: The Seven, all of them, had left the party an hour before Elizabeth had.

"We'd been hoarding beers all night without the parents or Coach catching on. Especially Coach. The man woulda freaked. When we had enough, we left and went to drink them."

"Where did you go?"

"Josie Bloom's basement. His parents were gone and we went down there and just got wasted."

"Was Jack Barrett with you?"

"I don't know where Jack was." Axelrod seemed serious for a moment, or as close to it as he could manage. "I never asked him where he was."

An instant later, he was back to his jovial self.

"I heard Jack was angry with Beth," I said.

"Nah, it was the other way round. Beth was getting all paranoid on him, accusing him of things, saying how he was sleeping with another girl, stuff like that."

"Was he?"

"If he was, none of us ever found out about it, and being as how Victoria was such a small town back then, we probably would have. I figure Beth saw the writing on the wall. She knew Jack was going to leave her for the U and this was a way of saving face. You know, dump him before he dumped her."

"They broke up?"

"Well, sure. It was inevitable. I mean, God, they were kids. If Jamie got involved with someone at that age, I'd whack her upside the head."

I flashed on Tapia, but said nothing.

Axelrod was laughing loudly again, or at least he increased the volume on the laugh that seemed never to end. I glanced about. No one was looking at us. I guessed that Axelrod's patrons were used to his outbursts.

"Jack left the party," I said.

"Yep.

"Then you and the others left."

"Yep."

"Sometime after that, Beth left."

"I guess."

"That's all you know?"

"That's it."

"Were you ever questioned by the Chief?"

"Chief Bohlig? No, why would I be?"

Before I could answer, a man appeared just inside Nick's heavy wooden door. His hair was parted crookedly and in need of shampoo. His complexion looked blotchy under a two-day growth of beard, and while he was clearly underweight, he was as doughy as unbaked bread.

"Nick," he brayed, suddenly the loudest man in the restaurant. "You no-good sonuvabitch."

"Hey, Josie, how are ya, man?" Axelrod called out. His voice was still loud and cheerful, but something had changed. There was an edge to it that hadn't been there before.

"I need a drink," Bloom announced, scratching first his hands and then his cheeks.

"You look like you've already had plenty, partner," Axelrod said. I agreed. Bloom seemed like a man who had been to hell and back and remembered every step of the journey.

"What're you, my mother?" Bloom said. "A drink. Rye."

"How 'bout something to eat first. We've got a great special tonight. Jace," Axelrod called.

A moment later the young woman was standing there with her pencil and pad.

"Good evening, Mr. Bloom," she said. "What can I get you? The special?"

"Hey, hey, hey," Bloom chanted. He stopping scratching long enough to wrap an arm around Jace and hug her shoulder. I don't know why I was annoyed by the gesture, but I was.

"Judith Catherine," Bloom said. "How's my sweetheart?"

"Just great," Jace replied.

"Atta girl."

"How 'bout that special?" Jace asked.

"If'n that's the only way I'm gonna get a drink in this dump, yeah, why not?"

"Sure thing, Mr. Bloom. Good to see you again."

She patted Bloom's arm and smiled before turning toward the kitchen.

"Hi, Mr. Bloom." I extended my hand. "I'm McKenzie."

He looked at my hand as though I had offered him the dirty end of the stick.

"Who the hell is he?" he wanted Axelrod to tell him.

"McKenzie's been asking about the Seven," Axelrod explained.

Bloom grinned, but there was nothing friendly about it. Maybe it was the teeth, I told myself. They were a ghastly shade of gray and his gums were bright red.

"Fuck the Seven," he said. "Where's the restroom? Hell, I know where the restroom is."

Bloom spun in the direction of the kitchen and staggered away.

"Charming," I said.

"Ah, that's just Josie," Axelrod said. "He's all right. It's just—I told you about Coach and the tournament? Same with Josie. Winning the championship was the highlight of his life. Ever since God's dealt him nothing but slop."

"Why would God do that?"

"Who knows why God does half the things He does? I'll tell ya, He's sure been good to Jack though, huh?"

I remembered something my dad used to tell me—"God helps those who help themselves"—but didn't mention it.

"It's this place, this town," Axelrod said. "Josie should live in the Cities, Mankato; live where people don't know or care that he stole the ball with eight seconds left on the clock and passed it to Jack so Jack could win the game at the buzzer. Only he can't seem to get away.

"I've been told he suffers from what psychologists call dual diagnosis depression, meaning he's not only clinically depressed, he self-medicates himself with alcohol, which makes it worse. Another guy, he told me Josie suffers from biological unhappiness, whatever that means. I think it's just that he's been unable to deal with the terrible fact that his life, his entire existence has been defined by something he did when he was only seventeen years old."

"What's he do for a living?" I asked.

"These days? These days he's—I'm not sure what you'd call him. Not a gambler, anyway. What Josie does, he goes around to all the bars in the county, every place that sells pull tabs. In Minnesota, the winning tabs must be posted—it's the law—so a guy can look at a box and determine how many winning tabs are still left to be pulled. Sometimes you can get a box that's maybe a quarter full or less, except the big winners, they haven't been pulled yet. What Josie does, he looks for these boxes. When he finds one, he determines if the total amount of the winners still left in the box is worth more than the cost of all the remaining tabs. If it is, well then he just buys the entire box, guaranteeing himself a nice payday.

"Problem is, it's expensive. A box, even a quarter box, might cost a couple of thousand dollars and it's illegal to buy pull tabs with a check or credit card, so Josie has to carry a lot of cash with him. Two, three, four thousand."

"Flashing that kind of money is dangerous," I said.

"Tell me about it. And Josie, he's not what you'd call retiring."

"I've noticed."

"People know him. They know what he does, and most people, the people buying the pull tabs, they don't like it much when he just swoops in and grabs all the winners. This one time these guys jump him in his driveway—he's got a place out on the county road, kinda isolated. One night these guys jump him, steal about a thousand dollars. Josie, though, he hid most of his money—as much as five grand he said—in his boots. Problem was, next day he goes around bragging about it, telling how he outfoxed the muggers. So, what happens . . ."

"Let me guess."

"Same guys jump him again a couple nights later. Only this time they take all of his money *and* his boots."

"Surprise, surprise, surprise," I said.

"Ah, Josie. What a guy."

"Where does he get his seed money?"

"Who knows? Hey, Josie."

Bloom had returned. If anything, he appeared even worse off than when he left. His face was paler, his eyes flat and expressionless, and he continued to scratch his hands and face. He looked as though he had as much future as a lighted match.

"Whaddaya say?" Axelrod said.

"It's a dog-eat-dog world out there Nick, 'cept when it's the other way 'round."

"I hear that."

" 'Bout that drink."

"Dinner should be ready in a jiff." Axelrod came around the bar and took Bloom by the arm. "I have a nice booth for you. Sit here and Jace will be with you in a minute."

Bloom pulled his arm away. Axelrod nudged him hard and Bloom half sat, half fell into the booth. He leaned both elbows on the table and held his head.

"Christ, Nick."

Axelrod excused himself so he could tend bar. At the same time, someone had pumped a fistful of quarters into the jukebox. The music—some country hokum about the appeal of women who drove pickup trucks—filled the room, causing everyone to raise their voices. Bloom sat unmoving in the booth, supporting his head with both hands. I glanced at Axelrod. As soon as his back was turned I motioned to the other bartender and asked him to pour a shot of rye whiskey and a beer chaser. I took both to Bloom, set them on the table in front of him. He looked at me, focusing his eyes like I was someone he'd met before but couldn't place.

"May I join you, Mr. Bloom?"

His little eyes blinked at me a couple of times without seeing me. Maybe he hadn't heard me. Maybe I wasn't there.

I sat across from him, setting my own drink on the

table's edge. He didn't seem to notice. Instead he took down the shot in one long swallow and sighed like a tire with a slow leak. I had pounded them myself from time to time, only not like that. Never like that. I wondered what kind of pain would make a man drink the way Josiah Bloom drank? Or was it pain? Maybe it was just habit.

"I'd like to ask you about Elizabeth Rogers," I said.

Bloom cupped both hands around the glass of beer, inhaled deeply, and drank. He drank half the beer and when he set the glass down again, he exhaled and coughed, as if the few seconds he had held his breath had nearly suffocated him.

"This can't go on," he said.

"What can't go on?" I asked.

In reply, Bloom drained the beer and motioned for more. I caught the younger bartender's eye and another rye and beer were served. Bloom guzzled the rye. I drank half my Scotch.

"You shouldn't drink like that," Bloom told me suddenly. "It's not good for you."

Like you should talk, I almost said, but didn't.

"You don't want to end up like me, do ya?" Bloom asked.

"You could quit, get treatment."

"I have. Many times. I once did 184 weeks and two days without a drink. I was younger then."

I did the math—three and a half years of sobriety out of how many? Over fifty? I nudged the remainder of the Scotch away.

"You drink and sometimes, not always, but sometimes, maybe once outta ten tries it all becomes perfectly clear, you understand everything and then"—he snapped his fingers—"it's gone. It just— It lasts a moment, then it's gone. But that moment, what a moment. Do you know what I mean?"

I didn't but said I did.

"It can break your heart," Bloom said. He drank half the beer in one gulp and set the glass carefully in front of him.

"Beth Rogers," he said.

"Yes."

"What do you know about Beth Rogers?"

"That's what I wanted to ask you."

"What?"

"Tell me about Elizabeth. Tell me about that night."

"The night when she— Oh, what did we do?"

"Tell me."

"I can't."

At that moment, Jace appeared. She set the platter of roast beef and garlic roasted mashed potatoes in front of him.

"Here ya go, Mr. Bloom."

Bloom stared at the food for a moment, then at the girl. Jace patted his arm and Bloom recoiled in fear.

"No, no, you're not Beth. You can't be Beth. Oh, Jesus."

Bloom hid his face in his hands. Jace set her hand gently on his shoulder.

"Mr. Bloom? Mr. Bloom? It's all right, Mr. Bloom. You have friends here."

Bloom dropped his hands from his eyes and looked hard at her.

He said, "You ain't her. Little girl all shiny and new, ain't got no scratches on you yet. Like you was, like you was—You ain't pretty like her, you know. You think you are, but you ain't. She was made of pure gold."

"Are you talking about Elizabeth?" I asked.

"She was—perfect. I woulda done anything for her. Anything."

"Mr. Bloom?" I said.

Bloom drowned a sob with the rest of his beer. When he finished, Jace took the glass from his hand. She looked at me then like she wanted to slap me. Jace gathered the shot and beer glasses onto her tray and took them away.

I leaned halfway across the table.

"It's been a long time, Mr. Bloom."

"Yes."

"What happened that night?" I asked.

"I don't remember," he answered.

The glaze in his eyes seemed to extend over Bloom's entire body. He slumped down and buried his head in his arms. I slid the roast beef clear.

"Mr. Bloom?" I nudged him. "Mr. Bloom?" I gave him a hard push.

A moment later, Jace returned.

"He's asleep," I told her.

She looked at the drunk with compassionate disapproval.

"Poor Mr. Bloom," Jace said. "He drinks like this because—because he's sad, I guess. The world isn't what he wants it to be. But he'll be all right. He'll find what he needs."

What a wonderful young woman, my inner voice told me. She possessed such faith in human nature. I hoped she'd never lose it. But given her clandestine relationship with a Hispanic boyfriend in a racist town, I figured she probably would. *You should have given her a bigger tip.*

Jace fetched her father.

"I'll take care of him," he announced. It was the first

time I had heard him speak quietly. "I wish you wouldn't have bought him drinks."

"So do I," I said.

"I'll take him home."

"Where does he live? I could drive."

"He's got a place near the fairgrounds. But I'll take care of him. You've done enough."

"I'm sorry."

"Hell, McKenzie. We're all sorry."

Chapter Nine

Snow was settling gently over Victoria by the time I left Nick's Family Restaurant. Over two inches of it had gathered on the ground, hiding all that was unpleasant and ugly and vile, painting the city in gleaming white.

I raised my eyes to the sky, closed them, and let the large flakes settle on my face; I opened my mouth and tried to catch them on my tongue. One of the things about fresh snow is its flavor. There is a goodness in it that you simply can't taste in any other season. It called to mind memories of long ago tobogganing on the steep hills at the Town and Country Golf Course, watching the Winter Carnival parade, ice fishing on Lake Mille Lacs.

Another thing I like about falling snow is how completely it absorbs sound, how silent it renders even the most intense traffic. It was because of the snow that I didn't hear them approach.

"You still here, shithead?"

He sounded so close that I thought he had shouted in

my ear. Yet when I opened my eyes, I saw that Gene Hugoson stood several feet away. Brian Reif was on his left.

"It's the Victoria nightlife," I said. "I can't get enough of it."

"Why don't you just leave?" Hugoson wanted to know.

"Sounds like a plan." I tried to retreat down the sidewalk. Hugoson cut me off. I slowly pivoted until the men stood at about forty-five-degree angles to my left and right. I tried to keep my eyes on both of them at the same time as they moved closer.

"Why are you guys so angry?" I asked. "What'd I do?"

"We don't like you, bitch," Reif said.

The slur was definitely a notch above the insult Hugoson had hurled at me, but I didn't like it any better.

"You say that like it's a bad thing," I said.

All the warning signs were there: Attack Is Imminent. They didn't even bother with the first stages. My muscles tensed.

"C'mon fellas," I said. "Can't we all just get along?"

"We ain't a couple of kids on the sidewalk," Reif hissed at me.

Hugoson was the closest, so I cheated to my left, waited for him to make a move.

"Sic 'im," Reif said. Or maybe he said, "Get 'im." I wasn't listening that close. As soon as Hugoson shifted his weight a fraction of an inch I kicked him just as hard as I could in the groin; disable the attacker in front of you as quickly as possible before turning to face the second, that's what I was taught.

Only there was a thin veneer of ice under the snow. When I kicked Hugoson, my back foot slid out from under me. I went down as violently as he had, my hip making solid contact with the frozen concrete sidewalk. Pain surged through me like an electric shock, and for a moment I forgot Reif. Only he didn't forget me. I heard him curse, felt his shadow move across my face. He raised his foot, tried to kick my head. I rolled away. Reif cursed again. I flailed at him with my leg. The heel of my boot struck his knee. That hurt him, but he didn't fall. Reif cursed some more. If words were sticks and stones I'd be dead.

I heard something else.

A voice calling loudly from behind me.

"Gun!"

I did a stupid thing. I turned toward the voice. Greg Schroeder was standing next to my car about a half block up the street. He was smiling. Fortunately, Reif was just as foolish as I was. He looked at Schroeder, too, the pistol that appeared in his hand pointed more or less at the ground.

I recovered more quickly than Reif and swung my legs, sweeping his feet out from under him. He fell backward, his arms outstretched. He landed first on his tailbone, then his back. I heard a dull thud as his head bounced off the concrete.

I lunged over his body, clutched the gun in both of my hands. I twisted it out of his grasp. He cried out. Maybe I had broken one of his fingers. I couldn't tell. I rolled to my knees, gained control of the gun, and pointed it in his face.

"Did you point a gun at me? Did you? Did you point a gun at me? Are you suicidal?"

Reif didn't look suicidal. He looked frightened as he gripped the fingers of his gun hand with his other hand and rocked back and forth.

I glanced over my shoulder. Hugoson was still holding himself, moaning quietly.

I turned my attention back to Reif.

"Don't shoot, don't shoot," he chanted.

I pressed the muzzle of the gun against his cheek.

"Please," he cried.

"Jerk," I said.

I stood up.

"What's your story? Why are you guys so pissed off?"

"Coach says you're spreading lies about the Seven."

"Ah, bullshit. What's it really about?"

Reif shook his head and it occurred to me that what it was really about was anger and disappointment and failed dreams. I was just the guy they decided to take it out on.

I told them, "I know a guy who always wears three-piece suits with an open shirt collar and plenty of gold chains. On occasion he'll float out on the middle of Lake Calhoun in a rowboat where he's sure he can commune with the spirit of Donna Summer. I assured him that as far as I know Ms. Summers is still very much alive and he told me, 'Disco is dead.'"

Hugoson raised his head, an expression of disbelief fighting through the pain.

"Disco's dead. Get it?"

"Huh?" said Reif.

"Hell with you guys."

The expensive Scotch I had consumed was now a faint, rhythmic pulse behind my eyes and a cardboard taste in my mouth. I felt very tired. I had nothing more to say to either man. I turned and started walking toward where Schroeder was standing. I took a half dozen steps before I heard Reif say, "My gun?"

"You want your gun back, you can come and get it any time."

Greg Schroeder had cleared snow off of the Audi and

was now sitting on the hood. He gave me a smile that was more in his eyes than in his mouth and one of those short, perfunctory waves Queen Elizabeth doles out to the commoners whenever she deigns to move among them. By the time I reached him, Hugoson and Reif were helping each other inside Nick's Family Restaurant. After they told their version of what happened, I doubted I'd be offered any more free dinners.

The gun turned out to be an older Colt .32, the kind generals in the army used to carry. As I walked to Schroeder I removed the magazine, ejected the round in the chamber, and field-stripped the pistol. By the time I reached the Audi, I had the Colt in pieces. I dumped them all in a trash container that the city fathers had the foresight to place on the corner.

"You're not going to keep it?" Schroeder asked.

"I hate guns," I told him.

"Yeah, me, too."

"You know, that's a $45,000 car you're sitting on."

Schroeder slapped it with the flat of his hand.

"You paid forty-five for this piece of junk?"

"What are you doing here?"

"Just hanging out. How 'bout you?"

"You followed me down here."

"Followed you? The way you drive? Get serious."

"This is intolerable."

Schroeder laughed at me.

"You know, McKenzie, watching you in action, first at the Groveland Tap and now with those two guys back there, it's a wonder to me that you've managed to stay alive as long as you have."

"I was lulling them into a state of complacency."

"Sure you were."

I grabbed two fistfuls of Schroeder's coat and yanked him off my car. I felt my lips curl over my teeth, felt my skin grow tight over my face. I leaned in close and snarled, "What are you doing here? Who sent you?"

Schroeder shook his head.

"Nope. Nice try, though. Maybe with a little work. You should practice in front of a mirror. And remember, less is more."

"Fuck you, Schroeder."

I pushed him away.

Schroeder smiled and shook his head like he felt sorry for me. He turned and began sauntering away through the snow. In the distance, I saw where he had parked his Ford Escort.

"Hey, wait a minute. I want to talk to you."

"I'll see you around, tough guy," he called over his shoulder.

"Schroeder."

He lifted his gloved hand and let it drop in a kind of backward salute.

"You sonuvabitch."

Schroeder thought that was awfully funny. He gave me another wave and continued walking to his car.

God, I hate that guy, I told myself.

The Victoria Inn was located on the edge of town off U.S. Highway 71 and boasted a cocktail lounge, indoor swimming pool, and $49 weekday rates. I decided to crash in Victoria overnight, meet with Dr. Peterson and Grace Monteleone in the morning, then try to speak with Josie Bloom again. That was as far as my plans took me.

"Will you be staying with us long?" the desk clerk asked as I completed the registration card.

"Just the night."

"I see." The desk clerk spoke in a way that caused me to look up from the card. The clothes the woman wore were too tight, and her face was made up as if she were intent on hiding all clues to her age, which I guessed was well over forty. She was grinning as if we shared a secret.

"Check or credit card?" the woman asked.

"Cash." I removed three twenties and a ten from my wallet, enough to cover the room rate and taxes. The desk clerk took the bills and examined them like she had never seen their like before. She worked the transaction on her computer and gave me a receipt.

"Luggage?" she asked.

I held up a paper bag. It contained a toothbrush, toothpaste, disposable razor, shaving cream, hairbrush, gel, cotton briefs, white socks—three pairs to a package—and an XXL Minnesota Wild hockey jersey. I had come to Victoria unprepared to stay the night and bought the items at a shop near the Des Moines River after first cursing myself for my lack of foresight.

"I see," the desk clerk said. Her smile came and went without touching the rest of her face as she studied the registration card.

"Is your license plate number correct?"

"Is there a problem?"

The desk clerk could see my Audi through the glass wall facing the parking lot. She matched the plates on the car against the number I had written.

"No, no problem."

I showered, put on a pair of fresh briefs, and pulled the large hockey jersey over my head. I went to the small table and worked my notebook for a while, adding impressions to the facts that I had written down after each interview. A few minutes later I was staring out my window at the parking lot beyond. It was still snowing.

I should have bought something to read along with my other supplies, I told myself as I flopped down on the bed with the remote control. The TV promised some distraction, about a dozen channels worth. However, I surfed through them and found nothing that interested me. Even ESPN was a washout, broadcasting a trick-shot pool competition. Curiosity caused me to linger for a moment to see what the adult pay-per-view channels had to offer. Somehow the trailers for *Sinderella* and *Naughty Nurses III* suggested that they were the same movie.

"Things will never get that bad," I vowed and quickly turned to CNN.

Still, the previews reminded me that I had promised to call Nina Truhler.

"Hey," she said after I identified myself.

"How's Prudence?" I asked.

"Prudence is a treat—as usual. How's Victoria?"

"It's snowing."

"Snowing in the Cities, too. I wish you were here to keep me warm."

"And shovel your sidewalks."

"That, too. When are you coming home?"

"I don't know. This favor I promised to do, it's turning out to be more complicated than I thought it would be."

"I have a question."

"Ask."

"When I spoke to you earlier, I said I loved you, but you didn't say that you loved me back."

"You know I do, don't you, Nina? Do I have to say it?"

"It's something a girl likes to hear every now and again."

"I love you."

There, I said it.

She exhaled like she had been holding her breath a long time.

"Nina?"

"I'm okay. It's just . . . after our last conversation . . . I guess I'm a little paranoid. I blame my ex-husband. 'Course, I blame my ex-husband for most of the things that are wrong with my life."

"I don't know about your ex, Nina. I'll tell you the one thing I do know: I really miss you when you're not around."

Nina hesitated, said, "I'll tell you the one thing I know for sure. You're both my lover and my best friend. Without you I'd be so absolutely, totally outnumbered."

"Well, then."

"Well, then, what?"

"Well, then, I'd better hurry home."

"Call me. We'll have dinner or something."

"Sure."

"Mac? I wish . . . I just wish."

"Good night, Nina."

"Good night, Mac."

I traded the cell phone for the remote and went back to CNN. There was unrest in Iraq. Wow, that's news, I told myself.

A few moments later, a hard knock brought me cautiously to the door of my motel room. I peered through the spy hole. City of Victoria *Interim* Chief of Police Danielle Mallinger was standing on the other side of the door. My first thought was that Hugoson and Reif had ratted me out. But then why was the desk clerk cowering behind Mallinger's shoulder?

I set the chain and opened the door, pulling the chain taut.

"May I help you?"

"Mr. McKenzie?" Mallinger said.

"If that's your real name," the desk clerk added.

"What do you mean, if that's my real name?"

"Could you open the door, please," Mallinger said.

"For what purpose?"

"Rushmore McKenzie," the desk clerk said. "It sounds like a phony name to me."

"What?"

"I'd like to check your identification," Mallinger said.

"You know who I am."

"Mr. McKenzie."

"I told you. He's a drug dealer," said the night clerk.

"Just a minute."

I closed the door, pulled my jeans back on, removed the chain, yanked the door open, and stepped into the hall.

"What did you call me?"

"A drug dealer."

I stepped toward the desk clerk and was immediately intercepted by Mallinger. She put a hand on my chest and nudged me backward.

"Look at the way he's dressed," the night clerk insisted.

"It's a hockey jersey."

"That's what the gang kids wear."

"Are you nuts?"

"Stop it, both of you," Mallinger ordered.

"Oh, you better have a good explanation for this," I told her.

"Look at him, Chief," the desk clerk told Mallinger. "He fits all the criteria you said to look for. He checks in alone, late at night, driving a flashy car—"

"Flashy car? It's an Audi."

"He doesn't have luggage, pays cash to use a room for only one night, uses an alias. What kind of name is Rushmore McKenzie?"

"It's the name my father gave me!"

"Yeah, right."

"This is intolerable," I shouted, then remembered what Greg Schroeder did when I said the same thing to him: he laughed.

"Dammit!"

I pushed past Mallinger into my room. A moment later I thrust my driver's license into Mallinger's hand. "My ID. Do you have an MDT in your cruiser? Of course, you do. You ran my ID and license plates this morning."

"I know."

"Then what the hell?"

"He's not a drug dealer?" the desk clerk asked.

"No. He's an ex-cop."

I glared at the desk clerk.

"Go away," I told her.

"Thank you for your help, Florence," Mallinger told the desk clerk. "I can take it from here."

"I only did what you said," the woman insisted.

"I appreciate it," Mallinger said. "Very good job."

"He's not a danger?" the desk clerk said, meaning me.

"No, he's fine, thank you. You can go now. Thank you."

Mallinger and I watched her leave.

"What was that about?" I asked.

"Just trying to keep the riffraff out of Victoria."

"Go away."

"No, really. I want to talk to you."

"Go away."

"C'mon, McKenzie. Where's your sense of humor?"

"In my flashy car."

"In Victoria an Audi *is* a flashy car. Seriously, I want to talk to you."

"What about?"

Mallinger gestured at the open door.

"If this is just a cheap trick to get me alone in a motel room . . ."

Mallinger removed her hat and dropped it on the small table, removed her bulky coat and draped it over the back of a chair, both without asking permission. She sat down.

"Comfy?" I said.

Mallinger ran long, slender fingers through her red hair. "We have a meth problem in Victoria," she said.

"Everyone has a meth problem."

"That's why I'm having Florence and the other motel managers take a hard look at strangers."

"Like me."

"Have you heard about those kids we busted?"

"I have."

"They were virgins, never tried the stuff before. Didn't know if they should sniff, smoke, or inject it. They bought it off a guy outside a bar near the county road. Only they couldn't ID him, the man who sold it. All they knew what that he was scary-looking."

"That pretty much describes every meth user I've ever seen."

"I want to arrest him. I want to put him away. That's what they pay me for."

"A drug bust would also go a long way toward removing the interim label from your title."

"There's that, too."

"Why are you talking to me?"

"You used to be a cop. A good one. I checked you out, first after your problems at the Rainbow Cafe this morning and then some more after your run-in with Reif and Hugoson."

"They file a complaint?"

"Not with me."

"Where are you going with this, Chief?"

"You've been running around town talking to a lot of people, asking a lot of questions."

"Not about meth."

"You want to know what happened to Elizabeth Rogers."

"That's becoming less and less of a secret."

"I can help."

"How?"

"I can show you the original incident reports, the supplementals, photos of the victim, transcripts of the Q&A's, the coroner's final summary—everything."

"I'd like to see the reports."

"Then give me something in return."

"Like what?"

"Whatever you find out. A smart guy like you, McKenzie, someone who keeps his eyes and ears open, he could do himself a lot of good."

"If I learn anything at all about your meth problem, I'll tell you."

"Then we have a deal."

"Why not? But you gotta know, Chief, meth is easy.

These people, they're so damn paranoid they're far more dangerous than any other people who use drugs. More guns, more violence. They love booby traps."

"You call that easy?"

"Because they're so outrageously paranoid you can get rid of them with a simple knock-and-talk. Just knock on their doors and warn them to shut down or prepare to be arrested and they'll be on the first stage outta Dodge. The trouble is, all you're doing is moving them down the road to another jurisdiction."

"The trouble is finding them, McKenzie. Help me find them and I'll help you."

Seemed fair enough.

Chapter Ten

Mankato was originally called *Mahkato*—meaning "greenish blue earth"—by its earliest inhabitants, the Dakota, although it didn't look any different to me. It became Mankato because of a spelling error that was never corrected, possibly made by the eighteenth-century Europeans searching for the Northwest Passage who settled there after getting lost on the Minnesota River. That's all I knew about the city except that it was where the Minnesota Vikings football team held its annual training camp.

About four inches of snow fell overnight, but the plows had been out early and I had no trouble holding the road even at fifteen miles above the posted speed limit. The sun was bright and the sky was unclouded and deep blue.

I easily found Dr. Dave Peterson's address, a red brick three-story building across from the River Hills Mall that he shared with several dentists, two psychiatrists, and an insurance agent. An assistant guided me to an examination room that I guessed also served as Dr. Peterson's office because of the family photographs and certificates hanging from the walls. I studied the photos while I waited. In their wedding picture, Dr. Peterson's wife was a petite brunette and he was tall with a full head of hair. She had become a plump blonde and he was bald by the time their photograph was taken at their daughter's high school graduation and I wondered if Nina's future and mine held a similar fate.

I glanced at my watch. Ten past eight. Dr. Peterson was late, but when was a doctor ever on time? I examined his certificates—Bachelor of Arts, Gustavus Adolphus College; Doctor of Medicine, University of Minnesota; Medical Specialist, Department of Ophthalmology, University of Minnesota; elected to the American Academy of Ophthalmology. That killed another five minutes. At twenty past eight, I returned to the receptionist to advise her that I was still waiting.

"I'm sorry. Dr. Peterson cannot see you today. Would you like to reschedule?"

"You don't understand. I'm not here for an examination. I came to ask—"

"I'm sorry, Dr. Peterson cannot see you today."

"Please. I'm here—"

"Would you care to reschedule your appointment? We have an opening in March."

I considered shouting. It's amazing how much grease a squeaky voice can get. Only the receptionist didn't look like a woman who was easily intimidated.

"May I leave a message?" I asked instead.

"Certainly."

On a notepad emblazoned with the doctor's name, address, and phone number, I wrote:

Since everyone has been so cooperative, I'm going to petition the Cold Case Unit of the Minnesota Bureau of Criminal Apprehension to immediately reopen the investigation into the murder of Elizabeth Rogers.

"Make sure he gets that," I said.

"Certainly," said the receptionist.

I found Mankato West High School on the other side of town near the Minnesota River. It was a midsize school, educating over 1,200 students grades nine through twelve, and it took its security seriously. I was intercepted first in the parking lot and then just inside the front entrance by people who were very keen to know my identity and business. After explaining, I was given both a visitor's tag that I wore around my neck on a chain and an escort to Grace Monteleone's office.

The years had not been as kind to Monteleone as they had been to Suzi Shimek. She was forty pounds too heavy, she had changed the color of her hair from auburn to a kind of orange-blond to mask the gray, and her face was etched with the lines of responsibility. Her eyes were clear, yet held the slightly wearied expression of someone who had been lied to often and was still having trouble getting used to it.

Monteleone's greeting was friendly, yet not warm.

"You have questions concerning the Victoria Seven?" she said, repeating what I told her over the phone. "I'm not sure I can help you."

I glanced around, trying to get a sense of the woman from the decor of her office. There was little to grab hold of. The carpet matched the drapes, which matched the chairs, which were made of the same wood as the desk, credenza, and file cabinets. Plaques testifying to Monteleone's competence were set at eye level and arranged eighteen inches apart. I could sniff the aroma of coffee, yet found no coffeemaker or mugs. Nor were there any unsightly stacks of paper or loose pads and pens lying about. The room could have been a display in an office furniture store showroom for all the personality it revealed, except for the few photographs arranged neatly on the desk.

"Your family?" I asked.

"Yes. This is my son and daughter-in-law." Monteleone held up the largest of the photographs. "This rapscallion"—she spoke the word proudly—"is my grandson."

"Good-looking kid," I said.

"Yes, and he knows it, too." Monteleone smiled proudly. "He's only twelve and already the girls are swarming around him. He's very bright, too. But you have to keep an eye on him. He's a Sagittarius like his father, and Sagittarians are adventurous, which means he can be a lot of trouble. Fortunately"—Monteleone set the photograph back on her desk—"that's my daughter-in-law's problem. I've already done my time."

I pointed at the third photograph. It was smaller, a three-by-five of a young soldier taken with a pocket camera, the color fading badly.

"Is that your husband?"

"Yes," Monteleone said.

"Suzi Shimek said he was killed in Vietnam."

"You spoke to Suzi?"

"Yesterday."

Monteleone nodded.

"Suzi never knew my husband. I hardly knew him. We found each other in June after I moved here from Victoria. We married in August, right before he shipped. He was killed on Christmas Eve."

"I'm sorry," I said.

"Thank you." Monteleone returned the photograph. "Why are we meeting?"

"John Allen Barrett. He was one of your students in Victoria."

"Governor Barrett. Yes, he was my student, I am proud to say."

"Why proud?"

"When a teacher sees one of her students become a success, she likes to think she played a small part in that success."

"Suzi said he was your pet."

"Teacher's pet?" Monteleone chuckled. "I suppose he was. I wanted him to do well. He was capable of doing so very well."

"He won the state high school basketball tournament."

"I don't remember him for that."

"What do you remember him for?"

"His kindness. His consideration. He had the gift of making the people around him feel better about themselves."

"Suzi said he was very intelligent."

"Oh yes. That, too."

"He dated Elizabeth Rogers."

"She was the prettiest girl in high school. Who else was he going to date?"

"I heard she and Barrett had a fight the night she was killed."

"I never heard that."

"That's why he left the party early."

"No, it's not."

"Why do you think he left the party early?"

"He was tired of it. Tired of the hoopla surrounding the team. Jack liked basketball. It helped him get noticed at an early age. It earned him a scholarship at the University of Minnesota. Yet it was never as important to him as it was to everyone else. He was smart enough to appreciate that it was just a game."

"Did he tell you that?"

"Yes."

"When?"

"Many times."

"Were you close?"

"No more than any teacher and student."

"The two of you spoke a great deal, I'm told."

"Jack had dreams beyond basketball. He was grateful to have someone he could confide in."

"What were his dreams?"

"To get as far away from Victoria as possible."

"Why do you say that?"

Monteleone glanced at the photographs of her family for a moment before answering.

"I suppose I'm being unfair. It wasn't Victoria that Jack despised. It was his father. Jack's mother died when he was a baby. When he was ten, Jack's father told him, 'When your mother died, they all said I should put you in an orphanage. I didn't, and it was the worst thing I ever did in my life.' Can you imagine that? A man saying something like that to his ten-year-old son?"

I flashed on my own father, who did everything for me after my mother died. *No, I couldn't imagine it.*

"Jack remembered the words verbatim," Monteleone said. "They haunted him. Because of those words, Jack never asked for anything from his father. The reason he spent so much time playing basketball was so he could get away from him. His father, for his part, never went to see Jack play. Not even the title game. Jack was a hero in Victoria, but not at home. I wasn't surprised at all that he refused to attend his father's funeral. Instead, he went to Europe to play basketball. Given his background, it's a wonder Jack turned out as well as he did."

"Perhaps you had something to do with that," I suggested.

Monteleone gave it a moment's thought before saying, "It's nice to think so."

"Have you seen him, spoken to him, since he left school?"

"No. I shook his hand once during a campaign fundraiser here in Mankato a couple of years ago, but he didn't recognize me."

I wasn't surprised. Monteleone no longer resembled at all the attractive young woman in the Victoria High School yearbook.

"I've been in Victoria," I said. "Some people blame Governor Barrett for Elizabeth Rogers's death."

"What nonsense. He couldn't possibly have known she would be killed when he left the party."

"Lynn Peyer—"

"Lynn Peyer." Monteleone spoke the name like it was an obscenity.

"She, for one, thinks Jack actually killed her."

Monteleone rose quickly to her feet.

"That's a lie. An absolute lie. A damnable lie."

"How can you be so sure?"

Monteleone slowly sat down.

"I just am," she said.

A few minutes later—after Monteleone decided she had more important things to do than speak to a muckraker like me—I was back on the road. Driving alone, I lapsed into a freeway fantasy. I had a fast car, plenty of money, and no encumbrances. I could go where I pleased, go where I've never been before, and do things I've never done. There was nothing holding me to the road I was traveling except a sense of duty, of responsibility, that I couldn't even define. Turn off at the next exit, I told myself. Or the next one. Or the one after that. Just turn off. . . .

A dozen exits later I was approaching Victoria. I was still way above the speed limit, but promised myself I'd slow down before I reached the city limits.

"No way I'm going to let that cowgirl give me a ticket," I said aloud.

What the hell, you'll probably never see her again, my inner voice reminded me. *Considering your relationship with Nina, that's probably for the best.*

My plan hadn't changed. I would find Josie Bloom in the hope that I could persuade him to tell me what he knew about the night Elizabeth was killed. I didn't expect much to come of it. "*Oh, what did we do?*" The line still hung in the air, demanding explanation. Only it could mean anything. From a chronic alcoholic? Absolutely anything.

Still, I'd love to get a long look at the case files. Maybe there was something there besides the unsubstantiated allegation that Elizabeth was killed by roaming transients. Something that would categorically clear Governor Barrett. Only I'd have to give Mallinger something in return, and I had nothing to swap.

The Bureau of Criminal Apprehension? That was just something to annoy Dr. Peterson and the boys. I had no intention of bringing official attention to Elizabeth's murder and subsequently to John Allen Barrett.

Which brought me back to Lindsey's elusive e-mailer.

"We're gonna have to do something about him," I said aloud.

I had been driving with both hands on the steering wheel in the ten and two positions, just as I had been trained. I took my right hand off the wheel only long enough to switch the radio to the classic rock station.

In that moment, the Audi lurched hard to the right.

Blowout, I told myself.

I gripped the wheel with both hands and twisted it to the left to compensate and removed my foot from the accelerator.

Only it didn't feel like a blowout.

A loud, high-pitched grinding sound added to my confusion.

The car edged closer to the shoulder and the ditch beyond.

I tried to pull it back.

It was like leaning against a moving wall.

A big blue wall.

A truck.

A pickup truck with a plow blade.

The plow blade was digging into my car just below the door handle, leaning against the Audi, pushing it toward the ditch.

I saw the truck, but not the driver. The driver was too high in the cab.

Doesn't he know I'm here?

I leaned on the horn and screamed at the truck to stop.

It didn't stop.

I downshifted and hit the brakes hard.

I felt the antilock braking system shuddering under my boot.

The pickup slowed as I slowed.

It wouldn't let me go.

I downshifted again and punched the accelerator. The Audi pitched forward. The pickup did the same.

I went for a matchup—wheel to wheel, bumper to bumper, trading paint as my father would say—my one chance.

Only I didn't have a chance.

If it had been another car, I would have been able to outdrive it. It wasn't.

The Audi was 53 inches high, 73 inches wide, and 159 inches long. The truck was at least 80 inches high, 80 inches wide, and 247 inches long. They did not match up wheel to wheel, bumper to bumper.

The Audi weighed approximately 2,650 pounds. The truck was four times that heavy. I had four cylinders and 225 horsepower. The truck was a V-8, maybe a V-10 with over 300 horses.

The numbers were not on my side.

I cranked the steering wheel to the left just the same, slamming into the truck.

The pickup rocked, but stayed its course.

I kept leaning against it, even as my fear grew that soon the front tire would fold, sending the Audi spinning into the ditch or under the truck.

Be afraid, be very afraid, my inner voice said.

Dialogue from SF movies I didn't need.

It was quickly replaced by something else, something inexplicable that I would noodle over for weeks to come—advice my father had once given me.

Never bet on professional boxing or amateur figure skating.

The truck had too much advantage. It was going to shove me into the ditch, probably roll me over. A bad thing, high-speed rollovers.

I knew of only one way to escape it.

I swung the steering wheel to the right.

The Audi flew off the highway at sixty-three miles an hour.

For an instant, I was airborne, the car soaring above the roadside ditch.

There was nothing for me to do except wait for impact. It seemed to be a long time in coming, long enough anyway for my inner voice to announce, *You love this car.*

The Audi splashed into the snow.

I felt the unyielding pressure of the seat harness on my shoulder and across my stomach, keeping me from leaping through the windshield.

The car skidded forward, losing speed rapidly as it plowed through the deep drifts. It reminded me of diving into a pool. The snow eased the Audi to a stop the way water slows a diver.

I bounced back against the bucket seat even as I gripped the steering wheel, still anticipating the sudden, excruciating jolt of collision. When I finally realized that the Audi was no longer moving, I leaned back against the seat, marveling that my air bags hadn't deployed. The engine had stalled, but the radio was working. Leslie Gore.

"It's My Party and I'll Cry If I Want To." I switched it off. An eerie silence enveloped the car. I sat there shaking for a full thirty seconds. I reminded myself to breathe. It took a few moments until I remembered how.

The nose of my car was now buried in snow; the silver hood and windshield were splattered with it. I was grateful for it. Grateful that it had snowed the evening before, grateful for all the snowfalls that had come before that one, and grateful for the snowplows that had pushed the snow off the highway into the ditch.

I glanced out my side window. I could see only the rooftops of the vehicles that passed me on the highway, oblivious to my predicament. I rested my forehead against the steering wheel. All those driving lessons that my father, that my skills instructor at the academy had given me—"We never covered this," I said aloud.

It didn't take long before my warm breath fogged the windows. I powered down the driver's-side window, letting clean, clear frozen air into the car. After a few deep breaths, I found my cell phone, dialed 911, and explained where I was.

"I need the police and a tow truck," I told the operator.

"Are you the driver of the vehicle?"

"Yes," I said, identifying myself.

"Are you hurt?"

"No."

"Was anyone else hurt?"

"No. There's just me."

"Police cars and an ambulance have already been dispatched. Are you sure you're not hurt?"

"Quite sure."

"I'll recall the ambulance, then."

"What do you mean police have already been dispatched?"

"Someone witnessed the accident and called it in a few minutes ago."

"Who?"

"The caller refused to give his name. He said he didn't want to get involved."

The light bars on two police cars flashed above me. The cars halted. Doors were opened and slammed shut. Someone shouted something at someone else. Danny Mallinger appeared on the rim of the roadside ditch. During my duel with the truck I had crossed into her jurisdiction. I gave her a wave. *How embarrassing.* She plunged into the snow and plowed toward me. I told the 911 operator that the police had arrived and thanked her. The operator told me to have a nice day.

I deactivated my cell phone and jammed it back into my pocket just as Mallinger arrived at my door.

"Are you all right?"

"Couldn't be better."

"There's an ambulance on the way."

"I've already canceled it."

"You're sure you're not hurt?"

"Help me out of the car."

I unlocked the door and tried to force it open, but it wouldn't budge. Mallinger frantically cleared the snow that was jammed against it. Finally, with her pulling and me pushing the door, we made an opening. She told me to be careful as she helped me from the car. I felt steady on my feet, but let her hold my arm just the same.

The second officer was now at the side of the car—a man even younger than Mallinger. Mallinger looked beyond him, following the long furrow the Audi had dug into the snow from where it left the highway to where it had settled.

"Going a little fast, were we?"

"I was under the speed limit," I told her. "Someone ran me off the highway. He did it deliberately. Just look at my car. Oh, my God. Look at my car."

The second officer was squatting next to the Audi, running his gloved fingers over a series of two-foot-wide grooves cut deep into the metal from the center of the car door to the rocker panels and all the way to the back bumper, the bumper nearly torn off. Most of the paint had been chipped and scraped off, replaced in a few instances with streaks of blue.

"Look at my car!"

"What hit him?" Mallinger asked the officer.

"Just look at my Audi."

"What hit you?" Mallinger asked me.

"A truck. A pickup. My car. I just bought it."

"What kind of pickup truck?"

"Blue. With a plow blade. I was a little too busy to get make and model."

"A blue pickup truck," said the young officer. "By the height of the grooves, I'd say it was a heavy-duty model. A lot of farmers with that kind of vehicle."

"Andy," Mallinger said, drawing out the name. "Andy?"

Andy wasn't listening. He pulled a plastic bag from the pocket of his bulky coat and a pair of tweezers. He began prying blue paint chips off my Audi and dropping them into the bag.

"Andy, what are you doing?"

Andy seemed surprised that Mallinger would ask such a question.

"Collecting evidence," he said.

"Evidence?"

"Paint samples for the PDQ."

"Don't waste time."

"Whoa, whoa," I interrupted. "PDQ?"

"Paint Data Query," Andy said, obviously pleased to demonstrate his knowledge. "It's a database of paint samples. The FBI and the Royal Canadian Mounted Police set it up about ten years ago. We send in an unknown paint chip and the lab will determine make, model, and year of the vehicle. We'll run that information through the DMV."

"Andy, the odds of getting a hit—it's a waste of time," Mallinger insisted.

"No, it's not. I have a girlfriend who works for one of the labs that collects paint samples for PDQ and she says—"

"Andy." Mallinger sighed impatiently and turned to me. "He's new."

"Hell with that." I looked directly into Andy's green eyes. "You collect all the paint samples you want. You get the sonuvabitch that wrecked my car and I'll make it worth your while."

Mallinger looked skyward and frowned.

"I need this," she muttered. "I really need this."

It took over an hour for a wrecker to get my Audi back on the highway. I warned the operator not to damage the car. He told me they could always wait until the spring thaw before trying to get it out of the ditch. I reminded him that it was a $45,000 car. He said, not anymore. I told him he wasn't very funny. Mallinger suggested I wait in her cruiser while they worked. I insisted on watching from the shoulder of the highway where I could get a better look. I cringed, closed my eyes, and more than once held my breath as the Audi was yanked, dragged, and generally muscled onto the pavement. I realized it was just a car, but still. . . .

I thanked Mallinger for her help and arranged to get a copy of the accident report for my insurance company. Man, were they going to love this. Afterward, I accompanied the tow truck driver to the garage. They put the Audi on a hoist and determined that there had been no damage to the undercarriage. After reattaching the bumper and engineering a temporary fix of the rear lights and filters—there was a lot of duct tape involved—they pronounced the car drivable as long as I didn't drive it too hard. They told me they'd be happy to fix the Audi "as good as new," but I would have to wait a good long time for parts. That didn't seem like an option to me. I paid with a credit card, thanked everyone, and drove off.

I still held to my plan, although it had been pushed back over four hours. Using my map and the address I had gleaned from the Internet, I found Josiah Bloom's place across from the Nicholas County Fairgrounds. There were no other houses in the vicinity and I wondered why it had been built there. Nor was there a garage, only a strip of asphalt next to the house. The strip was empty.

I knocked on the door and waited. After a few moments I knocked again. I tried the latch. The door was unlocked. I gave it a gentle shove and it swung open. I called Bloom's name several times. No answer. I stepped inside and was immediately seized by a sense of dread so deep inside me that it felt I had been born with it.

"Mr. Bloom?"

All the shades were drawn, turning the bright winter sunlight into gray shadows. I moved through a tiny living room filled with furniture that didn't match. There was a TV and a VCR. A long screwdriver had been jammed into the mouth of the tape machine—the sight made me consider returning to the Audi for my gun. Instead, I crossed into the dining room beyond. Through an open door on my right I saw a bathroom. To my left was a small arch and what looked like a kitchen.

"Mr. Bloom?"

I smelled something I couldn't place. It reminded me of cat urine, but what was that sweet smell mixed with it? It seemed to come from the kitchen, and smelling it did something to my body. I felt the hairs on the back of my neck rising, felt my lungs fight for air. Perspiration welled up under my arms and on my forehead and I swore I could hear—actually hear—the beating of my heart as I drifted toward the kitchen. I found a switch and flicked the light on.

Half of Josiah Bloom's body was in a chair, the rest slumped over a small wooden table. A puddle of rich, red blood nearly covered the table and dripped into another, much larger puddle on the pale yellow linoleum floor. I gagged when I first saw the small entry hole surrounded by burned and unburned gunpowder in his right temple. I gagged again when I discovered that the bottom left side of Bloom's head was gone, that his blood, bone, teeth, and brain were splattered on the kitchen wall, cabinets, and floor.

My gag reflex kicked in and I ran to the bathroom. I found the toilet, hovered above it, my body shuddering, until the gagging finally subsided. I took pride in not vomiting—the first time I came across a dead body I had. I rinsed my mouth and splashed cold water on my face. *Contaminating a crime scene, oh this is so smart*, my inner voice told me. *Wouldn't they be proud of you back at the St. Paul Police Department? Oh, wouldn't they, though?*

"Suicide," I told my reflection in the mirror. "I drove him to suicide."

Get over yourself, my private voice replied.

"Why then?"

The smell of cat urine was far greater in the bathroom and I began to look for the source. *Did Josie keep cats?* I found two large plastic buckets, one filled with empty cough medicine bottles and the other with batteries. The bathtub was hideously stained.

"Well, that might be a reason," I said aloud.

I forced myself back into the kitchen and examined Bloom's wound. Next I searched for the gun. I found it in an unlikely location—Bloom's hand. I looked at it for a long time. Then back at the entry wound.

"Danny isn't going to like this," I said aloud before I called 911.

Chapter Eleven

I gave my statement twice, first to Mallinger, then to the medical examiner, a local doctor who moonlighted for the county. Mallinger had made sure that no one entered the kitchen before the ME arrived, including herself.

"An apparent suicide," the ME announced. "However, there are some inconsistencies. For one, we have a footprint and some smearing in the blood on the floor." He held up his camera for us to see. "I have several shots of it."

"That was me," said I. To prove it, I showed them the tip of my boot, now stained red. "Sorry."

The ME took a photograph of my boot. Apparently he was a one-man forensics department.

"What else did you do?" he asked.

"I used the bathroom."

The ME had a disgusted look on his face. Mallinger nodded her head in understanding. She looked like she wanted to vomit herself.

We were outside, standing next to Mallinger's cruiser. She was pale and I noticed her breath was coming hard.

Other officers hung about waiting for instructions, but Mallinger waved them back. I suspected that she had never seen as messy a crime scene before. Unfortunately, I was about to make it worse.

"It wasn't suicide," I told the ME.

"Yeah, it was," the ME said.

"It wasn't."

"Since *CSI* everyone's a criminologist," the ME told Mallinger.

"Bag his hand, the hand holding the gun," I insisted. "Bag Bloom's hand so it won't rub against anything when you transport the body and test it for gunshot residue."

The ME glared at Mallinger like he expected the Chief to do something. Only the Chief was still too shaken to appreciate what I was telling her.

"Listen to me," I said. "The wound—it's a downward path." I pressed a finger against my own temple, pointing the finger at my jaw. "It's an awkward way to hold a gun. Usually, the path of the bullet is upward." I adjusted my finger accordingly. "There's tattooing around the wound, but no abrasion collar, which means the barrel wasn't pressed against the temple when it was fired. Something else. The gun."

"What about it?"

"It was large caliber."

"So?"

"He shouldn't be holding it. The gun should have fallen from his hand."

"Ever hear of cadaveric spasm?" the ME said. "I've seen suicides who go into spontaneous rigor mortis, who grip the gun so tight you have to pry it from their fingers."

"Only he's not gripping the gun. It's just resting in his hand like someone set it there."

The ME was looking at me now like he was amazed to hear that we spoke the same language. I've met a lot of half-smart people like him before. It was always difficult for them to believe that there were other people in the world just as half-smart.

"I'll bet if you try to lift fingerprints, you'll discover the gun has been wiped clean," I told him.

"Who's the professional here?" The ME was addressing Mallinger. "He's getting in the way."

"Maybe I'm wrong," I said. "Maybe I am. Will it kill you to find out for sure? If this were Ramsey County you'd have a GSR—a gunshot residue kit. Swab his hand and test it for gunpowder. What would it hurt?"

"What *would* it hurt?" Mallinger asked weakly.

"We don't have the facilities," the ME said. "I'd have to send it to a private lab and that's gonna cost the county a thousand dollars."

"Is that what we're talking about?" Mallinger asked. "A thousand dollars?"

"Chief—"

"Bag the hand."

"I'm telling you—"

"Bag the hand," Mallinger shouted.

The ME threw up his own hands in disgust.

"Something else," I said.

"What?" the ME asked.

"This is going to be even more expensive."

"What?"

I looked directly into Mallinger's eyes so she would better understand what I was telling her.

"There are signs of methamphetamine cooking all over the place. The odor of cat urine? That's what it smells like. Ephedrine from the cold medicine, lithium from the batteries—that's part of the recipe."

"Are you saying Josie Bloom was cooking meth?" the ME asked.

"Yes. In his bathroom. You can see the stains on his bathtub."

"No way. Josie wasn't smart enough."

"If you can make chocolate chip cookies, you can make meth."

"Are you sure?" The strength was returning to Mallinger's voice.

"Yeah, I'm sure."

"Then where is the lab paraphernalia?" the ME wanted to know.

"Good question," I told him. "I couldn't find any of the meth Josie cooked, either."

"How hard did you search?" Mallinger asked.

"Not as hard as you will, I bet."

"What should I do?"

"Call the Nicholas County Sheriff's Department."

"No, this is my case."

"This is murder, Danny. Don't make the same mistake your predecessor did."

"If the GSR test comes back negative, then I'll call the sheriff."

"Look, you're going to have to call him anyway. After you finish with Josie, you're going to need someone trained in dealing safely with meth to go over the scene. Then there's cleanup. For every pound of meth, there's six, seven pounds of hazardous waste. Josie could have poured it down the drain. He could have tossed it into his backyard."

"I understand," Mallinger said. "I'll take care of it. Thank you."

"Danny," I said.

She glared at me like I had just committed a cardinal sin using her first name.

"Chief Mallinger," I said. "Be smart."

"If you're so smart, maybe there's something you can explain to me," the ME said.

"What's that?"

"The screwdriver protruding from Josie's VCR. What's that about? Was he hiding his drugs in there?"

"People who use meth, they become so damned paranoid, they wonder where those people on the TV are. They attack the TVs and VCRs with screwdrivers and hammers to find them."

"Stay here," Mallinger said. She sauntered over to her officers and gave a few orders. They dispersed in opposite directions, each happy to be finally doing something, although what they were doing I couldn't tell you. The ME went back inside the house. Mallinger retired to the inside of her police cruiser and started working the radio.

I stood outside and shivered.

There was no traffic on the county road, and I was surprised when a battered SUV arrived, shuddering to a stop behind the ME's van. Kevin Salisbury stepped out of the SUV in a hurry, afraid he was missing something. Like the ME, he carried his own camera.

"Whaddaya got?"

"Are you talking to me?"

Salisbury glanced about, looking for someone to talk to. Finding no one, he returned to me.

"The police scanner said there's been a shooting."

"The ME's inside. You should talk to him."

"Yeah." Salisbury made for the house. Mallinger stopped him.

"Whoa, Kevin," she called as she left her vehicle. "Where are you going?"

"I want to go—"

"No, no, no. Come here."

Mallinger took the reporter aside and spoke to him like she had been doing it her entire life. For his part, Salisbury furiously wrote down her words in a notebook. After a few minutes Salisbury raised his camera. Mallinger shook her head. From his body language, I had the impression he was pleading with her, apparently without success. After a while, Salisbury began taking photos of the house, but he didn't attempt to enter it.

Mallinger rejoined me at the car.

"I don't want you speaking to Kevin," she said. "Okay?"

"Not a word. I promise."

"I appreciate it."

We watched the reporter circling the property, looking for an angle to shoot from that would make his photos seem ominous.

"What do you think happened?" Mallinger asked.

"You're not going to like it."

"I already don't like it."

"I think Josie's death is connected to the murder of Elizabeth Rogers."

"How could it be? That was thirty years ago."

"I spoke to Josie last night. He made some reference

to— When I asked him about the night Elizabeth was killed, he said, 'Oh, what did we do?' When I pressed him, he said, 'I can't tell you.' Then he passed out. I came here today to learn what he meant."

"Do you honestly think someone killed Bloom to keep him from telling a complete stranger a secret that he's managed to keep to himself for over three decades? That's kind of a reach, isn't it?"

"This morning I went to see Dr. Dave Peterson in Mankato. He was willing to talk to me yesterday. Now all of a sudden he's too busy to even say hello. That's when I did something foolish."

"No. Foolish? You?"

"I left a note telling Peterson that I was going to ask the BCA to reopen the investigation. The next thing I know, someone runs my car off the highway and puts a bullet in Josie Bloom's head. If it wasn't for the deep snow in the ditch, I'd be as dead as he is now."

Mallinger shook her head.

"I don't believe it."

"Chief—"

"I buy the first part. You started asking Josie a lot of questions, his partners found out about it, panicked, and kill him. I'm willing to accept that. Bloom was a weak sister and he was getting weaker. I think he was killed because his accomplices were afraid he would tell you something about their operation, and that's as far as it goes. The thing on the highway this morning—there's no evidence that that was anything more than road rage. The fact that you're asking questions about Elizabeth Rogers, that doesn't mean anything."

"You can't just eliminate the possibility."

"Sure, I can. You know, the guys in the truck, that could just as easily have been the two punks you punched out in front of Fit to Print. Did you ever think of that?"

"You know about them?"

"It's my town."

"C'mon, Chief."

"I'm lazy, McKenzie. I admit it. I don't like to work hard. That's why I want to be chief of the Victoria City Police Department instead of going to a bigger city. I was looking forward to a long, uneventful career. Now this." Mallinger sighed deeply and massaged her temples. "We'll test Josie's hand for gunshot residue. If it comes back positive, we're going to call it a suicide brought on by drug abuse."

"If it's negative?"

"If it's negative—ah, dammit. Wait here."

Mallinger disappeared into the house. The ME was following her when she returned ten minutes later. He smiled broadly as he approached Salisbury, as if speaking to the media was the most fun he could have. Mallinger flagged down one of her officers and spoke to him. The officer nodded his head like he was taking instructions.

"Come with me," Mallinger said as she approached her cruiser.

"Where are we going?"

"To our tiny, antiquated law enforcement center. I'm only doing this to get it out of the way, understand? We'll take a hard look at Elizabeth Rogers's file to see if there's anything that even remotely supports this goofy theory of yours."

I bristled at the word "goofy," but decided to let it slide. After all, it was nice of her to let me tag along.

* * *

Mallinger was a quick, assertive driver with even less regard for traffic regulations than I had.

"Have you ever been given a ticket?" I asked her.

"Of course not. I'm a cop."

Five minutes later we were walking under bright fluorescent lights through the bowels of the Victoria City Center, arms and legs moving in perfect synchronization, to a door labeled RECORDS. Along the way we passed Officer Andy.

"How's it going?" I asked him.

"I sent off the paint chips to PDQ. My girlfriend said she'd try to expedite the search. We should get a hit right away."

"Who the hell do you work for, Andy?" Mallinger wanted to know.

Andy looked from me to her like he wasn't sure.

"Wait here," Mallinger told me when we reached the door.

I waited.

And waited some more.

Finally, Mallinger reappeared.

"Let's go," she said as she brushed past me.

"Where?"

"To see Chief Bohlig."

"Why?"

"The file on Elizabeth Rogers. It's missing."

Chief Bohlig was a tall man, creased like old leather and wearing a thermal shirt that was faded from frequent washings and threadbare along the collar and cuffs. We found him chopping wood in the backyard of his lake home with a double-bladed ax. There was a pile of logs sawed into eighteen-inch lengths on his right. One by one, he split them into halves and quarters and tossed them into an even more impressive pile on his left. He chopped the logs on a thick, wide tree stump. The snow was trampled all around him and wood chips were littered everywhere.

Mallinger asked him why he didn't hire someone younger to chop his wood.

"I've seen it before," Bohlig said. "Seen it many times, how the soft life takes a man around the neck and slowly strangles him."

He looked at me.

"What do you think?"

"I never argue with a man who's holding an ax."

"Good idea," he said.

We watched him chop a few more logs. I grew impatient, yet said nothing. It was Mallinger's play. Finally, she asked, "Chief, what happened to the file on Elizabeth Rogers?"

Bohlig kept chopping as if he hadn't heard.

"Chief?"

"Why?" Bohlig asked in between swings.

"Josie Bloom is dead. Suicide or murder, we're not sure yet. We think it's connected to the Rogers killing."

"The murder was over thirty years ago."

"Where's the file?"

"Gone. Destroyed. When I retired I purged a lot of old case files. I figured you could use the space."

I couldn't contain myself any longer.

"The only murder committed in the history of Victoria, Minnesota, and you destroyed the file?"

Bohlig ceased chopping.

"Who are you?" he asked.

"I can't believe you threw away the file," Mallinger said.

Bohlig continued splitting logs.

"Probably shouldn't have," he said. "I didn't think it was important."

"Really?" I said. "Some people might think you knew exactly how important it was and that's why you destroyed it."

That stopped Bohlig in midswing.

"McKenzie," Mallinger called.

"McKenzie?" asked Bohlig. "Is that your name? McKenzie, you don't know what you're talking about."

"Enlighten me. What was in the file you didn't want anyone to see?"

"Nothing."

"Then why did you destroy it?"

Bohlig didn't answer.

"You covered it up, didn't you?"

"You have no right to say that to me."

"Why? Why did you do it?"

Bohlig continued to chop wood.

"Who killed Elizabeth?"

When he refused to answer, I stepped inside the arch of Bohlig's swing, like a boxer getting close to an opponent. Bohlig could have split me in half if he had wanted to.

"Who killed Elizabeth?" I repeated.

"It's in my report."

"What report?" Mallinger asked. "The report you destroyed?"

Bohlig didn't answer. Instead, he shoved me out of range. I nearly tripped on a log. Mallinger and I continued to watch him work. After a few moments he stopped and leaned on his ax.

"I don't know who killed Beth Rogers," he said without

looking at either of us. "The town is better off for my not knowing. Look at it. Look at what it's become."

"You sonuvabitch."

"McKenzie," Mallinger said. "Enough."

"You were a cop for forty years," I told Bohlig, "and the one time you had a chance to get it right, you sold out."

"You don't know anything about it."

"Then tell us." I waved at Mallinger. "Give us the benefit of your wisdom."

Bohlig continued to work on his woodpile.

"It's in my report," he said.

We drove back to town in silence. Not a sound emanated from the radio and for a moment I thought Mallinger might have switched it off. I had never heard a police radio so silent. But then we were in crime-free Victoria.

"I looked up to him when I was a kid," Mallinger said eventually. "I wanted to be a cop partly because of him."

I was too busy watching the trees whizzing past the window to reply. The sun was nearly down and the trees were like shadows.

"Did you have to accuse him like that?" she asked.

"Some days I just can't remember if I'm the good twin or the bad twin."

"Maybe the county attorney has a copy of the file," Mallinger said.

"Maybe."

"Maybe it's a moot point, anyway. Maybe Josie Bloom really did commit suicide."

"Take me to my car," I said.

Fifteen minutes later we stopped behind my Audi, parked across the street from Bloom's house. There was yellow tape all around the house, but no officers keeping watch. I asked her if that was a good idea. Mallinger was more interested in my future plans.

"What are you going to do now?" she asked.

"What makes you think I'm going to do anything?"

"Are you going home?"

"Do you want me to go home?"

"Chaos, panic, murder—I'd say your work here was done."

"I'm not going anywhere until I get the answers I came for."

"I was afraid you'd say that."

Mallinger waited until I started my car before driving off. I watched her taillights disappear around a corner while the Audi warmed. A second car, a smaller one moving slow, turned the same corner and approached from the opposite direction. I paid little attention until it abruptly veered out of its lane and accelerated toward where I was parked.

I brought my hand up to shield my eyes from the bright glare of the headlights.

The car came closer.

It's going to hit you, my inner voice shouted.

I lunged across the stick shift, half my body settling in the bucket seat next to me, the other half still curled beneath the steering column.

Only the car didn't hit me.

At the last moment it straightened and came to an abrupt halt next to the Audi.

"Hey, McKenzie," a muffled voice shouted.

I straightened in my seat and powered down the window. There were less than twenty inches between the two cars.

"How you doin', pal?" the voice asked.

"Schroeder."

"So," he said, "are you scared yet?"

"I'm getting there."

"Goin' into that ditch this morning, I thought I lost you."

"You saw it?"

"Oh, yeah. I called it in." He gestured in the general direction of Josie Bloom's house. "Now this. My, my, my, my, my."

I studied him for a moment. The hard, cold wind set my teeth to chattering despite the warm air that the car heater spilled over my legs and torso.

"Did you kill Bloom, Greg? Did you try to kill me?"

"What kind of question is that?"

A gun appeared in his right hand that I recognized only as an automatic. He pointed it at me, letting it rest casually against the crook of his left elbow.

"If I wanted you dead, you'd be dead. Bam, bam, bam, and I drive away. No muss, no fuss. As for Bloom, who the hell is Bloom and why should I care?"

I stared at the gun barrel. It seemed enormous.

After a moment it disappeared into the darkness of Schroeder's car.

"Don't worry about it," he said. "See you around, McKenzie. Oh, hey. Nice car."

A moment later, he sped off, driving at least one hundred yards on the wrong side of the street before returning to the proper lane. I watched his reflection recede in my rearview mirror. I closed the window and set the heat at full. It took a few minutes before my teeth stopped chattering.

Maybe I should go home, I told myself.

The job's not done, my inner voice replied.

What job?

You came here to protect Jack Barrett.

No, I didn't. I came here to find out who sent an e-mail.

Have you?

Dammit.

I opened the glove compartment, slipped out my Beretta, chambered a round, engaged the safety, and set it on the bucket seat next to me. Next, I retrieved my cell phone and punched in a number I've known nearly my entire life.

A young girl answered.

"Hi, Katie. It's McKenzie."

"Thank you, McKenzie, for the sno-cone machine."

"You're welcome."

"And the donut machine."

"Kate?"

"And the popcorn machine. I'm supposed to say that."

"You're welcome, Katie. Is your dad around?"

"He's watching basketball."

"Let me talk to him, please."

"But he's watching basketball."

"Katie."

"Okay. Dad."

There was a lot of fumbling before Bobby Dunston took the receiver from his daughter.

"I'm watching basketball," he said.

"Why? It's not the playoffs yet."

"What do you want, McKenzie?"

"I need you to do something for me."

"Why is it that whenever you agree to do these little favors for people, I end up doing all the work?"

"That's the way I plan it."

"What do you need?"

"I wouldn't have called if it wasn't important."

"Tell me what I can do."

"Thirty-some years ago a young woman named Elizabeth Rogers was murdered here in Victoria. The autopsy was performed by the Nicholas County Coroner. I need to know what's in the report and I need to know right away. Can you help me out? Call the sheriff's department? Take advantage of a little professional courtesy?"

"I can make a call, but thirty years? I don't know, Mac."

"Any help you can give me."

"It's getting late. If I can't get hold of anyone tonight, I'll try tomorrow."

"Thank you."

"Where can you be reached?"

"You have my cell number."

"I do. So, what's happening, Mac?"

"They wrecked my car, Bobby."

"No. The Audi?"

"They smashed it all up."

"How?"

"Some jerk in a pickup with a plow blade ran me off the road."

"Are you okay?"

"Yeah, but Bobby, they wrecked my new car."

"What's going on down there, McKenzie? What are you up to?"

"My neck, Bobby. I'm up to my neck."

There was a sign on the door to the Korn Krib, the tavern attached to the Victoria Inn. *NO GUNS ALLOWED ON THESE PREMISES*. Signs like that have been cropping up at public places, even churches, all across Minnesota ever since

Governor Barrett and the state legislature deemed it essential that any Clint Eastwood wannabe over the age of twenty-one who completes seven hours of training be allowed to carry a concealed weapon. I ignored the sign, carrying my Beretta in the inside pocket of my bomber jacket. Once I saw the karaoke machine next to the door, I was glad I did. Granted, no one was using it, but the night was young.

The Korn Krib was filling slowly. A pair of attractive women in high heels and dresses too thin for the weather were drinking and smoking cigarettes at the bar. They appeared to be waiting for someone. They could have been hookers. Or they could have been elementary schoolteachers from South Dakota. I didn't know and I didn't care. In the corner booth a man and woman in their early forties held hands across the table and spoke intimately to each other. They both wore wedding rings. I hoped they were married to each other but I wouldn't have given odds on it. Three guys, working stiffs who labored where a suit was the uniform of the day, shared a pitcher of beer at a nearby table. They kept glancing at the girls at the bar.

I found an empty table, slouched in a chair, and propped my feet on another. I waved at the waitress, ordered a Sam Adams from across the room. She stared at my feet on the chair cushion and frowned when she served the beer. Since she didn't actually say anything, I left them where they were.

I felt gloomy. Not Charlie Parker gloomy. Or even Billie Holiday gloomy. I was way down there at the bottom of the well with Tom Waits. I glanced back at the couple in the booth. They were still holding hands. I adjusted my chair so I wouldn't have to look at them.

I could have stayed in my room, but I wanted a drink, and drinking alone in a bar seemed less emotionally unsettling than drinking alone in front of a TV set, less like Josie Bloom. Besides, there was nothing on and I had run out of things to do. After I had checked back in—the desk clerk refused to speak a word to me that wasn't business related—I had taken up my notebook and started playing with what little facts I had gleaned during my time in Victoria. I played with them the way a child works with a Lego set, putting pieces together, taking them apart, rearranging them. I kept at it until the process had begun to repeat itself, yielding the same combinations and conclusions. Afterward, I had showered, dressed in the same jeans and shirt I had worn for the past two days, and jogged down to the Korn Krib.

I rested my elbow on the table and my cheek against my hand and slowly sipped the beer. Normally, I didn't care that much about the NBA. Pro basketball was way down on my list of favorite sports, somewhere between tennis and World Cup soccer. Yet I couldn't get enough of the game being shown on the big screen mounted above the bar. I had no idea which teams were playing. Hell, the only reason I was sure it was pro ball instead of college was because instead of the girl next door, the cheerleaders looked like women I had once arrested for solicitation.

"You seem tense," a voice said.

I looked up without adjusting my posture. Danny Mallinger hovered above the table. Instead of her uniform, she was wearing a green turtleneck sweater under a worn leather jacket that wasn't too different from my own. Her hands were thrust into the front pockets of her jeans, her jeans tucked inside long leather boots. I liked her. Liked her face. Her eyes. Liked her hair and the way she pulled it back behind her ears. I liked the way she spoke, too, and some of the things she said that were close to witty. I liked the way she seemed to swagger even when standing still—a rare gift in a woman.

"I'm not tense," I told her. "I'm just terribly, terribly alert."

"I can tell."

"Sit."

"Thank you."

Mallinger pulled out a chair opposite mine.

"There're a couple of girls at the bar you could roust if you're working," I told her.

"I came looking for you."

"Why?"

"To make sure you're all right."

"Why wouldn't I be all right?"

"Getting run off the highway, seeing a guy's head half blown off—it shook me up. 'Course, I'm small town. Might be you see a lot of that sort of thing in the big city."

I raised my beer.

"All the time."

And drank.

"Drowning your sorrows, are you?" she asked.

"Did you come here to give me a lecture on sobriety, facing my demons, that sort of thing?"

"No."

To prove it, she waved at the bartender. The bartender must have known her because he brought a vodka gimlet for Mallinger and another Sam Adams for me without being asked.

"I've been thinking about Chief Bohlig," she said.

"Oh?"

"I believe him. I don't think there's a cover-up. I think he dumped the file because it was thirty years old. He dumped a lot of files."

"You judge people according to your own behavior," I told her. "You can't imagine doing something like that, so you can't imagine why someone else would. Like most honest people, Chief, you think everyone is basically honest, too. They're not."

"That's a cynical attitude."

I watched her out of the corner of my eye.

"You're right," I said. "You are small town."

We sat silently, watching the game and sipping our beverages. After a few minutes, Mallinger asked, "What kind of music do you like?" I don't think she really cared. It was just something to say.

"Jazz mostly, but also blues, some rock 'n' roll. You?"

"You're probably going to laugh."

"Not even if I thought it was funny."

"I listen to Dvorak, Tchaikovsky, Beethoven, Mozart. . . ."

"Ah, the big bands. What's funny about that?"

Mallinger didn't say. Instead, she took another sip of her gimlet. Thus fortified, she said, "What happened today, do you want to talk about it?"

"Not particularly."

"No?"

"Talk, society tells us these days. Something upsets you, talk about it. Talk to family. Talk to friends. To qualified therapists. Whatever. Talk your problems away. Only the guys who fought World War II, the guys like my father who fought in Korea, who saw hell up close and personal, they didn't talk about it. Yet they built a nation of astonishing strength and vitality. Talk is overrated."

"That makes sense," Mallinger said.

I watched her while she took a sip of vodka.

"Do you want to talk about it?"

"Me? No. It's just . . ."

"Chief?"

"It's just that I don't know how to behave. No one ever taught me what I should do when I see—when I see things like that. Chief Bohlig, he never . . . I know you've seen things. I know you've done things."

"Yes, I have."

"The suspect you killed, with the shotgun . . . I've never killed anyone. I've never even discharged my weapon except on the range."

"That's a good thing."

"I've never even seen a man who was shot before—not until today. I thought . . ."

"You thought I could tell you what to feel?"

"Something like that."

"How do you feel?"

"I feel crappy."

"Okay."

"Okay?"

"I guess it's okay as long as you feel something."

"How did you feel? When you killed the suspect, what was it like?"

"Messy."

"No. I mean, how did you feel?"

"I just told you."

She thought about it for a moment, then said, "How do you live with it?"

"I remind myself that I did the right thing, that I saved

lives by killing the suspect. I remind myself that that was my job, to protect and serve the public. I remind myself that the world is a better place because I did my job. I remind myself that I'm doing good, that I'm one of the good guys."

"That works," Mallinger said.

"It works for me, Chief. The thing is, there is no answer, no formula, no set of rules to follow. It's like being an alcoholic. You deal with it day by day, some days being better than others, and any code, any philosophy that gets you from today to tomorrow is a good one."

"That's a hard way to live."

"Yes, it is."

We finished our drinks, ordered another round.

"For what it's worth, Chief, I thought you behaved very well today. You have nothing to be embarrassed about."

"You can call me Danny."

"I should have known Josie was on meth, Danny," I said. "The way he kept scratching himself, how his teeth were rotting out. Those are pretty obvious signs, but I didn't see them."

"Would it have made any difference?"

"Probably not."

We watched the game some more. At the same time, I was aware that something was happening between us. Something cellular. I felt my body vibrating like the strings of a harp. Suddenly, Danny seemed very sexy to me. It could be the alcohol, I knew. Or the incredible darkness that had seeped into my soul. I didn't analyze it. I didn't want to.

On the TV, a ref blew a whistle, signaling time-out. The game was replaced by a commercial.

"I'm not gay," I said.

"What?"

"I'm not gay. I'm not married or engaged. Just in case you were thinking that."

"Why would I think that?"

"Because I haven't hit on you yet."

"I noticed."

"I thought you might be wondering why."

"Why?"

"I figure everyone tells you that you're lovely, that you're beautiful. I figure everyone tells you that you could start a parade just by crossing the street and that you must get pretty bored hearing it all the time."

"Exhausting," she said, having fun with it.

"So I decided I would try to impress you with my maturity and intellectual depth. Only there's a problem."

"What's that?"

"I don't have any."

Mallinger laughed. She couldn't help herself.

I lifted my legs off the chair and swung them under the table, brushing her knee with my knee.

"Do that again," she said.

"Do what?"

"Make me laugh."

I did.

Yet it wasn't enough. Almost, but not quite. Not the laughter or the drinks. The gloomy feeling remained, fed by tiny reminders of Bloom and high-speed duels and fights outside restaurants and Greg Schroeder lurking in the shadows. It was still there when I announced that I was going back to my room and Danny volunteered to walk with me and I welcomed her.

Outside my room, I kissed her on the right cheek. I didn't say anything. I just reached my arm a little around her waist, not quite a hug, and I kissed her cheek.

She turned her mouth and kissed me back—on the lips. The kiss lasted longer than it had any right to, and near the end of it Danny moaned, not with passion or pain, but with relief. I broke off the kiss and examined her face—Danny's face. Not Bloom's. Not Elizabeth's. Danny's. It was a nice face. Without trickery, without guile or deceit. I kissed her again.

In my imagination, Mallinger's body was mostly muscle. In reality, there was a fleshiness about her that could easily turn to fat if she didn't exercise, and for a moment I actually considered telling her so before purging the thought from my head in horror. What was I thinking? *You're not thinking, that's the whole thing*, my inner voice told me. I felt giddy with excitement and at the same time felt that my excitement was somehow lewd, as if I was taking pleasure in a perversion—a thought probably caused by the knowledge that I was betraying Nina. I pushed that aside, too. Instead, I lost myself in the sights, sounds, smells, tastes, and feelings my heightened senses brought to me, the softness of Danny's skin and the scent of her and the surprising strength of her and the heat of her body when I entered her. I felt sensations—sensations gamblers must feel, sensations I found immensely pleasurable—and they kept coming and coming—until tenderness turned to sleep and night became morning.

Danny was standing at the window, looking out on the parking lot beyond. Early dawn circled her naked body.

"What is it?" I asked, just to be saying something.

"I should leave now."

"You don't need to."

"It wouldn't do for the chief of police to be seen leaving a strange man's motel room."

I objected to "strange man," but said nothing. I slid out of bed and came up behind her. I rested my hands on her shoulders.

"Don't do that," she whispered.

"Why not?"

"I can't stay. I have to go home. I have to put on makeup."

"I didn't know you wore makeup."

"I do. I do wear makeup. It comes with the job."

She turned and kissed me just as she had outside the motel room door several hours earlier. When she finished, she said, "Go back to bed." I did, but she didn't join me.

Chapter Twelve

I woke up feeling guilty as hell. Slants of sunlight fell across my face like the beams of interrogation lamps. I turned my head away. A song played in my brain, a song I knew as a child—the same song that was there just before I fell asleep after making love to Danny Mallinger. "The Teddy Bears' Picnic."

"You're one sick puppy, McKenzie," I told myself.

I went naked to the bathroom and splashed water on my face. That wasn't going to do it, so I took a shower, first cold and then as hot as I could stand it. Afterward, I swiped the steam from the mirror and stared at myself.

"Who do you think you are?" I asked aloud.

I thought of Nina Truhler. She deserved better than someone like me.

My cell phone played its tinny melody and for a moment I was seized with panic.

It's her. What should I say?

Only a glance at the numerical display told me I was wrong.

"Hi, Bobby," I said.

A fist of cold air gripped me as I stepped out of the bathroom. Goose bumps formed on my naked flesh and my body shivered.

"Good morning," Dunston said.

"What time is it?"

"Almost nine. Rough night, McKenzie?"

"Long night, anyway."

"I have the information you need."

"Hang on a sec." I went to the small table in the corner of the room where I found my notebook. "What do you have?"

"Want me to read it all to you or just give you the pertinent details?"

"Details."

"Let's see . . . Office of Nicholas County Coroner. Want the file number?"

"Not now."

"Decedent—Elizabeth Mary Rogers. Age—seventeen. Sex—female. Place of death—Victoria, Minnesota. Time of death—the coroner estimates death occurred between 2200 hours Saturday, March 15 and 0200 Sunday, March 16. Cause of death—she had a crushed larynx, resulting in acute asphyxiation. She died hard, Mac. The reports says, let's see—'indicates that the victim lived four to six minutes after the wound was received.'"

"Damn."

"Yeah. The coroner believes the larynx was crushed by hand—with the thumbs pressing inward—from the front—the killer was facing the victim—where is it?—skin and blood were found under the fingernails of the index and middle fingers of the victim's right hand classified as type O positive. She fought back, scratched him good."

"Just a second."

I wrote swiftly, trying not to see Elizabeth's face as I did. A hard rap on my door distracted me.

"Hang on, someone's knocking."

I carried the phone, pressed against my ear, to the door. I looked through the spy hole. I dropped the phone on the bed, grabbed my jeans, and slipped into them.

"Hey, babe," Danny Mallinger said when I opened the door. She was dressed in her police uniform and holding a cardboard cup holder containing two large coffees.

"I'm on the phone," I told her. I retrieved the cell from the bed, and retreated to the table.

"Sorry about that," I said.

" 'Hey, babe?' "

"It's not what you think, Bobby."

"Of course it is. You are such a slut, McKenzie." In Bobby's book, that was a good thing.

"Cut it out," I told him.

"Where was I?" He took a deep breath. "Indications are that the victim engaged in sexual intercourse with multiple partners shortly before she was killed. Less than an hour."

"Multiple partners?"

"Let's see. Presence of sperm—microscopic examination—she had intercourse with a type A negative and a type B positive secreter. They found male pubic hair, consistent with a type O positive, so that's three at least."

"At least?"

"There could have been more than three. Back in those days the best they could do was ABO blood typing.

They couldn't identify nonsecreters and they couldn't separate, say, one O pos from a second O pos."

"She was gang-raped."

The words tasted bitter in my mouth.

"Not necessarily. The report—the coroner said he couldn't determine whether the sex was consensual or nonconsensual. There was no physical trauma, Mac. No bruising, no contusions, or lacerations. Except for her throat, there wasn't a mark on her. There's one other thing to consider. An alcohol analysis was performed on spleen tissue and was 0.144 grams over 100 grams."

"She was drunk?"

"One hundred and twenty pound teenage girl? Oh, yeah, she was drunk. Does that help?"

"I don't know. Did they keep the samples?"

"No. My guy told me that samples in unknown suspect cases were not routinely held for any length of time in those days unless it was a high-profile case. There was no DNA testing, so there was no point."

I pivoted toward Mallinger. I looked her directly in the eye as I said, "Thanks, Bobby. I owe you one."

"You owe me a helluva lot more than one, but we'll talk about that later."

"Love to the family."

"Back at ya."

I deactivated the phone and set it next to the notebook.

Mallinger handed a cup of coffee to me and drank from the other.

"I thought you could use this," she told me.

"Thank you, Danny," I said while removing the plastic lid.

"That phone call—is there something I should know?" she asked.

"This is good coffee."

"Are you holding out on me, McKenzie?"

"Very good coffee."

"Uh-huh. I was going to ask you if you slept well."

"I did. How about you?"

"You were too much of a distraction. I had to go home, remember? It was lucky I did. The ME called at the crack of dawn. He was up all night trying to prove that you were wrong about Josie Bloom."

"Did he?"

Mallinger shook her head slowly.

"There was no gunshot residue on his hand, no fingerprints on the gun. The ME has classified it as a homicide. Once I heard that, I reinterviewed the kids we busted the other day. Did a photo array. They all picked Josie as the man who sold them the meth."

"What are you going to do now?"

"I've already done it. I called the Nicholas County Sheriff's Department. It's their case."

"How would you like to solve it?"

"What do you know that I don't?"

"Answer the question. How would—"

"I'd like it a lot. Of course I would."

"Could you get the rest of the Victoria Seven together, all of them together in the same room?"

"You think they killed Josie?"

"Get them together and we'll ask them."

"It's done."

"Done?"

"They're all over at Nick's even as we speak, planning Josie Bloom's funeral. That's where I got the coffee."

"Including Dr. Peterson."

"Everyone except Jack Barrett."

"Let me get dressed, we'll go over there."

"Before we do . . . About last night."

I didn't want to talk about last night and my reaction was probably more brusque than it needed to be.

"Let me guess," I said. "You're going to tell me that you've never done anything like that before and you're not that kind of girl."

"I haven't done anything like that before," Mallinger said. "But apparently I am exactly that kind of girl. The thing is, I'm pretty sure I'm not the kind of girl who does it a lot. McKenzie, I'm grateful to you. I needed comfort. I needed understanding and tenderness. I needed someone to care about me. You gave me all that. That's a lot to give, but . . ."

"But it's not going any further than last night."

"If it does, it won't be because I need comfort."

"Okay."

"Please don't be offended."

"I'm not offended, Danny. Honestly, I'm not. I suppose last night we were both using each other for the same reasons."

Mallinger nodded her head, but I don't think that was the answer she wanted to hear. Which was ironic, because that wasn't the answer I wanted to give. *Hell yes, I'm offended.* That's what I really wanted to say, but what was the point? At the first opportunity, I was leaving Victoria and I didn't plan on coming back.

"We should be on our way if we're going to catch the Seven," Mallinger said.

"Yeah, we should."

"I think from now on, you should call me Chief again."

"Why don't you wait outside while I get dressed, Chief."

* * *

It didn't take me long. Jeans, boots, the shirt and sweater I had worn the two previous days that now made me feel slightly soiled. I put most of my time into my hair.

I met Mallinger in the lobby. We left for Nick's in separate cars. Ten minutes later we walked through the heavy door of the restaurant. Axelrod, Hugoson, Reif, and Dr. Peterson were sitting alone in a room reserved for private functions just off the kitchen. I was pleased to see the splint on the middle finger of Reif's gun hand.

"McKenzie."

Axelrod seemed pleased to see me. The others said nothing. They were sitting at a long table, bottles of beer arrayed in front of them. I recognized Dr. Peterson from the photos in his office. He wore sunglasses—even indoors—that reminded me of the windshield of an expensive sports car. He was tanned, but it was man-made and didn't have the healthy glow you get from sun and fresh air.

"Have you guys met McKenzie?" Axelrod asked.

No one replied. The other men seemed more interested in Mallinger than they did in me.

"What's going on, Chief?" Hugoson asked.

"Good question," she replied. "What is going on?"

"Gentlemen, and I use the word loosely," I said. They all turned to look at me. "Which one of you has A negative blood?"

Dr. Peterson carelessly raised his hand.

Hugoson shot him a glance that could have frozen running water.

"Which one of you is B positive?"

"Shut up, you guys!" Hugoson told the room. "What are you doing here?" he asked me.

"How about you, convict? Are you B positive?"

"Who do you think you're talking to?"

"It's easy enough to find out. We'll just check your prison records."

Hugoson rose so quickly to his feet that his chair fell over.

"Going somewhere?" Mallinger asked.

"I don't need to listen to this crap."

"Aren't you curious?" Mallinger asked him. "Me? I'm curious. How 'bout the rest of you guys? Are you curious?"

"I am," Axelrod said and laughed. "Very curious." Only his laughter didn't have the same lilt as it had when I first met him.

"What's your blood type, Nick?" I asked.

"O positive. Universal donor." He answered like he was proud of it.

"What the hell are you talking about?" Hugoson wanted to know.

"You guys have been all hot and bothered ever since I began asking questions about Elizabeth Rogers. No one would talk to me except Josie Bloom, and you killed him for it."

"He committed suicide," Dr. Peterson said.

"No, he didn't," Mallinger told them.

They all seemed genuinely surprised by the news.

"I announce that I'm going to the BCA"—I was staring at Dr. Peterson, it annoyed me that I couldn't see his eyes—"and less than an hour later someone tried to kill me. Then someone killed Josie. Now we know why."

"Why?" asked Hugoson.

"Elizabeth Rogers was raped before she was murdered—raped by at least three men with type A negative, B positive, and O positive blood."

"Who are you, Kojak?" Hugoson wanted to know. "You expect us to jump up now and say, 'Yes, we did it, ha, ha, ha, and we're glad?' Get lost."

Here it comes, my inner voice announced. *The big bluff*.

"As soon as I leave here I'm going to visit the Nicholas County attorney and then we're going to visit a judge. We're going to get a search warrant and then we're coming back here and taking blood samples from each of you. Back when you killed Elizabeth, they didn't have the technology. All they could identify was blood type and that couldn't be used to differentiate between suspects with the same blood type. But a miracle has occurred since then, gentlemen. DNA testing. We're going to take your blood and match it to the semen you left in Elizabeth Rogers and then the mighty Victoria Seven, the do-or-die kids—you're all going to prison for the rest of your lives."

"I ain't goin' back to prison," Hugoson announced.

"If not for Elizabeth, then for Josie," I said.

"I had nothin' to do with that."

"Were you his partner, convict? Were you and Josie dealing meth?"

"Fuck no."

"How 'bout you?" I was staring at Reif. "Were you trying to pick up some extra cash to support your KKK club, or whatever it is?"

"No," he insisted.

"But you knew he was dealing."

"I knew," Hugoson said. "I seen enough crankheads in stir to know one when I see one, only I had nothing to do with it. That's bad shit and I had nothing to do with it."

"Who was helping him?" Mallinger asked.

"It wasn't me."

"Someone was helping him."

Neither Hugoson nor the rest had anything to say to that.

"It doesn't matter," I said. "When we get the search warrants for Elizabeth, all the rest will fall into place, too."

"We didn't kill Beth," Dr. Peterson said. He had a high, almost squeaky voice. It was the first time I had heard it.

"Shut up." Hugoson was snarling. "They don't have squat or they wouldn't be here. You think I don't know how things work?"

"We didn't rape her, either," Dr. Peterson said.

"Shut up, I tell you."

Hugoson went toward Dr. Peterson, but Mallinger stepped between them.

"It wasn't like that." Reif was doing the talking, now. "It wasn't like that at all."

"What was it like?"

"Beth, she found us. We weren't looking for her. She found us. We were in Josie's basement drinking beer, and we had a lot of it, and then she was there. She came over because she was looking for Jack. Jack Barrett. Only he wasn't there. We didn't know where he was and then—"

"She said she'd take us all on."

That from Hugoson. I spun toward him.

"What do you mean?"

"What do you think I mean? She said she wanted to fuck us all."

"Don't lie to me."

"It's not a lie," Reif insisted. "That's what she said. She said Jack was sleeping with another girl and that she wanted to teach him a lesson. So she, we . . ."

"So we let her," said Hugoson. "All of us. Together. We took her every way we could think of. A regular orgy."

I was forced backward by his words until my back was against the wall. My mind reeled at the information I suddenly didn't want to hear.

"All of you?" I asked.

I looked at Axelrod. He nodded.

"It was no big deal," Hugoson said.

I wasn't surprised that he thought so.

"She was seventeen," I said.

"So were we," Hugoson said.

"She was drunk."

"So were we."

"Beth came down to the basement and took off her clothes," Dr. Peterson said. "Just like that. She was standing there wearing nothing but her locket. A beautiful girl like her. What would you have done?"

Not that, my inner voice said. *I wouldn't have done that. Not even at seventeen and drunk with my friends urging me on.*

"You took advantage of her," I said.

"She took advantage of us."

"I don't believe you."

But I did.

"That's what happened," said Reif. "That's all that happened. We all did it and then she left."

"Just left?"

Reif glanced at Hugoson and looked away quickly.

"Yeah. She just left."

"It doesn't matter," Hugoson said. "You can't touch us. The rape thing has expired, the statute of limitations."

"But not murder."

"We didn't kill nobody."

"Tell us about the convenience store clerk you beat up," I said.

"Fuck you."

"It's true, though," Reif said. "We didn't kill her. We didn't touch her. We liked her. We really did."

"Then why was Josie Bloom so upset?"

"Because he *loved* her," Axelrod answered. There was fear in the voices of the other men. His was seasoned with regret. "He had loved her his entire life. That night in the basement, it wasn't fun and games for Josie. It was love. When she turned up dead the next morning, I guess he started to die, too."

"Oh, give me a break," Hugoson said.

"We didn't kill her, McKenzie," Axelrod said. "As God is my judge."

"She said, before she left . . ." Reif hesitated as if he knew he was saying something foolish and decided to say it anyway. "She said she was going to ruin everything."

"Shut the hell up!" shouted Hugoson.

"What do you mean, ruin everything?"

"She said—"

"Brian!" Hugoson shouted.

"She said she was going to tell Jack what we did. She said she was going to get her revenge on Jack and then see how well we all played basketball together."

Hugoson slumped in his chair. He knew a motive when he heard one.

"What happened next?" I asked.

"She left," said Reif. "We never saw her again."

"We were all together," Hugoson said. "We didn't leave each other until it was way early in the morning. If you want us to take a polygraph, we will."

Dr. Peterson nodded his head in agreement.

I knew it was unnecessary. The fact that Hugoson and others would even volunteer . . . I felt the need to sit down. I found a chair at the far end of the table. We sat staring at each other for a few minutes while Mallinger circled the room, not looking at anything in particular. The expression on her face—it seemed as if she had given up on civilization once and for all.

"You got nothing on us," Hugoson said.

"We didn't kill Beth," Reif said. "We didn't kill Josie."

"Who did?" I asked.

"I don't know about Josie, but . . ."

Reif didn't speak the words, but they hung in the air just the same.

Jack Barrett killed Beth.

"McKenzie?" Axelrod reached out his hand as if he wanted to touch me, then pulled it back again. "You'll never know how sorry I am. I could tell you and tell you and tell you and still you'd never know."

I was in the Audi, driving way too fast for the narrow county roads. I had ignored Mallinger's calls to wait when I left Nick's and sped to Chief Bohlig's lake home as quickly as I could. I found his driveway and turned in. The Audi slid on his slick asphalt and nearly rammed his trash bins before halting.

Mallinger arrived moments later. She ran to catch up as I approached Bohlig's door. He opened it before I had a chance to knock.

"I know what happened," I announced.

"Do you?"

"I read the coroner's report. I talked to the Seven."

"What did they have to say?"

"They said the sex was consensual."

"No way to prove it wasn't."

"They said they didn't kill her."

"They told me the same thing. Stuck together, they did."

"Did you interview Jack Barrett?"

"I did."

"What was his story?"

"Same thing. He didn't do it. Said he hadn't seen Beth since he left the party."

"Did he know about the sex?"

"No, and I didn't tell him."

"Why not?"

"If I could've baited him into admitting he knew about the gang bang, that would prove he had seen her after the party. He never tumbled."

"Did he have an alibi?"

"He said he went home, but . . ."

"But what?"

"I had the sense he was hiding something."

"You think?"

I stood on the front stoop, bareheaded, bare hands at my side, my bomber jacket hanging open, the lapels curling open in the breeze. Yet I did not feel the cold.

"What was his blood type?" I asked. "Did you at least learn that?"

"O positive."

"The same as the tissue found under Elizabeth's fingernails."

"Mighta been."

"Did you examine him for scratches?"

"He had some on his arms, but that coulda happened while playing basketball."

"He had motive, opportunity, scratches on his arms matching the blood samples, no alibi. . . ."

"No way he gets convicted."

"Did you even try to build a case?"

"Chief?" Mallinger was at my elbow. There was fear in her voice, as if she were afraid of the questions she was asking. "Did Governor Barrett kill Elizabeth Rogers?"

"I don't know."

"Did you try to find out?"

"To serve and protect," Bohlig told her. "That's what it says on the sides of our police cars; that was my job. I did my job. The town is a better place because I did my job. I protected and served this town and I don't lose any sleep over it. I picked you to replace me. Now we'll see how well you do."

"You're not a cop," I said. "You're a co-conspirator."

I sat at the small table in my motel room. I had a bucket of ice, a bottle of vodka, and a six-pack of tonic water—the Victoria municipal liquor store had opened at 10:00 A.M. and I was its first customer. Only I hadn't opened the bottle. When I bought the vodka it was with the intention of getting impossibly drunk. Now I wasn't sure I wanted to.

"What am I going to do?"

I had been asking myself that question since leaving Chief Bohlig. He was probably right. There was no way to convict Jack Barrett of murder. With the destruction of the samples, there was no longer evidence enough even to charge him. What bothered me the most, however, was that I had liked Barrett, genuinely liked him. I hadn't felt so utterly betrayed since my father died.

Outside the weather had turned nasty. The wind had whipped up and a hard snow was falling. Traffic moved cautiously on the county road beyond the motel parking lot. A couple of cars swung in, looking for refuge from the storm. I opened the vodka and a bottle of mix, built a stiff drink, and toasted the weather. Nature was cruel, but not vindictive, and never personal. "You might be a mother, but never a bitch," I said and downed half the drink. "You just don't give a damn." I told myself I didn't give a damn, either. I was lying.

I finished the drink in a hurry and built a second.

I hoped someone would tell me that everything was going to work out, that it would be all right. Someone radiant and entirely trustworthy, like Jessica Lange or Cate Blanchett. No such luck. Instead, I got Lindsey Bauer Barrett.

I had just finished the second vodka tonic when she called. At first I thought it might be Danny Mallinger and ignored her. After five rings my cell cycled over to my voice mail. Then it rang another five times. Then another.

"What?" I finally shouted into the receiver.

"Mac? It's Lindsey Barrett."

"Zee."

"Am I interrupting something? I can call back."

"No. I was just— Actually, I was thinking about getting drunk, if you must know."

"Why? What happened? Did you learn who sent the e-mail?"

"Not yet, no."

"What then?"

How do you tell your friend that you believe her husband is a murderer? Quickly, I decided.

"Jack could be guilty after all."

"What makes you say that?"

"I uncovered some evidence, talked to some witnesses. Zee, I'm sorry, it doesn't look good."

"Dammit, McKenzie. What are you doing?"

"What do you mean?"

"I asked you to learn who sent the e-mail, not investigate a murder."

"Zee?"

"Who sent the e-mail? That's all I want to know."

Once again my internal security system was on full alert. The alarm bells in my head were loud enough to blow out my eardrums.

"A lot of people could have sent the e-mail," I said. "A lot of people think Jack killed Elizabeth. The entire town has been pretty much covering up for him for the past thirty years. Even the former police chief thinks Jack did it and all but told me that he let Jack off to protect the community's reputation."

"What about evidence?"

"Evidence?"

"Could they arrest Jack?"

"I don't think so. All the physical evidence has been destroyed, and the witnesses—I doubt a county attorney would even consider the possibility. But, Mrs. Barrett, when am I going to hear some tearful denials? When is the loving wife going to come to the defense of her husband? When is she going to shout to high heaven that her man couldn't possibly be a killer?"

"My husband did not murder that girl," she said, but her voice was flat and without emotion. She could have been a checkout girl asking, "Paper or plastic?"

"Who knows what you know?" Zee asked.

The alarm bells became louder.

"What do you mean?"

"The details. Who besides you could really hurt Jack if he came forward?"

"There are maybe a half dozen people who could do more than just speculate. But they all have good reasons for keeping quiet, personal reasons. They don't want this to come out, either. Besides, most of them like Jack."

"Most, but not all. Have you forgotten the man who sent the e-mail?"

I had.

"I'm coming down there," she said.

"Don't, Zee. That'll only make matters worse."

"How could it make matters worse?"

"People will ask why you're here. What are you going to tell them?"

"I'll think of something."

"Zee, if you want my advice . . ."

"I do not want your advice, McKenzie. I want you to find the bastard who sent the e-mail. If you can't do that, go home."

She hung up on you.

I sat there, staring dumbly at the cell phone in my hand for a solid ten seconds as the realization sunk in.

She hung up on you, after everything you've done for her.

I set the phone on the table and watched it some more.

"I'll be damned."

I made a third drink.

The cell played its tune again. I was sure it was Lindsey calling to apologize. I was wrong.

"Hi, McKenzie. It's me. Danny."

"Hello, Chief."

"You can call me Danny again."

"Thank you."

She paused for a moment, said, "About what happened this morning. Do you want to talk about it?"

"No."

"I forgot. You don't like to talk."

"Talking won't change anything."

"It might help me decide what to do next."

"There's nothing you can do."

"I can go to the county attorney."

"With what, Danny? What evidence do you have? None. Your witnesses, they can't be relied on. There won't be any charges."

"We can at least get the allegation out there."

"What good will that do, besides getting you fired? Besides getting you trashed by every newspaper columnist, every TV pundit, and every radio talk show rabble-rouser from one end of the state to the other? This isn't some schmo off the street, Danny. This is the governor of the State of Minnesota. A popular sitting governor. You go after him, you had better have it wired seven ways to hell and back. We don't."

"We have to do something."

"Well, I for one am going to take a long nap. Care to join me?"

"I don't think so."

"Suit yourself."

This time I hung up.

Chapter Thirteen

The world had been transformed by the time I woke up. The storm had given way to bright sunshine, the wind had abated, and snow was melting along the edge of the asphalt where the plows had done their work. There was plenty of foot traffic, people walking about without hats and gloves and with their coats hanging open. I watched them from the window of my room, wishing for a moment that I was among them. I glanced at my watch. Only three hours had passed since the snow shower began, but most Minnesotans will tell you—if you don't like the weather, just hang around for a few minutes, it's bound to change.

So, what's next? my inner voice asked.

Go home, Lindsey Barrett had suggested. Why not?

You haven't done what you came here to do.

The world's not going to stop revolving if that happens.

It's not about the world. It's about keeping promises that you made.

My promise to Lindsey? I doubt any court would enforce it. A verbal contract isn't worth the paper it's written on, that's what my lawyer once told me.

Those are precisely the contracts you have to keep.

Who says?

You're the one who chose this life. Maybe it was out of boredom or a need to feel useful or the conceit that you can personally make the world a better place to live, but you chose it. You can't give it up because sometimes it's difficult.

I suppose that's true.

Winners never quit and quitters never win, remember? I'll bet you a nickel they have that posted on the Victoria High School gym somewhere.

Words of wisdom.

When the going gets tough, the tough get going.

Okay, now you're being annoying.

I closed my eyes and shook my head and rubbed my temples in an effort to quiet my inner voice. I had been spending way too much time in my head lately, too much time talking to myself. You live alone, do most things by yourself, it's probably inevitable. Yet at the same time, it couldn't possibly be healthy, could it? If nothing else, you lose perspective.

I thought about mixing another drink while I tried to determine my next step and quickly vetoed the idea.

"Maybe I should go for a swim, instead," I told the empty room. "Clear my head."

That would necessitate going shopping for a swimsuit, but so what? I needed clothes, anyway. The shirt, sweater, and jeans I'd been wearing for three days were starting to get ripe. Besides, unlimited pool privileges came with the room; Florence told me so when I signed the register.

When you signed the register.

Why didn't I think of that before?

* * *

Rufugio Tapia was behind the counter of Fit to Print. Jace Axelrod was on the opposite side, leaning against it while she spoke softly to him, and again I thought, *Romeo and Juliet:* "*See how she leans her cheek upon her hand! O, that I were a glove upon that hand that I might touch that cheek!*"

Tapia was inhaling every word the young woman had to say, oblivious to the older gentleman seated at one of his PCs. To the three women who fussed over a photo album near the copy machines. To the Hispanic man wearing a shirt identical to the one he wore who was operating a printer behind him. He slid his hand across the counter to Jace's hand. She welcomed it; their fingers curled and twisted into a tight knot—a knot they did not untie even when they saw me approaching.

My first thought—something had shifted in their relationship. They weren't hiding anymore.

My second was more paternal. Why wasn't Jace in school?

"Why aren't you in school?" I asked.

"Seniors get to leave campus if they want, and I had a free period."

"And you're spending it here?"

"I wanted to visit my boyfriend."

Neither Jace nor Tapia looked to see if anyone heard, but I did.

"What am I missing?"

"Nothing, we just decided not to keep our love a secret any longer," Jace said.

"Well," said Tapia.

"Well," Jace repeated.

"Well," I said. It was my turn.

"Well, it wasn't just our decision," Jace said. "My dad

said— This morning he told me if I liked R.T. I should date him. Openly. Just don't sneak around. 'No one likes a sneak,' he said."

As hard as I tried, and with as much reason as I had, it was difficult to dislike the man.

" 'Course, he still wants me to go to college."

"So do I," Tapia said.

"And leave you?"

"It is important to get a good education if you are to become wealthy and keep me in the style to which I want to become accustomed."

"You love me for my money?" asked Jace.

"Why else?" said Tapia before he kissed her.

"Don't mind me, kids," I said. "I'm just standing here."

"What can I do for you, Mr. McKenzie?" asked Tapia.

"*Señor Tapia*," I said.

"*Sí*."

"Last Friday night, during your anniversary celebration, did you happen to keep a guest book?"

"*Sí*."

"That you encouraged people to sign?"

"Of course."

"May I see it?"

"Do you think the person who sent the e-mail is in the book?"

"The e-mail was sent at 6:57 P.M. You said that you closed down at about five so you could throw a party for your regular customers. That means one of those people sent the e-mail. I'm just hoping that they signed the guest register."

"Would you know who just by looking at the name?"

"Probably not."

"I'll get the book."

"*Gracias*."

"So you're still looking for that person who sent the e-mail, the one R.T. told me about," Jace said while Tapia slipped into his office.

"I take it you two tell each other everything."

"We have no secrets, if that's what you mean."

"That's what I mean."

"Should we have secrets?"

"You wouldn't be the first."

"I wouldn't want to live like that."

I didn't blame her.

Tapia returned, carrying a leather-bound book with a spiral binding. "I want to thank you for breaking Brian Reif's hand," he said as he gave me the book.

"It was my pleasure."

I began flipping pages slowly. I was looking for a name, any name that I might recognize.

"Breaking his hand isn't going to make him any less of a racist," Jace told me.

"I didn't break it because he was a racist. I broke it because he was a stupid racist. It was the stupid part that got him hurt."

"There are a lot of stupid racists here," Jace said.

"Sometimes it feels that way," Tapia said. "But I'm not so sure. That group of Reif's, the Nicholas County Coalition for Immigration Reduction he calls it—it has only a dozen members. There are many more people like Mr. Axelrod than Reif."

"It's a good town," Jace said.

"Yes, it is a good town," Tapia agreed.

I found Tapia's eyes. He was looking at Jace so I looked at her, too. *For stony limits cannot hold love out; And what love can do, that dares love attempt*, Shakespeare wrote. Reif didn't live in the same world as these two kids. When all was said and done, I suppose I didn't, either. What a pity.

I went back to the book, studying each signature. Many were illegible, but then my handwriting wasn't so hot, either. Tapia took care of his customers while I studied the book, first the women, then the older man. His employee dropped a carton on top of the counter.

"Want me to take these across the street?" he asked.

Tapia told him he'd take care of it.

"These are nice," Jace said. The box was sealed, but a single printed sheet was taped to the top—the zodiac place mats meant for the Rainbow Cafe.

I went through the entire book, then started again. It was a long shot—worse than a long shot. It was impossible. Still, I kept at it until I discovered a name that I recognized, one that I had missed before.

"Troy Donovan." *I'll be a sonuvabitch!* "Troy Donovan was here?"

"Mr. Donovan?" said Tapia. "Yes, he was. Do you know him?"

"We spoke last Monday. How do you know him? Why was he here?"

"We're partners."

"Partners?"

"Yes. We have been for over a year."

"I don't understand."

"Fit to Print is a franchise, Mr. McKenzie. I have only one of seventeen stores. I bought the rights to operate Fit to Print in Victoria from the Donovan Printing Corporation. They're the franchiser. Mr. Donovan owns the company. It's his plan to put a Fit to Print in every small town in Minnesota."

"He came here to help you celebrate your first anniversary?"

"Oh, yes. Of course. Mr. Donovan is very hands-on. He visits all the stores a couple of times a year. I'm sure he'll return for our next anniversary."

"I don't believe it," I said aloud. Inside my private voice was chanting, *Dammit, dammit, dammit.* I knew Donovan was franchising Kinko's-like print stores in Minnesota. I read it on the Internet when I was researching him and the Brotherhood, but I was too damn lazy to dig deeper. *Dammit, dammit, dammit.*

"I bet Donovan used one of your PCs," I said.

"Just a minute," Tapia said. "You're not saying that Mr. Donovan is responsible for sending the e-mail you're talking about?"

Jace swung her head from Tapia to me and back to Tapia again, sensing trouble.

"Oh, I'm sure he's not," I said. "I'm just surprised to see his name in your book."

Of course, he sent the e-mail. He probably guessed someone would trace it to Victoria, as well—the scene of the crime. I bet he's also responsible for placing the fifteen roses at Milepost Three. He's been handling me from the very beginning, manipulating me to come down here and prove Jack Barrett killed Elizabeth Rogers. The incident in the skyway and the parking lot of International Market Square, the telephone call—reverse psychology at its finest. I know why he did it, too. It all makes perfect sense.

"Mr. Donovan is an important man," Tapia said.

I stared at Donovan's signature. I wondered what a handwriting analyst would say about it.

Such a small thing, writing his name down in a book. On

the other hand, they caught Ted Bundy because of a broken taillight. On still another hand, if I had known about his connection to Fit to Print, I wouldn't have needed Donovan's signature.

"He's been very good to me," Tapia said.

I bet the Brotherhood doesn't know Donovan is trying to sabotage Governor Barrett. I wonder what they'll do when I tell them.

"This is so wrong," Jace said. She was no longer interested in us. Instead, she was reading the place mat taped to the top of the carton. "This is a mistake."

"What? What is a mistake?" Tapia immediately moved to her side, forgetting me altogether.

"This horoscope. It says we're incompatible."

"*No lo creo,*" he cried, which my high school Spanish translated into "I don't believe it."

"It says Sagittarius and Capricorn are opposites."

"Oh, my, Judith Catherine." Tapia put his hand over his heart. "I thought you found a typo or something. I thought I was going to have to reprint the job." He circled her shoulder with his arm and kissed the top of her head. "Don't scare me like that."

"You should reprint these mats," Jace said. "Look at this. It says, 'When Sagittarius and Capricorn join together they may feel that they don't have much to gain from one another.' Are you sure you were born in November?"

"November 30," Tapia said.

The same birthday as John Allen Barrett, my inner voice reminded me.

" 'Sagittarius and Capricorn may not be able to see beyond each other's faults.' "

"I'll be damned," I said.

"Do you believe it, McKenzie?" Jace asked.

"I do not believe it."

"Neither do I."

Donovan, you bastard. Who's the schnook now?

I had not expected violence. There was a time back with the cops when that wouldn't have mattered. I would have responded quickly and efficiently just like one of those guys on TV who know exactly which way to roll when the bad guy leaps out with a lug wrench. Only not this time. This time I went into vapor lock. Norman probably thought I looked like a deer in the headlights when he pointed the Charter Arms .38 at me as we left Fit to Print. Only this time I knew Norman hadn't come to kidnap me. This wasn't a test.

Jace had stepped outside first; I had held the door for her. I offered to hold the door open for Tapia, too. He insisted I go next, even though he was carrying the carton filled with place mats for the Rainbow Cafe.

And there he was in the parking lot—Norman—dressed in his gray trench coat and black wingtips that were being ruined by the pool of slush he stood in.

This is not good, I told myself.

I had my gun. I had been carrying the Beretta in the inside pocket of my bomber jacket since my last meeting with Schroeder. Except my jacket was zipped halfway up. Why wouldn't it be?

Norman was holding his gun with one hand. *What a show-off*, I thought. He aimed at my head. He smiled. An amateur to the end, coming at me in such a public way. He did something you only see in movies and bad cop shows, too. He started talking. He said, "I'm going to enjoy this." That is what it took to kick-start me into action. His big mouth.

I seized Jace by the arm and shoulder and pulled her with me as I dove to my right behind the bumper of my Audi, parked in front of the building.

Norman fired twice. The bullets missed me and hit Tapia, catching him in the exact center of the carton he was toting. He staggered backward, hit the glass wall of his business, and slid into a sitting position on the sidewalk, still holding the carton in front of him, his eyes closed.

Jace screamed his name with such profound anguish, but at that moment it was merely noise to me. I pushed her down under the bumper and said, "Don't move," even as I unzipped my coat and found my gun.

I don't know if Norman was surprised that he missed me or that he hit an innocent bystander, yet for a precious moment he just stood there, looking down on Tapia, as paralyzed as I had been.

I circled to the rear of the Audi in a low crouch and brought my gun up.

"Norman."

He pivoted toward me, firing on the move. I yanked my shot wide, missing him completely, before I dipped back under the bumper of the car. I don't know where my shot went. Two of his slugs ripped into the body of the Audi.

I wished people would stop hurting my car.

Norman was on the run now. He dashed across the parking lot, hit the sidewalk, and kept going. I came up from behind the bumper and gave pursuit. Norman had about a thirty-yard lead and I wasn't sure I could catch him, wasn't sure I wanted to: He still had a shot left in his .38 and one was all it took. I was surprised when he decided to use it, when he brought his gun up to shoot over his shoulder.

I stopped chasing and went into a Weaver stance—a shooting stance with good balance. I brought the Beretta up with both hands, took two quick, deep breaths, and sighted down the barrel with both eyes open. I took a third deep breath, let half out slowly, and squeezed the trigger.

I fired one round.

It caught Norman high in the shoulder.

Yes!

The force of the bullet spun him in a complete circle and knocked him to the pavement. He rolled twice, yet managed to regain his feet. An amazing thing. He was staggering now instead of running, his pace much slower. I took aim, thought better of it. Norman was fifty yards away now and I didn't want to take the chance on a wild shot.

I gave chase again. A black Park Avenue sedan rolled past me and down the street. I had seen the car before. It outraced me to Norman's position. Norman cut across the boulevard to the curb. The car stopped and the passenger door flew open. Norman dove inside the car. The car sped off with as much acceleration as the tired sedan could muster.

I brought my gun up again, intent on getting off a few more rounds, but changed my mind. There were far too many people in the line of fire.

I watched as the car took a corner far too fast, nearly sideswiped an ancient station wagon, and kept going.

It's partly your own fault, my inner voice informed me. *If you had indicated that you could be bought or frightened when you first met Muehlenhaus, he might not have resorted to such extremes to get rid of you. Still, Norman got down here in one helluva hurry, didn't he?*

Tapia! I remembered.

I turned and began running back to Fit to Print, fumbling in my pocket for my cell phone as I went. I wanted to call emergency services. I had the phone in my hand, was bringing it to my ear by the time I reached the edge of the parking lot.

That's when I heard Chief Mallinger's voice.

"Halt, halt, do not move."

She was standing thirty feet away, sighting on me with her Glock.

"Drop the gun."

"Danny, it's me."

"Drop the gun. Drop it. Dammit, McKenzie, you drop that gun right now."

There are few people who enjoy a good argument as much as I do, but just then didn't seem like the time. Instead of protesting my innocence, I held the gun out in as nonthreatening a manner as I could mange and slowly lowered it to the ground. I set it gently on the asphalt and stood up, placing my hands behind my head, my right hand still holding the cell.

"Kick it away. Kick it away. Do it now, McKenzie."

I nudged the gun ten yards across the lot with the side of my boot.

"Put your hands behind your head, McKenzie."

"They are behind—"

"On your knees, on your knees."

I sank slowly to my knees. My jeans were instantly soaked with slush.

Mallinger was behind me. She locked one wrist with a handcuff, brought it down behind my back, and wound the cuff around the second wrist. She pushed me forward, so that I was lying flat in the slush of the parking lot, the cell still in my hand.

"Don't even think of moving," she told me.

I fumbled in my head for a few lines that might appeal to Mallinger's gentler nature. The best I could come up with was "You have nothing to fear from me."

"Shut up."

"See about Tapia," I said.

Mallinger rushed to the front door of Fit to Print. Jace was kneeling next to Tapia's body, hugging his shoulders and weeping. He was still holding the carton on his lap.

Mallinger took the place mats out of Tapia's hands and set them aside. She opened Tapia's jacket to examine his wounds. Only there were no wounds.

I watched as Mallinger sat back on her heels and contemplated the carton. She turned it in her hands. The bullets had gone in one side, but not out the other. She spun back to Tapia. She checked his pulse and smiled broadly. She began gently patting the back of his hands. Gradually, Tapia opened his eyes.

"What happened?" he said.

More statements. It seemed like I was making a lot of them lately, this time to Mallinger, an impossibly young county attorney, and a Nicholas County deputy with chevrons on his sleeve. With both Jace and Tapia backing me up, it was decided that I had probably not committed a crime, but I could be sure that all the parties involved would investigate thoroughly before they returned my gun. As Mallinger put it, "This used to be a nice, quiet town before you arrived, McKenzie."

I carefully explained that the man who shot at us—

whom I most likely shot in return, in case they wanted to check neighboring hospitals and emergency rooms—was named Norman—"I don't know if that's his first or last name"—and he was employed by Mr. Muehlenhaus of Minneapolis. Neither Mallinger nor the deputy tumbled to his name. But the eyes of the young county attorney grew wide and shiny. I knew phone calls would be made. I doubted that Norman would ever be found, much less arrested.

Kevin Salisbury, on the scene with his ubiquitous camera, had arrived before anyone else. He took photographs of Tapia, Fit to Print, the carton of place mats, Mallinger, the deputy and county attorney, assorted officers, me, and Jace—at least a half roll. Everyone gave him a statement but me. He was upset about that and reminded me that we had an agreement. I gave him a wink and a smile and brought my index finger to my lips in the universal sign of conspiracy. He whispered, "I'll talk to you later."

Eventually, Salisbury, the attorney, and the deputy left me alone in the parking lot of Fit to Print with Mallinger. The kids had been whisked off to Nick's by Axelrod, where, he assured Tapia, a cure for whatever ailed him could and would be found. I would have liked to go with them, but I wasn't invited.

I was cold and wet with slush and Mallinger asked me, "Are you satisfied?"

"Satisfied?"

"Do you have what you came here for?"

"Yes. Yes, I do."

"So you'll be leaving us soon."

Mallinger allowed me to take her hand in mine and bring it to my lips. I kissed her middle knuckle.

"I'm sorry I complicated your life," I said.

"I'm a big girl. I can deal."

"He didn't do it."

"Who didn't?"

"Barrett. He didn't kill Elizabeth Rogers. Chief Bohlig and the Seven and the rest of Victoria—everyone jumped to a conclusion thirty years ago, and so did I this morning."

"You think he's innocent?"

I nodded.

"Why?"

"Two reasons. First, Jack didn't have a car. How could he have dumped Elizabeth's body along the county road if he didn't have a car?"

"An accomplice?"

"That would suggest premeditation and we know there couldn't have been."

"That's thin, McKenzie. What's the second reason?"

"The second is a lot more conclusive. Unfortunately, I can't tell you. Not unless it is absolutely essential and it isn't because . . ."

"Because Barrett will never be charged, right?"

"Right."

"You don't want to embarrass the governor if you don't have to."

"That pretty much covers it."

"Whatever it is that you know, it can't possibly be worse than the rumor that he killed a girl."

"Sure it can."

"How?"

"Because it's not a rumor. Listen, I just wanted you to know that Barrett is innocent."

"So it doesn't haunt me that he got away with murder."

"I like you, Danny."

"I like you, too, McKenzie."

"I'm sorry about everything that's happened."

"I'm not. At least not about everything."

"I'd kiss you if we weren't in public—a nice, long, non-comforting kiss, if you get my drift."

"Maybe I should put the cuffs back on and drag you off to a holding cell."

"Maybe you should."

"McKenzie, if the governor didn't kill Beth, who did?"

"I have some ideas about that."

"Feel free to share."

"What are you doing for dinner, tonight?"

"That depends. Am I going to be in uniform?"

"Personally, I prefer lace. A pretty girl in lace can sell me anything she wants."

Mallinger fingered my soiled sweater.

"What about you?"

"Don't worry, Chief. I clean up real good."

"I'll meet you at the motel," she said.

"Sounds like a plan."

"I'm sorry I made you lie in the slush," she said. But the way she was grinning at the memory of it, I didn't believe her.

When I unlocked the door to my motel room, I found Lindsey Bauer Barrett waiting inside. I wouldn't have been more surprised if Hillary Clinton had come calling.

Lindsey was sitting at the small table; her hands were folded neatly on top like a schoolgirl waiting for the principal. The drapes were opened and I could see the motel parking lot over her shoulder. She had to have seen me coming and this is the pose she had chosen to greet me with.

"Hello, Mac."

"Zee."

I didn't bother to ask how she got in.

Zee gave me a quick inspection, wrinkling her nose at my appearance.

"What happened to you?"

"I was lying in a gutter. You should know something about that."

"It's going to be one of those conversations, isn't it?"

I set the shopping bag on the bed and removed my jacket. I've had it for many years—bought it long before I came into my money—and I hoped a dry cleaner could restore it. I hung it in the small closet and pulled off my boots while Lindsey watched me. There was a look of expectation on her face.

"I want you to do two things," I told her. "First, call your friend Muehlenhaus."

"He's not my friend."

"I don't give a damn what he is. Call him. Tell him there's been a terrible mistake. Tell him that I can prove Jack Barrett didn't kill anyone; I can prove it beyond a doubt, reasonable or otherwise. Tell him to stop trying to have me killed."

Lindsey didn't bat so much as an eyelash, which proved to me what I had suspected: She knew Muehlenhaus had sent Norman. She had probably been in cahoots with him since the very beginning.

"Second"—I pointed at the bucket near her elbow—"go down the hall and get some ice."

I took my time in the shower. Took my time shaving and brushing my teeth and getting my hair just so for my date with Mallinger. I had purchased a pair of black Dockers and a blue dress shirt with a buttondown collar and put them on. It was warm and damp in the tiny bathroom, so I waited until I was outside and had a chance to cool off before donning a black silk-blend sweater speckled with blue, red, and gold. I sat on the edge of the bed, quickly buffed my black leather boots with a towel and slipped them on.

"You look good," Lindsey said.

She was still sitting at the table. The ice bucket was three-quarters full and she had made a sizable dent in the vodka.

"I made you a drink," she told me.

I went to the table and picked up the short, squat glass that the motel provided. The drink was a bit stronger than I liked, but welcome nonetheless.

"Where's your driver?" I asked.

"He's around." Lindsey gestured at my room. "Not exactly a Barrett Motel, is it?"

"Did you call Muehlenhaus?"

"Yes."

"What did he say?"

"He said, 'Oops.'"

"You people."

"I hope you don't think that I—"

"You called him. You told him that I had information that might prove Jack killed his high school sweetheart. You probably asked him, 'What should we do?' What did you think his answer would be?"

"I didn't know."

"Fine, you didn't know."

"I didn't. You must believe me, Mac. I only wanted to protect Jack. That's why I called Mr. Muehlenhaus."

"The thing that bugs me—besides getting shot at and seeing an innocent kid almost killed—isn't Muehlenhaus. He's predictable. It's you, Lindsey. It's your willingness to believe that your husband actually murdered a girl. That just floors me."

"You told me he did."

"So?"

"What you said when you entered the room, that wasn't just to hold off Mr. Muehlenhaus, right? You really can prove Jack is innocent?"

"Yes."

She smiled, and for a moment she looked as she had when we were kids, when our lives were only slightly complicated.

"What proof? What do you know?"

"I'm not going to tell you."

"What do you mean you're not going to tell me?"

The smile disappeared. Lindsey was on her feet now and leaning heavily on the table. Her fingers gripped the edge of the table and I thought there was a good chance she would throw it across the room.

"I'm not going to tell you for the same reason that Jack never told you, or anyone else for that matter, the reason why he was content to let people whisper the word 'murderer' next to his name."

"Why?"

"I'm an honorable man."

Lindsey stared at me like she didn't believe it.

"You said so yourself, back at the Groveland Tap," I reminded her.

She still didn't believe it.

"Speaking of honor," I said. "Or the lack thereof. Tell me about Troy Donovan."

Lindsey regained her seat.

"I told you. I barely know—"

"Stop it, Zee. Stop lying. Just this once, tell me the truth. I've been shot at, my car has been forced off the highway, I've been assaulted in skyways, accosted in parking lots, received menacing phone calls late at night, and that doesn't count the dead bodies I've tripped over. I figured I earned the truth. Tell me about Troy Donovan."

"He's just an acquaintance."

"Tell me!"

"We were lovers. Is that what you want to hear, McKenzie? We were lovers, okay?"

"Ex-lovers?"

"Yes."

"Is that why he sent the e-mail?"

"He did send it, then."

"You know he did."

"I knew, but I didn't *know*. Not one hundred percent. That's why I sent you down here. To find out for sure."

"What then? Were you going to call Muehlenhaus? Have Donovan whacked?"

"I didn't know what I was going to do."

Lindsey finished her drink and poured another. She didn't add ice or tonic water. A grimace distorted her face as she took a long sip of the straight vodka and suddenly her perfect beauty seemed terribly brittle and easily shattered.

"It's my fault," she said. "Everything that's happened has been my fault. I know what I am, McKenzie. I'm an adulteress. I betrayed my husband's trust and his love just for the fun of it. Only I won't steal his dreams. That's one gutter I won't crawl into. That's why I broke it off with Troy. When it became clear that Jack was going to win the election, I told Troy I wasn't going to see him anymore. Only he wouldn't let me go. Even now he still calls. He sends e-mails. . . ."

I flashed on Nina Truhler's ex-husband.

"Some men need to own," I said.

"Troy thinks if Jack doesn't run for the Senate, we can still be together."

"He's afraid that if Jack wins a senate seat, he'll take you with him to far, far away Washington. I understand that. Only why send the e-mail to you and not to Jack?"

"It was a warning. I'm expected to talk Jack out of it, otherwise . . ."

"Otherwise Donovan will carry out his threat. Nice people you hang out with, Zee."

"We can't let it happen, McKenzie."

"We?"

"We can't let him hurt Jack like that. We . . . I love Jack. I love my husband. I know how that sounds after what I've done, but I do love him, McKenzie. We can't—we just can't . . . Oh, God."

Lindsey sighed as if all the air had left her lungs.

"What am I going to do?" she asked.

I poured a small amount of vodka into my glass, added both ice and tonic water. I sat across from Lindsey at the table.

"Why did you have the affair?"

"For the same reason I slept with you."

"To get back at your sister?"

"No. I mean . . . Have you ever done anything extraordinarily stupid, knowing it was stupid even while you were doing it?"

Images of Danny Mallinger flickered in my head.

"Do you mean recently?" I asked.

"We're supposed to become wiser as we grow older. Don't you believe it."

"Don't say that, Zee. It's the only thing that keeps me going."

"You never struck me as a man who makes many—what shall we call it—errors in judgment?"

"I can tell you stories that would bring bitter tears to your eyes."

Lindsey smiled briefly before drinking enough straight vodka that she coughed.

"Troy came along when I was feeling pretty sorry for myself," she said. "We had been married for seven years, Jack and I, and somehow our lives had come between us. Jack was busy doing Jack things—running his business, the charities, getting involved in politics, all the rest. Me—you know I had worked in advertising. That's how I met Jack. I was an associate creative director working on the Barrett Motels account, winning awards, making money, having fun. I quit after the wedding because—because of the resentment of my colleagues. It was as if by marrying a wealthy man I had somehow forfeited the right to work side by side with people who worried about mortgages and car payments and braces for the kids. Instead, I shopped. I lunched with women who shopped. Sometimes I did busywork for a couple of charities and nonprofit groups that would rather I just sent a check."

"You became desperately bored," I said.

"You know exactly what I'm talking about, don't you?"

I thought of Teachwell and the enormous amount of money that capturing him had brought me—the reason I had quit the cops.

"Yeah, I know," I said.

"Except that you found something constructive to do

with your time. I didn't. Instead, I found Troy." Lindsey shook her head sadly. "Sometimes we see things in people that just aren't there. Women do it more then men. Or maybe we're just more likely to admit it and be disappointed by it when we see that we're wrong."

"How did Donovan know about Elizabeth Rogers?"

"I told him. Jack has this recurring nightmare. It doesn't happen often. Couple of times a year at most. He has never told me what happens in the dream, but eventually I discovered what caused it—the murder of Elizabeth Rogers. I told Troy about it. I don't know why."

"Troy did some sleuthing, but not enough," I said. "He settled for the rumors."

"The rumors were all that Troy wanted. That's what he believed. It's what I believed. You must think me a fool."

"No. Foolish, maybe. There's a difference."

"What am I going to do?"

"What do you want to do?"

"I want to protect Jack. That's all I want."

"Okay."

"What does okay mean?"

"Now that we know Jack is innocent, the Chief and I are going to try to learn who actually did kill Elizabeth Rogers. Possibly we can remove the threat from Jack once and for all. As for Donovan—I'll take care of Donovan."

I told myself I was doing it for the governor, not for her. I still liked the governor.

"How?" Lindsey asked.

"Does it matter?"

"You're not going to . . . kill him?"

"Did you ask that when Muehlenhaus said he'd take care of me?"

"Yes."

"What did he say?"

"Said, 'Don't ask, don't tell.' "

"Sound advice."

As if on cue, there was a knock on the door.

"That's probably my driver," Lindsey said.

I yanked open the door and found Danny Mallinger on the other side. She was still wearing her police uniform.

"McKenzie, I have something you should know," she said. She saw Lindsey standing behind me. "I'm sorry, I didn't know you had company."

"Excuse me," Lindsey said. "I was just leaving."

I helped Lindsey on with her coat while Mallinger stood in the doorway watching.

"Are we still friends, McKenzie?" Lindsey asked.

I was still having a difficult time getting past Norman and Muehlenhaus.

"I liked your sister and then I stopped liking her," I said. "I liked you, too."

"But not anymore."

I didn't say no, yet the word hung there between us just the same.

"Let's just say that you used up your allotment of favors and let it go at that," I told her.

I led her to the door.

"It would seem that I'm the one who owes favors," she said.

"One day I may call to collect."

Lindsey kissed my cheek.

"Good-bye and thank you," she said, and slipped past Mallinger into the corridor. Mallinger let the door close behind her.

"Was that the first lady?" she asked.

"Don't ask, don't tell."

* * *

Mallinger moved deeper into the room.

"I like your sweater," she said.

"I wish I could say the same about your outfit. I thought we were having dinner."

"I thought you might like to take a little trip with me first."

"Where to?"

"You remember Andy, my rookie officer? I just met with him. Damned if he didn't get a hit after all. PDQ identified the color of the paint chips on your car as 'true blue.' They came from a 1999 Ford F-350 Superduty XLT pickup truck, and yes, it's available with a plow package. I just got off the phone with DMV. It seems there is, in fact, only one true blue 1999 Ford F-350 Superduty XLT pickup truck with a plow package in the county."

"Who owns it?"

"Eugene Hugoson."

Chapter Fourteen

The stars glistened in the night sky. They seemed to be considerably larger, brighter, and more numerous than they were in the Cities, where light pollution usually renders them as vivid as a flashlight with an exhausted battery. The moon, too. None of the songs I knew could do it justice. Mallinger was also gazing up at them. We were standing together next to the police cruiser she had parked in the space between the house and two outbuildings on Hugoson's farm.

"I wish I knew astronomy," Mallinger said. "If I knew astronomy I could be your guide. Instead, we're both lost in the night sky. Lost in the stars."

"Danny, you're a poet," I said.

"Nah. A guy used that line on me once and I've always wanted to give it a try myself."

"Was it successful?"

"You tell me?"

"We should have backup."

"I told you. All my guys are at the high school covering

the basketball game. Against Albert Lea. There's going to be five thousand people there. Besides, we're not going to arrest anyone. This is just—what did you call it before—a 'knock and talk'?"

Mallinger walked purposefully to the door. A light flashed on before she reached it. The heavy inside door opened. Hugoson stood behind the glass of the flimsier storm door. He made no effort to open it.

"Do you have a warrant?" he wanted to know.

"A warrant?" Mallinger said. "Gene, why do we need a warrant? We just came to chat with you is all."

"Chat about what?" Hugoson was talking to Mallinger while staring at me.

"Truth is, we wanted to take a gander at your Ford," Mallinger said.

"Why?"

"Just a quick look."

"Why?"

"Well now, Gene. We have reason to believe that it might have been involved in a traffic accident."

"Yeah? Who did I hit?"

Mallinger gestured toward where I was standing, my hands thrust deep into my coat pockets.

"No way," Hugoson said.

"We'll take a quick look. If we're wrong, if there's no damage, we'll apologize for disturbing your peace and be on our way."

"Yeah, I'd like to see that—a cop apologizing to me."

"Could be it's your lucky day."

Hugoson responded with an obscenity you don't hear on network television and slammed the door.

"Let's get a search warrant," I suggested. "Tomorrow we'll take this guy apart."

"Just wait," Mallinger said.

A moment later, Hugoson flew through the door wearing a bulky winter coat and thick boots. Mallinger arched her eyebrows at me. Her message was clear: I told you so.

"I knew you were coming," Hugoson said. "Sooner or later I figured. Chief, there's damage to my truck. You can see that for yourself, but you gotta know— Listen, Chief"—he jabbed a thumb in my direction—"I never touched this guy. I never went near this guy."

We followed Hugoson into his pole barn. He flicked a switch and a series of fluorescent lights blinked to life.

"I admit there's damage." He gestured at the pickup and stopped talking.

The truck shimmered beneath the lights. The plow blade was still attached. We eased to the right side of it with Hugoson trailing behind. Mallinger squatted next to the plow blade and front bumper. With a flashlight for help, she examined the blade, front grill, bumper, and side panel. After a few moments she flicked the light along the length of the vehicle. There were plenty of dings, dents, and rumpled metal.

"Look," she said.

I leaned over her shoulder. There were also plenty of dots and dashes of silver paint on the blade and truck body.

"I'll bet you a thousand dollars PDQ identifies it as Audi light silver metallic," I said.

"I know this looks bad," Hugoson claimed. "But we gotta be able to work this out. I'll pay to have your car fixed," he told me.

Mallinger pulled a plastic bag and a pair of tweezers that she had borrowed from Officer Andy out of her coat pocket. She dug chips of silver paint out of the plow blade and side panel and dropped them in the bag.

"This isn't right," Hugoson wailed. "I didn't go after this guy, Chief. You gotta believe me."

"You were correct before, Gene. This does look bad."

Hugoson glared at me like I was the source of all his problems in life. "What are you trying to do to me?" he wanted to know.

"Guess," I told him.

"You're trying to fuck me over cuz of what happened to Beth."

"If you want to tell that story in court, you go right ahead," I said.

"Goddammit, I can't go back to prison. I just can't."

Mallinger finished collecting samples and straightened up.

"I'm going back to the Law Enforcement Center," she said. "Do everyone a favor and turn yourself in early tomorrow morning. Otherwise, I'm coming back here with sheriff deputies and that kid from the *Herald*."

"You can't do this to me."

"The county attorney will begin with a charge of leaving the scene of an accident," I said. "I think he can make a pretty good case for felony assault, maybe even attempted murder."

"I didn't do it."

"It was your truck."

"I know, I know . . . Oh, shit. All right, all right, I know how things work. You gotta give me a deal."

"A deal? Why?"

"I'll tell you everything if you promise not to fuck up my parole. You can't send me back to prison."

"What are you talking about?" Mallinger said.

"Do we have a deal? I ain't talkin' unless we have a deal."

"I can't make a deal," Mallinger said.

"I can," I told him.

Mallinger scowled at me.

"I can only speak for the car," I told Hugoson. "Tell us something good and I won't file a complaint. I'll forget about the car."

"That's not enough."

"How much more do you need?" Mallinger asked.

Hugoson started walking in small, tight circles at the front of the garage, his hands squeezing each side of his head.

"I knew this would happen, I just fucking knew this would happen," he chanted.

Finally, he stopped. He moved to Mallinger and raised his hand like he wanted to set it on her shoulder, but didn't dare. Instead, he stared deeply into her eyes.

"You're a good cop," he said. "You got my respect. You do your job, but you cut people slack when there's slack to cut. You don't go around tryin' to break people's balls. If you promise to vouch for me with the county attorney, I'll tell ya."

"Tell me what?"

"Everything."

"For everything I'll cut you all the slack there is," Mallinger said.

"It was Coach."

"Coach Testen?"

"He came to me—"

"Coach Testen?" Mallinger repeated.

"He borrowed my truck. He said he wanted to move some stuff out of Josie's place. Later, when he brought it back, it was like this. I asked him about it. You gotta know I asked him about it. Look what he did to my truck.

I asked him and Coach says, he says, 'Looks like we don't need to worry about McKenzie anymore.'"

Mallinger grabbed my wrist and squeezed hard to keep me from speaking.

"When did this happen?" she said.

"Yesterday morning," Hugoson said. "He took the truck at about seven. He brought it back just before noon."

"He said, 'We don't need to worry about McKenzie, anymore.' Exactly those words."

"Yes."

"What else did he say?"

"He said to keep my mouth shut or he'd fuck me over, too."

"Coach said that?"

"Not those exact words, but that's what he meant."

"You didn't do anything about it?"

"No."

"What about Josie?"

"I didn't hear about Josie until—until later that night."

"What did you think when you heard about Josie?"

"I thought Coach must've fucked him, too."

"Still you did nothing?"

Mallinger scowled again when I asked, "What does he have on you, Gene?"

Hugoson began massaging his temples.

"A while ago, he and Josie—they asked me if I had— They said they didn't want to go through a dealer. They asked . . . shit. I gave them some anhydrous ammonia."

Shit is right.

"What is anhydrous ammonia?" Mallinger asked.

"It's a chemical fertilizer," Hugoson said. "Farmers use it in the spring and fall to add nitrogen to the soil."

"It's also a chief ingredient in the manufacture of methamphetamine," I added. "Did you know Coach Testen and Josie were cooking meth?"

"No, but . . ."

"But what?" asked Mallinger.

"I knew they weren't growing soybeans."

"Why didn't you come forward?" Mallinger asked. "If you knew they were cooking meth, why didn't you say so? When Josie was killed . . ."

"I couldn't. Don't you see? I gave Coach the fertilizer. Later, when he brought the truck back, he told me if I said anything, he'd take me down with him, claim I was in on it. What could I do? Tell me, what could I do? Even if I beat the meth rap, I'm not supposed to go anywhere near the bad thing. They would have violated my parole sure as shit. I can't go back to prison."

"Why did you give him the fertilizer in the first place?"

"He was my coach."

It was one of the few things Hugoson said that I understood. I've had coaches I would have walked through fire for.

"Josie and the Coach dealing meth," Mallinger said. "It doesn't make sense."

"It makes perfect sense," I told her.

"How does it make perfect sense?"

"People deal drugs for only one reason. Money. Josie needed a lot of cash for his pull-tab enterprises, and Coach—I saw his house, his car, his clothes. I didn't think of it at the time, but he does awfully well for a retired high school basketball coach."

"Not much money in coachin' high school ball," Hugoson said. "Coach had his pension—thirty years in the school system. He figured the town owed him more. He figured it shoulda done better by him. He had, whatchamacallit, illusions of grandeur."

"Delusions," I said.

"What?"

"Never mind."

Hugoson stood a few feet off. He was looking down at the toes of his heavy boots, probably wondering what was going to happen next. Mallinger gave him a hint when she went to the back of the pickup and examined the bed.

"We're going to impound your truck," she said.

"I need my truck," Hugoson said.

"I want the county lab to take a look, see if they can find anything, any residue, that could link it to a meth lab."

"That's why Coach borrowed it," I said. "To haul away Josie's lab."

"After I talk to the county attorney, you're going to come in, Gene. You're going to make a full statement—on camera—and then you're going to testify in court."

"I promise, Chief. I'll do everything you tell me that'll keep me from going back to prison. Only, beyond what I just told you—the truth is, I never saw Coach or Josie with meth, never saw them sell it or cook it or anything. So I don't know."

"Just tell us what you do know."

"Yes, sir . . . ma'am. Yes."

"In the meantime . . ."

Mallinger turned and walked out of the pole barn. Before following her, I turned on Hugoson.

"Listen to me." I was leaning so close to Hugoson that I could have kissed him. "Listen to me carefully. The night Elizabeth was killed—"

"I had nothing—"

"Shut up and listen! After you guys had your fun, after she left, what did you do?"

"Had a beer."

I was so angry now I was shaking.

"Don't screw with me, convict! Your life is hanging by a thread as it is. After Beth left, what did you do?"

"Nothing. The guys were all anxious about Beth and Jack, wondering what was going to happen and I guess we found out. We didn't do anything except . . ."

"Except what?"

"Josie."

"What about Josie?"

"He called Coach."

We were fast approaching Victoria and I was anxious. The left side of my brain wanted Mallinger to use her siren and light bar. The right side wanted her to stop the car and let me out.

"This is a mistake, Chief," I said.

"It might not be smart police work, but I want to talk to him tonight."

"You're right. It isn't smart police work. We should wait—see what forensics comes up with; see what CID pulls out of its hat."

"No, I'll talk to him tonight."

"Chief, if you want to lose the *interim* label, if you want the job permanent, you should do it by the numbers."

"This isn't about the job, and I resent it that you think it is."

"What then?"

"I'm tired of people fucking around in my town. If nothing else, I'll put the sonuvabitch on notice. He isn't welcome here."

Mallinger found a road that allowed us to circle Victoria and the traffic, such as it was. The downtown was a soft glow in the darkness.

"It was there in front of me all the time and I didn't see it," I said.

"How could you have guessed?"

"I shouldn't have had to guess, that's the point. When I heard the autopsy results I should have known. Skin and blood type O positive were found under the fingernails of Elizabeth's right hand. I've seen photos in back editions of the *Herald* taken at Elizabeth's funeral. Coach Testen was wearing a bandage over his cheek, his left cheek, the cheek Elizabeth would have scratched with her right hand."

"It's still circumstantial," Mallinger warned. "Since the samples were destroyed."

"You know about that?"

"I called the county coroner's office after your performance at Nick's. You did well getting those guys to talk after so long."

"Thanks."

"Still."

"Hmm?"

"I was thinking, we probably can't get Coach for Elizabeth. We probably won't be able to get him for Josie, either, unless we can connect the gun to him or he left something of himself at the scene. As for the meth, if he destroyed the lab—it doesn't look good."

"He did try to kill me with the truck."

"Why did he try to kill you? I'm playing devil's advocate here."

"To keep me from learning about Elizabeth and probably the meth."

"Yes, but if we can't connect him to Elizabeth and the meth . . ."

"I see what you mean. Most likely he'll be charged with hit and run."

"How do you know he tried to kill you? Did you see him? Did you see his face? That's what a defense attorney will ask."

"No, I didn't see his face."

"It'll be Coach's word against Hugoson's and Hugoson, the ex-convict who did time for armed robbery, car theft, and assault, *he* did have a motive for attacking you—the fight outside Nick's the night before, remember?"

"We do have one thing going for us. I haven't known him very long but I know this much, Coach likes to talk."

"He does indeed."

"Still, you should wait, Chief."

"I'm not waiting."

"Is there no way I can talk you out of this?"

"I'll drop you off at the motel."

"You could do that, Chief. 'Course, I'll just follow you to Coach Testen's."

"You would, too."

"Yes, I would."

"Does the term 'interfering with a police officer in the performance of her duties' mean anything to you?" Mallinger asked.

"Minnesota Statute 609.5—Obstructing Legal Process. It's a misdemeanor punishable by up to ninety days in jail. Since it's my first offense, I'll probably get a thousand-dollar fine. I'll take it out of petty cash."

"Let's hope that's all it costs."

* * *

I shouldn't have been there. Mallinger shouldn't have taken me. The Nicholas County sheriff told me so later, and the Nicholas County attorney agreed—oh, boy did he agree. It was foolish, reckless, and possibly even criminal; certainly it was against proper police procedure. 'Course, I knew that going in. I told myself I went because I needed to see Testen's face, I needed to look into his eyes. The evidence against him was so iffy, it was the only way I could be sure he was guilty, and I needed to be sure for Governor Barrett's sake. Yet, at the same time, I was aware of a curious mixture of fear and excitement twisting together in my stomach that I found exhilarating. It was like the time I buried the needle on the Audi, taking it up to 130 miles per hour. I didn't want to give up the feeling.

We parked in Testen's driveway. Mallinger stood for a few moments gazing across the street toward Jail Park. I wondered if she found it as forbidding as I had.

Without comment, Mallinger rubbed her gloveless hands together and headed for Testen's front door. There wasn't a single light showing in the house.

Mallinger rang the doorbell and knocked.

She rang the doorbell and knocked some more.

There was no response.

"He's not home," Mallinger said.

"It only now occurred to me, he's probably at the basketball game," I told her.

"Just as well. Now that we're here, we really shouldn't be doing this."

"Let's go talk to the county attorney," I said.

Behind us, we heard an unexpected voice.

"What would you tell him?"

We turned. The chrome and glass of the Crown Victoria police cruiser glistened under the bright night sky. Beyond that I could see nothing.

"Who's there?" Mallinger asked.

"What are you going to talk to the county attorney about?" the voice asked.

"Coach? Coach Testen?"

A shadow moved near the corner of the garage.

"Coach, I'd like to ask you a few questions."

"I know. I know what questions you wish to ask."

The shadow detached itself from the garage and drifted forward. Mallinger moved to meet it. Soon she was standing on one side of the cruiser and the shadow was on the other. I was standing behind Mallinger and to her right. The wind had picked up and was raking my face. *Don't you just love the weather in Minnesota?*

"I'm surprised you're not at the basketball game, Chief," Testen said.

"I could say the same thing about you, Coach."

"I've seen my share of big games."

"You were at the biggest game."

"That's right."

"Now that there are four classes, there'll never be a game as big again."

"I agree."

Testen was smiling.

"Why are you here, Chief?" he asked.

"Coach, I'm almost too embarrassed to tell you," Mallinger said.

"Please do. I won't be offended."

"There have been allegations, sir."

"From whom?" Testen nodded at me. "This gentleman?"

"Among others."

"Concerning what?"

"Josie Bloom's murder. A drug called meth."

"How can I ease your mind, Chief?"

"I'd like your permission—written permission, if you'll give it—to search your property."

"I'd be happy to grant you that permission," Testen said. "I have nothing to hide."

Nice touch asking for written permission, I thought. The way the chief was playing Testen—very professional. Yet it wasn't getting us anywhere. Coach was too smug, too sure of himself. He had been expecting us, which meant the lab equipment and everything else linking him to Josie—anything that would taint the shrine he had carefully built to himself—was gone, gone, gone. Still, I had a hunch and I played it.

"Chief Mallinger is looking for evidence of methamphetamine," I said.

Coach smiled at me.

"That is my understanding," he said.

"I'm searching for the silver locket you took off Elizabeth Roger's body the night you killed her."

The smile went away.

"You killed her," I said. "Elizabeth didn't find Jack Barrett that night. Instead, she found you. She told you what happened in Josie's basement and what she had planned. You strangled her to death for it. Didn't you?"

"There's no proof to support these spurious allegations."

"Yeah, there is. Add the locket and it's a slam dunk."

"Do you understand what is happening here?" Testen asked Mallinger, his voice climbing the ladder. "Do you fully appreciate what this . . . this gentleman is attempting? Do you, Chief?"

"Sir?"

"He's attempting to destroy the legend, the myth on which this town exists."

My stomach suddenly had that express-elevator-going-down feeling. There was danger here. I felt it. Mallinger had not. She had been correct at the motel when she told me that no one had taught her how to behave. She stood with her hands deep in the pockets of her jacket, not even thinking about her gun. I couldn't imagine a St. Paul police officer standing so casually before a suspect.

"Read him his rights," I said, frantic to get Mallinger's attention, trying to make her start thinking like a cop.

She glanced my way, but her attention was quickly drawn back to Testen.

"Rights?" Coach asked. "What about the rights of the people who live here? What about the rights of those people who were inspired by what was accomplished here? By what the Seven did, by what they represent? There is virtue here that the world does not often see. Sacrifice and commitment, perseverance and character, strength, and yes, integrity. It is what we teach our children. It is what all of us aspire to. Yet he would defecate on all that. And make us eat it.

"I cannot allow that to happen," Testen added.

"Coach?" asked Mallinger. She was smart, but not experienced. When the shadow raised its hand and pointed it at her—the hand holding something made of dark metal—she did not move.

"Gun!" I shouted.

That made her react. Mallinger quickly removed her hands from her pocket and went for her Glock. It was too late. Testen fired his gun. Mallinger was hit. She spun hard to her left and collapsed on the driveway.

I did a foolish thing. I moved forward. Not toward Testen, trying to get his gun—nothing as brain-dead heroic as that. I went toward Danny, wanting to help Danny. I might have even called her name.

Testen fired again. How he missed me from that distance I don't know. The explosion jolted me back into the reality of the moment. My fight-or-flight instincts kicked in. Outside Fit to Print I had been a deer caught in the headlights. Now I was a deer running, covering asphalt in a hurry as I dashed down the driveway toward the street.

The sound of multiple explosions followed me.

I wasn't running out of fear, I tried to convince myself. The point of running was to find a better place to fight, to give myself a chance. To give Danny Mallinger a chance. I couldn't help Danny if I was killed. I needed to escape so I could call for help. Yeah, sure.

I crossed the street and kept running toward Jail Park. Oak, pine, spruce, ash, and birch trees loomed above me, bending and swaying in the hard wind. The boulevard of snow between the street and the trees slowed me down. It filled my boots and immediately began to melt. Floundering, once falling, I pushed myself forward, knowing I made an inviting target in the bright moonlight.

I heard another explosion.

My heart beating wildly, breath coming in rasps, an ache in my side—*how is this possible*, I wondered. *I play hockey thirty weeks out of the year. I work out three-four times every week*. How could I be so out of shape? I pressed my hand hard against the ache and kept running.

Finally, I was there. Inside the park, surrounded by trees and underbrush. I squatted against an oak and searched for Testen. He was at the edge of the park and coming in. He was watching the ground, trying to follow my tracks in the snow. He seemed confused. The moonlight barely penetrated this deep into the forest and he was having trouble following my trail.

I fumbled for my cell phone, stopped. There was something on my hand. Blood. I didn't have an ache in my side because of running. I had been shot. I opened my coat, pulled up my shirt. More blood. I grabbed a handful of snow and pressed it against the wound. The snow quickly darkened. My body heat melted it and rivulets flowed into the waistband of my slacks. The damage didn't seem too bad in the moonlight, but what did I know? I gathered more snow and held it against my side while I worked my cell with one hand, using my thumb to punch the numbers 911.

"Officer down."

I spoke so quietly the operator had trouble hearing.

"Officer down," I repeated, forcing my voice higher. I gave the address, explained that Mallinger had been shot and by whom—that I had been shot—that I was being stalked by the shooter. The operator didn't seem to believe me, kept saying, "You're kidding." Still, she passed my call for help to both the City of Victoria Police Department and the Nicholas County Sheriff's Office without hesitation. She told me to stay on the phone.

Testen's head jerked up and he held it at an angle that suggested he was listening for something. I deactivated the cell phone. I was breathing deeply and rapidly and the noise distressed me. I covered my mouth with my hand, hoping my breathing sounds wouldn't be heard at any distance.

I wondered how long it would take for help to arrive. If it was the Twin Cities, the first squad would have been on the scene within two minutes. But this wasn't the Cities. There was no telling where the nearest cop could be.

The wound wasn't bad. Movie heroes would call it a mere flesh wound and then ignore it. Pardon me if I wasn't as hardy as those guys. I gathered up another handful of fresh snow and winced in pain as I pressed it against the injury. I started running some more, pushing deeper into the woods.

The snow didn't seem quite as deep under the thick trees, only about a foot. It was hard going, but not as hard as it had been. Still, after fifty yards I was breathing rapidly and I began to feel warm inside my coat. Soon I was perspiring freely. I had trouble seeing in the woods and tripped several times over branches hidden in the snow. I dug up one of them and began carrying it as a weapon—it was three feet long, two inches thick, and better than nothing.

The branch gave me confidence. My original plan was simple. Avoid Testen, cross the park, find a street, find a house, wait for help, don't get lost, stay alive—simple. Now I was thinking about taking the battle to him, wound or no wound. Circle around and attack Testen from behind. Or lie in ambush and hit him as he passed.

I paused for a moment to rest. The area around my injury had become numb and the bleeding had stopped, yet I kept the snow pressed over it just the same.

Again I searched for Testen. I couldn't see him, but I doubted he had given up the chase. It wasn't about money, or anger, or even survival with him. That's not why he killed Elizabeth and shot Mallinger. Coach killed for pride. He would never quit.

Dammit, you can never find a cop when you need one.

After a few moments, I continued walking, keeping low. I began to lose sense of both time and distance. I had no idea where I was. I halted, crouched in the snow. I was positive that the park must end just ahead with a street and houses beyond, except I had nothing on which to base that assertion except my own natural confidence. Or was it merely wishful thinking?

Where in hell was Testen?

I marched forward. Suddenly, I was out of the woods. Only it wasn't a street I had found, just a wide path. The path had appeared so abruptly that I was several yards deep into it before I shied like a startled horse and retreated back along my trail. I squatted behind a stand of spruce and examined the path. *It must lead to the street,* my inner voice told me, but that was just a guess. Still, it must lead somewhere. My concern was the light. In winter it's never entirely dark. The snow and ice always find one source or another of illumination to magnify and reflect, like the hundreds of stars in the night sky. The path seemed inordinately bright. I would be terribly exposed.

I watched the path for what seemed like a long time. Nothing moved on it except a few grains of ice and snow propelled by the wind. I could wait, I told myself. Go to ground. If Testen used the path, I'd be in perfect position to bushwhack him. Otherwise, the police and sheriff deputies were bound to arrive sometime—maybe after the high school basketball game. Except I really couldn't tell how serious the wound was. My hand holding the snow over the wound had become numb. So had my feet. My exposed ears and cheeks had become so cold they ached. Waiting didn't seem like an option.

I gave myself a slow count to three and dashed forward.

It was a mistake.

Testen had been waiting for me. Apparently he possessed greater patience.

He saw me, called out my name, and demanded that I stop.

I continued running along the path toward wherever it led. My legs ached and my lungs burned—you try sprinting through a foot of snow. I tripped, fell, skidded across the path, regained my feet and kept running.

Testen was shooting.

A bullet exploded snow at my feet; another whistled past my ear.

The snow was so deep.

I had no speed.

No chance.

I tripped and fell against the trunk of the tree. I couldn't run anymore. Not in the snow.

Testen was behind me, waving his gun. I turned to face him. He was as winded as I was. Worse. Yes, much worse. His breath came hard and fast and he was holding his side. There was a look of pain on his face.

He had the gun. I had only a branch hidden between my body and the tree. I gripped it tightly.

"Don't move," Testen shouted.

He was closer now.

Let him come.

If I could hit him and get past him, I could outrun him. Seeing him the way he was, I knew I could escape. If he came closer.

He did.

"It didn't have to be this way," he said.

He could barely get the words out.

He extended his arm, pointing the gun.

A target.

I brought the branch out from behind me and struck down hard at Testen's wrist.

He yanked his arm out of the way.

I missed.

Testen was startled by my weapon and took a step backward.

I swung again.

Missed again.

Testen brought his gun up.

I lunged at him.

He pivoted away and my momentum took me past him. I tripped and fell headlong into the snow. I dropped the branch.

Testen was there.

I attempted to crawl through the snow on hands and knees, trying to escape into the woods, knowing there was no escape.

Testen followed me easily, the gun leading the way. He seemed amused by my efforts.

A shout. From behind us.

"Halt. Police."

A silly thing to say given the circumstances, I thought.

Testen turned toward the voice.

Mallinger was staggering forward along the path, her left arm pressed hard against her side, her right hand holding the Glock, her face twisted with pain and effort. She brought the Glock up, pointed it more or less at Testen.

Testen stood straight. He held his own gun at his side and watched the Chief approach.

He might have surrendered, who knows? Except Mallinger collapsed. She pitched forward into the snow. The Glock slipped from her grasp and was lost. Mallinger was still alive, still trying to make headway, only it was like a woman thrashing in her sleep. Testen watched the Chief for a moment before turning toward me.

"This is your fault," he said. "None of this would have happened except for you."

He raised the gun until the barrel was pointing at my face.

My mind became a satellite dish—five hundred channels. I surfed through them all, holding no image long, never finishing a thought, until finally a stillness settled in me, the screen empty. I closed my eyes and braced myself for the impact of bullets.

Another shout.

"Hey."

I opened my eyes and saw Testen pivoting toward the voice, the gun still pointed at me.

Greg Schroeder stood next to Mallinger's prone body, her Glock cradled in his two hands. He was sighting down the barrel.

"Don't shoot me," Testen cried.

Schroeder killed him anyway.

It happened in slow motion.

Testen seemed to lean forward, crouching like he was about to spring into a dive. The bullets—there were four of them—hit him high in the chest and straightened him out. Some of the bullets went through him, and a spray of blood splattered both the snow and me. The force of the bullets lifted Coach up and away. His arms spread wide and then his legs, and when he splashed backward into the snow and came to a rest he looked like a man who was making angels.

A moment later, it was real time. Schroeder was standing next to me, the Glock resting against his thigh. He glanced at Coach Testen's body for a moment, then back at me. He opened my jacket, examined the bullet wound, grunted "hmmpf," like it was nothing to get excited about.

"How you doin', pal?" he asked as he helped me to my feet.

"Is he dead?"

"If he's not, he never will be. Are you all right?"

I heard him; I couldn't answer. I didn't know if I was all right or not. I felt my body shaking, yet that could have just as easily been the cold. I was so very cold. I stared at Testen's body, couldn't seem to pull my eyes away. *Should you laugh or cry or what?* my inner voice asked.

"McKenzie? Look at me!"

I looked.

"Are you all right?" Schroeder repeated.

"It was just a walk in the park, Greg."

Together we trudged back to Mallinger. The Chief was kneeling in the snow, her right hand clutching her left armpit. Schroeder opened her jacket to examine the wound. Over his shoulder I could see that Mallinger was much worse off than I was. She had lost an enormous amount of blood. I eased past Schroeder. I pulled my handkerchief from my pocket and pressed it into the bullet hole in the muscle between Danny's arm and her chest, trying to check the bleeding. She winced in pain, but said nothing.

Schroeder held out the Glock by the barrel.

"Take it," he told the Chief.

Mallinger seemed dazed. She stared at Schroeder for a moment like she was waiting for something to happen. When it didn't, she reached for the gun with her bloody hand, took it by the grip, and looked at it like she didn't know what it was.

"Screw it up and God knows how it'll end, Chief. If you play it smart and take the credit— Look at me." Mallinger looked. "Take the credit and you'll be a hero. Work it right and you'll be chief of police for as long as you want the job."

Schroeder patted my back. Maybe he winked at me, I couldn't tell in the darkness, although I was sure there was a smile.

Then he was gone.

CHAPTER FIFTEEN

Huge trucks and SUVs, their headlights blinding, came at me from the oncoming lane. They passed with a loud snatching sound, ripping the air around the Audi, creating tremors that I felt in the steering wheel. I was driving well beyond my headlights along State Highway 60, heading toward Mankato. I hadn't felt my fatigue until I started driving, and now it threatened to overwhelm me. I played all the tricks—slapping my face, powering down the window to let the frozen air do it for me, chewing gum, singing. I even poked my side, hoping the shock of pain would help keep my eyes open. Above all, I avoided staring at the white stripes, refusing to let them hypnotize me into an accident. Probably I should have stopped and rested. But I had to get shy of Victoria. I had to get home.

After I went to Mankato.

According to the Mankato phone directory, G. Monteleone, the only Monteleone in the book, had a house on Floral Avenue near the Minnesota State University campus. It was nearly ten P.M. when I knocked on the door. A light flicked on above my head. The door opened and Monteleone peered out. She saw my face, which I suppose looked frightening, and the dried blood on my jacket and slacks, which must have looked worse. A fearful expression formed on her face.

"Do you remember me?" I asked.

"What are you doing here?"

"I need to ask a few questions."

"I only conduct business at school. If you call tomorrow . . ."

"It's about your son."

Monteleone held tighter to the door.

"What is this about, Mr., Mr. . . . ?"

"McKenzie. You told me your grandson was a Sagittarius, like his father."

Monteleone hesitated.

"Yes," she said.

"That means he was born between November 22 and December 21, like his father."

"What is this about?"

"That means your son was conceived in March. You didn't meet your husband until June, after you left Victoria—do the math."

"Mr. McKenzie—"

"You didn't date anyone in Victoria, Suzi Shimek told me so."

"What has that got to do . . . ?"

"Tell me about March."

Monteleone answered with a blank stare.

"Jack Barrett is your son's father. Isn't he? You were having an affair with your student and you became pregnant and that's why you left Victoria—to keep it private. Not even Jack knows."

Monteleone continued to hug the door while her face came florid with anger.

"That's the most outrageous thing I've ever heard," she insisted.

"Jack Barrett was with you the night Elizabeth Rogers was murdered. You left at eight thirty. He left a few minutes later. That's what the fight with Elizabeth Rogers was all about, him leaving her for you. Only he never spoke of it. He could have used you as an alibi for her murder. He didn't. He cared for you so much that he was willing to protect you at his own peril. Because of that, for over thirty years the chief of police and nearly everyone else in Victoria was sure he had committed murder. For over thirty years the real killer got away with his crime."

"That's ridiculous."

"The truth often is. Ms. Monteleone, I'm not here to compromise you in any manner. I'll protect your privacy if for no other reason than that's what Jack Barrett wants. He's an honorable man, the only honorable man I've met in what seems like a good long time. But I need to know. I need to be sure."

"Why?"

"Why what?"

"Why should I trust you to keep my secrets?"

For an instant I flashed on Jack Barrett and Lindsey, I saw Donovan and Muehlenhaus and all the others, and I heard the words they emphasized during the meeting in Muehlenhaus's conference room. *You have already proven to us that you can keep a secret.*

"Because that's what I do," I said. "You don't know me, so you have no reason to trust me, but time will prove that I'm telling you the truth. I will never repeat to anyone what you tell me here, tonight. You have my word."

"I will answer one question. Only one."

"Was Jack Barrett with you the night Elizabeth Rogers was killed?"

"Yes."

"Good night, Ms. Monteleone. I'm sorry to have troubled you."

I was only a few miles north of Mankato when my cell phone played its melody. I fumbled for it in my pocket.

"Hello."

"Hey, pal. Nice night for a drive."

"Schroeder?"

"Yep."

"Where are you?"

"On your bumper."

I glanced in my rearview mirror just as Schroeder flicked his high beams at me.

"So, how are you doin'?" he asked.

"I've been better."

"How's the bullet hole?"

"Not a hole. A scratch. Granted, it took eleven stitches to close it, but a scratch just the same."

"Uh-huh. The cops held you for a long time. Nearly twenty-four hours."

"They're a thorough bunch."

"What happened?"

"What's the matter? Are you nervous, Greg?"

"Yes."

"Don't worry about it. Mallinger took the hint. Your name never came up. When her officers and the sheriff deputies finally arrived, she told them that she had shot Testen. She told them that she went to see Testen about a traffic accident involving me. She told them that she suspected that the accident might have been premeditated, that Testen had attempted to kill me, and that he might have killed Josie Bloom over a meth operation. She said she had no proof of these allegations beyond Gene Hugoson's testimony, at least not until Testen shot her when she started asking questions. She said she went to see Testen alone at night because Testen was an important figure in Victoria and she wanted to spare him from gossip in case the allegations proved unfounded. Eventually, they put her under anesthesia and took the bullet out of her armpit. Even doped up she stuck to her story. By then it sounded more believable. CID found Coach Testen's fingerprints all over Josie's place. Apparently he thought they would never even bother to look."

"What about the girl?"

"Elizabeth Rogers?"

"That's her name."

"I cornered Kevin Salisbury alone at the hospital. He's a reporter for the *Victoria Herald*."

"I know him."

"Of course, you do. I told Salisbury that Coach Testen killed Elizabeth. I couldn't supply him with a motive; I couldn't tell him what happened in Josie Bloom's basement—"

"What did happen in Jose Bloom's basement?"

"Never mind. I did tell him that the ME found skin and blood under Elizabeth's fingernails and that they match Testen's O positive blood type—God, they had better match—and that if he looked, Salisbury could see scratches on Testen's face in the photographs taken at Elizabeth's funeral. I also told him that Testen had probably kept a locket among his many souvenirs of the Seven's victory. Salisbury took the information to the sheriff—made it sound like he was the one who figured it out—and convinced the sheriff to search Testen's museum. Sure, enough, they found the locket at the bottom of one of the smaller trophies."

"Beautiful."

"So, you can tell your boss that come Sunday's edition of the *Victoria Herald* he should be free and clear of that particular problem."

"My boss?"

"The governor of the State of Minnesota. He hired you, didn't he, Greg?"

"Did he?"

"The only question I have is, Did he hire you to make sure I solved the case or watch my back?"

"Maybe both—if he hired me."

"The incidents on the skyway and in the parking lot, the telephone calls—the fifteen roses at Milepost Three. You arranged all that, didn't you?"

"I had to keep you interested, pal. You have to admit the roses were a nice touch."

"Very nice. Tell me something. Why didn't he send you in the first place? Why did he pick me?"

"The governor didn't pick you. The first lady picked you, remember?"

"Does he know why?"

"Of course he knows why."

"Then he knows about Donovan."

"That's my understanding."

"Why doesn't he do something about it?"

"He'd have to admit to his wife that he knows what happened, and he's not prepared to do that."

"Why not?"

"If he admits he knows about her infidelity, he'd have

to do something about it and maybe he doesn't want to do anything about it. Maybe he's content with his marriage, warts and all. Maybe he hopes to avoid confrontation so he can repair the damage quietly and in his own time. Maybe, despite everything, he loves his wife and doesn't want to lose her. This is all hypothetical, of course."

"Of course."

"Personally, I'd like to blow Donovan's brains out, but the governor won't have it."

"I'll take care of Donovan."

Schroeder chuckled loudly.

"You didn't get suckered into doing another favor, did you, pal? When are you going to learn?"

"I wish you'd stop calling me pal."

"McKenzie."

"Better. I spoke to Mrs. Rogers, Elizabeth's mother, before I left."

"Oh?"

"I told her that Coach Testen killed her daughter because he was afraid she would distract Jack Barrett from the big game. I didn't mention what happened to her before she was killed."

"What did Mrs. Rogers say?"

"She said she'd pray for him, pray for Testen. Can you imagine that?"

"Not really."

"She said something else that kinda threw me."

"What?"

"She said it looked like God picked the right emissary to do his will."

"She said that?"

"She believes in that sort of thing."

"What do you believe, McKenzie?"

"I pretty much make it up as I go along. How 'bout you?"

"I'm the same, I guess."

"I suppose I should thank you. For saving my life, I mean. I didn't get the chance before."

"It was my pleasure. Now I have a question for you."

"Sure."

"Why did you visit Grace Monteleone?"

"Are we about finished here, Greg?"

"Yeah, we're done. You have to admit—it was fun while it lasted."

"You have a strange idea of what's fun, Greg."

Schroeder chuckled.

"I suppose I do. I'll see you around, McKenzie."

"Not if I see you first."

I deactivated the cell and dropped it on the bucket seat next to me. I watched Schroeder through my rearview mirror as I gave him a backward wave. He flicked his high beams. I downshifted into fifth gear and accelerated, leaving him far behind me.

The streets of North Oaks all had soft names that made the place sound like a nature preserve—Wildflower Way, Birch Lake Road, Red Forest Heights, Long Marsh Lane, Catbird Circle, Mallard Road—and I doubted I had been the only visitor who questioned the sobriety of the men who had mapped them. The few times I had driven the streets I had become hopelessly lost. Members of the city's private police department were forced to give me directions—after first running my plates for wants and warrants and demanding that I explain exactly what I was doing in North Oaks in the first place since I wasn't sporting the tiny black reflector on my rear bumper that indicated I belonged to the exclusive community. Fortunately, no one stopped me as I negotiated the troublesome streets looking for Troy Donovan's address at nearly one in the morning, which made me wonder: They paid extra for this kind of security? Given the late hour, my appearance, and the condition of the Audi, the cops should have been on me like I was doling out free Krispy Kremes.

It took me awhile, but I finally located Donovan's house, a sprawling two-story, white, with black trim and shutters. I parked on the street and walked to his front door. It was late, yet there were plenty of lights burning inside.

"One last promise to keep," I said aloud before leaning on the bell.

Donovan examined me carefully through the spy hole before he opened the door, the safety chain in place.

"Mr. McKenzie? What is it? Do you know what time it is?"

"May I come in? There is something important I need to discuss with you, sir."

"With me? I suppose."

Donovan closed the door, removed the chain, and reopened it. I stepped across the threshold.

"Are you alone?" I asked.

"Yes, I am."

I hit him under the jaw with a palm fist, driving him backward into the house. I followed him inside, closing the door behind me.

At some point in his life, Donovan must have actually been in a fight because he didn't act surprised and indignant the way some people do when confronted with unexpected violence, demanding an explanation before attempting to defend themselves, asking "Why are you doing this?" while their opponent pummeled the hell out of them. Instead, after regaining his balance, Donovan actually threw a punch at me. It didn't amount to much, but I admired the effort.

I blocked the punch with my left forearm, stepped in close, slid my right arm under his left arm and around his body, swept his leg out and up, and threw him over my hip and down solidly on the hardwood floor. The move took his breath away, immobilizing him long enough for me to grab his right leg.

I hauled him across the floor to a chair while he gasped and coughed. I propped his heel on the edge of a chair and braced it against my leg so he couldn't pull it off. I removed my Beretta from my inside pocket, made sure he saw me chambering a round, and pressed the muzzle against his knee.

"Kiss it good-bye," I said.

"No, no, please, no," he screamed. "Stop. Oh, God. Why are you doing this?"

I ground the muzzle against his kneecap.

"No! McKenzie, please."

"Do I have your attention?"

"What? My attention? McKenzie, don't shoot me. Please. Why are you, why are you . . . ?"

I tried to keep all emotion out of my voice.

"You really want to stay away from Lindsey Barrett from now on," I said. "Don't see her, don't talk to her, don't write her, don't even think about her. These are the new rules you live by. Break the rules and one of two things will happen. Either I'll come back and put you into a wheelchair, or I'll inform Mr. Muehlenhaus that you've been endangering his investment. Personally, I think the second prospect is more frightening than the first, but that's just me."

"McKenzie, please . . ."

"Do you understand what I'm telling you?"

"Yes."

"Say it."

"I understand."

"Maybe you think you can say anything now and forget about it later."

"No."

I rapped Donovan's kneecap hard with the barrel of the gun. I didn't damage it permanently, but he'd be walking uncomfortably for a few days, and that would give him something to think about.

I released his leg. Donovan folded it neatly against his chest and caressed the knee.

"Why, why?" he whimpered.

"Just doing a favor for an old friend," I told him and returned the Beretta to my pocket.

I went to the front door, opened it, and stepped outside.

Two of North Oaks's finest were standing fore and aft beside my Audi.

"Is this your vehicle, sir?" the one in front asked as I made my way across Donovan's icy sidewalk. All things considered, I was surprised he wasn't shooting first and asking questions later.

"Yes, it's my vehicle," I said. "Such as it is."

"Sir, it is a violation of city ordinances to park your vehicle on the street."

"I apologize. I'll move it right away."

"Sir, may I see your ID?"

"Officer?" Donovan was calling from his front door. He

was leaning heavily against the frame, favoring his left leg. "Officer?"

"Mr. Donovan," the officer replied. I wondered if the cops knew everyone who lived in North Oaks by name or only the seriously wealthy.

"Officer"—I was sure that Donovan was going to burn me. He didn't—"it's all right, Officer. Mr. McKenzie is a friend of mine. I should have told him about the rules. I'm sorry."

"That's fine, sir." The officer nodded at me. "Mr. McKenzie, you're free to go."

I gave Donovan a nod. Apparently, Donovan got the message, which meant I could forget about him. And I so much wanted to forget about him, about all of them. I felt crummy about frightening him with the Beretta and wondered for a moment if I would have actually done what I had promised. In any case, he brought it on himself.

"Thank you, Officer," I said and climbed into the Audi.

"What happened to your car?" the officer asked as I fired it up. "There's a lot of damage here."

"I was sideswiped on the freeway by a snowplow."

"That's terrible."

"I thought so, too."

"It was such a nice car, too."

Was?

"Sir?"

"Yeah."

"Is that a bullet hole?"

"Don't be silly," I said before driving away. "Who would want to shoot at me?"

Just So You Know

On Saturday a few hundred people crowded into the St. Mark's Elementary School gymnasium to support about a half dozen nonprofit groups. There was a turkey dinner with all the trimmings, a raffle, cake-walk, something called a "bottle blast," various games of chance for the entire family, and, of course, sno-cones, popcorn, and mini-donuts. The corner where Girl Scout Troop 579 was ensconced had been hopping the entire day—we had to send Bobby Dunston out to get more paper bags for the mini-donuts, which gave me a great deal of pleasure.

"You scoffed when I bought the donut machine," I reminded him and Shelby. "Now what do you say?"

They admitted that making a hundred dozen mini-donuts per hour just about met the demand. On the other hand Shelby asked, "Have you ever even come close to making this many donuts before?"

I told her, "Just knowing that I could was enough."

On Sunday morning, I drove my Jeep Cherokee to Rickie's and had brunch with the boss. There was a jazz trio playing soft and mellow and they were pretty good. They were also college kids and you could tell they were itching to cut loose, only Nina wouldn't let them. Apparently she was concerned they would disturb the digestion of her older, after-church customers. She did promise them a Monday night gig to see what they could do and that seemed to encourage them.

While we ate, I told Nina everything that happened in Victoria, without pause or hesitation, starting with my meetings with Lindsey Barrett and the Brotherhood. The question Donovan had asked in Muehlenhaus's conference room—"Can we rely on your discretion?"—flashed in my brain without leaving an impression. It hadn't occurred to me to ask Nina the same question.

Nina seemed surprised that I had been so forthcoming.

"Usually you keep these things to yourself," she said.

"I met two kids in Victoria. They were young and they were in love, and the girl, who reminded me a little of your daughter, she told me that she and her lover had no secrets between them and I thought that's the way it should be."

Nina hugged me and kissed my cheek and thanked me for including her in that part of my life and I should have been glad for it, except I wasn't. Probably because I was holding out on her. I didn't tell Nina about Jack Barrett and Grace Monteleone or the child that they conceived together, a crime for which I easily forgave myself.

I also didn't tell her that I had slept with Danny Mallinger. Or that I had kissed her before I left Victoria and reminded her that we still had a standing dinner date. "Give me a week or two to heal and I'll call you," Danny said from her hospital bed.

No, I couldn't bring myself to tell her that.

On Monday I went to see Muehlenhaus. I entered his lobby and walked past the receptionist, through the glass doors into the inner office area, found the long corridor and marched to the conference room at the end of it. I did it without stopping—not even to admire the Degas—for fear someone would ask who I was or where I was going. Walk purposefully and with confidence, I told myself. You'd be surprised how far you can get.

I entered the conference room without bothering to knock. I was in luck. Muehlenhaus was there, along with Donovan, Glen Gunhus, Carroll Mahoney, Prescott Coole, and a half dozen other men I didn't recognize. If the room had been empty, I wasn't sure what I would have done.

"Hey, everyone's here," I said. "Good to see you all. No kidding. Troy, Mr. Muehlenhaus . . . Norman, how's the shoulder?"

Norman had been sitting in a chair near the door. He was standing now, his arm held in a white sling over his dark blue suit coat.

"No need to get up, I won't be staying long," I said.

Norman didn't sit down. He looked like he wanted to attack me. One thing you had to say about him, he was a gamer.

There was plenty of muttering. Someone wanted to know who the hell I thought I was. Muehlenhaus raised a fragile hand and silenced the table.

"Gentlemen, I apologize for interrupting your meeting," I said. "However, I think you should know that I am going to vote for John Allen Barrett. I am going to contribute money to his campaign. If I find the time, I'll even deliver campaign literature door to door. Unless he's weak on crime—an issue that's suddenly become quite important to me—I can think of no reason why he shouldn't be elected U.S. senator from the State of Minnesota. Maybe even president."

Troy Donovan was on his feet. He looked like he wanted to say something. I didn't give him the opportunity.

"There was a slight problem involving Mr. Barrett's wife that might have become an impediment to his campaign," I said. "However, I believe it has been satisfactorily rectified."

Donovan sat down slowly.

"What problem was that?" Muehlenhaus asked.

"Good morning, gentlemen," I said and left the room.

I retreated from the office along the same path I had come. When I reached the lobby I was stopped by the woman with the smart brown eyes that I had met, God, was it only a week ago?

"Mr. Muehlenhaus would like to speak with you," she said. "He's coming now."

"He's coming to me?"

"Yes."

That I wanted to see.

While I waited, I examined the Degas. I decided I understood the ballerina a little bit better than the first time I had encountered her.

A moment later, Muehlenhaus arrived. He offered his hand and I shook it. I was surprised by the strength of his grip.

"You did an excellent job in Victoria," he said.

"I didn't do it for you."

"Nonetheless, we are very pleased."

"Makes you wish you hadn't tried to kill me, doesn't it?"

I spoke loud enough for at least a half dozen people to hear me, yet no one behaved as if they had.

"I was wondering, Mr. McKenzie. How would you like to do a favor for me?"

You can guess what I told him.

DEATH IN PRECINCT PUERTO RICO

STEVEN TORRES

In the small town of Angustias in Puerto Rico, Sheriff Luis Gonzalo knows almost everything. He knows that Elena Maldonado's husband beats her. But when Elena is found dead, there's one thing Gonzalo doesn't know—who killed her. At first it seems like an open-and-shut case against her drunken husband, but with each passing day more suspects pop up. Soon Gonzalo feels like there's only one thing he knows for sure: he will not let Elena's murder go unpunished.

A New Leaf

A Cape Light Novel

THOMAS KINKADE
& KATHERINE SPENCER

JOVE BOOKS, NEW YORK
A Parachute Press Book

THE BERKLEY PUBLISHING GROUP
Published by the Penguin Group
Penguin Group (USA) Inc.
375 Hudson Street, New York, New York 10014, USA
Penguin Group (Canada), 90 Eglinton Avenue East, Suite 700, Toronto, Ontario M4P 2Y3, Canada
(a division of Pearson Penguin Canada Inc.)
Penguin Books Ltd., 80 Strand, London WC2R 0RL, England
Penguin Group Ireland, 25 St. Stephen's Green, Dublin 2, Ireland (a division of Penguin Books Ltd.)
Penguin Group (Australia), 250 Camberwell Road, Camberwell, Victoria 3124, Australia
(a division of Pearson Australia Group Pty. Ltd.)
Penguin Books India Pvt. Ltd., 11 Community Centre, Panchsheel Park, New Delhi—110 017, India
Penguin Group (NZ), 67 Apollo Drive, Rosedale, North Shore 0632, New Zealand
(a division of Pearson New Zealand Ltd.)
Penguin Books (South Africa) (Pty.) Ltd., 24 Sturdee Avenue, Rosebank, Johannesburg 2196,
South Africa

Penguin Books Ltd., Registered Offices: 80 Strand, London WC2R 0RL, England

A NEW LEAF

A Jove Book / published by arrangement with the authors

PRINTING HISTORY
Berkley hardcover edition / January 2004
Berkley trade paperback edition / December 2004
Jove mass-market edition / February 2006

For information, address: The Berkley Publishing Group,
a division of Penguin Group (USA) Inc.,
375 Hudson Street, New York, New York 10014.

ISBN: 978-0-515-14066-8

JOVE®
Jove Books are published by The Berkley Publishing Group,
a division of Penguin Group (USA) Inc.,
375 Hudson Street, New York, New York 10014.
JOVE® is a registered trademark of Penguin Group (USA) Inc.
The "J" design is a trademark of Penguin Group (USA) Inc.

PRINTED IN THE UNITED STATES OF AMERICA

10 9 8 7 6 5 4

A Letter from Thomas Kinkade

A *New Leaf*: The title of this Cape Light book suggests a fresh start, a new beginning. As a painter, I love new beginnings. One of my favorite moments is when I put my brush to a blank white canvas to begin a new painting. The precious newness of the moment is a thrill that is difficult to describe, but when people hear me say that, they often ask, "Don't you feel daunted by the blank canvas in front of you? Doesn't the task ahead ever seem too difficult, even frightening?" Truthfully the answer is no, for one simple reason: I have learned that no canvas is ever really blank. Every painting, every stroke of my brush, every glowing dot of light carries with it a little bit of me, everything that has come before. My task, and my joy, is to not hold back, to let the canvas fill with everything I have learned and seen and felt. My raw materials are not the paint and brushes and canvas cloth. My raw materials are my family, my friends, my joys, my sorrows, my faith in God, everything that makes up the color and form of my life. If I can embrace all of that, I know the painting will emerge.

For me, all of life is like that—a painting that we create and change and shape for all our years on earth. As you will soon see in *A New Leaf*, several of Cape Light's residents are facing a new white canvas. Some will feel the elation of love and others the sadness of parting. Some are hesitating to pick up a brush to let their new paintings take form. New relationships are begun and old relationships undone. Others are looking back on the canvases they have already filled and hoping to make sense of what they have created. But as they turn their new leaves and begin to allow their new paintings to emerge, they will certainly come to understand and appreciate anew the fullness that is a life lived on God's earth.

So join us now. Jessica and Sam, Dan and Emily, Sophie and Gus, and Molly are ready to welcome you to Cape Light. And I welcome you, too, with my thanks. Thank you so much for saving a small corner of the canvas of your life for the people of Cape Light.

—Thomas Kinkade

Chapter One

Molly Willoughby ran down the hallway, a radio tucked under one arm, a bucket of cleaning supplies dangling from the other. The vacuum followed like a dutiful pet, coming to a sudden stop beside her in the middle of the empty room.

She checked her watch. Nearly four and she had the whole second floor to finish: three bedrooms and two baths. Large rooms, too. And dirty. She'd never expected the place to take this long. The kitchen had been a nightmare. Scouring the stove and refrigerator had taken hours and worn out two sets of gloves.

She propped the radio on a window ledge and turned up the volume loud enough to be heard over the vacuum. The station was her daughter Lauren's favorite, one Molly usually avoided. But it was good cleaning music; the frantic beat kept her moving.

She covered the room in big strides, shoving the vacuum in all directions over the blue carpet, thinking how she'd never even wanted this job. She wanted to give up housecleaning altogether, but here she was, once again breaking her neck to finish on time.

Why do I let myself get talked into these things?

Because you need the money, a small, familiar voice answered.

True enough. Sometimes she felt like a hamster in a cage, racing endlessly on its wheel but never making any progress. There was the housecleaning, errand jobs, cooking for private clients, baking for restaurants. If someone offered her work, she couldn't afford to refuse. She took the job first and figured out how and when she would do it later. She worked hard to support her girls, though ironically, she knew they sometimes felt neglected. As if she didn't give them enough of her time and attention.

Well, maybe I don't, she admitted. If her ex-husband, Phil, would just grow up and help support his children in some consistent fashion, maybe she'd have some extra time to spend with them.

She hoped when they were older they'd understand. She thought she was doing a good job so far raising them. Hopefully, she'd send them to college someday. That was her real goal.

So they won't end up like me, racing from job to job, just to make ends meet, constantly juggling work and their needs, not to mention the often complicated child-care arrangements.

Her parents helped a lot, watching the girls while she worked. But Molly came from a large family, and her five other siblings needed help at times as well. Her parents were in Florida now with her younger sister Laurie who had recently given birth to twins. Her mother had called with a full progress report the other night, adding that she and Molly's dad planned to stay a few more weeks. Even though the babies and her sister were doing well, two infants at once were quite an adjustment. Molly remembered making some appropriately cheerful reply. She couldn't blame her parents for spending more time with their new grandchildren. And who wouldn't want to escape the New England winter? Though it was the last week of February, the cold and snow hadn't let up one bit. It felt positively endless. Still, Molly was unhappy to hear she'd have to get by without her mother for a few weeks longer than expected.

Her older brother Sam had always pitched in with the girls and still did, even though he had married a few months ago. Sam's wife, Jessica, had the girls now. Molly knew Jessica wouldn't mind if they stayed until she finished here. But Molly had promised her daughters pizza and a movie at the mall, and she didn't want to disappoint them.

I'll work until five, then come back real early tomorrow and finish up, she decided. *That should give me plenty of time to be in and out before the tenant arrives.* Fran Tulley, the real estate agent who'd handled the rental, had mentioned that the tenant wasn't due until noon.

Dr. Harding's arrival had been a hot topic around town. The village had been without a general practitioner since Dr. Elliot had retired last spring, almost a year ago now. Molly had heard Dr. Harding was a widower and a friend of Ezra Elliot's, and she pictured the new practitioner cut from the same mold, an elderly Yankee with a dry wit and a pragmatic manner.

She had never been a huge fan of Dr. Elliot, not like some in Cape Light. He was kind enough, in his way. But something about him had always intimidated her. He moved in a different circle, with the Warwicks and the rest of them, the kind of families in the grand old Victorians who might hire her to cook or clean but rarely acted as if she were their equal.

The window molding was coated with dust. She would need the brush attachment to get at that. The windowpanes needed to be sprayed and wiped down, too. Molly shut off the vacuum and looked for her spray bottle. Now the radio volume seemed deafening, and she rushed over just as the song was ending.

"*. . . Our love's down the drain. Ain't it a shame? You call to complain. . . .*"

Molly clicked off the radio, relieved at the sudden silence. "Give me a break. I'd complain, too, if I had to listen to you all the time."

"Me, too," a deep voice agreed.

Molly spun around to face the doorway. A man stood there, staring at her. Her heart jumped in her chest, and she took a sudden step backward. She had taken a self-defense course once, and her mind raced to remember the helpful tips. Don't scream? Or was it, scream your head off?

Hey, pal, I have a vacuum cleaner attachment here, and I'm not afraid to use it!

"I'm sorry. . . . I didn't mean to startle you," the intruder said gently.

"That's okay. I'm fine." *Good move. A stranger just broke into the house, and I apologize to him.*

"I called up the stairs to you, but I guess you didn't hear me."

"Apparently not," she agreed.

He had nice eyes, dark brown, and thick brown hair with a few silver-gray strands blended in, though he didn't look much older than she was.

Why was she even noticing this?

"I'm just bringing in some boxes. I know it's the country out here, but you shouldn't leave the doors unlocked."

"I thought I locked it," Molly replied.

Okay, he's a deliveryman. Or at least, that's what he says. Jeans. Work boots. A sweatshirt and a down vest. That's what they wear, right?

He wasn't exactly brawny, she noticed, but he did look fit.

He smiled again, then stepped back, raising both hands in a gesture of surrender.

"I'll back out slowly now, if you promise to lay down your weapon."

Molly didn't understand him at first, then realized she'd

been brandishing the vacuum attachment in a menacing fashion.

"Oh, sorry." She slowly let it slip down to her side but didn't let go altogether. She glanced at him again, still feeling uneasy at the way he was looking at her.

"Are you finished down there, yet?" she asked.

"Hardly. But don't worry. I can handle it."

She suddenly got it. Since the doctor was older, he probably needed help with items he didn't trust to the movers, which explained this guy. Well, that wasn't her problem. She already had enough on her plate cleaning up the place.

"I wasn't offering to help. I have plenty left up here to do, and it's almost five."

He looked surprised at her answer, then showed a neutral expression. "Sure, I understand. But maybe you can keep the music down a few decibels?"

"No problem," Molly returned, echoing his tone. "Would you mind wiping your feet as you go in and out? I just finished down there. I don't want to do it all over again."

He gave her a surprised look again, then nodded. "The place looks great. I'll be careful to keep it that way."

"I hope you're through soon. I need to lock up before I go." Molly turned and sprayed cleaner on the window. "The tenant won't be here until tomorrow, and I'm responsible for the place until then."

"The tenant?"

"Dr. Harding, from Worcester. Those are his boxes you're delivering, aren't they?"

He paused a moment, his expressive features warming with a slow smile of understanding.

"I *am* Dr. Harding."

Molly opened her mouth to reply, then abruptly shut it. Then she said, "Oh, I thought you were a deliveryman. Actually I didn't know who you were."

He looked as if he were about to laugh, but he was too

polite to embarrass her. She felt her cheeks grow warm and red. Then she felt like laughing at herself, too.

"One false move and I was going to brain you with the vacuum-cleaner pipe."

"I had a feeling that was your plan." He smiled again and then leaned forward to offer his hand. "Nice to meet you. I'm Matt Harding."

"Molly Willoughby." She met his gaze as they briefly shook hands, and she felt her knees get rubbery. She quickly looked away.

He's either really good looking, or I don't get out much, Molly thought, clearing her head.

"The real-estate agency hired me to clean the house for you," she said in a more professional tone.

"Right. They said they were sending someone over. You must have been working hard. It looks a lot better than when I was here last time."

"That's my job." She forced a smile. "I'm sorry for the mix-up. Someone told me you were a friend of Dr. Elliot. I guess I pictured you . . . differently."

He laughed. "Old and cranky, you mean?" When Molly didn't reply, he added, "I've known Dr. Elliot since I was a boy. He and my father are good friends."

"I get it." Molly nodded, feeling silly.

"I guess I'll go down and get the rest of the boxes."

"Sure. See you later." Molly looked away, suddenly engrossed in the contents of her cleaning bucket. But once she heard his footsteps disappear, she ran into the small bathroom that adjoined the bedroom and shut the door.

She stared at her reflection and gave a silent shriek. Her ponytail had exploded, and long, dark curls sprung out in all directions. A streak of oven grease marked her cheek and the tip of her nose. The mess trailed down her worn-out sweatshirt, which would not have been an entirely bad thing, Molly thought, if only the stains had blocked out the ridiculous saying printed across her chest: *Save a Chicken's Life. Eat a Lobster.*

Unfortunately, they did not.

For heaven's sake, he must think I'm a complete idiot, she thought mournfully. *And why did I wear these jeans today? They look terrible.* She surveyed her rear view and yanked the sweatshirt down over her hips, only to watch it immediately rise up again.

I've got to lose some weight. Get back in shape. I just never seem to have the time. . . .

A long dark curl flopped across her face, and she blew it away like a feather.

Oh, well. What's the point? He's a doctor, not a deliveryman. He isn't going to be interested in someone like me.

Molly wearily pulled out her hair clip and quickly combed out her hair with her fingertips, then rinsed the grime off her face and patted it dry with some tissues.

That will be enough primping for Dr. Harding, she decided.

The room had darkened with late afternoon shadows. She couldn't wait for spring to come. She was so tired of the short, dark winter days. Molly checked the time. A quarter past four. She considered staying longer, but her surprise meeting with the new tenant had thrown her off. She decided to ask if she could finish the rest of the work tomorrow and hoped he wouldn't mind.

As she came downstairs, she saw Matthew struggling through the front door with a stack of boxes. She ran down the last few steps and plucked a package from the top of the pile to help him.

"Oh, you don't have to do that." He set down his load and looked up at her.

"That's all right. It looked like it was about to slip. Is there anything else out there?"

"That's the last of it." Molly followed his glance to an impressive stack of boxes piled against one wall of the living room.

"The movers have the rest. There were some fragile things I didn't trust in the truck. Some medical instruments. And some family china that my daughter Amanda already has her eye on. I'd never hear the end of it if any of that turned up broken."

The tender note in his voice made her smile. "How old is she?"

"Fourteen . . . going on forty," he noted with a wry smile.

"I have one of those at home myself." He looked surprised, but Molly was used to that reaction. She had Lauren less than a year after graduating high school, and some people said she looked even younger than her age, which was now thirty-two. She kept talking, hoping he wouldn't make the usual comment. *Gee, you look too young to have a teenager. . . .*

"Lauren is my fourteen-year-old, and I have another who's eleven, Jill."

"Amanda is my one and only. I have it easy, I guess."

"Oh, I wouldn't say that. I think in some ways one is harder. With two, they have each other for company, so they go off on their own, and they're not always bugging you. And you have the older one to practice on, so you know what to do when the second one acts out."

He nodded. "A practice child. That's an interesting theory. I don't think I've ever heard that one before."

He seemed amused, and the way he kept gazing at her made her feel nervous again. She smiled, controlling the urge to tug on her sweatshirt.

"I guess I would have liked more kids myself," he admitted, "but life doesn't always turn out the way you plan."

"I know what you mean." She remembered he was a widower and guessed from his serious tone that his thoughts had suddenly turned to his loss. She glanced away, thinking of her own disappointments. "I hope coming to Cape Light works out for you. We're a little off the beaten track. But it's a nice place once you get used to it."

"Have you lived around here long?"

"All my life. That sounds horribly boring, doesn't it?"

"Not at all. I grew up in Worcester—which isn't nearly as scenic, I must say—and only left for medical school."

"But now you've come here."

"I have a sister in Newburyport, and I've always liked the area. Then word came through Ezra that he'd retired and the village needed a general practitioner, so here we are. It was time for a change, I guess." Matthew smiled but didn't say anything more.

Molly sensed that the decision to move had been hard for him, and he'd come with mixed emotions. She didn't know what to say. Then her phone emitted a long, shrill beep, saving her from having to make a reply.

"Excuse me. I think that's mine." She found her big black tote bag at the bottom of the staircase and dug out her cell phone.

Matthew turned his attention to the boxes on the other side of the room, sorting them into two piles.

"Molly! Thank heavens I caught you! I'm in a total panic. I had a closing today that was absolutely endless and now everyone will be here in two hours and I haven't even set the table or taken a shower and the mousse is a disaster—"

"Calm down, Betty. It's going to be all right," Molly said, soothing her.

It was her friend Betty Bowman, the town's leading real-estate broker and foremost female entrepreneur. Molly admired her tremendously, but Betty was easily the most domestically challenged person Molly had ever met. Their friendship had grown primarily from their common ground as single mothers and from episodes of Betty begging Molly to rescue her from some cooking or entertaining catastrophe.

Betty had a dinner party planned for that night for just four people, including herself. But that was more than enough to throw Betty, even though Molly had already cooked most of the meal and Betty was buying the rest prepared. All Betty had to do was fix the dessert, chocolate mousse. Betty was set on making that herself to impress her new suitor, Richard Corwin, since she knew it was his favorite.

"I followed your instructions exactly, but it looks like, well, like brown clay. I can move the spoon through it. That can't be right."

"Um, no. You shouldn't be able to stir it." Molly tried not to laugh.

"Could you run over for a minute and take a look? I don't even have time to run up to the bakery. . . ."

"Sure. Just for a minute. I'll be right over." Molly said good-bye and glanced over at Matthew.

"Something wrong at home?" he asked politely.

"No, thank goodness." Molly shook her head and smiled. "But I do need to run, if it's okay with you. A friend of mine is having a little crisis with some chocolate mousse—"

"—And you have to make a house call?" he finished.

"Something like that."

"You must be a great cook. I mean to get emergency calls on your cell phone."

Molly felt a warm flush creep into her cheeks again.

"I have my moments," she said lightly. His smile encouraged her, and she continued, suddenly wanting him to know she wasn't just a housecleaner. "I actually have a cooking business. Well, sort of a business. I'm just starting out really. But I bake for some restaurants in town and for private parties. Things like that . . ." Her voice trailed off quietly.

It didn't sound like much, she thought. Not very impressive compared to, say, saving someone's life.

Still, he nodded at her thoughtfully. "Sounds like you keep yourself busy."

Was he really impressed or just trying to be nice, she wondered.

"Your husband is a lucky guy, being married to a professional chef," he added in a teasing voice.

"He *was* a lucky guy . . . until I divorced him." She laughed at her quick reply but also heard the subtle note of anger there. "It was a long time ago," Molly added with a shrug.

She started to pull on her jacket and felt Matthew politely helping her. He met her gaze for a long moment, then stepped back. The room was dark enough now that she could barely read his expression.

She pulled out her bright blue wool gloves and matching hat and tugged them on.

"I'd better get going. I'll come back early tomorrow and finish up. You won't even know I've been here."

"Don't rush. Come whenever you like. Why don't you bring your girls? I know Amanda would love to meet Lauren. Then she'll have a familiar face in school on Monday."

Molly appreciated his offer. Most clients didn't welcome her children, and she hadn't quite figured out what she'd do with them tomorrow. Lauren sometimes watched Jill on her own, but it wasn't Molly's ideal arrangement, especially on a Saturday.

"Okay, I will, if you really don't mind," she said brightly as she pulled open the front door. "Thanks for the offer."

"Not at all. I'm looking forward to meeting them. See you tomorrow, then."

"See you." Molly smiled and walked quickly down the path to her car. He stood in the doorway and watched as she got into her aged hatchback. As she pulled away from the curb, she saw him wave and she waved back.

He was a nice man. An attractive man. Easy to talk to, she thought. Not at all what she'd expected. They seemed to have something in common, too, once they'd started talking about raising teenage girls.

And attractive, she noted again. *No doubt about that. I wonder when his wife died? Fran said a few years ago. I wonder why he's still single? He must have somebody,* she decided. *But if he does, why did he move here all the way from Worcester? Maybe he* is *unattached.*

But it could never work. He's a doctor and I'm just a jill-of-all-trades, master of none.

Don't even give it another thought, Molly, a sour little voice advised her. *He's out of your league.*

Ten minutes later Molly pulled up to Betty's house and parked in the driveway. Betty had a lovely home, a classic Federal-style Colonial on one of the best streets in town. Originally built for a ship's captain in the early 1800s, it was now a registered historic site. Molly secretly dreamed that one day she, too, might own a house like this. It wasn't just that the house was beautiful and spacious. More than that, it was a symbol to her of Betty's independence and success, the essence of what Molly aspired to.

Betty greeted Molly at the door dressed in a pale blue silk bathrobe with hot rollers sprouting from her short blond hair.

"I followed your directions exactly," Betty declared as she led Molly into the kitchen. "Maybe the chocolate was stale or something."

Molly peered into the makeshift double boiler and prodded the brown, sticky mass. "Looks like water from the boiler got into the chocolate. We have to toss it."

"Oh, drat. Is there time to make more?"

"We'll manage. I stopped at the store just in case." Molly opened the shopping bag and took out a box of chocolate, then found a clean pot.

"You're a pal, Molly. I owe you one." Betty stood at the counter and watched as Molly started cooking. "What can I do to help?"

"Just stand over there." Molly pointed to the far side of the room. "I don't want you anywhere near this stuff until it's time to eat it."

"Oh, you're mean." Betty laughed, shaking loose a roller. "Where were you when I called before?"

"At a cleaning job. Fran Tulley's rental on Hawthorne Street."

"Oh, right. The new doctor. Fran said he's quite good looking. And single," Betty said.

Molly slowly stirred the melting blocks of chocolate,

vigilantly searching for lumps. "He's not bad," she finally offered.

"You saw him? He's not due to move in until tomorrow."

"He stopped by the house to drop off some boxes. I didn't know who he was. I almost hit him on the head with a vacuum-cleaner pipe."

Betty sighed. "Sounds about right. Go on."

Molly shrugged. "There's not much to tell. He sounded a little sorry to be moving but said he needed a change. He has a sister in Newburyport and a daughter who's fourteen."

"Same age as Lauren," Betty pointed out.

"Yes, we covered that." With a deft twist of her wrist, Molly cracked an egg, separating the white from the yolk with one hand, then picked up another and cracked it.

Betty looked on in fascination. "I just love the way you do that thing with the egg."

"It's not hard. I'll teach you sometime."

"Deal, but let's get back to this doctor. He sounds like a possibility to me."

A *romantic* possibility, Betty meant. Betty had somehow deemed herself Molly's relationship coach, determined to find Molly a man despite her complaints of not having time to date. Molly always gave her a hard time when she slipped into this mode, but she had to admit, Betty often had some good advice.

Concerning Matthew Harding, Molly thought it best to shut Betty down from the start.

"He's not my type. Honestly." She beat the egg yolks with a fork and added a dash of vanilla.

"He sounds like anybody's type to me." Betty gave her a puzzled look. "What's going on with that guy Micky, your brother Sam's friend? Still seeing him?"

"No, thank goodness." Molly rolled her eyes. "He's nice enough, I guess. But he's just so dull. All he ever wanted to do was call out for pizza and watch sports on TV. One night he lost the remote, and I had to dial nine-one-one."

Betty started laughing. "He did not. You're making that up."

"How could I make up something like that? It was the end of the Super Bowl and the channel switched somehow, and he couldn't find the remote. He got so upset, he started getting dizzy and short of breath. I thought he was having a heart attack. The fireman said it was just a mild panic disorder."

Betty could hardly stop laughing. "I can see why that didn't work out."

Molly carefully poured the yellow ribbon of egg yolk into the melted chocolate and beat the mixture together with a wire whisk. "I'm glad you agree. My brother Sam thinks we were a perfect match. He claims I'm too picky."

It stung that Sam didn't think she could do any better than boring old Micky. But she didn't confide that part to Betty.

"You're the one who has to decide if it's right or not." Betty patted her shoulder. "It takes courage to drop a nice but boring guy. It's like clearing out your closet and giving all the dull, old clothes to charity. Now you've made room for something new and exciting."

Molly glanced at her and smiled. "Does that mean if I clean out my closet, I'll get a new wardrobe *and* a new boyfriend?"

"You never know." Betty stuck her finger in the satiny chocolate pudding, then popped it into her mouth. "Mmmm. That's scrumptious."

"I think you can take it from here." As Molly untied her apron, she reviewed the last steps of the recipe with Betty, who looked alarmed to be sent on alone.

"You can do it," Molly promised her. "Besides, you want to tell Richard you made it. You wouldn't want to fib about that."

"Me? I'd never do that. What a thing to say."

Betty grinned at her. Before they had become such good friends, Betty had often taken credit for Molly's cooking with dinner guests. They were close enough now to laugh about it.

"Who else is coming over?"

"Just Emily and Dan. Things are moving along for those two. I have a feeling they may have a big announcement soon. Emily doesn't say much, but I think they're going to get married."

"Wow! I didn't realize it was so serious. How nice."

Molly felt odd, even a little shocked, though she didn't know why the news should matter. She knew Dan by sight and Emily only slightly better. Dan had run the local newspaper most of his life and recently handed it down to his daughter. Emily Warwick was the town's mayor, and she was now related to Molly by marriage, as the older sister of Sam's wife, Jessica.

If there was ever a woman who seemed content with a solitary life, it had to be Emily. But now she was in love and might soon be married. Molly felt happy for her . . . and for some strange reason, sad for herself.

She picked up her bag and hitched it over her shoulder. "Got to run, Betty. Don't worry. The party will turn out fine."

"Oh, I hope so." Betty nervously plucked a few rollers from her hair and stuck them in her bathrobe pocket. "Thanks again, Molly. I owe you one."

"I'll collect." Molly was sure it wouldn't be long before she was asking Betty for some advice or favor. It was good to know she had a friend like Betty.

Molly left Betty's house in the village and quickly found her way through the side streets to the Beach Road. Driving beyond the town, she raced along to the turn that marked Sam and Jessica's house, which was hidden, even in winter, by trees and brush.

Molly had known Jessica Warwick since high school. She had always thought Jessica was Little Miss Perfect and a snob, just like her mother, Lillian, who had acted like a queen in exile since the Warwick family fortune was lost years ago. Jessica had gone away to college and then taken a banking job in Boston. But after Lillian had a stroke, Jessica moved back to town temporarily to help care for her mother. When Sam started seeing her, Molly was sure that Jessica was just using him for a summer fling. Even after the two became serious, Molly urged Sam to break off the engagement.

Okay, so she could be a little stubborn and narrow-minded at times. She'd be the first to admit it. But now that they were married, Molly had to confess Jessica was not exactly what she expected.

Despite her privileged upbringing, Jessica was happily married and content to live in this remote spot in a lovely old house that seemed a never-ending renovation project for her carpenter husband. Jessica also showed a real interest and affection for Lauren and Jill. Her hours at the bank made it easy for her to watch her nieces after school, and Molly had come to depend on her help, which was also a surprise.

As Molly walked up the path, the front door swung open. Jessica greeted her, wearing an apron over her office clothes, a satin blouse, slim-fitting skirt, and heels. An appetizing cooking smell drifted in from the kitchen.

"Lauren and Jill are upstairs getting their things together. Sam isn't home yet, though. Want to come in and wait for him?"

Molly was relieved to hear she'd miss her brother. She had escaped defending her decision to dump his friend Micky. This time, at least.

"Thanks but we'd better get going. I promised the girls a movie at the mall tonight, and I want to make the early show."

"Yes, I heard all about it. They can't wait." Jessica turned and called up the stairs. "Girls, your mom is here."

"Lauren, Jill, I'm waiting," Molly added in her "Commander Mom" tone. "Thanks again for minding them. I was in a pinch today."

"No problem. I love having them." Jessica smiled, and Molly felt her words were sincere.

As if on cue, Lauren and Jill galloped down the stairs, carrying their jackets and knapsacks. Jill jumped off the steps, hurling herself at Molly in a flying hug.

Molly grunted in reply. "Thanks, honey. I needed that."

"Hi, Mom." Lauren came down the last few steps more sedately. Molly kissed her on the cheek. Lauren was too old now to act so uncool, Molly thought with a secret smile. She watched as they both showed good manners, thanking Jessica, and each gave their aunt a hug.

"Sam will be sorry he missed you. But we'll see you on Sunday, right?"

Molly had almost forgotten. Jessica and Sam were taking the girls ice skating so she could work. Looked like she would have to face complaints about Micky and more advice about her life then.

"That's right." Molly nodded. "Well, thanks again. Tell Sam I'll call him."

"Bye, girls, see you soon." Jessica watched them from the doorway and waved as they all walked to the car.

VISITING HOURS HAD OFFICIALLY ENDED LONG AGO. THE hospital rooms were dark and the corridor nearly empty. Reverend Ben Lewis stood beside Gus Potter's bed. Gus gripped Ben's hand, his head resting on a pile of pillows. His skin was as pale as the white pillowcase, and it appeared almost translucent.

His blue eyes were bright, though, and his grip still surprisingly strong. He looked far happier than a man in his condition ought to, Ben thought. Far calmer, too, though he must realize what's happening to him. His wife, Sophie, knew only too well, and Ben could see her struggling to keep up a brave front.

"Thanks for coming, Reverend," she said. "You didn't have to trouble yourself. You'd better get home. Carolyn must be wondering what's keeping you."

"Carolyn is used to my late hours by now."

"How is she feeling?" Sophie asked with interest. "Is she still in therapy?"

A few weeks after Christmas, Carolyn had suffered a stroke and gone into a coma. That was over two months ago now, Ben calculated. He had nearly lost her. But she'd finally woken with few ill effects and was coming along with the help of medication and physical therapy.

"She's doing very well," Ben reported. "She still has some weakness in her left arm, though, and can't play the piano yet. But she wants to get back to her students soon. Maybe at the end of next month."

"Glad to hear it," Gus said. "Tell her we were asking for her."

"Yes, I will. Maybe she'll come with me next time I visit. I guess you'll be home again by then."

"The doctor said I can take him home in a few more days. Monday or Tuesday," Sophie said brightly.

She met Ben's gaze a moment, then rested her hand on her husband's shoulder. An array of tubes and monitors was attached to Gus's body, and Ben averted his gaze from the tangled paraphernalia.

"These doctors don't know anything." Gus waved his hand weakly. "Listen to them, and you'd be working on my eulogy right now, Reverend." Ben forced a smile at Gus's quip but swallowed hard. He knew he'd face that task soon enough.

"I'll spring right back. Always do. This is just another false alarm. I'd get up out of this bed and walk home right now if they'd let me."

"He must feel better. He's getting rambunctious," Sophie said with false cheer.

"Yes, very," Ben agreed wistfully.

They all knew the truth. The prognosis was grim. Gus's great and generous heart was finally giving out, his other vital organs rapidly failing. All the doctors in the world couldn't do much more for him. Sophie and Gus had decided that he would spend his last days at home on the orchard, in his own bed, rather than in a sterile hospital room.

Ben gave Gus's hand a final pat. "Bless you, Gus. I'll keep you in my prayers."

"Thanks, Reverend," Gus said. Sophie's eyes misted over. She nodded and blew her nose on a tissue.

A nurse briskly entered the room and picked up Gus's chart from the end of the bed. "How are you doing tonight, Mr. Potter?"

"Just fine. And yourself?" Gus sounded genuinely interested in her reply, Ben noticed. As if he was in the middle of a church picnic instead of a critical-care unit. Some people were just born with a certain buoyant spirit that didn't desert them, no matter what. Sophie was the same. They were made for each other and had lived together happily for nearly fifty years. They had that to look back upon at the very least.

"I'm just going to walk the reverend to the elevator, dear," Sophie told her husband. Gus, who had a thermometer in his ear, nodded and waved good-bye.

Sophie walked beside Ben, lost in thought. Ben waited for her to speak first. At times like this it was imperative for him to hold his peace and listen. Offering comforting words was important, of course. But listening, that was paramount.

"He's had a good day," she said finally. "His spirits are up. Did you hear the way he was talking?" she asked, shaking her head. "But he knows. He just acts as if it's all going to be okay. Like he can lick this somehow. Of course, he won't this time."

She pressed a tissue to her eyes. "Once I get him home, well, it will be easier for everyone. He'll have his family around him, and he'll have the orchard."

"That will be a great comfort to him," Ben agreed.

"I'm going to spend every minute with him from here on in. Luckily the TV show people have given me a break until the spring. We taped a bunch of shows right after Christmas, and they told me they're set for a while." Sophie released a long breath and shook her head. "Lucky for me. I wouldn't have the heart right now to get up in front of a camera. I might not go back after Gus goes," she concluded.

Ben swallowed hard. Sophie was talking about the cooking show she did for a local cable station, *A Yankee in the Kitchen: New England Cooking and Crafts with Sophie Potter.* The producer had spotted her at a fair on the village green last fall and the show had been a great success so far. Ben was sorry to hear she might abandon it. It would be a distraction for her after Gus passed on, he thought.

"It's probably best not to make any decisions about that now," Ben said gently. "What about the coming days, when Gus gets home. Do you have enough help?"

"My daughter Evelyn's made all the arrangements for the visiting nurse and home-health aid," Sophie said, mentioning her oldest child who lived in the area. "She and Una are taking turns helping with the housework. My son, Bart, should be in from Boston for a quick visit this weekend, and his daughter, Miranda, is coming in from New York. It should be a full house on the weekends. I hardly know where everyone's going to sleep."

It sounded like the typical Potter family reunion. But this time the gathering was for the most serious reason of all. If Sophie's entire family was coming together to spend time with Gus, she clearly didn't expect him to last long. Ben felt a sharp pang in his heart, and he reached out to take Sophie's hand in both of his own.

His gaze met hers, and her eyes filled with tears. "You'll get through this, Sophie. One step at a time. You have your family and all your friends. You have me," he reminded her. "Most important, you have the Lord."

She nodded. "Yes, I know. I'm grateful for our time together. Our blessings. I just wish sometimes . . ." Her voice caught and she couldn't go on. "It might be wrong to say it, Reverend, but I'm older than Gus. I always thought I'd go ahead. I didn't imagine living on without him. I know it's wrong to second guess, but I wish the good Lord had taken me first."

Ben didn't answer immediately. "I felt the very same way when Carolyn was sick," he said finally.

When Carolyn had been in her coma, there were a few days when it seemed unlikely she would survive, and Ben had entered the chilling dark places where Sophie now wandered. But of course, not fully, since the Lord in his mercy had spared him that irrevocable blow, the loss of his life partner. Barring a miracle, Sophie would not be spared.

"I felt . . . afraid. The greatest fear I'd ever known," he admitted. She glanced at him, then looked down at her hands. He knew he had voiced her deepest feelings.

"Yes. I am afraid. Terrified." She nodded her head. "I haven't said that many times in my life. But this . . . this is different."

"Very different," Ben agreed.

"It's as if my whole world is being pulled out from under me like a rug." Her voice held a note of amazement mingled with sadness and fear.

Ben didn't know what to say. Her whole world *would* be torn away once Gus was gone. Once a widow, she'd probably be forced to give up the orchard.

But first things first. She would face that road when she came to it.

"When Carolyn was sick and I felt the most afraid, there was a certain Scripture that came to mind and helped me through it. 'Be strong and of a good courage, fear not . . . for the Lord thy God, he *it is* that doth go with thee; he will not fail thee, nor forsake thee.' "

"Yes, I remember." Sophie nodded thoughtfully. "Deuteronomy. That's what Moses said to the Israelites when he knew he was going to die soon, and they'd go on without him."

Ben nodded and squeezed her hand.

"He will not fail me," she quietly echoed. "I know that's

so. Thank you, Reverend. And thanks again for coming by tonight."

"No thanks necessary, Sophie. You know that." Ben hugged her briefly, then stepped back. "Don't hesitate to call me at any hour, night or day. Even if you just want someone to talk to."

Sophie nodded. A small smile appeared on her lovely moon-shaped face. "I'll be all right."

He prayed that she would be. The elevator bell sounded. He stepped inside and hit *L* for lobby. Sophie stood watching him, framed like an image in a photograph. Then the elevator doors closed, blocking her from view.

Ben felt a heavy sadness nearly overwhelm him. He wished there was more he could do, more he could say to bring some comfort to Sophie and Gus at this dark hour. And there was so little. He'd counseled many families losing a loved one and knew that only too well by now. But he always wished there were more.

He pushed open the heavy glass doors of the hospital entrance and hurried to his car, feeling the stinging of cold air on his skin and in his lungs. The temperature hovered somewhere around twenty, he guessed. This was the toughest stretch of the winter, especially in New England. The holiday cheer long gone and so much cold and darkness to get through before spring.

But spring would arrive, Ben thought as he began the long drive home. Gus Potter wouldn't see it, though, his body returned to the earth, his soul hopefully home in heaven, well before the world grew warm and green again.

"DO WE *HAVE* TO GO WITH YOU?" LAUREN WHINED.

"Yes, you do," Molly said curtly. Molly somehow managed to get the girls home by nine-thirty after their pizza and movie at the mall. Getting them in bed with the light shut off was another matter entirely.

"We won't be there long. I just need to finish the second

floor. And you'll get to be the first one to meet Amanda. She'll be new at school on Monday, but you can tell everyone you've already met her."

Lauren sat back against her pillows, her arms crossed over her chest. The cat, Jasper, jumped on the bed and climbed into Lauren's lap, but Lauren barely looked at her. "I really need to go to the library and start my science project."

"Don't worry, we'll start the science project. Did you pick a topic yet?"

Nothing too ambitious please, Molly silently wished.

"The effect of electromagnetic fields on mealworms. This kid did it last year. It's really cool."

"Yuck! That's gross." Jill made a gagging noise.

"Come on, cut that out. It's science, for goodness' sake. Now get in bed," Molly coaxed her.

Worms? She secretly agreed with Jill and hoped she didn't have to handle any of the subjects.

"We'll go straight to the library right after Dr. Harding's house. I promise." Molly picked up a stray sneaker and set it next to its partner, then bent over to kiss Lauren good night.

Lauren didn't seem persuaded, Molly thought, but she had given up arguing at least.

Once the light was out in the girls' room, Molly went into the living room to fold a basket of laundry. When she was done, she peeked in again. They had both fallen asleep, and the cat was curled up in a snuggly ball at the foot of Lauren's bed.

Molly pulled up Jill's covers, gave her another kiss as she slept, then did the same to Lauren. They did her heart good, these girls. She loved them so much, sometimes it actually hurt. When she watched them sleeping like this, she didn't question working so hard and going to the limit to give them a good upbringing. Her daughters were everything to her. Maybe making up for a lot that was missing right now, Molly reflected as she left the room. But what could she do? This was her life. She had to make the best of it.

In the kitchen, she filled a bowl with her favorite ice cream, chocolate chocolate chip, then carried her treat into her bedroom. She picked up a thick paperback and stretched out on the bed. The book was a predictable but satisfying mix of romance and suspense and the ice cream, a guilty pleasure. She knew she shouldn't have it after promising herself just this afternoon to start dieting. Especially right after eating pizza.

But she was so tired and felt she deserved some reward after such a long day. Besides, she didn't need to squeeze herself into any Saturday night date clothes this weekend, she reminded herself, thinking of boring Micky and of Betty's pep talk.

When you got right down to it, Molly decided, men may come and go, but a good romance novel and some premium ice cream never disappoint. With a smile and a satisfied nod, she turned the page and savored another cold, sweet spoonful.

THE DRIVE FROM SOUTHPORT HOSPITAL TO CAPE LIGHT took more or less an hour. Ben found little traffic on the highway and knew the ride would be faster than usual.

In the dark, humming silence he mentally worked on his sermon for Sunday's service. He often found he got some of his best inspirations driving late at night on empty roads. The trouble was remembering them. His theme for this Sunday was connection, the web of friendships and family ties that supports us throughout our lifetime. He considered using the parable of the Good Samaritan, then remembered he would have that Scripture reading the following Sunday when he was going to talk about compassion. He would find some other Scripture to illustrate this Sunday's theme. He had noted a few already on a pad in his office. He'd stop off at the church tonight and pick it up so he could finish the sermon at home tomorrow.

Once off the highway, he drove down the Beach Road and into the village. Main Street was deserted, the old-fashioned gaslights casting a glow in the frosty night air. He'd lived here over thirty years but still found his attention captured by the charm of the Victorian homes, vintage storefronts, and the harbor view ahead. It was a timeless place, yet somehow ever changing, reflecting the mood of each season or hour of day. You'd have a hard time finding a prettier place to live—although the picture-book setting gave no one here immunity to life's challenges and sorrows. That was for sure.

At the end of Main Street, the blue-black water of the harbor stretched to the opposite shoreline. By Memorial Day, the inlet would be so full of boats, one would barely be able to see the waves in between. But the harbor was nearly empty right now, except for a few hardy, unadorned vessels belonging to the fishermen who worked year round. Still in a partially frozen state, the occasional boat stranded out in the ice looked like an odd decoration on the top of a frosted cake.

Ben turned on Bayview Road, which ran along the village green. At the far side of the green Bible Community Church stood, silent and dark, the steeple cutting a sharp silhouette against the clear, starry sky. Ben pulled into the lot behind the church and parked at one of the rear doors.

He unlocked the door and headed down the long dark hallway, past Sunday school classrooms. There was no need to turn on lights; he could find his way blindfolded. But just as he reached his office, he heard a strange sound. A muffled moan, distinctly human. Ben stood stone-still, his body tense and alert. There it was again, coming from the all-purpose room.

He approached cautiously, stopping in the doorway to turn on a light. "Is anybody in here?" he called out.

No one answered, and he glanced around. Then he heard movement coming from the kitchen area, a small room in the corner with a pass-through window. He wondered for a moment if he should call the police. But what if someone was hurt and needed help? Precious time might be wasted.

Ben walked slowly toward the kitchen, not knowing what he would do if the intruder was aggressive or carrying a weapon. He wasn't scared, though, feeling sure that the Lord would protect him.

"Is there anyone here?" he asked again at the closed kitchen door. "I'm coming in now."

He slowly pushed the door open and then felt it obstructed. Wedging his upper body through the opening, Ben saw a man's body sprawled out on the floor. The man was curled on his side, his arms clutching his stomach, his body quaking with chills. A booted foot blocked the door, but Ben managed to squeeze inside.

The man was filthy, his pants torn and his dirty coat ragged. Ben couldn't see his face, only a mass of long greasy hair and a full beard.

Ben knelt beside him, holding his breath against the stench, and touched the man's shoulder. Whatever the stranger had found to eat in the kitchen cupboards hadn't stayed in his stomach for long.

"Can you hear me?" Ben asked.

There was no movement at first, then the man slowly turned his head. His dark eyes met Ben's. One shoulder lifted, as if the man were trying to get up, but he crumpled back to the floor at once.

"Steady, my friend. It's okay." Ben touched the man's shoulder with his hand. "Don't be afraid. I'm going to get help."

Ben rose and removed his overcoat, then placed it over the stranger. He gently rested his open hand on the man's brow. "Don't try to move. I'll be right back."

The intruder stared up at him a moment, then closed his eyes. His chest rose and fell in a labored effort to breathe.

Ben ran to the phone in the far corner of the all-purpose room, dialed 911, and asked for an ambulance. After checking on the stranger, Ben went outside to wait for the ambulance. Though he was wearing only a shirt and wool vest, he was unmindful of the cold. He stared up at the cross on top of the church steeple, starkly outlined against the blue-black sky, then bowed his head in prayer.

Dear Lord, please help this stranger. Please let him get medical treatment in time.

The ambulance arrived a few minutes later, and the EMS workers followed Ben inside.

"He's back here. I'm not sure if he's fully conscious. He's having trouble breathing." Ben led them to the little kitchen and then stood to one side while they examined the stranger.

A few moments later, one of the workers opened a portable stretcher while the other spoke to Ben. "Hard to say what's going on. He definitely needs care. We're going to take him to Southport. I can't find any identification. When I asked him his name, I think he said, 'Carl Jones.' Are you sure you don't recognize him, Reverend?"

Ben shook his head. "I don't believe so."

He leaned over and took another long look. The room was fully lit now, and the man lay flat on his back. Ben stared at the stranger's face, just about to repeat that he'd never seen him. Then Carl Jones opened his eyes and looked up at Ben. His dark eyes were filled with anger and fear, like a wounded animal, angry at his captors and at himself for being too weak to get away and fearful of what would come.

Something clicked in Ben's mind. He knew this man. Or did long ago. Just about everyone in town would remember him.

But no one would ever imagine he'd dare to return.

CHAPTER TWO

TUCKER TULLEY GAZED OUT THE KITCHEN WINDOW, his thoughts wandering as he waited for the coffee to brew. An icy glaze, glistening in the early light, coated the shed and bench near the birdbath. Just enough ice to be a nuisance on the road this morning, Tucker gauged. He'd be called out for some fender bender before that stuff melted down. As a senior police officer, he didn't often pull Saturday duty. But ranks were thin because of a flu bug traveling around, and every officer left standing was pitching in.

He poured himself a mug of coffee and turned to the window again. A bank of blue-gray clouds fringed the eastern sky, a pale orange light barely visible where they parted. A few birds swooped down from the bare branches and flapped around the feeder. It was a dull winter morning, and he envied anyone still snug in his bed, like his wife and two children upstairs.

The phone's shrill ring broke the stillness. Tucker turned quickly to pick it up before it woke anyone.

"I'm sorry to call so early, Tucker," Reverend Ben said.

"But something important came up. I thought you should know about it right away."

"That's all right, Reverend. What is it? Are you okay?"

"It's not about me. I'm fine. Last night I found an intruder in the church. A vagrant, I guess you'd have to call him. He broke in and collapsed in the pantry. He was very sick. I called an ambulance, and it took him to the hospital in Southport."

"That's too bad. Would you like me to stop by so you can file a report?"

"I'm not going to report it. That's not why I'm calling you." The reverend paused. His silence made Tucker nervous. He sensed bad news on the way but couldn't imagine what it was.

"The man gave his name as Carl Jones. I didn't recognize him at first," Reverend Ben said. "Then later, I realized . . . well, I'm pretty sure he's your half brother, Carl."

Tucker blinked and took a deep breath. He felt as if someone had just slugged him in the stomach. "That's impossible. I mean, how could it be? Even if he's still alive, why would he ever come back here?"

"I asked myself the same question. I don't know why he'd come back here." The reverend's reply made Tucker feel relieved for a moment. "But I feel fairly certain he has. He's in terrible shape, too. I went to the hospital to make sure he was admitted. I'm going to call later this morning and find out how he's doing."

Tucker hesitated. Did the reverend expect him to drop everything and run down to Southport?

"I'm on duty today. I'll look into it, though, Reverend. . . . Maybe tonight, when I get off."

"All right, Tucker. I thought you should know."

The reverend's tone was mild, but Tucker felt the heavy burden of his unspoken assumptions. He knew the reverend expected him to visit this homeless man and find out for sure if it was his half brother. That was the right thing to do, the Christian thing to do. But if it *was* Carl . . . what then?

"Thanks for the call," Tucker added half-heartedly.

"That's all right. See you tomorrow." Reverend Ben said good-bye and hung up.

Tucker rubbed his forehead and took a deep breath. He felt a dull ache deep in the center of his head, the start of one of his tension headaches. Just what he needed today. He found a bottle of pain relievers and shook two tablets out into his hand.

Why in heaven's name would Carl come back here? It didn't make sense. It couldn't be Carl. *There's no reason to get so worked up,* Tucker told himself as he swallowed the medicine. *The reverend is mistaken. This is all a false alarm.*

Tucker hadn't spoken to his brother now in what—over twenty years? The last time he'd seen Carl was through a bullet-proof slice of Plexiglas in the visitors' room of the state penitentiary where Carl was serving fifteen years for manslaughter.

Once a month on visiting day Tucker would take the long drive across the state to see him. But Carl didn't want his visits or his letters. Tucker would show up, and Carl would meet him with cold indifference or acid bitterness. For a while Tucker kept going, out of pity or guilt maybe. It certainly wasn't out of love. The younger brother's hero worship he'd once felt for Carl had long since vanished.

"Forget about me," Carl had ordered him. "Don't come here anymore. I won't come out to see you, understand?"

Finally, Tucker gave up. But he'd never quite forgotten about Carl, the image of his renegade half brother always lingering on the edges of his memory.

Now he heard Fran's slippers scuffing across the floor, and he turned to see her standing in the kitchen doorway. She blinked sleepily at him, then walked over and kissed his cheek.

"Who was that on the phone, hon?"

"Reverend Ben." Tucker watched her pour a cup of coffee. She took a seat at the table and looked up at him.

"Is there a problem at the church?"

Tucker wondered for a moment if he should even tell Fran what the reverend had said. She'd get excited and worried, maybe over nothing. But finally he decided he had to tell her. Married couples shouldn't keep secrets from each other. It wasn't right.

"The reverend found a homeless man in the back of the church last night and checked him into the hospital. The man said his name was Carl Jones, but Reverend Ben thinks he recognized him. He thinks it's my half brother."

"Your half brother?" She set her coffee mug down on the table and shook her head. "That's impossible. The way he drank and carried on, I doubt he's still alive. Even if he is, why would he ever come back here?"

Fran's frank appraisal took him aback. But she was probably right. Of course, it wasn't Carl. "That's what I told the reverend. He thinks I should check though. Just to be sure."

"Oh, dear. I'm not so sure that's a good thing to do."

Tucker heard the note of worry in his wife's voice and realized that he didn't entirely disagree with her.

"Did this homeless man ask for you?" Fran peered at him over the edge of her cup.

"No. I just told you, he gave his last name as Jones."

"That should tell you something." Fran shrugged and took a sip of coffee. When Tucker didn't reply, she added, "I just mean, if he wanted to see you, wouldn't he give his real name? Maybe he's ashamed to get in touch. He doesn't want you to see what he's turned into. It might be kinder not to bother him."

"Maybe," Tucker said. "But I can picture Carl giving a fake name for any number of reasons. Maybe he felt guilty about breaking into the church. Maybe he came to town intending to get in touch but feels awkward after all this time. Maybe . . . maybe anything."

Fran took a deep breath and hooked a wayward strand of brown hair around her ear. When she spoke again, her tone was softer. "I'm sure whatever the reverend said made you feel responsible, honey. Of course you feel bad, thinking it might be Carl. Anybody would. But it's probably just some stranger. Nobody's seen Carl in years. How would Reverend Ben even recognize him?"

Tucker considered her words. "I don't know. He didn't say."

"Well, all I'm trying to say is that I don't see any point in stirring things up. I really think you ought to leave well enough alone."

Tucker sat down at the table across from her and sighed. Stirring things up was one thing Fran didn't like. He knew that by now. She was a wonderful wife and a loving mother. But she liked her world orderly, predictable. It didn't take much to get her worried or even frightened. That cautious side was what attracted him to her when they were younger. When she'd get this way, he'd find himself filled with an urge to soothe and protect her.

But by now Tucker knew her anxious nature sometimes made it hard for Fran to see things clearly. A person needed to put her fears aside and get some distance to sort out a tricky situation like this one, he thought.

"I don't know what I'm going to do," he told her honestly. "But it's not so simple. I'm not exactly overjoyed either to hear Carl might be back. But I don't know if I can just ignore it."

Fran sighed. She met Tucker's gaze and then rose from the table. She took a carton of eggs and the butter dish out of the refrigerator and placed them purposefully on the countertop. "Do you want some breakfast?"

"No thanks. I'd better get going. I'll grab something later at the diner. So what are you up to today?" He got to his feet and picked up his jacket from the back of the chair.

"Michael has basketball practice, and Mary Ellen has a party at the skating rink. I'll drop them off and run into the office for a while, then check on the rental on Hawthorne Street. That new doctor I told you about is moving in today."

"Oh, right. Don't forget his welcome basket and coupon book." Fran had gone back to work a little over a year ago at Bowman Realty. Tucker was proud of her, though he still had the urge to tease her about it from time to time.

"Don't be silly." She placed a frying pan on the stove and lit the burner. "Will you be home for dinner?"

"I'm not sure. I'll call you later." Tucker thought of the homeless man in the hospital again. If he didn't go to see him, what would he say to Reverend Ben tomorrow?

Tucker slipped on his jacket, buttoned up the front, then straightened his silver shield. He was a law officer, a father, a husband, a deacon in the church while his brother was an ex-convict and probably a homeless vagrant.

And there, but for the grace of God, go I, Tucker thought sadly. Life was strange. He knew the Lord had a plan for every one, but sometimes it just didn't seem fair the way things worked out for some people and not for others.

MOLLY ARRIVED AT DR. HARDING'S HOUSE BY NINE, cleaning supplies, vacuum, daughters, and all. While the girls worked on their homework downstairs, she worked on the second floor. The entire house was clean and ready by noon as she'd planned. Then she quickly made some repairs on her own appearance, changing into a blue velour top that was too good to wear for cleaning but didn't look that obvious, she hoped. She dabbed on some lip gloss and eyeliner, then combed out her long curly hair and pulled it back from her face with a thin tortoiseshell band.

Not bad, she thought, checking herself out in the mirror. She pulled the long top down in the back, wishing she hadn't indulged in that ice cream last night. She hoped the girls wouldn't embarrass her by shouting out something like, "Hey, Mom, why did you change your top and put on all that makeup?"

Why did I? Molly wondered. *Maybe just to feel more at ease around this guy, since I looked so awful yesterday,* she told herself.

Yeah, right. Tell me another one.

She heard someone pull into the driveway, and she walked to the window. It was the moving van, followed by Matthew's SUV. Molly felt her stomach do a flip, and she took a deep breath. *Get a grip, Molly. You're just the cleaning lady, remember? Say hello, help the man a little with his moving day and be on your way.*

MATTHEW PARKED HIS LAND ROVER IN FRONT OF THE house to leave the movers room to unload. He turned to Amanda and forced a smile. "Here we are, honey. We made it."

Amanda pursed her lips and fumbled with her seat belt without answering him. She didn't even look up at the house, he noticed. She'd already seen it once, about a month ago. But that was before it had been painted and cleaned up.

"It's a nice house, don't you think?" Matthew looked up at their new house, an ordinary but neat Dutch Colonial, newly painted in pale yellow with black shutters and white trim. "I mean, it's fine for now. Until we find something permanent."

"It's n-nice, Dad. It's fine." He could hear her speech faltering, a definite sign that she was nervous. Years of speech therapy had nearly rid her of a frustrating stammer. But whenever she was stressed, it cropped up again. A hard way to start off in a new school, he thought sympathetically.

"I w-wish Aunt Erica had come," Amanda said.

"I know. I do, too. But they needed her at the library. She couldn't get the day off."

Amanda sighed and leaned toward the backseat to get her backpack. He got out, opened the gate, and unloaded their suitcases. When he looked up at the house again, he saw Molly Willoughby on the porch, flanked by two girls, both with beautiful long dark hair, just like their mother's.

She smiled down at him and waved. "Welcome home," she called out. "You made it."

He smiled back, feeling instantly brighter. He'd almost forgotten she'd be here. And forgotten how pretty she was. Especially when she smiled like that. He was glad he'd asked her to come.

"Who's that?" Amanda turned to him, looking puzzled and even more nervous.

"That's Molly Willoughby, the woman who cleaned the house for us. She has a girl your age, and I thought you two should meet. It will be good to have at least one familiar face at school on Monday, don't you think?"

"I guess so," Amanda said doubtfully. She hoisted her knapsack to her shoulder and picked up a small duffel bag.

Matt thought Molly and her daughters were just what he and Amanda needed today, the perfect distraction from their moving-day blues.

Matt reached the porch with his bags and put them down near the door. "Well, here we are," he announced. "Amanda, this is Molly, and these lovely young ladies must be her daughters." He met the gaze of the older girl who looked determined not to blush at his gallantry.

"You must be Lauren." She nodded, and he turned to the smaller one. "And you're Jill."

"Wow, you're good," Molly said. She turned to Amanda and held out her hand. "Nice to meet you, Amanda. I hope you like Cape Light. It might seem tame compared to Worcester, but there's a lot going on at school. Lauren is going to electrify some poor defenseless worms for the science fair."

"Mom!" Lauren gave her mother an adolescent gasp of humiliation.

"Well, you are, aren't you? What did I say?" She glanced at Matt, who was struggling not to laugh, then turned to her daughter again. "Why don't you guys find some place to talk and you can tell Amanda about school and all."

"Okay." Lauren shrugged. She didn't look that excited

by the idea, Matthew thought, and he felt himself tense, worried about Amanda. He knew he tended to worry about her too much, especially since his wife had died. But this was one of those days when he couldn't help it.

Then he noticed Amanda's expression brighten. "I like your hair weave. It's cool," she said, complimenting the bright threaded braid in Lauren's long hair.

"Thanks. They do them at the mall. There's this booth."

"I know. We had one in Worcester. But my dad won't let me do it," Amanda said, casting an exasperated look at Matt.

"Don't worry. I'll work on him for you," Molly promised. "I want to get one myself. I'm saving up my allowance."

The girls laughed, and Lauren rolled her eyes. "My mom is a little weird sometimes. Don't give her too much attention. It only makes it worse."

Amanda met Lauren's knowing grin. Matt noticed how the girls' smiles mirrored each other with glittering mouths full of braces.

"Which is going to be your room?" Matt heard Lauren ask as they walked into the house.

"The one in the front. Come on, I'll show you." Amanda started up the steps and Lauren followed.

"Wait, I brought my CD player. I'll bring it up." Lauren raced back down the stairs and soon returned with her own knapsack. She ran around the adults and Jill like a light-stepping doe and bounded up the staircase again.

"Can I go?" Jill quietly asked Molly.

"Sure, go ahead, honey. I'll tell Lauren it's okay." Jill ran after the older girls, and Molly called up the stairway, "Lauren, your sister is coming. Don't be mean."

Molly looked over at Matt. "Well, let's get to work. What can I help you with?"

He stared down at her, feeling as if a mini-tornado had just breezed by. Did she have those big blue eyes yesterday? It was so dark in here, he hadn't noticed.

Although, to be honest, he really hadn't noticed women in general since his wife died. Not like this, anyway.

A moving man stumbled by, carrying two large boxes on a handcart. "These are for the kitchen, right?"

Matt glanced at them and nodded. "Back there, to the left."

"I can start unpacking the kitchen stuff," Molly said, turning to follow the moving man.

"Unpacking? I thought you were here to clean upstairs."

"Oh, I finished that. I can help you down here for a while."

"You don't have to. You probably have things to do today. I don't want to keep you." While he appreciated the offer, he didn't want Molly to feel stuck here, helping him unpack. She had only been hired by the Realtor to clean. He'd find a way to pay her extra for her trouble. He'd insist on it.

"I don't have anything special to do except work on Lauren's science-fair project, which I am *not* looking forward to. How did I ever get talked into helping electrify a bunch of mealworms?"

Matthew laughed. "Well, in that case, I guess the kitchen is a good place to start."

"Is there any special way you'd like me to organize things?"

"Whatever you think makes sense."

"Okay. See you later," Molly said brightly.

He followed her with his gaze until she disappeared, feeling strangely light-headed. The scent of her flowery perfume lingered in the air.

"Where would you like this, sir?" a moving man grunted, bumping into him. Matt turned to see two men staggering into the house, a long leather couch held up between them.

"In here, against the front windows. That's a good place," he said, hoping he was right. It had been a long time since he'd set up a house on his own.

The next two hours flew by as the movers emptied their truck into the house. Finally, they were gone and the rooms seemed strangely quiet. Matthew stood in the middle of the living room, staring around at the piles of boxes and the overall chaotic mess. Why had he done this? It seemed like a big mistake. He felt the sudden urge to cry, and he blew his nose hard on a hanky.

Then he heard Molly humming in the kitchen, a sweet, soothing sound. He took a deep breath, feeling suddenly calmer. He couldn't let her see him falling apart like this.

He picked up a box that read, "Kitchen," and carried it to her. He found her sorting out the silverware and arranging it in a drawer. She turned and smiled when he entered. "Don't mind me. I'm a champion hummer with a tendency for show tunes."

"I like show tunes. Perfect for humming. Who can ever remember the words?"

Molly laughed. "Not me, that's for sure. I could never be on Broadway."

Matt smiled. "Did you ever want to be?"

"Nope. Broadway star was never one of my job titles. Though there have been a lot of them, I must say."

"Really? How many?" He pulled open the box and pulled out some wadded-up newspaper.

"Oh, I don't know. Twenty or so at least since high school. I don't think I ever counted."

"Twenty jobs?" He looked up at her. She didn't seem the flighty type. "I don't know if I've ever met anyone who's had that many jobs. I'm not sure I believe you," he teased her.

"Well, let's see, I was a cabdriver, a school-bus driver, a waitress, a check-out clerk at the supermarket, worked in a doctor's office filing and answering the phone. That was deadly boring," she added, shaking her head. "I had to go back to the supermarket job after that."

Matt laughed. "Go on. That's only five."

"I'm counting the market twice. But never mind. The car wash, the dog groomer, the fast-photo place, the fast-food place, the slow-food place, baker's helper, mother's helper, hamburger helper—"

"Hamburger helper?"

"I just tossed that in to see if you were really listening." Her eyes sparkled, framed by thick dark lashes. He hadn't noticed those dimples before. Very fetching.

He looked back down at the box and cleared his throat. "Go on. I think that's twelve."

"Okay, let me see. I have more." Molly squeezed her eyes shut, thinking. "I nearly forgot, hostess at the funeral parlor." He shot her a puzzled look. "You know, arranging the flowers, showing people which room to go in, that sort of thing. I didn't really have the personality for it. It was the only time I was ever fired before for smiling too much on the job."

"Quite ironic," he agreed, with a grin.

"The delivery service, the shoe store, the movie theater, the answering service, one of those women in a department store who squirts you with a bottle of perfume. I had to quit that one before lunch hour. I had a monster allergy attack."

"That must have been rough," Matt said sympathetically.

"No great loss." Molly shrugged. "It was on to bigger and better things, the giant hardware warehouse—paints and floor coverings. How many is that?"

"Nineteen," he said, feeling awestruck.

"Oh, yes, census taker. That was actually fun. Once you get some people talking, it's hard to make them stop."

"I'm sure they must have enjoyed talking to you," he said sincerely. He caught her blushing again, and she turned back to the silverware.

"You have quite a résumé."

She shrugged. "That's what happens when you don't go to college. That's what I tell my girls. You have to stay in school. Get a good education. Find a real career. Don't end up like me."

He could see she was sensitive about the topic and felt

self-conscious with him now. She had no need to be. He didn't think any less of her for not having a college degree. Her persistence and willingness to try just about anything to earn a living was impressive.

"From what I can see, your girls would do very well to end up like their mother."

She glanced at him over her shoulder. "Thanks," she said quietly. "Oh, dear . . ." Molly stared down into the box she was unpacking. "I think something broke."

"My fault probably. I'm not a very good packer, I'm afraid."

Molly drew out the broken article, handing it to him with a look of concern.

It was a framed photo, one taken years ago when his family vacationed in San Diego, about a year before his wife got sick. Amanda looked so different then, like a little girl. They were all smiling brightly, the white-capped waves of the Pacific in the background. Were they happy then, he and Sharon? It was hard to remember now. Were they ever really that happy with each other?

Even on that trip, he remembered now, he was at a conference and had to attend meetings. Or he thought he did. Sharon wanted him to go sightseeing with them, but he let them go alone. She was mad at him after. He hadn't been a good husband to her. Not really. There was no making up for it now.

"It's just the glass. You can have it repaired in town," Molly suggested. He looked up at her. He'd almost forgotten for a moment that she was there.

"Oh . . . sure. I'll have it fixed." He wrapped it in another sheet of newspaper and put it aside. He felt Molly quietly watching him. She didn't say anything, but he felt that the light mood between them had suddenly shifted.

"I guess that's it for the kitchen. Let me show you where I put everything."

"Sure, fire away." He tried to concentrate but knew he wasn't going to remember half of it. The cupboards and drawers looked so neat and orderly, though, that he felt as if half the work of moving in was done.

"Thanks. This is great. It would have taken me a month to get it looking so organized."

Molly shrugged but he could tell she was pleased by the compliment. "No problem. It's just a kitchen."

The doorbell rang. Matthew was surprised. "I wonder who that is?" he murmured, stepping over a mound of newspaper as he went to answer it.

He pulled open the front door to find Dr. Elliot holding a large green potted plant decorated with a ribbon. "Welcome to Cape Light," the doctor greeted him.

"Ezra, come on in." Matthew felt happy to see his father's old friend. Happier than he would have expected.

"Well, looks like you've landed, bag and baggage," Ezra said, gazing around.

"It's a mess. But I'll get it sorted out."

"Moving—what a headache. I could never face it. I guess that's half the reason I stayed put so long."

Matt smiled. "What's the other half?"

"Oh, that's a secret," Ezra said, with a twinkle in his eye. "Everybody needs at least one to keep life interesting."

"I'll remember that," Matt said, grinning.

"Enough philosophizing. I just stopped by to see if you got in okay. Here's a little something to brighten up the place," Ezra added, handing him the plant.

"Thanks. Very thoughtful of you."

"Don't mention it. That's a philodendron, by the way. It can survive all kinds of neglect. A popular choice for waiting rooms, I might add. But you keep that one here. I've already put one in your office, which, I might add, is shaping up nicely."

"Yes, I know. I stopped by quickly yesterday. It looks great. Sorry I didn't get to call you."

Ezra had been kind enough to oversee the work on Matthew's office while he was still in Worcester. Matt knew the older doctor was eager to bring a new physician to the town. Still, his help had gone well beyond the call of friendship. Matt was starting to think that going out of one's way for a friend or neighbor was not the exception but the rule around here.

"That's all right. I'm glad you're pleased. What else does a fellow like me have to do? I like to make myself useful when I can," Ezra insisted.

Molly came out of the kitchen carrying a plastic bucket. She looked surprised to see Ezra, Matt noticed, and not very happy.

"Molly Willoughby, I didn't know you were here," Ezra greeted her. "Working hard as usual, I see."

While Matthew was sure Ezra's comment was innocent, maybe even a compliment, he could see Molly felt stung. She glanced down at the bucket with a tight smile.

"That's me. Have bucket, will travel. How are you, Dr. Elliot?" she asked politely.

"Fit as a fiddle. How are the girls? No colds this winter, I hope."

"Very well, thanks. You can see for yourself. They'll be down in a minute." She turned to Matthew. "I guess I'll go now," she said. "Unless you need more help. I can work upstairs on the linen closet or make up the beds."

He felt sorry to see her go but didn't want her to do more unpacking. She'd already been too generous with her time. "That's all right. Amanda and I can do all that. Would you like to take a coffee break, though? If I can find the coffee," he added with a smile.

She looked about to agree, but then he saw her reconsider. "Thanks, but I really should go. The girls have a ton of homework, and Lauren has to do some research at the library."

"Oh, yes, the electrified worms. Some other time, okay?"

"Sure, some other time." Molly nodded and dropped her bucket at the door. "Jill, Lauren, time to go," she called up the stairway.

The three girls quickly appeared, galloping down the stairs. To his amazement Amanda looked cheerful and relaxed. He'd envisioned their moving day as being difficult, even traumatic for her. Somehow it had turned out quite the opposite.

As Amanda swung by he noticed a long thin braid in her hair, a colorful bead fastened to the end. It wasn't exactly like the one Lauren wore but a homemade variation. He met Molly's amused expression, realizing she noticed it as well and had decided not to say anything about it.

As Molly said her good-byes and shepherded the girls toward the open door, Matthew found himself at a loss for words. He felt he should say something more than the usual, but what?

He suddenly spied her vacuum cleaner on the porch and jumped to pick it up before she could. "Here, let me carry that for you."

"Oh, thanks." Molly glanced at him, sounding surprised. They walked out together toward her car, a worn-looking blue hatchback. He loaded the vacuum into the trunk, then stood by Molly's open door.

"I know I keep saying it, but I really appreciated all your help. And talking with you, of course. I'll see you around town, I hope."

He inwardly cringed at his own words. As Amanda might say, how lame was that? Wow, he was rusty at this stuff. He hadn't had a date in decades. This was harder than he remembered.

"It's a small town. You won't be able to avoid me," Molly replied, with a wry smile.

"Right. Of course. Well, I wouldn't want to." He stared at her for an awkward moment, then realized he was holding on to the door and she wasn't able to close it. He let go and took a step back. "Well, good-bye now. Thanks again."

"Bye, Matt. Good luck with the rest of the unpacking."

Molly smiled at him, closed her door, then quickly pulled away.

He stood on the sidewalk and watched her drive off, sure he'd forgotten something important he needed to tell her. But he couldn't think what. Once in the house, he shut the door, then noticed the bucket by the stairway where Molly had left it.

He picked it up like a prize, realizing he now had the perfect excuse to call.

THE CLAM BOX WAS NEARLY EMPTY BY THE TIME TUCKER found his usual seat, a stool at the counter behind the grill. He'd purposely taken his lunch break late to miss the rush, but so far Charlie had been busy in the kitchen with some emergency, and Tucker hadn't spoken to him.

He ate a bowl of chowder, paging through a copy of the *Cape Light Messenger*. He stared at the front page, fantasizing for a moment that the headline read "Ex-convict Returns to Town, Breaks into Church," but he knew he was just being paranoid. Even if the paper reported the incident, they wouldn't word it quite that way.

They wouldn't need to, he thought grimly. That news would travel around town in no time.

Charlie appeared and set a dish down in front of him. "Are you sure I got this right? I've never seen you order a grilled chicken sandwich before."

"Fran's been after me to watch my cholesterol. Says I eat too many cheeseburgers."

"Well, you've got to eat something tasty. What's the sense if you don't enjoy your food?"

"Good point." Tucker stared at the sandwich, which did not look at all appealing. "This would go down a lot easier with a few slices of bacon on top."

"Coming right up." Charlie turned and arranged bacon slices on the grill, then set the metal press on top of them, making them sizzle.

"Listen, I had some news I wanted to tell you about," Tucker began. "A homeless man broke into the church last night. The reverend found him and took him to the hospital in Southport. Says he's real sick. The guy gave his name as Jones. But Reverend Ben thinks he's my half brother, Carl. He wants me to go down and see him."

Charlie turned and stared at him. "Your brother, Carl? That's a wild one." He shook his head.

Tucker knew Charlie wasn't much of a churchgoer and didn't have a high opinion of the reverend. Not the way Tucker did. But that was another matter.

"Well, what if it is Carl? I'm thinking I ought to at least find out."

"What the heck for? You don't owe him anything. All he's ever given you is trouble and aggravation." Charlie turned briefly to flip the bacon. "I thought you washed your hands of good old Carl years ago."

"I did. In a way," Tucker admitted.

"When did he get out of jail? Do you know?"

"A fellow I know in Paxton called me when Carl got out on parole. I guess that was about ten years ago."

"He never tried to get in touch with you, all that time?" Charlie asked, glancing back to check on the bacon.

"No, none of us ever heard from him. Not a word. I tried to find Carl when the old man died, but I didn't have any luck. I can't say I really blame Carl for not keeping in touch. The old man was too hard on him. I wouldn't treat a dog the way my father treated Carl. That was a lot of the problem right there."

Charlie laughed harshly. "Plenty of boys don't get on with their fathers. Plenty got disciplined with a belt or the back of a hand. But they didn't turn out like Carl. You can't blame your old man. Carl was a bad apple from the word go. Always in trouble at school. It's amazing he didn't wind up in jail long before he killed that man."

"Yeah," Tucker agreed. "He was always pulling some stupid stunt, and people always looked the other way, gave him another chance. Until he found a mess he couldn't talk his way out of."

"But how about the time he broke in here and emptied the cash register? You consider that just another stupid stunt?"

Tucker met Charlie's eye and looked away. "You know it was never proved Carl did that. It was just your father who suspected him."

"Everyone in town suspected him, Tucker. Except maybe you and your mother. Carl was just lucky there was no evidence and that the police back then were too lazy to follow up."

The bacon sizzled noisily, and Charlie turned again to check it. Tucker considered Charlie's words and decided it was wiser not to reply. This debate was decades old, and he knew he'd never win it.

Charlie was referring to the time years ago when the Clam Box was robbed. Tucker and Charlie were just kids, and Carl was in his teens, already known as the worst kid in town. There wasn't much in the till, so it wasn't a great loss that way. The police were never able to figure out who had broken in, but Carl had already been caught once that summer breaking into a house with his gang of friends, though he hadn't actually stolen anything. Otto Bates, Charlie's father, was convinced that Carl was the culprit. Otto had no evidence, just a gut feeling and a deep distrust of Carl. He'd told everyone in town that Carl was to blame, and everyone believed him. It was nearly as bad as if Carl had been arrested and convicted.

Charlie set the improved sandwich down in front of Tucker and disappeared to take a phone call. Tucker pushed the sandwich away, his appetite suddenly gone. It was easy to sit here and bad-mouth Carl. Other memories came to mind, though, images of his tough, older half brother scaring off a bunch of kids who were bullying Tucker after school. Or Carl tossing a game-winning pass on the high-school football field.

Due to their seven-year age difference, their relationship was never a close one. But they still spent time together, especially when their mother—who was actually Carl's stepmother—worked at the cannery and Carl was left in charge.

Tucker remembered now how he had once broken the windshield of his father's car when a baseball bat had slipped out of his grasp. He must have been about nine and Carl, who was pitching, about sixteen at the time. Tucker had been so terrified imagining their father's reaction, he'd thrown up on the spot. Carl calmed him down, saying he'd take the blame as long as Tucker would keep the secret. Tucker gratefully agreed. But when he saw his father lash into Carl that night, he couldn't keep the pact. By then, his father was in a mindless, drunken fury and hardly heard a word Tucker said. He felt grateful to this day for Carl's selfless action . . . and still a little guilty.

Tucker had looked up to Carl as a little boy, that was for sure. Then later, when he saw Carl's flaws all too clearly, he felt embarrassed by his misplaced admiration. Still, there was some spark of feeling left for his half brother, if only a sense of shared history and duty.

Charlie returned and started working on another order. Tucker watched him a moment before he spoke again. "Come on, Charlie. He wasn't all bad. The way he played football, we thought he was something else. Scouts from all the big schools came to check him out. They came as far away as Chicago," Tucker reminded his friend. "He had some arm. Could have made pro."

"He was good," Charlie acknowledged. "But they all knew he was trouble. Carl had a self-destructive streak a mile wide. You talk about your father mistreating him, but he gave Carl his fishing ticket," Charlie went on, referring to the lobster-fishing permit. "Would have set him up with a nice income if he worked at it. Carl managed to mess that up, too."

"Nobody ever proved Carl was poaching." Tucker found himself coming to Carl's defense again. "He was accused. It was never proven."

"Accused is as good as proved in my book. The state permit board seemed to think so, too. He lost his ticket, didn't he?"

Tucker didn't answer. Everything Charlie said was true. Carl's losing his lobster-fishing license wasn't the worst thing he'd done, but it was the beginning of the end, Tucker thought now.

The waters in New England were crowded with lobster men and the waiting list for a license was long. The valuable lobster-fishing permits were handed down from father to son. Each lobster fisherman marked his traps with a colored float, uniquely his and registered with his license. The float's design stayed in the family for generations, like a crest. The Tulley float was yellow with a white stem striped with pink, black, and green. When Carl lost his license, the colors were given to another fisherman. Losing the permit and the float for poaching—or even the accusation of it—was a family disgrace. That's the way Tucker's father saw it. His threadbare relationship with his firstborn finally reached an end. As far as Tucker knew, Walter Tulley gave up on Carl that day and never spoke to him, or of him, again.

It wasn't long after that, Tucker recalled, that Carl got into a fight in a bar that ended when Carl felled his opponent with an unlucky punch to the head. The man died in a hospital a few hours later, and Carl was arrested on charges of second-degree murder. He claimed he acted in self-defense, that the man had been coming at him with a knife. But eyewitness testimony was shaky and the case was prosecuted by an aggressive D.A. who was trying hard to win convictions and make a name for himself in the county. Tucker had tried to get Carl a good lawyer, but his brother had stubbornly chosen the court-appointed attorney who was well-intentioned but sorely inexperienced. Foregoing a trial, Carl entered a guilty plea. He was sentenced to fifteen years in jail and drew parole in ten.

Sometimes it seemed to Tucker that Carl had always drawn the bad breaks. Sure, he was responsible for his actions and the consequences, just like anyone else. Still, it seemed as if his half brother had been handed a heavier load than most and asked to walk a far tougher road. *If I'd been treated the same, constantly told I was worthless and would never amount to anything, maybe I would have turned out like Carl, too,* Tucker thought.

"You're awful quiet." Charlie scraped the grill with his metal spatula. "Strolling down memory lane?"

"I was just thinking how Carl and my father were exactly alike." Tucker shook his head and sipped his coffee. "Always angry, always blaming someone else for their troubles. Turning to drink when things didn't go their way. Always with some grand scheme that didn't work out. Ever notice that?"

"I know what you mean," Charlie agreed. "Meanwhile your old man ran around saying he wasn't even sure if Carl was his son."

"Oh, that old story." Tucker shook his head. "My father could never swallow the way his first wife ran off and left him with a baby. He couldn't get back at her, so he had to blame it on Carl. Carl was his boy, all right, when he was out on the football field scoring a touchdown. But when he got into trouble, my father would disown him. Walter Tulley was a hard man to live with. He was lucky my mother stuck with him."

"She was a good woman. She did her best by Carl, too. She tried to help him." Charlie wiped a spot on the counter with a rag and rearranged the napkin holder and sugar shaker.

She did try, Tucker thought. She always told Tucker that Carl was his brother, period. Never mind the "half" part.

Tucker knew his mother would have urged him to go to the hospital tonight and help Carl if he could.

"It might not be Carl. I might be worried over nothing," Tucker said, thinking out loud.

"Maybe. But if it is Carl, the only reason he'd come back is because he needs something, and he's got no one else to go begging to. He probably wants money or some place to crash awhile. It certainly isn't because he wants to visit with your wife and kids and see how your life is coming along."

Tucker had already come to this conclusion. He nodded and stirred a spoonful of sugar into his coffee.

"I'm telling you, Tucker. Don't get involved. Don't let that pushy preacher tell you what to do, either."

Tucker shook his head, his patience wearing thin. This conversation hadn't helped him one bit.

"So it's okay for *you* to tell me what to do but not Reverend Ben. Is that it?"

"Come on, pal. You know what I mean. I'm trying to give you some friendly advice. Some practical advice."

"You're not getting it, Charlie. I know Carl is trouble. I don't need you to tell me that. But what if it's him in that hospital?"

Charlie shook his head. "He'll just sucker you in. Mark my words. I know him and I know you."

A slow burn went through Tucker. He'd come to Charlie for some friendly sympathy—not to hear his brother's disreputable history recounted and then to be insulted.

He tossed some bills on the counter and pulled on his hat. "I've got to get back to work. See you."

Charlie looked surprised. "You hardly ate a bite. Want me to wrap this up?"

"No thanks," Tucker said, as he walked away. "The bacon didn't turn out to be such a good idea after all."

* * *

"Do you think they'll let me be in a few of Lauren's classes?" Amanda tugged her corner of the quilt, helping her father make up her bed.

"We'll ask the guidance counselor on Monday," Matt promised. He watched Amanda pick up a towel and her toothbrush and head for the bathroom. "Are you nervous about starting school?"

"A little," she admitted. "But at least I know Lauren. She's really nice. So is her little sister and her mom."

"Yes, they're a very nice family," he agreed. Amanda left the room, leaving him alone with his thoughts of Molly.

Molly was more than nice. She was bright and funny and a good mother, too. He thought she was beautiful, though he could see she felt awkward about her weight. She didn't have that starved, aerobically tortured look women seemed to think was ideal. But he didn't mind her curves. Not at all.

She was the first woman he'd really noticed since his wife's death, and he wasn't quite sure if his strong reaction to her was simply because Molly was so intriguing or because he was changing. Maybe something inside of him was waking up again.

But he wasn't sure he could handle dating. He had so much to do, getting Amanda adjusted to this new place and setting up a new practice. No, it wasn't the right time to start dating again, he decided as Amanda emerged from the bathroom. He wasn't ready.

With her face scrubbed clean and her long hair pulled back, Amanda slipped under the quilt. Matthew sat down on the edge of her bed.

"We got a lot done today, and we still have tomorrow to work on the house. We might be in pretty good shape by Monday."

"I guess so," she said. "Everything seems like such a big mess, though."

"We'll get there," he promised. "I thought we'd go to church tomorrow. We can try the one on the green, Bible Community Church. That will be a good way to meet more people, too, don't you think?"

Amanda nodded. Matt had never been very religious. He'd always left churchgoing to his wife and Amanda. But when Sharon got sick, he found himself more aware of his spiritual side and of his own mortality.

"Would you like to say a prayer together?" he asked.

Amanda nodded, then folded her hands and bowed her head. "You start," she said.

"Um, okay." Matt thought for a moment and then began, "Dear Lord, thank you for helping us find this new place to live and for a good moving day. We only found one or two things broken so far, despite my sloppy packing," he joked. "Please help us get settled here. Help Amanda make friends at her new school and help me with my practice." He turned to Amanda. "Anything else?"

She glanced at him, then lowered her gaze again. "Please bless Mom and keep her safe with you in heaven. We hope she knows we're thinking of her. We know she's watching over us."

Matt couldn't speak for a moment. "Amen," he said finally.

He stood up and kissed Amanda good night, then left the room.

Downstairs in the kitchen, he unpacked a sack of groceries. He found a bundle wrapped in newspaper on top of the refrigerator and opened it: the family photo, with the broken glass. He'd stashed it up there this afternoon to get it out of the way.

He stared down at the picture, thinking how unhappy his wife had been with him. She said he gave everything to his patients and left nothing for his family. They were often angry at each other, distant. They could never work it out and had nearly separated right before they found out about her cancer.

He'd tried hard to be a good husband to her then, but it was too little too late. When she died, he was left with a kind of grief that was like an overstuffed closet. Nothing had ever been resolved, and three years later, he still couldn't quite close the door.

He wrapped up the picture again and set it on the kitchen table so he'd be sure to take care of it. His own regrets and shortcomings were much harder to repair. He knew he was a good doctor, but maybe Sharon had been right. Maybe he couldn't be a good doctor and a good husband at the same time. Maybe he just wasn't cut out that way. He thought he'd done well with Amanda since her mother passed away, though he still had to be careful not to get lost in his work and shut her out, which was his automatic way of coping whenever things were difficult.

How could he think of dating again? Especially someone like Molly Willoughby. She was the type who would be looking for a serious relationship. Not just dinner and a movie on weekends. Matt couldn't imagine marrying again.

No, it would be better not to start anything. He'd drop off the bucket with an extra check for her, at the real-estate office. Like she said, it was a small town. If and when he was ever ready, he'd know where to find her.

THE MAN ASLEEP IN THE HOSPITAL BED LOOKED NOTHING like Carl, Tucker decided. This had all been a huge mistake. A false alarm.

A huge wave of relief washed over him. He watched the man sleep, breathing heavily, an oxygen apparatus hooked to his nose. His battered face told the story of a hard life, the heavy dark folds around his eyes, a squashed-looking nose that appeared to have been broken a few times, a jagged scar on his cheek. Carl was about fifty by now. But this man looked much older, in his sixties, Tucker would guess. Under the loose sheet Tucker caught sight of a swollen leg, puffy and discolored.

It wasn't Carl, thank God.

He took a deep breath and began to walk away. But then he felt as if he were being watched. He quickly turned and saw that the man in bed was looking at him. They locked gazes for a second and the sick man closed his eyes again, his expression unaltered.

But it was too late. Tucker knew. He felt his heart turn to lead. It was Carl. From somewhere down in that wreck of a body his half brother peered out with a familiar light. He'd been pretending to be asleep, waiting for Tucker to go. That was exactly the kind of thing Carl would do.

Tucker stood at the foot of the bed, tempted to walk out the door and never look back. Who would ever know? He wasn't even sure why he'd come in the first place. Still, he'd driven all this way. Might as well go through with it.

"Are you awake?" He waited.

Finally the sick man opened his eyes. "Who are you?"

"You know who I am. And I know you're not Carl Jones."

The man drew a raspy breath and glanced to the side. "I don't have any idea what you're talking about, mister. I ought to know my own name by now."

"Get off it, Carl. We're both too old for games."

"If you say so." The man sighed heavily and closed his eyes. Tucker waited for him to speak again, and Carl let him wait nearly five minutes before saying, "I tried to let you off the hook. But you never could take a hint, could you, Tucker?"

"Still playing the tough guy, huh?"

"Why not?" Carl shrugged. "You're still playing the Eagle Scout. Still got the uniform, I see. I didn't want you to come here. But I guess you couldn't help yourself."

Tucker took a step closer, feeling strangely immune to Carl's insults. Nothing Carl could say had the power to hurt him anymore.

"Why did you come back? Were you looking for the old man?"

"Are you crazy? What would I want to see him for?"

"He died about three years ago. I tried to get in touch with you before the funeral, but I couldn't find you."

Carl took another labored breath and shifted against the bed. "Doesn't matter. I wouldn't have come."

"So what are you doing here?" Tucker persisted. "I don't get it."

"There's nothing to get. I was on my way up to Maine to see this friend of mine in Portland. Figured I'd stop in Cape Light, see what's become of the place. I didn't plan on making any social calls."

"I see," Tucker said, wondering whether Carl was really passing through with no intention of getting in touch or whether this was yet another of Carl's stories.

Carl began coughing again, a choking cough that sounded as if he couldn't catch his breath. "Do you want a nurse?" Tucker asked quickly.

Carl shook his head and waved his hand. "It'll pass. Just let me be."

Tucker sat in the chair near the bed, his hat in his lap. The coughing abated, and Carl turned to him. "So, you found me. You've done your duty. You can leave now."

Tucker ignored him. "I heard when you got out. A guy I know called me. What've you been doing all this time?"

Carl grinned, showing a row of stained, jagged teeth. "I'm a big shot on Wall Street. Can't you tell?"

"I mean besides that," Tucker said, without smiling.

"Making my way. What difference is it to you? I kept myself out of jail, if that's what you're asking me."

Tucker felt weary. Weary and sad. He'd rarely seen a man who had done such a poor job of making his way in the world.

Carl started coughing again; this time the violent spasms forced him to sit up. His face grew beet red; his bloodshot eyes bulged. It sounded as if Carl were about to cough out his insides. Tucker quickly leaned over and pressed the call button for the nurse.

He stood up and touched Carl's shoulder. "Easy now. The nurse is coming."

"Water . . ." Carl managed.

Tucker poured out a cupful from the plastic pitcher near the bed, and Carl took it in a shaky hand. Only a few drops reached his mouth, the rest spilling on the sheet and hospital gown.

The nurse arrived, and Tucker stepped aside. "Just lay back, Mr. Jones. I'm going to turn up your oxygen. Just try to relax," she coaxed him, pulling the curtain around the bed. "The patient needs some privacy," she told Tucker. "You can wait in the hall if you like."

"I was just leaving."

Tucker tried to catch Carl's eye, but it was too late. The curtain was closed. He heard Carl continue to cough violently on the other side.

Finally he turned and left the room. Carl was in bad shape. He might even die. *That would let me off the hook real fast,* Tucker thought. Then he felt horribly guilty. He didn't want anyone to die. He just wished Carl hadn't turned up here after all this time.

Maybe Charlie and Fran were right. Maybe he should never have come here. He should have left well enough alone.

Tucker sighed and punched the button for the elevator. He had a problem now, and he didn't know what to do about it.

CHAPTER THREE

"I LIKE THE QUIET CHURCH BEFORE THE SERVICE BEGINS," Ralph Waldo Emerson once said. But Ben often thought of the quote as the service ended and he stood in the back of the sanctuary while the choir finished singing its response to his benediction. He loved the quiet in the church at that moment, as the voices harmonized and held one last note, the congregation standing with heads bowed having just received a final blessing. In that silent moment before the bodies began to stir and make their way back into the world, he felt the indescribable peace of the Lord, invisible yet tangible, filtering down on them all like shafts of colored light through the stained-glass windows.

Then the notes of the postlude sounded and the worshipers began to leave their pews, lining up to say good-bye.

He saw Tucker Tulley approach and greeted him.

"Thank you, Reverend, that was a fine service," Tucker said appreciatively.

"You're welcome, Tucker." Ben leaned closer, talking in

a more private tone. "I was wondering, did you have a chance to check on that man in Southport?"

Tucker nodded. "I went down there last night. It was Carl, just as you thought. We talked a few minutes. Then the nurse shooed me out."

Tucker's tone was not encouraging. Ben could see his brother's return was going to be a challenge for him—a great challenge. Ben hoped Tucker would turn to him for help. Yet he didn't want to press and have Tucker shut him out.

"Maybe you can visit again sometime. It sounds to me like he'll be in there awhile, from what the doctor said."

"I didn't get to speak to a doctor. What exactly is wrong with him?"

"Oh, a number of things. Emphysema, to start," Ben began. But before he could go on, Fran Tulley appeared. She quickly greeted him, then turned to her husband. "Excuse me for interrupting, honey, but I was just going out with Michael for those cartons for the food drive. Could you give us a hand when you get a chance?"

Each fall and spring, the church gathered donations of nonperishable food items and stored them in a pantry that was available to those in need. Reverend Ben now recalled that Fran was in charge of the spring collections and doing an impressive job.

"More donations?" Reverend Ben asked, pleased. "This could be the best drive we've ever had."

Tucker smiled at his wife with pride. "Fran's really put her all into it, Reverend. She's sending out flyers, knocking on doors. She even went up and down Main Street and got donations from all the restaurants and merchants."

Fran blushed, looking embarrassed by her husband's praise. "Oh, it's not such a big deal. Everyone's been very generous."

"Thanks to your efforts, Fran," the reverend put in. "We all appreciate it."

"No thanks necessary. I enjoyed doing it, honestly. Oh,

there's Michael coming in with a box. I'd better show him where to go. See you later."

"I'd better go help them," Tucker said. "See you, Reverend."

Ben said good-bye to Tucker, feeling it was unfortunate that they hadn't finished talking about Carl. But if Tucker was truly interested in his half brother's diagnosis, he could surely find out on his own. Ben wondered if he would make the effort.

Sophie Potter stood next in line. Her oldest daughter, Evelyn, and next born, Una, had brought her to church today along with another young woman whom Ben guessed must be a granddaughter. Sophie had so many, he could never keep track.

"Lovely service, Reverend," Sophie said. "I appreciate you mentioning Gus. I'll tell him what you said."

After asking the congregation to remember in their prayers those who were sick, Ben had talked about Gus Potter—his work for the church and his place in the community. He hadn't said much but Sophie had been deeply moved.

"I'll tell him myself. I'm coming to see him this afternoon. Can I bring anything?"

Sophie patted his arm and smiled. "You're the best tonic for Gus, Reverend." She turned to the young woman standing beside her. "This is my granddaughter, Miranda, my son Bart's girl. She's an actress in New York," Sophie confided with pride.

Ben noticed Miranda blush. "More of a wannabe," Miranda amended. "I'm mainly an office temp right now."

"If pretty counted for anything, she'd be in Hollywood, for goodness' sake. Why, just look at her," her grandmother insisted.

"Absolutely. She looks a lot like you, Sophie."

Now it was Sophie's turn to blush, but Ben thought it was true. Miranda had been blessed with the same lovely round face and reddish gold hair that had now gone white on her grandmother. Yet unlike Sophie, who was short and compact in build, Miranda was close to six feet tall. And she wasn't the wispy willowy sort that was in danger of being blown over by a stiff breeze. Miranda Potter looked strong and fit. She had the kind of looks they used to call statuesque.

"How long will you be visiting?" Ben asked.

"I can stay as long as I'm needed," Miranda said carefully. "Grandpa is coming home from the hospital, and there'll be a lot to do, a lot of visitors."

Miranda put her arm around Sophie's shoulder and met Reverend Ben's gaze. Her eyes were gentle, sea green in color. In her gesture he sensed her love and respect for her grandmother and realized that the Lord had a way of sending angels when they were most needed.

"I'll see you again then, Miranda."

"I'm sure you will." Miranda smiled and walked on with Sophie.

When Ben turned he was confronted by a new face, a dark-haired man with a teenage girl. Father and daughter, judging by their resemblance. He'd spotted them earlier, sitting off to the side, and wondered who they might be.

"I'm Reverend Ben Lewis. Welcome to Bible Community Church."

"Hello, Reverend. I'm Matthew Harding. This is my daughter, Amanda."

"Nice to meet you both." Ben shook Matthew's hand and then Amanda's. "Are you visiting us today?"

"More permanent than that, I hope," Matt said with a smile. "We're new in town. Just moved in yesterday. I'm a doctor. I'm going to open a practice here."

"You must be Ezra Elliot's friend," Ben said. "I do hope you can stay for the coffee hour. There are a lot of people here who are looking forward to meeting you."

"I'd like that very much." Matthew smiled agreeably.

He seemed a modest man, Ben thought. Not like some physicians he'd met.

"Well, here's a good start." Ben spotted Emily Warwick nearby. "Let me introduce you to our mayor . . . if I can catch her attention."

Emily stood with her mother, Lillian, whom she brought to church every Sunday. But today Emily was also accompanied by Dan Forbes, Ben noticed with surprise. He'd never seen the former newspaper owner and avowed cynic in church before. Of course, it had something to do with Emily. *Everything* to do with Emily from the looks of it. *God moves in strange ways indeed.*

Ben finally caught Emily's eye, and she approached with a wide, winning smile. "Good morning, Reverend. Did you want to introduce someone?" she asked, turning to Matthew and his daughter.

Ben made the introductions. Emily and Dan, of course, welcomed Matt warmly. Lillian, however, appraised Matthew in her usual manner. "You look a bit young," she said, fixing him with a sharp, critical gaze. "I won't go to a doctor under forty. Not nearly enough experience. I won't have physicians learning by trial and error on me."

Matthew smiled mildly. "I think that there are good and bad doctors of any age," he said diplomatically.

"That's just my point. You can't be too careful when it comes to choosing one, can you?"

"I'm sure there's no question about Dr. Harding's abilities," Emily said, casting a warning glance at her mother. Dan stepped up beside her and deftly steered the conversation on to other topics, and within minutes Matthew was soon surrounded by a circle of welcoming parishioners.

Digger Hegman and his middle-aged daughter, Grace, stood to one side, looking on. "What's going on here? A political rally in the church vestibule?" the elderly ex-fisherman asked Ben.

"Hush, Dad. That's not polite." Grace shook her head.

"It's the new doctor, Matthew Harding. Emily's just introducing him around."

"Hmmm . . . well, he looks like a decent fellow," Digger allowed. "I don't need to meet any more doctors, though. I think I'll wait to introduce myself if and when the need arises."

"That seems reasonable to me," Ben said, with a smile. All in all, he thought, Cape Light was going to be a good place for Matthew Harding and his daughter.

"COME ON, GIRLS. YOUR UNCLE WILL BE HERE SOON." Molly sifted through the open duffel bag on Lauren's unmade bed, checking the contents. "How about those waterproof mittens? Are they in here?"

Sam and Jessica were taking the girls ice skating and then entertaining them until the evening so Molly could catch up on her orders. She had a sudden increase in business, which was very encouraging. But now she needed to bake the entire day and into the night to make the deliveries on time.

The doorbell rang, and she started out of the bedroom to answer it but stopped as she saw Jill standing in front of the mirror, her hairbrush hopelessly tangled in her long hair. Molly groaned at the sight. "Lauren, help Jill with her hair, will you, honey? I think there's some detangle spray in the bathroom."

"Got any dynamite?" she heard Lauren mutter.

Oh, boy. That one is starting to sound just like me, Molly thought, as she left them alone to sort it out.

She pulled open the front door, expecting to find her brother, Sam. But instead it was her ex-husband, Phil Willoughby. Feeling shocked, her breath caught in her throat. Then she felt her anger rise.

"Hi, Molly." He smiled widely. Too widely, Molly thought, for a man with his track record. If he had any sense of decency, he'd be hanging his head in shame.

"What do you want?" She stood in the doorway, blocking his view. She didn't want the girls to catch sight of him. Then she'd really have a problem.

"Well, it's Sunday. I'd like to see my daughters." His calm tone annoyed her; he sounded as if he should have been expected and she was the one acting oddly.

There was a time, long ago, when Sunday afternoon was Phil's regular time with the girls. But in Molly's book, he'd long since forfeited that privilege.

Molly glanced over her shoulder, then stepped out into the hallway with him, closing the door behind her.

"You have some unbelievable nerve, I'll say that for you." Her tone was hushed but fierce.

"Molly, come on now. I thought about calling, but I knew you were going to act this way. You would have just hung up on me."

"You got that right."

He paused and looked her over. "You look good. Did you lose some weight or something?"

"Phil—" She shook her head, not knowing whether to laugh or scream. "You never change, do you?"

"Wait. Just stop right there, okay?" He reached into the front pocket of his jeans and pulled out an envelope. "Here, this is for the girls. I've got a good job now selling cars and trucks. It's a big dealership in Peabody. I'm living around there, too, now."

Molly considered this information. Peabody was about thirty miles southwest of Cape Light. The drive was mostly on the interstate, though, which was often loaded with traffic. He might get tired of that real quick, she thought.

"I made top salesman two months in a row," he added proudly.

"How nice for you, Phil." Her tone was flat and sarcastic, her expression blank. She took the envelope but didn't open it. She could guess a check was inside. "Fine. But it's a drop in the bucket, pal. You owe me so much child support at this point, I can't count that high."

"I'm going to make it up to you. Every cent," he promised. "That's just a start."

He'd said all this many times before, but Molly didn't bother to remind him of the fact. "Okay, you're going to start paying the child support again. Thanks a bunch. Do you think after all this time you're just going to buy your way back to see the girls?"

"Now, come on, Molly. That's not it all. I'm just trying—" He tried to explain, but Molly cut him off.

"What are you trying to do, Phil? Do you even know? Trying to disappoint them again? To confuse them and undermine their self-confidence, their sense of trust? You can't just walk in and out of their lives. I won't let you. Not for all the checks in your checkbook."

Phil nodded, his head bowed. "You were always like a mother lion with those girls," he said softly. "I bet if I tried to go in there, you'd claw my eyes out."

"You got that right." Molly felt like crying, but she didn't know why. She kept her hands crossed tightly across her chest and took a deep breath. She couldn't look up at Phil. She knew what she'd see. He wasn't a bad guy, really. Not deep inside. He'd never meant to hurt her or his daughters. But somehow, he always did.

"What do I have to do? Just tell me, and I'll do it. I want to see my girls again. I know I messed up, but it's different now." He paused, watching for a reaction while Molly tried hard not to show one.

"How is it different?"

"I've been thinking about things. I feel . . . older or something. I don't know." He shrugged and stared down at her. "I can't really explain it right now. But I promise, this time is different. It really is."

Molly took a breath. She hadn't seen him in months, not since last summer. He didn't look any different; Phil was still a big, broad-shouldered lumberjack type with blue eyes and thick blond hair. It wasn't hard to see why she fell for him in high school. His clothes looked a little finer, she noticed, the shearling jacket, for instance. But that didn't mean anything. Phil never minded blowing an entire paycheck on himself if some expensive piece of clothing caught his eye.

"I can bring you back to court, Molly. I have some rights, too," he reminded her quietly.

Now there was a threat she hadn't heard for a while. *He really must be planning to keep up the child support,* she thought, *or he wouldn't have the nerve to spring that one.*

But before Molly could decide how to reply, the door behind her swung open. She turned to see Lauren standing there with Jill still attached to a hairbrush, crying her eyes out.

"Mom, we really need some help here," Lauren moaned. Then Jill looked up and noticed her father.

"Daddy!" She immediately stopped crying and jumped into Phil's arms.

"Hello, sugar pie." Jill was big now, but Phil was still much bigger, Molly realized as she watched her ex-husband lift Jill off her feet in a tight hug, the brush dangling from her daughter's hair.

Lauren hung back, looking shy of her father, Molly noticed, or maybe just distrustful. But Phil smiled warmly at her and stretched open his free arm. "Get over here, Lauren Marie," he coaxed her. Molly saw her waver for a moment, then move toward him. He soon stood hugging both girls, one under each arm in a giant three-way embrace. Molly stood back, feeling invisible.

"Wow, I missed you girls so much," he said.

Right, so why haven't we seen you for months? And why just a five-minute call on Christmas? Molly wanted to say. But she bit her tongue. She didn't want to dash the happy reunion with cold water. She wasn't that mean-spirited. Part of her did believe that Phil was sincere. He was inconsistent and irresponsible, but in his own way, he still really loved them.

"Why don't we go inside," he said, ushering the girls

through the door. He glanced at Molly over their heads, and Molly had no choice but to let him in. She closed the door and suddenly smelled something burning.

She raced to the oven and yanked open the door. She grabbed some pot holders and pulled out the pans of muffins.

"Blast! Double blast!" She hated for Phil to see her out of control, but she couldn't help her reaction. The muffins were overcooked, too brown outside for her customers. She had to start over again with this batch. It was all Phil's fault for distracting her, of course. No doubt about it, the man was trouble.

She turned to him, feeling angry all over again.

"Something wrong, Molly? You look upset."

"No problem. Everything is under control," she insisted. She pulled off the oven mitts and tossed them on the countertop.

The girls were still hanging on him, and Phil looked awfully smug, his repentant attitude apparently wiped away with their greeting.

"Why didn't you tell us Daddy was here?" Jill's tone held a note of reproach. "We thought it was just Uncle Sam."

"I wanted to surprise you," Phil replied, and Molly didn't bother to contradict him. "How would you like to go out for the day? Do something special with me?"

"Yes!" Jill jumped up and clapped her hands. Lauren glanced at Molly. She could tell from her older daughter's expression that she wasn't totally buying this.

"Sorry, they already have plans. Sam and his wife, Jessica, are taking them out."

"Sam has a wife?" Phil shook his head in amazement. "I didn't know there was a woman alive that could hook your brother."

"Every man meets his match." Molly met his gaze for a moment, then looked away. She had once thought Phil was her match, but she'd discovered her mistake the hard way.

"Sam won't mind if the girls go out with their father," Phil said, gazing at Lauren and Jill again. "Just give him a call. He'll understand."

Sam and Phil had been friends in high school. Sam had been angry with him on Molly's behalf, but she knew her brother still had a soft spot for his old buddy Phil. That was just the trouble. It was hard for anyone to stay mad at Phil for very long.

"Please, Mom?" Seated on Phil's lap, Jill turned to Molly with a pleading expression. Lauren didn't say anything, though, and she looked a little sullen, Molly noticed.

"I can't call him. They're coming straight from church," Molly said curtly. "And you guys aren't even ready. Maybe you can see your father another time. You go finish up, and the adults will talk."

Jill got a grumpy face and didn't move from Phil's side. He gently patted her back. "Oh come on now, Molly. Have a heart. I'm here now. What's the point of making a big deal out of this?"

"The point is, you can't just fall out of the sky and expect us to drop everything. Especially since no one's heard from you for months. That's just like you, Phil." Molly heard her voice rising, but she couldn't help herself. "You say you've changed. This time is different. Well, that's no different."

Phil stared at her, his expression unreadable. Jill sat with a stricken look on her face. Lauren bit her nail, trying to look unfazed, but obviously disturbed as well.

Molly felt vaulted back through time, when her arguments with Phil left the girls frightened and confused. How did she fall into that trap again so quickly? She was ashamed of herself.

"A person has to start over somewhere, Molly. For pity's sake. Just give me a chance." Phil's voice was quiet and calm, a stark contrast to her own.

Molly looked at the girls again. She was between that

old rock and hard place. If she let them go with Phil, they might end up painfully disappointed and she'd be left to soothe their hurt feelings. But if she held the line and made him go, they would be mad at her, and she'd feel guilty for depriving the girls of a rare chance to see their father.

"Please, Molly? I'm going to toe the line this time. Honestly."

Jill turned to him and put her arm around his shoulders. "I believe you, Daddy."

"Thank you, sweetie." Phil smiled at Jill, then looked over at Molly. She knew she was beat. He always knew how to get his way, didn't he? No wonder he'd finally found his calling as a car salesman.

"All right. You can take them out. Just have them back by eight so they can get to bed on time."

"Yes!" Jill ran back into the bedroom, hairbrush flipping. Lauren turned and followed. "Should we bring that bag of stuff for ice skating?"

"Sure, I'll take you skating if you want. We can do lots of things." Phil came to his feet, all smiles again. "Thanks, Molly. I appreciate this."

"Don't thank me. Thank your girls. Just don't mess up this time, I'm warning you. There are no more chances after this one, Phil. I'm not kidding."

"I hear you." Phil nodded his head. "I won't need any more chances. This is it."

She gave him a look but didn't say anything. The girls rushed back into the room. Jill had managed to untangle the brush and had bunched her hair in a big clip. It looked a little funny, but Molly didn't have the energy to make any improvements.

The girls quickly kissed her good-bye while Phil looked on from the hallway. Lauren didn't look nearly as elated as Jill about the unexpected outing, but she didn't complain about it, either.

Once they were gone, Molly went inside and shut the door. The silence in the apartment seemed oppressive. She couldn't quite believe what had just happened, and she couldn't quite believe Phil had gotten his way, after all. The realization made her mad at him all over again.

She pulled Phil's envelope from her pocket and opened it. As she'd expected, it contained a check. But the sum, several thousand dollars, was far greater than she'd ever imagined, even as a peace offering. Phil owed her much more, of course. But this was an impressive start.

Molly sat down at the kitchen table and stared at the check. For most people she knew, this wouldn't be a lot of money. It wasn't exactly a lottery jackpot. But she could do a lot with this money. Buy the girls a good computer. Get some badly needed new tires for her car. Pay off the lingering bills from Christmas. Catch up at the orthodontist. Have a little money stashed in the bank for a rainy day. . . .

Did it make her think better of Phil? Only slightly. Did it make her trust him? Not one bit. If anything, it made her more wary. He was clearly trying to buy his way back into their lives, and she didn't want to play right into his tricks.

But he did owe her the money for child support, fair and square. And she did need it. So she folded up the check and put it in her purse so she could take it right to the bank tomorrow.

The doorbell rang, and Molly realized it had to be Sam and Jessica. She'd forgotten all about them.

She pulled open the door and let them in. "Hi, Moll." Sam leaned over and gave her a kiss on the cheek.

"Gee, it smells good in here," Jessica said, following him inside. "What are you making?"

"I just charred a bunch of banana muffins. They look awful but still taste pretty good. Anybody hungry?"

"No, thanks. We're fine. Are the girls ready?" Sam said.

Molly glanced at him. "They're not here, actually. I know you won't believe it, but they went out with Phil."

"Phil took them out? I didn't even know you were speaking to him again." As Molly expected, Sam looked amazed and confused by the news.

"I'm not. I mean, I wasn't. He just showed up here and wouldn't take no for an answer. Then the girls found out he was here, and Jill almost started crying when I said, 'No.' I'm really sorry you had to come all the way over, but there was no way to reach you."

"I get the picture." Sam shook his head. "A sneak attack. That's Phil." He glanced at Jessica who had taken a seat at Molly's kitchen table and opened her gray wool coat.

"He put you in a difficult position, asking right in front of the girls," Jessica offered.

"Exactly," Molly replied, feeling Jessica understood the situation perfectly. "What could I say? He claims he's changed. It's all going to be different. He even gave me a check." Molly pulled the check from her purse to show it to Sam.

Sam looked impressed when he read the amount. He handed it back to her. "That's a lot of money. Looks like he's serious this time."

"Or just feeling more guilty than usual," Molly noted. "I just hope he doesn't pull one of his vanishing acts. I'd never forgive myself for giving in to him. I told him this was his last chance. If he fails those girls again . . . well, he'll be sorry. Very sorry. I'll figure out some way to teach him a lesson."

"Molly, please," Sam coaxed her. "I know Phil wasn't the model husband—or the model ex-husband, for that matter. But he's not a monster. Maybe you should just relax a little and give him a chance. Maybe he's finally ready to grow up and face his responsibilities. Some guys are a little slow. But it can happen."

"Right, like snow in July," Molly said cynically. "I've heard all this before, Sam. Do you honestly think Phil Willoughby can ever change? I don't."

"Anyone can change, Molly." Sam shook his head. "You're so negative sometimes. Especially about men. We're not so bad, you know."

Jessica glanced at him. "Molly's been through enough this morning, Sam. She doesn't need a lecture about man bashing. She has every right to be concerned about the girls. Phil's been totally unreliable. Why should she believe him now?"

Molly was surprised to hear Jessica speak up on her behalf. Since the two had been married, she'd never heard Jessica and Sam disagree except about minor issues such as what color to paint the hallway. She'd never expect her brother to take Phil's side and Jessica to defend her.

Sam looked equally surprised. "No reason. Except to give the guy a break. That's all I'm saying. Is he going to pay his child support again?" he asked Molly.

"He says so. He has a new job selling cars or something."

"And apparently he's doing well at it," Sam added, nodding at the check.

Molly and Jessica shared a doubtful look. "It shows he made some extra money lately and he was feeling guilty," Molly said.

Sam sighed. He stuck his hands in his pockets. "I guess we all just have to wait and see."

Molly nodded. "I guess so."

She wished her brother was more sympathetic to her side of the situation. But Sam was like that; he always gave a person the benefit of the doubt. Even someone like Phil. It was a good trait in general, Molly thought, but awfully annoying at the moment.

As if guessing her thoughts, Sam reached over and gave Molly's shoulder a reassuring pat. "I guess we ought to go. You have work to do. Come on, honey," he said to Jessica.

Jessica stood up from the table and joined her husband. "Okay. But we ought to stop over at my mother's now for lunch."

Sam frowned. "I thought we ducked that invitation."

"Looks like it boomeranged." Jessica took her husband's arm as she turned toward Molly. "Emily brought

Dan to my mother's today after church. She could really use some reinforcements."

"Have some sympathy, Sam. Sounds like Dan is going to be your new brother-in-law," Molly said.

"Yeah, poor guy. I do feel sorry for him."

"Honey, please. My mother's not that bad." Jessica stared up at him.

"No comment. Especially since we were just in church." Sam grinned at Molly. He didn't have to say anything more.

Jessica's mother was a tough old bird, notorious for her sharp tongue. She had thoroughly disapproved of Sam and had put so much pressure on Jessica, it had nearly broken up the match. The fact that Sam was able to joke about Lillian was actually to his credit, all things considered. Lillian Warwick would be more accepting of Dan, Molly thought, because of Dan's stature in the town. Then again, she'd probably give him a hard time on sheer principle.

"So long, Molly. Good luck with your work." Sam touched her arm as he walked out.

"Call if you need me to watch the girls this week, okay?" Jessica said.

Jessica gave her a quick hug, and Molly found herself hugging back. She felt as if Jessica had understood how much Phil's appearance had shaken her—understood and sympathized with her. That was the second surprise of the day.

MOLLY WORKED ALL AFTERNOON AND INTO THE EARLY evening without taking a break, mixing up batches of muffins and pies, running between two apartments to check on the cooking. Her next-door neighbor often went away on weekends, and she let Molly use her oven when she had to do a lot of baking.

It wasn't a perfect solution, but it was the only way she

could even attempt to fill such big orders. If she wanted to go into this business full-time, she'd definitely need some other arrangement. Right now she didn't seem to have enough business to warrant renting out a real bakery or setting up a shop. But if she didn't get a larger, more professional work space, she'd never be able to handle more business. It was a circular puzzle she couldn't quite figure out.

She didn't have time to figure it out today, either. She didn't even have time to eat a real meal, but she sampled her wares so often, it didn't matter. She made a delivery to the Clam Box and another to the Beanery, a hip urban-style café in the village. Her last stop was a new client, the Pequot Inn, a fancy restaurant just outside of the village.

Back home again, she worked on an order for a dozen quiches with different fillings, which she would somehow manage to fit into her refrigerator tonight and deliver early tomorrow morning to the Beanery.

All the while she worked, Molly's stomach was twisted into a knot. She worried about facing Phil again and what would happen next. Sam had advised her to give her ex-husband time to prove himself. But all Molly could think about was all the times in the past that Phil had hurt and disappointed her.

Since they'd divorced seven years ago, Phil had never been a consistent presence for the girls or even consistent in sending support payments. He'd make an effort for a month or two, then the novelty of being a dad would wear off. He'd start missing his visits, calling at the last minute or, sometimes, not even calling at all. There were several times when they didn't hear from him for months at a stretch, and he seemed to move around so much that Molly was never sure of his phone number and address. Once they didn't hear from him for almost a year. Molly had learned through the grapevine that Phil had moved to Connecticut and tried to start a car-repair business with a friend. Again, he'd come back, insisting he'd changed, and he started visiting the girls and giving Molly support money. That was last winter. A little over a year ago, Molly realized.

By the spring, his old pattern prevailed, and he'd stopped visiting and sending checks, though he did call to say hello to the girls from time to time. He'd called on Christmas, though he did not send them any gifts.

He had probably taken them to the mall today, Molly thought. It would be typical Phil to try to make up for all the missed occasions in one extravagant shopping spree. The girls ought to be too old by now to fall for that tired trick. She was curious to see if it had worked this time. Curious and nervous. She didn't like the feeling and resented Phil for still being able to upset her like this.

Finally at a quarter past seven, she heard the doorbell ring, and she rushed to let them in. Lauren and Jill greeted her happily. They kissed Phil good-bye and went to their room.

"Good night, girls. I'll see you next week," Phil called after them. He met Molly's gaze. "That is, if it's okay with you."

Molly was relieved to hear Phil already making plans to see the girls again, but she remained wary. "What did you have in mind?"

"Well, a regular schedule, I guess. Two nights a week and every other weekend?"

"You are trying to make up for lost time, aren't you?"

"Yes, I am," he admitted. "If you'll let me."

Molly's first impulse was to answer in anger. No one had been stopping him all these months from seeing his daughters any time he pleased. But she remembered Sam's words and held her tongue. It was hard to give Phil another chance, but she didn't see that she had any other choice here.

"Did you open my envelope?" he asked her carefully.

She nodded. "I did. Thanks."

"I know it's not everything. But it's a start. I'm doing

pretty well now. I can give you more than the regular amount as a sort of back pay, okay?"

Molly nodded again. "That sounds all right."

"Listen, when we were talking this morning, there was something I forgot to tell you."

"Oh? And what was that?" She felt her nerves jump into emergency alert. Was this the part where Phil announces that he's leaving for Australia in a few weeks? Or something equally impulsive and thoughtless, proving that he'd gotten the girls excited over nothing.

"I wanted to tell you that I know now that I really screwed things up. I'm sorry for the things I did, the things I said to you. I was just . . . a fool. A total fool. I'm really sorry, Molly. I hope someday you can forgive me."

Molly was shocked by his admission and apology. But it would take more than remorseful words to heal the wounds from their marriage. Digging up their unhappy past was the last thing she wanted to do tonight.

"That's ancient history, Phil. It doesn't matter to me now one way or the other."

He was quiet for a moment. At first she thought her harsh reply must have upset him, but when he spoke, she could tell he wasn't mad—just ashamed of himself.

"I know you don't trust me anymore. I guess I deserve that. But I promise, I won't let you down this time."

"Don't worry about me. I'm immune to you. Just don't disappoint Lauren and Jill."

"I understand." He dipped his big blond head. "Good night, Molly. Good to see you again."

"Good night, Phil." She stood at the doorway and watched him walk down the hall. She couldn't say that it had been good to see him. It had been a shock, though. A real earthquake.

Molly heard the girls in the bathroom getting washed up for bed. She knew they would bubble over in describing their day with him. Though she was curious to hear how it went, Molly wasn't looking forward to hearing the girls sing his praises or show off all the presents he had bought them that she normally couldn't afford. Alone in the kitchen, she stood by the counter and mindlessly ate a banana-chocolate-chip muffin, one of the rejects from the order that had overcooked this morning. The cat appeared from wherever she'd been sleeping and twined herself around Molly's legs.

Molly was so tired, not to mention tense and angry. Why should Phil be able to drop down out of the sky and pick up where he left off? It shouldn't be so easy for him. It didn't seem fair. She knew she shouldn't still be mad at him for the way their marriage had ended. But she couldn't help it. The check would come in handy, but she felt mad about that, too. Mad at herself for feeling bought off. She wished she didn't need Phil's money and could just rip up that check and toss it in his face.

But the truth was she did need it. She was sure he could see that as soon as he walked in, but he was too smart to say anything. She was working hard but not doing all that well on her own. What was all this muffin baking and quiche making and backbreaking work adding up to anyway?

Molly sometimes imagined herself having her own shop, with loads of people working for her. She'd sit up front and be the boss, organized and smartly dressed. But that was just a fantasy, an imaginary carrot dangling just beyond reach that helped her get through the drudgery. It gave her some hope, some inspiration. But it would never come true. Who was she kidding? She could never start her own business. She never went to college. She just didn't have what it takes, the smarts and the confidence. Success took more than just making a good chocolate cake.

Jill walked into the kitchen, dressed in her nightgown. "Look at what Daddy bought me." She held out her arm, showing off a silver bracelet with a dangling heart charm. "He got one for Lauren, too. And some CDs and some other stuff. Want to see?"

Molly forced a smile. "Sure, honey. I'll be right in."

She put a dirty cup in the sink and shut off the kitchen light. Maybe she was lucky Phil had surfaced and would help out now. *I'll never do any better than this,* Molly thought sadly. *I'm a fool to try.*

Chapter Four

"Are you sure you're up to it? You can see just as well from the window in the kitchen." Sophie stood by her husband's wheelchair, which was parked in the living room, right next to his favorite armchair. He had the newspaper spread out on his lap, but it obviously wasn't holding his interest this morning. Miranda, who stood nearby, cast Sophie a concerned look over her grandfather's head.

"I need some fresh air. *Real* air," Gus insisted. "I've still got that blasted hospital smell in my nose. It's driving me crazy."

Sophie felt worried. He had only come home on Tuesday, the day before yesterday. Since then he had spent most of his time in bed. But this morning he'd asked to get dressed in his real clothes, his trousers, suspenders, and flannel shirt. That was a good sign, she thought. Except for his sallow complexion and hollow eyes, he almost looked his old self. But going outside? She didn't think that was a good idea. She glanced over at Miranda, who seemed to have the same reaction.

"It's cold out, Grandpa. It looks like it might snow any minute."

"Oh, that's nothing. A little flurry maybe. Bundle me up like a mummy, you two, if it makes you feel any better. I don't care. I want to go out and get some air."

Sophie sighed. Meeting her husband's watery gaze, she realized they had come to a point when she couldn't refuse him any request, no matter how extreme. Anything to please him now, to make the days he had left happier for him.

"I'll get his parka and scarf. Give him a thick sweater. That gray one on the chair in the bedroom should do."

Miranda nodded and disappeared to find the sweater while Sophie fetched the parka, scarf, and gloves from the mud room. They soon had Gus bundled up beyond recognition in his wheelchair. Sophie heard him chortling under the layers. "Where do you think you're taking me, girls, on an expedition to the North Pole?"

Miranda reached up and loosened his scarf. "Is that better?"

"A little," he conceded. "Okay, ready to roll." He jauntily patted the side of the chair.

Miranda pushed while Sophie went ahead and opened the doors. Gus was too weak to walk even the short distance from the bedroom out to the back porch. She could hardly believe it and willed herself not to cry.

Once outside, Miranda turned the chair to give her grandfather a sweeping view of the orchard and, in the far distance, the village below and the sheltered harbor. The sky above was heavy and low, gray clouds promising snow.

Miranda looked at Sophie. "Call me when you're ready to come back in, Grandma. Don't stay out here too long."

Sophie nodded. Her granddaughter understood that she and Gus needed some time alone right now. There were things to talk about, important things, with no time left to procrastinate.

"Warm enough?" Sophie pulled up a chair and sat beside him.

"Warm as toast," Gus replied. He held out his gloved hand, and she took it in her own. "We're sheltered from the wind back here, facing east. I see the snow coming down, though. It's just starting."

Sophie saw it, too, fat white flakes that slowly drifted down from the sky as if shaken loose from a flock of doves.

"I missed this place. It's good to be home. I don't want to go back to that hospital again."

"I know, dear. I don't think you'll have to," Sophie said honestly. The best they could hope for now was that Gus would be able to die right here in the comfort of his own home.

"In all the years since I came to live here, I don't think I ever spent more than a night or two in a row away from the trees. Or apart from you."

"Not a handful, by my count. We were never big on vacations, were we?" She smiled at him. "There was always something to do around here."

"We didn't need to go gallivanting around, honey. This was our world. God gave us plenty. As near to perfect as it gets, if you ask me. I couldn't ask for more."

"Me, neither," Sophie agreed. Born on the orchard, she had been living here so long, she sometimes imagined she would wake one morning to find roots sprouting out of her toes, like one of the apple trees. She often thought people must pity her, thinking she never did much with her life. But she knew in her heart she'd had a rich life—full of hard work and challenges, joys and sorrows.

If she died tonight, her spirit would leave this earth with a feeling of satisfaction; she had peace in her heart at a job well done. She glanced at Gus, his once strong profile worn down by sickness and age. But in his gaze there was a peaceful light, as peaceful as a calm blue summer sky. *He feels the same,* she realized. *He's not afraid of dying.*

"I've had a good life with you, Gus. You're a wonderful

husband and father. My best friend and the love of my life. . . ." Sophie felt her throat tightening, and she paused to take a breath. "I don't know what I'm going to do without you. I don't know how to keep going without you."

"Hush now, sweetheart. None of that." Gus leaned over and put his arm around her shoulders. "I was the lucky one. Everyone knows that. I didn't know up from down until I met you. You gave me children, this orchard, the kind of life a man could be proud of. You didn't even want me at first, remember?" he teased her.

"Oh, it wasn't like that. I liked you right away. I just couldn't see what you wanted with me. I'd been thrown over. I was practically a spinster."

Sophie's first love had left her at the altar, a public humiliation she had somehow survived. With her failed wedding day and the scarcity of eligible men after the war, she had lost all hope of finding another who would want to marry her.

"Prettiest spinster I ever saw." Gus laughed softly and shook his head. "I'll never forget that day your brother brought me here. I came to ask for a job and saw you, up in a tree, your arms full of apples. I felt my heart just jump out of my chest, I swear it."

He rested his hand on his heart and smiled. Sophie smiled too, remembering. Gus and her younger brother, Fred, had just come home from the army and neither had jobs. Tall and lean with a head of black wavy hair, Gus looked liked a movie star standing there in the dappled sunlight. She nearly fell right off the ladder the first time he spoke her name.

"You proposed pretty quickly, that's for sure. My brother said you were just after my property," she reminded him. "Tell the truth. It can't make any difference now. Was that your intention?"

Gus laughed and hugged her. "Yup, a gigolo. That's what I was. But you reformed me. A man needs a woman to improve himself, you know."

"I did reform you . . . almost." She sighed. "That feels like it was yesterday, doesn't it? Where did the years go?"

"They flew by. Season to season. Around and around we went. It felt like it would never end. Spring will be here before you know it. The trees will green up and the blossoms will come."

Sophie nodded, staring out at the orchard with him. She could almost hear that low hum of the bees right now and smell the moist earth coming alive again. Even the snow flakes clinging to the branches started to look like white blossoms.

"Every one will get to work again. Even your bees." Gus's voice held an optimistic note as always.

But they both knew he would not be out in the orchard working this spring. He would be gone by then. *Long gone from my side,* Sophie thought.

Her vision of spring suddenly melted before her eyes, and she began to cry. Gus patted her shoulder.

"There, there, sweetheart. I'm not going so far. It will be as if I'm sitting right here on the back porch, watching you."

Harder than that for her, Sophie thought. But she didn't disagree. There was a heaven, Sophie felt sure. And she was just as sure that Gus would be up there.

But where would she be? Away from the orchard by then, probably, if their children had a say in the matter.

"The kids don't think I should stay without you. Evelyn and Una had a little talk with me while you were in the hospital. Bart called and said the same thing, too."

"What do you want to do?" he asked her softly.

"They make some sense; I'm not saying they don't. Still, I can't imagine leaving here. I know it won't be the same without you. I might just hate it. But I was here on my own when we met, and I think I can do it again. I'd like to try, at least."

Gus didn't answer for a moment. He sat staring straight out at the trees and the low falling snow.

"I hate to think that my dying will force you off, Sophie.

After all the times we struggled to hang on to this place when it wasn't easy. But I guess I'm worried about you, too. I don't like the idea of you out here all alone. We're not young anymore."

"Oh, let's not talk about that now. Worrying is a waste of time. It says so right in the Bible," she reminded him. "The Lord doesn't want us to worry. He'll show me the right thing to do, I'm sure of it."

"I know He will. I just love you so much. And I promised I'd always take care of you." He wiped his gloved hand across his eyes, which were glassy with unshed tears.

Tears started trickling down Sophie's cheeks again. She couldn't help herself. She leaned over and wound her arm through his and put her head on Gus's shoulder.

"We'll be all right," she said finally. "He'll take care of us both."

"MOM, HOW DO YOU SPELL *HORRENDOUS*?" JILL SAT AT the kitchen table doing her homework, while Molly stood at the counter, chopping a pile of parsley. She paused, thinking, then shook her head.

"I'm not sure. You need to look it up in the dictionary. There's one right on your desk in your room."

"Never mind. I'll just say, 'It was really horrible.' "

Molly wanted her to get into the habit of using a dictionary, but she didn't push it. Jill was hurrying to finish her homework before Phil came by. He was due to pick up the girls at six, but Molly felt sure that with the snow he'd be late. He hadn't called to cancel, though, which was a surprise. In the past Phil had always grabbed the slightest excuse to postpone his visits.

Lauren didn't seem to remember that Phil was coming tonight, Molly noticed. But she was distracted by an unexpected visit with Amanda. Matthew had called in the afternoon from Southport and asked if Molly could pick up

Amanda after chorus practice since he didn't think he'd get home in time with the snow.

Molly didn't mind helping him out. She had to pick up Lauren anyway. He was also due to arrive shortly, and she felt undeniably nervous about seeing him again—and at the prospect of his visit overlapping with Phil's, though she didn't know why that should matter. Maybe because Phil brought out such a shrewish side of her personality? One she didn't want Matthew to see, that was for sure.

The sound of giggling came from the bedroom where Lauren and Amanda were holed up, supposedly doing homework. Well, that's how it was at that age. Somehow the homework got done.

Molly forced herself to focus on the task at hand. She had an important appointment tomorrow at the Beanery and was making several special dishes for the café owners, Jonathan and Felicity Bean, to sample. On Monday, when she had dropped off their order of quiches, they told her that they planned to expand their menu and asked if she could supply more lunch and dinner dishes. The order was potentially humongous, as Jill might say, and Molly felt both excited and nervous at the prospect. So nervous that she had only told Betty about the appointment.

Molly didn't want to get her hopes up, but she had already done some rough calculations, and if things worked out, she might finally be able to quit her cleaning clients to cook full-time.

Don't count your cupcakes until they rise, she reminded herself with a grin. But it was sure hard not to. Molly stirred a pot of seven-bean chili, a vegetarian entrée, and then checked the trays of beef empanadas and chicken pot pies that were baking in the oven.

Still feeling anxious, she went into the living room and glanced out the windows that overlooked Main Street. The snow was piling up out there. The forecast had predicted only flurries, but this was something more. Molly sighed. She had had enough snow this winter. When would it end?

It was already the first week of March. She hoped this latest addition would melt quickly.

An SUV-style truck slowed down and parked across the street. It was Matthew's Land Rover. She watched him get out and head for the door to her building. Molly spun around and quickly surveyed the room. She found a pair of slippers, an empty glass, and a magazine on the floor. She dumped the glass in the sink and brought the rest to her bedroom. She quickly checked her appearance in the mirror, pulling off her apron and adding a dash of lipstick from the tube on her dresser.

She paused and took a deep breath. She was getting too nervous. Exactly what she didn't want to do. She would act relaxed and friendly to him, but she didn't want to seem too interested. After all, Matthew clearly wasn't interested in her. He hadn't called during the past week, and he'd had the perfect excuse as she'd left her cleaning bucket at his house. But Fran Tulley had called to say he had dropped off the bucket along with an extra check at Betty's office. To Molly, his leaving the things with Betty was an obvious message: He didn't want to get involved.

She knocked on Lauren's door before heading back to the kitchen. "Lauren, Amanda . . . time to come out. Amanda's father is here to pick her up."

In the kitchen Jill looked up from her homework. "Is Daddy here?"

Molly shook her head as the doorbell rang. "It's Dr. Harding."

Then she turned and pulled open the door. Matthew smiled at her. His cheeks were red from the cold and his dark eyes were bright. Flecks of snow clung to his hair and coated his shoulders.

"Come on in," Molly greeted him. "You must be freezing."

"I'm all right. I'm used to the cold." He took off his gloves and rubbed his hands together. "Hello, Jill. How are you?"

"I'm good. Just doing homework. Do you know how to spell *cataclysmic*?"

"Hmm, that's a good one. I'm not really sure." He glanced at Molly with a helpless—and totally charming—smile. "Why don't you try the dictionary?"

"That's okay. I'll just say, 'It was really horrible.' "

"Right. And if you don't go into your room and get the dictionary, your grade on that story is going to be really 'horrible,' " Molly warned her.

"Okay, okay. I'm going." Jill sighed theatrically and picked up her notebook.

"Don't mind her." Molly turned to check the chili. "She gets a little cranky when she's hungry."

"Don't we all. Low blood sugar," Matthew explained. "Gee, something sure smells good in here. What are you cooking?"

"Well, let's see . . . we have some vegetarian chili up here." Molly gestured at the pot. "Some chicken and mushrooms crepes in this pan, and beef empanadas and chicken pot pies in the oven." She pulled open the door and took a peek. "Oh, and some string beans to make sure there's something green."

Matthew stared at her wide-eyed, looking as if he wanted to laugh, but he wasn't sure if he should or not. "Quite a menu. Are you expecting company?"

"I have sort of an audition tomorrow. At the Beanery. They're expanding their lunch and dinner menus and asked me to bring some samples for new orders."

"Oh, I see. Well, everything smells so good, I can't see how you could miss."

"Thanks." Molly smiled at him and lowered the heat on the oven. His expression peaked with interest, but he didn't say more. An awkward silence hung between them.

I'm sure I'll live to regret this, but what the heck, she thought glancing back at him.

"Would you like to stay for dinner? There's plenty here."

"Oh, no. We couldn't put you out like that. I wasn't hinting at an invitation," he added with a self-conscious grin.

"It's okay. I was going to ask you anyway. I need some more taste testers." That wasn't exactly true. But she was trying to make him welcome. "I can't trust anything the kids say unless the recipe involves pizza, peanut butter, or chocolate."

Matthew laughed. "Yes, the three major food groups as far as Amanda is concerned, too." He met her gaze again. "I'd be honored to be a taste tester. But I really don't want to impose on you, Molly."

"It's no trouble. You'd be doing me a favor, honestly," Molly insisted.

So much for her plan to act disinterested and not put herself out. But he looked hungry, and she really could use another adult opinion.

Oh, who was she kidding? She liked the guy. More than she wanted, and here she was giving in to that feeling after promising herself that she wouldn't.

But Lauren and Amanda seemed to have hit it off so grandly, Molly thought. Whether she wanted to or not, she would be seeing a lot of Matthew Harding. It was probably smart to try to work out a friendly relationship. Even if it never amounted to more than that.

"Well, okay then." He sounded doubtful but was smiling. "I'd love to."

"Great." Molly glanced at the clock. "My ex-husband is coming at six to see the girls. I guess we'd better sit down right away."

"No problem, I'm starved. What can I do to help you?"

Matthew washed up, then set the table. Five was a tight fit in Molly's small kitchen, but it would work out all right, she decided. The Hardings weren't going to stay that long.

While Matthew rounded up the girls, Molly set the bowls and platters of the various dishes on the table, along with a green salad and a basket of hot cheese biscuits she had baked to go with the chili. She had taken a course in food presentation and tried to add a professional finishing touch, sprinkling finely chopped herbs on the platter rim.

She was pleased with the way the table looked and with Matthew's reaction. "Wow, it looks like a restaurant in here," he said, taking a seat across the table.

"A very small restaurant," Molly amended. She was about to sit down between Lauren and Jill when the phone rang. Before she could answer it, the answering machine picked up. "Hi Molly, it's me, Phil. I got stuck late at work, and the turnpike is creeping because of the snow—"

Here we go again, she thought tiredly.

Molly picked up as he spoke. "Hi, Phil. I heard your message. So I guess you're not coming tonight. Is that what you're trying to say?"

"It's my own fault. I got a late start. I didn't think the snow would be so heavy." He sounded sincerely apologetic and disappointed. "Tell the girls I'm really sorry about tonight, but I'll see them on the weekend, right?"

"Sure. That should work out." Molly had lots of baking to do again, so Phil's visit would be a help to her.

"Are they around? Can I say hello?"

"We just sat down to dinner. I'll have them call you later at home."

They said good-bye, and Molly hung up. As soon as she returned to the table, she realized everyone had overheard the conversation. Jill sat with a long face, suddenly looking too listless to eat. Lauren looked subdued as well, though not nearly as crushed as her younger sister.

"I guess you guys heard the news. Your father can't make it tonight. He got held up with the snow."

Lauren shrugged. "That's okay. I didn't want to go anyway with Amanda here."

"Will he come on Sunday?" Jill asked.

"He said so." Molly wished she could sound more definite, but she didn't think it was wise. What if he canceled again? It wouldn't surprise her.

Part of her felt vindicated for distrusting him, while another part felt upset for her daughters, especially Jill. The weather *was* bad though. Maybe Phil wasn't falling back into his old ways so quickly. She would just have to wait to see.

"You can call him after dinner," Molly added.

"I'm not that hungry. I'll call him now." Jill started to get up from the table, but Molly stopped her with a look.

"We have guests, Jill. You can be excused when everyone is finished. Your father is still on the road. He won't be home for a while."

Jill sat sullenly, pushing chunks of the beef empanada around her dish with her fork. Molly felt embarrassed that Matthew had witnessed their little domestic drama but there was nothing she could do. She would need to talk with Jill alone later to soothe her hurt feelings. *See, it's already starting*. Molly sighed to herself.

"So how was school today, girls?" Matthew asked in a tone Molly thought determinedly bright. "How was chorus?"

"Mrs. Pickering drove us crazy," Lauren complained. "She made us sing the last bar of 'Oklahoma' about a million times. You know, that part when all the sections harmonize and get louder and louder. 'Oklahoma, o-kay, o-kah-ay . . . *O-kaaaay*!' " Lauren stood up from her seat, singing, waving her arms, and getting carried away.

Molly blinked, watching her daughter's outflung arms narrowly miss Matthew's head. Luckily he ducked in time, quietly laughing.

"I remember!" Molly interrupted. "You don't have to give a live performance," she added, sharing a grin with Matthew.

"Then Cheryl Nielsen said she had to go, and Mrs. Pickering totally freaked. Cheryl acts like such a big diva and always misses practice even though she has a solo.

And—" Lauren suddenly turned to Amanda. "Tell your dad what happened next."

Amanda seemed uncomfortable and wouldn't look at anyone. "You can tell," she said.

"No, *you.*" Lauren poked her friend with her elbow. "Go on."

Matt and Molly exchanged a curious glance. "What happened, honey?" Matt asked.

"It's no big deal," Amanda said, looking down at the table. "Mrs. Pickering got mad at Cheryl for talking back and said if she didn't stay, she couldn't sing the solo. It's in the finale, when we do this medley from *The Sound of Music.* Then Cheryl left anyway, so she picked me to do it."

"Wow! A solo part. That's wonderful. That's terrific news!" Matthew was beaming, and Molly felt happy for him. She wasn't surprised, though. Lauren said Amanda had a beautiful voice, despite her speech problem.

"When is that concert?" Molly asked. "Isn't it April something?"

"*Earth to Mom.* More like a week from Saturday?" Lauren reminded her tartly.

"Oops. I didn't realize it was so soon. Guess I'd better mark the calendar."

Matthew's eyebrows rose in surprise. "This is the first I've even heard about it. When were you going to tell me, Amanda? That day?"

Amanda gave him a casual shrug. "I just forgot. I wasn't even sure I'd be in the show since I just joined up."

"Well, sounds like you'll be there, front and center." Matthew paused and glanced at Molly. "Why don't we all go together, and I'll take everyone out to dinner after?"

Molly felt her expression freeze in shock and tried to quickly recover. "That sounds nice. But you don't have to take us out to dinner, Matt."

"I want to. I'd like to reciprocate for this . . . this absolute feast. I can't remember the last time I've eaten such delicious food. If the Beans don't hire you to cook truckloads of all this stuff, they're crazy, by the way. But I can't have you over to my house. I'm a terrible cook."

"He really is. You'd *better* let him buy," Amanda chirped up.

Lauren and Jill giggled. Matt looked about to reply then brushed it off. *I guess my feisty kids are rubbing off on Amanda,* Molly thought. *I hope he doesn't get annoyed.*

The girls talked more about the concert, and Matthew explained his frustrating delay in Southport regarding his privileges at the hospital. He'd thought that all the paperwork had been completed, and he would be able to sign in patients when necessary, but some form had been held up somewhere, and he'd spent the entire day there trying to figure it out.

"So finally, after about twenty phone calls back to my old hospital in Worcester, it was faxed over late this afternoon. I know I filled it out months ago."

"Sounds worse than the Registry of Motor Vehicles," Molly sympathized, but she was only half focused on the story. She couldn't stop thinking about his invitation to dinner next Saturday. The whole idea of it made her nervous—and excited. She started to reach for another biscuit, then folded her hands in her lap. *Get a grip,* she told herself. *The diet starts now.*

Don't make too much of this, she warned herself. *It's not a date. Not even close. He was just being friendly and polite, probably because he hasn't made any friends in town yet. And once he starts meeting people, he won't want to socialize with you. He's more the type for the other side of town, where Dr. Elliot and the Warwicks live.*

Matthew sat back and wiped his mouth with his napkin. "I know I said it before but I have to repeat myself. That was absolutely delicious, Molly."

Molly felt her cheeks flush. "Thanks. Glad you could join us." She rose to start clearing the dishes, but Matthew stood up and began clearing off the table, too.

"You sit. I'll clean up," he said.

Molly wasn't used to anyone telling her to relax and not work. She just couldn't do it.

"That's all right. It's getting late. The snow has stopped. You must be eager to get home."

"It's not late at all and I insist. I'm not going to freeload, then leave you with you a huge mess to clean up."

I never met a man who didn't, she was tempted to reply.

But she didn't say anything, distracted suddenly by the sight of Matthew yanking off his expensive-looking silk tie and rolling up his shirtsleeves. He looked even more attractive somehow. It was downright annoying.

"If you're done with dinner, bring your dishes to the sink," he told the girls.

Molly picked up the dishes of leftovers to be stored away. "Did you guys finish your homework? I heard a lot giggling in there before," she said to Amanda and Lauren.

"We didn't *exactly* finish," Lauren said. She and Amanda exchanged a secret glance, trying not to start giggling again.

"Why don't you get back to work?" Matt suggested. "We'll call you when we're done."

Jill brought her dish to the sink. "I'm going to call Daddy now," she said quietly.

"Sure, that's okay. The number is on the fridge," Molly told her.

"I know the number." Jill turned and headed for the phone in Molly's bedroom.

Molly sighed, and Matt glanced at her. "I guess she's disappointed that she didn't see her father," he said quietly. "Does he visit them regularly?"

"Not really," Molly murmured. "Well, he says now he wants to. But this is only the second time after a long break, and he's already messing things up again."

She didn't know Matthew that well. She didn't know him at all really. She felt upset about Phil but wasn't sure if she should confide in Matt.

"The snow really was heavy. I had trouble myself on the turnpike."

"I know. And I think he was telling the truth. But I hate to see the girls get their hopes up, thinking he's going to be a real father to them again and having it all come to nothing. I'd rather he didn't see them at all. I guess that sounds awful of me, doesn't it?"

Matthew wiped a dish with a soapy sponge. "You don't want to see them get hurt. I understand. I'm that way with Amanda. I get so overprotective . . . too much, sometimes. But it's hard not to be. You feel for them. It's only natural." He set the dish on the drain board and picked up another. "How long have you been divorced?"

"About seven years. We were married young. Things were always rocky between us. Then he met someone else. So we split up." Molly turned her back so Matthew couldn't see her expression.

Matthew didn't say anything for a moment. He rinsed off a dish and set it on the drain board. "What happened then? Did he remarry?"

Molly shook her head. "His fling didn't last that long. Just a way to get out of our marriage, I guess. He's still single. Moves around a lot. Changes his job a lot, too. He hasn't helped out much supporting the girls. He's around for a few months, then disappears. He always has some excuse when he comes back and makes big promises. The girls want to see him, so it's hard to say no."

"That's tough on you, too. I'm sure you don't want to be the bad guy and keep them away from their father."

"Tell me about it. Sometimes I think I should wear a T-shirt that reads, 'Big Mean Mom.' "

Matthew laughed. "I think you've got something there. You could sell a lot of those. Some that read, 'Big Mean Dad,' too, of course."

"I could have used one this Sunday. Phil showed up unannounced. I didn't even want the girls to know he was here, but they saw him and that was that." She took out a container of cookies and arranged them on a dish. "I'm just afraid he's going to pull his famous disappearing act again."

"It sounds like you're in a tough spot. But I think you're doing the right thing. Even if he does disappear again, at least you gave him a chance. You showed charity." Matthew glanced at her over his shoulder. "Jill and Lauren will remember that. I don't think you'll regret it."

"Thanks. I hope you're right."

Molly started a pot of coffee, and Matthew turned back to the dishes. "You're a good mother, Molly. You've done a great job with Jill and Lauren. You should be proud."

"I am proud of them," she said honestly.

Still his compliment didn't sit that easily with her. She knew that there were so many times when she showed the girls exactly the wrong example. Especially when it came to Phil. By now, she should have forgiven and forgotten all the slights, large and small, that had broken up their marriage. But the sore spots had never really healed, only covered over.

"So, how do you like Cape Light?" she asked, hoping to shift the conversation to less personal matters.

"So far so good. I'm really pleased to see Amanda adjusting so well to school. She's naturally shy, I guess, and her speech problem makes it even harder. She's had a lot of speech therapy, but it never resolves completely."

"That's too bad," Molly said sympathetically. "I hardly noticed it, actually. It's great that she likes chorus. Lauren says she has a beautiful voice."

Matthew smiled. "She really does. I think you'll be surprised." His expression grew more serious. "I can't tell you how happy I am that she joined up. It must have to do with Lauren. She joined at her last school, then dropped out. She wouldn't say why, but she's always so tough on herself. Amanda has . . . well, perfectionist tendencies. I'm trying to encourage her to open up, to relax about life a little."

"It's hard for kids at that age. They're so self-conscious.

If Lauren wakes up with a blemish, you'd think it was a world crisis. She actually begs me to let her stay home from school."

"Oh, yeah. I've heard that zit emergency myself. But this is different." He paused, and Molly sensed he was deciding whether to confide some deeper issue.

"My wife, Sharon . . . she was a good mother, don't get me wrong. But she could never really accept Amanda's speech problem. She could never just let it go. Sometimes I felt when she looked at Amanda that was all Sharon saw: that she stuttered when she was nervous. Not how bright and sweet and beautiful she is." He sighed and shook his head.

Molly didn't know what to say. She had imagined Matthew being married to someone who was perfect in every way. It was surprising to hear his wife had shortcomings and also to learn there had been friction in his marriage.

"I'm not sure how I would handle a situation like that," Molly admitted. "I guess there's a fine line between trying to solve the problem and paying too much attention to it."

"That was just it. Sharon kept finding new therapists, new treatments. I know she really believed she was just helping Amanda. But she couldn't see how she was hurting her at the same time. It made Amanda feel like something was horribly wrong with her. As if she wasn't good enough just the way she is."

Molly's heart went out to him. He loved his daughter so much. Strangely, she found she could also relate to Amanda, feeling she'd always been judged by her shortcomings and never her talents.

"I know this might sound a little crazy, but sometimes I think God sent Amanda into my life for a reason. She's made me a better person . . . and a better doctor. I think she's perfect just the way she is. I tell her that all the time. But I know she doesn't believe me."

Molly knew that feeling, too. If someone gave her even the slightest compliment, she couldn't help but contradict them.

"Keep telling her. Someday she'll believe you," Molly advised him.

Matthew stood drying his hands on a towel. He gazed at her and smiled. His warm brown eyes held a tender light. Molly wanted to look away, but she just couldn't quite. She felt a tug of attraction. Foolish, she told herself, but undeniable.

Lauren and Amanda ran into the kitchen. "We're finished with our homework, and we definitely need cookies. Please," Lauren announced looking around. She spotted the dish of cookies on the table and headed for it like a chocolate-seeking missile.

"She's part shark, I swear. She has the most amazing sense of smell," Molly said in amazement.

"My mom made these. They're awesome," Lauren promised, handing one to Amanda.

"They do look awesome," Matt agreed. He started to reach for a cookie then stopped, staring at Amanda.

"What happened to your fingernails?"

Molly looked, too. Lauren and Amanda had pasted on fake nails and painted them alternating shades of sparkle blue, lilac, and silver.

"They're just for fun." Amanda stared up at her father with a wary expression. "I think they look cool."

"They come off with a little nail-polish remover," Molly explained. Matthew looked relieved but still disturbed. "They'll probably fall off while she's sleeping," she added.

"With any luck," he said, giving the dazzling fingernails a resigned look.

"Would you like some coffee?" Molly asked politely.

"Yes, please." He nodded, unsmiling. The girls were uncharacteristically silent, munching mechanically on their cookies.

"Milk and sugar?" He nodded again, and she stirred some in. "How about some nail-polish remover?"

He stared at her for a moment, then his face broke into a

grin. She heard the girls laughing and hoped he didn't mind the joke at his expense.

"If you have an extra bottle, I'll take it to go."

"No problem." She set the mugs of coffee on the table and poured glasses of milk for the girls, then joined them at the table where the pile of cookies was rapidly diminishing.

Jill walked in, sat at her place, and took a cookie. She seemed to be in a better mood, Molly noticed. Her chat with Phil had definitely cheered her up.

A few minutes later, Matthew and Amanda were putting on their coats and saying good night. "Thanks again for dinner, Molly. And for picking up Amanda. Sounds like there's going to be a lot of chorus practice next week. Why don't we share the driving?"

"That would be a big help," Molly replied honestly.

"I'll call you tomorrow and we'll figure it out."

"Okay. Let me give you my cell-phone number. I'm always running around." Molly took one of her business cards from the basket near the phone and handed it to him.

" 'Molly to the Rescue. Cleaning, cooking, errands, and more,' " he read aloud. He looked up at her and smiled. "Not to mention the awesome cookies and sage advice."

"There's just so much you can get on a card," she said wryly. "Oh wait. Don't forget this." She grabbed the bottle of polish remover that Lauren had retrieved from the bathroom and handed it to him. He slipped it in his pocket, his eyes flashing appreciation.

They said good night again, and she closed the door.

So he was going to call her tomorrow. She'd be recharging the cell-phone battery tonight, that was for sure.

TUCKER LET HIMSELF IN THROUGH THE SIDE DOOR AND paused in the mudroom to pull off his wet boots, hat, and jacket.

"Tucker? I was wondering when you'd be home." Fran

came out of the family room to meet him. "Why didn't you call?"

"I left a message on the machine. Didn't you get it?" He kissed her cheek.

"You said you'd be a little late. It's after *ten*."

"That late already? I didn't realize." Tucker walked into the kitchen, and Fran followed. "Are the kids in bed?"

"Michael's still doing homework, but Mary Ellen just shut off her light." Fran watched as he sat down at the table and stretched out his legs. Tucker's dog, Scout, trotted over and licked his hand. Tucker scratched his soft head.

"I saved some dinner for you. Would you like me to heat it?"

"That's okay. I grabbed something on the road."

"How about a cup of tea? I was just going to make some. You must feel chilled from the cold."

"A cup of tea sounds good. I'll have some with you."

Tucker knew Fran was wondering where he'd been all night. Well, he had nothing to hide. "I went down to Southport to visit Carl again."

He watched her expression as she filled the kettle and set it on the stove. "I had a feeling that's where you were. Why didn't you tell me?"

Tucker shrugged. "I don't know. I didn't really plan on going to see him. But I had to drive down to Hamilton at the end of the day to interview a witness on a hit-and-run. So I was halfway there anyway."

Fran didn't reply. Tucker could tell from her expression that it bothered her to hear he'd been visiting Carl. Well, he couldn't help that. He could visit his brother in the hospital if he wanted to. He didn't need Fran's permission.

The kettle's shrill whistle broke into his thoughts. He watched Fran pour the water into two mugs, place them on the table, then sit down in her usual chair.

Neither spoke for a moment. Fran stirred some sugar into her tea. "So, how is he coming along? You never even told me what is wrong with him," she said.

He hadn't told her, Tucker realized. Mainly because, so far, he hadn't gone into much detail about Carl; it seemed a subject best avoided.

"Well, let's see. He's in pretty bad shape. He has emphysema, a collapsed lung, an ulcer, high-blood pressure, phlebitis, and a touch of diabetes."

"That's too bad. Has he improved at all since the reverend found him?"

"A little. He looks better, and they've pulled a few tubes out of him." Tucker blew on his tea and took a sip. He wondered what Fran was thinking. She didn't look happy; her pretty face was drawn into a tight frown.

"You must feel sorry for him. It's only natural."

"Of course, I feel sorry for him. Don't you?"

"Yes, of course, I do." She looked up at him, her brown eyes open wide. "But he never took care of himself. He never lived a normal life. Now he's facing the consequences, I guess."

Tucker sighed. "Some people just don't fit with a normal life. I see it all the time. You can't really blame them. That's just the way it is."

"I wasn't blaming him, exactly." Fran looked away and sipped her tea. "When will they let him out of the hospital? Did his doctor say?"

"He'll be released on Monday. You know how it is. They don't keep you very long in a hospital these days, no matter what's wrong with you."

There was a basket of clean laundry on one of the kitchen chairs. Fran came to her feet and started folding the clothes. "What are his plans? Is he still going up to Portland? Maybe that friend of his has a job up there for him." Fran matched a pair of socks and rolled them into a tight ball. "You'll have to give him some money, I guess."

"I thought I'd give him some," Tucker replied. "But I'm not so sure now what to do."

Fran stared at him curiously, a bath towel dangling from her hand. "What to do? What do you mean, Tucker?"

"The doctor says he's still pretty sick. Not well enough to work or travel around. I thought we should let him stay here awhile. In the spare room. Just until he gets back on his feet."

Fran's eyes widened in dismay. "Stay here? But he's been in jail, Tucker. He *killed* a man."

"That was an accident, self-defense. You know that." Tucker tried to catch her eye, but she wouldn't look at him. "I'm surprised at you, Fran. I thought you'd be more sympathetic to the poor guy. You've been running all over town for the past month collecting food for poor people. Well, now's your chance to really help someone who's down on his luck. Not just give him a few free cans of soup."

Fran's fair skin turned a mottled pink color. "That's not fair! One thing has nothing to do with the other. It's not that I don't feel sorry for Carl. I do. But he scares me, Tucker. He killed a man, and you're talking about bringing him into the house with our children."

"Come on, he's not going to hurt anybody. Carl's not like that. He's my brother, for goodness' sake."

"One that you haven't seen in over twenty years. He's been in jail a good part of his life and up to God-only-knows-what since. We don't know him anymore. We don't know what he's like."

Tucker pushed back from the table. He wasn't used to arguing with Fran. They hardly ever disagreed. He was tired from work and driving in the snow. He didn't want to say something he'd regret, but he could feel his patience unraveling.

"Can't you make other arrangements?" Fran pressed him. "There are agencies and public programs and all sorts of places that can take him in."

Tucker had looked into the alternatives, but they all seemed too grim. Too cruel. He knew how dangerous the shelters were. Most homeless people desperately avoided them. Besides, Carl was too sick now for any of those places.

"Even if I could get him into a shelter that was halfway decent, he wouldn't stay. He'd find a way out and start hitching rides again, living hand-to-mouth until who knows what happens."

Fran shook out a T-shirt and laid it flat on the table to fold. "He's been living that way for years, as far as I can see. Do you think a few days in our guest room is really going to change him?"

"I'm not trying to change him," Tucker assured her. "I just want to help him get back on his feet. I'm not thrilled to have him here, either. But there really isn't any place else he can go. Not until his health improves. I've looked into this, Fran. I really have. If there was some other way, I'd do it."

He watched her pick up a white handkerchief and fold it into a neat square. Her face was drawn into a tight expression.

"Come on, Fran. You're blowing this way out of proportion. I don't see that it's such a great imposition. It will only be for a few days. You'll hardly know he's around."

"Of course, I'll know he's around." Fran sat down at the table again and held his gaze. "I just feel as if your mind is already made up. You're going to do this no matter what I say. My feelings about it don't really matter to you."

Tucker sighed, feeling tired and frustrated. Still, he couldn't deny Fran's point. Driving home from Southport tonight, he'd considered the options and had pretty much decided to take Carl in. He just hadn't figured on Fran opposing him so strongly.

"I'm in a tough spot, Fran. I wish you could be a little more understanding. I'm asking for some patience. For my part, I wish the guy had never come back. But he did and he's here and I feel obligated to help him."

"Because?"

"Because the alternative is that I turn my back and get a call in a week or a month or whenever saying that he's been found dead somewhere and I didn't help him. Now that's something I just couldn't live with."

Tucker had been careful not to raise his voice. But the look on Fran's face made him feel as if he had all the same.

He stood up from the table. His shoulders felt stiff from too much driving, and he rubbed the back of his neck.

Fran looked up at him, then just shook her head. "Will you at least think about it a little more? Make a few more calls to places that would take him? There's probably a social worker at the hospital you can talk to. I'll call if you want me to."

He took a deep breath and then another, trying to use a stress-management technique he'd learned at work. Fran was quiet but doggedly persistent when she wanted something. Maybe that was why she was such a good salesperson.

"All right. I'll make a few more calls. I'll try to track down the hospital social worker. But I'm not so sure I'll come to any new conclusions on this, Fran." When she didn't answer or look up at him, he said, "I'm going upstairs. I have an early day tomorrow. Are you coming?"

She glanced at him briefly and shook her head. "I need to put the laundry away first. I'll be up in a while."

"Okay, then. Good night." He leaned over and kissed her cheek, but she didn't kiss him back.

It was going to be difficult around here for a while, Tucker thought as he climbed up the stairs. Carl wouldn't shower him with gratitude, that was for sure. And now he and Fran were at odds as well.

He'd made up his mind on the long drive home tonight that the only thing to do was take Carl in. Now he wondered if it was the right choice after all.

CHAPTER FIVE

TUCKER SAT NEAR THE BACK OF THE CHURCH, ON THE pulpit side, with Michael and Mary Ellen beside him. Fran didn't like to miss church, but she had to show houses today to a couple from out of town, and she had raced out to meet them at the train station while he and the kids were still eating breakfast.

The voices of the choir soared as they sang "Amazing Grace." The hymn was one of his favorites, but for some reason, the familiar lyrics failed to touch him this morning. Tucker's mind wandered, chewing over the same question about Carl and still feeling unsatisfied with the answer. Carl would be released from the hospital tomorrow, and a social worker had found him a space at a homeless shelter, a place run by a church down in Beverly. Tucker knew the shelter and didn't think it was so awful. A far cry from the comfort of his own guest room, but maybe not too bad for a guy like Carl.

He hadn't seen Carl since Thursday night so he couldn't say if his brother really planned on staying there or had only agreed to go in order to get released from the hospital. Maybe he didn't really want to know, Tucker realized. He'd told Fran on Friday night after dinner about his talk with the social worker and about Carl's plans.

She hadn't said anything at first. Then she dipped her head and said, "Well, that's good news, I guess. Maybe we could send him a care package or something. Some books and things he might need."

Her well-meaning suggestion had irritated him. Carl needed to rest up some place more hospitable than a shelter, Tucker thought. He didn't need chewing gum and a new package of handkerchiefs; he needed a good bed and a private room and some home-cooked food. But the look of sheer relief on Fran's face made it hard to open up the discussion all over again. She was genuinely afraid of Carl, no doubt about it, though it seemed clear to Tucker there was no reason in the world she should be.

Maybe it was just as well that Carl went to the shelter, that they didn't get any more involved, he had finally decided. Though that was back on Friday, and now, not even three days later, the decision didn't sit well with him, like something he'd eaten that just wouldn't go down.

Tucker focused again on the service. The Scripture readings had concluded, and Reverend Ben had started his sermon. Tucker shifted uncomfortably in his seat as he realized that today's Gospel was the familiar parable of the Good Samaritan.

"What is the reason Jesus even tells this story? He is first asked a question." Reverend Ben glanced down at the open Bible on his pulpit. " 'What shall I do to inherit eternal life?' " he read aloud. He looked out at the congregation again.

"In other words: How do we get to heaven? What do we need to do? Fair enough questions, I think. Jesus first answers that you must do two things: love God with all your heart and love your neighbor as yourself. Simple enough, you might think.

"But then the same man asks, 'Who is my neighbor?' " Reverend Ben paused, his gaze sweeping over his audience. "So in answer to this question Jesus tells the story of the Good Samaritan. A traveler is attacked by thieves and left on the roadside between Jerusalem and Jericho, half dead. Two men pass him, one of them a priest. Neither of them shows compassion or charity, neither of them stops to even see if the wounded man is still alive. Callous and indifferent, they move to the other side of the road.

"Then the Samaritan comes along. He binds the man's wounds and takes him to an inn, even though it means he has to walk while the wounded man rides. He then gives the innkeeper money, promising to pay for everything while the man recovers."

The reverend paused as if to let the words sink in.

"Is this wounded man a relative of the Samaritan? Is it his friend or someone from his town? No, of course not. The man is unknown to him, a traveler from Jerusalem, we are told. Yet, the Samaritan does what is necessary. He makes an effort, physically, financially, even emotionally, one might surmise. He puts himself out for this stranger. He doesn't fall back on all the excuses that seem to come so easily when we find ourselves in a similar situation. You know what I mean. We all do it, myself included." The reverend glanced around. " 'I'd like to help this man, but if I stop, I'll be late for my appointment. I really can't bother this time. Next time, I'll help.' Or, 'I don't really have much money myself right now. Someone else with more will probably help.' And here's a good one: 'Gee, I feel badly for the poor man, but what kind of person gets themselves into such a state? He should have known better than to drink, to gamble, to take drugs, to lose his job.' I'm sure you can fill in the blanks. 'I'd never get myself into a jam like that,' we tell ourselves. 'He pretty much got what he deserved.' "

Tucker sat up and crossed his arms over his chest. He felt his cheeks flush. He knew Reverend Ben hadn't written this sermon to send a message just to him—but it was starting to feel that way.

"Does the Samaritan ask the wounded traveler any questions? Does he try to figure out if the man is worthy of his aid? No. He finds a man in distress and immediately takes care of him. And so we find, at the end of the story, Jesus asks, 'Which now of these three, thinkest thou, was a neighbor onto him that fell among the thieves?' And of course the answer is, 'He that showed mercy on him.'

"So this then is the notion of a neighbor as set forth in this passage. A neighbor is the wounded one we find on the roadside, the one in distress who needs our aid without questions or judgments. Who needs our mercy . . ."

The reverend continued but Tucker stared down at the floor, hardly hearing another word. All through the story, he saw Carl's face on the wounded traveler. But he couldn't cast himself as the Samaritan. No, he was one of the men who had passed to the other side of the road. Or, rather, was just about to, he realized.

ON MONDAY MORNING TUCKER CHECKED IN AT THE STAtion house, took care of some paperwork, then prepared to go out on patrol. Just before leaving, he stopped in to see his boss, Chief Jim Sanborn.

"I need a few hours of personal time today, Chief. Say from about eleven to two?"

"Dentist appointment?" Jim glanced up at him and grinned.

"I wish. I'd rather have a root canal than sort out this piece of business."

The chief looked at him quizzically, then turned back to the papers on his desk. "Sure thing. Just tell Nelson at the desk so he knows you're off duty."

Tucker felt jumpy all morning but focused on his work. He was assigned to a speed trap near the elementary school. He ticketed a teenage girl flying through the stop sign and later stopped a guy in a panel truck doing close to sixty through the school zone. Tucker smelled the alcohol on his breath as soon as the trucker rolled down his window.

Tucker felt satisfied taking a drunk driver off the road. He had seen enough car wrecks to know that in a small but significant way, he had made the world a little safer today. But overall, day to day and hour to hour, he couldn't say he faced his job with the same eagerness he had felt years ago.

He'd never minded being a cop in a small town where the night police report often didn't amount to anything more ominous than raccoons rattling garbage cans. Lately, though, he'd felt restless. Bored perhaps by the sheer routine of ticketing traffic violations or taking down car-accident reports. He'd been on the force almost twenty years now and would qualify for early retirement in two more. He was starting to think he might be ready to quit the force by then, to do something else with his life, though he wasn't sure quite what. Being a policeman was all he'd ever really wanted to do. It was all he really knew.

At eleven o'clock he radioed the station that he was going off duty. With a sigh of resignation, he drove up to the turnpike and headed for Southport.

He wasn't sure why or how, but he had somehow decided to drive to Southport and see if Carl would come home with him. He thought about calling Fran at the real-estate office to give her some warning. *No*, he decided. *Better wait to see what Carl says.*

Despite his talk with the social worker last week and despite telling Fran that Carl was going to Beverly, Tucker had been seesawing in his mind all weekend about the situation. Sunday morning in church, though, was what ended the indecision. Reverend Ben's sermon had gotten to him.

Tucker reached the hospital at half past twelve. As he crossed the lobby, the elevator doors opened, and he spotted his brother being wheeled out of the elevator by a nurse. Dressed in ill-fitting secondhand clothes, Carl held a bunched-up plastic bag and a new set of crutches across his knees. *All he has in the world in his lap,* Tucker thought.

Tucker hurried to catch up with the wheelchair, aware that if he had been a minute later, he would have missed him. He wasn't sure if that was a lucky break or an unlucky one. Carl saw him and a bitter expression came into his eyes.

"What are you doing here?" Carl demanded. "Can't you give me some peace?"

"Simmer down. Just let me talk to the nurse."

The nurse pushing Carl looked Tucker over. "Are you here to pick up the patient, Officer?"

"That's right. I'm his brother," Tucker said. "Do I need to sign something?"

"Mr. Jones has to sign," the nurse told him.

"Hold up, here. I didn't give him permission to pick me up," Carl told the nurse. "You don't have to do what he says because he's wearing that uniform."

The nurse looked confused. She checked her clipboard, then looked up at Tucker. "The social worker has made arrangements for Mr. Jones to be transported to a shelter in Lowell. A van is coming soon to take him there."

"Lowell? I thought he was going to Beverly."

"There wasn't any room in Beverly. My travel agent had to switch my reservations." Carl smiled slyly at him.

Tucker didn't answer. The shelter in Lowell was awful, a real pit. If he'd had any doubts at all about taking Carl in, this clinched it. "Lowell is hours from here," Tucker said finally.

"What's the difference? You worried about visiting me or something?" Carl laughed, then coughed into his hand. "I've been to worse places than Lowell, believe me."

Tucker did believe him. That was half the trouble.

He paused for a moment, realizing that if he just let Carl go, all his problems would be solved. Carl hadn't asked him for his help. Quite the opposite. He was his usual surly, ungrateful self. But finally, Tucker just couldn't do it.

"You don't have to go there, Carl. You can stay at my house for a while in the spare room."

"Your house?" Carl shook his head. "That's not for me. What do you think you're doing anyway? Swooping in here like Superman, saving the day? You make me laugh, Tucker."

Tucker glanced at the nurse. "Will you excuse us a minute while we talk?" She nodded knowingly and walked toward the front desk.

"Stop arguing with me," Tucker said wearily. "It's a long drive back, and I don't have that much time. Now just sign the paper and let's get out of here."

"I know why you're doing this, Tucker. You can't fool me. You just feel guilty. Too much church, that was always your problem. You'd be just as happy to see the back of me than set me up in your spare room. Isn't that right?"

Tucker folded his arms across his chest. "Yeah, that's right. I'm not going to lie to you. But you have no money and nowhere to go, and the doctor says you're too sick to get a job or even travel. So either I can drive you to my house and give you a clean, comfortable bed and three meals a day or you can get on that van and go to Lowell," he stated bluntly. "What's it going to be?"

Carl stared straight ahead, his jaw set and a blank look on his ravaged face. He gripped his bag tighter. For a moment, Tucker thought he might choose the shelter just to spite him.

"All right," Carl said finally. "But I'm not staying long. A few days. Just until I get my second wind and this darn leg gets better."

"That's all I'm inviting you for. Just until you can travel," Tucker agreed, though he was sure it would take more than a few days.

"I'm due in Portland, you know. My friend is waiting for me."

"I know, I've heard all about it." Tucker wheeled Carl

over to the information desk and found the nurse with Carl's release form. Carl scrawled his name in the designated places and grumbled his thanks to her good wishes.

"I don't need this chair. I can walk out of here on my own," Carl complained as Tucker pushed him.

Right, that's why they gave you crutches as a going-away present. Because you're ready for the Boston Marathon, Tucker was tempted to reply.

He looked down at Carl. "It's an insurance thing. They don't want you to slip in the lobby and sue somebody."

Out in front of the hospital, he left Carl sitting in the wheelchair in the patient pick-up zone and went to get his car. As he drove back, he spotted Carl from a distance, huddled into his worn clothes, clutching the crutches and the plastic bag. He might have been a stranger, Tucker thought, the kind you don't want to look at too long. Tucker felt a twist in his stomach. His brother was a pathetic sight, a ruined man.

Tucker took the bags and helped Carl out of the wheelchair.

"Nice wheels," Carl said, nodding at the patrol car. "Don't you want to read me my rights before I get in?"

Tucker ignored him and stashed the crutches and folded wheelchair in the trunk.

"You might be more comfortable in the back. You can stretch out your leg," Tucker suggested.

"Yeah, I usually ride in the back of these taxis," Carl replied. "Cops don't invite guys like me into the front seat very often."

Tucker could well imagine his brother's many rides in police cars. He opened the back door without comment, and Carl hobbled over and fit himself inside. He clamped his jaw down hard as he settled in, and Tucker knew he was in pain.

As Tucker began the drive back to Cape Light, the only sound was the police radio with the volume turned low. Carl was quiet, and Tucker thought he had fallen asleep until he glanced into the rearview mirror and saw that Carl was wide awake, staring straight ahead.

"This spare room of yours, is it up in the attic?" Carl asked.

"On the first floor. It's half of the two-car garage. There's no climbing. You've got a bed, a dresser, and a little table with a TV. There's a bathroom with a shower there, too. Fran's mother uses it when she stays over."

"Great. I bet it even has wallpaper with little flowers," Carl grumbled.

"Yeah, there's wallpaper. And wall-to-wall carpet," Tucker noted.

"Just like the Copley Plaza Hotel. Remember when I brought you there?"

Carl's hard living had scrambled his brains, Tucker thought. Then he did remember. Carl was right.

"Yeah, I do. My wedding night," Tucker said.

He and Fran stayed at the Copley Plaza on the first night of their honeymoon, before they left for Bermuda. It was one of the best hotels in Boston. Charlie Bates had been best man, but Carl was the one who had driven them into the city after the wedding. Tucker had been just a rookie cop then, fresh out of the academy. Carl had already lost his lobster fishing permit, his life quickly sliding downhill.

Funny to think of that now, all things considered.

THURSDAY NIGHT'S SNOWFALL WAS NEARLY MELTED, A sure sign that spring wasn't that far off, Molly thought. Unmindful of the slushy pavement beneath her high-heeled boots, Molly nearly skipped up the path to Betty's real-estate office. She stepped inside and found Fran Tulley working at her computer. Fran looked up when Molly entered, greeting her with a wan smile.

"Are you here for your bucket? I think it's in the back. Betty has that extra check for you from Dr. Harding."

"Oh, that. I nearly forgot."

"He was certainly singing your praises," Fran added. "He would be a good client for you, Molly."

"I might be phasing out the cleaning business soon," Molly announced breathlessly. "But I can recommend someone. Is Betty here?"

"She's in her office. You can just go on back." Fran looked at her curiously.

Molly knocked on Betty's half-open door, then walked in.

Betty was on a phone call, but she quickly excused herself and hung up the phone. "So? How did it go? Did you get the order?"

Molly nodded and couldn't help but smile. "It's a whopper, as we say in the business."

Betty leaned back in her bouncy leather chair and clapped her hands together. "Bravo! The Spoon Harbor Inn, that's a big deal around here. You've got quite the client list now."

"I wouldn't exactly call it a *list*," Molly hedged. "More like a little lump of clients at this point."

"A list, a lump. What's the difference? You're really on a roll. So what about the cleaning business?"

Molly had mentioned to Betty last night that if she got a good order from the Spoon River Inn, in addition to last week's new order from the Beanery, she might be able to phase out house cleaning. But now that she had the order in hand, she was definitely getting cold feet.

"I'm not sure about that yet. I really have to rework the figures and check my expenses." Molly slipped off her good wool coat and left it folded on a chair. She wore black wool pants that she liked because she thought they made her look considerably slimmer and a turquoise-blue sweater set the girls had given her for Christmas. It was her favorite appointment outfit and also the only one she had in her closet.

"What about that money from Phil? That should help right about now." Betty sat up, talking excitedly, a bunch of gold bracelets on her arm jangling as she gestured. "You really need to take the leap, kiddo. You're definitely ready."

Molly sighed. She knew Betty was right. It was a now-or-never kind of moment when you got right down to it.

"Well, timewise it looks as if something's got to give," she admitted. "If I don't give up the cleaning, I won't have enough time to do the cooking and deliveries. So I guess I'll have to give up cleaning in the next week or so."

"Molly, that's great news." Betty popped out of her chair and gave Molly a big hug. "I'm so happy for you. I was hoping you'd make this kind of change."

"I've been thinking about it for a while. You know that."

And meeting Matthew had pushed her over the edge, Molly admitted to herself. Last week, when she'd first met him, she didn't want to tell him she cleaned houses for a living. It was odd; she'd never felt embarrassed about her work before. Even if nothing more came of their relationship, she'd always have him to thank for that sudden moment of motivation.

"I only hope I can get all this work done. I've bitten off a real big chunk here. I'm not sure I can do it."

"You have to hire a helper. This is just what I've been telling you. You're at the next level. You have to grow the business."

Molly laughed. "Thanks, but I don't think I qualify yet for business-school lingo."

"Of course you do," Betty insisted. "If you start thinking of your efforts as a real business, it will *be* a real business."

"How can I afford to hire someone? It's going to be a stretch just to stock up on all the ingredients."

"Find a teenager. You can afford that. Call up the high school. They have a list of kids who want part-time jobs. If you have some help, you can really increase your output and pay the helper from the profits, which should be double," Betty advised smoothly. "If it doesn't work out, you can cut back again. But it will work out. I feel really good about this, Molly. You're making a big move."

"I guess so." Molly had arrived feeling elated with her news, but now that they were discussing the practicalities, she felt a little overwhelmed. "I don't mean to sound like a wimp, but I'm scared. I don't know if I can do this. Maybe I should cancel the orders. . . ."

"Don't be silly." Betty put a settling hand on her shoulder. "Of course you can do it. You have to do it," she insisted. "If you want your life to be different, you have to make some changes, Molly. If you keep doing what you always do, you'll just get what you've already got."

"Who said that? Benjamin Franklin?"

Betty shook her head and smiled. "Another great American philosopher. Ann Landers. Oh, I nearly forgot. Speaking of profits, I have a check for you from that doctor. He couldn't stop talking about you. What did you do to that man?"

Molly felt herself blushing. "I just organized his kitchen, for goodness' sake. Besides, if he were really interested in me, he could have called and dropped the check at my house. He didn't have to leave it here."

"Some men are a little backward. They outsmart themselves. You know that. He may have dropped the check off here just because he *is* interested."

Molly did know. That was just the problem. Men were so convoluted sometimes. It hardly seemed worth the effort it took to figure them out. Molly bit her lip. She did want to talk to Betty about Matthew; she was dying to, actually. But she didn't want to make too big a deal about it. She could think of a thousand reasons why she wasn't right for him and it wouldn't work out. It was better not to get her hopes up, she thought.

"You could still hear from him. You never know," Betty said breezily.

That did it. Molly couldn't hold back anymore.

"I saw him last week. Thursday night. Lauren made friends with his daughter, so he came by to pick her up and ended up staying for dinner. You know, with the snow and all."

Betty's eyebrows went up in a knowing expression. "There wasn't *that* much snow."

"It was nothing. Just a last-minute invitation. But the girls are going to be in a chorus concert on Saturday, so he asked me to go with him . . . and we're all going out for dinner after." She saw Betty's eyes brighten at the news and quickly tried to discourage her. "But it's not a date or anything, Betty. Honestly. He's glad Amanda made a friend, and he's just trying to be nice."

"Nobody's that nice, Molly. He wants to spend time with you."

"It's not like that, really. Maybe he likes me as a friend, but I don't think it's anything more than that. He still misses his wife. And I'm really not his type."

"Okay, it's nothing." Betty shook her head and raised her hands in a sign of surrender. But Molly knew her well. She could tell from the soft expression on Betty's face that she sensed her real dilemma about Matthew. Molly was afraid. She had finally met a man she really liked, but what if he didn't like her? What if he didn't think she was good enough for him? That would really hurt, and she didn't want to get hurt anymore.

"So, I know it's not a date. But what are you going to wear?"

Molly sighed, surveying her friend's slim figure. "Hopefully something that makes me look ten pounds thinner."

"Molly, please. You have a great figure. Haven't you heard? Real women have curves."

"Yeah, they don't get more real than me." Molly smiled in spite of herself.

The phone rang, and Betty took the call.

Molly sat back, thinking that Betty was full of perky little sayings today. Not surprising from a former head cheerleader and high-school class president. Betty always managed to find a positive side to a problem and hardly ever seemed to let life get her down. Not that her success had been achieved without setbacks and hard work.

Maybe I should pipe down and listen more to Betty, Molly thought. *I could learn a lot from her.*

Betty hung up the phone and checked her slim gold watch. "Lunch time. Want to grab a bite?"

"Sure." Molly picked up her coat and her bag. "Where would you like to go?"

"How about the Beanery? We can grab a quick bite and then run over to that new store around the corner. They're having a big sale. I saw the perfect dress for you in the window."

Molly's first impulse was to refuse. She loved Betty, but she didn't need her to pick out her clothes. Even Lauren hated that by now. Then Molly realized Betty was only trying to help.

Maybe it's time I learned to accept a favor now and then, Molly thought ruefully. *It wouldn't kill me to see the dress Betty thinks is perfect. It might even be fun.*

"Okay, I'll take a look. You do have great taste."

"Yes, I do. Kind of you to notice." Betty smiled brightly at her as they swept out the door.

"TUCKER? CAN YOU HELP ME WITH THESE GROCERIES?" Fran called from the front door.

Tucker walked quickly to meet her. He took one bag from her hand and two others she had dropped just inside the door.

"You got home early," Fran remarked, dropping her load on the countertop.

"Where are the kids? I thought they'd be home by now."

"Michael has a game. I thought you were going to drop by and catch the last quarter."

"Oh, man. I guess I forgot." Tucker rubbed his forehead. "It was a hectic day." Fran didn't know the half of it.

"The coach will give him a lift home. Mary Ellen is at

chorus practice. She'll be there late a few nights this week—practice for the concert. Mrs. North is going to drop her home about six. It's our turn to drive tomorrow. Could you do it?"

"Um, sure. I can pick them up. Just write me a note or something so I don't forget."

He grabbed a box of rice out of a bag, confused for a moment about where it should go. He was relieved to hear the kids would not be home for a while, though if they were, it might help Fran keep her temper under control when he told her about Carl.

There was no good time for it. He really had to tell her. He had to do it right now.

"Fran, I have something to tell you, and I don't want you to get upset," he began.

She closed a cupboard and turned to him. "Did something happen at work? Are you okay?"

The concern in her voice was touching. Fran always worried about him getting hurt in the line of duty, even though it wasn't very likely in Cape Light. Tucker almost wished he had been in some dangerous situation. It would be easier to tell her that then his real news.

"Carl is here. I picked him up at the hospital around noon."

"Tucker, you didn't! I thought he was going to that shelter in Beverly."

"That one was full. They were sending him to one in Lowell. That place is a real pit. I couldn't let him go there," Tucker insisted.

Fran stared at him wide-eyed, obviously not knowing what to say. She abruptly turned her back and pulled a can out of a grocery bag. "How did you even know that?"

"I went down to Southport on my lunch break."

"So you intended on taking him home all along, I guess."

"Yes, I did. But I wasn't sure he'd come," Tucker slowly admitted. "When I heard where he was going, I knew I had to."

Fran turned to face him again. Her dark eyes were shining. At first he thought she was about to cry, then realized she was furious.

"Why didn't you just tell me this morning that you intended to do this? You could have at least talked to me about it."

"I wanted to, Fran. But I couldn't. I knew if I did, you might make me change my mind again, and I didn't want to change my mind. I need to help him. I really think this is the right thing to do."

"There are other ways to help him, Tucker. He doesn't have to stay here." Fran placed a can of coffee in a cupboard and slammed the door shut.

"Quiet down, will you? He's asleep in the spare room."

"You put him in my mother's room?" Fran was aghast.

"That's the guest room. It's not just for your relatives. Where did you think I was going to put him, in the toolshed?"

"I didn't think you were going to put him anywhere." Fran's voice rose on a shrill note. "It's my house, too, Tucker. I should have some say in this . . . this situation."

"Hello, Fran. Nice to see you, too."

They both turned and saw Carl in the doorway, leaning on his crutches, smiling bitterly. Tucker watched Fran's face go white as snow.

"Carl . . . I didn't see you there . . ." Tucker said, feeling his own face flush scarlet with embarrassment.

"Doesn't matter. I heard everything. We don't have any argument, you and me," Carl said to Fran. "I told Tucker this wasn't going to work."

"Go back to bed, Carl. Fran and I will figure it out."

"I heard what she said. I don't have to stay here. I should have gone to Lowell when I had the chance. I can probably get a bus there tonight, if you'll lend me the fare."

"Just give us a minute to talk this through," Tucker told him. "Besides, you've lost your place there by now. You'll just end up sleeping on the street."

Fran didn't say anything. She pursed her lips in a tight line and stood staring at Carl. "There must be someplace for him."

"There is. He'll stay here."

"Didn't you hear her? Your wife doesn't want me around. I told you this wasn't a good idea, but you—"

Carl began to cough furiously. His face grew beet red, and he gasped for air. He tilted so far forward on his crutches, Tucker was sure he would tumble to the floor.

"Oh no! Oh my goodness . . . Tucker, do something." Fran covered her mouth with her hand, frozen where she stood.

Tucker ran over to Carl, slung his brother's arm around his shoulders, then half carried, half dragged him back to the guest room. He set him down on the bed, propping him up against the pillows. Finally Carl's coughing spell passed, and he sucked in wheezy breaths of air.

"You still need the oxygen. I'll get some set up here for you tomorrow." Tucker stared down at him. The coughing had exhausted him; Carl leaned back, his eyes closed.

"Are you hungry?" Tucker asked.

Carl shook his head. "Just leave me be. Go on inside and talk to your wife."

"She'll be okay. Don't worry about her."

"Tell her I'm going in the morning."

Right, in the morning. Maybe some morning a month from now, Tucker thought. But he didn't reply. He left the room and closed Carl's door behind him.

In the kitchen, Fran had started making dinner. She glanced at Tucker, then set a pan down on the stove top.

"He's very sick. I told you he needs help."

"I can see that. He looks awful." She shook her head. "I would never have recognized him. How can a person let himself go like that?"

Tucker glared at her. "Quiet, Fran. He'll hear you."

Fran sighed. She put a bowl from the freezer in the microwave and set the timer. "I guess we're stuck with him for a day or two. But don't expect me to turn into Florence Nightingale."

He knew what she meant. He'd brought Carl here, and now Carl was his problem. She wasn't going to do much to take care of him.

Tucker heard the front door slam.

"I'm home. What's for dinner?" his son Michael called out.

"Hi, Mike. How was the game?" Tucker asked as his tall, rangy son came into the kitchen.

"It was okay." Michael took a banana out of the fruit bowl on the table and ate it in two large bites. "Coach has me playing forward."

"Pretty good. First season on varsity, and he's playing forward. Did you hear that, Fran?"

Fran nodded. "I heard. Very good, Michael." She spared a smile for her son, then turned back to the cooking.

"You'd better work on your fake shot," Tucker advised. "I think the snow has pretty much melted from the driveway. I'll practice with you out back on Saturday."

Fran glanced over her shoulder. "Go easy on him, Michael. Your father's not sixteen anymore."

Tucker shook his head. "Thanks, Fran. I almost forgot."

"This old guy? He's still got some moves." Michael slapped his father on the back as he passed his chair. "What for dinner? I'm starving."

"Just some stew I had in the freezer. It will be about half an hour before we eat. Do you have homework?"

"Yup. I'll do it upstairs."

"Wait a second. Your father needs to tell you something."

"Sit down, Mike," Tucker said. "This will only take a minute."

Michael stared at him curiously. He looked a little worried, Tucker noticed. "Am I in trouble or something?"

"No, nothing like that," Tucker assured him. "Why? Is there something you need to tell me?"

"No, sir." Michael looked at him, then up at Fran. "What is this about?"

"I've told you I have a half brother, remember?" Tucker began carefully.

"Right, his name is Carl. I've never met him. He went to jail or something, right?"

"That's right." Tucker paused, wondering if he should explain Carl's crime to Michael. They had never really discussed it in great detail. "He got into a fight with another man in a bar—"

"Oh, Tucker, do you have to tell him everything?" Fran cut in.

"Yes, I do. He's bound to hear it from some kid in school, so he might as well hear it from me first."

"I did hear it," Michael admitted. "Carl killed someone, right?"

Tucker took a breath and gave Michael the full story, concluding with his finding Carl in Southport Hospital.

"So what happened?" Michael asked. "Did he die or something?"

"No, he didn't die. He's still sick, but the doctors said he could leave the hospital. So I brought him here."

Michael's eyes widened. "He's here? In our house?"

"He's staying in the guest room."

"Can I see him?"

"Sure you can. Well, he's resting now. Maybe later. I'll see if he feels up to it."

"He's not feeling well, Mike. He needs his rest. We don't want you to bother him," Fran added nervously.

"Okay, I won't. But that's really cool. A real convict is sleeping in our house!"

"He's my brother, Michael," Tucker said in a warning tone. "I expect you to treat him with respect, the same way you treat me. You might hear some kids talking in school about this, but I want you to just ignore it. Carl's a sick man, and he needs some help. I want you to be nice to him."

"I will. How long is he going to be here?"

"Not long," Fran said quickly.

"Until he feels better," Tucker said, casting her a dark look.

Michael looked at both of them. "Can I go upstairs now?"

"Sure, go ahead," Tucker said. When Michael left the room he said to Fran, "See, that went okay."

But Fran just stirred a pot on the stove with a wooden spoon, and didn't reply.

Tucker got up from the table. "I'm going to bring Carl some dinner. He's got a list here of foods he's allowed to eat." He found the list on the refrigerator and glanced at it. "A bland diet, it says. Jell-O, applesauce, cottage cheese—"

"That's okay, Tucker. I know what a bland diet is. He can have some of these noodles." Fran shook her head. "There's some applesauce in the cupboard. We're out of cottage cheese, though. I'd better buy more tomorrow, I guess."

"I guess so." Tucker touched her arm gently. She had a right to be mad at him, he supposed, for not discussing this with her. But he thought it wouldn't take too long before she softened up about Carl. Fran could be stubborn but she wasn't heartless.

A short time later, he had assembled a tray and brought it to the guest room. Carl was awake, sitting up against the pillows. The radio on the bedside table was tuned to a sports news channel.

"Was that your boy that came home before?" Carl asked.

"You don't miss much, do you?" Tucker set the tray on the night table and sat in a chair by the bed.

"My body is shot, but the ears still work pretty good."

"Here's some dinner. I don't know what you like. I just picked some stuff off that list." Tucker eyed the bottles of pills on the nightstand. He'd have to check later to see if Carl was following his prescriptions. "You'd better eat something before you take those pills."

Carl glanced at the food but didn't move to eat it. "I heard you and Fran going at it pretty good in there. Why didn't you tell her I'm going tomorrow, like I said? I can't stay here."

"Look, let's not get into this all over again. I spoke to your doctor today, Carl. You need bed rest, and you have to go back for checkups and tests and whatever. You're going to stay here until you're fit and that's the end of it."

"Are you crazy? I'm not staying here that long. Your wife won't put up with it, for one thing," he joked bitterly.

"Don't worry about Fran. I'll work it out with her."

Carl turned away, facing the wall. "This wallpaper is making me dizzy."

"So stop looking at it."

Carl suddenly turned and met his gaze. "Sorry if I'm not oozing all over you with gratitude. But I never asked you to bring me here. You're doing it for yourself so you can sleep at night and face your preacher on Sunday. You don't have to phony up to me, Tucker. I see right through you."

Tucker's chin lifted, feeling the words like a slap across the face. It wasn't enough that neither his wife nor his best friend gave him any understanding or sympathy in this. Or that his own common sense was fighting him every step of the way. Carl had to fight him, too, paying back his kindness with bitterness, ingratitude, and contempt.

After twenty years his brother still knew how to push his buttons, he'd give him that much. Carl's words stung because they rang true.

"Tucker? Dinner's on the table. Everything's ready," Fran called from the kitchen.

"Wife's calling. You'd better run along now." Carl's expression was set in a grim line, and then he closed his eyes.

Tucker stood beside the bed, watching Carl. He smelled the hot food and heard his children and Fran gathering around the table. Carl might scorn and mock him. What did it matter? The blessings in his life were like a coat of armor. He thanked God for all he had compared to Carl, the simple things in his life that he took for granted, even his health.

Tucker left the room and quietly closed the door, his heart heavy with emotion. It was hard to imagine having nothing and no one—no job, no place to live, no one who cared whether you were alive or dead. He couldn't think of anyone he'd ever known like that, though as a policeman he'd seen his share of derelicts. But this was different. This was his own flesh and blood. What choice did he really have but to take Carl in?

Chapter Six

Tucker stepped out of his house and took in the clear sky and the bright sun that had just begun its climb. The wind was sharp and chilly, but the patches of snow that clung to the ground in icy clumps would not last the day, he predicted. It was the beginning of March, and though there might be more snow, the cold weather couldn't hold out much longer.

Fran and the children were just stirring when he left. Carl was still sleeping heavily. Tucker had set a tray of breakfast by his bed and a number he could call in an emergency. He would find some time today while he was out in the patrol car to stop home. He knew he couldn't count on Fran to help right now. But Tucker thought she might pitch in after a while.

He drove into the village and parked in front of the Clam Box. Main Street was nearly empty, the nearby bank and shops still closed. He usually loved this time of the day, starting off with breakfast at the diner and a chat with Charlie. But this morning his stomach grumbled acidly as he entered, his senses assaulted by the rich smells of coffee, bacon, and home fries on the grill.

Tucker had seen Charlie a few times since he'd told him he was going to see if the guy in the hospital was Carl, but they'd carefully tiptoed around the topic. Now that Carl was staying at his house, though, Tucker knew he had to be the one to tell Charlie—before he heard it from someone else in town.

Tucker took a seat at the counter. Charlie was nowhere in sight. But Lucy Bates suddenly appeared beside him, a wide smile lighting up her pretty face.

"Good morning, Tucker. Coffee, of course."

"Absolutely." Tucker smiled at her as she filled his mug. "I haven't seen you around much, Lucy. Busy with school?"

"I'll say. I have some really tough courses this semester. The reading list is just killing me. Though, I must admit, it still beats working here," she confided, in a teasing tone. "At this rate, I'll need a walker for the graduation march, but I'm trying not to think about that too much."

"Come on, now. You'll be done sooner than you think. I admire you, Lucy. I hope you stick with it."

"I'm trying," she said with a wistful grin. "Now, what can I get you this morning?"

Lucy was suddenly all business, pulling out her pad and scribbling his order, but he sensed his words had pleased her. He was sure she didn't get much encouragement from Charlie, who had fought so hard against her wish to go back to college that the conflict had nearly ended their marriage.

"How's your brother, Tucker? Is he still in the hospital?" Lucy asked as she put in the order.

"He came out yesterday. He still has a long way to go, though. He's got a pile of medications to take and needs to see the doctor for a while."

"That's too bad. Where is he staying now?" Lucy had

turned to pour two glasses of juice. Tucker paused a moment before answering her. He didn't know why it should be so hard to admit that Carl was staying at his house. But somehow it was.

"He's staying with me for now. Until he gets back on his feet."

Lucy glanced at him as she set the juice glasses on a tray. "That's good of you, Tucker. A lot of people wouldn't go out of their way like that."

"What else could I do?"

"What else could you do about what?" Charlie asked, coming up behind him.

Tucker hadn't even noticed him there, and he now turned in his seat to face his friend. Lucy hurried off with her tray like a small animal in the woods who had just heard a gun shot, Tucker thought.

Charlie moved to his place on the other side of the counter and stood facing Tucker, the look on his face still expecting a reply.

"We were just talking about Carl. He came out of the hospital yesterday." Tucker stirred his coffee. "He's staying at my place for a while."

Charlie's eyes widened. "You took him in? What did you do that for?"

"I didn't have much choice. I couldn't let him go to some shelter."

Charlie stared at him a moment, then turned to the grill, where he cracked open two eggs and set them to fry.

"I knew he would get to you. Like the frog and the scorpion. Remember that story?"

"No, I don't," Tucker said dryly. "But I'm sure you'll remind me."

"There's this frog about to swim across a stream. And there's this scorpion, sitting on a rock. He asks the frog for a ride across the water. Now the frog is a helpful guy. He doesn't like to see anyone else in a fix. But he's afraid the scorpion is going to bite him. So he says, 'All right. I'll give you a lift. But only if you promise not to sting me.' "

Tucker had an idea of where this was going and sighed. "Go on . . . and check on my eggs while you're at it. I don't want them cooked to rubber."

Charlie turned back to his cooking without missing a beat. "Well, the scorpion agrees to the deal, of course, and he jumps on the frog's back. Off they go, sailing across the stream. But once they get to the other side, the scorpion curls his tail and gives the frog a sting. The frog is dying; he doesn't know what to do. 'Why did you sting me? You promised not to,' he says." Charlie paused and flipped the fried eggs into a dish. "The scorpion just laughs. He says, 'Why did you believe me, you dumb frog? Because it's your nature to trust. That's why. And that's the same reason I had to sting you. I couldn't help myself. That's just my nature.' "

He set the eggs down in front of Tucker with a dish of rye toast on the side. Then he stood back, a satisfied expression on his face.

Tucker dug into his eggs and shook his head. "Okay, the scorpion stung the frog. It's a story about nature. What's that supposed to mean?"

"Don't you get it? If you let Carl ride on your back, you're going to get stung, my friend. He won't mean to. But he'll do it anyway. Mark my words."

Tucker stopped chewing, his mouth full of food. He tried to swallow, but it wouldn't go down. Charlie had some nerve, that was for sure. He was no stupid frog. And Carl . . . well, Carl could be nasty. But that wasn't the point.

"My brother isn't going to hurt me. That's ridiculous."

"That's what you think, Tucker. If you let Carl hang around, you're just asking for trouble. You think you're doing a good deed. But something bad is going to come from this." Charlie sagely nodded his head. "Carl Tulley is trouble waiting to happen. It's just who he is. And you should have wised up by now."

Tucker sat back and wiped his mouth on a paper napkin. "Thanks for the fable, Charlie," he said sarcastically. "But I can handle my brother. I'm not worried about it."

"Really? Well, what about your reputation in this town? People will be talking about him, Tucker. They'll be talking about you. You're not going to win any popularity contests around here by making it easy for Carl to stick around."

"That's all right, I'm not running for office. And you're no expert in that department anyway, as I recall," he added.

Tucker could tell in an instant his angry retort had hit its mark. Charlie had run for mayor last year against Emily Warwick and lost. The defeat had hurt Charlie badly, and now Tucker had rubbed salt into the wound.

Charlie spun around and attended to the grill. "If that's the way you feel, fine. Just don't bring him in here. I'll throw him out on his ear," Charlie stated flatly.

"All right." Tucker got up from his seat. "If that's the way you feel, I won't come in here anymore, either."

He pulled some bills out his wallet and slammed them on the counter. Charlie flinched, but he didn't turned around. Suddenly Lucy appeared beside Charlie. Tucker could tell she'd heard everything.

"What is this now? Don't fight like that, you two. For goodness' sake, you've been best friends since kindergarten." She touched Charlie's arm, but he barely glanced at her. "You're two kids in a school yard sometimes. Come on, Charlie. Apologize to Tucker. You can't let him leave like that."

Charlie sniffed. He pushed at a pile of potatoes with his spatula. "He's the one who should apologize. I was trying to give him some advice, and he jumps down my throat and insults me."

Tucker stood there a moment. He met Lucy's pleading

gaze, but he was too angry to even attempt to smooth things over.

"See you, Lucy," he said shortly. "I've got to go."

He walked to the door.

"Charlie, please," Tucker heard Lucy say again.

"Just let him go. Who needs him. . . ." Charlie muttered disgustedly.

The bells above the door jingled, the sound ringing in Tucker's head. The rest of Charlie's words were lost to him, but Tucker had heard more than enough.

He turned toward the station house and stopped. Reverend Ben was walking toward him. The reverend was another morning regular at the Clam Box, and running into him at this time of day was no surprise. Sometimes they even had a bite together. Tucker didn't feel like talking to the reverend right now, but he didn't see a way out of it. This was not turning out to be a good day.

"Tucker, I've been thinking of you," the reverend said in greeting.

Tucker forced a small smile. "Good morning, Reverend. What's on your mind?"

"Oh, nothing much. Why don't we talk inside?" the reverend suggested.

"I've already stopped in, thanks. I've got to get to work." Tucker shifted on his feet, impatient to go.

"Another time then." Reverend Ben nodded. "I was in Southport and tried to look in on your brother yesterday, but the nurse said he was gone."

"Yes, they finally released him. He's staying at our house in the guest room."

Reverend Ben smiled, but Tucker didn't smile in return.

"I'd like to visit him, if that's okay. How long will he be there?"

Tucker shrugged. "I'm not sure exactly. I thought he'd have to stay at least a week or two until he gets his strength back. But Fran . . . well, she really doesn't want him there. Even Carl has been giving me a hard time," Tucker admitted. He laughed sadly and shook his head. "It seems like I'm the only one so far who thinks it's a good idea."

"You're doing the right thing, Tucker. That isn't always easy. It seldom is, actually," Reverend Ben pointed out.

"Thanks, but the truth is, I'm not helping Carl because I really care for him. I don't even know the man anymore. I'm not even sure I like him," Tucker confessed. "I feel sorry for him, but it's not that either. Last night Carl said he knew I was only helping him because I felt guilty."

"Of course you do. He's family," Reverend Ben said quietly.

"But that's the *real* reason. The only reason. I know it looks like I'm a good Christian and all that, but I'm really just going through the motions. It's not in the right spirit . . . not like that parable you read on Sunday about the Samaritan." Tucker stared down at the puddles near his heavy black shoes. "I'm on shaky ground, if you know what I mean. So when Fran starts complaining or Charlie in there gets under my skin, I get confused. Why should I put up with all this aggravation? For what? What am I getting out of this?"

Reverend Ben reached out and touched Tucker's arm. "Frankly, hearing that you don't like Carl makes me think your actions are even more admirable, not less. It's easy to help people we like, Tucker. But to extend compassion, real charity, for someone we don't know or don't like, that's in a different league in my book."

"I'm not trying to show charity, Reverend. I just feel guilty, like I said. I know my conscience will get to me if I don't do something for Carl."

"I understand. But maybe pure motives are unrealistic. Like the idea of courage without fear. Think about it, Tucker," the reverend urged him. "If the world relied on pure motives for right action, I don't know where we'd be. Your intentions are good, and you're doing something to help. The results are the same and that's what really counts. Keep going. You might find the feelings you think you lack.

I'm sure that sooner or later—maybe even a long time from now—you'll feel truly glad you helped Carl. No matter what Fran or Charlie or even Carl himself has to say."

"Thanks, Reverend." Tucker rubbed the back of his neck. "I'm going to think about what you've said."

"Good. I'm glad I ran into you. But not surprised, actually. Sometimes my Boss schedules appointments for me without marking them in my book." The comment made Tucker finally smile. "If you ever need to talk more, Tucker, call me, okay?"

"Yes, I will," Tucker promised. "I'd better get to work. You have a good day."

"It's starting off pretty well." Reverend Ben patted Tucker's arm again and headed into the diner.

Tucker stood on the sidewalk and watched the reverend go inside. As Tucker had predicted, the large yellow sun had sailed up over Main Street and the morning sky had turned bright blue, and he suddenly noticed the sound of snow melting all around him, running down the drain spouts and dripping from rooftops.

Talking to Reverend Ben had not made him totally settled and resigned about Carl. But it had helped, Tucker realized. It had helped a lot.

MOLLY WOKE UP SLOWLY, A TANGLED DREAM CLINGING to the edges of her mind like a cobweb in a corner. She turned in bed and checked the clock. Five after seven. Why hadn't the alarm gone off? The girls would be late for school.

Then she remembered it was Saturday. She rolled on her back again, feeling an ache in her shoulders and back. Her legs felt leaden and sore. She had been cooking and baking all week—pushing herself to fill the new orders—and still had more to do over the weekend. She couldn't drop all her housecleaning clients with so little warning, either. She didn't think it was responsible of her. Besides, the same people who hired her to clean might call her for a catering job someday. So on top of all the new work, she'd somehow managed to fit in a few cleaning appointments as well.

She'd been so busy all week, she had hardly had a minute to spend with the girls, clean her own apartment, or even to eat. Which may have been a hidden bonus, Molly thought, since she felt as if she'd lost a few pounds without even thinking about it.

She glanced over at the closet door where a new dress, covered in a plastic bag, hung from the door. It was the one Betty had spotted. She had a good eye for clothes, no denying it. Just as she'd promised, the simple, tailored style did wonders for Molly's figure, and the deep blue color brought out the best in her eyes and fair complexion. The price was right, too, and Molly knew she would have treated herself anyway, even if Betty had not threatened to keep her trapped in the dressing room until she agreed to buy it.

Molly tried to think of the dress as a necessary purchase for all her new business appointments. She didn't want to admit she had bought it specifically to go to the school concert with Matthew tonight. She was trying to be low-key about this, but it wasn't easy. Luckily she'd been so busy all week, she didn't really have the time or energy to work herself up into a full blown, first-date frenzy.

"Relax, just be yourself. And try to forget all the reasons you think he wouldn't want to date you," Betty urged her.

Still, Molly found herself thinking about Matt a lot. Too much really. She finally had to give up telling herself she didn't really like him. She did like him. More than any man she had met in a long time. Which made her even more wary of getting her hopes up.

Molly sighed and forced herself to stumble out of bed and start her day. *If nothing comes of it, I'll be all right,* she told herself. *I just have to be.*

The doorbell rang at precisely five-thirty, just as Matthew had promised. Molly had already spotted his car pulling up on the street and had raced to the bathroom to check again on her lipstick, a bright new color she'd bought to go with the dress.

"Could you get that, Lauren? It's Dr. Harding and Amanda."

She heard the door open and the girls greeting each other with squealed compliments. "Okay, pal. It's show time," she whispered to her mirrored image. She shut the light and took a deep breath, then walked to the kitchen to see her guests.

"Hi, guys," she greeted Matthew and Amanda brightly. "Ready to go?"

"You look great." Matthew seemed unable to take his eyes off her and hurried over to help her with her coat.

"That dress totally goes with your eyes," Amanda agreed.

"Thanks." Molly's heart skipped with secret glee as she smiled up at Matthew. Dressed in a tweed sports jacket and coffee-brown sweater, he looked great, too. But she didn't have the courage to return the compliment. Not in front of the girls.

She glanced over at Amanda. "You look very pretty tonight. I like the way you did your hair."

Amanda had gathered her long brown hair into a single braid down her back. "Dad helped." She suddenly grinned. "It took a while, though."

"Hey, I did my best. I had trouble getting this thing to stay on." He pulled a small clasp with a velvet flower from his pocket. "Amanda wanted to wear it, but it keeps falling off."

"Here, let me." Molly took the clasp, quickly fit it to the end of the braid, and secured it in a neat, tight bow. "That should do it."

Amanda peeked at the braid. "Thanks, Molly."

Molly patted her shoulder. "No problem. Are you nervous?"

Amanda shrugged. "A little."

"Don't worry. You'll do fine. Lauren says you sound just like Julie Andrews. A real showstopper," Molly teased.

"Thanks," Amanda said shyly. When Molly looked up Matthew gave her a beaming smile. A silent thank-you for her attention to Amanda?

"I guess we'd better go. These performers need to warm up their voices, and we want to get good seats." He held up a camera. "I want to take some pictures."

"These school shows are always so crowded. We'd better go," Molly agreed. The group paraded out of the apartment and headed downstairs to the car.

Once at school, Lauren and Amanda ran off to join the chorus backstage. Matthew led the way into the auditorium, and they found seats down in front in the center section. Matthew sat next to Molly, and she was suddenly very conscious of his nearness, his broad shoulder brushing against her own smaller one and the spicy scent of his aftershave.

The house lights went down, the chorus filed onto the stage, and the music began. Although Molly loved watching Lauren and Amanda perform, she was finding it hard to concentrate on the show. Each time Matthew wanted to tell her something, he leaned close, his shoulder rubbing hers and his hushed words tickling her ear. Her senses befuddled, she somehow managed to say the right things in response.

Finally the show was drawing to a close. The chorus director, the infamous Mrs. Pickering, thanked the audience for coming. ". . . and for all your kind applause. Now, for our closing piece, a medley from *The Sound of Music.*"

Matthew straightened up in his seat, an anxious, excited expression on his face as he stared up at the stage. He didn't have to say a word. They both knew it was time for Amanda's solo.

The band swung into the bright notes of "My Favorite Things." Amanda stepped front and center, her strong soprano carrying the lilting verses, while the rest of the group sang a medley of other songs from the show in a soft harmonic background.

Amanda's voice rose powerfully on the final notes as the rest of the chorus went silent. Molly felt goose bumps on her arms, and she turned to see tears glistening in Matthew's eyes, his camera sitting untouched in his lap. He glanced at her a moment, then reached over and squeezed her hand, his gaze returning to Amanda.

The last note sounded, and applause suddenly roared through the hall. Matthew, Molly, and Jill all came to their feet, clapping.

"Wow!" Jill looked up at Molly. "I didn't know she could sing like that."

"Neither did I, honey," Molly admitted. Her eyes felt watery, and she quickly dabbed them with a handkerchief.

The chorus and their teacher took a few bows. The curtains closed and the house lights came on. Matthew turned to her, looking awestruck and very proud. Molly could see he was at a loss for words.

"She was wonderful. Really."

"I never heard her sing like that before," he said, sounding stunned. "She's really coming along. I wish her . . ." He stopped himself midsentence. Molly saw a faint flush cross his cheeks. "I wish I'd taken more pictures," he finished quickly.

Molly nodded, collecting her coat. She had a feeling that was not what he'd meant to say at all.

The crowd surged up the aisles toward the exits. Molly held Jill's hand so they wouldn't get separated. The lobby in front of the auditorium was packed with kids and adults moving in all directions.

"The girls said they would meet us here, near the water fountain," Molly told Matthew.

"There's their chorus teacher," Matthew remarked. "I'd like to have a word with her about Amanda. Do you mind?"

"Go ahead. We'll wait right here."

"Molly! I've been looking all over for you."

Molly felt her heart jump in her chest, and she looked up to find Phil standing right in front of her, as if he'd dropped down from the sky.

Dressed in a dark blue suit and yellow patterned tie, he looked so smart and polished that she barely recognized him. She'd never seen him look this handsome—not even on their wedding day, for goodness' sake. The flowers certainly added to the effect, she thought. Phil carried an armload of bouquets, enough to open a flower stand on the spot.

"What are you doing here?"

"I came to see Lauren. Didn't she tell you?"

"No, she did not." Molly guessed that the small detail had slipped Lauren's adolescent brain. Or maybe Lauren didn't think her father would really come. Molly was certainly having a hard enough time believing he was there.

"Daddy!" Jill ran over to give him a big hug, then gazed longingly at the flowers. "Are those for Lauren?"

"Hello, honey. Yes, there's one for Lauren. And one for you," he said, handing her a bouquet. "And one for Mommy." He smiled at Molly and held out a bunch of pink roses.

Molly didn't know what to do. She took the flowers without even looking at them.

"How thoughtful. Is this supposed to make up for all those times you forgot our anniversary?"

"Molly . . ." He smiled and shook his head at her.

Lauren suddenly appeared, her face glowing when she spotted her father. Molly stepped aside, feeling invisible.

"Dad! Did you see me?"

"Of course, I did, sweetie. I was sitting front and center. I even got a video." He held up a tiny expensive-looking camera. "You were great. I was so proud of you."

"Thanks, Dad." Lauren looked suddenly shy. "I didn't see you in the audience. I wasn't sure you would come."

"I promised you, didn't I?"

Lauren nodded but didn't reply.

"Here, I brought you some flowers." Phil handed her the bouquet, and her eyes lit with pleasure.

"They're beautiful, Daddy. Thanks." Finally, she glanced at Molly. "Look what Daddy got me. Aren't they awesome?"

"Absolutely," Molly agreed with a tight smile. She wondered now why she didn't think of flowers. Too distracted getting herself ready to see Matthew, she realized with a guilty twinge.

"You were great, honey. I loved the show." Molly reached out and stroked Lauren's hair.

But she wasn't even sure Lauren heard her. She had turned back to Phil, her attention totally fixed on her father. As was Jill, who stood on his other side, holding his hand.

Molly felt small and mean and overlooked. She sighed, thinking at least her daughters were happy. She had to give Phil a few points for tonight. He was clearly trying, and the girls appreciated his efforts.

"So where should we go for dinner?" Phil asked. "I made reservations at this terrific steak house, but I wasn't sure if that's what you'd all like to do." He looked hopefully at Molly. "I'd love it if you'd join us, Molly. I'm sure the girls would love it, too."

Molly felt thrown for a loop for the second time in fifteen minutes. This wasn't really happening, was it?

"Thanks, Phil. That's a nice invitation. But we have plans," she said quickly.

Phil's cheerful expression sagged like a sail that had suddenly lost the wind. She could see he had not anticipated this reply. Lauren and Jill clung to him, staring at her with downcast expressions. Molly just glared at them.

"But I want to have dinner with Daddy," Lauren complained. "Why can't we go?"

"You know why, Lauren. We've promised the Hardings. You don't want to disappoint Amanda, do you?"

Molly noticed Phil's gaze shift, and she looked up to see Matthew and Amanda standing beside her. "Sorry to keep you waiting," Matt said. "Mrs. Pickering had quite a lot to say."

Matthew looked at Molly and then around the group, his gaze finally coming to rest on Phil. The two men stared at each other for a minute, as if to say, "Who's *that* guy?"

Molly should have been horrified at the scene, but it suddenly seemed amusing. She hadn't been on a date with a man she truly liked in ages. Here she was, finally . . . and Phil shows up. If she didn't laugh at this, she would break down crying.

She quickly made introductions, summoning her best garden-party voice. The men briefly shook hands, and Phil shook hands with Amanda, as well, remembering to compliment her solo.

"That was lovely, Amanda," Molly agreed, catching the girl's eye. "I actually started crying," she admitted.

"Oh, Mom, you're such a waterworks sometimes," Lauren teased.

"She always gets like that." Phil laughed knowingly. "Cries at the drop of a hat. Even at TV commercials."

Molly glared at him. Matthew smiled in a tight, polite way.

Will this ever end? Molly thought desperately. She was not the praying kind, but she suddenly heard herself sending up a silent plea. Would somebody up there have pity on her and please get rid of Phil?

"We were just discussing dinner." Phil looked straight at Matthew. "I thought I'd surprise Molly and the girls. . . . But I guess they have plans with you."

Oh, Phil! How could you put Matthew on the spot like that! Molly wanted to shriek at him. He was as slippery as a bar of soap.

"Phil invited us out, but I told him we already had plans

with you and Amanda," Molly quickly explained to Matt.

Matthew looked confused, then glanced at Lauren, still standing beside her father, her arm hooked around Phil's waist. "That's all right," he said graciously. "Amanda and I understand if Lauren would like to see her father tonight."

Molly felt a little jolt. Did it really mean so little to him if she went off with Phil, or was he just trying to be nice?

"Don't be silly, Matt. We don't want to change our plans and leave you flat. That wouldn't be polite."

There was a moment of tense silence. Lauren looked disappointed but resigned, and Molly felt sorry for her. Still, this was Phil's fault. He should have checked beforehand and not assumed that they'd be at his beck and call.

Of course she looked like the bad guy again. Not him.

"Maybe we should all go out together?" Matthew suggested.

Molly stared at him. She knew he was just trying to be polite, but did he have to invite her ex-husband out on their first *almost* date? That wasn't a good sign at all, she thought dejectedly.

She looked over at Phil, sure he was going to say yes. He met her gaze and must have seen the silent scream of horror in her eyes.

"Thank you, Matt. That's nice of you to offer. But I don't think I'll crash the party." He hugged Lauren and Jill, one in each arm. "I'll see you two tomorrow. We'll have all day together," he reminded them. "You have a good time tonight and don't get to bed too late. I have a lot of plans."

The girls both nodded and kissed him good night. "Nice to meet you." Phil extended his hand and shook Matt's again. "I'll see you around," he added.

He cast Molly a knowing look, which she pretended not to notice. Phil knew she was interested in Matt. It was embarrassing being so transparent to him. Then again, he did know her well.

"Good night, Molly. See you tomorrow." Phil gave her a

lazy grin. "By the way, you look super in that dress. Blue is definitely your color."

"Good night, Phil." Molly kept her tone light. She secretly felt like flinging her bouquet at him but struggled not to lose her temper in front of Matthew.

THE THREE GIRLS CHATTED NONSTOP IN THE BACKSEAT on the way to the restaurant. Which was just as well, Matthew thought, since an awkward silence had fallen between him and Molly.

She stared out the passenger's side window, lost in thought. He couldn't help wondering if she was brooding over her ex-husband.

He was just as Matt had imagined—and even more so. Though he couldn't say why, Matt had not expected Phil to be so good-looking. Maybe he was just protecting his own ego. Molly was certainly lovely enough. She could attract any man she set her sights on, he thought.

Phil was a charming, smooth-talking guy. Whatever failings he may have had as a husband and father in the past, he now had Lauren and Jill wrapped around his little finger, though Matt could see he clearly loved both of them.

What about Molly? Was Phil hoping to win her back, too? Matt wouldn't be surprised. He glanced over at Molly, realizing he didn't like that idea.

"I'm sorry if Phil put you on the spot." Molly's quiet voice broke into his thoughts. "He's so . . . inconsiderate sometimes. Well, most of the time, actually."

"That's okay. I just didn't know what to say. I wasn't sure if you wanted to go with him. I'm happy you decided not to," he added.

He saw her smile and knew he had said the right thing. Finally.

"It all worked out, I guess." She settled back in her seat and sighed. "I thought he'd never get the hint. He really should have just let it go. He's going to see the girls all day tomorrow," she said. "He spoils them something awful. They're like little wildcats after a day out with him."

Molly shook her head, staring down at the flowers in her lap. "How can they forgive him so easily?"

Matthew looked out at the road. He didn't reply right away. "Children do have an amazing capacity to forgive and forget, God bless them. Especially a parent. It's a good thing, too. We do make so many mistakes."

Molly didn't answer right away. "Yes, that is a good thing. An amazing thing, really." She sighed. "I didn't mean to rant. He rattled me, showing up like that. I haven't seen him for months and now he's just popping out of the woodwork wherever I go. It's starting to feel like a bad horror movie."

Matthew laughed at the exaggeration. But he could tell that Molly still had some lingering feelings for Phil. Why else would she get so unhinged? She seemed to think it was all residual anger, but Matthew wondered if there was something more going on—something Molly might not even realize.

THE REST OF THE EVENING WENT SMOOTHLY. THE THREE girls kept the conversation lively. Molly quickly recovered from her distress over Phil and was her usual bright and vivacious self—times ten, Matthew thought. Or maybe it was just the candlelight flickering in her big blue eyes. Matthew knew he must be staring but found he could barely take his eyes off her.

Her emotions flashed across her lovely face like quicksilver, like sunlight sparkling on water. She was witty and irreverent one minute, tender and serious the next. She was warm. She was bold. She was outspoken, brimming with heartfelt emotion, then shy and suddenly self-conscious. She was honest and intelligent, totally without guile.

She was nothing like Sharon, he thought, who always

did and said just the right thing. No one would ever accuse Molly Willoughby of that, he thought, smiling to himself.

She was not like anyone he'd ever met before. If he wasn't careful, he would fall for her. Big time. By the end of the night, he felt lightheaded and happy, oddly at peace though he didn't quite know why.

After dessert, the three girls asked if they could take a walk around the restaurant, which had been a house. On a previous trek to the restroom they'd caught sight of the front parlor, which was filled with antiques, a game table, and a player piano. They were now eager to explore it.

"There's a Scrabble game in there with gold tiles," Jill told her mother in an awestruck tone.

"Go for it, Jill. Those vocabulary words are going to come in handy now," Matthew teased.

Molly glanced at him and laughed. "You're incorrigible," she said as the three girls ran off.

Matthew sat back, suddenly bashful at being completely alone with Molly. She looked so beautiful tonight. He felt a little dizzy every time he looked at her.

"I'm sorry about before," she said suddenly. "About getting all worked up over running into Phil at the concert." She shook her head; a silky curl fell against her cheek, he noticed. "He sure knows how to push my buttons. I guess he just knows me too well by now."

She glanced up at him with an uneasy smile. He could tell it was hard for her to talk about her ex-husband. Still, he was curious. He wanted to know more about her feelings for Phil. He suddenly wanted to know everything.

"When did you and Phil meet?" he asked quietly.

"I was fifteen years old, if you can believe that. A freshman in high school. I ended up marrying the first guy who ever asked me out on a date, for goodness' sake. I guess you could say I was a little insecure."

Matthew didn't mean to, but he couldn't help smiling at the way she told her story. "When did you get married?"

"Right after graduation. I was eighteen and Phil was

twenty. I didn't want to go to college, and I wouldn't listen to my parents. I thought I knew everything. I was a little wild. Had a bad attitude. I was every parent's nightmare."

"Oh, I'm sure you weren't that bad." Matthew *was* sure, too. He knew by now how Molly loved to exaggerate to make her point. She could never have turned out this wonderful if she was half as bad as she claimed.

"Oh, but I was. You have no idea. My parents should be awarded gold medals for putting up with me. I realize that now as Lauren is hitting that impossible stage." She sighed and took a sip of her coffee, glancing at him over the rim of her cup. "I bet you were a total angel. Honor roll, student government, all that stuff."

He smiled slowly at her. "Actually, I was pretty bad myself for a while. Had that bad attitude thing you just mentioned."

Molly's eyes widened in shock. "No, you didn't. You're just saying that to make me feel better."

He shook his head. "No, I'm not. I really did have a bad stretch there for a while. See, we have more in common than you thought."

"You're right about that." Molly still looked surprised, and he couldn't help grinning at her.

"I was rebelling against my father, I guess. It was always assumed I'd be a doctor, just like him. I was determined to show everyone I was different. Even if it meant ruining my chances to get into a good college."

Molly cast him a thoughtful look. "I get it. But what happened after that? I mean, here you are. You turned out to be a doctor, after all. What made you change your mind?"

"Well, something happened, something that changed my life, actually." Matthew paused and glanced away. "My best friend crashed his car a few weeks before high-school graduation. He died on the scene, almost instantly. It was a horrific bloody mess. I was in the backseat and somehow hardly got a scratch. I still have nightmares about it."

Matthew saw her draw in a sharp breath. "How awful for you." Her voice was warm with sympathy.

"It was awful, all right . . . but it made me wake up and realize I'd been wasting time. You see, I really did want to be a doctor. I had always wanted to do this, ever since I was a little kid. I would have wanted it even if my father had been a fireman or owned a hardware store. I just wanted everyone to realize that it was my choice. I wasn't just doing it because my parents wanted that for me."

Molly nodded. "I understand what you mean, and I'm glad it turned out okay for you. I'm glad you got what you wanted."

"Thanks," he said quietly. He met her gaze and held it. He felt she did understand. "How about you, Molly? Did you get what you wanted?"

She smiled softly and shook her head. "No, not yet . . . But I'm working on it."

He reached over and covered her hand with his own. "It will come to you. I have a feeling about that."

"I hope so," she said quietly.

Matthew didn't answer her. He didn't know what to say. He sat holding her hand on the linen cloth until Molly quite suddenly sat up and slipped her hand into her lap. He followed her gaze and saw the girls returning to the table. He glanced at Molly and shared a smile.

Well, there would be other times to talk to her alone like this, he thought. He hoped so, anyway.

On the drive home, she didn't say much. But she looked content—much more at ease than she had looked earlier.

Matthew drove down Main Street and parked in front of Molly's building. "I'll walk you to the door," he offered before she could say otherwise.

Amanda waited in the car and waved good night. At the door to their apartment building, Molly looked down at her daughters expectantly. They both responded to the silent prompt, turning to Matthew.

"Thank you for dinner, Dr. Harding," Lauren said politely.

"Yes, thank you," Jill chimed in.

He smiled at them. "You're very welcome. We must do it again sometime," he teased the girls in a formal tone.

"Indubitably," Jill said, and then she giggled, covering her mouth with her hand.

Lauren poked her with an elbow. "Come on, silly." They turned and ran upstairs.

Molly smiled up at him. "Well, thank you again. We had a great time. It was very, very nice of you."

"My pleasure. Honestly." He stared down into her eyes. "We *should* do it again . . . without the kids, I mean."

Molly's bright eyes widened. "Sure," she said slowly.

Her mouth made a perfect circle of surprise, and he wanted very badly to kiss her. But then remembered Amanda sitting in the car only a few feet away. She was watching them carefully, he was certain.

He leaned forward and quickly kissed her on the cheek instead. "I'll call you, okay?"

"Sure," she said again. He could tell she was wondering if he really would.

He suddenly wondered the same thing. This was hard, much harder than he remembered. Or was it only so difficult for him because of his past? He forced a smile and dug his hands in his pockets, taking a few steps away from her.

"See you," he called out as he got back in the car.

Molly lifted her hand and waved good-bye. Then she turned and went inside.

He started the car, feeling strangely unsettled. He could really care for her. He knew that now. Maybe he already did.

He just didn't want to be another man who let her down.

ON SUNDAY MORNING SOPHIE SKIPPED COFFEE HOUR AND left church with Miranda right after the service. She wanted to get home to Gus, of course. But she also knew that many friends from the congregation would soon be on their way to the orchard to visit.

Her daughters and their families were on hand to help out with the entertaining. As she gave her directions and did the little chores they permitted, she felt the familiar anticipation that came with expecting company tinged with melancholy, like a photo of happier days, browned and frayed at the edges. Their friends would gather in the familiar rooms as they had for years and years. The guests would talk and laugh and enjoy each other's company. Everyone would pretend it was a get-well visit. But everyone knew the truth. Sophie and Gus did, too. They were all really coming to say good-bye.

Gus was fading fast. Right before her very eyes it seemed. Sometimes, when she came upon him resting, drifting in his own thoughts, it seemed so clear that he was not there anymore. His spirit was testing the waters, venturing out beyond her husband's worn body, then drifting back again.

It was like watching the tide go out, each wave that comes in growing almost imperceptibly shorter. At first you can barely tell anything is happening. But over time, as an hour and then another slips by, you can see how the shoreline has pulled away.

That was how it was now, Sophie thought. Gus was moving away from her. Steadily, irreversibly. Like the tide in the sea.

"Should I put out the good china, Grandma?" Miranda called from the dining room.

"Yes, dear. And the silver flatware, too. The good everything. Take it all out," Sophie said with emphasis.

She set a homemade pie on a glass cake stand, sighing to herself. She wondered why she never realized before that life was so short, so precious. Why had she saved all these things? What for? So they could sit dusty and yellowed on a shelf? She should have used the good china every day. She should have dressed in her best clothes and dabbed on her treasured perfume just to go out and pick apples or dig in the garden. Gus's time had just about run out, and it felt as if her time had, too.

"I'll get the door," Miranda announced some time later from the front hallway.

Sophie was in the bedroom with Gus, making him presentable. He'd insisted on wearing a white shirt with a red bow tie and his favorite argyle vest. Gray trousers and his fancy black Sunday shoes completed the outfit. He hadn't been dressed up in real clothes for days. Sophie could see the effort had tired him but also lifted his spirits.

His normally ruddy complexion had taken on a yellowish cast. She knew what that meant. His liver and kidneys were giving out. If he noticed, he didn't say. He eyed himself in the mirror, combing his thin gray hair.

"Do I look okay?"

She stepped behind him and placed her hands on his shoulders. "Best-looking man in the room, as always," she assured him.

He turned his face to kiss her hand. "You're too good to me."

Sophie's reply caught in her throat, so she didn't say anything. He was mistaken. She could never be too good to Gus. It wasn't possible.

She rolled Gus out into the living room, into a circle of smiling faces and cheerful greetings. Jessica and Sam Morgan were there; Grace Hegman and her father, Digger; along with Harry Reilly, who owned the boatyard downtown.

"Gus, good to see you. You look swell," Harry said, shaking Gus's hand. "Better hurry up and get well. I've got myself a new boat. Did Digger tell you?"

"No, he didn't say. Trading up, are you? It's about time," Gus chided him.

"This rich guy had his boat in my yard, brand new. Had

it on the water one season. Then he gets transferred out to Arizona, and he can't wait to get it off his hands. He asks me if I can find a buyer. He was almost giving it away. I couldn't resist." Harry laughed. "It's top of the line. Practically catches the fish for you."

A few times each summer a group of the men from church got together to go fishing. They went out from sunrise to sunset, and the man who caught the biggest fish had to buy the rest dinner. Gus had always enjoyed those outings, Sophie recalled. It gave him a little break from the orchard.

"Remember that striper you hooked last summer, Gus?" Digger said. "Nearly broke my arm trying to help you reel it in."

"That was a beauty," Sam agreed. "I caught one half the size, and we still have plenty in the freezer."

"Oh, dear, tell me about it." Jessica sighed with a rueful smile. "How many ways can you cook bass?"

"I have a few recipes I can give you, dear," Sophie offered.

"He was a monster. Wait, I've got a picture of that guy right up on the mantel." Gus turned his chair and pointed.

Sam jumped up and took the photo down, then handed it to him. "That fish was almost as big as you are."

Gus laughed. "Not quite. Forty-six inches, if I remember right." He stared down at the photo, and Sophie noticed his smile slowly dissolve, like a lump of ice cream left out in the sun.

There would be no more fishing trips. No more mysterious tugs on a line. No more aching arms and a sore back from a battle with a big sea bass. No more unbelievable stories. That's what he's thinking, she realized. Her heart ached.

The doorbell rang, catching everyone's attention. "I'll go," Sophie's daughter Una offered.

Sophie heard the sound of Reverend Ben and his wife Carolyn coming into the foyer. She stepped out to greet them. The reverend's daughter, Rachel, and her husband, Jack Anderson, were also there, and Sophie was pleased to see them.

Carolyn gave Sophie a kiss and hug in greeting. "Mark wanted to come so much," she said, "but he volunteered to stay at Rachel's to watch the baby. He asked me to tell you he'll come by during the week to say hello if that's all right."

"Of course, it's all right. We'd love to see him anytime," Sophie said sincerely. She and Gus had known both Rachel and Mark Lewis since they were little children. So many friends, she thought.

As the Lewis family took off their coats, Emily Warwick and Dan Forbes arrived, along with Emily's daughter, Sara Franklin, and her boyfriend, Luke McAllister.

Sara handed Sophie a bunch of flowers. "These are for you," she said.

"Thank you, dear. How thoughtful." Sophie hardly had time to admire them before Miranda took the bouquet and went off in search of a vase.

Sophie followed Sara and Luke into the living room, remembering the day last fall that they had come apple picking in the orchard. Sara and Luke hardly knew each other at the time, but Sophie could tell something was simmering there.

I was right, too, she thought with satisfaction.

Luke had seemed such a mysterious figure when he first came to Cape Light. That was about a year ago now, Sophie realized. A former policeman, he had bought a piece of property from Dr. Elliot and decided to build a center for troubled teenagers on it. That had caused quite a stir in town. People were up in arms about it for a time, though she and Gus had always thought it was an admirable idea. When some of the kids came up from Boston to help build the place, there had been a terrible fire on the property. She and Gus had taken the kids in, and they all ended up working in the orchard when help was needed badly. Such a fortunate turn of events. *The Lord has a way of working these things out,* she reminded herself, *of untangling life's little knots when you least expect it.*

The construction at Luke's property was halted by the harsh winter but would start up again soon. Luke had told her it would open sometime in May. More kids from the city would come to stay then, and he'd offered to send more helpers her way. But with Gus sick and all, she hadn't made arrangements with him.

The orchard meant so much to so many people in this town. It held so many memories for the friends and family gathered here today, Sophie reflected. Even for total strangers just passing through Cape Light who stopped for a moment and found themselves in a tucked-away corner of paradise.

It won't be the same without Gus, Sophie reflected as she took a seat again among her company. She brushed the mournful thoughts aside and tried to focus on her guests. Her daughters, Evelyn and Una, along with Miranda, were taking care of all the kitchen work today so she could simply sit and enjoy herself. Sophie was totally unaccustomed to relaxing at one of her own parties, but she forced herself to stay put, knowing this could be the first and last time she'd have the opportunity.

Gus started telling a funny story about getting lost in the woods with his Boy Scout troop, way back when their children were all in grade school. Reverend Ben had been along, and he'd suggested they stop and pray for divine guidance.

"Oh, Ben, you didn't really?" Carolyn burst into laughter.

"Yes, I did. I didn't know what else to do. I'm not much of a woodsman, as you all know."

They all agreed, laughing loudly and long.

"It worked for Moses," Ben said.

"We did find our way eventually," Gus added. "Some ranger came along and took pity on us."

"You see? Our prayers were answered," Ben insisted.

The rest of the group continued laughing and teasing

him. *As it should be. This last get-together should be as happy as we can make it,* Sophie thought with a determined spirit. *We might as well be smiling. There will be time enough for tears.*

A light lunch was served—sandwiches, salads, and cheese—along with Sophie's famous scones with honey from her own bees and peaches and plums she'd canned the past summer. Everyone praised the meal lavishly, as usual, and just as predictably insisted that she didn't need to go to so much trouble. But they didn't leave much on the platters, she noticed with satisfaction.

After the coffee and Sophie's famous pies were served, guests began to bid farewell. First they found Gus, still sitting in the living room. It was hard for Sophie to watch them say good-bye to him, everyone acting as if they'd see him again soon, when they all knew that most of them would never see him again. Watching from the doorway, Sophie's eyes welled up with tears, and she had to turn away. She wandered into the foyer and composed herself, then suddenly found herself facing Emily and Dan.

"It was wonderful of you to have us all here, Sophie," Emily said. "And wonderful to see Gus. We don't want to make him too tired, though."

"Yes, of course. He was happy to see everyone. Thank you for coming. Both of you," Sophie said. Emily hugged her and then so did Dan.

"You take care of yourself," Emily added. "If there's anything you need, anything at all, just call me. Okay?"

Sophie tried to make light of her serious expression. "Well, it's good to know I have friends in important places. But don't worry, dear. We'll be fine. I have my children here now. It will be okay."

Dan met her gaze and forced a smile. They knew it would not be okay. Not entirely. But there was nothing more to say.

They said good-bye again and left. Then others began to drift to the door, and very soon, the guests had gone and only family remained. Evelyn's husband, Robert, took Gus into the bedroom so he could rest, then returned to sit in the living room with Una's husband, Ted. Some of the grandchildren wandered about, but most had settled into the family room to watch TV. Sophie's daughters along with Miranda were still in the kitchen, putting away leftovers and washing dishes.

Sophie felt alone in the crowd, outside of each circle. A sinking feeling had settled on her spirit now that the party was over. Her children had hinted that they wanted to have a family talk today, and she dreaded the inevitable debate over what she would do once Gus was gone.

She wandered back into the kitchen seeking some task to get her mind off her worries. "Need a hand in here?" she asked, her tone far brighter than she felt.

"We're all done, Mom." Una glanced at her. "Are you okay?"

"Just a little tired. That was a nice get-together though."

"Yes, it was very nice. Dad really enjoyed it." Una set a china saucer in a stack on the countertop, then looked at Evelyn.

"Would you like a cup of tea, Grandma?" Miranda asked her.

"Thanks, dear. That would be nice."

"Here, Mom. Sit down. I'll fix it for you." Una came up beside her and guided her to a chair at the table. Then Una and Evelyn sat down, too.

Evelyn was her oldest and the one who most resembled her mother. She wore one of Sophie's favorite aprons, and as Sophie looked across the table at her daughter, she almost felt as if she were looking in a mirror at herself . . . herself twenty-five years ago when everything had been ahead of her, so much life still to live, so much to look forward to.

"Mom, we thought we should have a talk," Evelyn began slowly. "We know it's hard to discuss it, but Dad . . . Dad is near the end. It won't be long now before you're on your own."

"Yes . . . yes I know." Sophie looked down at the table.

Miranda brought over the tea and set it before her without a word.

"You'll be alone here. It will be very hard for you," Una said.

"We know how you love this place. We all do," Evelyn added. "We've been trying hard to figure out some way around it . . . but we don't think you can stay here all alone, Mom. Una and I have talked with Bart," she went on. "We'd all be too worried about you."

"We know it's hard to face it. But you can't run the orchard on your own. These last few years, you and Dad could hardly manage it together," Una said.

Sophie didn't answer. She sighed and stirred her tea. "I think I could manage. I could hire some help. . . ."

"Oh, Mom. Even if you found good help, it would still be a lot of work for you. A lot of responsibility." Evelyn glanced at her sister. "Poor Dad, he worked so hard on this land all his life. We don't want to see you run yourself down out here, too."

"It's just not practical, Mom. Please be reasonable about this," Una implored her.

"I've lived here since the day I was born. That was a long, long time ago," Sophie said, shaking her head. "It seems very unreasonable to me to pick up and make a change at this late date. Impractical, too, come to think about it."

The two sisters shared a look. Sophie felt her eyes blur with tears, and she blew her nose on a paper napkin. Miranda reached over and patted her hand. She glanced at her aunts. "What about if Grandma leases out the land to someone who will work the orchard and let her live here?"

Una sighed. "That's a thought, dear. But she'll still really be alone in this big house. Anything can happen."

"Besides, bringing someone else into the business would be a big headache," Evelyn pointed out. "How would we even find someone to do it? It's almost spring. We'd have to sort it all out right away."

Sophie glanced at Miranda. "I've thought of that myself, honey. But it gets too complicated. It would be hard for me to see someone out in the trees who wasn't family. I've been here too long. Those trees are like my friends. I might not like the way someone else handled them," she offered with a weak smile.

"The thing to do is sell the place and then you can come live with me. Or Una. Or get a little apartment in town," Evelyn suggested.

"In town? Me?" Sophie scoffed as if Evelyn had suggested she move to Paris. "I'm just not a town-type person, honey. You know that. I need to be out in the open. I don't like houses and buildings blocking my view."

"I know it's hard, Mom," Evelyn persisted. "But try to be a little open-minded about what you might do."

Sophie pushed her empty teacup away and pressed her hands flat to the table. "I know you're only trying to take care of me. I know that, girls," she told her daughters. "And I appreciate it, truly. But I can't leave here. I'm just like . . . like a fish out of water away from this place. It's hard enough losing your father. I can't lose this place, too," she beseeched them.

She was trying not to cry but could feel the teardrops squeezing out from the corners of her eyes. "I really don't think I could survive away from here. Not for too long, anyway. I'd rather live on here for a month or a week or even a day than move away and live another ten years somewhere else. I'd rather the good Lord would just take me now. Can either of you understand that?"

"Oh, Mom . . ." Evelyn rose and stepped beside her mother to give her a hug. Una did the same.

"We didn't mean to make you so upset," Una said.

"Don't cry, Mom, please. We don't have to decide any of this now," Evelyn added.

They stood beside her for a second, comforting her while Miranda held her hand. "I'm sorry, Grandma," Miranda said simply. Sophie squeezed her fingers in reply.

Finally, Sophie sat up in her chair and wiped her eyes. "I'm going to look in on your father."

The bedroom she had always shared with Gus was on the second floor. But this time when he came home from the hospital, she had set him up in a hospital bed in the guest room on the first floor and moved in a twin bed from upstairs so she could be near him when he slept. The room was nearly dark, illuminated by a small night-light on a bed stand and the shine of a half moon.

Gus breathed heavily in his sleep with the aid of oxygen. Sophie sat in a chair near him and leaned over to touch the hand that rested outside the covers. He'd had a good day today, a happy day, with long moments of distraction, of being able to forget that he was so sick, so near death. As if he were ever able to forget that entirely.

She stared out the window at the orchard, the stark bare trees outlined in the moonlight. Such a sight, it nearly made her heart break. She had the urge to wake Gus up, just to show him, then thought that wouldn't be right.

Sophie squeezed her eyes shut, still holding Gus's hand. *Dear Lord, I know this is a lot to ask, but please help me. Please find some way for me to stay on this land. I know my children are loving and that's a blessing. They only want to take care of me. But you know my heart, Lord. You know why I can't leave here. People say that You won't send more our way than we can handle. I don't think I can face losing Gus and my orchard, too. . . .*

When she opened her eyes, Gus's eyes were open, too. "Sophie. How long have you been sitting here?"

"Oh, not long. Do you need anything?"

He shook his head. "I don't know why I woke up. Maybe it's the moonlight." He turned to the window, and she pushed aside the curtain so they could look outside.

"Isn't it beautiful," she said quietly. "I wanted to wake you up to see it with me."

"Maybe the Lord heard your thoughts, and he shook my shoulder, just to please you," Gus suggested with a smile.

Sophie felt her heart catch. "Maybe . . ." she agreed slowly. "I do hope He was really listening tonight."

She took his hand again, and together they watched out the window the fragile branches of the apple trees, waving against the star-filled sky.

Chapter Seven

Tucker smoothed his uniform jacket, then knocked sharply on the chief's door. He'd no sooner walked in the station house than he had been told that Sanborn wanted to see him.

"Come in," Sanborn called.

Tucker stepped inside and stood in front of the large wooden desk. The police chief was reading through some papers in a file and didn't look up right away.

"You wanted to see me, sir?"

"Yes, shut the door, will you?" Chief Sanborn sat back. The expression on his face made Tucker nervous. "Have a seat."

Tucker took the chair in front of the desk, the "hot seat" as his fellow officers called it. He wondered what this was all about. He'd taken a lot of personal time since Carl came to town. He suspected that his boss wasn't happy about that.

"How's it going, Tucker?"

"All right." Tucker shrugged, the chief's forced friendly tone making him even more uncomfortable.

"I know I've been taking a lot of personal time, Chief—" he began.

Sanborn held up a hand, and Tucker stopped talking. "Yes, you have. But that's not what I wanted to talk to you about. Well, not exactly." He shifted in his seat. "I know you have your brother at home now. That's quite a responsibility."

"I suppose. He's not much trouble. Stays in his room, watches TV. I do need to bring him to the doctor for checkups."

His boss nodded. "How is he coming along? Is his health improving?"

"He's making progress. Slowly but steady." Tucker paused, still unsure of the chief's motives for this private meeting. Was it to ask after Carl's health? That didn't make sense.

"So, what are his plans? Will he be staying around here long, do you think?"

Tucker blinked. Now he got it. "I don't think so. He talks about going up to Maine to live with a friend in Portland."

"I see." Chief Sanborn nodded. "I wanted you to know I'll be looking into Carl's records, his release records from prison and his parole, any recent arrests and so forth."

"Carl finished his parole without a problem, Chief. It's been a few years now."

Chief Sanborn didn't say anything at first. The look on his face made Tucker feel like a fool for taking Carl's word so easily.

"Well, I'm sure that's what he told you. What else would he say? But I do need to look into it officially. I know Carl is sick and not much of a danger to anyone except himself. But people get upset when they hear somebody with his history is back in town. I'm sure you've heard some of that already."

Tucker nodded. He'd heard it all right. Right under his

own roof, although Fran had calmed down considerably, and she seemed resigned to Carl's presence—for now, anyway. Why did people have to be like that? Didn't they have better things to worry about?

"I understand. Is that all you wanted to tell me?" he asked curtly. "I'm due on patrol in five minutes."

"That's it. I'll let you know what I find out," the chief added, dismissing him.

"Fine." Tucker came to his feet, turned on his heel, and left the office, feeling as if smoke were pouring out of his ears. As he went to the locker room, he could feel his fellow officers staring at him, speculating on his visit with the boss; all of them probably knew about Carl and felt the way the chief did.

I'm just imagining things now, he told himself. He picked up his hat and jacket and headed out the door to his squad car. Walking through the parking lot, Tucker passed two other officers and said hello. He saw them glance at each other, then one nodded, the greeting noticeably chilly.

Tucker tried not to show a reaction. He got in his car and drove out of the lot. An old saying came to him, one he'd never quite understood until now: "Just because you're paranoid, it doesn't mean they're not out to get you."

Were people turning against him now because of Carl? It was sure starting to feel like it. Even his boss seemed to think he was a fool for accepting Carl's story about his record. If Carl was violating parole, he could be sent back to prison. In his condition, that would most likely finish him off, Tucker thought.

Now he would have to wait to find out if Carl had lied to him. As if he needed something else to worry about right now.

"MOLLY! WHERE HAVE YOU BEEN? I LEFT TWO MESSAGES on your voice mail," Betty said in greeting to her.

"Racing around like a maniac, as usual. I had a lot of deliveries to make. It's Monday, remember?"

"Oh, right." Betty nodded. "No wonder you're so cranky."

Molly just grinned at her. Betty stood next to Fran Tulley's desk, peering down at two photos in her hand. It looked as if the women were trying to decide which photo to stick on the "House of the Week" poster that now sat on Fran's desk.

"Which do you like?" Betty asked. "This charming Cape? A steal at this asking price, believe me. Or this lovely Victorian? Needs a little TLC but could be a show place for a buyer with imagination."

Molly glanced at the photos. Neither of the houses looked very appealing, but Betty was a born salesperson.

"Whichever. You'll sell both in about twenty minutes," Molly predicted.

"Why, thanks. I think they will move quickly." Betty looked back at the photos. "I think we should go with the Cape. We did a Victorian last week." She handed the chosen photo to Fran, then turned to Molly again. "So how did it go on Saturday night? I'm dying to hear everything."

Molly was dying to tell everything, too, but didn't feel comfortable talking about Matthew in front of Fran.

"It was a very nice evening. The girls sang beautifully." She smiled at Fran. "I thought Mary Ellen did a nice job up there, Fran. I didn't get to tell you."

Fran looked up from the poster. "Thanks, Molly. Lauren sounded great, too. But Dr. Harding's daughter, she really brought down the house. I bet he was very proud," she added with a meaningful look.

"Yes, he was." Molly turned to Betty, who now looked about to burst from curiosity. "Amanda Harding sang a solo. She was amazing."

"Really? How nice." Betty clutched Molly's arm. "Come into my office. I want to show you something. Excuse us a minute, will you, Fran?"

Fran smiled knowingly, looking down at her work

again. Fran wasn't the gossiping type, but Molly still felt uncomfortable. That was the problem with living in a small town. Everyone seemed to know everything almost before it even happened.

Once inside the office, Betty quickly shut the door. "So? What's the story?"

Molly sighed and flopped into an armchair. "I had a great time. I think he did, too, but who can tell about these things? Men just . . . baffle me. He gave me one of those 'I'll call you sometime' good-byes. That's not a good sign, is it?"

Betty sat on the edge of her desk, her shiny, chin-length blond hair swinging around her face.

"Well, that depends. He doesn't seem like the type who would say that and not call. Maybe he just felt self-conscious around the kids. I think you should sit tight and give him time."

"Good advice. As if I have any choice in the matter," Molly added with a small laugh.

"I heard that his office was opening this week. I'm sure he's feeling stressed and expects to be very busy. Maybe he didn't feel able to make any plans right now."

"Maybe." Betty's explanation gave her a little hope but not much. "Wait, I forgot to tell you the funniest part. While I was waiting for Lauren to come out from backstage, Phil showed up."

"He didn't." Betty's eyes widened with astonishment.

"He did. With enough flowers for the entire Miss America pageant, playing his Devoted Dad act to the hilt. It's starting to drive me crazy." Molly's maddened expression made Betty laugh.

"He does sound a little over-the-top."

"Over-the-top would be an improvement. He just assumed that the girls and I would be free to have dinner with him. So that caused a big to-do with Lauren. Then Matthew felt awkward, I guess, and invited Phil to come along with us."

"Oh, no. You poor thing. A first-date disaster. I'd rather have spinach stuck in my teeth," Betty said decidedly.

"This was definitely worse than spinach. Phil finally took a hint and backed off. I guess I looked like I was about to strangle him. But that's what I mean about Matthew. I don't think inviting my ex-husband out to dinner with us was a good sign."

Betty gazed down at her a moment, then patted her shoulder. "Don't worry. I have a good feeling about this, honestly."

Molly felt cheered by her friend's words. "You were right about the dress, though."

"I told you that dress was perfect for you." Betty smiled in a self-satisfied way. "That proves you have to listen to my advice about these things. Don't get too distracted about Matthew. Just let it unfold." Betty gestured with her hands, the many rings on her fingers sparkling.

"Frankly, I'm so stressed about work right now, I don't have time to worry about him, too. That's what I really wanted to talk to you about, Betty. I'm getting cold feet. I think I made a huge mistake giving up all my cleaning jobs, and now it's too late to get them back."

"It's hard to make such a big change," Betty said sympathetically. "You're bound to have some second thoughts."

"I'd describe it more like sheer terror. I woke up at three A.M. in a cold sweat. I can't make a living on the cooking and baking alone. And even if I get more business, I can't handle it all. What was I thinking? It's just not going to work."

Betty rested a steady hand on her shoulder. "Take a deep breath, Molly. You're panicking. I think I need to have you breathe into a paper bag." Her tone was serious, but her eyes held a mirthful light.

"Of course I'm panicking! I'm just not like you, Betty. I just don't have what it takes to run a business."

"Now, now. None of that put-down talk. You're as smart as anybody, smarter than most people I know. So that excuse just doesn't work on me," Betty said sternly. "Let's talk about this logically, point by point. What exactly has thrown you into such a tizzy?"

Molly stared at her friend. As much as she felt like falling apart at the seams, clearly Betty wouldn't let her. She took another deep breath and tried to organize her thoughts.

"First of all, I don't have enough orders to make the amount of money I need."

"Okay, fair enough. But Phil is giving you support checks for the girls now, so that should help. More importantly, there must be loads more possible clients out there for you. Now that you're not wasting your time cleaning, you can go after new business—in that fabulous dress, of course," she added, making Molly smile again. "So, do you have any new prospects lined up?"

"Well, I do have an appointment tomorrow at the country club in Hamilton," Molly had to admit.

"Excellent. That horsie set throws tons of parties. You're bound to get a lot of contacts there."

"If I get the work."

"Of course you'll get it. Think positively," Betty urged her. "The first thing I want you to do after that is sit with the phone book and make a list of all the possible places you can call for work. Then try to set up some appointments. Mention your classy clients, like the Spoon Harbor Inn and the Pequot Inn. They'll be impressed. They won't want to miss out. If you don't have enough new clients after that, then . . . well, then we'll figure out some other strategy. Refrigerator magnets or sky writing, maybe," Betty said, waving her hands in the air.

"Betty, be serious. Besides, even if I get more clients, I can't fill the orders. I can't be cooking and baking night and day. And how about delivering all this stuff? I've been driving around all day as it is."

"Many hands make light work," Betty told her. "It's not

just a saying in a fortune cookie. Did you ever check into hiring a helper? I thought we already covered that."

"Oh, right. No, I guess I didn't."

Betty gazed at her and shook her head. "Listen, this is what I'm hearing: The old way was familiar and comforting, even though it wasn't getting you from point A to point B. The new path is scary, unknown. There are problems to solve around every corner, very discouraging. So it seems easier now—smarter even—to turn back and hide in your dark, cozy little hole. But that's not like you, Molly. You're not a quitter," Betty insisted. "I know this is what you really want, and I wouldn't be a real friend if I let you give up now, would I?"

Molly gazed at Betty for a long moment, then shook her head. "So you won't let me whine and wiggle my way out of this? Is that what you're saying?"

"See, you catch on pretty quickly." Betty smiled again. "Here's an idea for you. I'm going to teach an adult-ed course up at the high school about real-estate sales. Classes begin this week. There's also a course being offered about working in restaurants and catering, and I heard the instructor is great. I'm sure it would give you the nuts-and-bolts information you really need to get going."

"Take a course?" Molly considered the idea. Although she had thought of taking a class in starting a small business, it never seemed to be the right time. *But if not now, when?* she asked herself bluntly. Besides, what did she have to lose? She'd get an idea of the real problems she'd face trying to do this work full-time and possibly some of the solutions as well.

"That's a good suggestion," she said. "I'll go up to the high school today and look into it."

"That's the spirit. Don't delay; you might start getting second thoughts," Betty warned her.

Molly smiled. Sometimes Betty knew her too well.

"And I'll check the student job list while I'm there, too,"

Molly promised. She knew Betty was bound to mention that next.

When Molly was finally ready to leave, she gave Betty a huge impulsive hug. "Thanks. I guess I came unglued there for a minute."

"Yes, you did. Nothing I couldn't handle, though," Betty admitted with a grin. Then her voice turned serious as she said, "Just remember, 'Whatever you can do, begin it. Boldness has genius, power, and magic in it.' "

Molly blinked. "Don't tell me, Ann Landers?"

Betty shook her head. "Johann Wolfgang von Goethe, a German poet. The point is, I know you can do it, Molly. Trust me on this, okay?"

Molly nodded, suddenly feeling her throat too tight speak. She did trust Betty. Implicitly. She only wished she could trust herself as much.

FRAN MARCHED INTO THE FAMILY ROOM AND STOOD BEside the TV. Tucker glanced at her, then looked back at the set. He was watching some sporting event as usual—basketball tonight—and he had barely said hello when she came in.

At least Carl isn't in here, too, she thought. That would really be the icing on her cake today.

"I'm home," she announced, still wearing her coat.

Tucker gave her a confused look. "I can see that. Can you step to the side, please? I'm trying to watch the game."

Fran turned and clicked off the TV.

Tucker sat up straight in his armchair as if prodded by an electric shock. "What did you do that for? It's a big game, for goodness' sake. It's the Celtics, Fran."

"Sorry, Tucker. We have to talk." She took off her coat and sat down on the sofa.

"This is about Carl again. Isn't it?"

Fran nodded. She could see Tucker's expression change

and readied herself for another argument. She just had to make him see this time.

"Did something happen?"

"Yes, something happened. It was awful for me. You really have no idea. Or maybe you do but you prefer to keep your head stuck in the sand."

Tucker took a breath. She could see that he was trying hard to control his temper. "Let's see, you went down the street to Sylvia North's house for a PTA meeting. Is that right so far?"

Fran nodded. "The Teacher Appreciation Day planning committee. We talked for a while about the event. The luncheon plans, should we buy corsages or give plants, that sort of thing. Then Sylvia brought out the coffee and everyone started chatting about their kids and things going on in the neighborhood—"

"Okay, I get the picture. So, what was so awful that you turned off the Celtics with two minutes left on the clock?"

Tucker's impatient tone upset her all over again. "Sorry to bore you, Tucker. First my feelings aren't as important as your brother's and now I don't even beat out the Celtics."

"I never said that, Fran."

"You didn't have to say it. It's perfectly obvious." Fran sat back and crossed her arms over her chest. She could feel Tucker watching her, but she avoided meeting his gaze.

"Just tell me what happened at the meeting. Somebody said something nasty about Carl living here, is that it?"

"Brilliant deduction. You should be a detective. You're really wasted in uniform." Tucker took a sharp breath, and she knew that she had hurt him. Still, she pressed on, "I don't even want to tell you now. You don't care what I've been through over this situation. I lost a good client this week."

Tucker sighed. "You told me. But you don't know that for sure, Fran. They could have given the listing to someone else for a lot of reasons."

"It was because of Carl," she insisted. "I know you don't like hearing that, Tucker, but it's true. You know what they said at the meeting tonight? All the neighbors are concerned about Carl being here. They're afraid about getting their houses broken into and even their property values going down once the word gets out that the newest resident on our street is an ex-convict. Sylvia wants to put her house on the market soon. Not that I'll get the listing, believe me," Fran said, shaking her head. "She's the one who cornered me, asking how long he'll be here. 'Aren't you afraid to have him in the house with you like that?' she said. Well, what could I say? I *am* afraid sometimes."

"Oh, come on, Fran. Carl is no threat to anyone around here. That's just ridiculous. You have to just ignore that kind of talk."

"I'm sorry, Tucker. I just can't. It really upsets me." She shrugged. "Maybe I care too much what people think. Or maybe I'm not as good-hearted as you are," she said honestly. "But that's just who I am. I can't help it."

Her husband glanced at her, folding his hands together. He didn't say anything. He didn't have to.

The thing was, Fran knew she could help it if she really wanted to. She could try harder to live her faith. That's what the right attitude would be. But she didn't have patience or the energy for that. Not like Tucker, Lord bless him. Sometimes it seemed he had enough patience and integrity for both of them.

Her husband was special. He had a good heart; she'd always known that about him. *He's never changed but maybe I have,* she thought with a pang.

She could have married someone else, someone more ambitious, bound to achieve more material success in life. But she chose Tucker Tulley because of who he was inside. He wanted to do something meaningful with his life, and she had admired that. She'd been idealistic back then, with youthful values. Unrealistic ones, it now seemed.

"What do you want me to do, Fran?" Tucker asked

slowly. "Should I take out an advertisement in the *Messenger* and promise people Carl poses no threat to their safety? Do you want me to tell people that it's all my fault, that you have nothing to do with this?"

"Tucker, of course not. But—" Fran hesitated, wondering if she should just let it go. No, she had to be honest. "I want you to find other arrangements," she continued in a halting voice. "You said he'd only be here a few days. Well, it's been more than a few days now, and he seems to be improving. Maybe you can find him another place at that shelter in Beverly."

Tucker didn't say a word, but by the stiff way he was holding himself, she could see how hard she'd pushed him. She felt awful and nearly took back her demand.

"I'm sorry, Tucker. I just hate being talked about. Our own neighbors are mad at us. Maybe you don't mind that so much. Maybe you have thicker skin than I do. But it's hard for me. Don't you understand even a little bit?"

Tucker nodded and moved over onto the couch to sit near her. "Sure, I understand. I'm sorry, too, Fran. I don't mean to fight with you every night about this. We never really fight, do we?"

"No," she said bleakly. "Most of the time we're pretty good about talking things through."

Tucker put his arm around her shoulders, and the familiar gesture of affection made her feel a little better.

"This is a problem, Fran," he admitted. "I don't know what to do about it. I don't want you to think I don't care about your feelings in this matter. I do. But I promised Carl he could stay here until he recuperates, and I meant it. I promised him," he repeated.

Fran didn't know what to say. The same reply from some other man might not mean so much, but Tucker's promises were not empty words spoken lightly then broken on a whim. It would hurt Tucker to go back on his word to his brother. It would cut deep. *It would hurt our marriage, too, if I force him to do that for me.* And that, Fran realized, might be far worse than suffering the dirty looks of neighbors.

She felt Tucker watching her, but she didn't look up at him.

"All right," she said at last. "You promised him. You don't want to go back on your word. I have to respect that, I suppose."

He stared at her and blinked. She could tell he was surprised that she'd backed down, though his expression didn't show much.

"Can we at least figure out a time frame here? Something I can tell people?"

Tucker shrugged. "I guess that's a reasonable request. But it's not as if when the clock runs down, I'm going to throw him out. Carl's making good progress, though. I have to bring him to the doctor on Friday. Let's see what kind of report he gets. I guess it might be two or three weeks more?"

Fran felt deflated. Three weeks? It sounded like such a long time. But there didn't seem to be any help for it. She could manage, she decided. It wasn't as if Tucker was insisting that Carl move in with them.

Not yet, anyway. Thank goodness.

"All right. I just wanted some idea."

Tucker gave her a questioning look. "I suppose he could go sooner if he improves quickly."

"That's all right. I understand," Fran insisted. "I guess I could help you out by taking care of him a bit more. He could eat dinner with us, if he feels up to it. It's not right to keep him cooped up in that little room. He probably gets lonely."

"He must," Tucker agreed. "Even if he'd never admit it."

Tucker had been dutiful about taking care of Carl and spending time with him in the evenings. Fran suspected that Carl often chased him out of the room, always acting as if he didn't need anybody.

"You have a lot patience with him."

"Thanks. I try." Tucker dipped his head and smiled.

"And with me," she added with a grin. She paused and bit her lip. "I'm sorry I turned off the Celtics."

Tucker laughed and squeezed her shoulder. "That's okay. I'll catch the ending on the late news. Just don't try that again. I might not let you get away with it a second time."

"Fair enough. I wouldn't dare do it if the Red Sox were playing."

"Not if you know what's good for you."

Fran smiled at him. It felt good to laugh with her husband again, as if life were getting back to normal. She only hoped the rest of their time taking care of Carl would pass quickly so things really could get back to normal.

CHAPTER EIGHT

MOLLY STARTED OFF THE WEEK WITH A HECTIC schedule, though not busy enough to keep her from thinking about Matthew and from jumping out of her skin every time the phone rang. He was probably busy with work, this being the first week of his practice, Molly would remind herself. But as the week wore on, the thought became less and less consoling.

She was rolling out pastry dough for pie shells on Wednesday afternoon when the kitchen phone rang. Her hands were sticky and full of flour, and she nearly let the machine pick up. But thinking it might be the school nurse or something having to do with the girls, she scurried to answer it.

"Molly? Hi, it's me, Matthew." Molly was so surprised to hear his voice, she nearly dropped the rolling pin on her foot.

"Matthew . . . hi. How's it going?" Upbeat, casual, and friendly, she reminded herself. The attitude magazine articles about dating advise so you don't scare men off. As if an eligible male was a timid woodland creature. Like a chipmunk, for instance, Molly thought fancifully.

"I'm in a bit of a bind. I was hoping you could help me out."

"Sure, what's the problem?" Her heart plummeted. This wasn't about anything personal, like a date. He just wanted a favor.

"Do you think you could pick up Amanda today after school and keep her at your place for a while? I have an emergency. I have to check a little girl into the hospital. She needs surgery. It's pretty serious. Thankfully her parents brought her to see me in time. But I wanted to stay here with them, see how it turns out."

She could hear the tension in his voice now, even over the static-filled connection. She felt guilty for her snide thoughts. He was dealing with a life-or-death situation, and she was worried about her social life.

"Of course I'll pick up Amanda. Don't give it a second thought."

"Thanks. I knew I could count on you."

Molly didn't know what to say. At least he thought of her as a friend, someone he could turn to when he had a problem. That was something, right?

"Amanda is old enough to stay home alone, of course. But I have no idea when I'll be done here. Not before seven and it could be later."

"It's no problem, really. She'll be fine with us. Take all the time you need. And good luck with your patient. I hope it turns out all right."

"Thanks. Say a prayer for her, will you? The surgeon will need all the help he can get in there." He paused and she could hear him talking to someone else in the background. A moment later he returned. "I have to run. See you later."

Molly said good-bye but suspected he'd already hung up. She wasn't a prayerful person under normal circumstances. Growing up, she went to church every Sunday with her parents, who were still active at Bible Community

Church, as was her brother, Sam. But somehow, somewhere Molly had fallen off the track. She didn't have anything *against* church exactly. She just didn't have much time to go, it seemed. Or if she had the time, she felt too tired to get herself out so early on a Sunday unless it was for a holiday like Easter or Christmas.

She did believe in God . . . or something up there, watching over the whole messy works of the world. But as for prayer, Molly knew she was the type who only remembered God in a dire emergency. Then she prayed like a house on fire. She was sure the Lord found people like her annoying, like friends who only call when they need a favor.

She had even told that to Reverend Ben once. He had found it so amusing, he asked if he could use it in a sermon. The reverend had promised her that God wasn't like that at all. God didn't hold grudges and was interested in hearing her prayers no matter when she offered them. Molly found the words reassuring but had only half-believed him.

It seemed funny to her that Matthew would ask her to pray for his patient. The other night he'd mentioned he'd already joined Bible Community Church. She could tell he was a believer and seemed to assume she was, too.

We're going to need extra help tonight, he had said, recognizing that the fate of his young patient wasn't completely in his hands or even in the hands of the surgeon. It must help him as a doctor to believe in some greater power, she realized. Or maybe that's why he did believe. Because he dealt with life and death so closely.

Molly brushed off her hands on her apron, closed her eyes, and took a long, steadying breath. *Dear God,* she silently began, *please help Matthew's patient. I hope her surgery turns out all right. Please comfort her parents, and help them to stay calm. Please comfort that little girl, too. I'm sure she must be very frightened right now.* She thought for a moment, not knowing what else to say. *By the way,* she added, *I know you don't hear from me much, Lord, but Matthew asked me to call.*

She smiled to herself, realizing that she was being silly now. Yet somehow she had a feeling that the Lord didn't mind a little joke now and then. He had to have a good sense of humor in order to have created humans, she thought.

AS MOLLY HAD PREDICTED, AMANDA AND LAUREN WERE thrilled to spend some unexpected time together. By six o'clock there was still no word from Matthew, so Molly served the three girls dinner. Lauren had begged for tacos, not exactly a culinary challenge but appropriate for the setting and the impromptu guest, Molly thought, both of which are important considerations, as she'd learned last week in the first session of her catering course. "Let the food match the mood," her instructor had advised.

The mood seemed to be a free-for-all giggle fest, and it was survival of the fittest once Molly set the taco fixings on the table. Even Amanda forgot her impressive table manners and dove in up to her elbows, Molly noticed, which was probably a good thing. Amanda seemed to be growing accustomed to their chaotic household and though she was still shy and almost too well-behaved, Molly sensed she was opening up a bit.

As the girls chatted about a TV show they wanted to watch after dinner, Molly's thoughts wandered. She wondered what Amanda's mother had been like. From the little Matthew had mentioned, it sounded as if his late wife had been quite intelligent and accomplished, the well-bred type. You could see it in the way Amanda conducted herself, as if she had gone to an old-fashioned finishing school.

Molly bit into her taco, and it exploded in her hand. *Nothing like me, of course,* she thought, licking her saucy fingers. *No wonder he hasn't asked me out. No mystery there.*

"We're done, Mom. Thanks, that was yummy." Lauren spoke in a rush, wiping her mouth with a paper napkin. "Can we watch TV until Amanda's dad comes?"

"Um, sure. As long as the homework is done."

"Thank you for dinner. The tacos were great," Amanda said, carrying her plate to the sink.

"You're very welcome." Molly smiled at her. Maybe she and Matthew would never be anything more than friends, but she felt genuine affection for his daughter.

"I'm done, too. Can I go with them?" Jill asked, talking around a mouthful of food.

"Sure, honey. Go ahead." Molly finished the last bite on her plate and was tempted to fix another taco. She counted to ten and squelched the urge, chomping down on a carrot stick instead.

She had taken Betty's advice and made some cold calls, coming up with a few new prospects to see next week. She needed to look good in her new dress, and control-top panty hose could only get a person so far. Besides, after an hour or two, wearing control tops always gave her a whopping migraine. *Probably squishing all the blood up to my head,* she thought as she started the dishes, *like squeezing a tube of toothpaste in the middle.*

Molly had just finished cleaning up when the door buzzer sounded. "Who is it?" she called. She was surprised to hear Matthew answer. He was earlier than she expected. She had hoped to have time enough to change her shirt and put on some lipstick, but it was too late now.

What difference does it make? she thought, pulling open the door. *It doesn't seem as if this situation is going to take any romantic turns.*

"Hi, Molly." He glanced at her with a weary grin. "Gee, something smells good in here, as usual."

"We just finished dinner—tacos. There are leftovers, if you want some." Molly closed the front door and led him into the kitchen.

The look on Matt's face suggested that leftover tacos were the most appetizing offer he'd had in years. Then he shook his head and stuck his hands in his jacket pockets.

"No, thanks. I really don't want to trouble you."

"It's no trouble." Molly met his gaze, then pulled back. She didn't want to be pushy. *The man does not want tacos. What part of that sentence don't you understand?* she coached herself.

"How about some coffee? I was just making some."

"That would be great. I could use some caffeine just to get home," he admitted with a laugh.

Molly glanced over her shoulder and smiled. She took out two mugs and served the coffee with a dish of brownies she had on hand for dessert. She didn't feel like calling the girls in yet, though. She was sure Lauren would smell the chocolate and come streaking into the room soon enough.

"It was great of you to have Amanda over like this," Matthew said as she joined him at the table. "I hope I can repay the favor sometime."

"It was no trouble," Molly said honestly. "What happened with your patient? Did the surgery go okay?"

"Yes, as a matter of fact, she came through with flying colors. She's in the ICU tonight, but she won't be there long."

He looked exhausted but when he spoke about his patient, his smile widened and a light seemed to shine from deep within.

"That's good news. Her parents must be extremely relieved."

"Yes, they were. I was relieved to give them a good report, quite frankly. It's so hard when children are involved. My heart really goes out to the parents. You know they'd move heaven and earth to help their child and they feel so helpless. They look to a doctor as if he's a miracle worker. But sometimes, the miracles just don't happen."

"That must be tough. My kids have only had health emergencies once or twice so far, thank goodness. I know what you mean about that desperate, terrified feeling. But I never thought about the pressure on the doctor. It must be awesome."

Matthew glanced at her. "'Awesome' is a real good word for it." He picked up a brownie, looking lost in thought. Molly watched as he took a bite and chewed, his eyes slowly widening.

"Speaking of the word, these brownies are awesome, as Amanda might say. Just what I needed."

Molly laughed, feeling a chill when he suddenly winked at her. "Black coffee and brownies aren't exactly a balanced meal."

"Yes, I know. But it's been one of those days when you have to go straight for dessert, if you know what I mean."

"Do I ever," Molly commiserated with a laugh. She sipped her coffee, and their eyes met over the rim of her mug. A slow smile tilted up the corners of his mouth. She wanted to look away but couldn't. She felt sure he wasn't thinking about the brownies anymore. He was thinking about her and that was why he was smiling. She had promised herself she would be friendly to him and nothing more. This was starting to feel like something more . . . but she couldn't quite stop herself.

"That was fun last week, when we went out after the concert," he said suddenly.

Molly nearly choked on her coffee and set the mug down. "Yes . . . yes it was," she agreed. Then she stopped herself. She didn't want to start blabbing away and ruin it. Was he going to ask her out? Finally?

She held her breath, waiting to see what he would say next.

"I wanted to call you this week, but I got so busy with the office opening up—"

"Oh, sure. I understand. How is that going? You didn't even mention it."

"I've been swamped with patients. Ezra was right. People around here really have been waiting for a local doctor to move in."

The door buzzer suddenly sounded, and Molly jolted as if some invisible hand had reached down and shook her shoulder.

"Would you excuse me a minute? I'll just see who that is."

She rose and walked to the door, wondering who it could be. Her neighbor, maybe, needing to borrow something or dropping by to chat?

She pulled open the door and found Phil standing there. He smiled widely, not seeming the least bit embarrassed by or apologetic for the unexpected visit.

"Hey, Molly. How you doing? I was at my mother's house tonight, and on my way home, I saw your lights on. I just wanted to say hello to the kids for a few minutes."

"Phil." She stood in the doorway, blocking his entrance. "Don't you ever think of calling first?"

Phil peeked over her shoulder into the kitchen. She saw his expression change and was sure he had caught sight of Matthew sitting at the table. "Oh . . . sorry. I didn't know you were entertaining. I just want to see the girls for a minute. I won't be in your way at all," he promised, giving her a look.

Molly felt instantly infuriated. "You really need to call first, Phil. You can't just drop in here any time you're in the neighborhood."

He stared at her a moment, then dipped his head. "Sure. Sure thing. I know what you mean. I won't do it again, really."

Molly could see that despite his apology, he wasn't leaving. She sighed, not knowing what to do. She noticed Phil's gaze shift and looked up to find Matthew standing beside her.

"Hello, Phil," Matthew said cordially. "We met the other night at the chorus concert."

"Sure, I remember. Matt, right? Good to see you again." Phil leaned across Molly and shook Matthew's hand. "Sorry to interrupt your evening. I just wanted to say hello to the girls."

"That's all right. We really need to get going." Matt glanced down at Molly. She thought she saw a flash of regret in his eyes but then wondered if she had imagined it. "I'll just go pry Amanda away from the TV." Before Molly could protest, he turned and walked back toward the living room.

Molly glared at Phil, then turned her back on him and went inside. She didn't invite him in, but he followed her anyway.

"What? What did I do?" he asked innocently. "I didn't mean to chase the guy out." His tone was nearly a whisper, but Molly felt sure Matthew could hear. She felt doubly mad at Phil for the smirk on his handsome face. He seemed to be finding the entire situation highly amusing.

She crossed her arms over her chest, ignoring him. He stood beside her quietly for a moment, then leaned toward the table.

"Hmm. Brownies. May I?" he asked politely.

"Help yourself," Molly said tightly.

Matthew appeared with Amanda, who looked reluctant to go. Lauren followed, also wearing a long face.

"Hi, sweetie," Phil greeted her brightly. She barely glanced at him. Was the novelty wearing off? Molly wondered.

"Hi, Dad," Lauren replied. She quickly turned to Molly, grabbing onto her arm. "Can Amanda sleep over on Friday night? Pul-eassse?"

It was Matthew who answered. "I'm sorry, honey. Amanda and I are going into Boston for the day on Saturday. We need to leave very early so it wouldn't work out."

"Another time, I guess," Molly promised Lauren. "We'll figure it out."

Lauren refused to give up. "Maybe next weekend?"

"We'll see," Molly said almost automatically.

Molly followed Matthew and Amanda to the door. "Well, good night. Thanks again." Their eyes met briefly.

Molly felt odd. She yearned for some sign that Matthew intended on calling and finishing the conversation Phil had interrupted. But what could she say? Everything that came to mind seemed far too obvious.

"Have a nice time in Boston," she finally offered.

Wow, did that sound original and witty or what?

She watched briefly as they walked down the hallway, then closed the door.

Phil was sitting at the kitchen table with Lauren and Jill. Jill was showing him a report she had written on ancient Egypt. She had gotten an A on it and was very proud.

Phil was making all the right responses. "Wow, what a great cover. Did you draw that yourself?"

Jill nodded. "Look at this one." She flipped some pages to show a drawing of a mummy. "That's my favorite."

"It's beautiful," Phil said thoughtfully. He turned to his older daughter. "How about you, Lauren? Anything interesting going on in school this week?"

Lauren shrugged. "The usual. We had a big math test."

"How did you do?" Phil asked.

"Not too bad. B plus," Lauren reported.

"Can I see it?" Phil asked.

Lauren seemed surprised at the request, Molly noticed, but got up from her seat. "Okay. It's in my backpack." She left the room, and Phil looked up at Molly.

"Just trying to keep up with what they're doing in school. It's important, right?"

"No argument there," Molly said tightly. Had he been taking dad lessons in his spare time lately?

She was steaming mad at him but wasn't sure what to do about it. She didn't want to blast him right in front of the girls and look like the bully again.

But she still had to have a talk with him, a serious talk. Yes, she was angry because his surprise visit had interrupted her conversation with Matthew just as it seemed he was about to ask her out. But it was more than that. Much more. Phil couldn't just walk in here anytime he liked. He didn't live here anymore. He seemed to have suddenly forgotten that small important detail.

Molly decided to retreat and regroup. "I think I'll take a little walk while you guys visit. I could use some fresh air."

Phil and the girls looked at her curiously. "It's really cold out there," he warned her.

"That's all right," Molly said, heading for the door. "I really need to cool off. I'll be back in about twenty minutes and then you can go, Phil. Right?"

He met her gaze. "Uh, sure. That sounds fine."

Molly pulled on her jacket and stalked out of the apartment. She headed down Main Street at a brisk pace but felt a stinging cold wind as she neared the harbor. At the end of the street, the steamy windows and warm yellow lights inside the Beanery looked inviting. No, Molly thought. If she went in, she would surely run into one of the owners, Jonathan or Felicity Bean, or someone else she knew, and she was in no mood for small talk.

She turned and walked back up the other side of the street, the wind against her back. She was still so angry at Phil, she could hardly see straight. Walking seemed to help clear her head and slow her racing heartbeat. It didn't, though, change her determination to confront him.

When Molly came in she heard the girls and Phil in the bedroom. She slammed the door theatrically.

"I'm back," she announced, shrugging out of her jacket.

To his credit, Phil began saying good night and soon came out to the kitchen. He picked up his coat and pulled it on. "How was your walk? Your cheeks are sure red."

"My cheeks were red when I left, Phil. Probably because I'm so mad at you I could just scream."

He stared at her with a blank expression. "For interrupting your date, right? I'm sorry about that Molly. He really didn't have to go—"

"It wasn't a *date*. It's not about that at all. You are so dense sometimes, it's just amazing."

She glanced in the direction of the girls' bedroom, deciding that they needed some privacy.

"Come out in the hallway. I need to talk to you." Without waiting for his reply, she walked ahead and opened the door. He followed, looking curiously at her.

"Okay. What's on your mind?" he asked politely.

"Plenty. For starters, you can't just drop in here anytime you like. You don't live here anymore."

"I know." He raised his hands in a gesture of surrender. "I should have called. I won't forget next time."

His mild, nonchalant attitude annoyed her even more.

"You can't just drop out of the sky and decide you want to be a father again. You can't make up for all the time you missed in just a week or with a few trips to the mall."

Phil's mild expression hardened, like molten sugar cooling on a plate. "That's not what I'm trying to do and you know it, Molly. I think you're just peeved because I broke up your little coffee klatch with the doctor. Why are you hanging around in the kitchen? Why doesn't he take you someplace nice?"

Molly was so angry, she felt her head spin. "How dare you say that to me! I know what you're doing. You're just trying to distract me and it's not going to work. And that is not why I'm so angry." Molly took a long, ragged breath, her hands balled into fists at her side.

"What is it then? I just dropped in for five minutes to say hello to the girls. Now I'm leaving, just like you asked. I don't get it."

"Of course you don't get it. You have no idea, not the foggiest notion, of what it is to be a parent. A real parent. I've been taking care of your daughters on my own for a long time and doing a pretty good job of it. I don't need you to sweep in here, playing Santa Claus in July, and spoiling them rotten and screwing everything up. Maybe you can make them forget how you've ignored them all these years. But you can't make me forget, Phil. I'm a grown-up. I'm not fooled that easily."

Phil's eyes narrowed. He flinched for a moment, as if he had been slapped across the face. "Of course you won't forget, Molly, or forgive me. Not if we live to be a hundred and three. I'll tell you what I think. I think you're just jealous."

Molly gasped. "Jealous? That's insane! What would I be jealous of?"

"Jealous of me. Jealous because the girls do love me and want to give me another chance. You can't stand it. It's driving you up the wall. Go ahead, admit it. Be honest at least."

"You are crazy." Molly shook her head, feeling incredulous. "Where do you come up with this stuff?"

"You're an open book to me, Molly. You always were and always will be. You've had those girls to yourself for years, and you don't like sharing them. It's as simple as that. You don't like them looking up to somebody else now or seeing that they can love somebody else as much as they love you. Even if it's their own father."

His tone was low and grating, like an annoying appliance grinding away at her nerves. She felt raw and ragged, ready to lash out at him. Yet for some reason, she could hardly speak.

"That's a horrible thing to say to me. It's totally hateful. All the years that you ignored them, I've felt so awful that the girls never had a real father."

He didn't reply. His cold blue stare stated flatly that he stood by his accusation.

He's wrong, she told herself, yet deep inside, his words had struck home. She did feel jealous sometimes when she watched the girls with Phil. Pushed aside and displaced after all the years she had devoted to their needs and care.

She could be rational about it, of course. All this fuss over Phil didn't mean that they didn't love her anymore. Phil had appeared in a puff of smoke: Santa Claus, the Good Humor Man, and Dream Dad all rolled into one. How could they resist?

But in her heart it had all been very jarring. His reappearance had rocked her world. The deck was still rolling, and Molly felt as if she might be swept overboard.

"I'm here now, Molly. I'm here to stay, and you just have to accept it." Phil's tone was hard edged and maddeningly confident.

"Not so fast, pal. You want to be their dad again? Yippee. But that doesn't mean you can drop in here anytime the mood strikes. From now on, I'm in charge of the visiting schedule. One night a week. You can pick them up after school and have them home by seven—"

"That's impossible with my job!" Phil cut in. "You know that, Molly."

"As for the weekends, every other Saturday from noon to six P.M.," she continued, talking over his objections.

Phil's face turned an angry, mottled shade of red. "I'm their father. I have some rights."

"You gave up those rights when you walked out on us, Phil. If you don't like my schedule, take me to court. Let a judge hear what a model dad you've been all these years. Let him decide about your *rights*."

Would she really go to court over this? Probably not, but she could see her threat was working. Phil knew if they ever did go head-to-head in front of a family court judge, his track record would look awful. He had a better chance working things out with her—and that wasn't saying much.

Phil let out a long breath and stepped back, his hands on his hips. Molly watched him, feeling exhausted, as if she'd just run a marathon. She waited to see what he would say, sensing she had won this round.

"I know what you said is true. I know it better than anybody, believe me," he stated slowly. "I've been a washout as a father so far. Which is probably why I'm overdoing it a little now."

"A *little*? Try a lot, Phil. You're overdoing it a lot. . . ."

His sharp look silenced her. "I'm ashamed of myself. Is that what you need to hear? Okay. There, I said it." He leaned back against the wall, looking sad and angry and suddenly as drained as she felt. "I'm trying to do better. I'm trying to be a better man. Can't you see that? Can't you cut me a little slack here?"

To her surprise his honest admission of failure touched her. She would never have guessed he was capable of that kind of soul-baring confession. Still, she kept her arms crossed over her chest, not wanting him to sense her softening.

"Give me a chance. That's all I'm asking for. And how about I see the girls every weekend? Every other is a little harsh, don't you think?"

His persuasive salesman tone was back, a quick recovery, like one of those toy figures with the round bottoms. You push them down and they spring right up again.

"All right, every weekend," she consented, knowing that the girls would object to the limited schedule as well. "So, the ground rules are understood? Do you have any questions?"

Phil looked as if he were about to reply with some cutting remark, but he pursed his lips closed and shook his head. "No questions. I'll be back on Saturday, I guess."

"Yes, I guess so. Good night."

She turned and went back inside her apartment, shutting the door and leaning back against it for a moment. She wondered if the girls had been standing in this same spot, eavesdropping, moments before. She was sure that they must have been curious about what was going on out in the hallway between her and Phil. They wouldn't be happy to hear they'd be seeing Phil less. But she would deal with that problem when the time came, Molly decided. They couldn't go out with him so many nights of the week and get home late. It just wasn't practical. They were both falling behind in their schoolwork, and Lauren had barely touched the piano since Phil appeared on the scene. She would have to explain it to them and hope they understood. But of course, once again, she would be the one playing the villain in this domestic soap opera.

Might as well get myself a stovepipe hat and fake mustache, Molly thought wearily as she finally locked the door and turned off the lights.

Chapter Nine

Carl left the house and closed the door, then realized he didn't have a key to lock up. He looked under the mat, ran his hand on the ledge above the door, and even checked around the hedges for one of those fake rocks that people think are so clever for hiding spare keys. He was about to give up when his gaze happened upon a white flowerpot filled with yellow straw flowers on the top step. He picked it up and shook it. Just as he had suspected, the loose key in the bottom rattled noisily.

He tipped the pot, locked the door, and replaced the key, chuckling to himself. A flower pot, for pity's sake. A policeman ought to think of a better spot than that. Originality was never Tucker's strong suit, that was for sure.

He wondered what Tucker or Fran would think if one of them stopped home today for lunch and found the house empty. Fran would probably assume he was gone for good and start cleaning his room, as if he'd had bubonic plague. Then she would celebrate. He wasn't so sure about Tucker, though, and brushed the question from his mind.

It would be a while before he could leave for good. Though the swelling was down on his leg, he still needed something to help him walk. He hated using the crutches. It made him feel like a broken old man, but he knew he wouldn't make it too far without them. And he needed to get out. He was going stir-crazy in that flowered little tissue box of a room.

Hobbling along at a fairly quick pace, Carl reached the end of Tucker's street and turned onto Emerson. He paused and caught his breath. It was a fairly mild day, the sky clear and the air cool but humid with a hint of the spring weather soon to come. He wasn't having as much trouble breathing as he had expected, but he wondered if it was wiser to just take himself around the block a time or two and call it a day.

Then looking down to the end of the street, he decided what the heck, might as well try to make it all the way to town. It wasn't so far. Worse comes to worst, he would collapse on the sidewalk and someone would call Tucker.

He hadn't gotten a good look at the village that first night he landed here. Wasn't in much shape for sightseeing, he recalled. Now he was curious to see what the place had turned into. Tucker claimed it was almost the same as when he left years ago, but Carl had his doubts. Nothing stays the same. He didn't know much, but he sure knew that well enough by now.

He limped along, resting every few minutes to catch his breath. He had borrowed one of Tucker's jackets and a baseball cap and thought he looked fairly respectable, though he hadn't shaved for a few days.

He rounded the corner and found himself on Main Street. He stopped and stared down the street, feeling as if he had just walked onto a movie set. Everything looked so nice here, so pretty and clean. Like a picture postcard. The kind of town he could never afford to live in. He had never noticed that as a kid or even a young man. He'd just taken it all for granted.

He limped past a Victorian that held an antique shop. The Bramble, the sign read. He remembered that place. It was called something else in his time. An old man sat in a rocker on the porch, whittling a piece of wood. A yellow Labrador lay at his feet, as calm as a statue.

The old man stopped carving for a moment and met his eye, peering out from under the edge of his cap. Carl paused, leaning on his crutches. Digger Hegman, that was his name. An old fisherman, famous for clamming and predicting the weather. Carl was surprised to see the old geezer still alive.

"Hey, there," Digger called out to him. "Do I know you?"

Carl hesitated, not knowing how to reply. "I doubt it, mister. I'm a stranger here. Just visiting."

Digger kept staring at him, appearing unsatisfied with the reply. Finally, though, he returned to his carving.

Carl turned away and continued down the street. A short time later he spotted the Clam Box. He stopped, his body rigid as he recalled so many memories. After all these years, just looking at that sign still brought a sour feeling to the pit of his stomach. He remembered when old Otto Bates accused him of robbing the place. Though he certainly hadn't been any choirboy, he hadn't stolen so much as a teaspoon from that place. Didn't matter to Otto though. His mind had been made up, and he managed to convince half the town that he was right, too, no matter that the police said differently. Carl took a deep breath. Otto had barred him from going in there for years, as if Carl were carrying some contagious disease.

Some small voice still told him not to cross the street. But something else goaded him on. *Old Otto is dead and buried, and besides that, nobody would even recognize me now. Except maybe Charlie.* Charlie had never liked Carl, and the feeling had been mutual. Tucker and Charlie were still friends, Carl gathered from his brother's conversations. Though from Tucker's tone, it sounded like the magic was gone from that romance.

Carl wasn't sure what was pushing him to go in there; it certainly wasn't fond memories. But he was tired and wanted some coffee before he headed back to Tucker's. He pushed off on his crutches and hobbled across the street. He hadn't come this far to be scared off by the memory of old Otto Bates. *No sir,* he thought with a small smile, as he slowly opened the door. *Going in here after all this time, all things considered, might even be fun.*

It was midmorning and the place looked almost empty. A bell above the door jangled when he opened it, but no one paid him any mind. There were only two or three customers.

A waitress glanced up from behind the counter and smiled. "Take a seat anywhere. I'll be right with you."

He made his way to a booth by the window, slipped into the seat, and set the crutches on the seat opposite. There was a mimeographed menu in a plastic holder propped up between the salt and pepper shakers. It looked just the same as it always had. The same typos, too. "Fred Chicken in a Basket" was his favorite. *Poor old Fred,* he thought. *We're in the same boat now, pal.*

"So, what can I get you?" The waitress's voice interrupted his thoughts. He glanced at her under the brim of his hat, afraid she was someone he used to know.

"Just coffee, thanks," he mumbled. She jotted down the order, and he watched her walk back to the counter.

He did know her. Lucy Dooley. She had been a pretty one. Still had her looks, too. She would be Lucy Bates now, he suddenly remembered. She could have done better, that was for sure. Some women didn't have much sense when it came to picking men. A few had even latched onto him when he was younger.

A few minutes later Lucy returned with the coffee. He turned away, acting suddenly interested in the view out the window.

"Here you are, sir." She set down the coffee mug, a teaspoon, and a pitcher of milk with practiced efficiency. "Anything else?"

"Uh . . . no, thanks. That's okay for now." He coughed into his hand, and he sensed her looking at him. He looked away again, but couldn't help coughing.

She leaned over and gently touched his shoulder. "How about some water?" Not waiting for his reply, she went off to get it.

She soon returned and set the glass down in front of him. He thought she would leave again, but she stood there waiting for him to drink. He picked it up, his hand shaking a bit, and took a long swallow.

She was still there when he was done. There was a soft look in her eyes. He knew that look. She pitied him. He felt sure now that she recognized him but was too nice to say so.

"Thank you for the water, Lucy," he said slowly. Her eyes widened with surprise, but he smiled a little and pointed to the tag on her uniform. "That's your name, right?"

She smiled back. "Sure, that's me. Let me know if you need anything else, sir."

She walked away, and he breathed a sigh of relief. He had thought he was ready to face these people. Well, it appeared he wasn't up to it. Not today anyway, he realized.

A few minutes later, almost done with his coffee, Carl glanced around to ask for the check. The bell above the door jangled, and Charlie Bates stalked in, carrying a carton that appeared to be filled with cans.

He walked to the counter and dropped his load, then he turned and glanced at Carl. His gaze didn't linger, Carl noticed with relief. But then Charlie turned his head again and pinned Carl with a stare. Carl looked down at his coffee cup, burrowing into his coat and tugging the brim of his hat over his eyes.

Too late. Charlie started toward him with determined steps.

He stood at Carl's table, fists on his hips. "You have a lot of nerve showing up here. Didn't your brother warn you not to come in here?"

All heads turned in their direction. The other customers stopped talking and eating. Carl slowly lifted his head and met Charlie's angry stare.

"Tucker never said a word to me about you. What are you talking about?"

"He didn't, huh? Well, how about I don't believe you? I told him I didn't want to see you in here. Now I'm telling you."

Charlie leaned over, his angry face filling Carl's field of vision. "You know why, too," he added bitterly. "Don't play dumb with me, Carl. I'm not like Tucker. I see right through you. Now get out."

Carl didn't move a muscle. He didn't even breathe. He felt a surge of anger simmering up inside. Then he sat back and laughed like a crazy man until tears came into his eyes.

"You getting tough with me, Bates? That's a laugh. Places I've been, you couldn't scare a cockroach back into his hole." He shook his head, wheezing harshly between words.

"Why you—get up!" Charlie pushed Carl's shoulder.

Staring back defiantly, Carl barely budged.

Lucy rushed over and tugged on her husband's arm. "He's a customer, Charlie. Have you lost your mind?"

"Get away, Lucy. I know what I'm doing," Charlie snapped.

Carl came slowly to his feet, his stance shaky. "You want a fight? Go on, take the first swing. I dare you."

Carl felt his heart pound, the blood rushing into his head. He was a little dizzy and wasn't sure what he'd do if Charlie actually took a swing at him. Fight back as best he could, he guessed. He didn't care if he was half dead. He wasn't going to back down from this puffed up, bug-eyed bully.

Charlie stood staring at him, considering his next move. *He'll probably grab me by the collar and drag me out of here*, Carl thought. *Not without a struggle though.*

The bell above the door jangled and the door opened. Reverend Ben Lewis stepped inside and stared around. He spotted the two men and paused for a moment, then slowly walked over. "Hello, Charlie. Hello, Carl," he spoke in a normal tone, seemingly unaware of the tense standoff he had interrupted. "Glad to see you up and around, Carl. How are you feeling?"

"I walked into town to get some air," Carl answered awkwardly.

"That was ambitious. You must be hungry. Did you eat lunch yet?"

"He was just leaving," Charlie said flatly.

"Really? I hate to eat alone. Maybe you can sit awhile and keep me company," Reverend Ben persisted.

Carl glanced at Charlie's warning glare, then back at the reverend. Finally, he nodded. "Have a seat, Reverend. I've got all the time in the world." He swallowed a lump in his throat and sat down again, avoiding Charlie's scowl. "I guess I am hungry, after all."

Lucy stepped deftly around her husband and slipped the crutches off the seat opposite Carl, clearing the space for the reverend.

"I'll just put this aside for now," she said. "Your menus are on the table, gentlemen. Specials are on the board."

She glanced at Charlie's frozen expression, then went to get the reverend a glass of water and to refill Carl's glass. Charlie glanced at Carl a moment, then back at the reverend. Carl could see he knew he'd been beat.

"I'd better get back in the kitchen. See you later," he mumbled as he walked away.

Carl peered at the reverend from under the brim of his hat. Reverend Ben had pulled his fat from the fire just now, that was for sure. But he didn't know how to thank him. He pretended to read his menu, then stared out the window.

Lucy came by and took their orders, a grilled cheese and tomato sandwich for Reverend Ben and a burger for Carl.

Finally Reverend Ben slipped his menu back between the salt and pepper shakers. "I don't know why I spend so much time reading that thing. I could recite it by heart by now."

"I know it up and down, and I haven't stepped foot in this place for twenty years."

Reverend Ben grinned. "So, what do you think of the town, Carl? Does it look different to you?"

Carl shrugged. "Not as much as I expected. That was always the good thing about this place as well as the bad. It doesn't change much." He glanced over his shoulder at Charlie, who was working behind the counter. "The people around here don't either."

The reverend nodded. He removed his wire-rimmed glasses and polished them with a hanky. "Do you think people can change? Or that God just makes a person a certain way and that's it?"

Carl laughed nervously. How did God get mixed up in it all of a sudden? Leave it to a preacher to pull a fast move like that on you.

"I don't know. What do I know about God?" Carl shrugged but the reverend kept looking at him, as if he didn't accept that as a fair answer. "I guess people can change, sure. Why not?"

"Exactly. Why not." The reverend put his glasses back on and stared straight at Carl, a mild smile on his bearded face.

Carl felt the silence between them pressing him to speak.

"The question is, what's a guy going to get out of all the effort it takes to change. If there's no payoff, why bother?"

"That's one way of looking at it." The reverend nodded. "Of course, in my line of work, I see it from a different perspective. I see people struggling to change and sometimes failing at it, wondering, like you say, what's the payoff? Meanwhile they don't see that they already have the payoff in hand. Before they even try. And even if they never try at all."

Carl cast the reverend a puzzled look. He gave a nervous laugh and leaned back in his seat. "I'm sorry, Reverend. You lost me now. This kind of talk is getting a little heavy for me."

"It's simple, Carl. God loves us just the way we are. He loves us and forgives us, no matter what we do. That's the payoff I'm talking about."

Carl felt uneasy. He shifted in his seat, not knowing what to say.

"Sure . . . I get you," he finally replied.

Lucy brought their food, and the two men began to eat. Carl's thoughts wandered back to the days when his stepmother would bring him and Tucker to church on Sunday mornings. She would hold his hand when they walked across the village green, maybe just the way good mothers do. Or maybe because she was afraid he was going to take off on her.

He did remember some of this stuff. Of course in prison the ministers were always coming by, hoping you were so bored staring at four walls, you would try reading the Bible and talking with them, but they had never gotten far with him.

Carl set his hamburger down and wiped his hands on a napkin. "I never thanked you for taking me to the hospital. And visiting me there."

"That's okay. I'm glad I could help you." The reverend sat back. "I've been meaning to ask, Carl, why did you come back here?"

"I just wanted to see the place again. I'm not really sure why."

"Because it was home?"

"Yeah, maybe. For better or worse. I have more unhappy memories than good ones, I guess. But they're all mine."

The reverend took a sip of coffee. "I'm glad you came back," he said suddenly. "I think it's good for you and Tucker to see each other again."

Carl laughed. "Then you're the only one with that opinion. Tucker doesn't want me here. Neither does his wife. I don't even think the dog likes me."

"No, Carl. I think you're wrong. It might take time, but I think that eventually you'll see what I'm saying is true."

"Yeah, well, that's the thing. I won't be here for long. Not that long, anyway."

The reverend didn't reply, looking at Carl as if he knew something Carl didn't know. The look made Carl uneasy. *These preachers get ideas in their heads sometimes. Doesn't mean I have to listen,* Carl told himself. He wasn't going to stay around much longer. He'd been here too long already.

ON THURSDAY NIGHT, MOLLY DROVE HOME FROM HER second class feeling hopeful and energized. The instructor, a woman named Pauline Turner, spiced up her lessons with strange but true catering and restaurant adventures that were funny and instructive. She had started her own business in circumstances much like Molly's and was very successful, despite some struggles along the way. Her story gave Molly heart, and the practical how-to instruction—on everything from renting equipment to hiring helpers to timing each course—helped Molly feel that at some point, she too could manage her own catering business.

Still, she didn't feel ready to disclose her plan to the world-at-large. That would add too much pressure. What if she decided *not* to go through with it? Then she'd feel like a failure for not even trying.

She did have to ask Sam and even Phil to help her out by watching the girls while she was in class, but she had told them she was taking a first-aid course in CPR. She already knew CPR, but fortunately neither of them remembered.

Tonight at the last minute Sam got held up, so Jessica had come over to stay with Lauren and Jill.

"I'm home," Molly announced. She found Jessica in the living room, reading a book in the armchair. "How did it go?"

"Just fine. Your daughters are perfect angels."

"Right, tell me about it." Molly sat down on the couch and found a bunched-up sock wedged between the cushions. She plucked it out and tossed it on the floor. "They're so neat with their belongings, too. What are you reading?"

"Nothing special." Jessica held up her book so Molly could see the jacket. "Some historical for my book group. It's a little boring, actually . . . but I was also reading this, which looked very interesting."

Jessica leaned over and picked up a book from the side table. Molly recognized one of her textbooks from the class, the one she had forgotten to bring with her tonight.

"*Food with Flair: A Complete Guide to the Catering Business.*" Jessica looked up at Molly, then opened the book and pulled out Molly's registration card. "You're not studying CPR at the high school, are you?" she asked with a small smile.

Molly sighed and shook her head. "The canapé is out of the bag, I guess."

"I guess," Jessica agreed with a short laugh. "Why the big secret? Why didn't you tell anybody?"

"I don't know. . . . I'm thinking about starting up a little business. A shop, maybe, where I can sell stuff I cook and then use it as a home base for catering."

Jessica sat up with an excited expression. "That's a great idea! You'd be perfect for that."

"Not so fast, please. I'm just taking the course for now to see what's really involved. I didn't want to tell anyone because . . . well, if I don't do it, then everyone will be bugging me and asking why and making me feel dumb or something."

Jessica didn't say anything for a moment. She closed the textbook and put it back on the table. "I see what you mean. Sometimes it's better to plan something like this privately. What are you going to do for capital?"

Leave it to a banker to go straight to the bottom line, Molly thought. "Well, that's the problem right there. I have zero assets. Who's going to loan me enough money to get this thing off the ground?"

"A bank can make you a loan, even if you don't own a house or have a lot of assets. There are still ways to finance a start-up business. I can help you," Jessica offered. "I'd love to help you, really. That's what I do. You know that."

Molly was moved by the offer. She didn't have the best relationship with her sister-in-law; she never expected Jessica to believe that she could make a go of this catering idea. Molly had never felt that Jessica thought that well of her.

"A loan like that is a big commitment," Molly finally answered. "That part worries me, too. What if I screw up and the business fails? Then I'd be stuck with this huge debt." She looked up at Jessica. "I don't think I'm ready for that yet."

Jessica gazed at her a moment and then gave her small smile. "I understand." She looked back at the book. "I noticed the course doesn't cover the finance chapter until later. Maybe after you go over it at school, you'll feel more comfortable talking about it with me."

"Maybe," Molly agreed. She took a breath. It actually felt good to talk to someone besides Betty about this instead of keeping it all inside her head. She was still surprised, though, that her confidante turned out to be Jessica.

"You've met a lot of people who try to start a business. Tell me the truth, do you really think I can do this? My feelings won't be hurt if you say no," Molly added hastily, even if it wasn't entirely true.

"Absolutely," Jessica replied. "I'm sure you can. But you have to believe you can do it, even if other people don't. I guess that's the common denominator in the people who come to me and really make a go of it."

"Yeah, the confidence thing. I have trouble with that," Molly admitted. "I did find a great dress for meeting new clients. That's helped a lot," she joked.

"Hey, don't knock the clothes factor. There's nothing like a good hair day to make you feel you can take on the world. But everyone feels shaky from time to time, Molly. Nobody has it all together all the time."

"Sure, I know that. Not even Oprah," she said, making Jessica smile. "But sometimes I feel like other people have it together a lot more than I do. It's like, they know some trick that I don't know."

"You mean like in a self-help book?" Jessica glanced around and found one in a stack of books on the table. "I used to read these all the time, too. Some of them aren't so bad. Then I realized something that helps when I feel down about life and everything seems to be going wrong."

"Really? What's the secret?" Molly asked with a grin.

"That I don't have to do it all myself."

Molly knew Jessica was talking about God and felt distinctly uncomfortable. But she also knew that Jessica had not always been so spiritually minded. *When she came back to Cape Light last year to help take care of her mother, before she met Sam, she was like me,* Molly recalled. But Jessica had seemed much happier since then. Molly always thought the change was because of Sam. But maybe it was more.

"You mean thinking about God helps you have more confidence? Is that what you're saying?"

"Something like that. Let God into your life. Tell Him your problems, your worries about the future. Let Him help you. He created the whole world in six days. A little catering business shouldn't be so tough."

Molly laughed. "That's pretty odd advice from a banker."

"Maybe, maybe not." Jessica smiled and came to her feet. "You wouldn't think it was strange if I recommended some new self-help book, right? Well, think of the Scriptures as a really good self-help book."

Molly didn't know what to say. She knew she had a Bible in the house somewhere, but she'd probably get an allergy attack from the dust if she ever dug it out.

"I hope your plan does succeed, Molly. I really do," Jessica added sincerely.

Molly felt embarrassed. "Thanks . . . so do I."

ALL IN ALL, TUCKER THOUGHT, THE TALK WITH FRAN had helped. She wasn't walking around the house with that tight, angry look anymore. That didn't mean she'd changed her mind about Carl. The other night Michael asked Carl if he wanted to play a video game with him. Fran hadn't said anything, but she kept making excuses for Tucker to go into the den and check on them. Carl, it turned out, was good at video games.

On Saturday Tucker had the perfect excuse to escape the house for a while. He had promised Reverend Ben he would stop by the church and do some small repairs around the building. Gus Potter used to take care of those things. Since he got sick, there had been talk of hiring a regular groundskeeper, but so far nothing had been done and all of the deacons took turns. Today was Tucker's.

Reverend Ben was not very handy, but he liked to watch an ongoing repair. He seemed fascinated, always studying just how it was done. So Tucker wasn't really surprised when he heard the reverend's footsteps approach. The timing could have been better, though. Tucker was on his back, his head stuck under a sink as he attempted to repair a leaky pipe.

"How is it going, Tucker? At home, I mean." That question wasn't a surprise, either. "Is Fran getting used to the idea of having Carl around?" the reverend asked, handing Tucker a wrench.

"Things are better with Fran. We talked it out and she's resigned herself to the idea of him being there, at least for a while."

Tucker fitted the wrench to the pipe joint and gave it a yank. It didn't budge at first. He took a deep breath and pushed with all his might. It moved a fraction of an inch.

"I see. So Carl is accepted but not exactly welcome?"

"Pretty much." Tucker grunted, pushing hard on the wrench and finally unfastening the pipe section. "Fran's doing the best she can, but it's hard for her. She's like a lot of other people in this town. She thinks he's trouble." Tucker came out from under the sink and shook his head. "I feel for Fran. But I also feel bad for Carl. He knows she doesn't really want him there."

"That's not the best situation for either one," Reverend Ben agreed. "What do *you* want?"

"Search me," Tucker said ruefully. "All I know is Carl's got no other place to go, and I promised him he could stay with us until he's strong enough to be on his own."

The reverend reached out and patted Tucker's shoulder. "You're doing the right thing, Tucker. Don't forget that."

"Thanks, Reverend. I know you're in my corner. The problem is, I worry that maybe Fran, and even Charlie, might be right. Maybe Carl hasn't changed and never will. I could be the one making a big mistake here."

"If Carl hasn't changed, you'll find out and have to deal with it. But you can never make a mistake by sticking to your principles and showing compassion for your brother. Especially under such pressure."

"I'm feeling the pressure all right," Tucker admitted.

The reverend didn't reply. He watched as Tucker checked the threaded edges of the pipe, then eased himself back under the sink.

"I'm not that great a plumber, Reverend. I think it's fixed for now. But keep your eye on it."

"I will."

"Hand me that wrench again, will you?" Tucker called to him. The wrench appeared, and Tucker took hold of it.

"I think you've just given me an idea." The reverend stuck his head under the sink, looking surprised and happy. "If Carl feels good enough to walk into town, he's probably able to take a job. The church needs a handyman, and I have the authority to hire anyone I choose."

"You'd hire Carl to work here?" Tucker began to sit up

and hit his head on the bottom of the sink. He came out again, rubbing the sore spot.

"Exactly. Carl needs a real job, a sense of purpose—somewhere to go every day and money in his pocket. I think this is a good solution all around, don't you?"

"It could be if Carl wants to stay here," Tucker said cautiously. "He is feeling much better. And he had a good report from the doctor yesterday." Tucker rubbed his head again. "He's handy, too. Much better than me. I'll talk to him about it, see what he thinks."

"Tell him he can drop by anytime to see me. The job is his for the asking."

"Thanks, Reverend. I appreciate your help," Tucker said sincerely.

"No thanks necessary. You know that, Tucker." The reverend smiled. "Now about this sink . . . I don't know much about this stuff but what about this piece? Doesn't it go somewhere?"

He held up a thin metal washer, and Tucker groaned. "I forgot to put it back on. Now I'm going to have to take apart the whole thing and start over."

Reverend Ben looked contrite. "I'm sorry. I distracted you with all my questions."

"My fault," Tucker said. "I should have known it was missing. Carl would have. He would have had this fixed by now."

The reverend smiled. "Then let's hope he agrees to take the job."

Chapter Ten

On Sunday, after the service, Reverend Ben went to his office where Carolyn waited. A fresh, cool breeze filtered through the open window, ruffling his papers and nearly blowing them away. It was the first truly mild day the town had seen in many months, but for once the promise of spring did nothing to lift his spirits. Wordlessly, Carolyn helped him remove his vestments, then they walked out together to their car and headed for the orchard.

They drove out of town and along the Beach Road, the radio tuned to the classical station. Neither spoke for a long time.

"I might have to stay awhile. Sophie sounded as if he was very bad."

"I understand. I'll have Mark come pick me up later. I'll leave you the car."

"All right. I guess that would be best."

Carolyn sat with her gloved hands clutching her purse on her lap. It was good of her to come today, he thought. She knew that this visit was hard for him. Visits like this always were, but this one especially. He was sure that when she married him, she had no idea of what it would be like to be a minister's wife: the tedious hours of bake sales and the Christmas Fair committee spliced between life's most intense moments. Yet Carolyn seemed to sail through it all so smoothly. She kept him balanced and sane. She'd never know how much.

The Potter house was filled with people, food, and flowers, all the trappings of one of their famous parties, framed within a mournful, somber atmosphere. The living room was crowded with relatives. Ben recognized some of the grandchildren and Sophie's brother, Fred, who lived down in Florida.

Sophie's daughter Una came to greet them and take their coats. Ben and Carolyn embraced her, and he could see that her eyes were puffy from crying. Una led them to Gus, who lay in a hospital bed in the guest room on the first floor. Sophie sat by his side and held his hand. With her back to the door, she didn't even notice that Ben and Carolyn were there.

The smell of sickness filled the room. For a moment Ben felt as if he couldn't breathe. He stepped closer to the bed. Gus's eyes were closed. Ben wondered if Gus had already lost consciousness.

Sophie's daughter Evelyn and her son, Bart, stood on the other side of the bed. Evelyn walked up to him and took his hand. "Thank you for coming, Reverend."

"Evelyn, how are you holding up?"

"I'm managing. The waiting is so hard. It's very hard on Mom," she said, glancing at Sophie.

"Yes, of course. This is the most difficult time of all." It was true. Ben remembered when his own mother was dying, watching her cling to the last threads of life. He had been torn between desperate hopes that she would live just a little longer and equally desperate prayers for her painless release into the Lord's loving embrace.

"He goes in and out," Evelyn said. "The doctor said it would be like this. He's not in any pain, though, thank God."

"That is a blessing," Carolyn agreed.

Sophie turned her head, finally noticing Ben and Carolyn. Wordlessly, she held out her hand, and Ben stepped forward. He clasped her hand and then bent to kiss her cheek. Her skin was dry and papery, her stare, glassy.

"He can hear you if you talk to him," she said quietly. "I'm sure he can. He opens his eyes from time to time."

Ben nodded. There was nothing to say. He swallowed hard and glanced at Gus. His skin, which once glowed with health and vitality, was yellow and sickly, his face and limbs bloated.

He took Gus's swollen hand and sat at the edge of the bed. "Gus, it's Reverend Ben. Can you hear me?"

He didn't think Gus had heard at first. Then he saw the sick man's head move against the pillow. Gus's eyes fluttered open for a moment, and he stared up at Ben. "Reverend . . . good. I think I'm ready. . . . Will you send me off?"

"He wants to receive the sacrament," Evelyn said. "Can you do that for him?"

"Of course. I've brought everything." Ben swallowed hard.

He stroked Gus's hand. Gus had already closed his eyes, but Ben could see a peaceful expression on his face, and he knew Gus had heard him.

A short time later, Ben completed celebrating the sacrament at Gus's bedside. Sophie, her children, and a few of her grandchildren circled the bed, and Una led the group in a prayer. With their heads bowed and hands clasped, it seemed to Ben for a moment that they composed a circle of living, vibrating love, their final gift to Gus, a parting embrace as he journeyed on.

Ben felt witness to something awesome and powerful. *This is what life is all about,* he thought. *What love is all about. Forget the hearts and flowers. It's a mighty force, frightening in its power.*

Of all Gus had experienced in his long life, above all, he was loved, Ben thought. And that was saying a great deal.

Carolyn left a short time later. Ben sat with Sophie in

the room while others came in and out over the long hours. The afternoon faded black into night, and the night then crept along slowly.

Ben found himself dozing in a chair. Someone had tossed an afghan over him, Sophie probably. He sat up, feeling cramped and sore. He checked his watch. A little past five in the morning. The room was shadowy, the day's first light mingled with the glow of a small lamp by Gus's bed. Sophie still sat in her chair, holding Gus's hand, as focused and alert as when Ben had arrived that afternoon.

"Any change?" he asked, resting his hand on her shoulder.

"Yes . . . I think he's really going now." She rose and sat on the edge of the bed, then leaned toward Gus and placed her arm around his shoulders. "I'm here, Gus. I'm right here with you. Don't be afraid. Just let go now, darling," she whispered.

Gus didn't respond. Ben felt his breath catch. Was he already gone?

Then he saw Gus's hand stir, reaching to touch Sophie. She bowed her head to his chest, and his fingers found her hair. She was crying now, silent tears that fell from her eyes and dropped onto Gus.

Seconds later, Gus's hand fell limp and lifeless on his chest. Ben saw it and realized what had happened. No matter how many sick rooms he attended, no matter how many times he witnessed a person's passing, it was always so startling to him, the way the spirit of life leaves the body. When it finally happens, it's in the blink of an eye, as if someone had simply blown out a match.

Sophie seemed to stop breathing, too. For a minute everything in the room seemed to freeze. Then she released a long, keening wail that echoed through the house to the silent trees outside the window, to the very corners of the world beyond.

She collapsed in a heap on her husband as her children

rushed to her side. She clung to his body for a moment, then with resignation, bowed her head and kissed his cheek before allowing her daughters and son to help her to her feet.

"It's over, Mother. Dad is gone." Una sobbed, embracing Sophie.

"Yes, he's gone from us," Sophie managed between tears. "But I know he's at peace. He's with the angels now."

THE WEEKEND PASSED, AND TUCKER NEVER QUITE GOT around to telling Carl about the handyman job at the church. He wondered if he should tell Fran about it first, but he knew what her reaction would be: Why make it so easy for Carl to settle in? Wasn't the plan for him to go?

The truth was, Tucker felt the same way. He hadn't quite realized it when he was talking to Reverend Ben. But in the days since, he hadn't told Carl about the job because he wasn't sure he wanted Carl to stay. Carl had gotten a good report from the doctor on Friday. In a week or two, he would be well enough to travel. Considering all the upset he'd caused so far, did it really make sense for him to stay?

On Monday morning, Tucker dressed and went off to work, the guilty secret heavy inside him. He went on patrol, cruising around the village and mulling over the problem all morning. When it was time for his lunch break, he decided to stop at home. Maybe with no one else in the house, he'd find the courage to talk to Carl. There was always the chance Carl didn't even want the job, that he was set on moving on. Tucker tried to focus on that possibility. He felt bound by his talk with the reverend to say something though. It just didn't seem right not to let Carl know.

He let himself in through the side door and heard Carl in the kitchen. His brother looked startled to see him. Guilty even, though when Tucker checked to see what Carl was up to, he was only making sandwiches on the countertop.

A great many sandwiches, actually. It looked like half the contents of the refrigerator had been emptied out—packages of lunch meats, cheese, pickles, and other condiments. About twenty slices of bread were lined up. Some were covered with cold cuts, others with peanut butter, while another stack of bread slices stood waiting on the side.

Tucker was just grateful Fran never came home at this time. "What's going on?" he asked, keeping his voice casual. "Are you opening up a restaurant in here or something?"

Carl forced a smile but didn't look up from his task. "Nope. These are all for me. I'm going on sort of a picnic."

Tucker got it now. Carl was getting ready to leave. Right away, too. He felt a funny shock ripple through his body, as if he'd just been cut free from a tangled line.

Carl was leaving by his own choice. There wouldn't be any angry scenes or confrontations. No drawn-out stay. No more arguments with Fran. It looked as though he wasn't even going to say good-bye. To his surprise, Tucker realized he was hurt by that.

"You're leaving?" Tucker asked bluntly.

"That's right." Carl began slapping bread slices on the open-faced sandwiches, as if working on an assembly line.

"Weren't you even going to say good-bye?"

Carl glanced at him. "I was going to leave a note."

Right, about three or four words long, Tucker guessed. Carl never was a big one for letter writing.

He picked up the corner of a piece of bread and peeked underneath. "Can I have one of these?"

"Help yourself; they're your cold cuts." Carl gave a short laugh and shook his head.

Tucker took the sandwich and put it on a plate, then sat down at the table. "Why are you leaving? Because of what happened in the diner with Charlie Bates? I don't know how I stayed friends with him for so long. He's a troublemaker and a fool."

"I won't argue with that. But that's not why. I told you from the start I wasn't going to stay long."

"The doctor says you need more time to recover. At least a week more. I was right there when he told you."

"What does he know? I've been in worse shape than this and gotten along just fine, believe me."

Tucker did believe him. That was half the problem. He chewed on his sandwich, suddenly feeling reluctant to see Carl go.

"There's a lot of mustard on this," he muttered. "What do you use, half a bottle per sandwich?"

"Mustard's the best thing. Soaks into the bread. Ketchup and relish, too. Keeps it from getting too stale. You can't use mayonnaise. It can kill you, sitting there a day or two."

Tucker's stomach recoiled at the thought. Carl was planning on carrying this food around for a long time, he realized, a frighteningly long time.

"You can't go yet," he told Carl. "Fran is finally getting used to having you around. She told me this morning she was going to make meat loaf tonight, and she knows how I hate it. 'Your brother likes my meat loaf,' she said to me."

"She didn't say that. You're making it up." Carl pulled off a piece of plastic wrap and folded it around a sandwich.

"She did, too. My right hand to God." Tucker sat up, raising his hand.

"You're swearing now, see? My bad influence is rubbing off on you. I've got to go."

"Look," Tucker said, "I understand if you're tired of sitting around this place. You can get out a little now. Get a change of scenery."

"Right. And have some guy like Charlie try to push me around just to prove what an upstanding citizen he is? No, thanks. People in this town have short tempers and long memories, Tucker. Too many of them can't forget my past. I don't even know why I came back in the first place. And not to see you, if that's what you're thinking," he added gruffly over his shoulder.

"I wasn't thinking that." But now Tucker wondered about it. *Carl is such a twisted soul. Maybe he did come back to see me.*

"People like to gossip in this town," Tucker reminded him. "Before you know it, you'll be old news. They'll be on to something else."

Carl didn't look at him. He didn't even seem to be listening as he sorted the wrapped sandwiches, packing them into large plastic bags.

"Why give in to jerks like Charlie Bates? Why let him win? That's not the Carl I know," Tucker goaded him.

Carl turned to face him. "You hit the nail on the head right there, Tucker. We haven't seen each other in over twenty years. You don't know me anymore and I don't know you."

"Of course we know each other," Tucker protested. "Neither one of us has changed that much—except maybe we've both gotten more stubborn."

"For pity's sake . . . what difference does it make?" Carl's hands trembled as he jammed the last of the sandwiches into a bag. "Why do you want me here? What's in it for you? Your wife isn't happy about it. Neither are your neighbors. I just don't get it, Tucker. You ought to be offering me a ride to the bus station, not dredging up reasons for me to stay."

"I'll take you to the bus station, if that's what you really want," Tucker said slowly. "I just don't want to see you forced out. That's not right. It's not fair."

"Oh, no. Here we go again." Carl looked up at the ceiling and shook his head. "I'll tell you something, sonny. The word 'fair' isn't in my dictionary. I don't worry about fair and not fair. I'd go a little crazy if I did."

Tucker sat back and crossed his arms over his chest. He felt the heavy knot of his secret lodged at the bottom of his throat.

"Would you stay if you had a job?"

"A job?" Carl laughed and rubbed the back of his neck. "Who would hire me?"

"There's a job at the church. A groundskeeper/handyman kind of thing. Reverend Ben says it's yours for the asking."

Carl stared at him, then turned slowly back to the counter where he started to clean up the mess he had made. "When were you going to tell me about this? After I left?"

Tucker felt his face get hot. Carl was sharp, sharper than he liked to let on. "I'm telling you now, aren't I? This might work out for you. You were always good with your hands."

"I've had jobs like that. Plenty of them," Carl said gruffly. "No question I can do it."

Tucker wondered if he had insulted Carl. His brother used to have such grandiose ideas about himself. This job probably sounded too lowly to him. Well, it was, Tucker thought sadly. It was also as good an offer as he might get.

"It's kind of hard to imagine me going off to church every day," Carl said wryly. "But I wouldn't mind working for the reverend. He's not so bad—when he lays off the God talk."

Tucker was about to reply but held his tongue, waiting to see what Carl would decide.

"I don't know. People might not like it. They might cause more trouble for you," Carl added.

"I'm not afraid of that." Suddenly, Tucker really wasn't afraid. He recalled what the reverend had told him, and he felt himself on solid ground. "I wouldn't have told you about the job if I didn't want you to take it."

That was true, too, he realized. He had been waffling about this for days, but now that he finally put it on the table for Carl, he knew he had done the right thing. This job could change Carl's life. He would have steady work and be near family. He would be far less likely to slip back into the life of a homeless drifter.

Carl turned from the sink and looked at him. "I guess I could talk to the reverend about it, see what he says. If it doesn't pan out, I'll leave tomorrow. Or the next day."

"Sure, you go talk to him. You know the reverend. He's a good guy."

"Yeah, he's all right." Carl dried his hands on a paper towel, then tossed it in the trash. "You're not so bad, either, come to think of it. I give you a hard time, but you turned out all right, Tucker. You're a stand-up guy."

Chapter Eleven

On Tuesday morning the church was packed with mourners. Everyone in town seemed to have put their jobs and other responsibilities on hold in order to pay their last respects to Gus Potter.

Surrounded by her family, Sophie sat in the first pew, looking exhausted and bereft. Ben's heart went out to her. He had discussed the service with the Potters over the weekend, and they had chosen the hymns and Scriptures and designated readers from their circle of friends and relations. Gus had requested a favorite hymn, "I've Got Peace like a River," and Ben found his eyes filling with tears as the choir sang the familiar verses.

Finally, it was time to give the eulogy. Ben slowly approached the pulpit. The congregation sat in silent, sad attention. The task before him—to capture some sense of Gus's long virtuous life and somehow ease their sorrow—felt suddenly insurmountable. He glanced down at his notes and took a sip of water, then began.

"Dear friends, we are gathered this morning to celebrate

the passing of Gus Potter. Yes, I said 'celebrate,' not 'mourn.'" He paused and held Sophie's gaze for a long moment. "For those of you who believe the promise of almighty Jesus, our Lord and Savior, for those who have taken Him into your hearts as I know Gus Potter did, there really is no death. For true Christians, our earthly end is an illusion. It is a time to rejoice, not to weep, because at that moment that seems like defeat, an ebbing away of life, we are really victorious, delivered into life everlasting and God's abundant love and care.

"Death remains a fearful moment, a tragedy to us, a mystery that confounds our limited understanding. 'Poor Gus,' we say. But when we look at this mystery through the lens of faith, we see it differently. We see that we must put our limited, flawed logic aside and hold fast to our faith. Like a hand in the darkness, the Lord's hand will lead us forward into the everlasting light. Through the power of that guiding touch, that faith, we can believe and rest easy in our hearts, knowing Gus Potter is saved and waits for us at the hand of our Lord. . . ."

Sophie nodded and began weeping. Her daughters, Evelyn and Una, one on each side, put their arms around her shoulders.

Ben swallowed hard, fearful that he, too, might start crying and not be able to finish.

"As many of you know, I have stood up here and delivered many eulogies for beloved members of this congregation. But Gus Potter was special.

"By some standards, Gus was an ordinary man. He never ran for election or had his picture in the paper or made any startling discoveries. He worked hard all his life, finding great joy in caring for his family and tending the orchard. He was an honest man, a steadfast and loyal friend. A scout leader when our boys were young, a loyal Red Sox fan. Never a great fisherman, but sometimes a lucky one," Ben added with a small, sad smile.

"An ordinary man, some would say, but by the standards that really count, he was truly extraordinary. Gus was a man who lived his faith every day. He was a model of kindness and goodness to us all. Now he will live in our hearts and in our prayers. Let us give thanks today for having known him, for having been blessed by his grace and humanity. Let us also pray for the salvation of his eternal soul and his deliverance into the hands of our almighty Father. We ask this in the name of our Lord, Jesus Christ."

Ben paused but could not bring himself to look out at the congregation or even at Sophie and her family. He didn't know if they had found any solace in his words, but surely he had tried his best to comfort them and honor Gus's memory.

Gus was buried in the village cemetery outside town, on a sloping green hill studded with headstones that protruded from the ground like rows of crooked teeth. Some were so old that the names and dates carved in the stone were completely worn away.

After the burial, the mourners gathered at Sophie's house. Friends from the church brought food and cakes and helped to serve the Potters' guests. It was a somber gathering, as such events always are, Ben noticed. Yet, here and there, in a small child's laughter or when a happy memory about Gus was shared, Ben sensed the irresistible forward motion of life, pushing on, out of the shadow of death and loss.

As the house began to empty out, he looked around for Carolyn and found her in the kitchen, helping to clean up along with Jessica Morgan; her sister, Emily Warwick; and Grace Hegman.

He walked up to his wife and touched her on the shoulder. "I'm just going to speak to Sophie for a moment, and then we'll go."

Carolyn nodded. "All right, Ben. I'll be here. You come and find me when you're ready."

A few minutes later Bart Potter found him. "She's gone upstairs to rest, but I know she wanted to speak to you."

Sophie's son led the way upstairs to the master bedroom, the room Sophie and Gus had shared all their married life. Bart was a big man, dignified and elegantly dressed in a dark suit that looked custom-made. Ben knew he was a successful corporate attorney, a partner in a large Boston firm, but he could still remember Bart knee-high to a grasshopper, a mischievous boy with strawberry-blond hair like his mother's and a perpetually dirty face.

"I don't want to disturb her if she's sleeping," Ben said quietly, as they came to the half-opened door. "I can come back later, tonight perhaps, if she'd like to talk."

"Is that you, Reverend? I'm not sleeping," Sophie called out from the room.

Bart offered the minister a small smile. "She always had wonderful hearing. We could never get away with a thing." He touched Ben's arm briefly, then turned to go back down.

Ben entered the room slowly. Sophie sat in an armchair by the window. Sunbeams filtered through lace curtains, casting her in a golden light.

"I just needed to be by myself for a while."

"Understandably." Ben sat on the edge of the bed, facing her.

"Quite a crowd at the funeral. Everyone came to say good-bye. That was nice. Gus would have liked that."

"He was loved. We'll all miss him very much."

"I liked what you said at church, Reverend. It reminded me not to be so mournful. I'm mournful for myself, of course. But not for Gus. He's with the angels now, smiling down on me. I can feel it."

Her quiet voice was calm and confident and oddly reassuring. How ironic, Ben thought, that she should be the one comforting him now.

"Good. I feel it, too," he said honestly. He paused, wondering if it was too soon to ask her the question on his mind. On everyone's mind today, actually. He decided to go ahead with it. "What will you do now, Sophie? Do you know yet?"

She sighed and shook her head, looking more downhearted now than when she'd spoken of Gus moments before.

"My children think it's best if I leave and put the place up for sale. It's not what I want, of course. Everyone knows that. But they've got me in a corner. They're worried about me . . . and I am old. I feel about a hundred and one with Gus gone." She paused, her eyes moist with tears. "Maybe they're right. Maybe I'm not up to keeping this place going on my own anymore. They don't want to find out, anyway. That path is too dangerous, they say."

"I see. . . . That's too bad. But perhaps they're right."

Ben covered her hand with his own. It was hard to think of Sophie gone from here and the orchard gone, too, even though he knew it was probably the best and safest solution for everyone.

Sophie didn't look at him. She dabbed her eyes with a flowered hanky then stared out the window at the rows of bare apple trees.

"I'm going to live with Evelyn in a few weeks. Miranda is going to stay and help me pack up a few things. I'm not going to take much to Evelyn's, but I don't want to leave my good things around with the house empty."

"Yes, I understand." Though the situation was what he had expected, Ben felt a wave of sadness at hearing Sophie outline her plans so plainly.

"The place will go up for sale eventually. And that will be that."

The reverend didn't answer at first. Finally, he forced himself to say what seemed to be the right thing. "This is very hard for you. I'm sorry, Sophie. But your children want to take care of you now. They want what's best for you."

"I know. I know . . . I just wish it wasn't so."

They sat together for a few minutes more, and then Ben embraced her as they said good-bye. "You'll keep me up-to-date with what's happening here, right?"

"Yes, I will, Reverend." She sighed and glanced in the

mirror, adjusting a few pins that had come loose from her upswept hair. "I suppose I should go down now and say good-bye to everyone. This is the last gathering we'll have in this house, I guess. It's funny but somehow I always thought we would go out on a happier note."

So did I, Ben thought sadly. Without making any reply, he took her arm and escorted her from the room.

THE GOOD NEWS WAS THAT MOLLY'S PARENTS WERE FINALLY coming home from Florida tonight. A lot seemed to have happened to her since they'd left in mid-February. Though her mother could be intrusive at times—with the best of intentions, of course—Molly had really missed them.

The task of picking them up at Logan Airport in Boston had somehow fallen to her, which wasn't such good news. Molly didn't drive into Boston often, and the Big Dig project had made navigating the city a near nightmare. Add to that Friday night traffic. It wasn't going to be pretty.

But Sam had gone out of town for a few days to take a construction job in Vermont, and Jessica, who offered to go to the airport, wound up stuck with a business obligation. It was just as well, Molly thought. She was their daughter; it was her responsibility. The problem was, that didn't leave anyone to watch the girls. And with her parents and all their luggage, there wasn't room in the hatchback for two extra passengers.

Molly had not spoken to Matthew in over a week, but he did come to mind as someone who owed her a baby-sitting favor. Well, he came to mind a lot, she had to admit. But this seemed like a good excuse to call him.

When she explained her problem, he was more than happy to help her out. He'd even sounded happy to hear from her, she thought. Or maybe she had just been imagining that part? The question lingered as she took a bit of extra care on Friday night with her outfit and makeup.

The girls were waiting in the kitchen with their jackets on as Molly checked her purse one last time, making sure she had all the essentials: cell phone, flight information, change for tolls, a bottle of water, something to read in case the flight was delayed.

"You're just going to Boston, not the moon, Mom," Lauren groaned.

"Shush, you just made me forget something."

The phone rang and Molly stared at it. They really did need to leave. She didn't want to be hung up on a phone call with some client or chatty friend. Then she wouldn't have any extra time to see Matthew.

"Let's just see who it is," she told the girls. A moment later the machine picked up, and she heard Phil's voice on the line.

"Hi everybody. It's me. I wondered if I could take the girls out tonight instead of tomorrow. This guy at work gave me some tickets for the In-Tranzit concert in Southport. We can still make it in time. Give me a call on my cell phone right away, okay?"

Lauren jumped to pick up the phone, but Molly blocked her way. "Come on, let's go," she said curtly.

Lauren and Jill stared at her, not moving a muscle.

"What about Daddy? We have to call him back," Jill said.

"We'll call him later," Molly promised, "from the car."

"But what about the concert? I want to go." Lauren stared at her as if this had to be the most obvious thing in the world.

"You can't go. It doesn't work out."

"What do you mean? Why can't we go out with Dad while you're at the airport? What's the difference?"

Molly managed to keep her voice calm as she said, "The difference is we've already made plans. First of all, Lauren, Dr. Harding and Amanda are expecting you to visit them tonight. Second, it wasn't right of your father to call and invite you out at the last minute."

"But he just got those tickets, and everybody wants to see In-Tranzit," Lauren objected.

"I want to go to the concert, too," Jill chimed in. "This isn't fair. We'll never get a chance like this again. We have to go!"

Molly put her hands to the sides of her head, trying to clear her thoughts. Was this the right call? Was she being too tough on Phil about this scheduling thing? He had toed the line since their confrontation two weeks ago. But this maneuver was just like him; he was back to his old tricks. Even if he got the tickets on the spur of the moment, he should have never left a message like that. He was hoping the kids would hear it and wear her down. It was his usual game, and she wasn't going to let him win, Molly decided. The girls would be angry with her but what else was new?

"I'm sorry. I know you don't understand, but your father knows when he is supposed to see you. Tonight is not one of his nights." Molly spoke in a firm voice, glancing at each of the girls in turn, trying to give the look that said she wasn't going to change her mind. "We've made our plans and that phone call doesn't change them. Let's go."

With her head bowed, Jill sighed and shuffled toward the door. But Lauren didn't budge. She crossed her arms over her chest and met Molly's stare.

"You're so mean! You never want us to see Daddy. If it was up to you, he'd never be allowed to take us anywhere."

Molly stood openmouthed, feeling as if she'd been slapped. Somehow Lauren's defection made her even angrier at Phil. She struggled to hold her temper and not overreact.

"Lauren, that is not true and you know it. Any more backtalk like that and you're going to be in real trouble." Molly paused and took a deep breath. The girls stared at her. "Go ahead. I need to lock up."

Lauren made a sour face, pursing her lips in a frown, then stormed past Molly and out the door. Jill quietly followed.

As Molly had promised, she called Phil from the car. She was glad when his voice mail picked up so she didn't have to speak to him. The girls didn't say a word to her during the drive to Hawthorne Street. Their silent treatment worked. Though she was convinced she was in the right, Molly somehow felt awful.

As soon as they got to Matthew's house, Lauren and Jill ran upstairs to join Amanda in her room. Matthew and Molly watched them from the foyer, then Matthew gave her a quizzical look.

"Are you okay?" he asked quietly.

Molly wondered if she should tell him what was really going on. Men didn't like women who whined about their ex-husbands. Everyone knew that. But right now she felt like whining her head off, and the look of concern in Matt's warm brown eyes melted her reserve.

"No, I'm not okay," she admitted. "I just had this thing with the girls over Phil right before we left the house. It really rattled me. Lauren said I was mean and horrible and I never want them to see their father."

"Wow, that does sound bad. Here, come inside and we can talk." He put his arm lightly around her shoulders and led her into the living room.

Despite feeling so upset, Molly liked the feeling of Matthew's caring embrace and felt a little pang of loss when he stepped away.

She sat on the edge of the sofa. "We were just about to leave for your house when the phone rang. I let the machine pick up. It was Phil. He left a message that he had some free tickets and wanted to take the girls to a rock concert in Southport. But I didn't want them to go."

"Because you had planned to bring them here, you mean?"

"Well, partly. But also because I've told Phil that he can't just call up like that or drop in any time he wants and think the girls will always be at his beck and call.

We've worked out a schedule, and I want him to stick with it."

She let out a long breath, realizing that she'd been talking a blue streak.

Matthew sat in an armchair across from her, his brow set in a look of concern. He didn't seem bored with her venting, but his expression wasn't one of complete sympathy, either.

"So, what do you think? Am I a mean mother? I just want Phil to hold it together for five minutes and act responsibly. He shouldn't have left a message like that. He knew he would just be causing problems for me."

"Well, you're right. It was careless of him. Maybe he was so excited to get the free tickets, he didn't stop to think it through. He does seem . . . impulsive."

Molly glanced at Matthew, not sure he really understood why she was so upset and angry.

"I know it's hard when your kids get mad at you like that," he added. "It hurts a lot because you feel like you've been tying yourself in knots to do what's best for them."

"Yes, exactly." Molly nodded, feeling a bit calmer.

"Phil should be more mindful of his schedule and more considerate of you that way. You might need to talk to him again about it."

"Looks like I will. I'm not sure if he'll ever get it, though."

Matthew didn't reply. He sat looking at her, then glanced down at the floor.

Molly felt uncomfortable. "You look like you want to say something to me, but you're not sure you should."

He gave a short laugh. "You're right. I'm not."

"Go ahead. I'm interested in your opinion. Just say what's on your mind. I won't get upset," she promised, though she had the distinct feeling that she would.

"You've only told me a little about Phil, but from what I can see, there seems to be more going on here between the two of you."

Molly sat up straighter, suddenly feeling self-conscious.

"What are you talking about? I don't have feelings for him anymore—romantic feelings, I mean."

"But you're still angry at him. Not just about what he did tonight. About the past. And that's not good."

Molly felt stunned and embarrassed by his quiet words. It felt as if he could see right through her.

"Phil was a bad husband and a bad father," she said. "You don't forget that so easily."

"No, of course not. It sounds as if you had every right to be angry at him." Matt's tone was compassionate and understanding. "But you've been divorced now, what, seven years?"

Molly nodded. She met his gaze and looked away. It did sound like a long time when Matthew said it.

"I'm not trying to criticize you, honestly. But he's trying hard now. Anybody can see that. Give the guy some credit. Don't make it even harder for him."

Molly felt herself flushing with anger and disbelief. How could Matthew take Phil's side in this? What was going on here, some man club thing?

"I don't think you get it at all," Molly said curtly. "Phil can't just knock on the door one day and wave a magic wand and expect me to forget everything. He's done this before. Sooner or later he always gets tired of playing Dad and disappears again."

"Gets tired of it? Or are you trying to make it so hard for him that he gives up?" Matthew asked quietly.

Molly didn't know what to say. She had been wrong to confide in him. She suddenly felt wrong about a lot of things and didn't even understand why she was still sitting there.

"I'm sorry," Matt said, and she could tell from his expression that he knew he had hurt her. "I should never have said that, Molly."

"That's okay. I asked you what you thought. And you told me." She took a deep breath, not wanting him to see how upset she truly was. "Well, I've got to go. It's getting late."

She jumped to her feet and picked up her bag. "Thanks again for having the girls. It shouldn't take too long if the flight is on time."

Matthew followed her to the door. "Molly . . . please. Don't go like this. I'm sorry I said that to you. This subject pushes some buttons for me, I guess."

He paused and ran his hand through his hair. He was very handsome, and it annoyed her that now, after everything, she still felt so attracted to him.

"Do you have to go right now?" he asked. "I wish we could sit and talk more about this. I'm not sure you understand what I was trying to say."

Molly zipped up her jacket and opened the front door.

"I understand. But I need to go. Thanks for the advice." Then she turned and called up the stairs to her daughters, "Lauren, Jill . . . I'm leaving. See you later."

Nobody answered. "They probably can't hear you over the music. I'll go up and get them."

Molly shook her head. "That's okay. Nobody seems to hear me lately." She tried for a joking tone, but it didn't quite come out that way.

Then she pulled open the door and left.

MATTHEW FELT TERRIBLE WATCHING MOLLY GO. BUT there was nothing he could do to stop her. He watched her get into her car and drive away, then he closed the door and walked back into the living room. He had planned to catch up on some reading tonight—his medical journals were piling up to the ceiling—but he knew he wouldn't be able to concentrate now. He stretched out on the couch and stared at the ceiling, his arms folded under his head.

He cared for Molly. He had never meant to hurt her. He knew that under her tough, wisecracking act she was sensitive. It had cost her something to confide in him, and he had blown it. But he had to be honest with her. She clearly wasn't being honest with herself. She clung to her anger at Phil like a badge of honor. She was so worried about how Phil's behavior might hurt her daughters, she couldn't see how her behavior already was hurting them. And hurting herself.

But she wasn't ready to hear that, Matthew realized. *Not from me, anyway. Little did she know that I'm a specialist with that particular affliction. If only she had stayed, maybe I could have explained that to her, showed her that I now know that anger like that is quicksand. You can get stuck. You can go under.*

His marriage had been an emotional tug-of-war, too, the kind that nobody ever won. When he and his wife hit rough patches, he hadn't faced up to them. He clung to his grievances, just as Molly was doing, feeling totally justified and totally unwilling to step beyond that square on the game board. He retreated even deeper into his work, which was exactly what Sharon always accused him of doing. He stuck with the marriage for Amanda's sake while ignoring his wife's unhappiness . . . and his own.

But when he was finally ready to look beyond his anger and try to work things out, they learned that Sharon had cancer—the swift and vicious variety. Her illness became the focus of their life together, her futile struggle to survive, his even more futile one to help her. He did everything he could, and he realized that he still loved her. But it was too late. They never grew truly close again, not even at the very end.

Now he was left with regrets, a heart and soul full of them. He should have given up his resentment and anger and tried to simply be happy. Happy and grateful for so much that was right in their life together, the blessings they did enjoy. It seemed so simple now. Why had it seemed so difficult then? So obscured?

Almost three years had passed since Sharon's death. He thought by now he would have worked this all out. Everyone told him he had to forgive himself; he had to let go. But he couldn't forgive himself. He couldn't forget. He felt stuck, unable to change the past and undeserving of a future where he could be happy and feel love again.

He did what he could to get out of his rut. He moved from Worcester, changed his job, cut back his working hours. But they were all changes to the surface of his life. It was like getting a haircut to cure a headache, Matt thought cynically. And of course, what he really needed was some sort of spiritual healing.

He put his hand over his eyes to block the light from the reading lamp. With his eyes shut, his thoughts turned toward praying. He hadn't done too much of that lately. Maybe that was part of his problem right there.

God, I'm sort of confused right now, he began. *I didn't mean to hurt Molly tonight. Please give me the chance to make it up to her somehow. Please let her be ready to listen when I talk to her, too. She's such a wonderful person. I do care about her, more than I even want to sometimes. I hate to see her eaten up by her anger. Show her how to find forgiveness for Phil and freedom for herself. I know that's what I need, too. But I can't seem to get there either. Please help me. Show me what to do.*

Chapter Twelve

Whenever Molly saw Emily Warwick around town, she would say hello but would rarely stop to chat. Molly didn't have much time for small talk, for one thing, and Emily was . . . well, Emily. She was the mayor of Cape Light, and Molly had always found her intimidating. Emily had manners, poise, and a certain way of speaking that made Molly feel like she was back in school, forced to talk with one of her teachers. Emily had, in fact, been a high-school English teacher before entering politics. Even having her brother Sam married to Emily's sister hadn't done much to dispel Molly's apprehension.

But when they came face to face outside the Beanery on Monday afternoon, it just didn't seem right to pass by without acknowledging the news of Emily's engagement to Dan Forbes.

"Emily, congratulations! I saw Jessica over the weekend. She told me your good news."

Molly wasn't just trying to say the right thing. She did feel genuinely happy for Emily. It was hard not to once you saw her smile. "So, where's the ring?" she added in a teasing tone.

Emily held out her hand, looking as if she felt silly but also proud.

It was stunning, Molly thought, a square-cut blue sapphire flanked by two small diamonds. Impressive yet tasteful, just like Emily. "It's beautiful. I wish you the best."

"Thank you, Molly. I appreciate your good wishes." Emily smiled at her, then looked down at the ring. "I didn't even think I wanted an engagement ring, but Dan practically dragged me to a jeweler and insisted I pick something out."

Molly shook her head in mock sympathy. "I know what you mean. I hate when that happens." Emily just laughed. "Have you and Dan set a wedding date?"

"Not yet. Sometime this summer, probably. Dan wants a honeymoon trip on his sailboat, so it can't be too long off. I'm not much of a sailor, though," she admitted. "But 'in sickness and in health' covers seasickness, too, I suppose."

Now it was Molly's turn to laugh. "Are you going in for lunch? I'm meeting Betty here. Want to join us?"

Now, how did that happen? Molly wondered. *I guess I'm not as intimidated by Emily as I thought. Or maybe she's nicer than I realized, once she relaxes a little.*

"Oh, thanks, Molly. I can't today. I have to get back to the office. But you just reminded me of something I want to ask you."

What would Emily Warwick want to ask her? A recommendation on the best brand of silver polish?

"Betty told me you were starting a catering business, and I wondered if you would do an engagement party for me and Dan. It wouldn't be anything huge. We were thinking of about fifty people. Well, maybe more like seventy-five. We both know so many people in town, it's hard to keep control of the guest list."

Molly felt her eyes widen in shock but forced herself to keep a lid on her reaction. Which was, in fact, sheer panic. She couldn't cater a party for seventy-five people. Especially the seventy-five people that Emily and Dan would invite, the cream of Cape Light society . . . if there was such a thing.

It was flattering, though, that Emily had even thought to ask her.

"It's nice of you to think of me, Emily, but I really haven't started the business yet. I'm just in the planning stages. I probably won't be ready in time to do it for you."

"Oh, that's too bad. Are you sure? You did such a great job with Jessica's shower. The food, the flowers, everything was so beautiful. Are you sure you couldn't manage it?"

Emily's tone was so flattering and hopeful, Molly was tempted to reconsider. But Jessica's bridal shower had only been a small gathering of women in Emily's living room. Not a full-blown formal affair for seventy-five, which would probably grow to a guest list of over a hundred before Emily and Dan were through with it.

Molly glanced up at Emily, searching for the right words to politely decline. But before she could speak, Emily continued, "We're flexible about the date. Maybe we could figure out something that works with your schedule. What if I call you during the week?"

"All right. That's a good idea." Molly nodded, not sure what she was getting herself into. Part of her wanted to jump for joy. If she could pull this off, it would be a quantum leap forward for her. But the other part of her, the larger part, shrank back in pure terror.

"Great. I'll talk to you soon." Emily gave her another cheery smile and headed up Main Street to the Village Hall.

Molly was just about to go in the Beanery when she saw Betty's white Volvo pull up and park nearby.

"Sorry I'm late," Betty said. "Waiting long? I tried to call you, but your phone isn't on—"

"Just answer one question. Have you been telling everyone that I've started a catering business?"

Betty shrugged. "I may have mentioned it to a few people."

"Like Emily Warwick?"

Betty looked so pleased with herself, Molly knew for sure it had been one of her little schemes. "Did she call you already? She's so efficient. No wonder she's mayor."

"Look, I know you're just trying to help me, but I can't do a big party like that. I'm nowhere near ready for it."

"Now, now. Just calm down. You need some lunch. Let's go inside and talk about this." Betty took her arm and led her through the door. Molly felt like a small child being coaxed out of a tantrum. She had a feeling that once Betty was through with her, she would be eating all her vegetables. Or rather figuring out the roasted vegetable platter for Emily's party.

They were soon seated at a small table in the back of the café, and they quickly gave their orders.

Plenty of privacy, Molly thought gratefully. She hated to argue in public, and the look in Betty's eye told her she wasn't going to give up that easily on this.

"Did you see Emily's ring?" Betty started off in a chatty tone. "It's a beauty."

"Absolutely," Molly agreed flatly.

"She looks very happy. Dan does, too. For Dan, I mean."

"And I'd hate to be the one to ruin it for them with an awful party. Why am I even discussing this at all? I couldn't even attempt to do that party, Betty. You know that."

"Of course you could. You just have to think big, Molly. You can't live your life on a small-screen TV, you know. It's a great opportunity for you. Everyone in town will be there."

"That's exactly what I'm thinking. If I screw up, it will definitely be on a big screen. That's not exactly a great way to launch a business."

"Okay, I understand." Betty reached over and patted her hand. For a moment, Molly thought she might relent. "This is a big risk for you. But you have to leave your comfort zone if you want to succeed. You have to put yourself out there and risk being a big flop."

"All right, point taken . . . but can't I be a big flop a few months from now? And in some other town, where they don't know me as well? This all seems just a little too rushed for me."

"That's the way life is. Opportunities like this don't always come around at your convenience, Molly. I really think you're ready for this. I wouldn't have recommended you to Emily otherwise. Stop thinking about being a failure and focus on the payoff if you do a good job. It could launch your whole business plan like that." Betty snapped her fingers, which sounded like a tiny firecracker exploding at the table.

"I don't have a business plan," Molly reminded her.

"Well, then you need one. I'm sure it's covered in your text books somewhere. You'll need it to get financing, you know."

"What financing?"

"Well, you need some capital to get started. Emily will give you a deposit, of course. But there's going to be some outlay of funds for your supplies and wages and all. You'll have to hire help and rent tables and chairs, that sort of thing."

Molly sighed as the waitress set their orders down. She knew if she let Betty proceed on this track much longer, they would wind up their lunch with a walk down to the bank.

"Why don't you talk to your sister-in-law about it? She does small-business loans, right?"

"I just knew you were going to say that." Molly forked up a bite of salad, tempted to confess she and Jessica had already sort of started talking about this, but Molly knew that would only encourage Betty more.

"You definitely ought to talk to Jessica," Betty was saying. "She might have some ideas for you. And just promise me that you'll talk to Emily and see what kind of party she wants before you flat-out refuse? Will you do that one thing for me?"

Molly sighed, unable to avoid Betty's pleading gaze. "All right. I'll talk to both of them. Happy now?"

"Perfectly. You're going to thank me for this someday. I guarantee it."

Betty began eating her salad with a pleased expression on her face. Molly didn't answer. She hoped Betty was right. Her friend's unflinching confidence in her boosted her spirits. But she still struggled with a voice in her head that insisted she couldn't do it and was a fool to even try.

It was hard to change. It was hard to leave her comfort zone, as Betty had said. That was the bottom line here. It was easier to stay in one place and complain and remind herself of all the reasons she couldn't get ahead.

And maybe that was also true for the way she dealt with Phil, she thought, remembering what Matthew had said.

But that was another matter entirely. *One crisis at a time,* she decided. *Your other worry goblins will have to take a number.*

Now a real chance to get her business started had been thrown in her path, and Betty wouldn't let her ignore it. But Molly still wasn't sure she had the courage to pick up the prize and run with it.

"GOOD MORNING, CARL. UP AND AT IT ALREADY, I SEE." The reverend shielded his eyes from the sun with his hand.

Carl stood high upon a ladder, working on a gutter pipe that ran down from the church's roof. Patching a leak with some tar, it looked like to Ben. His nose wrinkled at the smell of it.

"I heard it might rain again on Thursday," Carl said. "I wanted to fix this pipe while we had some dry weather."

"Good idea. That's been bad for a while. Well, when you're done come into my office, will you? I wanted to have a word."

Carl looked down at him. Even from the distance between them Ben could see a look of alarm on his face. "I'm just about finished if you want to wait a minute," Carl said.

Ben nodded. "All right. Don't rush."

He hadn't meant to make Carl worry. Ben wondered if the poor man thought he might be getting fired. Of course, it was nothing like that. He had started at the church last Tuesday, exactly a week ago, and so far his work had been exemplary.

"There's no problem, Carl," Ben called up to him. "It's nothing urgent."

Carl began the descent down the ladder. He still favored one leg but never complained. He actually looked somewhat healthier, Ben thought, since he had started working. Maybe the fresh air and exercise had done him good.

"I wanted to talk to you anyway, Reverend. I'm just about done with this list you gave me last week." Carl fished in his shirt pocket and pulled out a grubby piece of paper, the list of repairs that needed to be done around the building and grounds.

"Done already? That was fast." Ben took the list in hand and reviewed it, noticing Carl's scrawled notes and check marks, as well as the careful accounting he had kept of the costs of supplies. The reverend had given him two-hundred dollars in petty cash. The church had an account at the hardware store in town, but he thought that it would do Carl good to see that he was trusted with the money. People tend to live up to the expectations others have of them, Ben had always noticed.

"What's this note here about the window?" Ben squinted through his glasses, unable to read Carl's writing.

"Oh, that . . . that was the window I busted when I broke in that night. I thought you ought to take the cost of fixing it out of my pay." Carl shrugged, as if it were unimportant.

The reverend looked at him a moment, then back at the list. He wanted to keep this as a reminder, to show the naysayers in the congregation—a small but vocal contingent who had come to him after service on Sunday, unhappy to learn that Carl had been hired. Ben had stood his ground, reminding them of their Christian duty, exhorting them to take a more compassionate attitude toward their unfortunate brother. They had backed down, but Ben knew they were watching from a distance, waiting for the slightest excuse to make Carl go.

The list gave Ben heart. It renewed his faith in the capacity of people to grow, to turn over a new leaf. Not only had Carl completed the tasks in record time, he had chipped in money from his own pay to make amends for his mistake.

"All right, Carl. Thanks. I'll put that on the record." Ben looked up at him. "You're doing a fine job here so far. I'm pleased with your work."

"Um, thanks. Is that what you wanted to say to me?"

"Actually, I wanted to talk to you about Easter. It's coming up about three weeks from now."

Carl laughed. "I remember Easter, Reverend. I'm not that far gone."

"Good to hear it. My prayers are working then. The thing is, the church should really look picture-perfect on Easter Sunday. I mean, as close as you can get it. I know we've let things go around here. But I've seen what you can do in just a week. I have a feeling you'll pull it all together beautifully."

Carl looked pleased by his praise, Ben thought, but also as if he now felt a bit of pressure.

"Well, I'll do what I can, I guess. It depends on what you have in mind. This is a pretty old building, Reverend."

"That it is. There's always something in need of repair. The first church was built here, oh, around 1660. Right after the town was founded. It was just clapboard, and at some point, it burned down. This church was built to replace it in the early 1800s. They say right after it was finished a huge blizzard hit, and the minister was trapped inside for a week with only a bag of clams. He came out promising he'd never eat a clam again."

"I can believe that." Carl grinned and looked up at the church steeple. "The place sure could use a coat of paint. But I don't know how my leg will hold up on a ladder all that time."

"Painting wasn't even on the list. It's a good suggestion, though. Maybe during the summer we can get to that, when your leg is feeling better. I guess I'm talking more about a general sprucing up—waxing the floors, some new varnish on the pews, cleaning the windows, that sort of thing. You could paint just the front doors, I suppose."

"Sure, I can do that. You just write it all down, and I'll get to work on it."

"All right, I will. I'll see you later then." Ben nodded at Carl and continued walking down the path that ran along the side of the church.

When he reached the side door, he turned and looked back. Carl stood by the ladder, carefully stirring the unctuous black mixture in the can. Dressed in his painter's cap, coveralls, and sweatshirt, he looked like any workman, starting off his day, focusing on the task he'd been set, putting interest and heart into the work of his hands.

That was good, Ben thought. Carl had come to this place a rootless wanderer with no purpose or direction. Now he was evolving into something else altogether.

MOLLY HAD NOT SPOKEN TO MATTHEW IN A WEEK, NOT since the night she'd gone out to the airport to pick up her parents. He had left a message on her machine on Wednesday, but she didn't call him back. That was amazing to her, when she stopped to think about it. She figured he was calling to apologize, and she hadn't been ready at the time to talk to him about their confrontation.

But now it was Friday night. Amanda was coming for a sleepover, and Molly knew she had to face him.

Amanda walked in, toting her duffel bag and looking as

relaxed as if she lived there. "Hi, Molly. Sorry I'm late. Dad got stuck at the office."

"That's okay, honey. Lauren's waiting for you. She's in her room."

Amanda sauntered off, and Molly was left alone with Matthew. He stood in the doorway, looking hesitant. He looked handsome, too, she couldn't help noticing, dressed in a gray suit and blue shirt with an expensive-looking silk tie that hung loose around his neck.

"Would you like to come in for some coffee or something?" Molly asked politely.

"Uh, no thanks." He smiled, looking uneasy. "I have to get over to the hospital and check on a patient."

"Oh, sure." Molly nodded. She felt nervous seeing him again but glad at the same time. It was strange. She had expected to still be mad at him, yet she wasn't.

"I need to pick up Amanda on the early side tomorrow. We have to drive out to Worcester for a family party. My dad's going to be seventy."

"How nice. That's a big event."

"My mother seems to think so," he noted with a laugh.

"What time would you like to pick her up?"

"About nine? I promised we would be there in time to help set up. Oh, she has a special outfit to wear in that hanging bag. I'm sure she'll remember. But just in case."

"I'll do my best." Molly had to smile. "You know how they are. I can barely get them to go to sleep before sunrise."

"Sure, I understand. Let her have a good time. She can sleep more in the car."

"I'll set a few alarm clocks," she promised. "That usually works."

"Oh, sure. Good idea."

He smiled back at her, looking as if he wanted to say something more, something important.

She didn't know what to do. He didn't seem to be leaving, but he didn't seem to be staying, either.

"It's good to see you," he said finally.

"Um . . . thanks. It's nice to see you."

Another long awkward pause. Now he was staring at the carpet in the hallway. He was driving her crazy. She wanted to just shake him, but she didn't have the nerve, of course.

Finally, he looked up at her again. "Listen, Molly . . . I tried to call you this week. Maybe you didn't get the message or something."

"Oh, right." She felt instantly embarrassed. "I'm sorry. I was in such a rush this week, I guess I forgot to get back to you."

"That's okay. I just wanted to apologize again for the other night. What I said to you about Phil—I should have never spoken to you like that. I'm truly sorry if I hurt your feelings. I know you're just trying to do what's best for the girls."

She didn't know how to reply. She didn't want to start imagining things again, but it really seemed as if he'd been thinking about this a lot. Thinking about her.

"It's okay, Matt. I have to admit I was a little miffed at you. Well, a lot miffed. I nearly broke the sound barrier driving down to Logan," she admitted with a small smile. "But a funny thing happened this week. Phil did it again. He called on Wednesday, which isn't his night, and asked to take the girls to his mother's house for dinner. I nearly said no, just on principle. Then I looked at the way Lauren and Jill were staring at me, and I said okay."

"You did?" Matthew looked surprised.

It had taken a few days of licking her wounds, but she realized there was some truth to what Matthew told her. When she took a good look at Lauren and Jill's sullen faces, she knew that she had to lighten up on their father.

"Even if Phil hasn't really changed, I have to give him the benefit of the doubt for now. At least, I have to try. And you were right. I have to stop reacting to him the way I did seven years ago." She shook her head and grinned at him. "For one thing, it's not very attractive to get hysterical all the time."

"Oh, I don't know," he joked. "I like to be around women who can really express their emotions."

"That was diplomatic," Molly said with a laugh.

"Well, it's true. . . . I like to be around you, right?"

She met his warm gaze, then looked away, a firm grip on the doorknob. She hoped he couldn't tell that she suddenly needed the solid support.

"Mom, did you order the pizza yet? We're totally starving." Feeling dazed, Molly turned around to find Lauren, Amanda, and Jill staring at her.

"In a minute. I'll be right there," she promised. She turned back to Matthew, feeling three sets of eyes boring into her back.

"I guess I'd better order the pizza."

"Looks like you might have a mutiny on your hands otherwise. Well, good night. See you tomorrow," he said lightly. "Good night, Amanda," he called to his daughter.

"Good night, Dad. What are you still doing here anyway?"

"Just talking to Molly." Molly glanced at him, noticing the color suddenly rise in his cheeks. She was totally charmed.

Matthew disappeared down the hallway, and Molly shut the door with a sigh. She wished she had time to sit and analyze his behavior, word by word, look by look, hitting the mental replay button freely. But that would have to wait. Right now, she had to order a pizza and referee a sleepover.

MOLLY WOKE TO THE ANNOYING BUZZ OF HER ALARM clock. She peered at it with one eye and slapped the off button. It was Saturday. She didn't need to get up. She closed her eyes, instantly falling back to sleep again. Until a second alarm clock went off on the other side of the bed. She scrambled toward it like a crab, scuttling under the sheets, then realized Jill was sleeping in her bed, hidden under the blankets. She must have wandered in during the middle of the night, probably to escape the teenage talk fest in the other bedroom.

Molly reached over her and grabbed the second alarm clock, amazed that Jill didn't budge an inch. This one made a nature sound, like waves lapping on a shoreline. Sometimes it sounded more like water sloshing around the washing machine, but what do you expect for seven ninety-nine at the discount store?

She sat up and sighed, finally silencing the sound.

Then she remembered why she had set two alarm clocks. Matt was coming in less than an hour to pick up Amanda. She had to wake her up and get her ready.

Molly got out of bed and grabbed her robe. Her eyes felt scratchy. She had managed to stay up until about midnight reading a book, then finally drifted off to sleep.

The girls were still awake when she fell asleep. She was sure that they had stayed up into the single digit hours. Well, it was only once in a while, she thought, as she quietly entered Lauren's dark room. It was nice to see that they were such close friends. These are the memories you treasure and look back on—staying up all night with your best friend, trying on each other's clothes, and talking about teachers and boys or whatever.

She lifted a shade to let in a little light, then turned to Jill's bed, where Amanda was curled up in her sleeping bag. "Amanda, honey. It's time to get up. Your dad will be here soon."

Amanda rolled over and stretched, her eyes still closed.

Molly's eyes widened as she stared at Amanda's hair. What in heaven's name? She ran to the bed, silently praying that she didn't really see what she thought she saw.

No, it was true. Amanda's beautiful auburn hair was chopped into a ragged chin-length bob and colored a hideous, iridescent shade of red. Or maybe it was really more of a purple, Molly thought, feeling her stomach knot with nerves.

She quickly turned to look at Lauren. Just as she feared, an almost identical makeover.

"Amanda. Lauren! Wake up this instant! What in the world have you two done to your hair?"

The two girls sat up and stared at her groggily. Amanda focused on Molly and a look of sheer panic took hold of her.

"It's henna, Mom," Lauren said reassuringly. "It's not like dye or anything."

"Does it wash out?" Molly asked.

"Um, well it's supposed to. But I'm not really sure."

"We really thought it did, Molly. Lauren read the box, and it sounded like you could wash it right out."

Oh, dear. They must have tried already. That isn't a good sign.

"Where's the box?" Molly asked desperately.

"It's in the bathroom somewhere, I guess." Lauren shrugged her thin shoulders under her T-shirt.

Molly ran into the bathroom. It was strewn with wet towels that had purple streaks. She found the box on the floor and snatched it up, searching for the instructions. Yes, it did say it washed out—in four to six weeks.

"Four to six weeks!" She screamed the words out loud.

She ran back into the bedroom and glared at the girls, waving the box in the air. "Four to six weeks. It says so right on the package. How could you do this to yourselves? And what about those haircuts? What did you use, Lauren, a grapefruit spoon? What in the world possessed you?"

"I'm sorry, Molly. We just wanted to do something fun. My dad's going to have a fit," Amanda said.

Yes, he was. Molly felt like crying herself just thinking about facing him. Amanda's eyes were brimming with tears, and Molly knew she couldn't be too hard on her. Besides, she was sure this whole thing was Lauren's idea.

She spun around to face her daughter, who was scrunched

in the corner of her bed, her back against the wall, as if she wanted to melt right through it.

"Lauren Marie, how could you? Look at Amanda's hair. Her father is going to be furious!"

"But I did it, too," Lauren pointed out.

"That is not the point! You know you shouldn't have done something like this without my permission. And you know I never would have let you dye your hair."

"It's not dye, Mom. It's henna. It's all natural, no chemicals. They used it all the time in ancient Egypt," Lauren informed her, sounding like a TV infomercial.

Molly felt her head pounding, as if the top were going to blow right off. She took a deep breath and closed her eyes.

God, give me patience, she silently prayed.

When she opened her eyes, they were both staring at her, looking suitably terrified.

"Into the bathroom, both of you. I'm going to see if I can get that stuff out."

Lauren and Amanda glanced at each other. They slowly slipped out of their beds and headed toward the bathroom. Lauren glanced over her shoulder at Molly. "You can try if you want," she said in a small voice. "But I don't think this is going to work."

Molly had a feeling Lauren was right. Still, she had to try. She wondered if Matthew would notice if she sent Amanda home in a big, floppy hat. . . .

MATTHEW ARRIVED PROMPTLY AT NINE. THE GIRLS SPOTted his car driving up and parking in front of Molly's building. Amanda was ready and waiting in the special outfit she had brought for her grandfather's party. She looked lovely, Molly thought.

Except, of course, for her hair.

"Oh, no. My dad's here." Amanda turned to Molly, looking stricken. "Would you just tell him what happened before he sees me, Molly, please? Like sort of break the news to him?"

Molly swallowed hard. The old story about the messenger who brings bad news came to mind. Especially the ending.

Last night she had once again imagined she had some chance of dating Matt. But this unexpected calamity would put them back to square one, she expected. Or even further, into a negative zone, if there was one.

The door buzzer sounded. Molly gulped. "Okay, you two stay in here," she said to the girls. "I'll go talk to him first."

"Thanks, Molly." The look of gratitude on Amanda's face bolstered Molly's courage.

"That's okay, Amanda. Don't worry. I have on my bulletproof vest."

She heard them giggle nervously as she headed for the front door. She took a deep breath and pulled the door open.

"Good morning. Sorry to make everyone get up so early on Saturday." Matt smiled at her, but she could hardly smile back. "Is Amanda ready?"

"She's all dressed and packed," Molly reported. "Come on in a minute."

"Sure." Matthew stepped inside. He, too, had dressed up for the occasion in a navy blue blazer, khaki pants, a white shirt, and a red-patterned tie. He looked like one of those ads for men's clothes where the guys are always hopping off sailboats. His dark hair was still wet from the shower, slicked back on his head.

Of course, they'd have to be going to a major family party today on top of it all. Just my luck.

"So, where is she? Does she know I'm here?" He rubbed his hands together and looked down at Molly.

"Yes, she saw you drive up. She's in the living room with Lauren. . . . It's just that I need to talk to you a minute."

He stared at her. She could tell he suspected this was something personal, about their relationship—or about the relationship they didn't actually have, Molly corrected herself.

"It's about Amanda," she said quickly. "She and Lauren were up very late last night. I must have fallen asleep. I didn't hear a thing—"

"She's not hurt or anything?" he broke in.

"Oh, no, nothing like that. But they decided to give themselves new hairdos." She swallowed hard. "With henna, actually."

"Henna? What in the world is that?"

"It's all natural, a plant extract. The ancient Egyptians used it."

His expression changed from mild alarm to what Molly would describe as Code Red. Sirens screamed and red whirling lights flashed in his eyes.

"Let me see her, will you?" he said curtly. He nearly pushed Molly aside as he made tracks for the living room.

Amanda sat in the corner of the sofa, her hands pressed between her knees. She peered up at her father.

"Hi, Dad," she said weakly.

Matthew's face turned pale as paper. "Amanda . . . *what* in the world did you do to yourself?"

"It's only my hair. It will grow back, you know." Her voice trailed off, and tears squeezed out of the corners of her eyes.

"Your beautiful hair! For goodness' sake, we have to go to Grandpa's party! Doesn't this stuff wash out?"

"Well, it did wash out a little," Molly put in.

"You mean it looked worse than this?"

"A little brighter, I guess. The box said four to six weeks. But if you work at it with strong shampoo, I think you can get it out quicker than that. Or you could have Amanda's hair dyed her regular color so you wouldn't notice it so much."

"Great!" Matthew took a deep breath. He looked down at his daughter again, then back up at Molly.

She braced herself for what was coming next.

"How could you let this happen? I send her over here, trusting you to take care of her. This is totally irresponsible!"

Molly nodded, realizing she did deserve to take some of the heat for this episode.

"I'm sorry, Matthew. Really. But I had no idea that they were still even up—"

"You should have had some idea. What would it take? Maybe if they'd shaved their heads bald, you would have heard the electric razor?"

"Now, please. Try to calm down. Lauren did the same exact thing to herself," Molly pointed out. "I was furious at first, too. But really, it's just hair. It will grow out."

"Sure, maybe by the time she's in college," he railed.

Molly was shocked at his temper. Matthew was normally so easygoing. She knew the hair thing was bad, but he was overreacting just a bit, wasn't he?

"Matthew, girls do things like this to themselves from time to time. It's really just part of the territory."

"Not my territory! This wouldn't have happened if they had been at my house, I'll tell you that much."

"Oh, really?" Now Molly felt angry, too. He wasn't such a perfect parent. If anything, he didn't give Amanda enough breathing room. "You know, after a certain age, parents really don't have all that much control. But I don't think you've really faced that. Maybe Amanda just needed to experiment, to express herself."

Amanda and Lauren glanced at each other, shocked to hear Molly defending their case.

Matthew's face turned red, either with embarrassment because he knew what she said was true or because he was now even madder at her.

"Thanks for the insight. I didn't know you were a psychologist now, too. I guess the advice comes with the new hairstyle—a package deal?"

"No charge," she snapped back.

"Come on, Amanda. Where are your things?"

"By the door," she squeaked.

"Okay, let's go." He glanced at Molly. "I'd thank you for having her over, but—"

"Skip it. I won't tell Miss Manners on you."

Molly stood with her arms crossed over her chest. She didn't even look at him as he walked past.

Matt picked up Amanda's duffel and sleeping bag. "Say good-bye, Amanda. I'll be waiting in the car." With that he swept out the door.

Amanda glanced back at Lauren, who now trailed behind her.

"Bye, Lauren. See you in school Monday . . . if my father doesn't ground me for the rest of my life."

"He won't." Despite her mood, Molly had to smile.

"Don't worry," Lauren reminded her in a whisper. "You know how they get. He'll get over it in a day or two."

"I hope so." Amanda stopped in front of Molly. "I'm sorry he yelled at you. But thanks for telling him for me."

"That's okay, honey." Molly reached out and touched her hair. "It doesn't look so bad. I'm kind of getting used to it."

Amanda smiled, her braces glittering. "Thanks. I am, too."

A few moments later Molly and Lauren stood by the window and watched the Land Rover disappear down Main Street.

She wasn't sure if she should laugh or cry. *Well, another relationship goes down the drain,* Molly thought. *If only the henna had disappeared so easily.*

Chapter Thirteen

FRAN DECIDED TO WEAR HER NEW SUIT TO CHURCH. It was linen and had a long jacket in a tasteful toast color that went well with her reddish-brown hair. She buttoned the jacket, smoothing the edge of her silk blouse underneath. It would do, she thought. She had to run an open house today in the estate section near Lilac Hall, the old Warwick mansion. She still had a million things to do: set up the signs, check to make sure the house was in order, set up the flowers, and study the specs one more time. Wealthier buyers asked more questions, she noticed.

Betty had asked her to handle the property at the last minute. Not that Fran was complaining. Although Betty had brought in the listing, she promised Fran a full percentage if she sold it. Betty was good that way.

Besides, Betty had other worries right now. She had to drive down to Connecticut this weekend to visit her son. Fran felt badly for her. Betty rarely let on, but Fran knew that it had been difficult for her ever since her son asked to live with his father. She didn't know what she would do if she and Tucker ever split and the kids had to live away from her, even on weekends.

She slipped on her rings and her watch and a gold bracelet, then checked her appearance in the mirror. All she needed was her diamond stickpin, the perfect touch for this outfit. She found the velvet box in the top drawer of her dresser but opened it to find the box empty. She checked the other boxes carefully, one by one, but didn't find the pin. She didn't keep much jewelry in the house. Most of it was at the bank in a safe-deposit box. There weren't too many boxes to look through.

Fran removed the boxes and searched the drawer, thinking it could have fallen out somehow. She shook out a few scarves and a pair of gloves. But then the drawer was empty and, still, no pin.

Her best piece of jewelry. She felt panicked. Tucker had it specially made and gave it to her for their anniversary two years ago. Tucker would be so upset if she had lost it somewhere.

"Fran, what's taking you so long? We're going to be late."

Tucker stood in the doorway, an impatient look on his face. He wore a sports jacket and gray pants; a tie hung loosely around his neck. "The kids are already outside. Mike's going to start shooting baskets, and he'll look like a mess in no time."

"Come in a second . . . and shut the door," she said quietly.

He looked puzzled but did as she asked. "What is it? What's the matter?"

She picked up the empty case and showed it to him. "I wanted to wear my stickpin today. But look, it's gone."

Tucker glanced at the box for a moment. "Well, maybe you just put it someplace else. Did you check?"

"I looked through everything. I took everything out of the drawer. It's not here. I'm positive."

Tucker's mouth tightened to a thin line. "Maybe you

took it off someplace. You could have left it at work. Or it might be stuck on some other dress in your closet."

"I'd never take it off and just leave it somewhere. Don't be silly." She was very careful with her belongings, especially jewelry. "It was right in that box. I'm sure of it."

"What are you trying to say, Fran? It didn't disappear into thin air."

"It's perfectly obvious," she said. "Carl took it. He must have. Nobody else has been here."

Tucker's reply was immediate. "You don't know that. Maybe you just put it someplace else. Or brought it down to the bank."

"I'd remember going to the bank with it, Tucker. The pin was right in my dresser drawer." Fran paused, trying to calm her rising frustration. What would it take to get through to Tucker? He was completely blind where his half brother was concerned. "It's got to be Carl. I can't see any other explanation for it."

Tucker looked angry now, his jaw set in a tight line. "You're just mad because Carl is staying here longer. That pin could be anywhere. Maybe you lost it."

"I didn't lose it."

"Well, I'm not going to accuse Carl of something like that without a shred of proof. So maybe you ought to look harder."

TUCKER MARCHED OUT OF THE BEDROOM, NOT KNOWING what to think. The trouble was, he could imagine Carl taking the stickpin. Yet he drew back from that image. He wanted to believe his brother had changed. But Fran sounded so sure that she had left the pin in the box. What else could have happened to it? There weren't too many explanations left.

He felt his gut clench as he saw Carl standing at the bottom of the stairs. He must have heard every word, despite the closed door. It was a small house with thin walls; voices carried.

Carl stepped aside to let him pass. "I'll go. You don't have to say anything."

Tucker turned to him. "Did you take that pin, yes or no?"

The second he asked the question he knew he had made a mistake.

Carl's head jerked back at a sharp angle. "Why even ask? Sounds like you already know."

"What's that supposed to mean?"

"I didn't take your wife's jewelry. But you think I did. Same difference to me."

Tucker was instantly sorry. But it was too late. The damage was done. "I didn't mean it like that. Fran is upset up there. I was only asking you."

"Sure, who else would you ask? Tell her I'm leaving. That should cheer her up again."

Carl started walking back toward his room. Tucker wanted to tell him to wait. But he didn't. He would talk to him later, after church. When they had all calmed down.

BEN WALKED INTO HIS OFFICE, PICKED UP A LETTER HE wanted to answer, and slipped it into his jacket pocket. He didn't notice Carl sitting in the straight-backed chair by the door until he turned to go, and when he did, he jumped back in surprise.

"Carl . . . in heaven's name. You startled me."

"Sorry. The door was open, so I came in here to wait. You took a long time out there."

"There was a meeting of the youth group after coffee hour. What are you doing here? Is something wrong?"

"Well, yes and no. See, the thing is I need to go. Leave town, I mean. I thought you might give me some of my pay if you have any cash on hand, Reverend."

"Oh. I see." Ben suspected it was something like that.

He had noticed the tattered pack leaning against the chair. But why so suddenly? Just yesterday he had seen Carl and everything seemed fine.

"Of course. I don't mind giving you your pay. But first, will you tell me why you're leaving so suddenly? You didn't mention a word about this yesterday."

"Oh, I don't know. It just seems time. The weather is warmer and all. I feel better, too."

Ben caught his eye. "The weather has been warmer for a while now, Carl. Did something happen today? Did someone say something to you?"

Carl looked down at the floor for a long moment and rubbed his chin. "Fran thinks I stole a piece of jewelry out of her dresser drawer. I didn't. . . . But that's what she thinks."

Ben felt the words like a blow. No wonder he was leaving. Ben could hardly blame him.

"What about Tucker? What did he say?"

"He asked me if I did it. Not exactly saying I did. But what's the difference? He wouldn't ask you."

Ben knew that was true. He paused, wondering what he should say. It seemed so wrong for Carl to leave this way.

Help me, Lord. I need some words here. He's doing so well. I need to persuade him to stay.

Ben sat down in a chair next to Carl. "Listen, Carl. I know you're angry. You have every right to be. But if you go now, Fran will only think she was right to accuse you. Don't run away as if you were guilty."

Carl considered his words, then shook his head. "What's the difference? There's only going to be more of this."

"There is a difference, a real difference. You said before Tucker wouldn't ask me if I stole the jewelry. That's true. What would I do if he did? I wouldn't run away, right?"

Ben watched Carl think about the question, then he slowly nodded. "No, I guess not."

"Well, it's the same for you, Carl. You have nothing to

be ashamed of, nothing to run away from. But you do have a reason to stay. You've got a job here, and you're good at it. I don't want you to quit on me now. We were just getting started. What about Easter?"

Carl frowned. "What about it?"

"You were fixing up the church for Easter. You still have a long list."

"Oh, yeah, the list."

"You like the job, right?"

"Sure, I like working here. It's quiet. Nobody's breathing down my neck every minute, getting on my case."

Ben's hopes sparked. "You do have your autonomy. That's hard to find."

"Tell me about it." Carl shifted in his chair. "The thing is, I can't go back to Tucker's house anymore."

Ben understood, but he felt bad for Tucker. He had tried hard. It just hadn't worked out.

"Maybe it's time to find your own place. You can stay here tonight if you want. There's a cot in the infirmary, over near the classrooms. You can make yourself something to eat in the pantry. I'm sure there's plenty of food. Tomorrow I'll help you find a room to rent in town. I know a place or two we can try."

Carl glanced up at him, looking pleased with the suggestion. "All right. That might work out."

"I'm sure it will. I know you're angry, Carl. But it's better not to run. You'll just take all of this with you. If you stay, you have some chance of moving beyond it someday."

Carl nodded. "I know what you mean. I'm not surprised at Fran. But Tucker . . ." He shook his head.

"I know. But think of all he's done for you since you got here. That should count for more than a few words spoken in anger. Everyone loses his patience once in a while."

Carl chose to ignore that. "I guess you need to get home, Reverend. Just show me where the cot is. I'll be okay."

Feeling relieved, Ben silently thanked the Lord for his help. It was disheartening to see that after all Tucker had done, Carl was now mad at him. But at least Carl was staying. There was still a chance they would make amends. Ben would pray for it.

AFTER CHURCH ON SUNDAY, MATTHEW DROVE OUT TO the beach with Amanda. It seemed the perfect day to walk to the lighthouse on Durham Point Beach. The warm sunshine beat down from a clear sky, and the breeze from the water was soft and mild. Amanda was so elated, she immediately kicked off her sneakers and ran down to the shoreline. Then she pulled off her heavy sweatshirt and tossed it on the sand.

"Look at the water, Dad. Isn't it great?" she called back to him.

"Yes, it's beautiful here today," he agreed.

Worcester was so far inland, they hardly ever got to an ocean beach. There were lakes, of course, but nothing compared to this.

Amanda seemed to think so, too. He saw her lean over to roll up the legs of her jeans and suspected she was going to get her feet wet. He started to call out to her, then stopped himself. She could get her feet wet if she wanted to. She wasn't going to catch pneumonia. He was too protective sometimes.

Watching her from this distance, it was startling to him to see that she was quickly evolving into a young woman. Some traces of the little girl remained but fewer and fewer every day. With her hair cut short like that, she resembled her mother, especially from far away.

He wondered how Sharon would have reacted to the new hairdo. Probably better than he had, he thought. A chest-beating father gorilla would have handled it with more sensitivity. He sat on a driftwood log that had washed up above the shoreline and watched Amanda amble along, squealing at the cold water every time her feet touched the foam.

He had tried to have a father-daughter talk with Amanda

on the way to Worcester, but it ended up as a screaming match—their first. He had been nearly as shocked by her temper and rebellious attitude as he had been by the new hair color. For heaven's sake, what was in that stuff? he wondered.

By the time they had reached his parents' house, Amanda wasn't speaking to him, and he was almost too exhausted to explain her appearance.

But then his sister Erica reminded him of the time she had actually burned off chunks of her hair with an iron, trying to make it straight. Remembering that event did give him some perspective.

He expected his parents to be appalled, especially since they loved to show off their granddaughter to all their family and friends. But they seemed to find Amanda's outrageous behavior absolutely charming. His mother made a great fuss, saying Amanda looked very exotic, like a cover girl on a magazine.

"Don't worry, dear. She's just acting her age. It's good to see her misbehaving a little. I think it shows she's getting past her grief a little. I do worry sometimes that she's too perfect," his mother had confided to him.

Interesting . . . Molly had said just about the same thing. He hadn't given her any credit for the insight, though. Just the opposite in fact. *Maybe I should have thanked her instead of blaming her,* he thought, feeling badly.

Now he realized it was one of the first times Amanda had ever gotten into real trouble and acted like a regular kid, not some robot child, shy and uptight and too worried about the rules to have any fun. Wasn't that one of the reasons he had moved to Cape Light, so that Amanda could make a new start and open up a little?

He saw her coming back, chasing some birds down at the water's edge. Her beautiful long hair didn't trail behind anymore, like little girls in picture books. She looked more like a rock singer on the cover of a CD.

But maybe that was okay. More than okay, it was the

way it should be right now. He couldn't keep Amanda from growing up, from moving away from him. They both had to move forward, to embrace the new—even if it meant strange hairdos. At least she'd found the courage to try, he realized.

Amanda ran up to him and flopped on the sand at his feet. She looked breathless but happy. "What are you doing up here, Dad?"

"Oh, I don't know. Just thinking."

"About Mom?" she asked quietly.

"A little," he admitted. "I was thinking that she'd probably like your new hair."

"I don't know," Amanda said. "It's not exactly . . . perfect."

"Maybe not," he allowed, "but your mother knew that thing that all women seem to know: It's only hair. It grows back. It's not the end of the world if you have fun with it." He smiled at her. "So, I was wondering what I would look like in a pink Mohawk and maybe an earring or two?"

Amanda stared at him a moment, then shook her head, her face deadpan. "Uh, no. I don't *think* so."

Her tone was so purely teenage sounding, he just had to laugh.

SOPHIE WOKE EARLY, WELL BEFORE HER USUAL TIME. SHE wasn't sure why. It was almost as if a hand had jostled her shoulder, which was an uncanny feeling. What day was it? Tuesday, she realized. A week since Gus's funeral. She bowed her head and said a silent prayer.

Then she climbed out of bed, scuffing to the kitchen in her slippers as her hands automatically pulled some pins from her robe pocket and pinned up her hair.

She heard people needed less sleep when they got older, but that had rarely been her experience. *Maybe it's getting to me now,* she thought. She set up the coffeepot and peered out the window. It was not quite light out. A heavy mist settled among the trees, making the orchard look dreamlike.

Sophie poured a cup of coffee and took a sip, her gaze still fixed on the trees. Then she turned and walked to the mud room. She pulled Gus's old green barn jacket from a peg and put it on over her robe and nightgown. She sat on the bench and stuck her bare feet into a pair of work boots. She found some gloves in the pocket and put those on, too, then covered her head with a wool cap. She opened the side door, the cool moist air shocking her fully awake. She paused for just a moment, then stepped outside, breathing in the rich, misty air.

It was chilly now, but it would warm up nicely today, she predicted. Sunlight glowed on the far horizon, dabbing the gray predawn sky with a rosy hue. The sun would burn off this mist in a few hours. It would be a clear, sunny day. A spring day, she realized, walking toward the apple trees.

There was so much to do out here. The trees needed attention, a knowing hand. There was pruning to take care of and the ground to clear. Fertilizer was needed. She should do a check for cocoons and insects.

Sophie reached up to touch a branch as if she were reaching for the hand of an old friend. It didn't make much sense to do any of that now. Not with the land going up for sale soon, and someone coming along and knocking all these trees down to build houses, most likely. There was slim chance of finding a buyer who would keep the orchard running. Her son, Bart, had told her she had a better chance of getting hit by lightening.

Sophie sighed. That was probably true, though he didn't have to put it so bluntly. She noticed a rake on the ground and bent to pick it up. Had it been out here all winter? She and Gus had grown careless last fall with Gus's health failing. They never would have forgotten a good tool like this otherwise.

She picked it up and began raking the ground around the tree roots, gathering the dried leaves and winter's debris into a small pile. Without thinking, she moved on down the row, raking another area. She lost herself in the rhythm of the work, not noticing the sun rising or the time passing. She lost herself in thoughts of the past and found herself humming a familiar song as she worked along.

"Grandma! What are you doing out here?"

Sophie looked up to find Miranda staring at her. Her tall, long-limbed body looked hastily dressed in sweats. Her long thick hair was a mess, making her appear as if she had just tumbled out of bed.

"Oh dear, you startled me." Sophie stood back, leaning on the rake. She pressed her hand to her chest and laughed.

"Are you okay, Gram?" Miranda's concerned look made her want to laugh even harder.

"Of course, I'm okay. I just woke up early for some reason and felt like getting some air. I saw this rake on the ground and thought I would make myself useful." She sighed and looked around at the apple trees. "There's so much work to be done out here—spring work. I know nobody is going to buy this place and keep the trees, but I hate to neglect them."

Miranda gently took the rake from her grandmother's hands. "Let's forget about the packing. We can work out here today, if you like. You never know. Someone might want the orchard. You don't want the trees to look shabby. It would bring down the price."

"I'll say it would." They both knew Sophie didn't care much about the price. But she did take great pride in her trees.

"Just tell me what to do. I always used to come and help you and Granddad when I was in high school."

"I remember." Sophie glanced at Miranda, then back at the row of trees. "It would be nice if we could just prune back some of these stray branches and maybe clear up the ground a bit. So the roots can get the fertilizer."

"All right. I'll go get a wheelbarrow and some tools from the shed."

"Get some for me, too, honey. I'm not a bit tired."

Miranda smiled at her over her shoulder. "You don't look tired, Grandma. You look raring to go." Then she stopped and turned to face her. "I do think you ought to go back inside and put some clothes on, though. Just in case somebody stops by to say hello."

Sophie glanced down at herself and laughed. "I'm out here in my nightgown, for goodness' sake. I almost forgot." She looked up at Miranda and shook her head. "Guess I got carried away."

"I guess so," Miranda agreed. She looked up at the sky which had turned a deep shade of blue. "It's going to be a great day. We can get a lot done."

"Yes. We'll get a lot done out here today," Sophie agreed happily. She turned and headed for the house, eager to change into her clothes and get back to work.

"HERE ARE SOME SAMPLE MENUS I'VE PUT TOGETHER FOR you. This one is mainly seafood," Molly pointed out. "This one is a little more gourmet—more exotic ingredients, different sauces. This one is pretty standard, a lot of all-time crowd pleasers. But you can switch things around if you like. Or if there's something special you have in mind, we can figure that in, too."

Emily glanced at the menus with interest, her reading glasses perched on the tip of her nose. "Hmmm, these look good," she said.

Molly took a breath. She had been talking nonstop since she arrived and hoped she didn't sound as if she were babbling. They sat in Emily's living room, with Molly's papers and photos of table settings spread out on the couch and coffee table. Molly had arrived at five. Her mother was at her place, visiting with the girls. It was now after six, but they weren't quite done. Emily had some idea of what she wanted the event to be like; so far, though, she seemed to be an easygoing client.

Which was a good thing, Molly knew, since she wasn't sure how she would handle anyone tougher. She was barely out of Catering 101. Preparing for this appointment had been a do-it-yourself crash course. Thank goodness her teacher had given her lots of advice about what to bring along and key points to discuss. She even loaned her a book with photos of table settings and told her where she could find samples of table linen and flatware to show. Lauren had helped her type out menus on the computer. Her teacher had also encouraged Molly's classmates to help out to gain some practical experience, so there was her staff . . . if she needed one.

"Just try to play the part," Betty had advised in a last-minute pep talk. "I know you feel like you're faking it, but you're really not. It's just a new side of your personality, one you're going to see a lot more of."

Molly did feel a little as if she were acting. So far Emily hadn't asked any questions she couldn't answer, but she kept waiting for Emily to see through her act. It was funny how now she wanted this job so much when last week the entire idea seemed horrifying.

Finally Emily looked up, holding the menus out in front of her. "I like the idea of doing something a little different, not the same old buffet you see everywhere. I think most of this will be wonderful," she said, pointing to the gourmet choices. "And maybe you can add the ubiquitous ham or turkey, tucked away in the corner for the less adventurous eaters."

Molly laughed at her analysis, surprised to realize she even knew what *ubiquitous* meant, thanks to Jill's vocabulary list.

"I think we can do that. No problem." She jotted a note on a pad: *Add boring roast entrée.* Wow, this was really happening.

They went on to talk about the decor. Molly had a lot of ideas for creating an atmosphere that was both sophisticated and festive and even had suggestions for making the invitations match the party ambience. Emily seemed to love her ideas.

"I could have it here if we keep the guest list down. But the party seems to be growing by the hour." Emily gazed around. "It might be more comfortable at my mother's. The rooms are so much larger, especially if we're going to set up small tables at dinner time."

Molly gulped. Lillian Warwick's house? Now there was an unexpected speed bump. She didn't get along with Lillian Warwick. Last summer, after Lillian's stroke, she was hired to clean for her and bring over meals. The job came to an abrupt end when Lillian insulted her brother Sam, and Molly stomped out in a fury. Molly was sure Emily would remember and tried to keep her own expression blank. She couldn't risk making any waves. She was lucky to get this job at all.

"You know my mother's place. But maybe you'll need to look the house over again sometime. Just let me know," Emily suggested.

"Uh, sure. Once we get closer to the date." *If the old dragon will even let me in.*

Emily glanced at her, and Molly could tell she had guessed her thoughts. "Don't worry about my mother. I'll handle her."

"I'm not worried," Molly fibbed. She *was* worried about dealing with Lillian Warwick, but she was also worried about so many other issues that Lillian seemed just one hurdle among many.

Emily had some questions about the flowers, which distracted Molly from her worries about Lillian. The meeting wound up a few minutes later. Emily sat back on the couch and slipped off her glasses, looking pleased.

"Well, it takes a lot to put together a big party, doesn't it? I wouldn't really know where to begin on my own."

"You just have to show up and be the hostess—with your fiancé, of course."

"Oh, Dan hates parties. I'm surprised he even agreed to

this one. But he's a lot more social than he lets on once you get him out of the house."

Emily smiled at her, and Molly could see that she was really in love; her expression took on a glow just talking about her husband-to-be.

The two women parted with Molly agreeing to send Emily an estimate of the cost by the end of the week. As she walked down the path from Emily's house to her car, she felt like jumping in the air and shouting, "Yes!"

But she was afraid that someone would see, so she just smiled and said it softly to herself.

TEN MINUTES LATER MOLLY ARRIVED HOME AND WAS MET at the door by her mother. "How did it go?"

"Pretty good. Thank goodness, I can finally take off these shoes." She kicked off her dressy pumps and sighed with relief. Her poor feet were used to spending the day in cushy old sneakers. They were totally in shock.

"All we did was talk. I don't know why I'm so exhausted." She dumped her portfolio on the kitchen table and dropped down into a chair.

"Don't worry, dear. I know you can do it. Think of all the cooking you've done for our family parties. It's not so different."

Molly's father was a professional cook, and her mother was quite impressive in the kitchen as well. With her five siblings, there had always been something to celebrate. Or maybe her family just liked having big parties. Like her sisters and brothers, Molly had learned to cook from her dad. He always made it look easy and fun. It was true in a way; preparing for a party wasn't a big deal. It shouldn't be with her experience, anyway.

But there seemed to be so much riding on this. Molly almost felt as if she couldn't breathe if she thought about it too long.

"This is different, Mom. It's not just our family. I'm trying to start a real business here."

"Yes, dear. I know. Just don't let yourself get too stressed about it. That's not going to help you." Marie Morgan picked up a pot and dried it with a dish towel. "Emily's a nice lady. I've always liked her."

"Yes, she is nice," Molly agreed. "I was pretty surprised to hear she was getting married, though. She always seemed the forever-single type to me."

"Every pot has a lid." Her mother gave her a meaningful glance. "Even—"

"—yes, even the bent one," Molly finished for her. How many times had she heard that one? Clearly, she belonged in the bent-pot category, though her lid had yet to proclaim himself.

Her mother kept looking at her, making Molly feel distinctly uncomfortable. "What's the matter, Mom? Why are you looking at me like that?"

"You must be tired. You didn't even notice the flowers."

Molly followed her mother's gaze and suddenly saw a huge bouquet sitting on the counter by the phone. She got up to take a closer look.

It had to be Phil, always going for the grand gesture. What he was trying to trick her into now? Or was he apologizing for some slip up she didn't even know about yet?

"Where's the card?" she asked, looking around.

"I left it there by the phone book." Molly could feel her mother watching as she pulled the card from the tiny envelope.

Dear Molly,
So sorry I lost it on Saturday. You were right. It's a girl thing, and it's only hair. (I'm actually starting to like it . . . but don't tell Amanda.)

Thinking of you, Matthew

Molly laughed a little at his message, and her mother gave her a curious stare. "Who was it? I'm dying to know," she admitted.

"Oh, just this guy, the father of one of Lauren's friends." *Keep it vague,* she advised herself. *You'll have fewer questions to deal with later.*

"That new doctor?" Marie's eyes were bright with interest. "I've heard he's quite nice. People seem to like him already. Why did he send you flowers? Did you go out with him or something?"

"Mom, slow down." Molly gave her mother an exasperated look. "He got a little upset when Lauren and Amanda dyed their hair, and he just wanted to apologize."

"Oh. Well, that was considerate." Her mother looked a little disappointed, Molly thought, but not without hope.

Molly gazed at the flowers. It was a thoughtful gesture. That "thinking of you" part had given her hope again, too, though she hated to admit it.

Molly knew she had to call him now. The idea made her nervous. She would just thank him and see if he had anything more to say. *Like finally inviting me out on a date, for instance.*

"Dinner's almost ready," her mother said. "Why don't you call the girls? They're doing their homework."

"All right. What did you make for us?" Molly peeked under a pot as she passed the stove.

"Spaghetti and meatballs. Jill wanted it."

"Looks yummy. I'm starved." Molly touched her mother's shoulder as she left to get the girls. As much as she liked to cook, it was a sweet break when someone else did it so she could just relax and sit down at the table.

After the girls were in bed and her mother had gone, Molly made herself a cup of tea and took the phone into the living room. She had promised Betty she would call after seeing Emily. But first, she thought, she ought to call Matthew.

She felt silly, noticing how her hand shook as she

pressed the numbers. She hoped her voice wouldn't betray the butterflies in her stomach.

When was the last time she had called a man she really liked? She wasn't sure. Boring Micky didn't count. *When was the last time I even* met *a man I really liked, come to think of it?*

"Hello." Matthew's voice came on the other end of the line, and she coughed to clear her throat.

"Hi . . . it's me, Molly. Thank you for the flowers. They're really beautiful. You didn't have to go to all that trouble."

"Yes, I did. I was totally over the top. Amanda told me she was mortified. She had to have a long talk with me in the car about my behavior."

Molly laughed. At least he was starting to see the humor in the situation. "Sorry to hear it. I hope she wasn't too hard on you."

"Not so bad. She did let me watch TV tonight."

He sounded really happy to hear from her—and relieved. He must have thought she was angry at him. She had been so distracted getting ready to see Emily, she hadn't really had the time to dwell on it. Well, not as much as she had expected to.

"How was your father's party?"

"It was fine. It was good to see everybody. But I don't miss Worcester much. I guess Cape Light is starting to grow on me. Amanda and I went to the beach on Sunday and walked to the lighthouse. It was a beautiful day."

"Yes, it was almost like summer," she agreed.

He was prolonging the conversation. That seemed a good sign. For some reason, she didn't want to tell him about her appointment with Emily. It was all too new and tentative.

They talked about some events going on at school, safe topics, Molly thought. Then the conversation seemed to dwindle. Molly felt awkward, wondering if she should be the first to say she had to go.

"I noticed that there's some good music in Newburyport this weekend. On Saturday night at Bay Street Café," Matthew said suddenly. "It's jazz, a pianist who's really great. I know this is short notice, but I wondered if you would like to go with me?"

Molly couldn't answer. Had he actually asked her out on a real date, no children involved?

"Um, sure. I'd love to. That sounds like fun." She actually hated jazz but knew she couldn't say that. She also didn't think she would notice the music too much. She'd be too distracted by Matthew.

"Great. I think the first set starts at nine, but we can grab dinner first. How about we say around seven?"

"Seven sounds fine."

Molly hung up the phone, totally elated. Now she did jump up from the couch and pump her fist in the air. "Yes!" she said out loud.

She sank back onto the couch, quickly dialing Betty. She had a lot to report.

Chapter Fourteen

"So, you've finally got a Saturday off. What are you going to do today, honey?" Tucker bit into a slice of toast, looking interested in her answer.

Fran shrugged. "Just some spring cleaning. I guess I'll start in our bedroom. The curtains need to be washed. And maybe this afternoon we can give Scout a bath together. He's been looking a little scruffy lately."

"Poor Scout. I didn't realize he was on the list, too. I just don't have the heart to tell him. You'd better." Tucker's glum expression made her laugh.

"Come on, Tucker. It's almost halfway through April. You know I always do heavy cleaning in the spring."

"I remember. It's serious. Guess I'd better take the dog and clear out for the day."

"Good idea," she agreed with another laugh. She didn't often have a Saturday off from the office, and even though she knew it sounded terribly boring, she was secretly looking forward to a cleaning spree and having the house to herself for the day.

Fran cleared up the breakfast dishes, then headed for the master bedroom. She took the curtains down and washed the windows. The closet was next. There was a rummage sale coming up at the church, and she was sure her closet was stocked with donations.

She sorted out her clothes quickly, making piles on the bed for the cleaners and the rummage sale. Then she used the step stool to get at the handbags on the top shelf. There were so many dusty old bags up there, most of them totally out of style. She had to be careful with what she wore to work. She had to make a good impression on her clients.

She pulled down an old straw bag with a broken handle and tossed it on the floor. A suede fringed number followed; Mary Ellen might like that one, Fran thought. There was a leather bag behind that one, a shoulder bag she used to like a lot. She smoothed her hand over the leather flap. It still might do after a polish, she thought. She lifted the flap, noticing some loose change on the bottom, along with a pen that read Bowman Realty.

Then something else caught her eye. A small white box, the kind that jewelry comes in. She took it out and opened it.

Her diamond stickpin. She was so happy to see it. Then she felt a clutch in her chest, remembering how she had accused Carl. She was so sure he had stolen the pin. But here it was, sitting in her bag all along. How had it gotten in here? She stepped down from the stool, her legs feeling shaky.

She suddenly remembered. Months ago they'd had the bedrooms painted, and she had to leave the painters alone in the house all day. She brought most of her jewelry to the bank, but at the last minute realized that the stickpin was still in her dresser drawer, so she rushed around looking for a place to hide it.

And then she forgot all about it, obviously. She hadn't had a reason to look for it until that open house.

She sighed, looking down at the pin in her hand. Carl had moved out because she accused him of stealing it. *I panicked,* she realized. She sat on the edge of the bed, not knowing what to do. *Should I go see him at the church and apologize?*

She really didn't want to do that. She and Carl hardly spoke, even when he lived there. It would just be so awkward for both of them. She had to admit that she was afraid of what he might say, especially if she went on her own.

Maybe Tucker could speak to him and apologize for her. She would tell him later, when he came back to wash the dog. Then they could decide what to do.

She put the pin back in its box and tucked it away in her dresser drawer. She did feel guilty about accusing Carl. But she was still relieved that he had moved out.

"DO YOU WANT TO PACK THESE TEAPOTS, GRANDMA?"

The teapot collection. Sophie had nearly forgotten about it. It had been there for so long, she almost stopped seeing it. Late afternoon sunlight slanted through the kitchen windows, falling on the row of china. The teapots were all shapes, sizes, and colors. Two had glazes that were quite unique: a shiny, obsidian with white peonies; and an iridescent gray-blue with a spray of plum blossoms.

Although Sophie had rarely set foot beyond Cape Light, her teapots had come to her from all corners. Her brother Fred and others would buy them for her in far-off places, souvenirs of their travels. She did love them all. Looking at them was like a trip around the world.

But what would she do with them now? They wouldn't fit in at Evelyn's house. Her oldest daughter was particular about her decor. Maybe Una would like them or even Miranda. Still, Sophie didn't feel quite ready to give them away.

"I'm not sure, dear," she finally answered Miranda. "We don't have to pack up everything right now. There'll be time later."

After the house was sold, Sophie meant. It was still too hard to say the words aloud. The poor house. Sophie wondered if it would be knocked down to make way for something more modern.

Oh, she couldn't worry about that now on top of everything. Not with all three of her children coming tomorrow—coming to settle things before she moved to Evelyn's house.

She suddenly felt so overwhelmed, so distraught. She felt light-headed and clammy, too. She held on to the back of a kitchen chair and abruptly sat down.

"Grandma, are you all right?" Miranda hopped off the step stool and ran to her side.

"I'm fine. Just a little winded. All this packing. It gets on my nerves," Sophie confessed.

Miranda brought her a glass of cold water, and Sophie drank it thirstily. "The dust bothers me, too," she added with a small smile. "I guess I let things go a bit once Granddad got sick."

"What's the difference? Don't worry about that now." Miranda touched her shoulder.

Truly, what was the difference now? She never heard anyone at her stage in life say, "Gee, I don't think I dusted enough." With Gus gone, the simple things that had once ordered and organized her life, like keeping up with the housework and deciding what to cook for dinner, seemed to have slipped away.

This was just a phase, people told her, part of the grieving process. "You'll get through it," they said. "Things will get back to normal, little by little."

But she knew they were wrong. She was leaving the orchard. Her life would never get back to normal or anything like it.

"Grandma, do you feel okay? Maybe I should take you over to the doctor. There's a new one in town. He might have office hours on a Saturday."

"No. I don't need a doctor." Sophie forced a smile and patted Miranda's hand. "I need a time machine."

One that could take me back ten or twenty years, so I could live my life all over again, Sophie thought. *I don't think I would be bored one bit.*

Miranda sat watching her for a long time. "Why are you leaving here?" she asked finally. "I know you don't want to."

"What a question! Everyone seems to know why I have to go. Ask your father, he'll tell you." She didn't mean to snap at Miranda, but her nerves were raw; she couldn't help herself.

"It just seems so wrong."

Miranda's gentle tone nearly made Sophie cry, but she wouldn't let herself break down that way.

"It feels wrong to me, too, I have to admit. But there doesn't seem to be any other way. Your father and your aunts won't allow me to stay here alone. That's what happens when you reach a certain age—everything goes in reverse, and you get ordered around by your children. Next thing you know, they'll be setting my bedtime and telling me I've had enough TV."

"I know how they're pressuring you, Gram. But there must be a way you can stay. You can't give up so easily."

"Oh, but there isn't, dear. We've been over and over this. It just pains me now to keep talking about it. Honestly."

Sophie knew Miranda meant well, but she wished she would just give up. Still, she had only herself to blame for the Potter stubborn streak. She was the one who taught her children and grandchildren to be persistent, to fight to the very end. "A diamond is just a lump of coal that stuck to its job," she would tell them, quoting one of her favorite sayings. Still, she didn't see how persistence or even sheer stubbornness would help her now. Miranda was so young. She didn't understand.

"Listen, I've been thinking about this," Miranda said. "What if I stayed here with you? Moved in permanently, I mean. You could tell me what to do, and I could run the orchard for you."

Sophie felt her heart catch. *If only,* she answered silently.

"Oh, my. That's a lovely offer, Miranda, and I appreciate it. But what about your career, your acting? You can't give that up and come live out here in the middle of nowhere."

"I don't think I'm cut out to be an actress, Gram. The auditions are like cattle calls, and I never get called back. Well, not enough to make it feel worthwhile. I've been plugging away at it for a while now, and I'm tired of it. I guess I didn't even realize that until I came up here to see you and Granddad. Even if I go back to New York, I'm going to give up acting."

She sounded so definite. Sophie had a lot of respect for that. It was good to see that despite the stubborn streak, her granddaughter was flexible and wouldn't stay stuck in a rut.

"Well, it sounds as if you've thought about it and made up your mind," Sophie said. "But I don't see why you would want to stay up here. It's so isolated and you're so young."

"I'm twenty-five, Grandma. The same age you were when you took over."

"Yes, that's true. But things were different then. There was a war going on. We got old fast back then."

"Oh, Grandma. Come on, you know that's not true."

Sophie laughed. "I can't help it, honey. You do seem so young to me. And it's such hard work to run this place. I'm not sure you really know what you would be getting into."

"I'm not afraid of hard work. I worked here every summer when I was in high school. And I've loved working in the orchard with you these last weeks. We got a lot done out there. Don't you think?"

Sophie bit down on her lip. So many times she had seen her granddaughter out there and thought she was seeing an old movie of herself. Only Miranda was so tall and fit, she hardly needed a ladder to reach the branches.

"Yes, we did get a lot accomplished," Sophie admitted. "You're a good worker, too. You've got a real feel for the trees. I always said that to your grandfather, even when you were in high school."

"Grandma, please. Just think about it, okay?" Miranda leaned closer and squeezed her hand. "I don't want to see you leave here. Not yet. I know we could do this together. I really do."

Sophie couldn't help it. The touch of Miranda's hand and the light in her young eyes sparked hope in her heart.

"Well, you've given me a lot to consider, young lady. I'll be up half the night probably . . . but it might work out. If we can persuade my children."

"We will. We won't take no for an answer," Miranda promised.

Sophie just smiled. In her heart, she quietly spoke to Gus, for she suddenly felt sure he was nearby, listening.

Did you hear that, Gus? Didn't I tell you that if the Lord wanted me to stay he'd send a way? Well, here it is. Our own Miranda. My prayers have been answered. Then she decided to say a few words to God, too.

Thank you, Lord. She was right under my nose, and I didn't even see. But we're going to need your help tomorrow. It's not over yet. . . .

"WELL, HERE THEY ARE. THANKS AGAIN FOR HAVING them over." Molly led Lauren and Jill into Sam and Jessica's house.

Jessica stood in the front hall, taking the girls' backpacks. "Gosh, you look gorgeous. I love that outfit."

"Thanks. I bought it in sort of a rush at one of the outlet stores. I need some more good clothes for appointments."

Jessica's remark made Molly feel self-conscious. They both knew she had run out the day after Matt had called to get something new to wear. She had found a peach-colored sweater set with a matching paisley skirt in a sheer layered material. It floated to a graceful length that was flattering to her figure.

The high-heeled sandals, though painful, helped a lot in that department, too. Luckily, Matthew was tall, and she could get away with such tricks without towering over him.

Sam appeared on the stairway. "I thought I heard you

come in." He stepped over and gave her a quick kiss on the cheek. "Looking good, Molly. So, what's going on?"

"I told you, she's going out with Dr. Harding." Something in Jessica's tone made Molly blush.

"Oh, the doctor. Yeah, I heard all about it." Sam stuck his hands in the pockets of his jeans. "Where are you guys going?"

"Dinner and then to hear some jazz at Bay Street Café."

Sam looked amused. "You hate jazz. You always say it gives you a headache."

"I do not say that. I like jazz. I like all kinds of music." Molly knew she sounded huffy, but she was a little nervous tonight. She didn't need Sam's teasing.

He probably didn't think Matthew was a good match for her—not like his couch-potato friend, Micky.

"I like it a lot better than watching sports on TV, I'll tell you that much," she said brightly.

Sam didn't answer, but she could tell by his expression that he caught her meaning.

"Oh, don't pay any attention to him. You never took me on such interesting dates, pal, come to think about it," Jessica reminded her husband.

Sam turned to his wife and flashed his notoriously charming smile. "I must have done something right. You married me, honey."

Jessica looked as if she didn't want to smile back at him but finally couldn't help herself. "Yeah, I did, didn't I?"

"Have a good time, Moll," Sam said.

"Thanks, I will."

"Yes, have a great time. And don't rush," Jessica added. "The girls can sleep in the guest room if they get tired."

Molly thanked Jessica and said good-bye. Then she stepped carefully in her high-heeled sandals down the gravel driveway to her car. She slowly eased herself in so she wouldn't wrinkle her skirt on the way to Matthew's house.

Her hands were sweating on the steering wheel. *It's ridiculous to be so nervous,* she told herself. It wasn't as if they had never spent time together. By now she felt she knew Matt pretty well. But they had never really spent time alone together. She wondered if it would be hard to keep up a conversation without the girls constantly distracting them.

Was he too good for her? Too smart, too sophisticated?

She was feeling a lot better about herself lately and about her life . . . but this was different.

"Don't turn this into some kind of test," Betty had wisely advised. "You're not going to an audition, for goodness' sake. Try to figure out if he's good enough for you."

He's good enough, she thought. *He's just right.*

Molly turned off the Beach Road into the village. Just as she passed the harbor on her way to Hawthorne Street, her cell phone rang. She dug in her bag with one hand and answered it. Was it a call from Lauren or Jill already? She hoped they weren't going to haunt her all night.

"Molly? It's Matthew. I'm glad I caught you. Where are you?"

"In the village. On the way to your house."

"I'm not at home. A patient needs to be admitted to the hospital. I'm on my way to Southport now to meet her."

"Oh . . . that's too bad." She meant it was bad for his patient, but she also felt bad for herself.

"I know. I'm so sorry. It's a really rotten break. But listen, the table is still reserved. Why don't you take a friend or something?"

A friend? She didn't want to take a friend. She wanted to go with him. Molly swallowed hard, fighting back tears.

"Um, thanks. Good idea. I'm not sure who I could ask on such short notice, though."

"Well if you can find someone, it should be a great show. I'll try to . . ." The connection began to break up, and Molly couldn't hear what Matthew said next.

"Matt? I can't hear you." She listened to the static for a moment, then shut her phone. The car seemed to drive itself down Main Street. Molly saw an empty space in front of the movie theater and pulled over.

She had a few single friends she could call, but she knew that most of them wouldn't be able to run out at a minute's notice, anyway. She didn't really feel like calling anyone; she had told Matthew she would just to be polite. And to save face, too. She didn't want him to know how disappointed she felt. He said he was, too, but he didn't really sound it.

She sighed and looked out the window. Wrong place to park, she realized, watching couples walk hand in hand into the movie theater. She felt her eyes fill up with tears again. This time she pulled out a pack of tissues and let herself cry.

She permitted herself a few moments of abject misery, then blew her nose and rallied. This wouldn't do. It was just a canceled date, not the end of the world. He did have a good reason, not some lame excuse—and she had heard enough of those to know the difference.

She fixed her runny eye makeup with a tissue, then took a deep breath. She didn't really relish the idea of going back to Sam and Jessica's and explaining what happened. Hiding out at a movie for a while was an option. But that was silly. Matt was a doctor. He had emergencies. She had nothing to feel ashamed of.

She started her car and headed back to Sam's house. The ride on the Beach Road, with its lush greenery and sea breeze, calmed her a bit more. When she reached the house, she gritted her teeth and climbed up the gravel driveway again, nearly tipping over in her heels. Jessica answered the door, looking surpised.

"Molly, are you okay? Did you have car trouble?" she asked with concern.

"I'm fine. Matthew had an emergency. He had to admit a patient to the hospital and had to cancel on me."

Though she tried to sound matter-of-fact about it, she knew she really sounded glum.

"Gee, that's too bad." Jessica's sympathetic look nearly made her come unglued again. Molly smiled wanly, struggling not to start crying again.

"I'll survive. I don't really like jazz anyway. I guess I'll take the girls home."

"Sure. We were just about to have dinner. Would you like to stay?"

Molly considered the invitation. On one hand, it would give her something to do; on the other, it would be too depressing.

"That's nice of you to offer, Jessica, but I think I'll just take them out somewhere."

Just as Molly was about to call the girls, Sam walked into the living room. "Hey, Moll. What are you doing back here?"

"Matt had to go to the hospital on an emergency," Jessica explained.

"Oh, that's a tough break."

Molly glanced at him, daring him to say she'd been stood up. Sam just crossed his arms over his chest and gazed at her with a sympathetic expression that made her feel even worse somehow.

"Oh well. He couldn't help it, I guess," Sam said finally.

"Of course, he couldn't help it," Jessica replied.

Sam was caught off balance by his wife's defensive tone. "Well, that's too bad. The hazards of dating a doctor, I guess. Want to hang out with us tonight? We rented a movie."

"Thanks, but I think I'll just take the girls and go. You've been helping me out so much with the kids lately. You guys deserve a Saturday night alone," Molly said sincerely.

Jessica smiled at her. "You know I never mind having them here but thanks."

A few minutes later, Molly had Jill and Lauren back in the car, and they headed toward the village.

"Are we going home already?" Jill asked.

"What happened to your date with Matthew?" Lauren asked bluntly.

Molly didn't answer right away. "I guess you guys didn't have dinner yet, right?"

"No, and I'm starving I might add," Lauren answered.

"I might add that, too," Jill said in a serious tone.

"I might add that three," Molly replied, starting to smile again. "Tell me what you think. The barbeque chicken place on the turnpike and then we try out that new tropical mini-golf with the waterfalls?"

"Yes!" Jill answered.

"I'm getting a little *old* for mini-golf, Mom, in case you haven't noticed."

Molly met her gaze in the rearview mirror. "I hear you, honey. It's not my first choice, either, to be perfectly honest. But the palm trees and waterfalls sound like fun."

Lauren sighed, sparing a small smile. "Okay, if you guys really want to."

"I want to," Jill said.

"I do, too." Molly summoned up a burst of enthusiasm she didn't know was in her. It was the old "making lemonade from life's lemons" trick. *I've had a lot of practice at that one,* she realized.

"Let's go," she said. She turned the car around and headed for the turnpike, trying not to think of how her feet would feel in her fancy shoes at the end of a night of mini-golf. Or how her new outfit would look after the barbeque. At least Lauren and Jill thought she was a great Saturday night date.

As for Matthew's opinion, it didn't look like she was ever going to find out.

THE NEXT MORNING, MOLLY WOKE TO THE SOUND OF rain spattering against the windows. The change in the weather seemed to mirror her dark mood. She rose and made the girls' breakfast, then got them ready for a day out with Phil.

It was a relief to have the apartment to herself. Still, facing a full day's worth of baking left her feeling depleted and depressed. A new helper, whom she had found through the high school, was due to start today but had left a message last night canceling on her. *It seems to be my weekend to be stood up,* Molly thought, as she put on her apron.

She worked through the morning, focusing on her orders and trying not to think about Matthew. He *would* call, right? It was hard to guess. Maybe he would wait a day or two. Maybe he didn't want to ask her out again and wouldn't call at all.

After pushing herself through several hours of baking, Molly needed a break. She was exhausted. She hadn't slept well and even an entire pot of coffee hadn't burned through the dense fog in her head.

She went inside and allowed herself to lie down on her unmade bed. *I never do this,* she told herself as her head hit the pillow. *What's wrong with me today? Maybe I'm coming down with something.*

Right, that little bug women get when they've been rejected by a man.

The steady patter of rain quieted her scattered thoughts as she drifted off to sleep.

BART POTTER SAT AT THE END OF THE WORN KITCHEN table. He had his father's build, tall and broad shouldered, though he was carrying some extra weight around the middle as he moved into middle age. In his fancy sport clothes, her son still looked every inch a corporate lawyer, Sophie thought, as if he were sitting at the head of a boardroom table instead of in her old homey kitchen. He frowned at his daughter.

"I'm surprised at you, Miranda. If you're disappointed with your career, that's one thing. But you can't hide out here. Your grandmother has to move. You have no right to talk her into staying."

"She didn't talk me into anything. You sound like I was hypnotized or something," Sophie grumbled.

"What I said was that I'm done with acting and I like it

here and I'll stay if Grandma wants us to run the orchard together," Miranda explained.

"But you can't stay. Neither of you can. That's just my point," Bart said firmly.

Evelyn and Una sat together on one long side of the table, opposite Miranda. The two sisters glanced at each other and then at their brother.

"Calm down, Bart. Let's not lose our tempers," Evelyn said. "Miranda's been here with Mother through the worst of it. I'm sure she's feeling some strain after the last few weeks, too. We all know how distressed Mom is about leaving."

"I'm sure Miranda feels badly for her grandmother and just wants to help," Una added. She gave Miranda a sad smile. "We all feel badly about Grandma having to leave here, honey."

"We grew up here. We have so many memories. It's hard for everyone in the family to give up this place," Evelyn agreed.

Bart shook his head and exhaled noisily. Snorting like a horse, Sophie thought. Normally, she was proud of the way he had turned out. But this was one argument he wasn't going to win.

"All right. She just wanted to help. It was a nice gesture. And we all feel badly about giving up the orchard. But these matters have been discussed and decided," Bart pointed out. "I don't see any purpose in backtracking again. It's been hard enough to get Mom this far." He stared around the table. Una and Evelyn avoided his gaze, Sophie noticed, but she met it head on, unflinchingly. He finally looked away.

He sat back and cleared his throat. "I thought we were going to talk about how and when we'll put this place up for sale."

Sophie sat up straight and folded her hands in front of her on the table. She took a breath and was surprised to feel a small smile forming on her lips. "I'm not selling."

"Oh, Mom . . ." Una shook her head and glanced at Evelyn.

"Mother, please. Be reasonable now." Evelyn's tone was coaxing.

"Of course you are," Bart said flatly. He frowned at Sophie, a cold blue-eyed stare. "This has already been decided."

She remembered that look from when he was a little boy and didn't want to clean up his room or finish his homework before he could go outside and play.

It was suddenly very quiet while Sophie met Bart's gaze and held it. Outside, the wind picked up, spattering raindrops against the kitchen windowpane. Finally, Sophie answered her son. "No, I'm not. And you can't make me."

Sophie noticed Miranda smile and duck her head. *Yes, Grandma sounds like a rebellious child,* she thought, enjoying the irony. She kept a straight face, though, and went on in a measured tone, "This property is still in my name. While I'm still alive and sane, I decide when and if it goes on the market. Not you three."

Una tilted her head in Sophie's direction. "But, Mom, you know that we're just concerned for you—"

"It seems to me that if you're that worried about me, you would see that I can't leave. Not yet. It would break my heart, even worse than it's already been broken by losing your father."

Sophie reached over to pat her granddaughter's hand. "There's only one person who understood that—and who offered real help to me. Why, we've been taking care of the place together for the past few weeks now and doing just fine. She wants to stay, and I'm glad to hear it. I'm taking this girl up on her offer no matter what the rest of you think about it."

Her children looked at each other nervously, feeling shamed perhaps by her words. She could see that they were giving up on changing her mind, even Bart. She could tell by the way he sat back from the table and took a deep breath.

"Frankly, I don't see how you're going to make this work." He fixed his daughter with a stern glare. "I told you the same thing when you said you wanted to go to New

York and be an actress. Maybe you always need to find out the hard way."

"Maybe we do," Miranda shot back. "If we fail, it won't be for lack of trying, right Grandma?"

"That's right." Sophie nodded emphatically. " 'Whatsoever thy hand findeth to do, do with thy might. . . .' I'm not afraid of this not working out. All things are possible with God's help."

Bart laughed nervously. "Oh, dear. She's starting to quote the Bible at me. I guess it's time to give up."

"You ought to try it in court sometime, son. It will definitely get people's attention," Sophie advised.

"Well, Mom, looks like you got your way." Evelyn smiled ruefully and shook her head. "You know we're nearby if you need anything," she said to Miranda.

"Me, too, dear," Una said to her niece. "I can't say that I'm entirely in favor of this plan, Mom, but I am glad you're not leaving here yet." She glanced at her older sister and brother. "I suppose we'll just have to wait and see."

"Thank you, Una. Thank you, Evelyn and Bart. I know you all have my best interest at heart. But this is best for me. Miranda and I will make it work. I know it in my heart."

Sophie sat back in her chair, smiling with satisfaction. She felt as if she'd just come home after a long exhausting trip. She was back where she belonged, finally, and didn't plan to leave any time soon.

THE SOUND OF THE DOOR BUZZER WOKE MOLLY FROM A deep, dreamless sleep. She opened her eyes to find the room steeped in shadows. She turned and picked up the clock. Half past four? How could that be?

She sat up and rubbed her forehead, then launched herself toward the front door. "Be right there," she shouted.

Phil and the girls, back early. She hated for anyone to see her looking such a mess, rumpled and wrinkled, as if she had just rolled out of bed, which, come to think of it, she had. It was only Phil, though. It didn't matter.

But Molly pulled opened the door to find Matthew instead. Dressed in a yellow slicker, he stood with his face and hair wet from the rain. He held a bunch of daffodils wrapped in paper in his hand, their droopy yellow heads looking half-drowned.

"Matthew . . . hi." She tucked a thick lock of hair behind her ear, wondering now why she hadn't even bothered to stop and splash her face.

"I hope I'm not bothering you. I knew you were probably home working today. . . . I just wanted to say hello."

Molly was sure her shock at his unexpected appearance showed all over her face. She ducked her head and stepped aside to let him in.

"Come on in. I was just taking a break." *Sleeping away the afternoon, if the truth be told,* she silently added.

He handed her the bouquet. "These are for you. A little soggy though, sorry."

"Thanks, they're very pretty. I love daffodils. They always look so optimistic."

"Yes, they do seem that way, now that you mention it."

He hung his slicker on a row of hooks near the door and followed her into the kitchen. He stood in the doorway, watching her place the flowers in a vase. The expression on his face made her uneasy. It was a sad, thoughtful look that didn't bode well.

"Can I make you some coffee or tea?" She carried the small vase to the table. "I have loads of muffins and stuff," she added, pointing to the trays she had already baked.

"Um, no, thank you. I'm fine."

"I think I'd better have some coffee to wake up again," she said honestly. "I don't know why I'm so sleepy today."

"It must be the rain."

"I suppose." *More likely feeling blue over you,* she wanted to add. She poured out a cup of coffee from what was still in the carafe from that morning and stuck it in the microwave.

"Did you get over to Newburyport to hear the music last night?"

"Um, no, I didn't after all." The microwave beeped, saving her from facing him. She carefully took out the hot cup and blew on it. She was about to tell him what she did end up doing, but she caught herself. Tropical paradise minigolf with her kids sounded so pathetic.

Matthew nodded politely. "Well, it's too bad you couldn't go. I'm sorry again I had to cancel on you like that."

"That's okay. I understand, honestly." Molly pulled out a chair and sat down at the table with him. "How is your patient doing?"

"Oh, not too bad. It was an older woman, lives alone, not taking care of herself properly. She came in complaining of stomach pains. It turned out to be her gall bladder. She needed surgery right away. I went down to the hospital today to look in on her. She seems to be feeling a little better."

"Well, that's some good news," Molly said sympathetically.

She knew that he hadn't been lying to her last night. She'd never suspected that. Yet, something about his mood right now made her uneasy. She couldn't quite put her finger on it.

Maybe he's just tired, she thought. He handled an emergency last night and drove to Southport and back today. But that didn't seem to be it, either. She felt herself sitting there, sensing she wasn't going to like whatever he had to say next.

Matthew cleared his throat and rubbed his hands together. *Here it comes,* Molly thought. She tried but couldn't stop herself from filling in the heavy silence, just to change the subject and forestall the inevitable.

"Where's Amanda today?"

Matthew looked up suddenly. She could tell his thoughts

had been wandering. "She's visiting her grandparents, Sharon's folks, in Amherst. I was supposed to drive out there today actually, but I decided not to."

"To pick her up, you mean?"

"Yes. And to visit Sharon's grave. It's three years this week since she passed away."

Molly felt a sudden jolt. She suddenly had some clue to his strange withdrawn mood. She didn't quite know what to say to him, though. "I'm sorry. It must be a hard day for you."

"It is. I feel sad, of course, thinking about the past. But it stirs up a lot of questions for me." He paused and met her gaze. "About starting a relationship again, for one thing."

Molly swallowed hard.

He sat silently again, but Molly couldn't stand the suspense.

"Like . . . with me for instance, you mean?"

He nodded and forced a small smile. "Yes, exactly. Who else would I be talking about?" He reached across the table and took her hand.

"Oh." That was all she could manage to say. She felt the warm pressure of his hand on hers and squeezed back.

"The problem is, it's hard for me, Molly. Thinking about the past makes me remember that I wasn't very good at being in a relationship."

Molly waited, but he didn't say more. She felt uneasy about pushing him, but she couldn't help herself.

"When you say you weren't good at it, what do you mean?" she asked gently.

He glanced at her and then looked away. "I mean I didn't have a happy marriage. My wife felt neglected. She felt I worked too hard and gave my best to my patients. I tried to work things out with her, but I don't think I ever really pleased her." He shrugged. Molly could see it was hard for him to continue, and she willed herself not to interrupt him.

"I don't know," he said finally. "Maybe Sharon was right. Maybe I'm not really cut out for marriage, for giving another person all they need. Maybe I do give my all to my work. In all this time, I haven't been able to figure that out. To get past it, I guess you'd say."

"Oh. I see." Molly continued to hold onto his hand, but suddenly his touch meant something else entirely to her, not a hint of things to come but a bittersweet ending to something that had never quite begun.

Matthew shook his head, looking frustrated with himself. "I'm saying this all wrong. The thing is, I wasn't lying last night when I had to break our date—"

"I know that," Molly cut in.

"Well, okay then. But afterward and today, I've had a lot of time to think about this . . . you and me dating, I mean. It's hard to say this to you, but I know I'm just not ready to start seeing someone again. Not even you. Especially you, in some way. There's so much that's good between us now, just the way it is. I don't want to lose that."

"Being friends, you mean," she said abruptly. *Oh, so this is the "let's just be friends" speech,* she realized. She felt she might cry and slipped her hand from his grasp.

He stared at her a moment. "Sure, I think of you as a friend. But I really care for you, Molly. I think you're amazing. Absolutely great in every possible way. The problem is, I've been through a lot the last few years. Moving has been another big upheaval. I need to focus now on the new practice and on Amanda, making a home for her here. I don't want to start something with you and end up disappointing you or leading you on. When I look into the future, I really don't see myself getting married again."

He'd been staring down at the table, delivering his words slowly and carefully. Molly took them in, one by one, feeling her heart drop by degrees. She felt too sad and stunned to speak.

Finally Matthew looked up at her, his dark eyes shining with emotion. Molly realized she didn't feel mad at him. She felt embarrassed. Had she been so obvious? It made her cringe now to see herself that way.

"Matthew, it's okay." She forced her voice to sound

even and light. "It was just a date. I wasn't expecting a marriage proposal. Maybe on the third date or so. But not on the first one."

He looked at her, trying to smile, but not quite managing it. He ran his hand nervously over his damp hair, pushing it back from his forehead. "I guess I really meant you're not the kind of woman *I* could take lightly. If we ever did get involved, I know it would be serious for *me*."

His honesty was startling. It gave her hope and at the same time, made her feel even sadder and more frustrated.

"Well, that's nice of you to say."

"I'm not just saying it. It's true." His voice was quiet but emphatic.

But the other part—the more important part—was also true. He didn't have to repeat those words again. They still hung in the air between them, changing everything.

She stared at the vase of daffodils, their green stems looped over the edge, their golden heads sagging. Disappointed and dispirited, exactly the way she now felt.

But she knew she had to rally, at least for the few minutes he would remain here. *I can put the pillow over my face and cry my heart out later.*

"I understand what you're trying to say. Thanks for being up front with me."

His dark gaze sought hers out, but she avoided looking at him. "I know it doesn't sound like much," he said, "but I wish this could have worked out differently."

"It's all right. Maybe it's better this way. At least everything's out in the open now, right?" Her voice sounded a bit sharper than she intended, but she couldn't help it.

"Yes, I guess it is." He sighed and looked down at the table, then pushed himself up from his chair. "All right then. I guess I'd better go."

"Matt . . . please. We'll still be friends. It's okay."

She didn't know why she found herself suddenly trying to reassure him, to make him feel better, when she was clearly the injured party here. But he looked so forlorn as he rose from the table, almost as if he might be having second thoughts about what he'd just done.

She stopped herself. More wishful thinking. That was her problem—what had gotten her into this spot in the first place.

He walked over to the door and grabbed his rain jacket. She followed from a safe distance.

"Don't work too hard. I'll see you around, I guess," he said gently.

"It's a small town. You won't be able to avoid me."

Her tart reply reminded them both of the time they'd met. He gave her a brief smile, one that didn't quite touch his eyes.

"I wouldn't want to. You should know that by now."

Molly watched him walk down the hall, then closed the door. She immediately felt tears welling up in her eyes and then streaming down her face. She tried to hold them back but couldn't. She covered her face with her hands a moment, briefly considered running back into the bedroom and flinging herself on the bed, then shook her head.

No, she'd lost too much time over this already. She had to work. She wasn't half through on her orders. Lauren and Jill would be home in an hour, she realized. She couldn't let them find her looking so upset.

"I'M SORRY, BETTY. I JUST DON'T WANT TO TALK ABOUT this anymore. Can we change the subject, please?"

Molly sat at a table in the Beanery with Betty on Tuesday afternoon. Betty had been quite sympathetic as Molly related the story of Matthew's broken date and his heart-to-heart chat on Sunday. But despite Betty's sympathy and sound advice, she just didn't want to pick it apart anymore. The whole topic was still too painful.

"How did it go in Connecticut? How's Brian doing?" Molly asked suddenly.

"Oh, well now. There's a fresh topic for you."

Betty pursed her lips and stared down at her salad. Molly could tell that Betty didn't like the attention deflected to her own problems.

A few months ago, Betty's sixteen-year-old son, Brian, had more or less demanded to leave Betty's custody and live with his father. Betty's ex-husband had recently remarried and moved to New Canaan, Connecticut. At first Betty had refused to let Brian go, but finally she decided she had to give in.

"Brian is doing fine. He seems happy to be with his father," she reported. "I have to admit, I miss him a lot and feel badly that he didn't want to stay here with me. I'd be lying if I said differently. But it's good to be getting along with him again. We actually had fun together. So that's some benefit, I suppose."

Molly felt a wave of sympathy for her. She knew Betty had gone through a lot lately over Brian. She had also handled the news that her ex-husband was now the proud father of another baby with his second wife.

"How does Brian feel about the baby?" Molly asked.

"He's wild about the baby apparently. But I'm not surprised. The baby was part of the draw. I think Brian was afraid Ted was going to forget about him once he had another child. Ted, of course, is not quite *that* bad," Betty added with a short laugh. "But Brian didn't want to get shut out. He wanted to stake his claim in the new family."

"That's probably true," Molly agreed. Meanwhile, she could see that Betty was the one who felt shut out. Not that Betty held any grudges against her ex-husband; she seemed genuinely happy that he had started over. But Molly could see that Ted having a baby made her feel older, and now she felt rejected by her son, who seemed to prefer Ted's new family circle. The music had stopped, and Betty had found herself without a chair.

"How's it going with Richard?" Molly asked, hoping to steer the conversation in a more positive direction.

"Oh, Richard. That fizzled out." Betty sighed and put her

napkin on the table. "We get along well enough, I suppose. We have the same interests and all that. He's a really nice guy, very thoughtful. But there wasn't much chemistry." She shrugged. "It was a mutual decision. We'll still be friends."

"Sounds like you feel okay about it."

"I do," Betty assured her. She glanced up at Molly.

"You can't expect every relationship to work out. Few do, actually."

Molly took a long sip of her diet soda, remembering the way Matthew had looked at her, saying he wished it could work out differently for them. She wanted to believe that he meant it, even though it didn't change anything.

No, she didn't want to think about that anymore. It didn't help one bit.

"What's going on with Emily's party? Did you give her your estimate yet?" Betty asked suddenly.

"Oh, I've been working on that. I'm not sure I'm going to do the party, though." Molly braced herself for Betty's reaction, sure of what would come.

"Molly, what do you mean? I thought it was all settled."

"It was never settled, Betty. I had a good meeting with Emily. But I never agreed to do it. We didn't even talk about a date."

"But I'm sure she's counting on you. You can't back out now."

"I'm not backing out, for heaven's sake. I didn't get far enough to be backing out. The more I looked into what was really involved in pulling this off, the more I could see that right now it's beyond me. I need to be more realistic. I can't do it."

"More realistic. Okay." Betty paused, nodding to herself. "I know what's going on here. You can't fool me."

Molly felt her mouth go dry. She never could fool Betty. But she could try.

"Okay, I'm game. What's going on? I don't have a clue."

"You do, too. Or maybe you're just so deeply in denial, you can't see it."

"See what Betty?" she asked a bit impatiently.

"It's because of Matthew. That's what made you suddenly 'realistic.' That's what made you think you don't want to do Emily's party."

"Oh, Betty, that's not true. I've just thought about the work involved, and I changed my mind."

"You can't do this to yourself. I won't let you."

"You won't let me do what?"

"Use this rejection—from some guy who doesn't appreciate you or is just in a bad place emotionally right now—as an excuse to throw away everything you've been working for. Forget about Matthew. You have a really great chance to get your business going, and you can't lose confidence in yourself and toss it away because this romance didn't work out. One thing has nothing to do with the other."

"I know that," Molly answered.

She stared down at her plate and pushed a bit of lettuce around with her fork. All last week she had felt wary but excited about the opportunity. It was Sunday night and Monday when doubts started moving in like storm clouds—just after her talk with Matthew, she realized. She couldn't help it. Nothing seemed right since then.

"What have you done so far? Did you figure out your costs and overhead and that sort of thing?"

Molly nodded. "I called up Pauline," she said, referring to her instructor. "We went over everything on the phone."

"That's great. Then you must be ready to give Emily an estimate."

Molly didn't answer for a moment. "I could be."

"Look, I'm sorry to be so hard on you about this." Molly noticed her smiling a little. "Think of it as a tough love kind of thing."

Molly smiled, too. "If you say so."

"I do. I know you had your hopes up about Matthew. I'm sure you feel like your heart has just been tossed in a food processor or something."

She did. With the setting on puree.

"But working hard is the best revenge, Molly. It's the best way to get over anything—a failed romance, a bad haircut. Even your ex-husband having a new baby," she added with a wry smile. "I've been through this a million times. Believe me."

Molly looked up and met her friend's sympathetic gaze. Betty was a fighter, that was for sure. She didn't let anything hold her back.

"You've already done all the groundwork, Molly. It would be a shame to just let this go."

It would be a shame. Betty was right. One thing didn't have anything to do with the other, though somehow in her mind, they had gotten all tangled up. She had to hold fast to some idea of herself, of what she could do. She couldn't let herself be so affected by other people's opinions—even Matthew's.

"All right, I'll meet with Emily again. I'll give her the estimate," Molly agreed with a long sigh. "Are you happy now?"

Betty sat back, quietly beaming. "Yes, very. Just for that, lunch is on me. And let's get dessert. Not one of yours, though. We need to check out the competition. And don't worry about your diet. This is market research."

"Right. The calories don't count then, I guess."

Betty nodded. "Exactly. Like writing it off on your income tax."

Molly laughed and shook her head. "Betty, you're too much."

Betty raised her hand, waving the waitress over. "Thanks. I'll take that as a compliment."

BOLSTERED BY HER LUNCH WITH BETTY, MOLLY CALLED Emily later that afternoon. Emily sounded happy to hear from her and eager to see her estimate for the party.

"When do you think you'll have it ready?"

"I guess I can drop it off at your house sometime tomorrow."

"Great, but don't bring it there. I won't be home tomorrow until very late. Come by my office. I'm eager to see it and talk it over with Dan."

"Um, sure. No problem. I'll drop it off at your office sometime tomorrow," Molly agreed.

They said good-bye, and Molly had a sudden moment of panic. She gulped it back, thinking of Betty's advice. The best cure was just to get at it.

By working late at night after the girls had gone to sleep and calling her course teacher with a few more questions, Molly managed to pull together a professional-looking estimate. She arranged it in an attractive glossy folder—a discard from one of Jill's many school reports—then packed it in a manila envelope. She even whipped up some attractive letterhead on the computer, though she still didn't have an official name for her business.

As promised, she drove over to Village Hall the next day and walked back to the mayor's office. Emily's secretary was out, and Molly wondered where she should leave her package. Then she heard Emily call to her through the half-open door of her office.

"Molly, come in. I'm glad I spotted you out there."

Molly went into Emily's office and handed her the envelope. "Here it is. If you have any questions, or if I misunderstood anything we talked about, just give me a call."

"Yes, I will." Emily opened the envelope and then drew out the sheaf of papers from the folder. Molly felt a little twist in her stomach. She didn't want Emily to read it right in front of her.

Emily must have sensed her dismay. She glanced at Molly and smiled, then stuck the papers back in the folder.

"I've come up with a date." Emily picked up a calendar from her desk and flipped the page. "Dan and I thought May seventeenth could work out well. What do you think?"

"May seventeenth?" Molly looked down at the calendar

to the little square where Emily now pointed. She suddenly felt so nervous, she practically couldn't see straight. It seemed as if Emily had glanced at the price quote on the top page and was going to agree to it.

Molly felt terrified. This was really happening. The party would be a month from now. Plenty of time to get ready, and yet it felt too soon. Way too soon.

"It's a Sunday. Do you have anything else scheduled that day, do you think?"

"Um, no. I don't think so." Molly took a breath. Her calendar was clear. Completely clear. Emily was her first and only client. Didn't she know that?

"I'll check to make sure, though." Molly forced her voice to sound more professional.

"Great. You check and see if that date works out. I'll look over the estimate and get back to you promptly." Emily smiled at her. "Thanks for coming by. I appreciate it."

"That's okay. I guess we'll talk later in the week then."

Molly said good-bye and left Emily's office. She had the strangest feeling that Emily and Betty were in this together somehow, a conspiracy to help her out, whether she liked it or not. Jessica might even be in on it, too, she thought vaguely.

No, that's just plain silly. I'm being paranoid about people being too nice to me and treating me so respectfully. I always have to think there's some catch. That's just like me, isn't it?

Chapter Fifteen

A week of solid rain finally abated, and on Easter Sunday a brilliant sun rose against a spring blue sky. The air smelled of moist earth, green buds, and new grass. The cleansing breeze flowed through the open windows and wide open doors at the rear of the sanctuary.

As the choir sang the first hymn, Ben gazed out at the congregation. The church was full today. The men were dressed in their best suits and ties, the women in bright colors and flower patterns, and the children looked scrubbed and fancied up to within an inch of their lives.

The church was decked out in its own Easter finery, the altar covered in an abundance of white lilies and baskets of blue hyacinths, filling Ben's head with their heavy scent. More than that, the pews and floors were polished and the windows bright. Carl had completed the list and more, and Ben was sure the Lord was pleased with his efforts. He told Carl as much yesterday afternoon. Carl accepted the praise in his typical taciturn manner, but Ben could see that he was touched by the words.

Ben saw Carl sitting in a pew with Tucker and his family. His dark jacket and white shirt had been borrowed from Tucker, no doubt. But he was there, gazing down at the hymnal and mouthing the words along with everyone else. Tucker sat beside him, staring straight ahead, as did Fran and their children. Ben was sure they had weathered some curious stares that morning. He knew it took courage on Carl's part to brave this crowd. He was so reclusive. Maybe that was slowly changing, too.

Ben had asked Carl if he had plans for Easter Sunday. If Carl was going to spend the day alone, Ben intended to invite him to his own home for Sunday dinner, but he had been pleased to hear that Carl was going to Tucker's house. Considering the hasty way he had left the Tulleys, this seemed a step back in the right direction. Ben asked God to bless them all for their efforts.

Soon it was time for the sermon, and Ben took the pulpit, his notes in hand. "Welcome, everyone. My heart is full with the good news. Like the angel said, 'He is risen.' Let us rejoice and give thanks for this message and the mystery that redeems us.

"And let us pray that this miracle lives in our hearts, not just today, on Easter Sunday, but every day. Let us be mindful of this fantastic event, which not only promises us forgiveness and salvation for all eternity but new life in this life here on earth, as we struggle with our human frailty and imperfections.

"Each time we feel discouraged and wish for a second chance, let us look back on this day and remember the story of Easter morning, the good news that comes to us in the Scriptures. Yes, we do have another chance. Let us put our faith in the Lord and the power of prayer and we can experience the miracle of change and rebirth, just as surely as spring stirs life in the earth again after the long, deadening winter."

As the service continued, Molly shifted in her seat,

willing herself not to glance to the side where Matthew sat with Amanda farther down the pew.

She usually didn't attend church but Easter was special, like Christmas. You just had to go. Now that she was here, she wasn't sorry. The short sermon, powerfully spoken, really struck a chord. She could see herself in the reverend's words, despairing as she struggled to start a new life and chase after her dreams, losing her energy and faith. But maybe she could do this. She squeezed her eyes shut and sent up a quick prayer. *Please Lord, help me get things moving in the right direction. Help me with my plans and all I'm trying to do.*

Down the pew, Matthew thought about the sermon, too, and how he had come here, to Cape Light, hoping for a new life, for renewal that hadn't yet come to him. Maybe he just needed more time here. Maybe the spring would help, though in some strange way the new season only made him sadder.

Part of it was Molly. She was so much like spring—so full of life—it hurt to see her here. More than he ever expected.

He missed her and thought about her and almost called her up to say hello a dozen times. Of course they had run into each other a few times during the past weeks because of the girls. But it wasn't the same between them anymore, and Matthew regretted that. He missed the easy banter and warmth.

Like the reverend said, he was discouraged. He felt stuck. But he knew in his heart that he had never really called upon the Lord to help him. He was still too scared, afraid of failing Molly, disappointing her the same way he had disappointed Sharon—and of disappointing himself. He had missed his chance with Molly, the chance of a lifetime. Mainly because he just couldn't get out of his own way.

Sophie Potter listened attentively as Reverend Ben concluded the service with the benediction and response. The choir sang the final hymn, and Miranda smiled at her. "Ready to go, Grandma?"

Sophie nodded. "That was lovely. I do love church on Easter morning. All the flowers and the sunlight. It's my favorite holiday."

"I know what you mean. It doesn't feel like it's really spring until Easter, does it?"

Sophie followed the others down the aisle. She held Miranda's arm but thought of Gus, missing his presence beside her even though she felt sure he was up in heaven, celebrating with the angels. She thought of Reverend Ben's words and thanked the Lord again for answering her prayers and granting her a new life at the orchard. *I know this isn't a permanent thing. I'll keep working hard, Lord, and try to live your Word. I won't squander the time I have left here, believe me.*

THE MORGANS GATHERED AT MOLLY'S PARENTS' HOUSE after church. It was a small house in the section of town that had once been a community of summer cottages. The Morgans had expanded it over the years, but the cozy little Cape was never ideal for raising so many children or feeding so many at a sit-down dinner. Somehow, though, they all managed to squeeze together every holiday around the dining-room table.

Sam and Jessica were there along with Molly's younger brother Glen and his family, who lived in Burlington. Molly's younger sister Laurie and her oldest brother Jim were at their in-laws' houses, but Molly's mother couldn't abide a holiday gathering with fewer than twenty, so she had invited other relatives to fill the gaps—Molly's aunt Mary and uncle Lou along with Molly's cousin Beth and her husband and children.

Molly was so busy catching up with her siblings that she nearly forgot about Phil. She had agreed he could stop by and take Lauren and Jill to visit with his parents today.

They were all finishing the main course when Molly suddenly noticed the time and sent the girls upstairs to wash their faces and brush their hair. Playing with their cousins had left both girls looking rumpled. Not that Phil would mind; she knew he would show them off as proudly as if displaying two princesses.

Moments later the doorbell rang. "I'll get it. It's just Phil," she announced as she left the table.

"Phil? Phil Willoughby is here?" Her father sounded dismayed. Then she heard her mother shushing him.

"He's coming to get the girls, Joe. I told you that."

Molly knew that while she left the room her mother would be filling in her aunts and other interested guests on the news that Phil was trying to clean up his act and be a real dad again. She wasn't sure how her family would react. They hadn't seen Phil for a long time, and she knew that her father, at least, was still angry with his ex-son-in-law for the way he had treated Molly.

"Come on in," Molly greeted Phil. "The girls are upstairs, cleaning up. I'll try to hurry them along."

"No hurry. That's okay." She could tell from his voice that he was apprehensive about facing her family. Well, he should be.

Molly walked into the dining room while Phil hung back in the doorway. "Hello everyone. Happy Easter," he said politely.

Her father continued to chew his food, glancing at Molly's mother.

"Happy Easter, Phil," Marie replied. "It's beautiful out there, isn't it? I thought the rain would never stop."

"Yes, it's a beautiful day," Phil agreed heartily, seeming relieved to have something so mundane to talk about.

"Phil, how are you doing?" Sam walked in from the kitchen and shook Phil's hand.

"Sam, good to see you." Phil smiled widely at his old friend. "I heard you got married. Where's the lucky girl?"

"She's right here." Sam proudly rested his hand on Jessica's shoulder. "Jessica, this is Phil. Do you remember him from school, honey? We were in the same year."

"Nice to see you again, Phil." Jessica's tone was diplomatic. Molly couldn't tell if she remembered Phil or not.

Molly heard Lauren and Jill come down the stairs. Phil turned to greet them, holding out his arms. "There they are, my two beauties. How lucky can a guy get?" Phil asked, kissing them each on the cheek.

Molly saw her mother and father exchange a look as the girls both hugged Phil, obviously thrilled to see him. "I have some Easter surprises in the car for you," Phil confided in a whisper.

Jill's smile widened, her eyes alight with greed. "Bye, Mom, see you later."

"I'll walk you all to the door," Molly told her. "Say good-bye to everyone, girls. Show some nice manners."

Her daughters politely bid the group good-bye, running to the head of the table to kiss their grandparents, then back to Phil. Molly followed Phil and the girls out to the foyer.

"We won't be too late," Phil told her. "What about next week—don't they have off from school?"

"Spring break," Molly groaned. "I have so much work right now. I need this school vacation like a root canal from the Easter Bunny."

Phil laughed. He always did like her stupid jokes. "Don't worry. I can take some time off. I'll take them off your hands for a few days. It will be fun now that the weather is warmer."

"Would you? That would be great." Molly smiled at him with relief.

"As long you don't mind if I change my schedule," he added. "Maybe you have some stone-carving tools handy?"

"Okay," she said, returning his smile. "I'll see what kind of stone-carving tools I can find. Just call ahead and give us fair warning?"

"Sure. I can do that." He smiled widely and touched her shoulder. "Happy Easter, Molly. You look good in that color, sort of a peaches-and-cream thing going on there."

"Right. Thanks, Phil." Molly nodded and stepped back into the door. "I'll see you. Have fun with your family."

"Sure, see you." He smiled again and walked down to his car where Lauren and Jill were already waiting. Phil was a character, Molly thought, watching them pull away. At least he did show up here today, as promised. It scared her to even think it, but he was *practically* getting reliable.

When Molly returned to the dining room, dinner had ended. The guests had dispersed, waiting to be called back for dessert and coffee. Jessica and Sam were among the helping hands clearing the table.

"Funny to see Phil after all this time." Sam stacked some dinner dishes, putting the silverware on top. "He looks like he's doing well. It's good to see him pulling himself together and doing right by you and the girls."

Molly picked up some glasses. She felt an impulse to make some disparaging remark about Phil but caught herself. She didn't want to be like that anymore.

"So far, so good," she said. "We've hit a few bumps, but we're managing to work things out."

"That's great. Maybe you guys will get back together again."

Molly turned her head to look at him, thinking he had to be joking. "Are you crazy? I'd never get back together with Phil. Not in a million years."

Sam stood with his stack of plates. "What's so crazy about it? It happens to people all the time. The kids would be happy. Maybe Phil's finally grown up. He's always been a good-hearted guy, even though he messed up with you. You could do a lot worse than him, Molly."

Molly stood there, stunned. The entire idea was so unthinkable to her that she couldn't reply.

Yes, I could do a lot worse than Phil Willoughby. He's not the most awful man in the world. But I could do a lot better, she thought, turning toward the kitchen. *Though I seem to be the only one who thinks so.*

When it was time to serve dessert and coffee, Molly was

still helping out in the kitchen. She had made a number of desserts for the party, including a cheesecake, a lemon meringue pie, and for the younger members of the group, a rabbit-shaped cake covered with coconut icing. She finished decorating the platter, adding a few jelly beans for color around the edge. Jessica swept by and popped one into her mouth.

"Wow, that looks beautiful. What's inside?"

"Chocolate cake. Well, more of a fudge cake, actually."

"I'm not sure I could tell the difference. But I'm willing to try." Jessica smiled and took another jelly bean. "I hear you're going to do my sister's party. You must be excited."

"More like terrified," Molly confided. She shook some powdered sugar on the cheesecake then took another critical look at it. "The woman who teaches my course is giving me a lot of help, but I'm still sort of nervous."

"How about your financing? How's that going?"

Molly laughed. "So far I'm working off my Visa card. . . . That's not the way you're really supposed to do this, right?"

"Well, it's one way, I suppose. I can give you a few more ideas if you come down to the bank sometime." Jessica smiled at her, then stole another bean. "You're in business now, Molly. You can get a line of credit or a loan."

Molly didn't answer right away. She concentrated on arranging a cluster of strawberries on top of the cheesecake. "I don't know. Do you really think the bank would loan someone like me money?"

"You're not so bad. I'll put in a good word for you, promise," Jessica gently teased. "Just call me next week, okay?"

Molly met Jessica's gaze. Her smile was so sincere, it was hard to refuse. *She really does want to help me,* Molly realized. *I've really haven't been fair to her.*

Jessica brushed off her hands. "Can I help you put these cakes on the table?"

Molly nodded. "Sure. The bunny cake is ready to go."

Jessica picked up the platter and gazed down at it. "That's one thing I dislike about Easter," she said, walking slowly into the dining room. "Decapitating these poor, defenseless chocolate rabbits."

Molly had to laugh. When she stopped to think about it, that part always made her squeamish, too.

MATTHEW HAD SPENT THE DAY AT HIS SISTER'S HOUSE. He and Amanda had come home in the early evening. Amanda quickly changed into her jeans and now sat glued in front of the TV. He sat in the living room, trying to read a book but not quite focusing on the story.

His parents had been at Erica's house, too. Erica was divorced and didn't have children so it had been a quiet afternoon but a pleasant visit with his family. Erica was a good cook.

Not as good as Molly, of course. He had been thinking of her a lot today. She hadn't been far from his thoughts ever since he saw her in church that morning. The truth was, she was never far from his thoughts. He missed talking to her. He missed the way she smiled, the way she moved, the way she just lit up a room. He missed her smart-aleck sense of humor. His life seemed dull lately without Molly.

He had been tempted to talk to Erica today when he helped her in the kitchen. But just as he worked himself up to asking for her advice, his father had come into the room.

What could Erica tell him anyway? He had to figure this out himself. It didn't take a rocket scientist. He was stuck on Molly Willoughby.

But what to do about it? He had backed himself into a safe, comfortable little corner with that "let's just be friends" speech. He could kick himself now, just thinking about it. *She must hate me now. Or at least think I'm a jerk.*

Which I have been. Totally, as Amanda would say.

He glanced at the phone and took a deep breath. What if

he called her right now? He could say something like, "I saw you in church today, and I didn't get to say much. I just wanted to wish you a happy Easter. . . ."

He shook his head. That wouldn't work. She was mad at him. She had a perfect right to be. He had hurt her feelings. She might not even talk to him. He had to do better than that.

Not tonight, he told himself. He was too tired. It wouldn't come out right. He needed to go to bed and get some sleep. He had a big day tomorrow, booked solid with appointments and a patient going in for bypass surgery.

Matt closed his book and put it aside. *Molly, Molly, Molly. What did you do to me? Even thinking about work can't make me forget you entirely.*

He sighed and rubbed his eyes with his hands. He thought of Molly again, how lovely she looked in church today. What had she been thinking, sitting there so close to him? She had said hello, then barely glanced his way, her attention fixed on Reverend Ben.

The sermon had touched him, and the message came back to him now, along with his fears. Matthew swallowed and whispered a prayer. "Dear Lord, I'm sort of a mess tonight. I think I've finally found someone I could truly love. But I'm afraid to move forward, afraid to disappoint her and fail her, like I failed Sharon. Please help me change. Give me a second chance to do better."

He took a deep breath, then opened his eyes. He didn't know what else to say. He hoped the Lord had heard his words, but he also knew that praying wasn't like waving a magic wand. For his prayers to work, he would have to do his share.

TUCKER WAS OUT ON PATROL MONDAY AFTERNOON WHEN the call came in, a break-in on North Creek Road. Kevin Degan, the homeowner, had called to report it. Since Tucker was the nearest car, the dispatcher directed him to the property.

Tucker pulled into the driveway, parking behind an SUV. The open hatch revealed a jumble of suitcases, pillows, and golf clubs—the usual paraphernalia from a family car trip.

The Degans were waiting for him at the front door. "Officer, we've been robbed," Mr. Degan began. "We just pulled in from a few days in Vermont, visiting relatives. We opened the door and found this." He gestured to the living room behind him, where an end table had been knocked over and sofa cushions lay scattered on the rug.

"I'm going to take a full report," Tucker assured him. "Let's just go step by step. What time do you think you got in?"

"It was half past two. I know because I checked my watch."

"Kevin always checks to see if we've made good time," Mrs. Degan added. Her face was tear streaked as she pointed to the back of the house. "They came in through the glass door in back. It's broken in a million pieces."

"It must have happened last night. The rain got in and wet the carpeting," her husband said.

Though it was clear and sunny now, it had poured the night before. "That's a good guess, sir," Tucker said. "But just to be on the safe side, I'm going to have a look around and make sure the intruder is really gone."

Mrs. Degan gasped, and her husband put his arm around her shoulder. "That's fine. My boys are back in the kitchen, having a snack. Nothing stops teenagers from eating, right?" He shook his head. "Should I call them in here, too?"

"That's all right. They're okay. I'll start upstairs."

Tucker checked the house, jotting some notes on a pad. It was a messy job, amateurs. It looked as if they'd been in a rush but hadn't taken anything too big—no computer monitors or TV sets. They had torn the bedroom apart, especially the woman's closet and dresser. Looking for jewelry, he figured. He felt a twinge, remembering Fran's stickpin. She still hadn't found it.

He checked the house room by room, then returned to

the Degans and took down their story. He called the station from his car radio and made a quick report. Mr. Degan had some pull in town, and the chief was sending another car over with a team that would dust for prints, question the couple more closely, and talk to the neighbors about anything they might have heard or seen.

Tucker continued his part of the process, finishing up the standard questions he needed for his report. When his colleagues arrived, he was free to go.

He got back in his car and radioed the station, then resumed his usual route around familiar village neighborhoods. The Degan's break-in nagged at him. He couldn't remember the last time he heard of a robbery like this in Cape Light. It was unlikely the thieves would be caught, he knew. That was just the way these things usually went. The family would collect on their homeowner's insurance and probably install an alarm system.

Back at the station, he began to type up his report. The other officers at the Degan house had come back earlier; he had seen them leaving Chief Sanborn's office.

He was nearly done with his paperwork when the chief stopped at his desk.

"I'm almost done with the report on that break-in on North Creek, Chief. Is that what you're looking for?"

"Yes, I'd like to see that as soon as you're done. Bring it into my office, will you?"

Something in the chief's tone and expression set off silent alarm bells, but Tucker showed no reaction. He checked through the document quickly, fixed a messy spot with white out, then carried the papers back to the chief's office.

Sanborn beckoned him in. "Shut the door, will you, Tucker?"

Tucker closed the door and gave the chief his copy of the crime report, then took his usual seat. "The Degans were pretty upset. There wasn't much to go on out there, though. Looks as if it happened last night."

"Yes, so I've heard. Myers and Paretsky talked to some

neighbors. One of them says he saw someone in the Degans' backyard. Claims he got a good look at him, too."

"Really? In the rain and all? He must have good eyesight."

"It didn't start raining until about midnight. This was around ten. The neighbor took out his newspapers for recycling, says he saw some guy running through the Degans' backyard."

"Well, that's something I guess." Tucker wondered what this was all adding up to.

"I like to think I'm a fair man," Sanborn said. "I checked Carl's record. You were right. He served his time, had no parole violations. But this neighbor's description fits your brother, fits him to a tee."

Tucker didn't say anything at first. It couldn't be Carl. This was just Sanborn needing to make a quick arrest.

"That's interesting," Tucker said finally. "Did this neighbor see the guy breaking into the house?"

"No, just running out of the yard." The chief leaned back in his chair. "He claims he got a good look at his face, though. The guy taking off nearly ran right into him."

"Did the neighbor hear anything, the glass door breaking, for instance?"

The chief shook his head. "He couldn't say. It appears that whoever broke the door may have cut his hand on the glass. There were also some fingerprints around the place. Myers sent them to the county, so they can run them through the computer."

Sounded as if he was talking about laundry being sent out to the dry cleaners, Tucker thought. Not something as weighty as Carl's guilt or innocence.

Tucker's heart felt like a brick in his chest. He was not really surprised that Sanborn would suspect Carl, but a cold dread filled him as he wondered if Carl really did it. They had just had Carl over Sunday night for Easter dinner. Could he possibly have robbed the Degans' house that same night? Tucker still didn't have a high opinion of Carl, but he truly doubted he would do something like that. Carl had been doing so well, working at the church and living on his own, not causing any problems for anyone.

"I'm going to bring him in for questioning," Sanborn went on. "I've sent out a car to pick him up. They should be back any minute. I wanted you to know that."

Tucker held his tongue, not trusting himself to speak. Chief Sanborn almost seemed to be enjoying this. He couldn't wait to prove that he was right about Carl and that Tucker was wrong.

"What's your plan here, to see if the neighbor can I.D. him?"

"Something like that."

"That doesn't mean much, Chief." Tucker swallowed back a hard ball of anger in his throat, struggling to keep his voice even. "Witnesses like that make ridiculous mistakes all the time. You know that. Just because some neighbor identifies Carl doesn't mean he did it."

The chief let out a long slow breath, rubbing his chin with his hand. "I knew you were going to say something like that. Your loyalty is admirable, Tucker. But I think it's been sadly misplaced."

Tucker stood up from his chair, though he hadn't been dismissed. He was so angry, he could feel himself shaking with it. "I guess we'll have to wait and see, Chief."

The chief glanced up at him. He had already begun reading the report. "Yes, we'll see. You ought to go now. I'll let you know what's happening."

"Fine. But I'm going to stick around until Carl is done here tonight."

They both knew Tucker meant to see if he needed a lawyer.

"We're just going to talk to him."

"Yeah, I know. I know the drill by now." Tucker knew his tone was a shade disrespectful and wondered if his boss would call him on it.

Chief Sanborn didn't look up again. "Suit yourself."

* * *

Tucker was sitting at his desk when Carl was brought in. He felt the other cops looking at him as he went over to the desk Sergeant, who was checking Carl in.

"They just want to talk to you, Carl. There's nothing to worry about," Tucker promised. "Just answer their questions and they'll let you go."

Carl, flanked by his two police escorts, gave a short, bitter laugh. "Sure, that's what they always say."

Tucker suddenly noticed a large bandage on Carl's left hand. "What happened to your hand?"

"I cut myself fixing something at the church. What's the problem? Didn't you ever see a bandage before?"

Tucker swallowed hard, still unwilling to think the worst.

"You don't have to say anything without a lawyer present. I'll call one for you."

"I don't need no lawyer. I can speak for myself. I'm not afraid."

Carl needed to have an attorney present, Tucker thought with alarm. There was no telling what he might say once he got angry. Tucker had questioned his share of suspects. He knew the tricks. Carl might incriminate himself without even realizing it.

"Hold up here awhile. I'm going to get him a lawyer," Tucker told Tom Schmidt, one of the officers with Carl.

"We're just delivering him to the questioning room, Tucker. They'll read him his rights, like always. He's got to ask for the lawyer. Not you."

"The man is right," Carl said. "I been through this before. I remember how it goes." He turned to Schmidt. "All right, lets get this over with. I don't have all night to hang around here. I'm a busy man."

Tucker waited at his desk, pretending to be working while Carl was questioned. He called home and left a message for Fran, warning her that he was held up at work and would be late. He didn't explain what was going on with Carl. He wanted to wait to see what happened before he told her anything.

Two hours passed. Tucker walked back to the interview room and asked what was going on. An officer standing near the closed door told him a detective from the county was still questioning his brother and taking his statement. They were waiting for the Degans' neighbor to arrive to see if he could identify Carl.

Tucker nodded and headed for the locker room, where he got a soda from the machine. Frank Myers, who was on the team sent to the Degans' house after him, was in there, pulling on his jacket.

"Tough break, Tucker. I heard they brought in your brother."

"Yeah, some county detective is talking to him now. I just hope they don't get him talking, make him say something stupid."

Myers stared at him, and Tucker suddenly felt a cold distance between them. "Like what? A confession, you mean?"

"There's no proof Carl did this, Myers. Not a shred. Just some neighbor who *might* have seen some guy who *might* look like my brother on a pitch-black rainy night."

"It wasn't raining yet. But I get your point. I'd feel the same if one of my relatives was brought in." Myers touched Tucker's arm in a gesture of camraderie, but Tucker shrank back.

"See you around," Myers said softly.

"Right, see you." Tucker turned away and headed back into the station. As he passed the front desk, he saw a man walking in and gazing around, looking confused. He guessed it was the Degans' neighbor, coming to view Carl through the one-way window.

Well, at least this would be over soon. He sat at his desk again, forcing himself to look busy and unconcerned.

The truth was, he felt torn apart, seesawing between believing Carl was innocent and feeling as if he'd been played for a fool.

Carl was once picked up for breaking and entering, back when he was a teenager. It had to be thirty-five years ago by now. But Sanborn would find that on his record, if he hadn't already, and jump on it like a dog on a bone.

Tucker wondered what Carl's alibi would be. He remembered the bandage on Carl's hand. The burglar had cut his hand on the glass door, Sanborn said. They would probably match the blood type, though that didn't mean much unless they used DNA testing, which Tucker knew was so expensive it would never be used on a case where there was only property damage. Carl could have cut his hand at work, like he said. But it didn't look good.

He thought of the missing stickpin again and felt as if its needle point had jabbed right into his heart. Maybe he should have known back then. Maybe Fran was right.

Still, Tucker found himself wanting to believe Carl was innocent. It seemed as if he had really changed these last few weeks. Was that all just an act?

Tom Schmidt stopped by Tucker's desk and spoke in a confidential tone. "I wanted to tell you. I was just back there. They're going to let him go."

"The neighbor couldn't I.D. him?" Tucker asked hopefully.

"It was shaky. The guy got rattled, kept wiping his glasses. That doesn't look so good in court. Sanborn got annoyed. The blood on the door was a match—O positive. But everybody's got O positive, even Sanborn's mother."

Tucker forced a smile. "How about the fingerprints? Did they hear back yet on that?"

"No, the prints they had weren't clear. Sanborn's sending someone back to the house tomorrow to see if they can find more."

That was unlikely, Tucker thought. By the next day,

with the family walking around carrying on with their lives, they wouldn't find anything matchable. He felt relieved—until he realized that feeling this way must mean he thought Carl was guilty.

Tucker rubbed the side of his cheek and looked up at Schmidt, thinking, *He thinks Carl is guilty, but he feels badly for me and is trying to help me out.*

"Will he be out soon?"

"Sounds like it." Schmidt glanced over his shoulder, then moved closer to Tucker and lowered his voice. "They were trying to get a warrant to search Carl's place for stolen goods, but the judge wouldn't sign off. Not enough cause."

Tucker hadn't even thought of that. A search through Carl's belongings might explain everything—or not. He could have hidden small items anywhere, not just in his room. He could have hidden things at the church, for instance, Tucker thought. He pulled back from the idea; it seemed too sad and cynical.

"Thanks, Schmidt. I owe you one," Tucker said quietly.

"That's okay." Schmidt rested a heavy hand on his shoulder. "See you tomorrow. I'm checking out."

Nearly an hour later, Carl emerged. He looked even more worn and haggard than usual, with deep, dark rings under his eyes and a glassy angry stare as he approached Tucker.

"Well, I'm out of here. I told you I didn't need no lawyer."

Tucker felt every eye in the station house watching them. "Come on, I'll give you a lift home."

Carl nodded and followed him, seeming oblivious to the attention. "A police station has a certain smell. Ever notice? I sure hate that smell."

Tucker didn't answer. The truth was, he was starting to dislike it, too.

They got in Tucker's car and started toward the house where Carl now rented a room. It was an old-fashioned building outside the village, three stories high and squarely built. At the turn of the century it had been a boardinghouse for summer visitors. The present owner, an elderly lady, rented furnished rooms at cheap rates. Tucker knew what it looked like inside, though he'd never been to see Carl there. The rooms were small and dark, hot in the summer and cold in the winter. But the place was clean overall, not a complete dump.

He pulled up outside and parked. "So, I heard the neighbor couldn't really identify you. Were you even there?" He tried to sound mildly curious, no pressure.

Carl's back went up at once. "I just sat through umpteen hours of questions. Now you're starting in on me, too?"

"I'm just curious, Carl. You might have been there. It doesn't mean anything."

"It seemed to mean a lot to that county detective."

Tucker felt his gut clench. "You told him you were there? Did you put that in a statement or something?"

Carl shook his head. "Oh, man. Let me out of here. I got nothing else to say to you, Tucker. Maybe I *do* need a lawyer."

He started to open the car door. Tucker touched his arm. "Look, Carl, this is serious. They tried to get a warrant to search your room tonight, but the judge wouldn't give it to them. Tomorrow, though, they might find one who will."

"You know what they say, if at first you don't succeed." Carl laughed bitterly at the expression on Tucker's face. "What do you think they're going to find up there anyway, Tucker? Besides a bunch of dirty laundry and soup cans, I mean. Why do you look so nervous, man?"

"I'm concerned for you. Can't you see that? I don't want you put away for something you didn't do."

"Neither do I, when you put it like that." Carl stared straight ahead. "You act as if you think I did do it. That's what is sounds like to me."

Tucker felt as if his head might just explode. "Stop talking in circles for a minute, will you, please? Did you do it? Is that what you're trying to tell me?"

Carl leaned back, laughing quietly. "You're the cop, what do you think? Some neighbor says I was running through the backyard but face-to-face doesn't recognize me. I cut my hand, see?" He raised his bandaged hand. "And I did time for killing a man and have a record of breaking and entering—"

"Did you give a statement? Did you sign anything?" Tucker interrupted him.

"Sure I did. They wouldn't let me out otherwise."

"They can use that in court against you. Don't you know that?"

Carl turned and looked at him. "Who says I'm going to court? They've got nothing on me."

Tucker sighed in frustration, not knowing what to believe.

"You're the one who's in hot water," Carl taunted him. "I saw the way you were moping around the station house, Tucker. You had a bad day at work. You ought to get home."

"Right, I need to go home." Tucker felt totally frustrated with Carl. Not that he ever expected a thank you. He'd had enough of talking in circles for one night.

"Good night, Carl. I'll speak to you tomorrow."

Carl slipped out of the car and closed the door. He leaned in through the half-open window. "So long, Tucker. Take it easy." Then he turned and walked toward the boardinghouse, looking like a man who didn't have a care in the world.

TUCKER WALKED OUT TO HIS SQUAD CAR THE NEXT morning, eager to leave the station house and get out on duty. He unlocked the door and looked up to see Reverend Ben crossing the parking lot.

"Reverend, good morning," Tucker said as Ben approached him.

"Sorry to bother you at work, Tucker. I hoped to catch you before you left the station. I need to talk with you."

"This is about Carl, right?"

The reverend nodded. "I went down to the church this morning and found this note." He reached into his jacket pocket and pulled out a folded sheet of paper. He handed it to Tucker, but Tucker didn't even bother to open it. He had a feeling he already knew what it said. "He's gone, right?"

"Yes. He left for Maine to see that friend of his. He says he'll call when he has an address so I can send some back pay. But I don't understand what he's talking about in the note. What robbery? When did the police question him?"

Tucker felt his body sag. Whether it was with sadness or relief, he couldn't tell. He took a deep breath before he answered the reverend's question.

"Two nights ago there was a break-in on North Creek Road. A neighbor claimed he saw a man who fit Carl's description. So they brought Carl in for questioning."

"I see . . . and you were there, too, I gather?"

Tucker nodded. "I wasn't allowed in the interview. But I waited for him. I drove him home last night."

"Do the police think he's guilty?"

"Well, he's the only suspect so far. It's all circumstantial evidence—not even a fingerprint to go on. But Carl did admit to being in the neighborhood that night. His alibi isn't strong."

He had finally heard Carl's story this morning from another officer on the case. The story made Tucker cringe with embarrassment. It seemed so trumped up and transparent.

"What was it?" the reverend asked with interest.

"Carl says he was walking a dog down North Creek Road. Says he takes out the trash and walks the landlady's dog some nights as part of the deal on his rent."

"Yes, I know. I helped him find that room. That was the arrangement," the reverend confirmed.

Tucker paused. So Carl hadn't been lying about that part.

"Well, he said the dog spotted a cat or a raccoon or something and ran away from him. So he chased the dog through some backyards and wound up coming back out to the street through the Degan's yard. That's why the neighbor saw him, he said."

The reverend nodded. "That makes sense to me. But you don't sound as if you believe him."

"I don't know what to believe, Reverend. I tried to believe he's changed . . . but yesterday I felt like a fool, trying to defend him. Now he's taken off, run away from this whole mess, which definitely makes it look like he's guilty. If they get some solid proof, they'll go looking for him."

"Carl's leaving town doesn't prove anything. And even if he is guilty, you have nothing to be ashamed of, Tucker. You tried to help him. You went out of your way to give your brother a new start here. You acted with kindness and courage."

"Thanks, Reverend," Tucker said, feeling better about sticking up for Carl and looking out for his rights. He'd probably do it again, given the chance.

It didn't look like there would be another chance, Tucker realized. Carl was gone. He'd probably never see him or even hear from him again. Tucker had a strange feeling and swallowed back a lump in his throat. When he looked up, he realized the reverend was still standing there, watching him.

"I better get to work. Appreciate you stopping by, Reverend."

"That's all right, Tucker. If you want to talk about this some more, you know where to find me."

"Yes, I do." Tucker nodded and jammed the unread note into his pocket. He doubted he would want to discuss Carl anymore with anyone. Just thinking about Carl made him confused and depressed. He wished he could forget his brother ever existed.

Chapter Sixteen

"Are you sure it's safe? I mean, the water isn't very deep, is it?" Molly stood in the middle of her kitchen, clutching a knapsack of extra clothes she had packed for Lauren and Jill in case they got wet. They were going kayaking today with Phil down in Essex, but now Molly felt reluctant to let them go, even though they were on spring break and she needed to work. "How do you know there won't be any rapids or currents or things?"

Phil and Lauren stood staring at her. Lauren rolled her eyes, then glanced at her father.

"Really, Molly. It's very safe," Phil said.

"Really? Then why do you need all these extra clothes? Don't those boats tip over a lot?"

"It will be fine, honestly. They're going to love it."

"It's not too cold out for this?"

"Perfect weather. You don't want it too hot." Phil took the knapsack from her grasp and hooked it over his broad shoulder. "Listen, if you're so worried, why don't you come with us? You need a day off, Molly. You've been working too hard."

She had been working hard. She had a lot of new clients and had started training her helpers from the high school. She was also preparing for Emily's party and had just seen Jessica at the bank yesterday, where she had applied for a small-business loan.

She was worn out from work and all the excitement. But she still didn't feel right just goofing off.

"I can't. I have too much to do. It does sound like fun, though." She picked up her apron from the back of a chair.

Phil reached over and snatched it out of her hands. "You won't be needing that today. They do make you wear something called an apron, but it's a part of the boat that keeps you dry."

"Mom's going with us? Great!" Jill walked into the room, beaming at Molly.

"Mom in a kayak?" Lauren rolled her eyes again. "This I've got to see."

"Why, don't you think I could do it?" Molly challenged her. "I would probably be great with a paddle. All this baking builds up arm muscles, you know." Molly flexed her biceps, and the girls started laughing.

"Not bad," Phil nodded, looking impressed. "I think you ought to have Lauren in your boat. She's the heavier freight."

"Thanks a lot, Dad!" Lauren gave her father a playful nudge.

"Oops. Guess I said something wrong."

"Yeah, I guess." Molly said dryly. She sighed and glanced around the kitchen, her work pulling her in one direction and Jill tugging her arm in the other.

"Come on, you're going with us," her younger daughter insisted. "You need some fresh air and exercise."

"Besides, our vacation is almost over and you haven't done anything fun with us all week, Mom," Lauren added.

Molly glanced at Lauren, then back at Phil. The girls were right. She needed to take a break and be with them. Even if it meant spending the day with her ex-husband.

ALTHOUGH MOLLY WAS APPREHENSIVE AT FIRST, SHE found the hardest part was getting herself into the boat. Once they were out on the water, a smooth quiet inlet near the Essex River, Molly felt an extraordinary sense of peace. They paddled out across the smooth blue surface that showed barely a ripple in the morning light. Except for the slap of water against the hull and the dip of the paddle, it was silent. Birds balanced gracefully on long stalks of marsh grass, and fish wriggled past under the boat, their slick silver bodies darting through the clear water. The two kayaks glided across the calm inlet, and Molly fell into a smooth rhythm both with her own breath and heartbeat and with Jill, who sat in front of her, also paddling.

At one point they got their signals crossed and the boat started to tip to one side. "Jill, watch out!" Molly cried. She tried to reach forward to her daughter, which only made it worse. Then somehow she managed to get them righted despite Jill's screeching. Phil paddled over to check out the fuss, and the two boats bumped together, making the girls laugh out loud.

"Aren't there any brakes on this thing?" Molly called out as her boat collided with Phil's.

"Dad, for goodness' sake. You're such a bad driver. You need to let me steer on the way back," Lauren told her father.

"Great. I'll just rest. My arms are getting tired already," Phil complained in a good-natured tone.

Molly glanced at him. His muscular arms were bared by a T-shirt under his life vest, and he didn't look the least bit tired. Attractive, yes. Tired, no. She looked away, surprised that she had even noticed him that way. Well, he always was a handsome guy. There was never any question about that.

Finally, they paddled up to a beach that appeared to be a sandbar. The sand was nearly white, covered with shells, and Molly felt as if she were paddling up to a deserted island. They pushed their boats up to the shoreline and hopped out.

It wasn't really warm enough to swim, but the girls were so hot from paddling in the strong sun, they jumped into the water with their shorts and T-shirts on and splashed around wildly.

"Now you see why you need all the extra clothes," Phil said.

Molly stood on the edge of the water, watching with a smile. "They have the right idea. It gets pretty hot out there." She tipped her head back and took a long drink from a water bottle.

Phil thoughtfully waited until she was done, then gave her a hard shove, pushing her in with her daughters. "I was hoping you'd say something like that."

"Phil . . . you're horrible." Molly couldn't help laughing at him. She climbed out of the water, soaked to the skin. She came after him, but he was too quick and dashed away, laughing.

"Get him, Mom! You can't let him get away with that," Lauren called out. Then Lauren and Jill joined in the chase, and Phil let himself be caught. With each girl tugging an arm, they pulled him into the water.

"Oh, man, that is cold!" He jumped out like a pop-up toy. "I can't believe you guys did that to me. Three against one, no fair. Just for that, I'm going to hide your paddles. You'll be stranded out here."

"No way!" Jill shouted at him.

"Yes, way. Just try me," he warned her. But the girls pounced on him as he hurried to get out of the water and pulled him down again.

Molly was laughing so hard, she couldn't speak. She couldn't remember the last time she had this much fun. For an instant, she felt as if they were a real family again.

Sam's words suddenly echoed in her mind. *Maybe you guys will get back together again.* She pulled out a towel from the pack and dried off. Was it even remotely possible?

They ended up at the Woodsman, an Essex landmark that offered no-frills seafood and a rustic ambiance. Everyone wanted the same lunch, a cup of chowder and a lobster roll. They carried their trays of food outside to the wooden tables set up under long awnings. Molly felt tired, and she ached in places she didn't even know she had. But she was hungry, and the tasty food and view of the open meadow behind the restaurant took her mind off her pains.

The girls finished quickly and went for a walk in the meadow. "I can't believe they have any energy left after all the paddling. I can barely chew," Phil confessed.

"Me, either, but it was fun. Thanks for making me go with you. It's been a great day."

Phil smiled at her. "It would have been fun with Lauren and Jill. Having you with us made it really special. I'd forgotten how much fun you are, Molly."

"So did I," Molly said with a small smile. "Sorry you got dunked by my assistants."

"That's okay. I deserved it. I did it to you first."

"So you did. I almost forgot about that."

Phil was quiet for a moment. "I almost forgot how pretty you look when you're smiling like that."

Molly glanced up at him quickly, then looked out at the meadow. What was going on here? She didn't like that look in his eyes.

"I've been thinking about you, Molly. I've missed you."

"Oh? Really?" Molly coughed. She didn't know what else to say. She picked up her soda and sipped from the straw.

Phil's blue-eyed gaze became intent. "I know this probably sounds crazy, but I think we should get back together."

Molly put the cup down abruptly. She started to speak, but he interrupted her before she could get any words out.

"I know we had some bad times. But we're older now. We're calmer. Well, I am," he added. "We were happy together sometimes, Molly, really happy, like today. It wasn't all bad times—"

"No, it wasn't, Phil," she cut in. "I would never say that. But that doesn't mean we should get back together again."

"The girls would love it. I've never seen them as happy as they were today. Well, not recently anyway."

She couldn't argue with that. Still, getting back together for the sake of the girls wasn't a good reason, was it?

"Just think it over. I have a good job now. We could buy a house. You wouldn't have to work so hard. A lot of our fights were about money. It wouldn't be like that anymore."

He met her eyes, trying to persuade her to see the reason in his unexpected proposal. Molly stared at him, stunned. *He's a born salesman,* she reminded herself. *A few minutes more of this and I'll start to agree with him.*

Well, almost.

She saw Lauren and Jill walking back toward them and breathed a little easier. He wouldn't keep this up in front of the girls. He had better sense than that. She hoped so, anyway.

"Hi, guys. Ready to go?" Molly's voice was bright.

Phil rubbed his chin, looking as if he realized he hadn't gotten very far but wasn't going to give up quite so easily. The look in his eyes made her nervous. She couldn't quite believe this was happening.

MOLLY WAS RELIEVED WHEN SPRING BREAK ENDED AND the girls went back to school. As of tomorrow, she had two weeks left to prepare for Emily's party, which wasn't long at all. And she had cold feet again about applying for the small-business loan. Jessica was calling regularly, gently pressuring her for the paperwork. It just seemed like an awful lot to bite off, Molly thought, especially since Emily was her first and only client and could be her last if it didn't go well.

Of course, if she didn't get the loan, she might not have the means to do this right, so there was another dilemma.

She had also been putting off the visit to Lillian Warwick's house to check the rooms and plan the setup. But on Friday she realized she had to face the inevitable. She called Emily, and they made a plan to meet there at two.

Molly was apprehensive enough about facing Lillian with Emily by her side, but just as Molly was about to leave the house her cell phone rang.

"Molly, it's Emily. I'm stuck in a meeting. I'm not sure when this will be over. My mother is expecting us. Why don't you go on over, and I'll try to catch up?"

"Um, sure. I was just leaving to go there," Molly told her. "See you later then."

She hung up the phone, feeling her stomach twist into a knot. *You're a businesswoman now,* she told herself. *You have to be polite to the client's mother. Even if it is Lillian Warwick.*

Molly arrived at Lillian's grand old house on Providence Street a few minutes later. She rang the doorbell and glanced around. The place looked deserted. Then again, it always looked like that. The curtain in the front window stirred. Still, no one came to the door.

Molly rang the bell again, then knocked. Finally, she turned around to go, and as she did, she heard the door open behind her.

She whirled around to see Lillian peering outside, her mouth set in a frown. "I thought my daughter was coming with you."

"Emily got held up in a meeting. She told me to come ahead since you were expecting us."

"I was expecting my daughter . . . but never mind, come in."

Lillian pulled open the door and stood back, taking in Molly with an appraising glance. Molly felt as if she didn't quite pass muster, even though she had pulled her wild, curly hair back into a neat upswept hairstyle and wore a dress and heels. She also carried a professional-looking black portfolio, hugging it in front of her now like a shield.

"Let's see, where should we start?" Molly tried for a light yet professional tone.

"How should I know? I really don't want this party here in the first place—strangers tramping through my house, breaking things. I wish they would have it in a restaurant or an inn. I'm not running a catering hall here, you know."

"Of course not." Molly struggled for a pleasant tone. "But house parties are so much more personal and comfortable than something in a restaurant."

"How preposterous. Emily has no nostalgic feelings for this house, believe me. She was never happy one minute under this roof. It's just for convenience's sake. Her convenience . . . and my inconvenience."

It was a wasted effort trying to be pleasant to Lillian Warwick, that was for sure. Molly decided it was best to just do what she'd come to do and get it over with.

"May I see the dining room?" Molly asked.

"You know where it is. You don't need a tour guide."

Molly thought Lillian would stay out of her way after that, but she followed her, walking carefully with the use of her cane. Lillian stood in the doorway while Molly surveyed the room. The heavy drapes were drawn, and the room was so dark Molly could hardly get a good idea of the size.

A long banquet-sized table took up most of the space. It was really too large for the room and must have been brought from Lilac Hall, the old family estate.

"Can this table be closed to a smaller size?" Molly tried to check to see if it could, but the table was covered by a lace cloth.

"Why ask me? I thought you were the expert. Though I don't see how one can make such a leap, from cleaning girl to party planner or whatever it is you call yourself now."

Molly felt stung. She held her breath, not permitting

herself to react to Lillian's barbs. She had done more for Lillian than clean house. She had also made meals for her, though Lillian never thought much of her cooking.

"I'm starting a catering business, Lillian. It's not brain surgery."

"I'll say it's not." Lillian tugged on the edges of her cardigan sweater. "That's my daughter for you, always doing people favors, even at her own expense. This party will humiliate her, mark my words. She hires a cleaning girl to stage an engagement party for a hundred guests. At her stage in life, mind you. I must say, I'm aghast."

Molly had rarely heard that word used but didn't need a dictionary to gather its meaning. She felt her face turn beet red, and she swallowed back an angry response.

The problem was, Lillian's cruel taunts had hit a nerve. She was a cleaning girl trying to stage a formal party for the town's mayor. She wasn't fooling anybody in her stylish new clothes and upswept hairdo, least of all, Lillian.

She couldn't let Lillian see that she had rattled her. Determined, Molly strode into the living room and started a quick sketch, noting the arrangement of the heavy old pieces of furniture. Later she would figure out how they might be rearranged to make more room for the guests and extra tables.

Lillian peered at her sketch. "Don't tell me you're going to redecorate in here as well. Or is that another sideline for you?"

The place could use a little freshening up, Molly thought. It looked as if Lillian had hired Teddy Roosevelt to do her decorating.

The doorbell rang, and Lillian glanced at Molly. "That must be Emily, late as usual. She'll be late for her own funeral," she complained as she started toward the foyer.

Molly sighed with relief. She never imagined she would be so happy to see Emily Warwick enter a room. She had been a heartbeat away from losing it and congratulated herself now for keeping her temper.

"Hi, Molly, sorry I'm late." Emily walked into the room and bent to kiss Lillian's cheek. "Hello, Mother."

"Since you're finally here, I'll let you handle things," Lillian said with a last disparaging glance at Molly. "I'm going upstairs. I find this all very tiresome, Emily."

Emily ignored that and turned back to Molly. "So, what are you up to? Any questions so far?"

Just one. How have you survived with such a mother? Molly wanted to ask her. Of course, she didn't.

"I was just doing a sketch of this room to figure out how we'll set up the tables. Isn't there a patio outside?"

"Yes, the patio is right off the kitchen. Would you like to see it?"

"Let's take a look. If the warm weather keeps up, we can set up cocktails and hors d'oeuvres out there."

"That's a great idea." Emily led the way through the kitchen to a back door. Molly followed, grateful that Lillian had retreated for now. Still, Molly couldn't help feeling a little battered by Lillian's cutting words, in part because of her own doubts. What if she couldn't pull this off? What if Lillian was right?

MOLLY LEFT LILLIAN'S HOUSE FEELING WEARY AND stressed but also encouraged. Emily had seemed pleased with her ideas for the setup and decorating.

Checking her watch, Molly realized she needed to rush over to the middle school to pick up Lauren, who had stayed late for lacrosse practice. Her mother had already picked up Jill and brought her to her own house.

Molly pulled into the parking lot by the athletic fields and soon spotted her daughter, standing in a cluster of other girls. Amanda Harding was there as well. Lauren ran over to the car and bent down to talk to Molly.

"Can Amanda come home with us? She's not feeling well."

"Um, sure. Of course she can. Where's her dad?"

"We don't know. She tried to reach him on his cell phone, but he hasn't gotten back to her yet."

"No problem. Go get her." Molly wondered about Matthew. It wasn't like him not to answer his cell phone. She knew he'd been working long hours the last few weeks. She had seen a lot of Amanda lately. During the vacation, Amanda had hardly been home at all, shuttling between Molly's and her aunt's in Newburyport.

She hadn't seen much of Matthew since their talk. She told him they would still be friends, but it was too hard for her. She still had feelings for him—deep feelings that wouldn't go away that easily.

The two girls jumped into the backseat. Molly stopped at her mother's house and picked up Jill, then took everyone home.

Amanda seemed subdued during the car ride. When Molly asked if she was all right, she just nodded.

There seemed to be something else going on; Molly knew that look on Lauren's face by now. She would get to the bottom of this sooner or later.

Once they got home, Molly suggested that Amanda call her father again. Amanda got a machine this time and left a message that she was at Molly's house. Jill ran off to watch TV in the living room, pleased to have the remote all to herself. The two older girls started toward Lauren's room, but Molly stopped them.

"Dinner will be a while. How about a snack—some popcorn?"

Lauren and Amanda glanced at each other. "Okay," Lauren said.

Molly slipped a bag of popcorn in the microwave and took out a big bowl. "Eat in here, okay? I don't want a lot of crumbs in your room."

"I'll get something to drink," Lauren said, going into the refrigerator. Amanda sat at the table, and Molly joined her.

"So, how was school today? Anything interesting going on?"

Molly waited. She wasn't sure this would work. Sometimes the direct approach was best, though, catching them off guard.

Amanda swallowed and shook her head no. Molly could tell that really meant yes, and whatever had happened wasn't all that easy to talk about.

Lauren came to the table with a carton of orange juice and a funny look on her face.

"Amanda had this . . . thing happen to her today." She rested her hand on her friend's shoulder. Amanda sat staring down at the table, and Molly saw her eyes glistening with unshed tears.

"Was she hurt at practice or something?" Molly asked with concern. "Amanda, can you tell me? You don't have to if you don't feel like it," she added.

Amanda lifted her head and rubbed the back of her hand across her eyes. "N-n-no . . . it's okay." She winced, hearing herself stutter.

Molly hadn't heard the speech defect in a while, and though it wasn't terribly obvious, she could tell it upset Amanda.

"Amanda had to give a book report today in English, and she had trouble talking," Lauren explained. "And when the teacher left the room for a minute, this dumb guy in our class, Ricky Hanratty, started imitating Amanda, and she got really upset."

"Oh, Amanda, honey. That's just awful." Molly rose and went over to Amanda. She put her arm around Amanda's shoulder and gave her a hug. For a long moment Amanda sat stiffly; then the tears came, and she seemed to melt. She turned and pressed her face against Molly's hip.

Molly leaned over and stroked her hair. "That was such a cruel thing to do. What a creep," she stated flatly. "You just can't pay attention to dumb kids like that."

She hugged Amanda. After a moment, Amanda pulled away, collecting herself. Molly got the popcorn from the microwave, poured it into a bowl, and brought it to the table. Amanda was drying her eyes with a tissue, but she still looked shaken. *Maybe I helped a little,* Molly thought, *but what she really needs is her father.*

"I'm so sorry, dear. You had a really bad day. But soon everyone will forget all about it. You'll see."

"I hope so," Amanda managed to say.

Lauren glanced at her mother. "Can't we take this stuff in the bedroom? I don't see what the difference is. I eat in there every minute of my life."

"That's just the problem. Okay, take it in if you have to. Just try to pick up the crumbs later so they don't get smashed into the carpeting."

As if Lauren would remember to do that, Molly thought, shaking her head.

Molly started to fix dinner. She was rinsing some lettuce in the sink when the door buzzer sounded. Wiping her hands on a towel, she went to answer it. Phil was coming tonight to visit the girls. She had felt a little uneasy about seeing him ever since he had made his wild proposal to get back together again.

She took a breath and pulled open the door—and found Matthew on the other side.

"Molly, hi. I'm sorry I didn't call first. I picked up Amanda's message, and I came right over."

Molly stepped aside to let him in. "That's all right. You didn't have to rush. She just wasn't sure where you were today. She couldn't reach your cell phone."

"I was having some trouble with the phone today. I've been running around, as usual. A patient had to be taken by helicopter to Mass General this afternoon for emergency heart surgery."

He sat at the kitchen table, looking beat, his handsome looks marred by dark circles beneath his eyes.

Molly felt sorry for him, yet she could also see now what had been going on between him and Amanda. She sat down at the table across from him, determined to have a talk.

"Amanda had a problem at school today. That's why she came home with us."

"What happened? Is she okay?"

"She's fine . . . or she will be. A boy in their English class made fun of her speech problem after she gave a report. She's very upset. It must have been quite painful for her."

Matthew looked alarmed and angry. "Why do kids act like that? Don't they know any better? You would think they were old enough by now to understand and have some consideration." He shook his head. "I'm going to call the school. No kid should get away with behavior like that."

Molly reached over and lightly touched his arm. "Matthew, I know you're upset, but making a big deal about this might upset Amanda even more."

He glanced at her, then nodded. "Good point. I didn't think about that."

Molly withdrew her hand. He seemed very conscious of her touch and of her taking it away from him. "You told me once you came here to make a new start, so you would be able to give Amanda more time and attention."

Matthew looked puzzled. "Yes, that's true. But what does that have to do with it?"

Molly sat back. "You haven't been around much these last few weeks. Not that I don't love having Amanda here. I do. But I feel as if she's here more than at your house lately."

He frowned at her. "I've been busy with work. I can't help my difficult hours."

"Maybe not," Molly agreed mildly. "Or maybe you just can't help falling back into old habits again."

"You're saying I'm doing the same thing I did when I was with Sharon?" he asked sharply.

She shrugged. "I don't know. You're the one who told me that you have a way of disappearing into your work. And I watched you disappear on me." She saw that he was about to interrupt her, and she silenced him with a look. "That's okay. I'm fine," she said calmly. "But it's not okay for Amanda. She needs you, and you're not there for her lately. You ought to think about it. That's all I'm saying."

Matthew looked blindsided. "I guess we ought to go now." His voice was quiet.

Molly stood up. "Okay, I'll go tell Amanda you're here."

Matthew watched as Molly disappeared down the hallway that led to the bedrooms. He let out a long breath. She had all but accused him of running away from her. Had he? He had thought he was doing the honorable thing, trying to protect her feelings, to keep himself from disappointing her. Apparently it added up to the same thing.

As for Amanda, Molly was right on that score. He had fallen into his old workaholic habits again. Even his sister had noticed it on Easter Sunday and said something to him. He had to break out of these tired patterns. It felt as if he was coping, but it caused more damage in the long run.

He could get back on track with Amanda. He was sure of that. But he didn't think he could ever fix things now with Molly.

TUCKER WAS ALONE IN THE LOCKER ROOM, GETTING ready to go home, when Chief Sanborn walked in. "Tucker, glad I caught you. I wanted to have a word."

Tucker closed his locker door. "What's up, Chief?"

"It's about North Creek Road. The Degan house."

Tucker had already guessed that would be the topic. "Did you find more evidence?"

"Not really." The chief's tone was vague. The crime had been reported nearly two weeks ago, but Tucker knew from gossip around the station house that no real progress had been made since then.

"We're still looking at Carl. The neighbor wants another chance to identify him. If we do get a clear I.D., I think Carl will give us a confession."

Tucker laughed; he couldn't help himself. "If he did it, that is, and if you can find him. He could be anywhere by now."

"That's why I'm talking to you, Tucker. Any idea of where he went?"

Tucker considered his boss's question for a moment. "I have some idea," he admitted. "But I don't have an address, if that's what you're asking for. You can't have him picked up without any hard evidence, Chief."

"I know that, Tucker." Sanborn's tone was harsh and impatient. Tucker realized he'd gone too far, but somehow he didn't really care anymore. He respected Chief Sanborn a lot more, he realized, before this whole business with Carl.

The chief stared at him a moment. "When the time comes, I expect you will be more forthcoming."

Tucker leaned back and squared his shoulders. "*If* the time comes, you mean," he corrected, and he left the station without waiting to be dismissed.

TUCKER ARRIVED HOME TO FIND FRAN COOKING DINNER. He brushed by her without a greeting, took some headache medicine from the cupboard, and poured himself a glass of water.

"You don't look well," Fran said sympathetically. "Did you have a hard day?"

"They all feel hard lately." Tucker swallowed the pills and drank some water. "The chief stopped me on the way out. He wants me to tell him where Carl is. He has absolutely no hard evidence, but he wants to make that arrest." Tucker's tone was bitter as he sat down in a kitchen chair.

"Tucker, calm down. You're taking this so hard." Fran rested her hand on his shoulder.

"How am I supposed to take it? First Carl is accused of robbing a house, then he disappears and Sanborn is after me as if I'm some kind of accomplice because I won't tell him where Carl is. I don't even know where Carl is."

Tucker shook his head. "I still can't believe he robbed that house."

Fran sighed. "I think it's fairly likely he did. A neighbor saw him running from the yard. He even had that cut on his hand from breaking the glass."

"You sound just like Sanborn now, Fran. Whatever happened to innocent until proven guilty?"

Fran sat down near him. He could tell she felt sorry for him, but that seemed to make it even worse, as if she felt he were a naive fool to believe Carl could be innocent.

"I have a feeling no one will ever know for sure, Tucker. He did run away though," she reminded him. "That should tell you something."

Tucker didn't know what to think anymore. One minute he believed Carl was unjustly accused, the next he believed he was the guilty culprit who had played him for a fool.

"There was your diamond stickpin." Tucker's tone was reluctant. "Maybe I should have known after that."

Fran got up from the table and checked a pot on the stove. "I finally found that. It was the funniest thing. I hid it in an old handbag and totally forgot about it. I thought I had told you."

Tucker turned to look at her. "No, you didn't tell me that. I would have remembered. I *definitely* would have remembered."

Fran stirred the food in the pot with a wooden spoon. "I'm sorry. It just slipped my mind. But honestly, Tucker, one thing has nothing to do with the other. So, he didn't steal the stickpin. That doesn't mean he didn't rob that house."

"It means a lot to me, Fran," Tucker practically shouted at her. He was so angry, he could barely see straight. "You should have told me you found the pin, Fran. How could you *not* tell me such a thing? Why, we practically chased Carl out of the house over that. Doesn't that mean anything to you?"

Fran stepped away from the stove. "You're right. I should

have told you, Tucker. I don't know why I forgot. I was embarrassed, I guess, for making such a fuss about it at the time. I even thought one of us should apologize to Carl for the things I said." She sighed and looked down at the floor.

"Well, we can't now. Nobody can apologize to him," Tucker said. "It would have made a big difference to me, Fran, knowing you found that pin. I would have treated him differently that night he was at the station house. I wouldn't have doubted him the way I did. Maybe he wouldn't have run away. It wasn't just about you being embarrassed. Don't you understand that?"

"I-I guess I didn't think of it that way." Fran looked up at him, her expression remorseful. "I'm sorry, Tucker. I wasn't thinking."

"I'll say you weren't."

Tucker came to his feet. He was stunned and furious and sick at heart. He had more to say to Fran—a lot more—but he felt himself choking on his anger. He strode past her and into the mud room, then pulled open the side door and left the house. He heard Fran calling after him, but he didn't turn around. His mind was whirling. Carl hadn't stolen that stickpin, after all. It seemed to change everything.

Chapter Seventeen

"Molly . . . wait!" Molly heard the sound of Matthew's voice calling out to her from down the street. She turned slowly, her arms filled with the sample books of linen swatches she'd borrowed from her teacher.

Matthew walked up to her, looking breathless and happy. She hadn't seen him for over a week, since he'd come to pick up Amanda and they'd had words about his long hours.

"What are you up to? Did you just rob the library?"

"I'm meeting with Emily Warwick here." She tilted her head toward the door of the Beanery, which was a few feet away. "I'm catering her engagement party."

"Wow, that's great. It sounds pretty involved."

"You have no idea." Molly rolled her eyes. "Neither did I, or I probably wouldn't have gone through with it."

"When is the party?"

"A week from Saturday." She paused, unsure of how much she wanted to tell him. "I'm trying to start a new business. Emily is my first client."

"I'm impressed—the town's most prominent personality. That's quite a start." Matthew smiled at her. "Here, let me help you with that stuff."

She let him take some of the heavy books, feeling as if they were suddenly in high school.

"I'm a little early for my meeting. Would you like to have some coffee?" She felt nervous asking him, wondering if he was mad at her for the unsolicited advice she had given him.

"I would love to," he replied. "I don't want to interrupt your business meeting, though." So, she was a businesswoman now, having meetings that shouldn't be interrupted. She rather liked that idea.

"It's really fine. She's not due here until four, and Emily's always late," Molly added with a grin.

Matthew opened the door for her, and they went inside and found a table. The both ordered espressos. Matthew glanced at the desserts in the glass display case. "Those chocolate chip cookies look good—and familiar. Did you bake those?"

Molly nodded. "A standing order."

He smiled. "You're going to be famous someday, Molly. I just have a feeling."

"You can say you knew me when." Her tone was light, but her heartbeat suddenly raced, set off by the look in his eyes.

"I'm hoping I'll *still* know you then, to be perfectly honest."

He caught her gaze, and Molly again found herself at a loss for words. She was relieved when the coffee arrived, and she stirred her cup with the pretty stick of crystalized sugar that came with it. *A nice touch,* she thought. *I'll have to remember that.*

"So, how is your practice going?" She meant it as a neutral topic of conversation, then realized he might think she was checking up on him after their talk about Amanda.

"It's fine. I've figured out a way to cut back on my hours a bit. I guess I was overwhelmed at first. The town hasn't had a local doctor in so long, people ran in with everything from a hangnail to acute appendicitis. And I tried to accommodate them all—even the hangnail." Matthew gave her a wry smile. "But I've found a doctor in Essex who will see my patients on my off hours."

Molly nodded. "That sounds like a good arrangement."

"Yes, it should work. I probably would have done something like this sooner or later, but I have to admit talking to you gave me the push I needed to look for someone right away."

Molly took a sip of coffee, still unsure of what to say.

"You were right. I was letting the practice take over my life. That's not why I came here. It's not fair to Amanda."

"I didn't mean to be hard on you, Matt. I just felt badly for her. She was so upset."

"Yes, she was. She's better now, and she's getting some speech therapy again, too. I know she loves living here. It was a good move for her."

How about for you? Molly wanted to ask, but she didn't have the courage.

"So, this business of yours . . . have you come up with a name yet?"

Molly shook her head. "Lauren suggested Awesome Food. No, I got that wrong, *Totally* Awesome Food," Molly corrected herself in a serious tone that made Matthew laugh. "Jill came up with a good one, Incredible Edibles."

"I vote for Totally Awesome Food. Maybe you should have a contest. It could be good publicity."

"Good idea. I'll make a note of it."

Molly enjoyed talking and laughing with him like this more than she wanted to admit. She had missed him. Matthew was special to her, different from all the men she had met after her divorce. He had somehow won a place in her heart. She couldn't say how that had happened, only that mysteriously it had.

"You're going to be a big success, Molly. I just know it." His tone was quiet but sincere, and Molly felt her spirits lift with his praise.

"Thanks. I'm trying," she said with a small smile.

He reached over suddenly and took her hand. Molly's heart skipped a beat. He sat staring at her hand in his, seeming lost in thought. When he looked up at her, his gaze wandered over her face, resting on her mouth. She felt as if he wanted to kiss her. He wouldn't do that here, in the middle of the Beanery, would he?

Not that she didn't want him to, she suddenly realized.

"Mayor Warwick, good to see you." She turned to see that Emily had just walked in, and Felicity Bean was talking with her. Felicity and Jonathan Bean had given Molly's baking business—and her confidence—a big boost that Molly would always be grateful for.

Matthew eased his hand away and sat back in his chair. "I guess your four o'clock is here, Ms. Willoughby."

She laughed at his secretary impersonation. "The mayor again. Guess I have to take a meeting." Her blasé tone made him smile.

Then she paused before speaking again in her own voice, which emerged sounding a bit shaky and shy, she noticed with dismay. "It was good to run into you, Matt."

He stood up and sighed. "Good to see you, too. Don't work too hard, okay?" Then he did lean over and kiss her, a quick hard kiss on her lips that stole her breath away. As he pulled back, the look in his eyes was challenging, as if to say, "I really wanted to do that. So I did."

Molly took a deep breath. "See you," she said quietly. He nodded and walked away.

Molly felt stunned. What ever happened to his "let's be friends" agenda? That kiss—which was definitely more than friendly—seemed to cancel out that plan, though Molly wasn't sure what was left in its place. He had her guessing, as usual. But she had hope again, hope that something more would come of the connection between them.

Maybe it's not just me, she realized. *Maybe Matt couldn't just let it go, either.*

* * *

REVEREND BEN SAT UP ON THE EXAMINING TABLE, THE sleeve on his left arm rolled up to his elbow. A bloody, makeshift bandage covered a deep, jagged gash on his forearm.

Matthew leaned over him, carefully cutting off the bandage. "You've got quite a cut here."

"I thought you might say that."

"How did this happen, Reverend?"

"I was just working around the church, trimming back some bushes on the side of the building. I lost my balance and scraped my arm on the edge of the shears."

"That's a bit more than a scrape." Matthew surveyed the cut once it was exposed.

"I shouldn't have been out there. The deacons usually take care of those things. We had a good handyman for a few weeks, Carl Tulley. But he had to leave the job rather suddenly."

"Yes, I heard about that." Matthew had heard all about Carl Tulley, though he didn't believe half of it.

He turned to the cabinet behind him and took out some gauze and tape. "You're going to need some stitches. When was your last tetanus shot?"

The reverend shrugged. "I don't remember."

"You'll need one today. Just to be on the safe side."

Matthew assembled the materials he needed and started to work on Reverend Ben. "Ever had stitches before?" he asked as he quickly pulled the needle through.

The reverend glanced briefly at his arm and then away again. "Once or twice, years ago."

"These are the melt-away kind. You won't have to come back to get them out. I do want you to watch for any signs of infection, though."

The reverend nodded. "So, how do you like it here so far, Matthew? Are you and Amanda settling in okay?"

Matthew smiled. "I'm the one who's supposed to start in on the small talk—to distract you."

The reverend smiled. "You forgot to ask me what I do for a living. Isn't that the standard question?"

"More or less," Matthew admitted with a short laugh. He applied a strip of adhesive on the gauze, then turned to cut another. "We're doing okay, I guess. This office is extremely busy. Sometimes I think I could stay open twenty-four hours a day."

The reverend gazed at him. "I think you mentioned that you came here to work less, not more."

"That was part of the reason." Matthew had finished with the bandage and turned to put the materials away in the cabinet.

When the reverend didn't say anything, he added, "My wife died about three years ago."

"Yes, I know that. I'm sorry for your loss."

"I've never quite gotten over it. I guess I moved here for a change. To see if it would help."

The reverend leaned forward, folding his bandaged arm across his chest. "Has it helped you, Matt?"

Matt looked at him, then shook his head. "Not completely. Not as much as I had hoped. But that's my own fault, too."

"How so?"

Matthew shrugged. "It's just hard. Even moving to the moon might not really help me."

"What part is hard, Matt? You still grieve for your wife—is that what you mean?"

Matt didn't know how to explain it. He wondered now how he'd even gotten so deeply into this subject. There was something about Reverend Ben that made him want to talk, to unburden himself.

"We had an unhappy marriage. My wife felt neglected. She said I worked too hard." Matt paused and shook his head. "Maybe I did. I know I could have been a better husband to her. But when I finally tried, it was too late. Sharon was sick. We didn't have much chance to make it better. I never got the chance to make it up to her."

"And you feel sad about that."

Matt nodded. "Yes, and guilty, too. I feel sort of stuck, to tell you the truth. Like I can't fix the past and can't do any better in the future, so I'm afraid to even try."

"But you would like to try, I gather. Or else you wouldn't even be thinking of it."

Matt thought of Molly. Yes, he would like to try. If she would give him another chance. If it worked out between them, it would be like a new life, he thought.

"I have tried, in a way. But I keep slipping back. Until I resolve my feelings about my wife, I can't seem to move forward, and I just don't know how to do that."

"I see." The reverend nodded. He met Matt's gaze. "You believe in God, right?"

"Yes, of course I do."

"Do you believe that God alone has the right to judge us? That we don't have the right to judge each other—or even to judge ourselves?"

Matthew considered his words. He didn't answer at first. "It's hard not to judge myself, Reverend. Very hard."

The reverend nodded in agreement. "Yes, I know. I feel the same way myself at times. What about your wife? Would she have wanted you to feel this way, so burdened and stuck, so unhappy?"

"No, not at all. She wasn't like that."

"She would have forgiven you then?"

Matthew glanced at him, unsure of what to say. "I guess so."

The reverend didn't say anything for a moment; he just looked over his bandage again and started rolling down his sleeve.

"You know the Lord's Prayer, of course. I bet you say it often, maybe even every day. Some people say that prayer alone summarizes the entire Gospel."

"I never heard that," Matthew replied.

" 'Forgive us our debts, as we forgive our debtors.' The key, you see, is forgiveness. There's so much of Christianity in that single word." The reverend looked up at him. "God forgives you, Matthew. That's a given. He asks that you reflect that forgiveness to those around you—even to yourself. Forgiveness is a virtue, no doubt. But it's also medicine to a troubled soul. It can heal and bring resolution and tranquility."

Tranquility. There was a sweet-sounding word. Matthew swallowed hard. Could he forgive himself? he wondered now. He'd never really tried, he realized.

"You've given me something to think about, Reverend."

Reverend Ben smiled and hopped down off the table. "Not the usual distracting small talk?"

Matt shook his head. "No, not in the least, sir."

The reverend didn't say anything. But Matthew could tell by his small smile that he felt quite satisfied with that reply.

"LILLIAN? I KNOW YOU'RE IN THERE. YOU REALLY NEED to just open the door now and let us in." Molly's tone wavered between a sugary, coaxing voice and one edged with the anger and frustration she truly felt.

She listened again at the thick wooden front door, wanting to stamp her feet in sheer outrage. But she controlled the impulse, well aware of the eyes on her of the group of helpers she had hired for the day. They were watching her from the sidewalk, where they stood by a rented van loaded with party supplies, waiting for her instructions.

Molly knew Lillian was in there. She just wouldn't answer the door. Oh blast! What else would go wrong? It was hard enough to do this party, the event that was supposed to launch her new business. Now she had Lillian to contend with. How could she have everything set up in time if she couldn't even get inside?

Molly sat down on the top porch step and put her head in her hands, feeling as if she were about to cry. One of her helpers, a girl named Christine whom Molly had hired from the high school, walked up to her. "Isn't anybody home?"

"She's home. She doesn't want us to *think* she's home. But she's in there, believe me. She just won't let us in."

"Oh." Christine gazed up at the house. "What about a back door?"

"I tried. The house is locked tight as a drum."

"Is there someone you can call? How about Mayor Warwick?" Christine persisted. Molly sighed. As if she hadn't already thought of these things. Still, the kid was only trying to be helpful. "I left a message on her cell phone. I think she's off at a day spa in Newburyport or something."

And Jessica went with her, Molly added silently. She had left a message at Jessica's house, too. Now there was no one left to call and, short of breaking and entering, no way to get in the house and set up for this party. Every minute spent melting out here in the hot sun was time wasted. It had taken all morning to pick up the tables, chairs, linens, and tableware and to assemble her crew. It was already one o'clock, and Molly knew she was an hour behind schedule.

Christine walked up the steps and stared at the front door. "Gee, too bad you don't know where she keeps a spare key. There must be one around."

Molly blinked and suddenly sat up straight. She did know where Lillian left her spare key. She had used it when she used to come here to clean. Working for Lillian had been so miserable, she'd blocked the entire episode out of her mind.

She jumped up, hoping the key was still in the same place, inside a cushion on a wicker rocking chair out on the porch. As Christine watched, Molly grabbed the cushion and unzipped it.

She pulled out the key and held it in front of her like a prize.

"Yes!"

"Is that the key?" Christine asked.

"Yes, for the front door." The question was, did she have the courage to use it? Molly took a breath. What was the worst that could happen?

Lillian could call the police and have her carted away for breaking in.

Knowing Lillian, it was definitely a possibility. Molly glanced over at Christine. "You go down and tell the others to start emptying the truck. I'll leave the door open. Just start coming in with the stuff."

Christine nodded and skipped down the steps. Molly took a deep breath and approached the door. Lillian would put up a fuss, she was sure. But maybe if the crew started marching in with all the equipment, she would feel outnumbered.

Molly hoped so. She slipped the key into the lock and slowly turned it, then pushed the door open. The house was silent and dark. The foyer felt cool, despite the heat outside.

"How did you get in here!" Molly looked up at the top of the stairs to see her nemesis dressed in a long robe and leaning on her cane.

"I used the spare key. I guess you didn't hear me knocking," Molly said diplomatically.

"I heard you." Lillian shifted on her cane. "I'm not feeling well. I can't have all this hubbub in the house today."

"I'm sorry, Lillian. We have to start setting up. I need a few hours to get everything ready."

Lillian peered down at her, then slowly began to come down the steps. "But you can't start working in here. Don't you understand me?"

Lillian's tone was sharp, her voice piercing. Molly felt intimidated but forced herself to keep her own voice steady and calm. "But Emily must have told you I was coming—"

"This is my house, not Emily's." Lillian stood at the bottom of the steps now. "I've already told you. Your presence here is most inconvenient and unwelcome. I won't have it!"

Lillian's eyes widened in astonishment as Molly's helpers began to troop into the house, carrying stacks of rented chairs and folding tables.

"Who are these people? Where do you think you're going? Get out! All of you!" She turned to Molly and glared at her. "Stop them. Stop them immediately!"

Molly's crew paused, looking from Molly to Lillian, their faces growing red and strained as they held their heavy loads.

Molly quietly nodded and waved her hand. "Go on in. It's okay. I'll work this out."

At Molly's last remark Lillian's face grew pale. Her mouth opened to speak, then closed again. Molly suddenly worried that the old woman might make herself sick over this.

She didn't know what to do. Should she stay out and keep trying to get in touch with Emily? But that might take all day. She wouldn't be ready in time, and this party would be the disaster Lillian had predicted.

"Mother, what in the world is going on here?"

Molly suddenly turned to see Jessica in the doorway. She had never been so happy to see her sister-in-law. "Jessica . . ."

Jessica glanced quickly at Molly. "Sam picked up your message and found me. Thank goodness." She looked back at her mother. "What's the problem here, Mother? You knew Molly was coming today."

Lillian swallowed and sniffed but looked her daughter straight in the eye. "Yes, your sister talked me into having this debacle of a party at my home. But I never agreed to having it torn apart by this band of riffraff." Lillian stood up straight. "I'm not at all well. I need my rest. I can't have these people milling about, tearing the place apart."

Jessica moved toward her mother. "Mother, you knew what was going to happen here today. Molly needs to set everything up."

"A professional party expert could manage in far less time with far less fuss, if you ask me. Not to mention her employees. Why, there's a girl in there with an earring in her nose!"

She referred to Christine's unfortunate nose piercing. Christine had promised to take the nose ring out this evening for the event; it never occurred to Molly that it would be a problem during the setup. She was such a good kid, Molly hardly noticed it anymore.

Jessica ignored the comment. She took Lillian's arm and began to lead her back upstairs. "You need to have your hair done, Mother. You're practically the hostess tonight, you know."

"The hostess? I'll probably be up in my room with a horrid migraine."

"Of course, you won't. You don't want to embarrass Emily and Dan like that. I have an appointment for you at the beauty shop in town. Now, what are you going to wear? Is the blue dress back from the cleaners?"

Molly heaved a huge sigh of relief as she watched Jessica and Lillian disappear down the upstairs hallway. The coast was clear for now. Molly turned her attention back to the business of getting this party together. She had a little over four hours to set up. She just hoped she could do it all in time.

MOLLY WAS OUT ON THE PATIO, CHECKING A FLOWER arrangement, when she spotted Emily and Dan inside. She could tell immediately from the look on Emily's face that the preparations had been a success. More than a success. Emily looked absolutely astounded.

"Molly, the house looks beautiful! The flowers, the tables—everything looks great." Emily beamed at her. "How long have you been here?"

"Oh, a few hours." Molly wondered if Jessica had told Emily about Lillian's behavior. It seemed almost beside the point now. The setup phase was over. All she had to do was serve the food.

"Molly, can you come in the kitchen a second?" Nick, one of her helpers, stood in the doorway to the kitchen, his eyes wide with alarm. *This is not good,* Molly thought.

"I can see you have a lot going on. I won't keep you," Emily said to her. "I'll see you later."

"Absolutely." Molly smiled mechanically at Emily, then did a speed walk back to the kitchen to find a minor crisis. The crab spread had not completely jelled. Instead of artful swirls, it had turned into ugly misshapen globs as her helpers squeezed it out of the pastry tube and onto the rounds of garlic toast.

"It looks awful. Should we skip it?" Christine asked.

Molly took a breath and stared down at the crab spread. She had never had so many people looking to her for directions—and expecting the right answers. She had raised two children. But that was different. Her kids didn't listen to half of what she said and argued with the rest of it.

This crew was listening and really expected her to know what she was doing.

"Is there any extra cream cheese from that spinach thing?"

"A bar or two," Christine reported.

"Okay. Get the cream cheese, and mix some into the crab spread, about half a bar to start. It should start molding. Test it with a spoon before you put in the bag again. And add a little dill if it starts to taste too watered down."

Christine's expression brightened. "Extra dill. Got it." She raced off to find the cream cheese, and Molly felt quietly pleased to have solved the problem.

She turned and surveyed the kitchen. The rest of the crew was hard at work, some preparing the hors d'oeuvres, others working on the entrées and side dishes. She walked around with her list in hand, making sure everything was on track.

The hands of the kitchen clock approached six. Molly

called her group around the table. "You're all doing a great job. Emily is very pleased with the setup, and the food looks terrific. All we have to do now is serve it," she added, making them laugh.

"Don't worry. It will all be fine," Molly promised them. She was in charge now, like a general going into battle. Even if she had her private doubts, she had to give her crew confidence. "We can do it, no problem."

They smiled and nodded at her. Nick poked Christine in the ribs with his elbow. The clock struck six, and Molly took a deep breath. "Okay, guys. Back to your stations. It's show time."

The rest of the night flew by as one course led to the next. Molly's inexperienced crew made a few slip ups—a tray of glasses crashed to the floor, a batch of canapés caught fire, setting off the kitchen smoke detector. Molly leaped up on a chair and yanked the batteries out of the alarm. Luckily the jazz trio in the backyard was playing a loud number that covered the noise. And as the entrées began to come out of the kitchen a short time later, a roast fish flew off its platter when one of her helpers tripped. Molly miraculously caught it midair. She quickly set it back on its platter, artfully covering the damage with some creative garnish. She never realized how much you had to think on your feet in this business—or how resourceful she could be.

After the dessert had been served, Betty snuck into the kitchen. She walked straight up to Molly and gave her a huge hug. "Everything is fabulous! I knew you could do it!"

"Thanks, Betty. I couldn't have done it without you."

"Without my nagging and pushing, you mean?" Betty gave her a knowing grin.

"Well . . . that, too," Molly admitted.

"You didn't need me. You did this all on your own and don't forget it." Betty patted her on the shoulder. "I did find the blue dress for you, though. I'll take credit for that."

"Okay," Molly readily agreed. "You get credit for the dress—and a whole lot more."

A short time later, the guests had departed and her crew was busily breaking down the tables and chairs and putting the house back in order. Emily and Dan found Molly in the dining room, packing up the rented dishes and flatware.

"Molly, we just want to thank you again," Emily said. "And I'm sorry my mother gave you a hard time earlier. But you know, when she finally came down for the party, she actually *almost* looked like she was enjoying herself."

"That's a lot for Lillian," Dan assured her. "I'm not big on parties, Molly, but this was a great one."

Molly felt pleased by their compliments—pleased and proud.

"Thanks for hiring me. You knew this was my first real job and well . . . you didn't have to take a chance."

"Oh, I knew you could do it." Emily smiled at her, her blue eyes warm with affection.

Molly smiled back, feeling suddenly shy. It seemed everyone in town—except Lillian, of course—believed she could do it. She was the only one who had doubted herself.

MOLLY ARRIVED AT HER MOTHER'S HOUSE ON SUNDAY afternoon, feeling exhausted but victorious. It was Lauren's birthday, and her mother had invited them over for cake. Molly had taken the girls out to dinner beforehand, letting Lauren choose the restaurant.

She usually did something even more elaborate for a birthday, hosting a party or taking a group of kids on an outing. But Lauren was going to have another party with her friends next weekend; Phil had offered to take a group to a water park.

Molly knew Phil was coming later. Lauren had invited him. It was only right, Molly thought, now that he'd become such a big part of their lives again. Still, she felt apprehensive about seeing him. They hadn't really talked since the kayaking trip almost three weeks ago, but something in the way he looked at her lately suggested he hadn't forgotten his question.

"Where's Lauren's friend, Amanda?" Marie carried out a pitcher of lemonade and set it on the picnic table alongside a platter of appetizers. "Isn't she here, yet?"

Molly didn't realize Amanda had been invited. But she'd been so busy with Emily's party, she had let her mother take care of all the preparations for this small one.

"I just spoke to her yesterday. She's definitely coming," Lauren said, pouring herself a glass of lemonade.

"I just spoke to her father on Friday," Marie added. "I'm sure I told him the right time. Well, no problem really. The cake won't be out for a while. I'm sure they'll be here by then."

Molly's ears perked up at the plural noun. It sounded as if Matt had been invited as well. A cherry tomato lodged in her throat. She coughed before she was able to speak again.

"Did you invite Matt Harding, too?" She tried to sound casual, but her mother glanced at her sharply.

"Of course I invited him. . . . Did you not want me to?"

"Uh, no, that's okay. I just didn't realize." Molly turned to Lauren, hoping to quickly change the subject. "Go help Grandma carry out the rest of the snacks, will you, honey?"

While I duck behind the garage and scream, she thought.

Lauren complied and followed her grandmother back into the house. Molly had barely checked her lipstick when Matthew and Amanda appeared at the back gate.

Molly walked up to them and met Matt's gaze. His dark eyes studied her and his smile widened. Slightly unnerved, Molly took the gift Amanda was holding. "Here, let me add this to Lauren's pile of loot. She's in the house with Jill. Go right in."

"Thanks. See you." Amanda ran off, leaving Molly with Matt.

"So, you had your big debut last night. How did it go?"

"Fine. Great actually. There were a few speed bumps, but overall it was a success."

"Glad to hear it, but I'm not surprised. Sounds like you're on your way."

"I hope so. I did get some interest from other guests. I'll have to see how it goes, I guess."

"Did you decide on a name yet? Or are you going to stick with Totally Awesome Foods?"

Molly laughed, surprised he'd remembered. "Still working on it." She looked up at him and smiled. He looked different somehow, more relaxed and happy. He was tan, as if he'd been out in the sun. His warm brown eyes were brighter, too, framed by crinkly lines at the corners when he smiled.

"Sorry we're late. Amanda really wanted to try sailing. We rented a boat and were out on the water all day."

"That sounds like fun. I didn't know you sail."

Matthew grinned. "I don't really. I only know enough to get us in and back and not capsize. But it's a wonderful break. I can see how people really get into it. Amanda is already trying to talk me into buying a boat."

"You ought to try Reilly's boatyard. He's always got a few bargains lying around," Molly advised him.

"Maybe I will. Do you like to sail?" he asked.

"I love it. I haven't been out on a sailboat in years, though. I'm not sure I'd remember what to do."

"Maybe we could go out sometime and figure out the ropes together."

Molly laughed. "That sounds like fun. And by the way, they're called lines."

"Right, the lines, I mean. See, you're ahead of me already."

Molly's father had just returned with a tray of cold drinks, and she could tell he had overheard a bit of their conversation. She saw her father look at her, and she felt her cheeks get warm, matching her pink sweater top.

"Have a soda, Matt." Her father politely handed his

guest a tall plastic cup. Then he turned to Molly. "Phil is inside, with your mother. He's asking for you."

Molly felt her stomach drop. She glanced up at Matthew and could have sworn he paled a bit under his bronze complexion.

"Lauren wanted her dad here for her birthday."

"That's nice. It's good of him to come." Matt's tone sounded bright, but his expression didn't match it.

"Excuse me, I'd better go say hello." She turned away from Matt, feeling flustered. For goodness' sake, she had thought she could just kick back and relax today. Now she had to play dueling single dads. This was a twist. Not uncommon for some women, maybe, but she had never had this much attention from men, at the same party no less.

Inside, Phil greeted her happily. "Wow, you look great. Pink is your color, Molly."

"Thanks, Phil." It occurred to her that no matter what she wore, Phil told her it was her color.

Lauren rushed into the kitchen with Amanda and Jill. "Hi Dad." She jumped up and gave Phil a big hug.

"How's the birthday girl?" He held her at arm's length and took her in, then slowly shook his head. "Fifteen. I can't believe it. It feels like yesterday me and your mom were just waiting for you to be born. . . . Remember, Molly?"

"I remember. The car was out of gas. We had to call Sam."

"Oh, boy. She'll never let me live that down, will she?" Phil shook his head, laughing with Lauren. "I was so excited to be having a baby, I just couldn't see straight. It was a good thing I didn't have to drive, after all."

Everyone in the kitchen laughed at Phil's story—even Molly. It used to be that whenever she thought about that bit of their history, she felt a spurt of residual anger at Phil's thoughtlessness. Now, she saw it differently. They had been so young. He had been nervous and excited. His forgetfulness seemed touching to her now.

"The car we had back then was such a wreck. It probably wouldn't have made it in time anyway," Molly remembered.

"Probably not," Phil agreed. He glanced at her and caught her eye. Molly smiled briefly and looked away. She could tell he was thinking about them getting back together again.

She suddenly noticed Matt standing in the doorway and wondered how long he'd been there. Long enough to hear her and Phil reminiscing?

Phil seemed surprised to see him. "Hello, Matt. Good to see you." His voice held a questioning note, as if he doubted his own words.

"Nice to see you, Phil." The two men briefly shook hands.

Squaring off before a duel, Molly thought. Now what was she supposed to do? *I'm not exactly Scarlett O'Hara, able to entertain a circle of gentleman callers with my wit and charm.* She just didn't feel up to it after yesterday.

She quickly turned to her mother, who looked delighted at what was going on right in her very kitchen. Annoyingly so, Molly thought. In fact, she realized her innocent-looking mother had cooked up this whole thing by inviting Matt here and not telling her.

"Can I help you with anything, Mom?" Molly asked.

"No, dear. I'm fine. You go entertain the guests."

"No, Mom, I really want to help you. You've done *enough* already, honestly."

Molly gave her mother a look, and Marie finally seemed to get the message. "Well . . . if you insist. Why don't you bring those dishes and things outside and set everything up?"

Molly grabbed the tray of tableware and stalked outside again. She stacked the dishes and paper cups, then looked around to see what Phil and Matt were up to.

Phil suddenly appeared beside her, slipping his arm around her shoulder in a proprietary manner. "How are you doing, Molly? Need any help?"

"It's just a stack of paper plates, Phil. I think I can handle it."

Phil laughed and squeezed her shoulder. Molly felt Matthew watching from a distance as he chatted with her father. She tried to wiggle away, but Phil's arm felt glued to her shoulder.

"I wanted to tell you what I got Lauren—" He leaned closer, attempting to whisper in her ear.

Molly quickly slipped out from under his arm. "That's all right. Surprise me."

Phil was unconscionable at times. He knew she liked Matthew but obviously thought he could scare him off. She wasn't sure what she was going to do to stop him, but she definitely was not going to let Phil get away with it.

Five minutes later, while clearing the way for the birthday cake, Molly spotted Phil and Matt off in a corner and had a sudden awful thought: Phil was telling Matt how they were going to get back together.

He wouldn't do that, would he? Molly realized with horror that he would.

She ran across the lawn to where they stood. "What are you guys talking about?" she asked breathlessly.

Phil glanced at Matt and back to Molly. "I was just telling Matthew about that time Lauren got out of her crib and left the apartment all on her own. She went downstairs in the elevator. We didn't even think she was tall enough to reach the buttons. Luckily, a neighbor found her in the lobby and brought her back."

"Luckily," Molly agreed. A walk down memory lane. How charming for Matthew.

Matthew smiled politely. "It's amazing that kids survive to be teenagers considering some of the stunts they pull."

"Yeah, I know what you mean." Phil nodded sagely. "That probably wouldn't happen now, though. I mean, if Molly and I were still married and say, had another baby or something. First of all, we'd be a lot more careful, childproofing everything. And we'd probably live in a house and all. It will be a lot safer."

Molly stared at him, wide eyed with shock. "*Would* be a lot safer you mean, not *will* be."

Phil smiled slowly and shrugged. "Sure, would be. What did I say?"

Molly was about to explain it to him when she caught Matthew staring at her. She decided it was best to just let it go.

"Forget it, Phil." She took a step back and shook her head. "The birthday cake is coming out in a minute."

She turned and walked back to the house, feeling two sets of eyes boring into her back.

Later, as Molly sat with her mother, sipping coffee and watching Lauren open her gifts, Matthew came over to them.

"Marie, thank you so much for having us. I had a great time and so did Amanda."

"Oh, thank you for coming, Matt. It was so nice to finally meet you."

Molly could tell her mother was totally charmed. She was practically batting her eyelashes at him. Molly cringed with embarrassment.

"I hope you'll come again soon," Marie added.

"I hope so, too." Matt turned to Molly, and she met his smile. *Now it's my turn to feel watery knees,* she realized as she looked up at him.

"Good to see you, Molly. Sorry we didn't talk more. Don't forget our sailing idea, okay?"

She hadn't forgotten but was surprised to hear him mention it again. Maybe Phil's tactics hadn't scared him off.

"No, I won't forget."

"Maybe we can go out next weekend—if you're not catering any celebrity parties."

She smiled at him. "I'll check my book."

Before she could say anything more, Phil suddenly appeared.

"Leaving, Matt?" Phil stuck out his hand. "Good to see you again. Good night, now."

Molly shrunk into her folding chair. *Why don't you just push him through the gate, Phil?* she wanted to ask.

Matt glared around, looking as if he was ready to give up for the night. "Good night, everyone. Thanks again."

He glanced one more time at Molly, but she couldn't quite interpret his look.

Molly stayed on to help her parents clean up. And so did Phil. As Molly gathered a stack of paper plates and tossed them in a bag, Phil walked up beside her.

"Your parents always did know how to throw a nice party."

"Lauren seems to have enjoyed it." She glanced at him. "She liked having you here, Phil. It's been a while since you've been to any of their birthday parties."

"Yeah, I know." He rubbed a hand through his thick blond hair. "We had some cute ones when they were little. Remember when I got dressed up as Barney? 'Hi, kids!' " He waved, doing a voice that made her laugh.

"Stop . . . I remember." She collected the plastic forks, shaking her head. "That was fun."

"Except the suit was so hot, I nearly fainted." He sighed. "Sometimes I think about having another kid. I know I would be a better father. I'd appreciate it more, you know?"

"Yes, I do. We had our kids so young. We didn't realize what we had."

She thought about having another child sometimes, too. But she never pictured Phil as the father.

He didn't speak for a minute, and Molly guessed what was coming next.

"Did you think anymore about us getting back together?"

No beating around the bush with Phil. She had to say that for him.

"Yes. I did think about it." He stared at her intently, looking uncharacteristically nervous. This really mattered to him; she hadn't realized how much.

"And what did you decide?"

"I'm flattered, honestly. I know the girls would be in favor of it, too. . . . But I don't think it would be the right thing for us to do. For either of us."

"Speak for yourself, Molly. I know what I want."

"Do you really?" she asked him gently. "I know you want to make amends, Phil. The girls forgive you. And I do, too. You've shown a lot of character coming back here, trying to face up to your mistakes. When you first told me you had changed, I didn't believe you."

"Tell me about it."

"But you did change. Even I can see that now."

He nodded, his expression serious. "But not enough to win you back, I guess."

"That's not it, Phil. We can't turn back the clock and rewrite history. We shouldn't try. I don't think it would work out in the long run. We were young when we got married and we made some mistakes. That's okay. Let's just turn the page and try to do better now."

Phil let out a long slow sigh. Then he put his arms around her and gave her a big hug. A friendly hug, she thought. Well, mostly friendly.

He stepped back and smiled. "Okay. I understand. I thought that's what you would say, but I couldn't help giving it a try. And listen, I want to wish you luck on your new business."

"Thanks, Phil. That's good of you to say."

"I know you'll do well at it. You're such a hard worker. I can't see how you'll miss. I want to help you. If I had given you more support for the girls all these years, maybe you wouldn't have waited so long to start this."

That was true, Molly thought, though she didn't openly agree with him.

"I have some money saved for the girls' college fund. I want you to have it."

Molly was stunned by his generous gesture, which seemed even more poignant considering that she had just turned him down.

"Phil . . . you never fail to surprise me."

He seemed pleased with the comment, taking it as a compliment.

"The girls have turned out great, just like you, no thanks to me. I owe you for that alone."

"I've done what I could for them because I love them, Phil. You never have to repay me for that." She smiled at him. "I appreciate your offer, honestly. But I really don't need the money. I have my own banker, and I've made arrangements to get things up and running. Save the money for college, the way you planned. That would mean a lot to me."

Phil nodded. "All right, if that's what you want. Consider it done." His expression turned mischievous. "A banker, huh? Gee, you are going places."

"It's my sister-in-law," she admitted with a grin.

He shrugged. "That still counts."

Yes, it did, Molly thought, feeling pleased with herself. Maybe she really was on her way.

CHAPTER EIGHTEEN

TUCKER HAD JUST FINISHED HIS PATROL WHEN, DRIVing up Emerson Street, he spotted another police cruiser coming in the opposite direction. The officer signaled with his lights for Tucker to pull up and talk. It was Tom Schmidt.

Schmidt walked over to him after they'd both parked. "I've got some news for you, Tucker. I just heard from this friend of mine on the job in Hamilton. He collared some kids breaking and entering at about two A.M. last night. The silent alarm went off, and they were caught red-handed. My buddy says they found a load of stolen goods back at the ranch, including some trinkets from the Degan house. How do you like that?"

Tucker's mouth went dry. He had mixed emotions about the news, that was for sure: happy to hear Carl wasn't the guilty one after all but feeling even guiltier now for having doubted his brother.

"Thanks for letting me in on this, Schmidt. I appreciate it."

"Some of the guys have been hard on you. I don't think that's right. Sanborn, too. He owes you an apology in my book."

My book, too, Tucker thought, though he doubted he'd ever hear it. The two police officers parted, and Tucker drove on, with a lot to think about.

Once he went off duty, he called a friend at the Hamilton police department and got the full story. The thieves were two teenage boys with a history of truancy, shoplifting, vandalism, and a general all-around bad attitude. Future Carls. After their cache of stolen property was found, they confessed to the North Creek Road burglary, which was just one among many.

Fran was up in the bedroom, putting laundry away, when Tucker got home that evening. Things had been strained between them ever since her revelation about the stickpin. He knew she was sorry. He kept reminding himself that he loved her—he knew he did—but he just felt hollow and sad inside. Something between them was injured and neither one knew how to heal it.

Now she looked at him, and he could tell from her reaction that he had a strange expression on his face.

"What is it, Tucker? Are you all right?"

"I had some news today." He took his shield off his shirt and dropped it on his dresser. "They caught some kids in Hamilton who have been robbing houses. They did the Degan house on North Creek Road. Confessed to it and everything."

"Oh." Fran looked surprised. She sat down suddenly on the bed, a bundle of towels in her lap. "That is news."

"I'll say." Tucker turned to her, feeling angry all over again. "Everybody around here had Carl made out for guilty, and he was telling the truth all along. We weren't fair to him."

Fran sighed and shrugged. "Well, we tried, Tucker."

Tucker glared at her. He felt suddenly as if he were

about to explode. "That's supposed to be okay? That's a good enough excuse for you? That we tried?" He laughed harshly and shook his head. "We didn't try hard enough. We were ready to believe the worst of him the first chance we got. Both of us."

Fran lifted her head, looking indignant at his accusation. "I know I was wrong to think he took my pin. But honestly, Tucker, given his history . . . even you suspected him."

"You see, that's it exactly." Tucker heard his voice rising on a note of anger, but he felt so frustrated with Fran all of a sudden, he couldn't control it. "It's not fair to have suspected Carl of taking your pin or of the robbery. It's not right. We didn't treat him like other people—like a decent human being ought to be treated. We never gave him the benefit of the doubt. And he's my brother, besides. Don't you see? It makes me sick to think about it. And I'm as guilty of it as you are."

He stared at her, breathless from his outburst. She shivered, looking suddenly fragile. Then she met his eyes.

"You're right," she said. "We were terribly unfair to Carl."

Just hearing her say that eased something in Tucker's heart.

"It's a shame Carl isn't around to hear about those kids in Hamilton," she went on.

Tucker turned suddenly and yanked his blue shirt out of his pants. "I'm going to take a few days off and go look for him. He should know his name has been cleared around here, and I'm going to tell him."

"Where will you look?"

"Up in Portland, Maine. Reverend Ben gave me an address where Carl asked him to send a paycheck. I can start there, I guess. I'll take some personal time and leave tomorrow."

"How long will you be gone?"

Tucker shrugged and pulled on a sweatshirt. "I don't know. As long as it takes. I hope he hasn't gone too far by now."

Fran was quiet for a moment. "I hope so, too." She touched Tucker's arm as she walked by him. "I'll get the small blue suitcase. It's in the hall closet somewhere."

TUCKER WAS PACKED AND READY EARLY THE NEXT MORNING, dressed in his sports clothes. After Michael and Mary Ellen left for school, he put his coffee cup in the sink and kissed Fran good-bye.

"Okay, I'm going. I'll call you from the road."

"Yes, don't forget. I like to know where you are." Fran gave him a small smile. "Take care of yourself. Drive safely. Don't eat a lot of junk food on the highway."

Tucker didn't answer. He could see that she didn't know what to say.

"I love you, Tucker," she said quietly.

"I love you, too. You know that."

She nodded, looking suddenly as if she were about to cry. Then she kissed his cheek again, her hand lingering on his chest. "Good luck. I really hope you find him."

"I do, too," he answered.

Tucker reached Portland about two hours later. He hadn't been up this way in years and was surprised to see how much the city had changed, especially down on the waterfront. The rundown wharf areas were filled with restaurants, condos, and hotels. The old warehouses across the way held slick-looking office space, fancy shops, and designer coffeehouses for the tourists who roamed the winding cobblestone streets, toting their shopping bags.

He didn't know the city very well, but with the aid of a map, he located Carl's mailing address. He was not surprised to find himself in a rundown neighborhood, one that had been bypassed by the development boom. Here the houses looked old and badly in need of repair. Some were squat single-family homes on tiny patches of property, others were semidetached two-family homes of post–World

War II vintage. It was the kind of neighborhood Tucker more or less expected.

He finally found the address at the end of the street, a larger three-story building that looked as if it was once an old apartment house. Judging from the sign in front, it appeared to be a shelter now, run by some charitable organization.

So, maybe Carl really didn't have a friend up here after all, Tucker realized. Or maybe Carl hadn't been able to find his friend. Whatever the reason, the bottom line was Carl had been reduced again to shelter life, which upset Tucker even more.

He got out of his car and went inside. The place was dark and depressing. He walked into a common room furnished with broken-down armchairs and a slip-covered couch that sagged in the middle. A group of men sat watching a big TV, most of them smoking. A window fan circulated warm air and cigarette ashes.

Tucker scanned the circle of faces but didn't see Carl. They each stared back at him suspiciously. Even out of uniform, Tucker guessed many could still tell he was a cop. Carl once said he could just smell it on him.

Tucker walked farther down a main hall. The scent of pine disinfectant was nearly overpowering. He found an office and, in it, a paunchy middle-aged man with a long, stringy ponytail sitting behind a desk. The name tag on his T-shirt read, "House Manger, Ralph Newman." The guy had a look about him, Tucker thought, as if he'd been through it all and had come out the other side, calmer, wiser, looking to help men like himself find their way back.

"I'm trying to find my brother," Tucker explained. "He gave this place as a mailing address. Can you tell me if he's still here? Maybe you have some log book or records I can look at."

"We don't ask the men to sign anything. It seems easier for most of them that way. Do you have a picture? Maybe I'll remember him."

"No, I don't." Tucker felt bad that he didn't even have a single photo of Carl. He had tried to include him in one on Easter Sunday, but Carl was terribly camera shy.

He ended up describing Carl's physical appearance as best as he could. The man gave him a thoughtful look.

"I think I remember that guy. He looks something like you, now that you mention it."

Tucker felt his face flush. He never thought of himself as resembling Carl, but he supposed it was true.

"Right, Carl Tulley. He was waiting for a letter, and once it came, he left. That was about two weeks ago. I haven't seen him since."

Tucker didn't answer. That must have been the letter from Reverend Ben with Carl's back pay. By now Carl could be anywhere.

"Sorry I couldn't help you more." Tucker could tell from the man's expression that he must look awfully disappointed.

"That's all right. Do you have any suggestions about where else I can go? Some other shelters in the city, maybe?"

"Sure. I have a list somewhere around here. I'll get it for you. It's the cold weather that drives them indoors, though," he added while riffling through a desk drawer. "Once it warms up, he really could be anywhere. You should check the parks, especially along the waterfront. The hospitals and police stations, too. But I guess you already know that."

Tucker knew he would find Carl quickly if his brother had either gotten sick again or arrested. But he hoped that wasn't the case.

Ralph handed Tucker the list. Tucker thanked him and said good-bye. Then he remembered to leave his name and cell-phone number just in case Carl returned.

"I haven't found a motel yet. But I'll call you later today with a number where you can reach me in case the cell phone doesn't work. I'd sure appreciate a call if you see him around again."

"Sure, I'll do that. Should I let him know that you're trying to get in touch?" The man's look was curious.

"Uh, no. I'd rather you didn't. It's hard to explain."

"Okay. I understand." Tucker thanked him again and left the shelter. He stood on the sidewalk a long time, clearing his head with the fresh air. On a scale of one to ten, the shelter was about a negative five kind of place to live in, Tucker thought. But right now, Carl might have it even worse.

Tucker grabbed a quick bite at a drive-through window, gobbling the food in his car with one hand while he navigated more of Portland's back streets. He spent the rest of the day checking the shelters on the list and the parks he noticed along the way.

At six o'clock he wasn't close to finished, but he decided to find a motel room. He let himself in and dropped his bag near the door, not even bothering to put on the lights. The day had been exhausting. Despite his best intentions to call Fran, he dropped down on the big bed and closed his eyes to rest.

His determination of last night had been boiled down during the day to a layer of gritty resolve. The faces of the homeless men he'd seen today loomed up before him, their expressions blank, their dark stares accusing.

The task seemed hopeless, but he wasn't going to give up. He would call the police stations and hospitals tonight and try the other shelters tomorrow. Eventually he had to get some lead on Carl. Somebody somewhere had to remember him.

Tucker closed his eyes. *Dear Lord, wherever Carl is tonight, please give him comfort and shelter. Please let me find him and try to make things right.*

MOLLY'S FATHER ALWAYS SAID, "IF SOMETHING SEEMS TOO good to be true, it probably is." A cynical point of view, perhaps, and she'd been making a conscious effort to be more positive lately, but on Saturday morning, she couldn't get that bit of wisdom out of her mind.

Matthew called the day after Lauren's birthday party and invited her to go sailing with him, just as he promised. That was the "too good to be true" part.

On Saturday morning at about six o'clock, Jill shook Molly's shoulder, waking her from a sweet dream.

"Mom, I feel sick. I think I'm going to throw up."

Molly sat up in alarm and felt Jill's forehead. She was burning with a fever. She needed a cool bath and some medicine. The look on Jill's face told Molly that she needed to take immediate action. "Okay, let's get into the bathroom, honey."

It was soon clear that Jill was quite sick. Too sick for Molly to leave—even for a date with Matthew.

Lauren and Amanda were going with Phil to a water park for Lauren's belated birthday celebration. Jill was supposed to go along, too. The poor kid was so miserable that Molly couldn't even feel sorry for herself.

Molly sighed and picked up the phone to call Matthew. So much for the long-awaited date. The fact that she was the one canceling this time did little to help her feel better. *It feels as if this relationship just wasn't meant to be,* she thought dismally as she punched in his number.

Matthew picked up on the second ring. "Molly, hi. I was just going to call you. The weather looks perfect. You'd better bring a hat and wear a lot of sunblock. But don't worry about lunch; I've already taken care of that."

He sounded so excited, as if he was really looking forward to this. Molly hadn't even thought that he might be disappointed, too.

"I'm sorry, Matt, but Jill's come down with some bug or something. She has a high fever and all the classic symptoms. I can't leave her like this. I really have to stay home."

"Oh, I'm sorry to hear that. There's something going around the elementary school. I had a lot of calls this week."

"There's *always* something going around the elementary school." Molly suddenly felt so blue looking ahead to the long day she would spend alone with Jill.

"I'm sure you know what to do. But why don't I take a quick look at her later when I bring Amanda? I can hang out and keep you company awhile."

Molly thought he was just trying to be polite. "It's okay, Matt. You don't have to do that. I'm sure you would rather get outside today."

"Really, I want to. I can stay with Jill awhile if you need to go out anywhere."

If you're here, why would I want to go out? Molly nearly answered.

Finally, she said yes, then raced around trying to quickly ready the apartment and herself and at the same time take care of Jill and get Lauren ready for her outing.

A short time later she opened the door to find Matt and Amanda. Amanda was ready for the water park, wearing her bathing suit under her clothes and carrying a knapsack. Matt still looked as if he were going sailing, wearing a T-shirt, baseball cap, khaki shorts, and boat shoes. He stumbled into her house carrying a large blue cooler.

"What's in there, your medical kit?" Molly couldn't help teasing him.

"Lunch. I packed some food for our trip. I thought we could have a picnic in your living room or something."

"Oh, that sounds fun. No bugs to worry about." Molly stepped aside to let him pass. "Well . . . not too many."

Matt laughed, carrying the cooler into the kitchen. "There's a lot of ice in here, but I'll put the food in the refrigerator anyway."

"Go right ahead." It looked like he planned on staying awhile. This was getting interesting.

She was just about to close the door when she saw Phil coming up the hallway.

"Hi, Molly. Are the girls ready?"

"Lauren and Amanda are. But Jill is sick. She came down with something this morning."

"Gee, that's too bad. Can I see her?" Phil stepped inside, and Molly closed the door.

"Sure, she's in bed, but I know she's not sleeping." Molly followed him to the kitchen. "It's just a little bug. I'm sure she'll be all right in a day or two."

"But you called the doctor anyway, I see." Phil smiled at Matt, who stood at the kitchen counter emptying containers from his cooler into the refrigerator. "I didn't know doctors still made house calls—and stocked refrigerators, no less."

"This one does. Only for special patients, of course." Matt turned and looked at Phil. He smiled, but in his eyes Molly noticed a challenging light, one that suggested he didn't realize that Phil wasn't his competition, after all.

"We had a date to go sailing today. Matt offered to come here and visit for a while instead."

"Oh. I see." Phil nodded. "I'll just run in and say hello to Jill for a minute. Then we'll get going."

A few minutes later Phil left with Lauren and Amanda. *Amazing,* Molly thought. Phil seemed to be accepting Matthew's presence with far more grace than she expected.

Matthew waited in the kitchen. He stood leaning against the counter as she entered, making her feel self-conscious.

"I was just going in to check on Jill. Have you taken her temperature lately?"

"About an hour ago. It was a little over one hundred and two."

"That's not too bad. I brought her some ice pops. They're a good way to get fluids in her if she can keep them down."

He had thought of everything, hadn't he? Molly watched him retrieve an ice pop from the freezer and pick up a napkin from the counter.

Molly led the way to Jill's room, where Jill looked up from her pillows, her small pale face surrounded by dark hair.

"How do you feel, honey?" Matt asked.

"Terrible." Jill crossed her arms over her chest and looked away. Matt glanced at Molly, suppressing a smile.

"What's wrong, Jill? Does your stomach still bother you?" Molly sat down on the edge of her bed and felt Jill's forehead.

Jill shook her head no, nearly shaking Molly's hand away. "Everybody went to the water park without me. That's not fair." She was about two seconds away from bursting into tears.

"That was a tough break." Matt nodded in agreement. "It really stinks to be left behind like that. Is that park fun? I've never been there."

Jill looked at him in disbelief. "Yeah, I'd say it's fun."

"Jill, don't be fresh." Molly gave her a warning look.

Matt touched her arm. "Well, your mom and I didn't get to go, either. Maybe we could take you and a few of your friends sometime."

Molly turned and stared at him. She had heard he had a nice bedside manner, but he really didn't need to go that far.

"Could we, Mom?" Jill's expression brightened so dramatically, she hardly looked sick anymore.

"We'll see. You just get better for now, okay?"

"Yes, let's get you better. Let me take a look down your throat, Jill. Say 'ah' for me. Nice and wide now."

Matt gave Jill a quick examination then took her temperature. He diagnosed the problem as a virus, hopefully the twenty-four-hour kind and recommended bed rest and lots of fluids. He offered Jill the ice pop, and she ate it eagerly.

Molly rose from the bed, preparing to leave the room. "Would you like to read a book or watch a video?"

"Would you play a game with me, Mom?" Jill asked hopefully. "Can we play Bamboozle?"

Normally Molly would. What else was there to do with a sick kid? But now she had Matthew to consider. She didn't think it was fair to subject him to board-game torture.

"What in the world is Bamboozle? I've never heard of that one." Matthew smiled at Jill, and Molly waited for her explanation.

"It's really cool. It's like a trivia game where you have to answer these hard questions about stuff . . . you know, geography and history and stuff. But if you don't know, you can make up an answer, and if you trick everyone you get points. But if you don't trick them and they know they answer instead, they get points. Or if you don't want to try to trick people, then you have do something stupid. Like balance stuff on your head or something. Or you lose points."

Matthew frowned at Jill. Molly could tell she had lost him early in the explanation and nearly laughed out loud at his polite, perplexed expression.

"I see," he said slowly. "Sounds like fun." He glanced at Molly. She could tell what he was thinking.

"No, really. You don't have to play. It's okay. She can watch TV."

He shrugged. "Why not? Just for a little while."

"Please, Mom? Dr. Harding says he wants to." Before Molly could stop her, Jill hopped out of bed to get the game.

"I'm great at trivia games. You guys don't stand a chance," Matthew bragged.

"Really?" Jill returned to the bed with the game and began to set up the board. "Mom says people who know a lot of trivia have their brains stuffed with useless information."

Matthew laughed and glanced at Molly. She could feel her cheeks turning red. "I never said that."

"Yes, you did," Jill insisted.

Matt grinned. "She might be right. Your mother usually is."

Molly smiled back at him. "How true. You get extra points for that." *In my book, anyway,* she thought.

They gave Matthew a few more instructions and began to play. Jill won the first round, and Molly won the next two. Matt seemed dumbfounded. He clearly wasn't used to losing.

"Okay, I guess that's enough for now." Molly tried to end the game, giving Matt an easy way out.

"Just one more?" Jill pleaded.

"I'll play again."Matt looked determined to win.

"Okay, one more." Molly shrugged and set up the board again. For a while it seemed as if Matt would finally win, but then Molly impressed them all by not only seeing through Jill's bluff but also knowing the name of President Harding's dog.

"Laddie," Molly announced.

Jill suddenly looked sleepy and decided she wanted a nap. "We'll play Monopoly later, okay?" she asked as her eyes began to close.

"Sure. I'm even better at Monopoly," Matt promised.

"That wouldn't take much," Molly teased him. She kissed Jill's forehead, then followed Matt out of the room.

Once they were alone, the glow of her board-game victories faded, and Molly felt nervous. "How about some lunch?"

When in doubt eat something. That was her motto.

"Sounds good. I'll take care of it. There's all that food I brought over in the fridge. I have a cloth for the floor, too."

"A cloth for the floor?" Molly didn't have the slightest idea what he was talking about.

"We're having a picnic in the living room, right?"

She had thought he was joking about that this morning. It seemed he was perfectly serious.

A few minutes later she and Matt had set up a picnic lunch on her living-room floor. Molly sat back, leaning against the couch. Sunshine streamed in the window, warming her face, and she closed her eyes, pretending she was outside in a sunny meadow.

"Take a nap if you like." Matt walked in with cans of soda and sat down nearby. "You must have gotten up early."

Molly opened her eyes. "I was just pretending I was outside."

"That reminds me. I forgot my recording of nature

sounds." She could see from the look in his eyes that he was joking.

"I have an alarm clock that's supposed to sound like ocean waves . . . but it's more like the washing machine on rinse cycle."

Matthew smiled, handing her a plate and a sandwich. Molly took it from him, feeling a little thrill. She wasn't accustomed to being served, especially by a man.

"Maybe we can go sailing next weekend. Or out to the beach or something."

She liked the way he said that *or something* part. As if it was a definite idea in his mind that they'd see each other, one way or another. Still, maybe he was just trying to make up for another fouled-up date.

"It's nice of you to stay today like this, Matt. You probably have lots of things to do."

She was trying to give him an out in case he didn't want to hang around after lunch.

He stretched out on his side, eating his sandwich. "I'm in no rush. They'll be other sunny days around here. Besides I wanted to spend time with you today. The sailing didn't matter to me, really." He glanced up at her and smiled. Molly felt her breath catch at his words.

He speared an olive with his fork and popped it into his mouth. "So . . . how's it going with Phil these days?"

Molly was surprised at his sudden change of subject. "About the visiting you mean? We've worked it out. He's trying not to be so last minute about calling and coming over here, and I'm trying to be more flexible."

Matt nodded. "That sounds like a good compromise. He looked pretty comfortable at Lauren's party."

Comfortable? Now what did that mean? Molly felt herself flush. Did Matt think there was something going on between her and Phil?

"He always got along well with my family. They were mad at him for the way he acted after the divorce. But they can see he's trying hard to make it up to the girls."

"And make it up to you," Matt added.

Molly paused, not sure how to answer him. "Yes, to me, too. He even offered to help finance my business."

"He did?" Matthew suddenly sat up. He looked upset or as if he had bit into something that didn't agree with him. "That was big of him."

"I thought it was good of him to offer. But I didn't accept. I just didn't think it was right. And I didn't want to give him the wrong impression," she added.

Matthew didn't answer at first. He sat back against the couch and stretched out his legs on the checkered cloth. "What impression was that?"

Molly turned to face him, suddenly distracted by his nearness. "Oh, I don't know. I think Phil had some expectations or something, some fantasy that we might get back together again. I know he really wanted to help me start the business. But I also think he thought it would get us more involved with each other, more tangled up beyond the girls."

"And that's not what you want?" Matthew's dark eyes held a serious light.

"No, not at all. I mean, I'm glad he came back and that we've worked things out. I think we can be good parents together for the girls now and even good friends. But nothing beyond that."

"Well, I'm glad to hear you worked that out with him. I couldn't really tell what was going on at Lauren's party. I thought maybe you two were getting back together. Or at least, you were thinking about it."

Molly felt her heart skip a beat. "Maybe Phil was thinking about it. But I never gave it a thought. Not really."

"Good. I was hoping that's what you'd say." His tone was even and nonchalant, but the corners of his mouth turned up in a smile. Then he reached over and wiped his thumb across her cheek. Molly felt mesmerized by his touch.

"Just a dab of mayonnaise. You're perfect now." He met her gaze with an intense stare, and Molly's mouth went dry.

He was going to kiss her again. She just knew it. She held her breath, unable to move.

"Mom! Can I get up and watch TV now?"

Jill's voice broke the spell, and Molly jumped back, as if waking from a dream. She glanced at Matthew, and he shook his head, nearly laughing. She could see a faint hint of color high on his cheeks, and she knew she had guessed his intentions.

"I'll be right there, honey. Just a minute."

Molly got up and left the room, hoping Matt didn't notice how her knees were shaking.

Well, I guess he's definitely had a change of heart from the "let's be friends" conversation, she thought. Though at this rate it might take years to figure out what—if anything—was going on between them. But it was encouraging to realize that, even though he saw Phil as competition last weekend, he was still eager to keep this date with her.

Very encouraging, Molly thought.

Jill came in to watch TV, wondering about the picnic cloth and the food on the floor in the middle of the living room. She flicked on her favorite kids' channel, and the sound of the kids' show totally dispelled the last trace of romantic ambience. Molly and Matt picked up their mess and carried everything back into the kitchen.

"That was fun. Thanks," Molly said quietly.

He glanced over at her. "It was just practice. We'll have the real thing next time. Promise."

Molly met his gaze and smiled back at him. She warned herself not to get her hopes up again. But she couldn't help it now.

She heard the sound of Matthew's beeper and watched him fish into his pocket for it and check the number.

"My service. I'd better call in." Using Molly's phone, he called his answering service. Molly could only hear half of the conversation, but it sounded as if Reverend Ben Lewis needed Matthew's attention.

Matthew hung up from the service and then called Reverend Ben. They spoke for a few minutes, with Matthew asking a few questions. "I think you ought to have me take a look, Reverend. Can you meet me at my office in, say, half an hour?"

They ended the conversation, and Matthew turned to her. "Sorry, Molly. I have to run. Reverend Ben has some stitches on his arm. It sounds as if they might be infected. I have to see him right away."

Molly felt a pang of disappointment but said, "That's all right. I understand."

"I'll talk to you soon." He stared down at her, looking like he was unwilling to go. He moved toward her and cupped her cheek with his hand. Molly held her breath, bracing herself for another of his quick exciting kisses.

"Mom? Can I have something to drink?" Jill's voice, calling from the living room, broke the heavy silence between them. "And can we play Monopoly now? There's nothing on TV."

Molly sighed and shook her head. "Sure, honey. Just a minute." She looked up at Matthew. "I've been summoned."

"So I noticed." Matt smiled and stepped back. He picked up his cooler and headed for the door. "By the way, you can't lose if you build a hotel on Park Place. That's the whole trick."

Molly walked him to the door and opened it. "Thanks for the tip. I'll try to remember that."

She smiled to herself, watching him walk down the hallway, tilted sideways to balance the cooler.

It had *almost* been like a real date. Good practice at any rate, she thought, remembering his words.

BY MONDAY, TUCKER FELT NO CLOSER TO FINDING CARL than when he had arrived in Portland five days ago. He had visited every shelter and soup kitchen in the city; he'd checked with the police, the hospitals, and all types of offices for destitute men and women. He'd done all he could think of and then some but still had no clue to Carl's whereabouts.

On a tip from a social worker in one of the city offices, Tucker went to an empty lot on the east side of the city where men who were looking for day work gathered early in the mornings. Many were immigrants without working papers and many looked like Carl, lost souls hanging on by their fingernails, desperate for a day's wages. Trucks would drive by, and foremen would pick out a lucky few.

Tucker stood in the lot, sipping from a cup of coffee, trying to blend in, though he knew very well that he didn't. He waited for several hours, searching the faces that moved through the gates, looking for Carl but not finding him. The place felt to him like a phantom world, a depressing scene that made him feel both more discouraged about finding his brother and, at the same time, even more determined.

He returned to his motel room that night, feeling exhausted. The desk clerk passed him two pink message slips. As Tucker expected, the first was a call from Fran. The second, though, was from Ralph Newman, the man who ran that first shelter, Tucker recalled. Hoping for good news he returned to his room and quickly dialed the number.

"I saw your brother," Ralph Newman told Tucker. "He stopped by late this afternoon to see if there were any more letters for him. Then he gave me a forwarding address. Have a pen handy? I'll give it to you."

Tucker quickly scribbled down the address, wondering who Carl expected to hear from. *Was he expecting another letter from Reverend Ben? Or did he think the reverend passed along the address and perhaps I would write?* Tucker felt a pang of guilt. He'd had the address for almost two weeks and had never gotten around to contacting Carl, though he meant to. *This would have been so much easier if I had,* he realized.

Tucker thanked Ralph and hung up the phone. He

grabbed his car keys and headed out again, stopping to ask directions from the desk clerk.

He drove for about fifteen minutes, heading into a neighborhood of brick and brownstone row houses. Most looked rundown, some were abandoned with boarded-up windows, and a few showed signs of hopeful renovation.

Tucker wondered if the address Carl had given was another shelter, but he soon found himself in front of a three-story brick building with a long flight of steps leading up to the front door. He climbed the stairs and peered through the glass on the outer door. Checking the names on the mailboxes, he finally spotted a strip of tape with the name "C. Tulley" and realized Carl was living down in the basement.

His heart hammering, Tucker went down the front steps again to the sidewalk. Under the staircase he saw a battered black metal door. He rang the buzzer and sent up a silent prayer. *Please let Carl be all right.* A few moments later, the door swung open, and Carl stared out at him.

"Tucker? What are you doing here?"

"I missed you, too," Tucker replied. "Can I come in?"

Carl hesitated, and Tucker wondered if, after all the time and trouble he'd gone through, Carl was now going to slam the door in his face. *Not that I don't deserve it,* Tucker thought.

Carl stepped back and let him in. Tucker followed his brother into a small room where high basement windows let in a little of the day's dwindling light. The room was sparsely furnished with a table, two chairs, and a cot covered with army-issue blankets. A sink and an old refrigerator with duct tape on its handle took up most of the opposite wall. A counter held a hot plate and a small portable TV tuned to a baseball game.

Carl stared at him, his arms crossed over his wide chest. He was clean shaven with a recent hair cut. He looked healthy, too. Tucker felt almost weak with relief to see him looking so well and sent up silent thanks to God.

"Who's winning?" Tucker nodded at the TV.

Carl ignored the question. "How did you find me?"

"It wasn't easy." Tucker glanced around. "When did you move in here?"

"A few weeks ago. I'm the janitor for this building and the one next door. The room is part of the deal."

"You got a job pretty quickly. That's good."

The haunting faces of the indigent men and women he had seen that week rose up to taunt him. Again Tucker sent up thanks that Carl hadn't been living in the shelters or out in the open all these weeks. This room was hardly a palace, but it was safer and cleaner than the places he'd visited the last few days.

"The reverend sent me a letter to show around saying what a good worker I was and so on. That helped some." Carl sat down in one of the two kitchen chairs but didn't offer a seat to Tucker. "So, you found me. What now?"

"I came to tell you something, Carl. They caught the kids who broke into the house on North Creek Road. They confessed to it and everything. Your name is cleared. You can come back to Cape Light. No one will bother you."

Carl squinted up at him, then shook his head. "Did you come all the way up here just to tell me that? I know I didn't do it. I don't need you to tell me I'm innocent."

Tucker felt his jaw go tight. He deserved that. He sighed and sat down at the table across from Carl. "I'm sorry I doubted your word that night, Carl. That wasn't right. I believed you mostly. But there was a lot of pressure in the station, and I didn't know what to believe there for a while. That was wrong. I should have taken your word and not let it sway me."

Carl stared at him, his expression unreadable. "All right. You said your piece. I got the news."

Tucker wasn't sure what to say. Carl didn't seem to get his point. "The reverend is saving your job. You can come back. You can stay with us again until you find another place of your own."

Carl gave a short, bitter laugh. "Why would I ever go back there, Tucker? Use your head, for pity's sakes. Those people will never accept me. They'll always be whispering behind my back, suspecting me of everything. You're dreaming, Tucker. I can't go back there. I don't know how I ever ended up in that town again in the first place."

Tucker took a breath. Carl's expression looked determined, his mind made up. "You came back because Cape Light was your home and still is. You didn't do anything wrong, Carl. There's no reason to run away. You have a job there and a place in the world there. You have connections—a family."

Carl frowned at him, shaking his head, but Tucker sensed that he was making some headway.

"I want you to come back, Carl. I don't want you to live out the rest of your days alone, down in some cellar room. I'm your brother. I want to help you. I know I messed up, but I am trying my best. I really am."

Carl didn't speak for a long time. He just got up and fiddled with the TV dials, finally turning the set off. When he faced Tucker again, Tucker thought he saw his brother's chin tremble.

"You did okay by me, Tucker. I know I never thanked you, either. You didn't have to come up here and look for me and all that, just to tell me about those kids."

Carl nodded, looking almost as if he were talking to himself. "I can't go back, though. But it's good of you to ask me. Maybe this place doesn't look like much, but I'm okay here. It's all right for me. And say I get in a jam sometime down the road, I know I can call you. So that's something, right?"

Tucker looked up at him. The room was darker now, and he could barely see Carl's face, only his dark eyes that looked like bright bits of glass.

"Yes, that's something. Don't forget it, either." Tucker stood up and coughed to clear his throat, which felt suddenly thick. "I'm going to try to stay in touch. I know you're not much for that, but just a card or a call from time to time would be enough, Carl. If you move from here, you let me know."

"I will." Carl nodded. He suddenly stuck out his hand, taking Tucker by surprise. Tucker stared at his brother's hand a moment, then took it in his own and shook it hard.

"So long, Tucker. We'll hook up again someday, I guess."

"Sure. I'll see you, Carl. You take care."

Tucker finally let go of Carl's hand, wondering when and if he'd ever see him again. It seemed a sad irony that, after all these years, he finally felt reconciled with his brother, and they were parting with no real hope of ever seeing each other again.

Chapter Nineteen

Tucker packed up and drove back to Cape Light that same night, stopping once on the road for fuel and a bite to eat. He had called Fran from the car as he left Portland, telling her he found Carl and was on his way home again. He also told her not to wait up for him, but when he drove up to the house, he saw that the lights were still on in the family room.

Tucker entered the house quietly. Scout, who had been sleeping at the top of the stairs, ran down to greet him, wildly wagging his tail and jumping up to lick Tucker's face. Tucker patted the dog, then went back to the family room. Fran sat in her bathrobe, watching TV. She looked half asleep and blinked when she saw him.

"Tucker. I didn't even hear you come in." She got up and kissed him hello. "I thought you would be later."

"I made good time. Not much traffic at this hour." Tucker nodded, forcing a small smile.

"Do you want anything? A sandwich or something? There are some leftovers from dinner I can heat for you."

Tucker shook his head and sat down on the couch. "No, thanks. I'm fine." Scout sat at Tucker's side and leaned against his leg. Tucker patted his silky head. "Looks like Scout missed me."

"We all missed you, Tucker." Fran gave him a small smile and sat down in the armchair. "So you found him. I'm surprised."

"It was a lucky break, I guess. Carl went back to some shelter he'd been in to see if he had any mail. He left a forwarding address and this guy who ran the place called me."

Fran didn't say anything for a moment. She picked a thread off the edge of her robe. "Where is he living now? Is it . . . decent?"

Tucker shrugged. "He got a job as a janitor at an apartment house. He gets a room in the basement for free. It isn't much, but it's better than a shelter by a long shot. And it's good to see that he's settled down and working." Tucker paused and leaned back against the couch. "I asked him to come back here again. But he doesn't want to."

"Oh." Fran took a breath. "Why not? Did he say?"

"He's had enough of this place. He says no one here will ever accept him. I don't know. Maybe he's right. I just hated to leave him there, all alone like that. I'm afraid he might get sick again or get into trouble and not let us know."

Fran looked at him a long time. "Maybe if you keep in touch with him, in time, he might move down here again."

Tucker had secretly hoped for the same thing but was surprised to hear Fran say it. She sounded as if she wouldn't mind.

"I don't know if he'll stay in touch. But I'm going to try."

"Tucker, I did a lot of thinking while you were away. I need to apologize to you and not just about the stickpin. I was wrong to give you such a hard time about Carl, about letting him stay here. You were right to help him. I can see that now."

Tucker sighed. He felt so drained. Her words helped, but only a little.

"Thanks, Fran. Thanks for saying that."

"No, I really mean it. I'm truly sorry for the way I acted. It wasn't right. You're a good man. You have a good heart. You've gone the limit for Carl—anyone can see that. It counts for something, even if he doesn't come back. You've been a good brother to him and a wonderful example to our children."

Tucker felt his throat go tight, almost as if he might break down crying. "Thanks," he managed. "It means a lot to me that you would say that."

"Are you okay?"

"I'm spent," he said honestly. "And I'm disappointed in this town, Fran, in the way people acted. They were just too hard on him. That's why Carl's gone." He paused for a moment, collecting his thoughts, ideas he'd been mulling over on the long drive home.

"I don't like the way they acted down at the station house. The way they treated Carl and treated me, too. Especially the chief. It wasn't right."

"I know what you're saying. I'm one of the guilty ones. I know I was too quick to judge him," Fran said, an embarrassed expression on her face.

Tucker reached over and patted her hand. "At least you figured it out, finally. I knew you would. I was thinking more about Charlie and some guys at the station. I'm not even sure I want to be a cop anymore. Isn't that something? After all these years. It's all I ever wanted to do with my life, since I was a little kid. But after that night with Carl, it just doesn't seem the same to me. I've been thinking about an early retirement. I can do that, you know. I'm coming up to twenty years."

Fran got up from her chair, sat beside him, and put her arm around his shoulders. "You're tired now, Tucker. And you feel badly about Carl. Give it some time, then if you still want to quit, fine. Whatever you decide is okay with me."

Tucker sighed and put his arms around his wife. They sat together without talking. Fran was right. He was tired. He wasn't thinking straight. He would let all of this settle and see how it felt once he was back on the job. He would take it one step at a time. But it was good to know Fran was with him again, understanding his problems, trusting his judgment. That was one good thing to come of this, he thought.

BETTY WAS TALKING SO QUICKLY, MOLLY COULD BARELY keep up with her. She did manage to scribble down the address, 53 Mariner's Way, as Betty rattled on.

". . . and I got the key as a special favor from the landlord. You'll be the first one to see it. We can put a binder on it tonight and sign a lease by the end of the week. Oh, I nearly forgot, there's even a brick oven in the basement. Can you beat that? You'll need to get permits and such. But I can work out good terms on a lease, and the zoning is right, too, if you want to put in some little tables eventually. But you really need to get over there right away, Molly. This one will go fast. It's a prime location. The other brokers in town are already breathing down my neck."

"Okay, I'm going. I'm leaving right now. Right this minute." Molly held the phone to her ear with her shoulder and raced around the apartment, grabbing things with both hands as she located her purse and car keys.

She wondered if she looked all right. She didn't want to run into the landlord and make a poor impression. The black capri pants seemed fine, and the sleeveless striped T-shirt was still clean. She switched her sneakers for black slides, swiped on some lip gloss, and yanked a brush through her hair with one hand.

"Call me right away once you see it. I have this walk-through on another property I can't postpone—the closing is tomorrow. It could take a while."

Molly could tell Betty really wanted to see the vacant shop with her rather than keep her appointment. Maybe it's just as well, Molly thought. As much she valued Betty's opinion, Molly wanted to see the place for the first time on her own.

"That's all right, Betty. I understand totally. I'll call you first thing."

"Okay, dear. Good luck. Oh, rats, I'm breaking up. . . ."

Betty's voice dissolved into a blur of static, and Molly sighed with relief, finally able to hang up.

Ten minutes later, after picking up the key from Betty's office, Molly parked on Mariner's Way. Although not a main street, there were quite a few stores here as well as the post office, so everyone passed this way sooner or later.

Molly jumped out of her car and gazed at the storefront of the vacant shop. It was a medium-sized shop, not too narrow and not too wide. There were plate-glass windows in front with window boxes at the bottom that now stood empty. A sign above the door read Shoe Stop, and just below that a canvas awning, dark green with white stripes, stretched out, half open and sagging in the middle.

Molly pictured the storefront painted a cream color with a new sign, a burgundy background with gold lettering: Willoughby's Fine Foods & Catering. That was the name she finally decided on. It sounded solid to her, established, as if she'd been in business a long time and would continue even longer.

Her fantasy renovations continued as she added a matching awning and some interesting swoops of fabric across the windows inside. The window boxes would be full of flowers—bright, eye-catching colors and long trailing vines.

Though she hadn't seen the inside yet, the place already felt good, as if it might work out just right.

Her hand trembled with excitement as she opened the door with her key. The place smelled musty but was full of light. She walked around slowly, picturing where she would put a counter and glass display cabinets. She pulled up a corner of the worn blue carpeting and saw a beautiful wooden floor that only needed some light refinishing. She saw a door in back and entered what appeared to have been a stockroom.

Betty said there was a sink and gas hookup for a stove back there someplace, Molly recalled, as she investigated further. According to Betty, the place had quite a history. It had once been a bakery and before that a tearoom back in the nineteenth century. Molly wondered if she could find some old photographs of how it looked back then and hang them on the walls.

She saw another window and a door to the back of the store. She knew she could make a good working kitchen in this space.

It was perfect, she thought, just as Betty had promised.

Molly walked out of the dark back room into the front again, her eyes blinking against the sudden light. She could make out the silhouette of a man standing in the doorway, though she couldn't see his face.

"Molly?" She recognized Matt's voice and stepped closer, shading her eyes with her hand. It was him, for sure. She could barely believe it.

"I was down the street at the post office. I thought I saw you come in here."

"I'm just looking around. I might rent it for my shop, Willoughby's Fine Foods and Catering. What do you think?"

"I think that's a classy name." Matt took a few steps inside and glanced around. "It has a lot of light. I like the look of the place from the street, too. Old-fashioned and sort of classic. Or it could be." He looked at her and smiled. "I think you could do a lot with it. I know you could."

"I have a few ideas." Molly stepped closer.

"You always do."

His encouraging words made her feel good, as usual. She liked the way she felt about herself around Matt. That was part of the attraction, she realized. When he looked at her that way, she felt as if he saw the best she could be and anything was possible.

"It's funny to run into you like this," he said. "I was going to call you when I got back to the office."

"Oh?" Molly stopped short, not daring to add, "About what?" It had been three days since their picnic in her living room. She had been hoping to hear from him, all the while warning herself not to get her expectations too high again.

"I wanted to ask you out to dinner actually." He shook his head, smiling with a baffled expression. "But I was almost afraid to. Every time we make plans, some disaster strikes and it doesn't work out."

"Tell me about it." Molly felt a tight, forced smile stretch across her face. She braced herself for another one of those "I think you're swell but looks like this just isn't meant to work out" speeches.

Could he possibly do that to her? She was sure her heart would break.

Something in her expression must have given her away. Matt suddenly stepped closer and put his hands on her shoulders. He stared down into her eyes.

"I was just thinking about you this morning and realized that I've known you for, well, almost four months now, and we've never had a real date. Without any adolescent chaperones, sick children to care for, or Phil showing up, I mean."

Molly took in a shallow breath, unable to look away from his dark, tender gaze. "And?"

She knew she sounded nervous, but she couldn't help herself.

She saw Matt swallow hard, looking unable to answer for a moment. "The thing is, I realized that I'm in love with you, Molly, and we've never even been on a real date." He paused. "Don't you think that's funny somehow?"

His voice trailed off to a near whisper. Molly couldn't answer. She was sure she hadn't heard him correctly, but the look on his face left no doubt. She didn't know whether to laugh or cry. It was all she could do to nod her head.

"Well, what do you think? Did I mess up totally by being such a jerk and not getting out of my own stupid way? Could you give me one more chance to show you how I really feel about you? How I've always felt . . . but just couldn't figure out."

She paused and took a deep breath. "I love you, too."

The look of relief on his face was astounding; Molly knew she would never forget it. He pulled her close for a long, deep kiss, and Molly melted in his strong embrace.

When they finally broke apart, she stared up at him, unable to believe this was really happening. "Are you sure about this?" she asked quietly. "I mean, I'm just a cook and you're a doctor and everything. We aren't a very good match. . . ."

Matt pulled back, his expression astounded. "Molly, please, don't say another word. I never once thought of you as less than my equal in any way." He grinned at her. "Actually, there are so many times when you're clearly the superior one that I may have to make sure I don't get an inferiority complex."

"But—"

"You're perfect for me." He cut off her objections, laughing. "Perfect, period." He pressed his cheek against her hair. "All this time, I've been worried that I wasn't good enough for you. That I couldn't give you enough, give you what you deserve in a relationship."

He leaned back again and looked down at her, a soft smile on his lips. "But I know it will be different with you. I love you so much. I know we'll be happy together."

Molly felt every cell in her body trembling with joy—and shock. This was so much more than she had hoped for. She never in a million years imagined that Matt would have such feelings for her. But it seemed he really did.

She sighed and dropped her head to his shoulder, clinging to him. "I think you're pretty near perfect, too. . . . But I'll let you know if I see any room for improvement."

Matt laughed and held her close, nearly lifting her feet off the ground. "That's just what I expected you to say."

His mouth sought hers, and he kissed her again for a long time. When Molly finally opened her eyes and looked around, she blinked at the sunlight, feeling dazed, as if she were an entirely new person who had woken up in a whole new world.

TUCKER WAS WALKING THE BEAT ON FRIDAY AFTERNOON. Just as he passed the Clam Box, Charlie appeared in the doorway, carrying out a big white laundry bag. "Tucker, how are you doing?" he called out. "Want to come in for some coffee?"

Charlie had never really apologized for the argument he'd started weeks ago. They had barely said hello to each other since.

"No, thanks. I just took my break about an hour ago."

"Ah, come on. Just for a few minutes. What's the matter, don't you like my cooking anymore?"

Tucker gave him a reluctant smile. "What do you mean, 'anymore'? I'm not sure I ever did."

Charlie's face fell, then he forced a smile. A nervous smile, Tucker noticed, as if eager to show he got the joke.

"Okay, then. Suit yourself." He hefted up the laundry bag and tossed it over his shoulder as he headed down the sidewalk to his car.

"See you, Charlie," Tucker called after him.

Charlie raised one hand, his back now turned. "Sure, see you around, Tucker."

Tucker continued walking toward the station house. He guessed that now that Carl was out of the picture, Charlie had decided they should forget their argument and be friends again. It was the same way at the station house. Even Chief Sanborn was now acting as if he had never doubted Tucker's judgment, never pressured him about Carl. It was as if the whole thing had never happened, which made Tucker feel odd and unsettled.

Maybe everyone else could forget that Carl existed now that he had left town, but Tucker couldn't. He refused to. Even if he never saw Carl again, he wasn't going to deny his brother just to keep things smooth and easy. For so many years he had pushed Carl to the back of his mind, almost pretending he didn't exist. He had been embarrassed to admit that he was related to someone like Carl, a convict who had served time in jail. But he couldn't do that anymore. Carl was part of him, part of his family, his history. He could see now that denying Carl was like denying part of himself.

Carl had shown real character in the way he'd pulled himself together, Tucker thought, the way he'd made a new life for himself up in Maine even after being treated so badly down here. Tucker admired that, though he was sure people like Charlie Bates and Chief Sanborn would never understand.

He wasn't sure yet what he would decide about staying on the police force. But he knew his lifelong friendship with Charlie Bates would never be the same. *How could it be?* Tucker wondered. *It would deny Carl and deny so much of me.*

THE PHONE RANG EARLY SUNDAY MORNING. TUCKER HAD just come in from walking the dog and no one else in the family was up yet. He answered it and heard Reverend Ben on the line.

"Sorry to bother you, Tucker. But I see it's your turn on the fix-it list. Could you come over to the church a little earlier this morning? There's a problem with the side door. It seems to be jammed. It happens sometimes in the warm weather. I'm not sure what to do about it."

"That's all right, Reverend. I know what to do. I'll bring the WD-40 and some silicone spray."

The reverend didn't answer right away. "Sounds good to me, Tucker. Whatever you said."

Tucker laughed in reply. He showered and dressed quickly, then arranged for Fran to come to the service with the children later in her car.

The village green was nearly empty at such an early hour, with only a few joggers loping along the harbor. Tucker parked on the far side of the green and walked toward the church. The tall oak trees were covered with early green leaves, the shade was cool, and the air smelled of damp earth and freshly mown grass.

He found the side door of the church open, but a ladder stood blocking the entryway. *Maybe the reverend called another deacon who got here before me,* Tucker thought with surprise. He stepped up to the doorway and looked around.

"You looking for somebody?"

Tucker turned at the sound of Carl's voice right behind him. Carl was dressed in his work overalls, carrying a screwdriver and a tiny oil can.

"Carl . . . you came back. Why didn't you let me know?"

Carl shrugged. "I figured you'd find out soon enough. It's a small town. News travels fast, you know."

"Yeah, I know."

Carl walked past Tucker and climbed up the ladder.

Tucker took a few steps back and watched him work. "How long have you been here?"

Carl shrugged. "Day before yesterday. I got a room in that same place where I was living before, and I got my job back here, too. I've been settling in."

"Sure, I understand." Tucker paused. He wasn't surprised that Carl had not called him straight off, all things considered. But he was still surprised that he'd come back to the village.

"Why did you come back? I thought you said you never would."

"Oh, I don't know." Carl shrugged. "I thought some about what you said. I wasn't guilty of nothing. I should have stuck it out here instead of running. The reverend said the same thing to me. He wrote me a letter a day or two after you left. I would have liked to have seen those cops' faces when those kids were picked up in Hamilton. I missed out on that."

"Yeah, you did," Tucker agreed, thinking there would be no lack of surprised looks once people saw Carl around again.

Carl put down the screwdriver. "And I guess it meant something to me, the way you came to find me, to tell me what went on down here. You went the distance for me, Tucker. I don't think anyone's ever done that before."

Tucker didn't know what to say. He looked away from the ladder, relieved that Carl couldn't see how his words had affected him.

"You were right, too. I have a good job here, better than up in Portland. And I got ties, family ties. For better or worse, as they say. So . . . here I am."

Tucker watched him climb down the ladder. Carl kicked the doorstop away and tested the hinges. The door opened and closed smoothly without sticking.

"You fixed that pretty good. Better than I would have."

"It needs to be planed a little on the bottom. I'll get to that tomorrow. I didn't want to take it down today with the service and all. The reverend likes the church to look nice on Sundays."

Tucker met his brother's dark eyes. "I'm glad you came back, Carl. I'm happy to see you."

"Likewise, I guess." Carl's voice was gruff. He coughed into his hand.

Tucker suddenly leaned over and patted Carl's shoulder. It was not quite a hug but certainly more than a handshake.

He pulled away and faced him again with a small smile. "Why don't you come by for dinner this afternoon? I think we're having baked ham."

Tucker knew how much his brother liked ham. He doubted Carl had eaten a decent meal since he'd left town.

Carl laughed. "Maybe you should clear it with Fran first. She's probably still counting the silverware from the last time you invited me."

"Don't worry about Fran. She's all right. I think she'll be happy to see you."

Carl squinted at him with utter disbelief. "Sure, when pigs can fly she'll be."

"No, I'm not kidding. People can change, you know."

Carl stared at him a moment, then nodded. "If you say so."

"I do."

Tucker knew he would never doubt that again.

SOPHIE WASN'T SURE SHE COULD DO IT AT FIRST. BUT something inside had pushed her beyond her sadness and regrets, beyond her mourning of Gus's death. Maybe it was Gus's spirit, willing her to carry on without him. He would have wanted her to have the Memorial Day picnic at the orchard, just as they did every year for so long now that she couldn't even remember when the tradition had started.

Sophie sat at her dressing table, working on her hair. Through the bedroom windows she had a bird's-eye view of the setup for the party, the long cloth canopies, the tables already laden with food. A number of guests had already arrived and were helping with the last of the preparations.

It was going to be a big crowd this year, maybe the biggest ever. That would be hard to gauge, though, since they never kept records of these things, only photographs. Maybe next winter when the cold set in again, she and Miranda could dig out the old albums and check. But they were far too busy now. Too much work filled every hour of every day to wonder and worry about the past.

Miranda had lit up when Sophie said that the picnic tradition would continue. Sophie knew Miranda would not have argued if the decision had been otherwise, but she could see how Miranda had put her heart into the preparations this week. She found special paper garlands and lanterns to hang from the trees. She gathered pitchers and vases and filled them with flowers. She found a crew of helpers to set up the tables and made phone calls for hours, figuring out the menu and the shifts on the barbeque.

"We'll hold it in honor of Granddad," she had suggested, and Sophie had liked that idea.

Sophie had baked and cooked all of her specialities, her apple pies, Poppy Seed Cole Slaw, Johnny Cake, and Twice-Baked Beans with Seven Secret Spices.

She stuck one last pin in her upswept hair, smoothing back wisps of faded strawberry blond and gray. She took a necklace from the jewelry tray, a gold heart locket with Gus's photo inside, a picture taken on their honeymoon. She always wore it close to her heart now.

Sophie knew she shouldn't dawdle, fussing over her appearance so. She ought to be downstairs with the guests by now. Still, she felt no hurry. It felt as if Miranda were the real hostess this year, even taking precedence over her aunts Evelyn and Una. That was as it should be, Sophie realized. Miranda had earned that right, the way she fought to save the orchard. Sophie was happy to step back and watch her granddaughter shine today.

Day by day, Miranda was becoming more a part of this place and the orchard, more a part of her. Sophie had not expected their plan to work out nearly so well. But Miranda had been right. She really did belong here.

Sophie rose from her dressing table and gave her reflection a once over. "You'll do," she heard Gus whisper in her ear. "You'll do just fine for me, dear."

She nodded and said a small silent thank you. It was time to go down and join the party.

REVEREND BEN FOUND HE HAD TO PARK SOME DISTANCE down the road from the orchard. It was always this way when you were a latecomer. He had dropped Carolyn off at the house and now walked alone toward the party. He could already hear the music drifting over the trees and smell the appetizing barbeque. The big yellow house came into view, a grand old Queen Anne, its wraparound porches filled with lounging guests. A few called out greetings, and he waved back. He was not surprised to see Jessica and Sam Morgan here or to see Sam's sister Molly. But he did take notice of Molly walking hand-in-hand with Matt Harding, his daughter Amanda and the two Willoughby girls trailing behind. They both looked happy, Ben thought, happy and totally at ease with one another. It appeared that Matt Harding had found a way to forgive himself and move on. Ben felt truly pleased for him and for Molly, too, who had certainly weathered her share of difficulties.

Ben walked on, noticing Tucker and Carl Tulley standing together in the shade of a large oak talking to Digger Hegmen. Carl looked fascinated as the old seaman spun one of his many yarns. Ben was glad to see that Carl had come, marveling that Tucker had been able to persuade him.

Strange things had happened around here lately, he realized. Strange and even miraculous. The silent answers to so many prayers.

He walked through Sophie's garden at the back of the house, heading toward the tables and canopies. He glanced across the rows of blooming flowers. Emily Warwick and Dan Forbes sat together on a stone bench. Dan had his arm around her, and they looked as if they were off in a world of their own, more like two teenagers than people in their forties. Ben felt cheered to see Emily so radiantly happy.

Only a year ago her life had been so different. She had had no one in her life, just strained relationships with both her mother and Jessica. She hadn't been reunited with her birth daughter, Sara, and had never imagined such a relationship with Dan.

He thought of his own life, how much had happened in such a short time. Carolyn's illness and accident, the birth of their first grandchild, his own crisis of faith, and the return of his son, Mark. He had married Jessica Warwick and Sam Morgan and eulogized Gus Potter. It seemed inconceivable that so much had happened in such a short time, and yet it was all just part of the steady, unexceptional stream of life.

The distant view of the village below captured his attention. Ben stopped and stared out at the town and harbor. It looked like a miniature village from this distance, a Christmas decoration in a shop window. Sometimes it seemed as if nothing ever changed here, and yet the village was really more like the sea, with so much churning under the surface.

What would the coming year hold for him and everyone here, he wondered. Only God in his heaven knew the answer to that. Ben only knew that acceptance was the key—acceptance, faith, and compassion. *To live without fear and to trust in God's love and in his promise to take care of us.*

Today was a time for celebration, a well-deserved rest from the daily routine. There would be music and dancing, eating and laughter. When darkness dropped like a heavy curtain over the horizon, a hush would fall over the crowd as everyone settled back to watch the fireworks light up the sky over the harbor.

Ben knew he, too, would watch and marvel at the sight, knowing all the while that mere fireworks could never match the majesty of the natural world, the miracles God sent us everyday in a grain of sand, a clap of thunder, or the petals of a flower.

Still he would end the day content and smiling, like all the rest, thankful for the simple pleasures of this life and the endless blessings of this single day.